*Also by William Kelley*

GEMINI

WILLIAM KELLEY

# THE GOD
# HUNTERS

SIMON AND SCHUSTER
NEW YORK . . . . . 1964

LIBRARY OF CONGRESS CATALOG CARD NUMBER: 64-10625
MANUFACTURED IN THE UNITED STATES OF AMERICA
BY H. WOLFF BOOK MANUFACTURING CO., INC., N. Y.

FOR MY MOTHER

*Alethea Kelley*

While I certainly hope that there is some similarity between my characters and real people, it is necessary for me to state that any painful correspondences between them and actual persons living or dead are purely matters of coincidence.

I owe thanks to my editor, Bob Gott-
lieb, who lent money, patience and
brilliance whenever needed, which in
all cases was damned often.

I owe thanks, especially, to my marvelous wife, Nina, who endured while I
was prevailing around for four long
years.

. . . but found not God
Nor whirlwind's voice to cry
Them welcome,
Or to weep the hunters home.

# THE PROLOGUE

# • ONE •

HE ENTERED THE HOUSE at the kitchen door. One of the German nuns was kneeling on the floor in front of the huge cookstove, head bowed. The only sound was issuing from a caldron that occupied most of the stovetop, its lid doing a ponderous plop-plopping steam dance.

Aubrey sniffed the air once, delicately.

Ah, gristle stew. The glory of thy people. They all do it well, even stupendously, one might say. The German sauerbraten nuns, the Italian pasta nuns, the Polish head cheese nuns, the Bavarian blood sausage nuns—all are expert at making gristle stew. It's a mystic talent breathed into them at the taking of the veil. Go ye forth, sisters, and bestir until you have come upon forty-two pounds of perfectly fresh and prime stew meat, and take it up in both hands and you will find lurking within you the power to render it instanter a foul and gummy and malodorous abomination, the vapors of which shall rise in a uniformly poisonous cloud to the lingering consternation of the American Brotherhood of Meat Packers. Good Sister Gregor of the Gridiron, be of good cheer. Your prayers are having their effect. What you've got there, from the smell of it, is a ruddy gristling wonder.

Grinning then, he went on his toes soundlessly across the kitchen, pushed through the swinging doors into the corridor, came down off his toes and his grin suddenly, continued heavy-footed—his tennis shoes squeaking on the hardwood-bright parquet as if in pain—down the corridor to the back stairs, and mounted them slowly, as one might a scaffold.

His room opened off the first landing: a long, narrow, low-ceilinged cubicle, one of the two singles in the house. It had three unusual and redeeming features, all windows. He let the wind slam the door behind him and sort of fell away, elbows first, to his closet, sorted among the hanging garments, withdrew the newest of his white habits, the one whose whiteness had not yet been pressed yellow, and donned it ceremoniously, kissing the collar of the soutane, the black plastic ring of the cincture, the neck circlet of the scapular, and the top of the capuche's bib, saying the prayers prescribed for each as he did so, and then sat down and put on black socks and his first-line black shoes. He stood up and went to a small hand mirror fixed with scotch tape to the inside of the closet door. He squinted at himself. If I only weren't such a handsome devil, he thought. Brown hair, blue eyes, perfect nose, cleft chin, big handlebar ears—why I think I'll have to grow a beard by tomorrow morning, before I go out into that world full of rapacious women, if I'm to be safe at all. He grimaced at himself, shook his head, and went to the door. He pulled it half open, hesitated, pushed it shut again and, without releasing the knob, fell to his knees and closed his eyes.

Dear Lord Jesus Christ. You see me kneeling here, and You know my heart and what is in it. If what I am about to do is clearly wrong, prevent it. But if it is merely rash, ill-considered, and has only a slight chance of success, do please permit me to proceed.

Then he went quickly out, skipped up the stairs to the second floor, and walked around the banistered balcony to the Father Master's door. He knocked.

"Who is it?" The voice within was sharp and clear.

"Mr. Strycker, Father. I'd like to see you, if I may."

"Can it wait for an hour?" Now the voice was plaintive, suggesting that damned near anything conceivable could wait for an hour.

"Yes, Father, certainly."

"Good. Come back then. I'm soaking a boil."

Aubrey winced, staggered back slightly from the door. "Yes, Father." He turned and walked back to his room. That was your Father Finnegan. Disguise nothing, ask no quarter, give none, and let delicacy take the hindmost. A man of parts, all of them crusty.

In his room, he removed his capuche and scapular, laid them neatly on the bed, walked to the east window, opened it, stared for a moment at a large chicken hawk circling over the four pine trees on the hill above the house. Then he said aloud, "All right, all right. The letter has to be written, so write it now. Now!"

He eased himself to the edge of the marred wooden desk, took a pad of writing paper from one drawer and a well-chewed Wearever from another, and arranged both neatly on the desktop. Then, lips pursed, he stared down at the pen and at a fly that was now crawling its length, and went on staring until the fly had flown east out the window, until his expression had become an agitated scowl. His arrival on the hard, slat-backed chair was the result of a snarl, a desperate half-gainer lunge, and some accomplished footwork. He snatched up the pen as his rump struck, and had the cap off in his mouth and the point to the paper before he was done hitching the chair into position. Very rapidly, he wrote:

*St. Titus' Novitiate*
*Chelsea, New York*
*Ascension Thursday*

*Director of Vocations*
*The Society of the Sahara*
*Southampton, New York*

DEAR REVEREND FATHER:

Then he held the pen poised, worked it in a series of fast and tight circles over the paper, heaved a couple of sighs, looked out the window once, said Dear Reverend Father several times, and finally seized a handful of his hair savagely with his left hand, and started to write precipitately and without pause, chewing the Wearever cap furiously as he went.

*I hope you will excuse the scrawl and informality of this letter, but I have tried to write it at least a dozen times with attention to round and proper phrasing and have gotten nowhere. So, if you will suffer me, I will simply blurt out what comes, in the order in which it* comes, and hope that it will add up to something intelligible when I'm done. It takes the primitive form of an application to your holy Society as a candidate for the priesthood.

I am a candidate for solemn vows—a novice—in the Order of Anchorites of St. Titus, presently in the ninth month of my novitiate. You may not know that the Titan Order is constituted rather like your own in that the novitiate year follows the study of scholastic philosophy. My scholasticate was completed last June with a degree of Bachelor of Arts in Philosophy after a four year course at St. Titus' College, near Boston, Massachusetts. Simple vows are taken by Titan scholastics at the end of the first year of the scholasticate, for a period of three years. Hence, I am no longer in simple vows, their term having expired in July of last year. I am free to leave this novitiate, and the Titan Order, at any time.

I realize that certain canonical difficulties are raised by the fact that I have already made part of my novitiate. If it becomes necessary that I begin the novitiate over again, should I be accepted by your Society, I will be happy to do so.

I expect to be on my way to New York City, where my father lives, by early tomorrow morning. I would, then, be available for an interview in Southampton as early as Saturday, or any time thereafter. I can be reached, at your convenience, through my father's business office, that is, in care of Mr. Kermit Strycker, President, Kaatskill Productions, Inc., Rockefeller Center, 630 Fifth Avenue, New York City.

It is entirely possible that the name Strycker is familiar to you. I am the fraternal twin of Mr. Arnold Strycker, who applied as a candidate for the priesthood in your Society four years ago. He was then, also, a member of the Order of Anchorites of St. Titus. The fact is that Arnie and I, after a year in the Titan Order, decided that we had made a mistake and should have entered the Saharan Fathers. During our vacation home at the end of our first year, Arnie, without my knowledge, went to your motherhouse in Southampton and presented himself as a candidate. He had decided that I didn't really want to leave the Titans. In any case, he was told by the Saharan Father who interviewed him to think it over for a few months. Arnie and I returned to the Titan seminary, spent most of the summer at the Titan summer house in Maine, and were back at the Boston house in late August, preparing to pronounce our simple vows, when Arnie was, for psychiatric reasons, withdrawn from the Order and removed by my

14

father to the Horton Farm, Shelter Island, New York. Arnie was then under the delusion that his body had been possessed by the Holy Ghost and the Devil at the same time. He has been at the Horton Farm ever since, except for a yearly absence of approximately one month's duration in the care and legal custody of my father. Arnie's particular mental difficulty has been diagnosed as schizophrenia of the type having to do with delusions, or fantasies, concerning the reconstruction, or restitution, or salvation of the world. Sometimes he believes he is God's agent, and sometimes the Devil's. It is very complicated and my account of it is based upon the most fragmentary possible reports, contained in letters from my father, or imparted during his very occasional visits (he is in the motion picture-television industry and travels a great deal), or in even more occasional and almost incomprehensible letters from Arnie himself. He has moments or days or even months of complete sanity, I am told, but apparently he never writes letters during these sane periods.

I should point out, I guess, that my own sanity has been attested to by a psychiatrist who examined me at my insistence after Arnie was committed. The Titan Fathers did not request this examination, but there certainly was occasion for uneasiness and I wanted to put the matter as safely beyond question as I could.

The psychiatric report, and all the other documents and transcripts you may require, are obtainable, I feel sure, from The Very Reverend Eli Tyman, O.A.S.T., Provincial of the Eastern Province, at St. Titus' College in Boston.

I think you should also know that my parents were married in the Dutch Reformed Church, and have been divorced since 1955. My mother was converted to Catholicism in 1944 and had all three children baptized in the Church at that time. My younger sister, Aline, has been in a Carmelite cloister in the Bronx since July, 1958. My mother has not remarried, and has lived with her mother in Fort Lee, New Jersey—where I was raised and educated—since 1937. My father did remarry, in 1956, but has been separated from his second wife since 1957 or thereabouts. I have not met my father's second wife or her daughter by a previous marriage.

It occurs to me that I am trying to say too much here. Perhaps all that really needs saying is that I have been certain for the last four years that my true vocation lies with the Society of the Sahara, that I have finally found the courage to leave the Titan Order, and that I would be most grateful if you should see fit to invite me to Southampton to present my case in person.

Yours truly in Christ,
AUBREY STRYCKER, O.A.S.T.

He jammed the pen into its cap, still held in his mouth, and used the pen to tap his way through the letter, twice, groaning in exactly the same places the second time as he had the first. Then he quickly addressed an envelope, sealed the letter in it, tossed it with the pen to the top of the desk, and regarded both for a time. It was done. Or half done. He glanced around at the clock. It was time. He got to his feet slowly, put on his scapular and capuche with ceremony, went to the door, paused there, and looked back at the letter.

An undisputed world's record. Who else has ever taken four years to write a four-page letter?

He shook his head, turned away and seized the doorknob.

I will go now unto Finnegan. Unto Finnegan who gives joy to my youth.

And went out stiffly, forcing himself at the knees. He almost stopped at the corridor window, but only slowed, looking out and down at the front lawn and its screen of birches and the blue river beyond, half turning as he passed to hold the view as long as possible.

Bright day, breeze in the birches, and stride on, Mr. Strycker, stride on. Forge fire in the eye and summon up the sinew, for exactly here, in this quintessence of river valley, is where it begins. And if you step out briskly, that lawn will become sand, that sky pure heat, those birches tamarisks, that river cracked earth. And if you listen with a cleansed ear you may catch out the sweet sound of the trumpets of the kingdom.

And he strode on, the skirts of his soutane whipping busily about his knees, and came at the Master's door resolutely, fist poised, jaw set. And bent his knuckles to the wood almost harshly, after the slightest of hesitations, and rapped loudly, as if this were a door that had long been closed to him.

# · TWO ·

FATHER FINNEGAN was a tall, grayed, slat-nosed, stoop-shouldered, twanging down-easter with narrow-set polar eyes and the complexion of a dried pinecone. His aspect was dartive and elusively criminal, and this was only indifferently dissembled by a pseudo-benign smile and a sort of ready-mix titter, without the first of which Father Finnegan was almost never seen, and without the second of which he was certainly never heard. The smile was known as Finnegan's Rainbow and the titter as Finnegan's Wake. Not that he was ill-intentioned or unfair: quite the contrary. Aubrey thought him far and away the most unimpeachably objective judge of humanity he had yet encountered, and his appointment as Father Master of Novices had to follow upon a rather firmly established personal holiness. Still, the Master was definitely a moral pessimist, and had a nicely developed talent for making you feel that it was surpassingly stupid of you to pretend that any least one of your motives had anything even remotely good about it, his attitude being, to state it mildly, that men had been falling daily for thousands of years and weren't likely to start floating or rising in *his* lifetime, no matter how sanguinely canonical the appearances. He looked upon mankind as an overgrown gaggle of Israelites, utterly incapable, as Harnack put it, of traveling nine feet in any direction without falling among abominations.

17

Out of this attitude came the first of Father Finnegan's working principles: the overwhelming majority of men have to be surprised or shocked into being just approximately honest about any sublunary thing. And there followed from this—because he dearly loved to experiment—a whole Gladstone bag full of sinister little tricks calculated to startle truth from the mouths of sinners. Since the old man had had a full hour to sort among his psyche shakers, and since he knew who his visitor would be and could, therefore, fine the thing down precisely, and since, as was obvious from past performances, he looked upon Aubrey as an especially devious and even challenging prevaricator, Aubrey expected a truly inspired exhibition, and the Master did not let him down.

The priest rose as soon as Aubrey arrived in the doorway, gave him the so-you're-ready-to-confess-at-last-Shagwell stare, smiled suddenly, even gaily, abruptly frowned as if he had just recognized his visitor and had been expecting someone else, and said, "Oh, it's you, Mac-Iver." Then he waved off Aubrey's attempt to identify himself and staggered hazardously into backward motion toward an inner door, indicating, by a series of ineffable flutterings of jowls and hands, a call of nature, and managing to convey, as he exited center rear with flourish, that nothing could be so natural as that the sudden appearance of MacIver should bring on a bowel movement.

Aubrey sat his straight chair tensely. Round One to Finnegan on footwork and some smashingly deceptive head fakes. He is a shrike, no question about it. The world's oldest gray shrike. I hope he's in there a long time and gets some of the vitriol out of him.

Father Finnegan was at it an uncommonly long time, so long in fact that Aubrey was beginning to fancy that the priest had succumbed in one of those fabled occurrences known as total passage of the innards, when, his survival and approach heralded by the flushing of a toilet, Father Finnegan fell gauntly flapping back into the room, thrashing his capuche in the air as he came, thereby creating his own wind and beating noisily before it, like a derelict albatross in a gale with ragged wisps of molting feathers slapping along its whited spine.

He fell away toward his desk and came about listing abjectly to port, put his hands on the desktop and leaned himself passably upright. He worked his eyelids funerally, made a noise like a death rattle, and croaked out a few words about being sorry for the delay but he was suffering from a full-blown case of the Fundy Flux.

Aubrey's inward groan got away from him but he covered the audible portion with a sickly, sympathetic murmur. It won't work, you old predator. I've been armed against the Camille act for years. My mother is an expert. You'll have to stretch out on that desk and die before you reach me with that one. And even then I may only pause long enough to lift the lid and tumble you into it.

Aubrey had long regarded the desk with suspicion; a boxish mahogany monstrosity polished to a sheen like patent leather, its top kept bare of any object whatsoever. It was decorated here and there with little carved convexo-convex Oriental eyes, Semiramic if not Sennacheribdic in their flat, fatalistic meanness, and Aubrey was apprehensive, especially in times of stress, that the desk was something out of Finnegan's nineteenth reincarnation, and really the sarcophagus of one of the Master's ancient friends—perhaps Ashurbanipal of Nineveh, or another of those innocently brutal Assyrians. Aubrey fixed his gaze on one of the eyes and, to his own satisfaction, stared it down. Get back in there, you dirty old Ninevite, before I put the acid to you.

Father Finnegan, seeing that he had lost his effect, cleared his throat, licked his lips once, and leaned toward Aubrey threateningly. "Yes, yes, MacIver. What is it? What's on your *mind?*" His eyes, quick and flicking and sub-zero gray, moved on the novice penetratingly, and he repeated, "What's on your *mind?*" suggesting that only an extravagant and holy charity allowed the imputation of mental processes to this wretch, MacIver.

"Well, Father, I want you to know at the outset that I have given this matter the most serious and prayerful consideration."

"Come to the *point*, MacIver. The point!"

"Yes, Father." Aubrey said it all in one breath. "I've decided to leave the Titan Order in favor of the Saharan Fathers." He regretted his choice of words immediately and started to correct himself, but the Master, who had allowed himself the merest flash of surprise, was already talking, shaking his head as if in severe pain.

"MacIver, you appall me." And he looked appalled, his eyes like black ladles dishing up astound and consternation with marvelous facility, his jaw munching like a Roman eagle chewing buckshot; and no place to stare or spit any of it except right back at Aubrey. And he did, vehemently, as if he truly were outraged, as if this were the first novice who had ever suggested departure to him rather than (as Aubrey guessed) the four hundred and fiftieth, or thousandth, or who the hell knew? And came around his desk unbending like a bird into flight, waving both hands for silence as Aubrey continued to splutter, and took his position insessorially high on the balls of his feet not a yard in front of his victim and peered down at him along the ridgebone of his ancient beak and, refusing to acknowledge objection or interruption, holding Aubrey impaled as on wire barbs with the bitter force and butchery of his words, proceeded, in nearly a half hour's catbird screeching of truth and sarcasm, blithely, inextricably mixed, to enlighten that victim forever and indelibly as to the fury of a religious order scorned.

And, at one point, the Master said, "You would leave us in favor —in favor—of the Saharan Fathers? By what mad logic do you conclude, MacIver, that the bestowal of your inept person upon any organization of rational men would be a favor? A calamity, yes, but a favor? Never! You? You who have preconized time and time again by your aberrant behavior to fellow novices and superiors alike that you are about as precisian with regard to the Holy Rule of our Order as might be a baboon in a grove of forbidden bananas? You? You who are probably the last novice in the community who should be considering anything else now or at any future time but the extraordinary generosity of God and the Titan Order—not to say the *rash* generosity—in your being offered an opportunity of solemn vows and the priesthood in *this*, one of the ancient orders of the Holy Roman Catholic Church! You! Who should be doing nothing but thanking God and this order for tolerating you as long as we have. You who have been in this order—a *guest* of this order—for how long now? For five years! Five years! During which you haven't had to pay for a meal or a shirt or a bed or a book. Four of those years in college, absorbing free one of the best classical and philosophical educations available today. At the end of which you were awarded your bachelor's degree in philosophy! Do you know what that degree is worth? Do you appreciate what it is worth? And *this* year, this year of meditation and quiet on a beautiful Hudson River estate—a time of uninterrupted peace that most men can only dream about? *And* all of your summers at your leisure on the Maine coast—something only the wealthiest of men can afford? Have you any appreciation of what you are sitting there flatly repudiating, MacIver? Do you understand you are repudiating this order's entire investment in you? Don't nod at me, MacIver! For, as heaven is my witness, I submit to you that you have lost all appreciation of the meaning of the word appreciation!"

And he said, "I hope, MacIver, that you aren't so deluded as to think you are a fit candidate for the missionary life. You who constantly talk during Great Silence, sleep during meditation, neglect your assigned jobs, are known by everybody as a dreamer part of the time and as a smart aleck the other part—you now think you are ready for a higher, more difficult life? For a life of physical sacrifice and self-abnegation? Why, only fraternal charity prevents me from laughing out loud!"

And he said, "The Saharan Fathers are an intense and devoted group of religious. They have chosen one of the most difficult missions in the world. They need pious, zealous, wholly dedicated men for their priesthood. Does that describe you, MacIver? If you think it does, your self-delusion is only exceeded by your pride and effrontery. You are so obviously unfitted that any discussion of your fitness would be nothing less than ludicrous."

And he said, "I've had serious reservations about you since you came under my jurisdiction. I'm not speaking now of your conduct. I'm speaking of your religious faith, or lack of it. I have the reports that came down here with you from Boston. All about how you troubled your way through scholastic philosophy, questioning virtually every article of faith and doctrine in the canon of the Church. No doubt you thought that clever and sophisticated and, apparently, the Master of Professed was not alarmed by it. But I am alarmed by it! I find it dismaying in a religious who is supposed to be ordained a priest in four years. And, most important, I think there is a strong possibility that all of your questioning, however dialectic or academic in tone, springs from an area of very real and dangerous doubt in you, doubt of your faith and doubt of yourself. I'm especially worried about this when I add to it your well-known interest in every sort of religious deviation and quackery, from Zen Buddhism and yoga to black magic, spiritualism, alchemy, the raising of the dead, and I don't know what all. I'm sure you're aware, MacIver, that my judgment of your fitness for solemn vows may very well be definitive. I can assure you that this foolishness about the Saharans has severely damaged your candidacy as far as I am concerned. My advice to you is to set about repairing that damage, if you can, before it comes time for me to pass final judgment. I suggest you get busy being a

Titan novice, and a far better one than you've been to date."

The priest's sneer had gradually faded into a quite sinister frown. He turned slowly, dramatically, walked around behind his desk and stood there facing Aubrey, his eyes lean and eager, his attitude that of a perched bird. The novice sat in the silence, looking at the old priest in glances, casting about for a beginning to his reply, certainly daunted by the force and flow of the Master's attack and pained by its accuracy. And a first sensation of unreality began to visit him, a dim image of himself actually seated there requesting his release, actually preparing to quit. He thought of all the time between his first day as a Titan and this final day, and of all those who had begun with him and of all those who had left before him—all those who had done that incredible thing (that act that was always more distressing to those who remained than to him who went away, or so it naturally seemed, that act that haunted those who remained yet was no more admitted by them to consciousness than it was forgiven, was for those who remained as nearly unthinkable an act with reference to themselves as was deliberate mortal sin) and realized that he had always known this final day would come for him but had never allowed himself to imagine its sense of loss, its threat, its very finality, its pain.

And he thought, Dear God, yes, how easy to remain here. How easy to wrap myself in my median mantle and climb into my cozy little choir stall beneath that golden dome and take my vows with the rest, and move to another mansion in good time, and go on moving from mansion to crenelated mansion, up one side of the good Hudson and down the other and beyond, but not far beyond, and pass my days in Gothic, overstuffed comfort, letting discipline and fervor slip away until I am fat and lazy and lukewarm beyond warming, until I have blown my soul into mediocrity in the smoke of ten thousand clear Havana cigars. Dear God, why not? Who will say me nay? Unless I say me nay.

And he said, "Father, I'm sorry, but I am as near to certain as I can be about my vocation to the Saharan Fathers. I realize my shortcomings as a religious, and I appreciate your summation of them, your very accurate summation. But I still must go."

The priest waited a few seconds, as if he expected more, but then said, "Well! Of course, you are quite free to go, MacIver. But you distress me! Is that all you have to say?"

"Father, I *had* more to say, but I don't see how I can make my explanations acceptable to you. Or my motives."

"How is that? It would appear you have little faith in your supposed decision if my poor words could so disconcert you." Aubrey held his silence, looking down. Then he peeked up to see Father Finnegan taking a long smiling look at his fingernails as he said through a long, wearied sigh, "May I remind you, MacIver, that I am your lawfully constituted superior in religion—the voice of God as far as you are concerned, according to canon law and our Holy Rule."

"You are my lawfully constituted superior, Father, as long as I am a member of this community."

"And you are *still* a member of this community, MacIver."

"Not in intention, Father. That's the whole reason I'm here." Aubrey spoke quietly, but with gathered firmness.

Father Finnegan, for the first time since the interview began, experienced difficulty with his condescending smile. It waned for an instant, clung precariously to dry lips, went atremble, nearly vanished, and never afterward regained its full wattage. Aubrey watched, seeing the first touch of surprise, even confusion, arrive in the priest's expression, the rare sight of the Master coming to loose ends, searching for what to try next. And Father Finnegan's hesitation ended in a heavy, surrendering blow. He fell backward into his chair, leaving eight long streaks across the shining desktop after his dragging fingers. He observed the streaks, leaned forward, and rubbed at them vigorously with the sleeves of his habit. Then he looked up at Aubrey, and his expression, his mood, seemed suddenly to change. "Has it gone that far, then?" he asked quietly.

"Yes, Father."

"I'm very sorry to hear it. Perhaps if you had come to me sooner . . ." But he dismissed this, almost sheepishly, with a toss of his choir sleeves. "All right, MacIver. You were obviously aware that I was rather more forceful than good manners or charity ordinarily would have permitted. As you know, my duty is to test, and to discourage, if possible, any decision to leave the Order. However, while I apologize for the bluntness of my delivery, I retract none of my judgments. You are far from exemplary as a religious. You are bright and apparently blessed with an indestructible vocation to the holy priesthood, indestructible considering its survival of all the callous-

23

ness with which you have treated it. God, quite clearly I would say, wants you a priest, and I would be less than candid if I told you I thought otherwise. But I must tell you, with equal candor, that if the Saharan Fathers should ask me for an opinion as to your short-comings—which they certainly will do—I will not only report on them with exactitude, but will also suggest they put you on bread and water for a year or two until some of your insouciance has been, shall we say, neutralized."

"I understand, Father."

"You understand nothing, MacIver. Let me explain. And, allow me to ask a few questions. I am fully aware that your father is a famous and wealthy man, and that he has made generous gifts of money to our order. If the expenses of any Titan have been more than paid, yours have. I was hoping you'd bring that up, but you were too—how shall I put it?—shifty." Father Finnegan frowned. "And I know your right name but, for some reason, I see you as MacIver. Now, that's very strange, because I don't ever remember knowing a MacIver. But there you are." The priest gazed out the window, blinking.

There was a prolonged silence. Aubrey stirred on his chair. "You'll want me to leave in the morning, Father?"

"I don't want you to leave at all." The Master joined his hands palm to palm, folded his fingers, then raised a steeple with his fore-fingers and put his nose in at the front door. "Tell me. Has it occurred to you that this desire to go somewhere else, especially to such a roman-tic place as the Sahara—the long-flowing white robes and the ladies peering through their fascinators and the Riff song playing in the background—have you thought that it might just all be a temptation from the devil? Here you are, about to take solemn vows, begin your theological preparation for the priesthood. Can you imagine to what lengths the Devil would go to prevent you—particularly you, with your academic brilliance?"

Aubrey approached his barricade cautiously and peeked over it in certain astonishment at this new Father Finnegan. What's upon us? The father-son approach? Careful, now. Thumbs in cummerbund, boy. Formality does it. "I've considered that it might be a temptation, Father. But I don't think so."

Father Finnegan ripped his chapel into two hoary fists and brought both down shatteringly on Ashurbanipal's tomb. "You don't *think* so! What you mean is, you don't *think!*" He leaped to his feet, took two turns around his chair, and marched to the window, still rubbing his fists together. Then, abruptly, he relaxed. Perhaps he caught a reflection of himself in the sunlit glass. For whatever reason, he closed his eyes, pressed his lips firmly together, and was silent. Aubrey decided to sit the interval out. The priest turned, finally, took his chair, and laid his hands, palms down, flat out on the desk. He raised his eyes slowly and spoke with the rasping weariness of an old man.

"I'm sorry, Strycker. But, you see, I'm an historian by training and avocation. I'm even supposed to be writing a book about the Borgias, or something equally frivolous. If history has taught me anything, it is this: most human beings think, not with their brains, but with their genital organs. Freud confirmed it, but no good historian needs his confirmation. The whole history of Christianity is nothing more than a record of the Church's attempt to raise the human thought center from the bowels three feet—give or take a few inches—straight up. Up to somewhere near the cranial cavity. And a cavity it usually is. Some men, and very few women, are able actually to raise the thought center a foot or so to somewhere near the heart, but most of them, especially those who become religious, never seem to succeed in raising it beyond the abdominal cavity. Now, you are a very young man, Strycker, and, though intelligent and perhaps very intelligent, I doubt seriously that you have gotten your motivating thoughts out of your pubic area yet. At the risk of sounding prurient—although at my age prurience is a difficult matter, I assure you—I would guess that at least half, if not three-quarters, of your motivation is sexual. Oh, nothing directly sexual, please understand. But obliquely so. You must see that I am being extremely frank, probably too frank. But I want you to examine yourself carefully in the light of this possibility. I don't mean that you are leaving this novitiate with the formed intention of seducing a woman, or anything like it. But I do mean that you are leaving with thoughts of adventure, of the impression you will make upon your family and friends, of a sea voyage perhaps during which you will parade the decks in somber black to the titillation of all ladies within eyeshot, of a warm reception among the Saharan Fathers here and abroad, of the adulation of the natives on that day you arrive among them, especially when they discover— which you are secretly certain they will—that your father is a famous man, a man of the movies. And so on. And before you answer, Strycker,

25

let me say this: Whether or not any of these things are now in your conscious mind, whether or not you acknowledge any of these, or their like, as present now within you, they will rise up sooner or later to haunt and distract you. And I, an old and much-traveled man, can assure you that because you are intelligent, because you do apparently have at least an intellectual awareness of what Jesus Christ came down here to impart, you will one day know—know, as surely as you know that you are often tempted to unchastity—that the only important thing is to meet the Christ of the New Testament head on and courageously, and that this can be done—this immense, incredible, transcending thing—as well right here on this Hudson River hillside as it can in Algiers. It is all just earth, Strycker, spinning like the eyeball of an idiot, and if it's the sand you want, with the hot sun on it, may I suggest that you wait until next summer when you'll be back at St. Titus' Bay?"

Aubrey decided his best answer to this was silence. And there was a silence that seemed to get shorter as it went on. It folded back upon itself, gathering its seconds into a single bright moment of utter clarity. Aubrey sat in it strangely light-headed, weightless, acutely conscious of the turning of the earth. And his whole thought was: only man is free. Only man can choose between yes and no. Only man can choose to be or not to be, to stay or to go. The rest of nature is bound, by law, by instinct, by habit; only man can form the intention to run contrary to, or with, any or all of these. Listen to the old earth, groaning down there on its axis. Listen. Leap into the air and hang there a few minutes, and the old earth must inevitably bring your chair right back around under you again. But you—you can drop into it, or you can wait until the Sahara comes around and fall into the first oasis. And, for a time, it seemed to him that he was suspended in air, beyond gravity, held aloft by the simple awful power of his free will, and he kept watching the world and Father Finnegan and the Sahara go by, and kept waiting for someone to tell him what to do.

But Father Finnegan was motionless in his chair, his nose back in the chapel of his hands, staring out the window. And the silence went on. From far down on the river came the whine of an outboard motorboat. A breeze moved the curtains at the window, and invaded the giant oak tree on the back lawn, and he watched the dark green of it shiver and flash in the sun. The smell of moist earth came into the room, and the world seemed warm and familiar, and he felt an inchoate desire to go out and wrap his arms around a tree.

"All right!" Father Finnegan said suddenly. He didn't look at Aubrey, but went to the window, raised it a bit higher, and leaned his hands on the sill. "Fine day," he murmured, peeping out of the tops of his eyes at the sky. "Never wear sunglasses, Strycker. They prevent you from seeing things as they actually are." He drummed his fingers on the sill with startling force. "But it may be that in the Sahara . . ." He turned and crossed to Aubrey and stood over him, arms folded, bouncing lightly on the balls of his feet. "You have made up your mind, have you?"

"Yes, Father."

"You're concerned about the salvation of the Arabs?"

"I think less that than about the salvation of myself."

"Good answer, boy. You should have said that sooner. Now. Why do you feel you can't save your soul in the Titan Order?" Father Finnegan's tone was soft, almost benign.

"I didn't say that, Father. It's just that I think I would be a more effective priest, and a holier priest, with the Saharans. And, therefor, more likely to—to persevere." Aubrey hated the word persevere, but it had trapped him.

"Why do you think you'd be more effective or holier?"

"It's very hard to explain, Father." Aubrey saw his hands begin to move expressively in front of him before he started to speak and tried to haul them in, but didn't succeed. Then he forgot his hands and listened, aware that, as happened so often with him—as, in fact, he so often planned it—he was likely, under this pressure, to come closer to the truth in his rushed words than he ever had been able to do in his meditations. And suddenly, effusively, he began to talk.

And, near the beginning, he said, "My brother Arnie, my sister Aline, and I were brought up in the thirteenth century. In a great fenced medieval close of a house by my mother and my grandmother. Both of them dying, my grandmother of old age and my mother because she's a fanatical convert and thinks that dying is the sole business of the good Catholic. *Except* in so far as she believes that the good Catholic mother has the additional duty of settling her children safely into religious life. All that keeps her alive, I think, is the hope that she'll see me ordained, and the hope that Arnie will recover well enough to have another go at it. The house used to be

27

full of religious statutary, medals, crucifixes, holy pictures, rosaries, prayer books, missals, Bibles, and volumes on religious subjects. My mother had, and still has, a shrine in her room, complete with candles, crucifix, holy water font, an incense pot, scarlet and gold hangings, and a color photograph of my father. Every night in my memory, after my mother's conversion, I knelt with her and with Arnie before that shrine, sometimes for an hour, praying for my father's salvation. Religion became very nearly the sole acceptable topic at table, although my grandmother, who is neither Catholic nor religious, occasionally introduced discussion of her childhood, so that we might be suddenly swooped into the nineteenth century. But seldom beyond it. It was, always, a house in which few were welcome and no single thing less than most rigidly formal and invariably ordained— a house from which, even when we got outside the gates to go to school, there was really no escape. Such an atmosphere made it predictable that neither Arnie, nor Aline, nor I would ever seriously entertain any other ambition but the religious life; predictable that seminary life would hold no terrors for us; and predictable too, that the three of us would become insufferable little sanctimonious snobs. And we did. Precociously pious and too precious for words, the model children, the untouchables, the rich kids who had oh such noble intentions of throwing all our daddy's money away in the name of Jesus. My grandmother hated our guts by the time Arnie and I were eleven and might still if my father hadn't come home from war. He took one look at what had happened to us, and declared the Reformation, the Renaissance, and the Age of Enlightenment all in one afternoon. Arnie immediately sided with my father, and, somehow, I sided with my mother. Eulalia, my grandmother, acted as referee. And whenever my father would visit, the battle would be on. My father would have read up on Darwin or Marx or Freud or some topic he thought would be good for us, and would have bought every book available on that topic, and would attempt to deliver us a lecture on it while my mother screamed at him from the sidelines. Arnie would scoop up the books and take to the upstairs, and I would stay with Aline—who usually sat there crying quietly—and I would listen and issue an objection now and then but mostly just look on as the three of them went on drinking and arguing for hours. Until things got too bitter, or my mother ran crying from the room, or until they were all too drunk or exhausted to

28

continue. Then, after an hour's rest, we would have dinner, and it would start all over again. And go on into the night. I'm not exaggerating. Not a bit, Father. And this went on, off and on, for seven years, until I left for the seminary with Arnie."

"Your mother won all those arguments?"

"No, Father, not at all. She won the war but not the arguments. And she didn't so much win the war as she starved the troops into submission. My father had us only one day a week. On that seventh day my mother rested and came on so strong and diligently that during those other six days there was scarcely a moment of our lives when Rexfordia was not within swooping distance."

"Rexfordia? Your mother?"

"Yes, Father. My father did all he could. He took us to fights, taught us to drive, box, fence, shoot, skate, ski, and whistle at girls. He even taught us to drink, starting when we were fifteen—beer, wine, whisky, liqueurs. He was delighted when we managed to get drunk with him. He didn't allow us to smoke, however, until we were sixteen."

Father Finnegan's eyes were wide with surprise, but his sarcasm had not deserted him. He said, "Well! Obviously, your father didn't want you to stunt your growth!" He snorted out a smile.

"What I want to emphasize, Father, is the anger of my family," Aubrey said quickly, ignoring the priest's levity, "the pride, ruthlessness, bitterness, the vicious tongues of all of us, including even Aline when she got old enough to get into it. The pattern was thirteenth-century piety except on Wednesday nights, when my father came to dinner, and Saturdays, when he would either deliver his lecture and stay again for dinner, or else take us kids into New York for lunch and a show or something. When my father was around, it was strictly nineteenth- and twentieth-century recrimination. And, of course, the piety and the recrimination were complementary. Piety taught us that we were evil fallen creatures, and recrimination put that theme to music. Both, as a matter of fact, were long-standing traditions in the Strycker-Milligan complex, but we kids had no way of knowing that beforehand. We listened and learned and, finally, participated and attacked one another. Every meal was a mere accompaniment to a running quarrel, a continuum of nourishing and negating on the way to indigestion. Food and uproar went together, as did Strycker and Milligan, which is to say not at all, but inevitably.

Suddenly, the cathedral would give way to catharsis, the pursuit of perfection would give way to the pursuit of imperfection in one another. Everything was challenged, ridiculed—from table manners and slips in grammar to the shape of one's face—often good-humoredly but always with a sort of mocking promise of anger to come. And it always did come. There would be the most vicious possible accusations—lying, cheating, stealing, adultery, madness, homosexuality, cowardice, cancer, syphilis—everything from my mother's once ordering me to put my hands on the table because she was certain I was playing with myself during dinner, to my father's once accusing my grandmother, quite seriously, of poisoning her husband to death."

"Wait, wait," Father Finnegan said, waving the flat of one hand agitatedly, his expression informed with shock. "In the name of heaven, why? Why would such things go on?"

"Well, Father, I think it began as a kind of game on the part of my mother's mother. A test of toughness, a contempt for conventional forms and acceptance, and an extremely high regard for wit and vituperation. My father and Eulalia made a fine art of the game."

"Some game. But what's the point here, Strycker? Most of us who go on to the priesthood manage to overcome defects in our backgrounds, more or less severe."

"The point is, I didn't, and haven't, overcome the defects in mine. Arnie and I came to the seminary antisocial, belligerent, convinced of our intellectual superiority. We were Darwinians. We believed in the privilege of the bright. We believed that to be charitable was to encourage stupidity. We were almost incapable of living together with others in harmony. There's no doubt that Arnie was the leader, my mentor. But even after he left I wasn't able to beat down family pride, to become a member of the community. The idea that I am exceptional, privileged, apart, is so deep in me that I've never been able to come anywhere near humility. It is always a concession, a betrayal of my background. I can respect humility, but not unless it is accompanied by brains. Otherwise humility might be simplemindedness. How can you tell? If a man is academically bright, I figure his humility is a clever sham. And if he isn't bright, I figure that in acting humble he's just making the best of a bad situation. When I have found brains and humility together, unmistakably, I've stood in awe of the possessor. And I've gone back to try again. But brains and humility in concert, in one person, are very rare,

Father, as you well know. So rare that I hold out little hope of my being swept away on a tide of good example."

Father Finnegan laughed shortly. "No. I wouldn't say you were in great danger of that. But you still haven't gotten to the point. The Saharans live a community life and, I daresay, have a certain regard for humility among the members of their society."

"I'm sorry to be taking so long, Father. I'll try to be brief."

"No Titan ever, in the history of the Order, has been brief. I wouldn't want you to shatter any precedents."

"Seriously, Father, if I were to remain with the Titans, I'd be living a much closer community life than I would with the Saharans. In the Saharans, I'd be put out on a station for months at a time alone or with one or two other priests at the most. Also, the chances are strong that in the Titans I'd end up going on for a higher degree, going on to teach, and so on, and all I can see in that is a reinforcement of intellectual pride . . ."

"Unless somebody should pin your intellectual ears back." The priest smiled evenly, neither confirming nor denying the pleasure this thought seemed to give him. "But go on, go on. You're finally getting to the point."

"The chances of my being asked to teach, and write books, and get near academics at all in the Saharans are slim. And even if it happened that I were assigned to a Titan parish, I'd be dealing with the same sort of people I'm now having, and always have had, such trouble dealing with, on anything like a charitable basis. The people in this very community. That is, with Americans who resent my attitude, my damned condescension, on sight. Who sense it in me despite my best efforts to conceal it, and who, therefore, finally succeed in bringing condescension out of me full-blown. In the Saharans, I'd be dealing with simple people, who will look upon me as an exceptional being in the first place, as privileged, so that we would start, you might say, even. And my hope is that those simple people would shame me into some idea of what pure humility, under God and nature, means. There would be no occasion among those simple people for exercise of my reputed expertise in insult and wit and conversational subtlety. Everything would be boiled down to the essentials, and I'd live in their poverty with them, and deal with life and death, hell and heaven, and look right into eternity every day of my life. I'd move out of the sphere of my mother's influence. She wouldn't be

31

able to make any more of her grand, chauffeured, gift-laden arrivals, which have been affronting me and my classmates for almost five years. Also she might begin to understand at long last that I have no wish to become a secular priest in the New York archdiocese."

The priest chuckled as Aubrey fairly shouted the last words of this sentence. "It would seem, if I may judge by the tone of your voice, that your mother is a real issue here."

"She's real enough, Father. But I don't think she's a major issue."

"All right. I'll accept that. Now, could you sum up?"

"I—I don't know that I can sum up, Father. But whatever else is true, this is true. I want to go to a place where life is not easy, where pleasures are few, where my life will have a single, hard, unqualified purpose, and where any ambivalence or deviation on my part will stand out in sharp relief. In the Titan Order there are too many legitimate ways to waste time. Even in the seminary. In Boston there was the Literary Club, the Catholic Action Club, the Dramatic Club, the Seminary Guild, two or three kinds of discussion clubs—all of them legitimate and even useful. And I belonged to every one of them. Only when I got here, where there are none of those things, where the life is much more quiet and more regular, was I able to see that I had dabbled away four years. And I'm convinced, if I stay with the Titans, I'll go right on dabbling years away. I think to be a good priest in this order—or any noncloistered American order—requires an iron will. I haven't got an iron will, Father."

"Damned few of us have. Nobody of my acquaintance. But you have a good argument. Not that you're telling the whole truth, by any means."

"I'm telling it as best I can," Aubrey said defensively.

"Of course you are. I mean that the whole truth is just not known to you. Your deepest motives are hidden from you. As I said before . . ." The priest pulled at his nose. "But I did say it before, so never mind. However, one possible hidden motive, as an example. Didn't your brother Arnold—before he left us so unfortunately—didn't he have the Saharan Fathers in mind?"

"Yes, Father. That's when I first thought of it. How did you hear about that?"

"It's a small order, Strycker. I hear everything. Now!" he said, rising, coming around in front of his desk with measured step, pulling at his nose, snuffling. "I wonder if it has occurred to you that you might, unconsciously, see yourself as Arnold's surrogate."

"It has, and I don't. I admit that Arnie thought of the Saharans first and all that. But I would have thought of them on my own. Eventually."

"How can you be sure?"

"Because they are the right choice for me."

Father Finnegan shook his head. "Ah, youth." He smiled down, much mellowed; a great gray benevolence. "Why not a cloistered order?"

"I don't think I'm suited for it."

"Neither do I. Tell me this. Does it bother you that, in effect, you are running away from a whole infantry of difficulties? Surely you know you will take them with you?"

"I'll take them with me, sure. But they'll starve for want of material objects. If it made sense for me to run away from the distractions of the world when I came to the Titans, doesn't it make even more sense for me to run farther away from them by going to the Saharans?"

"Well, it's not a perfect syllogism, Strycker, but I take your meaning." The priest grinned and tapped one finger against his teeth. "One last thing. How about your family? What will they have to say about this?"

"They won't like it."

"Does that bother you?"

"No, Father. Because it won't really bother them, once they get used to the idea. My father gets to Africa once or twice a year anyway."

"What on earth for?"

"Hunting, Father. Big-game hunting."

"Oh yes. Of course. I've seen pictures in the papers. Big beard, big hat, big horns." He pinched his nose. "Ah, the animal's horns, of course." He turned slowly. "Yes, yes." He walked back behind his desk very deliberately. "So! You'll be going south, Strycker?"

"South? Oh yes, Father. New York."

"Train tomorrow at—well, Brother Leo will know. He's still chauffeur?"

"No, Father. Mr. Kipp and I—this month."

"Kipp? Oh, that won't do. No. We can't have your Boswell taking you down to the train. How did I happen to assign you two to the same job?"

"I don't know, Father."

"I wish that fellow would get his hair cut short! Well! See Leo Stuckey. I think he's out fiddling with the tractor today. Arrange for him to take you down. Tell him he's excused from office this afternoon so he can help you get your trunk down. Oh!" Father Finnegan grabbed at his buttocks with both hands, then dug through the side vent of his soutane to a hip pocket, and brought forth a wallet. It looked like a withered monkey's paw. The priest touched his nose once, glanced at Aubrey, licked thumb and forefinger, brought the wallet up close to his face, scowled into it. "Will five dollars be enough?"

"I think so, Father. I'll return it by mail as soon as I get home."

"Oh, well!" Father Finnegan said, issuing the first laughter Aubrey had ever heard from him—a sound like a hatchet sliding on ice. "In that case," he cackled, "take ten!" Expansively, he counted out a five and four ones on the desktop. Then he frowned, grunted, thumbed impatiently among the cards and worn papers in the wallet, glanced a couple of times at Aubrey, who had come to stand by the desk, closed the main section of the wallet, turned it endwise and went to a small, cleverly concealed zipper pocket, started to unzip the pocket, but, suddenly, shot his eyes around at Aubrey with a look of such black accusation that Aubrey, caught in the act and wholly guilty, looked immediately away. But Aubrey contrived to watch out of the corner of his eye as Father Finnegan extracted two half dollars from the side pocket, placed them side by side on the bills, and pushed the money slowly across the desk toward him. "There you are," said the Master grandly, as if he had just discharged the national debt. "Ten dollars!"

"Thank you, Father," Aubrey said meekly; and, with what innocence he could muster, trying not to observe the restoration of the pawlike exchequer to its sanctuary, he pocketed the money.

"Now! Have you mentioned your departure to any of the novices?"

"Ah, yesterday I told Mr. Kipp I was coming to see you, Father."

"Hum. Too bad, too bad." The priest went to the window. "Well, say no more to him about it. Don't even say goodbye to him. Say goodbye to no one. There's nothing more distracting to a community, as you must know, than the defection of one of its members. Just steel yourself against whatever sentiment you might feel. The novices will understand. Or if they don't, I understand. Goodbyes

34

in these cases do nothing for anybody. Except harm. I'll speak to Kipp tomorrow. Buck him up. Give him a tot of rum or something." He turned to Aubrey, his eyes softened and kind. "You understand. Just disappear."

Then he was walking toward Aubrey with his right arm half raised. Aubrey realized that the priest was giving him his blessing, and fell to his knees. The Master's hands rested briefly upon his head, and Aubrey heard the benediction pronounced slowly and distinctly, the voice ancient and gentle, the words so familiarly spoken that one might have thought the priest was talking with God about the weather.

Then Aubrey was backing out of the room and Father Finnegan was by the window, nodding and wishing him good luck, and just as Aubrey was closing the door the priest was saying, "Yes, yes, they'll accept you, I'm sure. They need priests as badly as we do. And if God is with you, and you keep your mouth shut, MacIver, you might amount to something after all."

# THE FIRST PART

# · THREE ·

AND THE SIXTEEN following hours, between the moment he closed the door on Father Finnegan and that quiet time when the New York Central local gave a whistle and a lurch and started out of Chelsea station, were unreal, nearly sleepless, and flew off up the pipe to eternity as if aware he wanted them gone. Which he did, yet somehow enjoyed them, their certain easy melancholy, their readily bearable regret about leaving behind the people and things of his almost five years.

Somewhere near the end of the first hour, after a wide-ranging and profane search, he found Brother Leo Stuckey—the only candidate for the Titan Brotherhood then at the novitiate, and not a shiningly representative one—on the afterdeck of the Fordson tractor, dragging a double plow up and down a thirty-acre field just inside the front gate. Leo, almost obscured by a vast cloud of oil fumes, rode sidesaddle on the tractor seat with the trip rope for the plow in one hand. He was frowning down at the plow, because, as even Aubrey could see, the shares were not taking a deep enough bite. Aubrey walked over to one end of the field and watched the tractor come on and smelled the sweetness of the open ground, and felt the impatience drain out of him. Because, what the hell, there were more important things than helping a novice escape. So that he was entirely amiable about Leo's almost running him over, and about his slowness to believe that Aubrey was really really leaving for good, and about his little homily on how Aubrey should think twice, and about his request that Aubrey stand on the plow for a couple of runs to see if that would make the shares bite deeper. The which he did, and it did make the shares bite deeper, so that Leo, who was redheaded and from Dodge City, Kansas, and had the plainsman's syndrome of reckless caution in all things, allowed as how he would try some sandbags on the plow the next day. Aubrey rode the tow bar back to the barn and got there hoarse from trying to talk to Leo over the grating thunder of the engine, and very nearly asphyxiated from its fumes. But there was finally an end to the clamor and clank, and a period of conspiratorial waiting until the others should have gone to chapel for Divine Office, and then they climbed to the second floor of the barn and brought down Aubrey's black trunk and three suitcases, and carried them up to Aubrey's room, with Leo, now full of angular, Adam's-apple eloquence, informing Aubrey that he was making a great mistake and that the Titan Order was destined to rule the Church, having made great strides in Kansas since the Depression. He got rid of Leo only by promising to look over Kansas if he should ever find himself at loose ends in the Middle West.

He went then to his packing, and had filled the bottom of the trunk with shoes, boots, shower clogs, galoshes, a raincoat, and a suit of levis, and was about to dump in a drawerful of socks and underwear, when it came to him that he had no need of any of it. Most of it was fairly new. Rexfordia the Shopper was always sending him boxfuls of things from Abercrombie and Fitch (even after he had precipitated a four-letter exchange by telling her he approved of Abercrombie but didn't want another damned thing she got from Fitch), but almost none of it would be right for Africa, and Rexfordia would insist on buying him all new things anyway, so why the hell cart it home? He'd just drop the word to Leo, Leo would tell a few close friends, there would be a brief trampling rush, and within an hour of his departure his chattels would have new caretakers.

The idea pleased him inordinately, and he whistled a *Salve Regina* as he emptied bureau, closet, and bookshelf into the trunk and two suitcases, and stacked the suitcases on the trunk, and stacked what was left over on top of the suitcases. It made a nice substantial mound of worldly goods there between the two north windows, and he was pleased with it, and patted it on the snowshoes several times out of pure satisfaction. He had withheld his tennis racket, a Tad Imperial that had become practically an extension of his right arm, and a thin-paper Spanish edition of *Don Quixote* that he was not sure could be replaced, and hesitated over them now, but finally threw both up on top of the snowshoes and tossed the third suitcase after them. The only thing he could not bring himself to sacrifice was a red high-school letter sweater with a single white stripe on the left sleeve and the legend STA (St. Titus Academy) on the back. He did toss it up on top of the third suitcase, and stood there looking at it for a time, testing how he felt about it, working his mouth and shifting his shoulders as if he were about to make a speech, until it occurred to him that no honorable novice would wear another man's letter sweater anyway, and he snatched it jealously back from receivership. He located a large shoe box, stuffed the sweater into it, put the shoe box on the bed next to his black suit, white shirt, black tie, black hat, shaving kit, journal, and a small bundle of letters and papers, stepped back smiling, clapped his hands once, rubbed them together, and said, "Why, I'm virtually divested of vested things. Divestment's just what I needed. Yes, indeed."

Then the community came marching into the dining room from the chapel with a sound far below like cows coming home; and after that the Latin growl of the grace before meals, and the scraping back and forth of chairs, and Henry Fowler's voice taking up the reading of the *Autobiography* of a holy woman called Venerable Anne of St. Bartholomew. Then Father Finnegan remembered it was a free day and rang the bell, releasing the immediate roar of several dozen spontaneous conversations. He could still go down and eat, and was tempted, but rallied his resistance around his nostrils and the lingering smell of the gristle stew, and decided in favor of a shower and shave.

He extracted a clean towel and his bathrobe from the chattel pile, patted it on a protruding fishing rod, and assured it that towel and robe would inevitably be returned. He stuffed what he had on, including the tennis shoes, into a bag of dirty clothes and added the bag to the pile. He went out frowning at the bathrobe as he knotted it around him, it being a large, white, becollared and becrested garment of inch-thick terry cloth, weighing a half stone dry and at least two stone wet, sent to him airmail special delivery (as if there had been some rush about it) by Kermit from the Hotel George V in Paris three years before, with a note saying that Kermit had paid the concierge for it and that, therefore, Aubrey could wear it in good conscience, and that he (Kermit) thought it just the thing to protect one's monastic nethers during those ball-curdling Boston winters. Aubrey had written back, thanking his father for the bulletproof winding sheet, saying that it was the very thing to wear to his martyrdom (which would occur as soon as they found some more lions for Boston Garden). But Aubrey had worn it for Kermit's sake and because he figured the itch it gave him was good mortification. He was now perversely warmed by the thought that both robe and itch would soon be the sovereign property of Brother Leo Stuckey.

An hour later, bathed, beardless, and combed, he went down to the chapel, and remembered, as he approached the side door through the runway from the back of the main house, that there would be a Holy Hour in progress. He opened the door to the sound of Father Finnegan's voice, made a double genuflection, and got to his choir stall with a minimum of noise—causing only two or three heads to turn to note his late arrival.

Father Finnegan was reading from a spiritual volume about how the true Christian believes that God's providence either ordains or permits everything that takes place among men for the spiritual good of all, and how the true Christian must submit his will to the will of God even with reference to the evil visited upon him as effects of the sinful acts of others—wars, persecutions, famine, revenge, and so on —because this evil comes to him under the seal of God's wisdom and through His inscrutable, permissive providence. It was one of the Master's favorite themes, and, much as it appeared to sadden him, he hammered away at it on almost every public occasion (leading Aubrey to believe that permissive providence had unloaded an extraordinary amount of gratuitous evil effects upon the old gentleman at various times in his life, and that the good priest was simply doing his best to convince himself of the inherent justice of it).

The Master was kneeling at a prie-dieu in the sanctuary half turned toward the novices, ancient face bent to the open book, eyes blinking in the blaze of electric and candle light from the altar and from the shimmering golden sunburst around the sacred pyx, white hair tumbled forward to touch the steel rims of his glasses, his voice strong but somehow caustic and raw, as if vital parts of the speaking apparatus had been torn and shredded and were vibrating now painfully, the nerve ends exposed; or as if he could no more speak than swallow the doctrine of permissive providence without a throaty clutching of gall, without a lifting of vocal hackles and a tearing of all words that sought passage.

Aubrey closed his eyes and listened and thought that some enterprising record company ought to sign the old man to make an album of readings from the Book of Job, or from the Lamentations of Jeremias; a voice to speak, to and for all ages, the weary litanies of human pain; a fit figure for an apocalypse, a man and a voice to protest the crack of doom. And he thought of his own will to the priesthood, which he had always understood primarily as a will to reduce the sum of human pain in himself and in others—as a gesture, if only a gesture, toward silencing the great sad sound of the human midge —and he felt his soul already shrinking back from the first ordeal of pain his decision would present, and wondered if it were necessary he endure it, wondered, a first time, if he required himself to go home to say his goodbyes.

And he considered this until the sounds of the closing ceremonies brought his eyes open. He looked up; watched the last vagrant wisps of incense lift high above the altar toward the round pietà window, its lower hemisphere tilted open so that the Mother of Sorrows appeared to be holding only the upper half of the dead Christ, the metallic diameter of the window (a representation of the Guenther sculpture) dividing the corpus above the loincloth, and he saw the incense hang for a time in the opening, saw it lighted into a deeply rubescent haze by the long final reaches of sunlight from the west, its redness precisely that of the stained glass at the wound in the chest of Christ, and its motion giving the wound movement and the blood of it gentle flow; and he thought of his mother and his brother and saw them there, and called his seeing right and just, and saw himself in the angled lower hemisphere, out of joint, the dispensable legs and belly of his twin, but no more; an adjunct his mother might kiss and anoint as might that other Mother the wounds in the feet, but an adjunct nonetheless; a completion that only could add areas of pain, a complement that gave mild but acknowledged offense; and watched the ruddled incense disperse and drift in its tatters at last out into the still May twilight, and rose with the others to sing "Holy God, we praise Thy name," and thought, as he jerked the sleeves of

43

his habit free of the sweat at his wrists, that he could go out to Africa without saying goodbyes, without raising new fire to burn and bleed them and him again, without stirring those damned hot ashes again, but knew, even as he opened his mouth to sing (even while Billy Kipp tossed the skirts of his capuche up onto his shoulders and leaned into the console of the organ and sounded the lead notes just as Father Finnegan's lead foot struck the tiled floor of the sanctuary, and the thirty-four novices, arranged seventeen to a side in their white oak stalls, and the three servers at the altar, and the Master, and Billy Kipp as well, came, all of them, out of their hour's silence lustily and with the fervor of release) that he had neither the courage nor the cowardice for such a departure, knew that he wanted to see Arnie and Aline again if all it meant was a joining of injuries, that he wanted to see his mother again if all it meant was a meeting of mutually enraging disappointments, that he wanted to see his father again if all it meant was a lancing of old resignations; knew as he sang "Lord of all, we bow before Thee," that in order to begin again, he would have to return and face his beginnings once more, would have to bleed himself in his blood once more, would have to offer them one last chance to destroy him, and himself one last chance to understand and love them, would have to face his living as if they were not his dead, would have to take himself once again among them with a fixed smile, exactly as though his presence were welcome and salutary and somewhat anticipated, exactly as though his presence were an assuagement instead of an irritation, a diminution and not a summation of old and ragged wounds; and he sang "Everlasting is Thy name," and thought of Christ saying, "Leave the dead to bury their dead. It is for thee to go out and proclaim God's kingdom," and he protested with that other, saying, "Lord, I will follow Thee, but let me first take leave of my friends," and heard Jesus answering, "No one who looks behind him, when he has once put his hand to the plow, is worthy of the kingdom of God"; and knelt in his place and thought of the fierce young Jew who had spoken those words, and nodded at their truth, yet was aware that he could not begin to be so fierce; knew, even as he stared at the tabernacle and felt the divine presence of the speaker and prayed for the gift of indifference to family, that he would go home to take his leave, that he would look back from whatever plow, would take his surest direction from a short look back; and went on kneeling in his place until the others were gone and the chapel lights off—until the chapel was empty except as the final lighted turnings of the earth brought those saints in the west windows to vivid, prismatic life, a life of burning, blue-veined, nearly antic disturbance, during which each without exception put forth hands, tears, and dreadful eyes, making gestures at first benevolent but finally imprecatory, pleading with him, and then warning him to stay where he was rather than return to any least earthly affection—but held out against all of those imaginings and impulses that would have him surrender his blood to his bond, and turned his face from the sun-shot windows and from the curtained tabernacle and looked east, out through the bottom of the window at his left, its lower tenth hinged and open to the back lawn, to the extravagant fragrance of the grass, mowed that afternoon for the first time since the abrupt and insistent coming of winter in the middle of the preceding autumn, open to a clear view across the lawn of the screen of birches along the path to the convent, young trees all proudly barked in their white as he in his, their leaves close and delicate and beginning to stir in the first evening breeze, giving back a sound like nuns at prayer, and listened and watched as the day gathered one last flush of light, sending it up from the valley below, roseate and glowing and touching all the air for a long moment before it suddenly faded and night came rapidly on; and thought of the single given life of man and the awful finalities that attended it; the finality of time past (the passing of this latest of my eighty-six-hundred twilights, and how many more, how many); the finality of time to come (I am now nothing, and I attain to what I have been only as I reach to the future and seize it coming on and stamp it with the stuff of me before it, too, is merely past); the finality of space (of goings away and the land between, and the time it might take to return, so that in every step of your going out you die somewhat and go on dying as you go on stepping, and the same with your return, for space between is never really regained, nor time between ever made as never was, and so that the turning of a shoulder is a finality and a death, and, dear Christ, the burden); the finality of goodbyes (even if I should come back, and even if all concerned laugh off the affront of my going, and forgive, the goodbye shall have left its mark upon the bidder and the bade, a mark indelible and not available to recall, for no goodbye, for whatever reason, is ever really forgiven); the finality of love (whether given or withheld, the most exquisitely tuned moment tendered the human heart is that moment when the choice is made and somehow, and inevitably, revealed, and neither lover nor loved, unloving or unloved, can control the degree or the direction of the elation, or of the pain); the finality of any mortal act whatsoever (nothing done undone, nothing said unsaid, nothing thought unthought, and the consequence of each least of these susceptibly eternal); the finality of death (mine and anybody's, but mine day by day); and the terrible finality of judgment after death (that judgment being perhaps nothing more than the fixation of my mind, character, personality precisely as they were at the moment of my death, an eternal fixation, never to be any better and never to escape what I shall have made of myself—a just judgment, and judgment enough); and he measured his going away and the desert against the terms of all of these finalities and found that they simply became part of the single great finality—that he would go away and remain there until fixed in death—and glanced up at the darkened pietà window and saw that it was closed, that the belly and the legs and the wounded feet of Christ had been restored to Him, and to him and to them, and he took this as his point of departure, and looked away and stared into the hard oak of the stall in front of him until an image of his father came and quickly went, so that the image (and the trinity) was complete, and then put his face to his hands and said, "I am a forked futility except as I reach out to others, except as I reach out to Christ, except as I become a third point in that desperate triangle formed by God, man else, and I; that sorrowfully sounding triangle ever loathing to be flatted, that geometry of redemption ever seeking to strike its angularity, not to the awful collapse of the straight line vanishing at both ends to nothingness, but to that blessed round of perfect and unending love, that divine and infinite circle of love given and love received, that trinity of points upon a circumference of mutual affection with which this universe was meant to be girdled round from the time this time was decreed; and went on with a prayer (from A Manual of Sacred Chant by Joseph Mohr, printed in Germany, its imprimatur given at Ratisbon on the fifth of December, 1898, the stern and Germanic eloquence of which touched him more deeply and gave him more meaningful and properly dreadful dialogue for God than any other prayer book he had come across) "to Secure the Blessing of God in the Choice of a State of Life," and prayed: "O Jesus, Eternal Wisdom and most charitable Counsellor of

46

all who apply to thee, I come to consult thee, and to ask thee for light and direction. Let me see, I beseech thee, how I am to act, and what is most agreeable to thy will. Let me see, by means best known to thyself, what it is that thou requirest of me. Teach me in what manner I am to conduct myself, and the means I am to make use of, that all I do may succeed to thy glory, and the welfare of my soul. I offer thee a heart—a heart prepared to follow thy divine directions and to execute thy orders; because it is in thee that I place all my hopes, and I desire nothing more than the accomplishment of thy will. Let, therefore, thy divine light shine upon me, and do not abandon me to my own darkness."

He got up then and let himself out at the front door of the chapel and went down in the night to the terrace near the Virgin grotto, and stood there and listened to the sounds of the crickets and the night birds, and to that mysterious nocturnal hum of the Hudson, which, he thought, was perhaps only water moving on tamely within its banks, but was possibly, too, the river gods holding tenebrae, and grand council on such portentous matters as acceptable high-water marks, tugboat noises, and the coming of the ducks. There was no telling about the Hudson, what with its troll under every bridge.

He stood attentive, for a long time, making notes against a memory of the night. Then he walked very slowly back over the wet lawn to the circular driveway in front of the white statue of St. Titus and looked up at the great hulking packing-crate of a house. He waited until he had the words, then spoke softly, just above a whisper.

"Everybody knows that the best time to say goodbye to people of the race of men is when they are asleep. So, goodbye to you, each and every, and goodbye especially to you, Billy Kipp. And if Father Finnegan should—however wildly improbable it might sound—offer you a tot of rum tomorrow, make sure he tastes it first."

Then he went into the house and up to his bed and watched the four pine trees out his east window until they were hung with the stars beyond; watched until he fell aselep.

And he slept intermittently, falling in and out of an insistent technicolor dream, complete with camels, minarets, Sigmund Romberg's music, and a hot sweat, and featuring the blessed Charles de Foucauld and the unblessed Aubrey Strycker, both of whom, after an inflammatorily spiritual hour over mint ices in downtown Oran, were chased over, under, around, and past every sand dune from the

Algerian border to the Nile, by El Krim himself at the head of about forty thousand itinerant Berbers, all on horseback and displaying an incredible excess of murderous U.A.R. good spirits and small arms fire, until, just short of El Shab oasis, the unblessed Strycker was shot through the oblongata, and the blessed de Foucauld ran on ahead, crying, "In the name of the chased Christ, A.S.! Arise and sprint! Gamal Abdel Nasser is on his way to rescue us with the Stern gang!" And the dream ended with Aubrey's ambescent skull, still grinning piously and enthusiastically, if quite conscious and thirsty after more than ten years of sunshine, being approached by the first jeep of the *Cinerama Visits Jesus Christ* company, and the last mortal words Aubrey heard—just before his bone was ground under wheels, down and down irrevocably beneath the indifferent sand—were spoken by one of the principals in the jeep, who said, "Christ Jesus, Morris! Don't run over that skull! You'll puncture a tire!"

# · FOUR ·

HE WAS UP EARLY, clothed in his best white habit, seated on the springs of his stripped bed, thinking—for no reason he could discover —about the problem of evil. And it seemed to him that he was a Pfc. in the Third Crusade under Richard the Lionhearted, and that he had charged upon Acre with the rest, but had fallen long before he had gotten to the walls, and yet knew, as he lay there dying, that he was contributing to the peace of Christ, that his dying would diminish the power of the Devil.

Then a knock at his door, and there stood Billy Kipp. And Billy said not a word, in deference to the Great Silence. He just hung there, solemn-lipped and huge-eyed, his face an ethereally tragic poster in favor of not putting war orphans in gas ovens or something similar, and, for a time, Aubrey, sad and sympathetic and sentimental though he felt, had no notion of what to say or do. He murmured a goodbye as Billy's eyes left his face once, very briefly, and traveled over to the large pile of chattels and returned full of the awful certainty. Then Billy's arm came up out of the folds of his habit like a clapper on a turnstile, stiffly and resolutely, the hand dangling there unattended for a split second before Aubrey, seeing the thumb tremble and the tears start, seized and shook it with great and athletic vigor. When it was done and both had let go, Billy stood for a final despairing moment, then turned and dived off the landing toward the bottom of the stairs.

Leo was waiting for Aubrey at the entrance to the chapel, his eyes snapping back and forth, from the gathering novices within to the corridor, as if he suspected that Aubrey had either already sneaked by him, or was about to, subtly disguised, maybe, as a hymnbook. Aubrey presented himself boldly, causing Leo to issue a little cry of alarm. But he recovered handsomely, leaned to Aubrey with dissimulatory abandon, his eyes going one way and his mouth the other, and whispered hoarsely, "Leave right after communion!" Aubrey nodded and gave the countersign—an extended wink covered cunningly by the right hand just out of the font and moving, palm wide, to the forehead (a maneuver done with sufficiently debonair accomplishment only by those agents raised as Roman Catholics)—and went to his stall.

And although he chanted them, he spent Prime and Tierce listening and looking around at the others, and telling himself that God had been good to him in giving him these five years, if He never gave him another. And attended the Mass as devoutly as he had ever done, and dedicated his communion to the intention of the Society of the Sahara, asking as objectively as he could that his application to its service be turned down out of hand if it had more of his will than God's in it.

He dearly wished to beat Leo out of chapel, just to disconcert him, but he was still saying his thanksgiving after communion when Leo hit center floor, went swooping through his solemn choir bows, and strafed his way out, elbows working. Aubrey waited a moment, saying, Goodbye, old man, and continued success at scaring novices into men; and Goodbye, novices, and God speed you; and Goodbye, Billy, my good friend, and may all your errors be in center field. Then he stood up, missal and prayer book and pars verna of his breviary in hand (the telltale sign of the departing novice), and heard a little gasp as he went into his profound bows, and said to himself, May God bless you all. Left and right and down the middle. He went out with a strained lifting in his walk, and a choking in his throat, and a prayer that God was with him.

And was standing in the driveway, waiting for Leo with the pickup truck, and listening to the first antiphons of Sext, hearing the choir take up the cry and chant the first psalm with a great and smashing

50

and dawn-pure ferocity, before he realized fully what he had done, and felt the first acute and sincere pain of going away; and it closed his eyes and held them closed until Leo arrived, tires squealing. He threw his door open, stood up, peered over the roof of the pickup, and said, "You could have at least brought the suitcases down." He was smiling, but not highway beam. Aubrey opened the door on his side, placed his shoe box neatly on the seat, and got in after it. Leo ducked back into the cab.

"Hey, Aub! We got to get the suitcases and the trunk! That's the way Father Finnegan says to do it."

"No suitcases, no trunk," Aubrey said, staring straight ahead.

"What?"

"No suitcases, no trunk."

"Ah, c'mon, Aub. All the stuff you got?"

"It's all here in this shoe box."

"Now, look, Aub. I got to drop you, pick up the mail, gas the truck, and get back in time for meditation. That's Father Finnegan's orders. Now, c'mon, will you?"

"The way I look at it, Leo, if it won't fit into a shoe box, it just gets left behind."

"But you got that trunk, Aub! And those three suitcases!"

"The way I look at it, Leo, if it won't fit into three suitcases and a trunk, to hell with it. Saving your presence."

"If *what* won't fit?"

"My belongings, my gear, my worldly goods, my vested things."

"Well, what are you going to do, *leave* them here?"

"There's nothing else for it, Leo. As I see it."

Leo's shock of recognition was infinitely craftier than befitted a man of God. "You mean, Aub, you're leaving all that stuff behind?"

"Like I say, Leo, if it won't fit into a trunk or three suitcases, or else, if its essence cannot be boiled down, so to speak, to a shoe box, it just gets left behind. I, for one, simply lose interest."

Leo had heard all he needed to hear, and hit the seat, the gear-shift, and the accelerator in rapid order and tore off down the driveway, eager and bright-eyed, his glance sliding to Aubrey and away as he went, as if afraid the madman would change his mind before Leo could get out beyond the three-mile limit. And Leo's conversation, after they had turned the county road, was confined to a series of rather sentimental, if very particularized, inquiries.

"You mean, you didn't take the snowshoes?"

"They're between the second and third suitcases, Leo."

"And the ski boots?"

"In the bottom of the trunk, Leo. Size ten and a half."

"Perfect," Leo said. "And how about the suit of levis?"

"Right in there somewhere, Leo. You'll find it all rather messily stacked, if I do say so."

It was clear, however, even after forty-odd questions, that as they neared the railroad station, there was still something very much on Leo's mind. He started twice, hesitated, and as they came to a stop behind the ticket office, he got it out. "What's in the shoe box, Aub?"

Aubrey took up the shoe box with some ceremony, lifted the lid, and held it out toward Leo. Nodding solemnly, Leo approved the choice. Then he extended his hand, said a grim-faced goodbye, and asked, "What about the pith helmet?"

The train ran down to Grand Central with little speed and less determination, halting approximately wherever anybody had hung out a sign, but he enjoyed the ride and the strangeness of running alone and free after so long in the crowd of the cloister. And he felt high and full of certainty, wrapped in that cloak of serene gravity which the practiced religious takes with him into the world, and pushed himself back happily into the straw-yellow seat and watched the river go by. Watched its smooth mile-wide surface, its smugness, its aristocratic content within the grand banks it had, in other centuries, carved out for itself. He inspected its regal width critically at Haverstraw Bay and issued a statement to the press to the effect that the sun had never had a finer mirror and that the Tappan Zee Bridge was an atrocity. When the train paused at Ossining, he surveyed Sing Sing carefully and gave out another statement—this an exclusive to Dorothy Kilgallen—that the hard cases would very shortly be removed by the state to that well-known privately owned maximum-security prison near Chelsea, New York, run by none other than the prince of all penologists, warden and chief psychologist, Sennacherib "Fingers" Finnegan.

At Grand Central he mailed his letter to the Saharan Fathers and, reluctantly, went into a telephone booth. He disliked telephones, having gotten nothing but disaster out of either end of the best of them since boyhood. He misdialed once and got a camera store. He dialed correctly the second time and got somebody's chain of movie theaters. He went out for some more dimes, telling himself to stick with it: he was getting closer to show business all the time. He took it somewhat stoically because, after all, he'd frustrated the telephone company's conspiracy against him for nearly four years by making no calls at all. He got ten dimes for Father Finnegan's two half dollars—a very poor exchange—went back to his booth, and found a female slate-colored junco in it, leafing through his breviary.

"What language is *this?*" it demanded, its false teeth clicking fiercely.

"That's Latin, madam."

"What's the matter with ya? Can't ya read English?"

And it slammed the book down on top of the missal, informed him that damned foreigners ought at *least* to learn the language, and went clicking away, doing a sort of common two-step in march time. Aubrey made a mental note that slate-colored juncos are sometimes found in telephone booths.

The third dialing did it. He asked the girl for Mr. Strycker's office.

"You want TV?"

"Well, if he's in TV, yes."

"Look, mister, we got two departments, TV and Movies."

"I know that, but he can't be in both places at once."

It was the kind of conversation that might still be going on. He finally got through to Kermit's secretary's secretary, a Miss Taylor. She didn't know about Aubrey, and Aubrey didn't know about her. But he finally discovered that Kermit was not in, that he might be at home or just *might* be out at Belmont Park ("Please don't tell him *I* told you") where he had just purchased a racehorse.

Aubrey took the Madison Avenue bus, got off at 79th Street, and walked around to Kermit's house, a tall, narrow, gargoyled graystone just below the Metropolitan Museum on Fifth Avenue. The front door wasn't locked, nor was the inner gate—a huge business made of fat fourteen-foot black iron spears. He put his hat, shoe box, and books on the hall table and went to the elevator. It was on the ground floor, door open. He stepped in, feeling vaguely like a jackass private detective who walks obliviously into trap after trap, never pausing to wonder who unlocked all the doors. He pushed the button for the top floor, where Kermit had his office, and the elevator rose with a click-clicking noise, like teeth breaking. The gentlemen with brass

53

knuckles and truncheons are waiting just above. Welcome, Brother Gummer of the Dunes.

The car reached the top floor, the door opened without a sound. He stepped out cautiously toward a short wall that had formerly been oak-paneled but was now covered with sections of full-length mirror, edges decorated in pink. He turned right, moving uncertainly along the short corridor of mirrors, turned left at the end of it, and stopped short, finding himself in a pink-pocked bedroom filled with a long-haired girl, standing stage left facing him, right arm and hairbrush suspended in midair, mouth open, and naked but for a pair of fluff-toed pink slippers.

## · FIVE ·

THEN A FROZEN MOMENT, murmurous with perfume and the last failing notes of the song the girl had been humming, and he stood as a statue to another, she moving only her eyes, lifting them into an intense wideness, and her mouth, not yet to speak but to round her lips into a perfect ought of surprise, but she standing there otherwise in the hue and stillness of bronze, half turned, her breasts beautifully formed and incredibly presented (like nothing seen before or imagined; a largesse and a symmetry and an assertion that peeled his eye and held it stunned, as might any natural wonder), and incredible her whole body, the swells and flutes of it, and the clear certainty that it was warmed and poised by blood, and held there motionless by the will of the she who informed it, and incredible that such a marvel should have been given by God into the sovereign control of a single human will.

After how long a time of dumb staring he had no notion then or later, whatever had been holding his vision abstract abruptly left him, and he felt a split second of voluptuous response before he was able to snap his head around and go stumbling backward, all confusion, walking his hands down the mirrors toward the elevator doors, hearing the girl call out, "Hey, wait! Aren't you Aubrey?", but clutching onward until his hands were at the control panel searching out buttons. And pausing then to question his first wild thoughts—that he

55

was in the wrong house or that Kermit had moved out of this one—as he realized she had called him by name. His right name. He stared at his reflection in the mirror opposite and nodded. Yes, I'm Aubrey. But how does she know? Who in hell is she?

"Hey, you out there," she called, her voice calm, even friendly. "You can come on back in now. I'm all covered."

Covered? Dear God, that must have taken some doing. She could get along with just one of those. He swallowed, cleared his throat, swallowed again, gave his inquiry his best diaphragmatic bass. "Who are you?" It came out an intonation, echoing lugubriously in the brass-lined elevator. Then, suddenly, not having made a sound in her approach, she was standing in front of him, covered, smiling, her huge green eyes amused and measuring him—measuring him with such wide-open, straight-on, flat-out boldness that he felt he was offending strict purity merely by glancing back at her. He kept his eyes moving—telling himself the real danger lay in fixing one's gaze—and thought, Good Lord. Doesn't she know she shouldn't go around looking at men like that? Apparently she didn't know. She flounced her hair from under the collar of her robe, batted her eyes (not a blinking bat, he adjudged, but a bat impure and simple) at him once, tossed her head in a sort of amiable defiance of original sin, and ran the tip of her tongue wetly along her lower lip (moaning slightly as she did as if to suggest that her lip had an extraordinarily fine taste about it), and said, "I'm Julie. Julie Chace. And I know you're Aubrey from Kermit's pictures of you." She moaned again but confined her tongue to peekings here and there along her now wide, brilliant grin. "But I'd have known you anyway, you look so much like Arnie. Except you're much more handsome." She cocked her head, surveying him topknot to toe with nearly obscene care. He strove to hold himself upright and undaunted, stiffening his legs, particularly the muscles to the rear which were fluttering toward retreat. He tried not to gulp, but did gulp. She was tall—a big girl all around—and was holding herself erect right along the line, from her high-heeled slippers to the point of her chin, which was slightly lifted so that she appeared to be pouting in spite of her grin—rather, he thought, like a Bengal tigress complaining that her lance-corporal lunch had been quite delicious but distinctly inferior to the succulent sergeant major she'd had last week. And before he could remove the debris from his gulp and summon the crisp tone her

56

superior attitude demanded, she was speaking again, softly, insinuating somehow that he ought to do better. "Don't you recognize me, Aubrey?"

He ordered his crisp tone to report at once, but it was cowering down somewhere south of his larynx, pushing an unarmed quaver out to face the onslaught. And this quaver was already protesting, Your stepsister? That can't be. Stepsisters are knobby little wretches with braces on teeth and ears, and always popping bubble gum and skinning cats, and the like. How could this be your stepsister? But he found voice enough—a squeaking that had no interest in becoming vocal—to say, "I—I've never seen a picture of you."

Her eyes narrowed just slightly, to mere enormousness. "You mean you don't believe I'm who I am?"

"What?"

"Don't you believe I'm your stepsister?"

"I've never seen a picture of my stepsister, either."

"Well, okay, but who else would I be?" She giggled delightedly. "I tell you true. We are steps!"

She made this announcement with an excess of familiar and even possessive exuberance that affronted him. Even if she was his stepsister—and he supposed he was ready to acknowledge it as soon as he could summon the proper tone out of his laggard voice box—she didn't have to trumpet it as if she'd just planted her flag in his sternum. "But I thought," he said, now producing a sound like a rasping of parched tubers, "I thought my stepsister was only about sixteen."

"Well I was only about sixteen. Four years ago." She knew she had him—he could tell—and she began to sort of voluptuate herself, in half steps or less, into the elevator. His thumb hung dead on the first-floor button. He tried to reactivate it but it just hung there, nailed to the quick.

And after that, after she had occupied the threshold of the car, there was nothing to be done. Nothing to say except yes, you must be my stepsister and I'm sorry I invaded your bedroom in the dead of day while you were nude and brushing your auburn hair, and sorry that I've never seen a picture of you, and sorry that I didn't recognize you at once—but he really got none of it said what with her moving right in on him, taking him by the arm and leading him into the bedroom, talking and smiling the while, going on nonstop with apologies, throaty giggles, proclamations, and the reading of vital statistics, such as "I can understand your hesitance, but I really am Julie Chace, daughter of Karen Van Hatten Chace Strycker by her first marriage, and your stepsister by her second marriage to your father, Mr. Kermit Strycker. I don't have a birth certificate with me, but I'd be glad to show you my birthmark." In other words, laughing at him all the way, saying that the pleasure was all hers because he'd accepted her at last (this after a very dubious handshake), saying that she hadn't meant to be naked but that he appeared far more embarrassed by it than she was, saying that she had a wide Cinemascope screen she could dress behind so that he wouldn't see a thing unless he was fairly shifty about it, saying that he looked very tired and lamb-white and even a little horrified but that he had vast amounts of holy charm about him without even trying, saying that he shouldn't look so absolutely compromised because she had no designs whatever on his virtue as yet, and saying, most offensively, that he reminded her a little of a young fat boy she'd seen in an Italian movie who'd gotten seduced by his aunt who was a Poor Clare nun and had wandered around like a sick calf for the last two reels.

He tried desperately to rally himself, to summon up, stiffen, and snap the sinews, but it was no go. He moved like a monster with his electrodes clogged, sternly, giving motor orders from the hips. He sat in a pink wicker chair she indicated, watched her pluck dress, other bits, and shoes from bureau and closet and go behind her screen, and listened while she delivered a monologue on the subject of their unexpected encounter, and all that. His mind was full of ejaculations about clerical chastity, everything from warnings to keep a table between yourself and any manner of female mammal to pragmatic reminders about how the most unsuccessful fathers in the world are priests, hermits, and constitutional virgins of any description. And out of this proceeded a comic desperation.

Here I sit, he thought, in my stepsister's boudoir. Is this likely to do anyone any good? Certainly not. But if no good, then, by moral definition, harm. Nothing stands still in this world. All things to all women, of course, but the ecclesiastical etiquette here is what I'd like to hear about. Will Monsignor Amy Vanderbilt please step forward, right up here, girl, into the decision area. Mink and all. That's right. Thank you. What's that you say? Run like hell? Would you put that in Latin, please?

And he sat there feeling completely obligated, yet threatened, and moved from one side of his chair to the other in short, purposeful surges, concluding now to flee, then to face it out, but actually concluding nothing.

And Julie was observing all manner of things with uniformly cheerful condescension. "Why, I never expected I had such a *handsome* stepbrother. What have you been doing behind those walls?"

Leaping, sister, leaping.

"I've just moved in. Well, halfway. It used to be Kermit's office, you know. He had it fixed up for me when I started at Barnard. Most of my stuff is still in the apartment. On the Drive."

The sex drive, no doubt.

"What are you doing here, anyway? Aren't you supposed to be confined up on the Hudson?"

"I broke out," he said quietly.

She peeped over the top of the screen, laughing. "Oh, I can tell— I can just *tell*—you're not as pious as you pretend to be, step."

I'm every bit as pious as I pretend to be, step. And what would you know about piety anyway?

"So, you really didn't answer me. About what you're doing off the reservation."

That's what *I* would like to know. More like off limits. I shouldn't be *here*, that's for damned sure. Too much going on back there. I am not St. Anthony. "I quit," he said and, prying himself from between the arms of the chair with virtuous resolution, he fled the room and dived into the elevator. Yet hesitated, thumb poised over the down button, and shouted, "Where's Kermit?"

"Out at Belmont with his horse. He'll be in this afternoon. Hey! Where'd you go, step?"

He took monkish satisfaction in punching for the first floor and calling out loudly, "I'll see you downstairs! Step!"

But went down accusing himself. For Pete's sake, have you no social presence at all? You acted like a twelve-year-old with the bollicky hives. A little holy, debonair aloofness is what's needed here. You should have kissed her. An impeccably chaste kiss, of course, but it might have put her off balance. That's the trick in these cases, MacIver. Crowd a boxer always, and keep your trunks up at all times.

About one minute later he was seated in a tufted leather swivel chair in a first-floor room that Kermit had made his office. Straight ahead was a huge walnut table, and all around were various dead things, from lionskin rugs with hoary heads attached, to heads of the big African five without rugs attached hoary or otherwise, but all staring down from the oak-paneled walls. Aubrey was on long-term acquaintance with most of them, but there was a new and especially shaggy-eared Cape buffalo whose eyes were some kind of antipathetic and novaculitic agate, clearly reflecting no least use for Aubrey. And Aubrey was returning the buffalo glance for baleful glance when, suddenly, Julie's voice attacked him. "Well, damn it, I'll track you down if it takes all day." He jumped several inches straight up, elbows flailing, but recovered quickly, and had just located the intercom transmitter, when she spoke again, mockingly. "Look, step, don't be such a damned coward. I know you're down there. I can hear you palpitating."

He depressed the top-floor button. "I'm here. In Kermit's office."

"Well, welcome to the network," she said gaily. "What happened to you? Short taken?"

"I'm sorry. I didn't mean to be rude."

She hesitated. "I guess I'm the one who's been rude. I can't help it. I was born rude." She giggled. "Have you any plans for lunch? I've got a fitting at noon, but then I'm free."

"Well, I—I'd *like* to . . . but . . ." But what? Good Lord, man, trippingly, trippingly! "I'd like to, but I thought I'd better get over to Fort Milligan and see my mother. She doesn't even know I'm out—home—yet."

"You mean, you haven't told *any*body?"

"No. It happened sort of suddenly."

"Not even Kermit? I mean, you *are* going to Alaska with us, aren't you?"

"Alaska? Are you going to Alaska?"

"Sure, didn't you know? Next week—a week from today. The bear season closes on the thirty-first."

"I didn't know. I haven't thought about it. You mean, you personally are going bear hunting with Kermit?"

"Hell yes. I love to hunt bear. I also *swim* bare." She laughed, but managed to keep talking. "Seriously, step. It'll be great now with the Lodge all finished."

"Oh. Where's the Lodge?"

"Out on the Alaska Peninsula. At Cold Bay. Doesn't Kermit ever

60

write you letters, for God's sake? He's been going to Cold Bay for the last two years, or something."

"He did mention Alaska once."

"Well, look. I'd better call Kermit's secretary and get the reservations changed. You know?"

"Well, I don't see how I can do it, Julie. I've got this interview and all."

"Interview for what?"

"For admission to a seminary. The Saharan Fathers."

"I thought you quit."

"Well, I'm sort of—between seminaries."

"I'm between hangovers myself."

"Look, is Arnie going? To Alaska?"

"Well, I *think* so. If he's *feeling* well enough. He—went with us last year, and with Kermit the year before that. It's sort of his vacation. Doesn't *he* write you either?"

"Not too often. And his letters are usually about other things."

"Listen, Aubrey, you've *got* to go with us. Kermit would be heartbroken. Won't they give you time off? I mean you've been cooped up about ten years, haven't you?"

"Almost five."

"Well, Christ! So they won't give you two weeks off?"

"Well, it's sort of complicated. I'd like to go."

"That's what you said about lunch."

He explained about Rexfordia again, and threw in Eulalia this time for emphasis, and Julie begged his pardon for being pushy, and he said she wasn't being pushy, and rubbed his forehead with his free hand and wished the conversation would somehow get to an end because the intercom reminded him too much of a telephone. And it finally did end with Julie deciding that she and Kermit would come over to Fort Milligan as soon as Kermit got home and stay there for dinner. And the last thing he heard from Julie was "Tell Rexfordia to sic the Cardinal on that seminary so they'll let you go to Alaska. You're just what the damned expedition needs."

He was in a cab before he realized that he didn't have enough money to pay the fare to Fort Lee. He told the driver at a stoplight, and the driver turned, fairly intensively dismayed. "Well, look, buddy, jeez. I'm the best Jewish-Catholic you'll ever meet, but Fort *Lee!*" But the driver decided, after questioning Aubrey acutely, that he would take a chance that somebody would be on hand and moneyed at Fort Milligan when they got there, and Aubrey thanked him, and said a prayer for all Jewish-Catholics north of the Battery. Then he sat back and thought about Julie.

Her beauty was not a matter of perfect features—her lips and mouth and eyes all seemed too large. It was rather an extraordinary effect of vital power, an ambience of self-confidence, a nearly mocking manifestation of feminine force and sexual assurance. It came out of her unmixed, unstrained, raw-pure; so elemental it could have little or no guile behind it. Clearly, Julie got what Julie wanted, and if Julie didn't, he imagined her claws would come snapping out her fingers automatically, like switchblades.

And her eyes aren't quite right. They look like they've got little people dancing in them. Dwergers and sprites. She is just like the rest of the Strycker-Milligans. How did she pick it up so fast? Pixies, every one of them. Down from the mad side of the moon. From between Mount Atrabilia and the Valley of Vitriol. Not an unfrantic head in the carload. Greeting any one of them is like taking a straight shot of Tabasco. Lord God of sublunatics, shine thou gently upon us, strike the blood from the moon, and give us this one season of peace.

He was thinking about Aline as they went up onto the George Washington Bridge, and looked back over the Bronx and wondered in what part, in what building, she was enclosed, and wondered if he would be permitted to see her and if he would recognize her if he did. He'd seen her last when she was thirteen—a sweet, abstracted, unnaturally solemn child, with large black eyes that seemed to reflect more than they saw, a child of long silences and quiet voice and a wistful manner that suggested a fairy queen who had misplaced her wand, or a little girl always about to leave on a long journey: and he had talked and she had listened whenever they had been together, and he realized now that he scarcely knew her at all, that he knew her primarily as she reminded him of Rexfordia.

And he thought of Rexfordia, and hoped she wouldn't scream or faint when she saw him and not threaten suicide when he told her about the Saharans; thought of Arnie, and hoped he would be well and able to come home for a time and be able to talk about something other than his breakdown ("Goddammit, I'm *not* broken *down*, Mother! I'm broken *up*! My pieces are rising on high! Look, look!

Like a goddamned flock of red-shafted flickers!"); thought about Kermit and knew that he longed, just then, to see his father most, and hoped that Kermit had forgiven him the priesthood by this time; thought about bear hunting and Alaska and told himself he couldn't possibly go; and thought, sadly and finally, of Fort Milligan and of the forlorn growing up and of the pain that had come out of it—and of the pain that might yet come.

And looked downriver from the height of the bridge to the good ships wattled snug and waiting the land, waiting him; and promised himself that no one, no affection, no pressure would prevent him from making one of those ships his ship. He would go, by God, and His grace, in a blown-out inner tube, dragging the whole Strycker-Milligan complex like a sea anchor behind him, if it came to that. But how fine it would be to go out to Africa in a ship; to go slowly down the Hudson, very slowly, and on out the Narrows, taking a last long lingering ecstatic look at this world's greatest heaping of cantilevered crap, waving it goodbye and goodbye and goodbye, joyous to be departing all in one sweep of the eyes so mammoth and reasty a conglobation of garbage, waving and laughing and jigging on the deck to know that you were free of it all in one brief hour, to know that you were shat of it forever in one monstrous turdweight, to know that you were outward bound to solitude and God's own ever and would never, if you were crafty about it, have to clap eyes upon it again.

And he would be crafty. Oh, dear and sweet Lord, yes. Shifty, persistent, obnoxious, and crafty. Seriatim and simultaneously. And one fine waking-up morning, he would take ship fiercely, as a lover takes revenge, and begin at once to wrap his solitude around him like Christ's own battle banner.

But first, he thought, the battle. Reel Two, Scene One.

## · SIX ·

HE POINTED OUT Fort Milligan to the driver as they descended the slope of the bridge into Jersey, and the driver said that he'd noticed it dozens of times on his runs to the airport because of its red-tile roof but had always figured it belonged to some tycoon or hood, but that it made just as much sense that it belonged to the Church, because, after all, as he'd heard the other day, the Pope held the mortgage on the Lever Building. "That's right. Why the hell *wouldn't* he own that there house?"

"You don't really believe that?" Aubrey asked, smiling.

"Hell yes, bud. It's a fact. The Lever Building. And who the hell knows how many others? Except the Pope himself."

Aubrey thought to argue but decided his black suit limited his acceptance as an unprejudiced witness. And how did he know that the Pope *didn't* hold the mortgage on the Lever Building? A good investment, to be sure, and a clean one. He took another look at Fort Milligan. Designed for misery (actually, for Eulalia, in 1902), it was a vast, ramble-gabled, gray-boarded, enshuttered blockhouse, with towers, colonial pillars, a random assortment of glassed-in sun porches indiscriminately appended, marble front steps and adjoining marble lions, the steps leading majestically downward from the front door to a sheer drop, off the top of the Palisades, of about a hundred

64

and seventy-five feet. Just where these front steps had been intended to lead no one seemed to know. Kermit had once told Aubrey that they were used for the extermination of unregenerate bill collectors in the lean years prior to World War I. And the rumor was that the iron fence across the bottom step had been installed only after a New York State Supreme Court justice had gotten drunk during a party one night and had mistaken the steps for a short cut to the Fort Lee ferry.

The grounds were spacious and full of trees, shrubs, and flowers, the whole encircled by a fifteen-foot-high iron spike fence. There was just one gate in this fence, a medieval wonder bristling with pointed knobs and bosses and always locked so that it was impossible to come or go without strenuous effort on the part of chauffeurs, without, in fact, a solemn high ceremony that involved much rattling of keys, clanking of drawbars, and the negotiation of a series of cunning iron baffles that would have preserved Tutankhamen inviolate if the Egyptians had been as clever as Eulalia Milligan. Only once, in a long history of assaults upon it—before they discovered a loose spike behind the garage—were Aubrey and Arnie able to open the gate without detection from the house, and then the operation required two hours, a rubber-headed ball peen hammer, and an unsolicited short circuit in the warning system.

Within, the house looked like a cross between the felon reception rooms at Dartmoor and a charity bazaar at Northanger Abbey. A more formidable, closely packed, disintegrated collection of rummage could only have been duplicated at, say, an auction of the personal effects of Trismegistus, St. Elizabeth of Hungary, Pepin the Short, David Belasco, Aaron Burr, Rodrigo Borgia, Paul Revere, and Little Nell's grandfather in his salad days.

"Says Milligan," the driver said, reading the name-plate fixed to the gate. "You mean this ain't a convent or a what-the-hell?"

"It's a what-the-hell, but it ain't a convent," Aubrey said. He got out and rang the bell. Roger, the chauffeur, appeared at the door of his apartment over the garage, did not recognize Aubrey, and came reluctantly down the steps and the driveway, squinting, and was within six feet of the gate before he made out who it was. Then all was Hungarian rhapsody, and he unlimbered the gate and came through it flair-britched, puttees flashing, and with a flood of language that, however incomprehensible, unmistakably made Aubrey welcome from Budapest to the sea. He left Roger dickering with the astounded driver over the fare, and started the long walk toward the house.

And walked slowly, thinking then about Rexfordia. About Rexfordia the beautiful, Rexfordia the girl. Remembering her most clearly as she had looked in 1932 when, for a brief time, she had been a photographer's model. (Eulalia had raised hell, and had made her stop, even though it had been all very respectable, posing in and around Packard motorcars.) Remembering her from an old *Good Housekeeping* magazine, from his favorite picture of all time, in which she is leaning against the front fender of a 1933 Chummy roadster. She is wearing a two-piece dress of bright yellow with a matching cloche. Her very white face framed by her very black hair, pushed out in curls all around the edges of the hat, and a filmy white scarf at her throat. She is smiling gently, one hand on hip, and her eyes are dark and enormous. The scene is autumnal. Around her on the ground the leaves are yellow and brown and red, and the leaves of the great-trunked chestnut tree behind and over her still have touches of green here and there. The small sky is sunlit, but a somber, wintry blue, and the car gleams rich black, its white top down, its chrome brilliantly silver.

Yet with all this—all the color and contrast—the center of the photograph is, for anybody, Rexfordia's eyes and face; in them all the wistful hope, the wan innocence, the eager, sweet, yielding, glad femininity that are girl becoming woman. She is fawn, nymph, princess, eternal gamin. Whenever he thought of what the world might have been, thought of an age of innocence, he thought of that photograph. There would never be a better autumn than that one, there would never be a better-looking automobile than that Packard, there would never be a girl more immediately and innocently and subtly desirable than Rexfordia in her twenty-first year.

Another image of her came to him out of the years near the end of the war, after the final separation from Kermit. (The years of what Eulalia still called "Rexfordia's decline.") At thirty-one, she had simply retired from the world, had walked weeping back in among her memories and drawn the curtain. There was no insanity, no immobilizing despair. But there was an immense, crushing melancholy that moved with her, informing everything she did, settling finally in her eyes.

66

She is at the piano dressed in a flowing white silk robe with a broad sash belt, her hair loose down her back in shining curls. She is playing Grieg's "Nocturne" or Massenet's "Meditation" or Debussy's "Reverie" or Schumann's Traümerei or the Élégie from Les Erinnyes by Massenet, or something similar. Aubrey is seated a few feet from her in his uniform: a black suit with short pants and a white frill collar, white socks to the knee, black shoes, hair combed out sheepdog-long in the British manner, and a flower in his lapel—a fresh flower every day chosen for each of the children from the greenhouse by Rexfordia—and the scene is out of Botticelli's La Derelitta or something grimmer, with the room dark, crowding with gloom (the shrubs around the house having gone unattended throughout the war, now filling the windows, already ivied and draped), the music flowing around him like old moonlight through a graveyard, Rexfordia bent to the keys reverently, sounding each note as if to signal the first act of the Apocalypse. And invariably ends in one of two ways: either she stops abruptly in the middle of the piece and walks rapidly from the room, or else raises her slim white fingers from the final notes, puts them to her throat, stares at him intensely while the echoes die in the draperies, then comes to embrace him and takes him in her arms and says something like "Oh, Aubrey, someday we will go to Zermatt and I will show you where your father and I stayed once and picked flowers in the snow."

And he was listening for piano music as he walked in under the porte-cochere, up to the front door. But what he heard was the voice of Solly, the outsized maid, and saw her standing in the hall with her huge, white-starched, Irish-stout barrel of a rear end to him, talking loudly on the telephone.

". . . a Christian bone in you, you goddamned Grake blatherskite, you'd know better than to send carp into a daycent Christian home. And I'll have the salmon by five o'clock—cold fresh from the wather, mind—or I'll be down and have the oily nose of you!"

He waited just inside the screen door until she slammed the receiver down. "Sure," he said quietly, "and listen to the viper's tongue of her."

She didn't turn at once, but hunched her shoulders in huge anticipation, then came violently about, red-platter face shining like a sunburst. "Sweet risen Jaysus! Aubrey! Will you look at the darlin' bye!"

She trundled down the hall to him, her arms outstretched, and just before she engulfed him, he saw his mother enter the far end of the hallway from the living room, and hesitate there. He watched her as best he could over one or the other of Solly's shoulders (Solly batting his head back and forth as she kissed him repeatedly on either cheek), and Rexfordia, still beautiful, ethereal, clothed in an ankle-length white robe, began to move slowly, seeming to glide, and her eyes larger and more brilliant as she came on, and she was crying freely when he took her in his arms.

And he thought, My God, my God, haven't four years gone by? Can four years go by and nothing change?

She said nothing but his name, over and over, and so woefully that Solly, who had been smiling, began to look as if she might cry. Aubrey eased his mother away from him and started to speak, but she lifted her face, awash with tears, and whispered, "No, Aubrey. Oh no. You haven't lost your vocation. Please God, Aubrey, it isn't that? It isn't that?"

"No, Mother. It isn't that."

Her extraordinary eyes told him he was lying. "But how can you be home, Aubrey? They don't permit vacations from the novitiate."

"No, Mother. I've left the Titans. I . . ."

"Left? Left the Titans? Oh, Aubrey, why? They asked you to leave?"

"No. I left of my own free will."

"Oh please, Aubrey. Please don't try to protect me. Did you do something? Something wrong?"

"No, no. Now, Mother, I can't explain it all at once. Let's go in and sit down."

"Oh, it was that way, wasn't it? There was trouble like there was with poor Arnold?"

"No, there was no trouble, absolutely no trouble. Like Arnie's, or any other. I just left, that's all."

"You'd tell me the truth, wouldn't you, Aubrey? You'd tell me the truth? Even if there was trouble like Arnold's?"

"Mother, there was no trouble. I didn't hit anybody, or throw any fits, or break any windows, or blow up the chapel. I simply left. I left to go . . ."

"But why? Why, Aubrey? It isn't that girl?"

"Girl? What girl?"

"That—that girl from Cliffside?" Her eyes narrowed.

68

Aubrey almost laughed. Rexfordia had reference to a certain Mary Elizabeth Conroy, virgin of Cliffside, who had once—just once—accompanied Aubrey and Arnie to a movie in Fort Lee. Rexfordia had espied them coming out together, laughing and performing other such lascivious acts. "For God's sake, Mother. I wouldn't know her if you served her for dinner. I'm still going to be a priest. Now, come on. We'll go sit down."

And he refused to explain further until they were seated in the claustrophobic living room, side by side on one of the six sofas. Then, with Solly standing across the coffee table hands on hips, told her about the Titans and why he left them, and about the Society of the Sahara and approximately why he had applied to it for admission. When he had done, Rexfordia was weeping quietly but firmly. Solly was indignant. "Well, may Jaysus presarve us from blackamoors! Africa, is it? Why, billy-be-damned, I'd as liefer you went to the Jesuits! What in the name of the bleedin' lamb do you want any truck with all those Africans for?"

Rexfordia touched his hand. "But you still want to be a priest, don't you, Aubrey?" Her voice was a whispering, just slightly more than silence, something less, or more, than mortal.

"Of course I do, Mother."

"Even if you hadn't thought of Africa?"

"Yes. But Africa, the Society of the Sahara, is where I should have been from the beginning. It's my vocation."

"Well, dear, we can't always be so sure about that, can we? Arnold, poor dear, thought *his* vocation was to Africa. You remember?"

"Sure I remember. We decided on the Saharan Fathers together."

She closed her eyes and shook her head very gently. "Sometimes I think that's what upset him so much. The thought of going so far away from home and those he loved." She smiled sadly. "Oh, Aubrey, do you realize that the American Church is desperate for good priests? Especially secular priests. Just last Sunday, Monsignor Allen—oh, he's a brilliant young man—was telling me how urgently in need of candidates the New York archdiocese is. Especially the kind of young man who could become an administrator."

"I wouldn't make an administrator, Mother."

"Charity begins at home, dear. I know the African Church must be very short of priests. But don't you think they would do better in the long run training their own?"

"Sure. And I'll help them train their own."

69

"That would be very worth while, I'm sure, dear, but don't you think there are great sacrifices to be made here in America, too? Don't you think that, after all, there are others really better qualified for that sort of work than you are? I mean, young men who could meet the poor people of other countries much more nearly on their own level and, therefore, with more understanding than you would be able to do?"

"I'm poor myself. I'm right down there in the lowest bracket."

She blinked at him. "Secular priests take no vow of poverty." Then, as if to press an advantage, "And, I must arrange for us to have dinner with the Cardinal while you are here. Perhaps next week. Oh, he's such a spiritual force. He's in touch with American Catholics in every walk of life! Business, education, politics—there are such exciting things happening in American Catholic politics, Aubrey. It would be such a shame if you were to go away now. Just wait until you talk with the Cardinal!"

"Mother, I may sound ungrateful, and I apologize for it, but I don't want to have dinner with the Cardinal, or to talk with him. It's not only not my place, as a seminarian, to be dining with cardinals, but I don't know what possible good it would do either the Cardinal or me. Once I say that I'm bound for the Saharans, and he says, That's fine, my son, I hope you make it, what more is there?"

"Why, much much more, dear. He will inform you, stimulate you, make you see what it is to be a prince of the Church, a statesman of Christ."

"Mother, please listen, and understand, and believe me. I've had four years to make my decision, to think out all possible alternates, to eliminate every other possibility but Africa. In other words, Mother, whether by a cardinal or the Pope himself, I do not intend to be recruited. I am given, body and soul, if they will have me, to the Saharan Fathers."

And just here she decided to sound retreat for the day. She signaled her bugler, sheathed her sword, struck her battle flag, and withdrew. Yet her will to destroy him was in no way diminished. Rather, it increased, this manifested in a sudden brightening of eye, a new fixity and depth of stare, a squaring of chin. What she had ordered was a strategic withdrawal, a delaying action. She had not given up. She was merely taking his new measure, calculating the grown thickness and height of his ramparts, and raising her sights

70

accordingly. She would reserve her fire until the light was more, or entirely, in her favor. She was a past mistress of the warlike art of lulling an opponent into an illusion of security, into feeling that an issue had been resolved, only to resume hostilities at a time long after the enemy had put the cosmoline back in his cannon. Wait, she was thinking, don't press. He still wants to be a priest. That's the important thing. Arrange dinner with the Cardinal, chip away subtly at this wild idea about Africa, cry a little every other evening, and you'll soon have him in the archdiocesan seminary. There he sits, your future Archbishop of the City of New York. And, as he read these thoughts in her eyes, Aubrey was impressed, as he had always been, and even put into slight apprehension by her determination, utter and irrevocable, to have her own way; but he was still tempted to tell her not to dedicate herself so overwhelmingly to winning this particular battle because he would become a Trappist before he became a secular, and did start to say this, but she interrupted. "Oh, I'm so glad you haven't lost your vocation. I was so worried." She smiled weakly and dabbed at her eyes with her handkerchief. "I came out into the hallway and saw you, and knew you weren't supposed to be home, and I was sure it was just one thing. And I've carried on so. You do forgive me, don't you?"

Aubrey nodded and smiled. She took his near hand and squeezed it, and, her artillery concealed to her satisfaction out there among the weeping willows, ran on to other topics. And talked most eagerly, on and on.

About Arnie, and how she had gone out to see him about a month before, and how he had seemed perfectly normal and had not had a major disturbance in a long time and yet had said to her as she left, "Here, Mother, let me wring out your handkerchief. I'm fresh out of holy water."

About Aline and her visit to her at about the same time, and how she had seemed very happy, and was looking forward to taking her temporary vows in September, and how she had told Rexfordia that she was praying very hard for Kermit's conversion.

About the impending wedding of Philip Cherry, Jr. (the son of one of Kermit's business partners) to a darling girl from San Francisco named Prissy Cullenly, and about how everybody—Rexfordia, Kermit, Julie, Arnie, and, of course, Aubrey—would attend the wedding on the way up to Alaska ("Of course I'm not going to Alaska, and I

71

hope you don't either"), and how she was so happy for her dear friend, Mrs. Cherry.

About her mother, and how she had been feeling a bit run down lately and had to have a registered nurse with her all the time these days—a sweet person named Magda, who, unfortunately, did not get on at all with Solly—to give her shots of whatever when needed, and how Eulalia was upstairs resting just now, but would be down for dinner because Uncle Peter (who owned a medium-sized New York trade book publishing company) was coming over to talk with her about the story of her life, and how Kermit and Julie would certainly be welcome for dinner, but she did hope Kermit would be sober, and remain sober, and not start any arguments with Eulalia. (Aubrey made a mental note here that anyone who could start an argument with Eulalia—her instincts being all antagonistic, her five senses delicate antennae cross-wired to a self-starting disputor which could pick up the slightest impulse of contrary opinion anywhere within two hundred and seven yards of her acid tongue—that individual who could beat Eulalia to the draw should be awarded all seven degrees of the Royal Order of the Wasp.)

About Julie, and how she was such a beautiful thing but, unfortunately, falling more and more under Kermit's sway, and how it was definitely a mistake for her to have gone to Barnard where she would be so available to his corrupting influence, and how Kermit had done absolutely nothing to have her introduced properly into New York society, which, one would have thought, was the least he could have done.

About Karen Van Hatten, Kermit's second and wandering wife, and how she was in Rome making movies and scandal and was just the most abandoned creature since Salome, and how she had tried to commit suicide by slashing her wrists in Las Vegas in 1958, while Julie was staying with her for the Christmas holidays, and how Julie had wandered into the bathroom and found her mother bleeding into the tub and had called the police, which was the only thing that saved us all from the worst kind of publicity, because, after all, the suicide of the most wide-ranging, indiscreet, and energetic adulteress in the history of Los Angeles County would be certain to make all the headlines, even if she weren't Mrs. Kermit Strycker.

About Julie's father (this at Aubrey's request, because he knew next to nothing of her background), and how he had been handsome,

72

dashing, Oxford, proper, and mad for airplanes, and had met Karen Van Hatten when she was still in her teens and Miss Netherlands or some such, and married her, and got her with child, and had taken his commission in the R.A.F. late in 1939, and how he had been killed in the raid over London, December 29, 1940, just after Julie's birth.

About Kermit and the way he had always been so wild (now that Solly was bringing on the martinis) and the old story about how he had once taken an oath to be a great man, and God alone knew what had happened, and how he had playboyed his way in and out of four colleges in one year, and spent another two as a merchant seaman, and had presented himself one day at the Long Island studio of D. W. Griffith, then—in 1925—engaged in making a motion picture of Marie Corelli's *The Sorrows of Satan* and got himself signed on as an assistant carpenter and helped to build a stairway to heaven up which Lucifer would climb to do battle with the Archangel Michael, and how he was noticed in due course and taken to Hollywood with the blessings of Jesse Lasky and presently put under contract to Famous Players Corporation, and stood around and flexed his muscles in several of Cecil B. DeMille's productions until he was noticed again by a leading lady and invited to share her sheets, and did, and starred as a Viking in the same lady's next picture, and how he was never an actor, nor happy at it, but yet liked the money and the roaring around in large motorcars and sailing parties on steamships and the general notoriety that, more and ever more, attached itself to his brooding, handsome, stone face, and how, when the novelty and charm of all of this began to wane—and he was asked or required to play gangster after pimp after Viking after playboy after pirate after Hun after popinjay—began to wonder where he was going and what all this had to do with his greatness, and decided to get out and, on his twenty-eighth birthday, gave out a now-famous interview in which he stated that Hollywood was made up of whores and whoremasters, all of whom could be bought, and those who couldn't could unfailingly be rented, and thereupon departed for Manitoba to hunt the great elk, and how thereafter he wandered the world for years and years, returning to Hollywood now and then, but mostly hunting and hunting, pausing once to go into partnership with his brother Jan to found Strycker Lines in memory of their father, but was never satisfied until, in 1934, at the christening of a ship, he met Rexfordia

73

Breesvort Milligan, photographer's model and socialite, and asked her to marry him. "And, Aubrey dear, I married him because I loved him. And I love him still. What he was then. And what he might have become. Oh Aubrey, dear, we must pray constantly for his conversion."

About Kermit again (Solly having brought on more martinis, and Aubrey, on his second—at, strangely enough, Rexfordia's urging— now entering into the spirit and romance of Rexfordia's recital, and the shadows in the room now partly obscuring her remarkable face, and his love for her not diminished one whit by her unconscious self-revelation), and how he had asked her to attempt a reconciliation with him in 1956 (something, until that moment, unknown to Aubrey), and how it had been an abysmal failure because of Kermit's behavior and attitude, beginning with the fact that Kermit kept insisting that they were living in sin, which was, of course, ridiculous (or was it? Married in the Dutch Reformed church, wife converted to Catholicism after separation, husband obtains very quiet Mexican divorce—where *did* that leave Rexfordia's moral integrity?), and how she had moved bag and baggage over to his house in New York— paintings, furniture, *everything*—and renewed her contacts with the Manhattan social set, only to have Kermit begin to act at once like a caveman, and how he thought nothing of belching and picking his nose in public, and how he had once passed air very loudly and then announced to the distinguished company that a good "fart" (Aubrey's interpolation) now and then clears the pipes, and how he frequently got drunk and recited passages from the books of Hemingway out the windows at passersby on Fifth Avenue, and how he was always firing his revolver into a toilet bowl and missed one night and put a bullet into the left eye of General Cornwallis, whose portrait hung in the drawing room immediately below Rexfordia's bathroom and then would use no other bathroom because, as he claimed, he enjoyed knowing while seated there that the "Old limey bastard's head" was directly beneath him, and how he had never really given up any of his mistresses after their reconciliation and took one or more of them on a hunting trip to the North Woods, and crash-landed an airplane near Rangeley Lakes, Maine, and got photographed with a blond actress, one of the mistresses, as he came out of the wreckage, and then tried to tell Rexfordia that the blonde was not an actress at all but a famous woman guide by the name of Diana of Umbagog, and how he had once said to a certain Monsignor Twill at a reception

74

that he (the Monsignor) was suffering from a social disease called virginity for which there was only one cure and that he (Kermit) would be glad to recommend a certain brunette panacea if the Monsignor were interested, and how Kermit had worked for a year on his book about Hollywood and produced rather less than twenty typed pages, fourteen of which consisted of the word "bullshit" repeated in neatly spaced lines, and how he had finally left her one morning, after only two months of their experiment, having been brought home by the police dead drunk, apprehended after a ninety-mile-an-hour chase down the Major Deegan Expressway, Kermit driving a hearse he had appropriated (there weren't any cabs around, Kermit said) in front of the Cathedral of St. John the Divine just as the pall-bearers were arriving at the rear of the vehicle with the casket (and Kermit's comment on this had been that the pallbearers were daw-dling and that he'd waited for them as long as he could), and how, after that, he had gone back to Hollywood and made a bad picture (as producer-director) about Baranov, who had managed the plunder-ing of Alaskan furs for the Russian Czars, and had gone on location at Cold Bay, Alaska, and had got himself clawed up by a big brown bear, and had built a lodge there, and had been practically living at Cold Bay ever since.

So that Aubrey was about one-third drunk with badly suppressed laughter, and about one-third drunk from one and a half martinis and about one-third drunk with longing to see his father again, when he heard Kermit's gloriously sonorous voice sounding in the kitchen: "Jesus Christ, you goddamned old sow-bellied harpy! I don't want to know where he's going! I want to know where he *is!*"

## · SEVEN ·

THE CHANGE in Rexfordia was electric. "He's here," she said, her martini glass just touching her lower lip and held there, her eyes glowing and fixed wide on the door he would enter, her lips slightly parted and whispering again, "He's here." A child in awe. "Oh, good Lord! They're so early! I must look terrible!" And lightly, swift as a fawn, she was out of the room and up the stairs.

He turned then to watch Kermit enter; smiling, hearing him in the hall, waiting for his father's presence to fill the room.

Kermit came through the door as he always came through doors, even in his movies: listing slightly to port, right forearm raised nearly to chest level, the fist doubled, surveying the new scene tentatively over his knuckles with his head cocked somewhat left; and, having decided he was safe from immediate attack or having sighted his objective, lowering his guard and charging. He bore down on Aubrey gleefully, his hands outstretched, his famous shaggy head tossing from side to side, his jaws working, making a noise in his throat that was a compromise between a chortle and a happy growl, and saying, finally, as he seized Aubrey under the arms and lifted him two feet off the floor, "Jee-sus Kurr-rist! It's my Aubrey!" He held Aubrey up there for a time, beaming at him, then lowered him, and shook his hand crushingly, and went on a little tour of inspection of Aubrey's person, clucking the while, poking with a knuckle here, chopping with the

76

side of his hand there, feeling his muscle, punching him in the gut, and, at last, facing him and bringing both of his huge hands down open and hard on Aubrey's clavicles, shouting, "By God, you're in good rig, Aubie! If you were a bull moose, I'd shoot you!"

"You look good yourself, Pop." Aubrey was grinning delightedly.

"I am! I am!" He stepped back and clapped both hands on his stomach. "Two hundred and twelve this morning, Aubie. Lowest in ten years." Then, excitedly, conspiratorially, shooting his fist to Aubrey's chest and holding it there, "Oh, by God, let me tell you. I've started to grow again! Yes, I have! I'm within an ace of six feet one, and I figure I'll be right up there with you by duck season." He nodded sharply to show that he meant it.

"If anybody can do it, you can, Pop."

"Goddamn right. When the beast charges, drop it on him!" He turned an imaginary rifle on a footstool, then glanced up quickly. "Where's your mother?"

"Ah, she went up to dress for dinner."

"Good, good. She looking well?"

"She doesn't look like she's eating enough."

"Eating enough! Jesus Christ, the Milligans don't eat! Don't you know that, boy? Never have! Isn't a goddamned one of them could boil water in a steam-heated pisspot! How in the name of Christ any of them grew up, don't ask me! When I first met your mother, I used to come over here for dinner and there they'd all be sitting around sucking on old bones!" Kermit was walking around in a tight circle, gesticulating freely, doing what he enjoyed most in life next to hunting: working himself into a state of mock outrage. "Don't ask me what bones. Probably some old Eulallylip saved up after the Little Big Horn!" Sudden alarm and lowering of the voice. "Where's she?"

"Grandma?"

"Yes, yes, Grandma."

"She's resting, Rexfordia said."

"Resting? Jesus Christ, she hasn't taken up sleeping, has she? Who'll shoot the process servers?"

"Rexfordia says she isn't feeling too well. She even has a nurse."

"Oh well, that's happened before. Christ, yes. Old Rimfire will recover and the nurse will die." Aubrey burst into laughter and sat down on the sofa. Kermit continued his pacing. "Hell, yes, you wait and see. You know how old she is?"

Aubrey pretended to calculate, playing the game. "She must be over eighty, now."

"Over eighty my ass! She is ninety-seven years old! Wait! Ninety-eight, by God! You think I'm kidding? Well, a couple of years ago I looked it up, and Eulalia Xanthippe Breesvort was born in Kaatskill County, New York, shortly after four A.M. on the morning of April 12, 1861. Yes, by God! And you know what else happened that morning?" Dramatic pause, no slightest betrayal of dead seriousness as he stared into Aubrey's joyous smile. "They fired on Fort Sumter, that's what! At *four-thirty* A.M. Just time, I figure, for Old Rimfire to mount her broomstick and fly down to Charleston and put the torch to the touchhole!"

Aubrey laughed delightedly. This was a new story, which was rare for Kermit, he being entirely devoted to his old stories, finding in their frequent repetition the opportunity to embellish delivery and make subtle changes in content. But, having scored resoundingly with a new one, he seemed enormously pleased with himself, and stood over Aubrey, bearding himself into a small grin, as he nodded and lit a cigarette. Then issued a single bark of a laugh, and was off again.

"What we ought to do, I figure, is truss her up on her one-hundredth birthday, float her around in Charleston Harbor and let Fort Sumter fire on *her!*"

Julie put her head in at the door and shouted over their laughter. "Hey, you old bastard!"

Kermit turned, smiling, and bowed his head to her. "Look at her, Aubie. Isn't she beautiful?"

Aubrey looked, and she was. She was wearing a white suit with a large jade pin in the right lapel, the pin almost covered by a vagrant swatch of dark brown-red hair. She touched her throat with one hand and tossed the hair back. "Hi, step. Don't let the old boar trample you." Aubrey made motions and murmurs. Her presence virtually paralyzed him, yet he couldn't look away from her. "Listen, we're going to eat at eight. Would you like a snack before . . ."

"Snack my ass! I want a drink! Christ! I brought six bottles of Old Fitzgerald!" Julie shot her tongue at him, and went away. "I always bring my own, Aubie. If I didn't, they'd have me drinking water! Oh, this is a great house, this is. I was telling you, Aubie, no Milligan was ever known to feel like having a drink or a meal, *anytime.* I used to come over here to see your mother and they'd all be sitting around

78

—in here! This same room! Hasn't changed a goddamned iota since the year one! And they'd be squeezing their tea bags and blowing bubbles, and six o'clock would come and go, and seven, and eight, and I'd be about ready to start foaming at the mouth, and presently here would come old Rimfire with a cupful of her goddamned dried Indian bones and announce spareribs for dinner! Spareribs! Jesus Christ, there wasn't even any goddamned marrow in them! About the third time around it'd all been sucked out! Use those goddamned bones for peashooters if you wanted to! And I finally, I *finally* came to grief one night—I mean, it just got to be too damned much for human endurance—when I rose up and told old Eulallylip that she really ought to take mercy on that poor old long-suffering Indian, and bury his goddamned spareribs, and *leave* 'em buried! Well, I want to tell you, I was ordered out, and it was five or six weeks before I was allowed back." He turned to Aubrey and pointed a finger. "But then—*then*, I was ready for them. On my way over, I stopped by a butchershop and got me about twenty pounds of the best damned top sirloin steaks I could find and four or five quarts of good pre-Prohibition bourbon whisky, and I just left them out in the car. Well, the *same*—goddamned—dunk-and-fart contest goes on until eight-thirty! Even Old George—she starved him to death, you know—was beginning to look peaked. Old George was a grand man, Aubie, but for a multimillionaire, he took more crap than the pull drawer on a birdcage. Anyway, it's getting on toward eight-thirty before Grandmugger makes her entrance and there's been, lo and behold, a change of menu! Now she's got a rasher full of *liver* paste. And it is the foulest goddamned brackish—I mean, it tastes like ground essence of mule tit! So I rise up and I say, very politely, that I'm terribly sorry, ma'am, and all, but my doctor has put me on a strict diet with special instructions as to how it must be cooked, and would the old prune mind if I used her kitchen to prepare what I've brought along? Why, no, that would be fine with her. Then I say that, as a matter of fact, I've brought along quite a bit more than I can eat by myself, and I wonder if any one of them would care to join me. Oh, no, no. All seven of 'em stuffed to the nose rings. Well, I want you to know, Aubie, when I brought out my twenty pounds of rare-cooked steak and five bottles of bourbon, by God, I had to *fight them off!* Why, I reached out once and didn't see old Rimfire forking in from the flank, and goddamned near lost a hand!"

Julie came in toward the end of this recital with an ice bucket, some glasses, and the whisky. She poured Kermit a tall glassful of whisky over ice, and waited with it until he had finished, watching Aubrey, smiling easily at him, her eyes unwavering, familiar. He couldn't keep himself from glancing at her, and almost failed to laugh when Kermit had finished.

Kermit turned on her at once. "Do you have to stand there, distracting my audience?" he said softly.

She gave him the drink. "Your audience is distracting me," she said, sweeping her eyes back to Aubrey. "I didn't know you had such a handsome son hidden away."

"Now, none of that, daughter. He's spoken for. Jesus Christ Himself has him under contract." He looked inquiringly at Aubrey. "What's this about another seminary, anyway?"

"Haven't you asked him about that yet?" Julie said.

Kermit looked sheepish and sat down beside Aubrey. "No. I was just so glad to see him. God, it *is* good to see you, Aubie. You got all summer?"

Then Aubrey explained, knowing before he started that Kermit would not really hear what he was saying. The heart of the matter, for Kermit, was that Aubrey was free, and free to stay free—if he chose to—for as long as he liked, and, therefore, any talk about his possibly not going along to Alaska just failed to reach Kermit, as did his attempts to dim Kermit's enthusiasm over the idea of a safari in Kenya later in the year before or after, or whether or not, he reported to the Saharan Fathers in the North. Kermit heard what he wanted to hear. His ears, he was fond of saying, were highly selective instruments, the whole basis of his success in the motion picture and shipping businesses. Kermit, moreover, was a man of the moment: Aubrey was there, talking, within touching distance. Kermit's consciousness refused to permit entry to anything that might suggest that somehow, five minutes, five hours, five days, or five years from that moment, Aubrey might not be there. The only concrete response Aubrey was able to get out of him followed from the facts that the Saharan Fathers had their place in Southampton and Kermit had a place in Southampton. If Aubrey did happen to be called for an interview, they would all go out together and get in some trapshooting on the sand dunes.

"You're not getting through to him, step," Julie said at one point. She had a way of smiling with a pout that made her lips, her whole aspect, so entirely sensual that it moved him directly in a place in which he had trained himself not to acknowledge movement. She was all eyes and pout now, and he couldn't have answered her to save his virtue. Kermit answered for him.

"What the hell do you mean, daughter? I understood every word he said, perfectly."

"Maybe. But you don't *believe* he's really going to Africa? Except perhaps to hunt with you."

"Believe? How the hell can you believe something that's still in the future? I believe that Aubrey believes he's going to be a priest in Africa. That's all anybody can ask me to believe. Especially since I'm going to do my goddamnedest to talk him out of it." He turned to Aubrey, smiling, his eyes, overshadowed by a thicket of brows, flowing over his son with hope as if looking for a sign.

"Me too," Julie said, and she winked at Aubrey and crossed her legs in the same instant.

And though he looked back immediately at Kermit, he heard one of her legs sliding over the other.

Kermit was saying, ". . . Shelter Island and get Arnie in the morning. Would you like to go along?"

"I—ah—I don't think so. You'll be bringing him back anyway, won't you?"

"Hell, yes. I just thought you'd want to see him as soon as you could." Kermit's tone reproached, but gently.

"Well, I think I'd rather avoid Shelter Island."

"I'll tell you what. I'll be bringing him into the city for lunch, anyway. Unless he's really bad. . . ." Kermit looked into his drink, sipped it, glanced at Julie, then took a large gulp. In the silence, Aubrey kept his eyes on his father, aware that for the moment Julie was outside, looking in. "Why don't you join us for lunch? Arnie likes the Edwardian at the Plaza. We ought to be there by one or so."

Aubrey understood then that Kermit had gone it alone for maybe a hundred Saturdays, and was asking for support. "Sure. I'd like to very much. That's where we used to go before the fights."

"That's right!" And his eyes, which had been tight and close, were eloquent of his gratitude. And Aubrey was suddenly thinking about the ridiculous ease of the religious life.

"What fights?" Julie said.

"Boxing, at Madison Square Garden. Saturday was my day with

the boys. And Aline used to go along now and then, too, and sometimes Rexfordia would eat with us. Then she and I would fight the main event before we ever got to the Garden."

Aubrey smiled, and found his eyes on Julie's knees. He moved them to her eyes. She was pouting at him, and winked again. He turned quickly to Kermit. "How's Aline?"

"Well. I'm ashamed to say I haven't seen her since Easter." He shook his head. "Oh, she's fine, the poor little thing. Every time I see her in that goddamned crazy-house, locked up, and her tiny little voice . . ." He drained his glass and changed course. "Half the time those goddamned harpies won't even let me see her! They've got this goddamned divided room with a screen in the middle, and she comes out with the chains rattling and sits on her side and you sit on the other. For Christ's sake, more than half the time! I think I've only seen her face to face three or four times since she went in! Your mother saw her around Eastertime. Didn't she tell you?"

"Oh sure, but I thought you might have seen her more recently. Mother says Arnie has been doing very well."

"Yeah. Well, I think he does better with her than he does with me. They have more in common." Kermit's hands tightened on his glass. He glanced at Julie again, then frowned and pulled at his nose. "I'm sorry. I didn't mean that the way it sounded. Or if I did mean it, I apologize. Your mother and I . . ." His voice trailed off and he stared down at the rug.

Aubrey chanced a look at Julie. She was staring down also, at her hands folded in her lap, her pout gone. This reassured him. She could be reached, and he wondered why he had been so sure she couldn't. Maybe because a ruthless, sensual exclusivity seemed to proceed from her, seemed to come out of her right at him, like a threat. And now that he knew she could be reached, that something entirely external to her could touch or move her, was she more or less a threat? He had no idea.

Then Rexfordia came down the stairs and into the room, beautifully turned out in a white dinner gown, and Kermit went to her gallantly, and kissed her hand, and their mutual tenderness lasted until Rexfordia happened to ask if Uncle Peter had arrived yet.

"What?" Kermit roared. "Is he coming tonight?" He recoiled from her confirmation of it and staggered over to his bottle. "Jesus Christ," he muttered, "Uncle Numbnuts is coming."

82

"Now, Kermit, be nice. Uncle Peter has not been feeling well. He looks twenty years older than he is."

"Numbnuts *is* twenty years older than he is! The son of a bitch would *have* to be to get that goddamned miserable in one lifetime!"

Rexfordia raised her voice a full note. "Really, Kermit. He's here to discuss something very important with Mother, and I'd appreciate it if you'd just—act civilized for once."

"I've got a better idea, by God! I'll leave! I'll leave right now before Numbnuts gets here!"

And he started from the room, but the doorbell was already ringing and Rexfordia was telling him to be quiet, and then there was Uncle Peter Breesvort standing in the doorway, peering in at them over his pince-nez, his fat round little mouth wide open, his shock at seeing Kermit manifestly intense.

Kermit stood this gaping as long as he could—about four seconds—then bellowed, "Well, Uncle Numbnuts, are you going to walk in freely, or do I have to get the hog hook and drag you in!"

# · EIGHT ·

THE EVENING was a predictable disaster.

Hostilities commenced as Eulalia came down the stairs and into the living room with Magda, the nurse, just behind her, and Eulalia —not more than five feet tall, her hair startlingly white, tied in a neat bun at the nape of her neck, her face an aristocratic and awesome gathering of deeply etched contour furrows, her eyes stunningly blue and ageless and flashing to the heart of all they lighted upon, her smile rarely shown yet so genuine when it was that the only false thing about it was the teeth, her voice thin with the rattle of death but full of the lean magnificent arrogance of command, and her whole presence so informed with belligerence and defiance and human pride that you first suspected, and then you knew, that swooping death had tried her often but each time had been sent limping off wingless to await Eulalia's chosen day—looked right at Kermit and said, "Where's that goddamned Strycker, and who the hell invited him anyway?"

Kermit rose up immediately from a sofa in a far corner, where he had been taking refuge from the living sight of Uncle Peter (whose capacity for absorbing abuse without the slightest attempt at retaliation had been proved limitless in the first three minutes of conversation with Kermit, until Aubrey had taken pity upon Peter and asked him if he'd published any good books lately), and waved a bottle, and shouted, "Here I am, Grandmugger! Congratulations on your six-hundred-and-sixty-sixth birthday!"

At which Eulalia smiled a millimeter or so, and the happy exchange might have gone right on if Magda hadn't intervened.

"Mrs. Milligan," she said, "really, if you don't permit me to give you your sedative, I can't be held accountable."

"Accountable!" Eulalia snapped, turning to glare at her. "Why, you goddamned idiot, on the day you prove yourself accountable, I'll sign your papers for admittance to human society." Then, to Kermit, "Strycker, will you come over and throw this Amathon out? She's worse than my doctor. She cajoles me into bed, claps a thermometer in my mouth, fastens an ice bag to my forehead, props my behind up on a bedpan, and tells me to relax! The woman is out of her head, Strycker, and I call upon you, ignorant brute that you are, to deal with her as you best know how."

"Glad to, Grandmugger! Magda! Stick her with the needle!"

"Hah! Listen to him! The bastard speaks from his heart! You'd like to see me dead, wouldn't you, Strycker?"

"Hell no! I hope you outlive me, and I mean that sincerely."

"You lie."

"Well, good Christ, do you think I want you haunting me?"

"Don't flatter yourself."

"At least this way I can see you."

"I won't pretend that I harbor any similar affection for the sight of you."

"But your face is so much more interesting than mine. I mean, who else has powder burns on her nose from shooting her mouth off?"

"Don't talk, you bearded vacuity. You midair full of bristles!"

"By God, you ought to grow a beard. I'm sure you could. Cover up all of that corrugated brimstone!"

"And you ought to give your face to medical science."

"And you ought to give yours to archeological science! Even then they'd have to give you a face-lifting before anybody would believe it! And lifting your face would take four small burros and Lipchitz the sculptor!"

". . . leave your body to a zoo! As the first known example of a hairy-forked baboon that passed its life walking around backward on its forepaws talking about Lipchitz and like matters, and finally died during an enema when it choked to death on the tube!"

85

Kermit opened his mouth to make answer; then, beginning to acknowledge a masterstroke, went to a grin. Eulalia, holding tense and preying, breathed once and laughed derisively: a wineskin being squeezed for last drops. Then both began to guffaw.

"Mrs. Milligan, please," Magda said, whining, persisting. "It's only a small pill, and with a bit of water you'd never . . ."

"Water! Why, you damned idiot, the doctor said whisky! Get out! Out! Where's Rexfordia? Rexfordia! This damned female you hired hasn't stopped pouring water into me since she arrived. She treats me like a ship's boiler! I declare she has a bet with the chambermaid that I can fill the bedpan. Strycker! You drunken fool, come forward and restrain this creature. I asked for a registered nurse and got a wet nurse instead!" Then, pointing dramatically, "Out, you damned Aquaria! I'll not drink any more water, and I'll not pass any more, either! I'll be damned if I'll be primed like a bilge pump!"

"Now, Mrs. Milligan," Magda said—and Aubrey's heart went out to her, this stout, bewildered woman who had no idea what manner of windmill she'd hired herself out to—"That's strict doctor's orders. I'm just trying to do my job."

"Your job! Your job, you ignorant woman, is to do what I tell you to do. Where did you train?"

"Mother Cabrini."

"I thought so. Another damned Roman Catholic. So that's what you've been knitting. My shroud!"

"Mrs. Milligan, I've been knitting a sweater!"

"A sweater! For whom, may I ask? Fatty Arbuckle?"

"It's for you! I was knitting it for you!"

"I knew it, by God! Don't you know any better than that? You get the hell upstairs and unravel that monstrosity before I unravel you at the withers!"

Magda opened her mouth to speak, then closed it, let it go to quavering at the corners, and uttered a gullish wounded cry as she turned away and ran—clumsy white shoes and poor fat ankles—out of the room.

Eulalia looked after her a moment, then turned to the company. "She's really a sweet girl, but she needs to learn discipline."

After which Aubrey took a deep breath, or tried to, and settled back into the wings of the most defensible chair he could find, but Eulalia was upon him almost immediately.

"Aubrey! What's all this I hear about Africa? In the name of God, child, don't you know those nigras are profoundly savage people, respecters of neither God nor man?" Aubrey tried to say something about all men being equal before God, and something simultaneously about Muslim Arabs, but Eulalia advanced two steps on her short-heeled strapped shoes, stabbing viciously at the air with a bone-inspired forefinger: "Let me tell you a story, child, about a girl I had. Her name was Ella, with me all her life, and I thought the world of her. And she up, after twenty-three years with me, and married a big black West Indian six and a half feet tall by the name of Russell. And he took to beating her. He would beat her every night, up there in the nigra quarters over the coach house at Arthur Avenue. Well, I got tired, child, of hearing that poor little girl scream, and I took my gun, my .44-caliber cavalry revolver, and I went out to the coach house and up the outside steps, and I rapped on the door, and I said, 'Russell, you open the door or I'll shoot my way through.' Well, he knew I could shoot, and he said, 'Mrs. Milligan, have you got your gun with you?' And I said, 'I have, Russell, I have.' And he said, sort of snippy-like, 'Have you got your gun all loaded, Mrs. Milligan?' And I said, 'I have.' And then he said, 'Well, Mrs. Milligan, I've got my gun, and it is all loaded, too, and if you don't go away, I'll be out to meet you.' And I said, 'Come out, Russell. Come out here with your gun.' And so out he came with his gun, a small silver pistol not as big as his aboriginal hand. And I didn't even look at him, child. I just walked down those stairs in front of him and drew a line with the toe of my boot in the dust of the driveway, and I said, 'This is your line, Russell.' Then I paced off the proper distance, ten paces, from his line and I drew my line. And I toed it and said, 'All right, Russell. Stand up to your line, facing me. When I count three, you may begin to fire and I will begin to fire.' Well, Russell stood to his line, and I said, 'One.' I held my pistol down, pointing at the ground, child, and I knew it made him nervous, and he had *his* gun pointed right at me. He knew that *I* knew I could bring my gun up at the count of three and blow his left eye out without touching the socket. *That's* what he knew, child. He'd seen me shooting acorns many an afternoon. And I said, 'Two.' And Russell said, 'Mrs. Milligan, I'm leaving.' And he did leave, but he took Ella with him, and I never heard from her again."

And Eulalia stood in front of him, as skirmisher, her old arm half raised, her eyes immensely sad, whether at the loss of Russell as a target or Ella as a maid Aubrey couldn't tell, and Julie was asking her about how she had outshot the Fort Lee police force for six years running in much-publicized old-woman-against-Fort-Lee's-finest pistol matches, and Eulalia was saying, Yes, that was true, and that she was seventy-four on the day of the first match, but that she had posted her best score on her seventy-seventh birthday and had fallen into some kind of an unaccountable decline thereafter; yet Aubrey could see that Eulalia wasn't really interested. Russell had gotten away. He had not stood to the test. That was the real regret of it all. And, looking at her, Aubrey gave her tribute, tribute to her great and indomitable belief in her destiny and in the rightness of her will. He remembered her saying to him, "Child, I can make this body do whatever I want it to do. And when this body is worn out, and when it is dead, it will be I alone who shall have worn it out, I alone who shall have killed it." And, as she said it, her eyes had been hard and bright and calm, and he had known exactly what she meant, which was that she had not come upon this earth to trifle: if you chose to stand against her in a matter of ultimate importance you were, patently, choosing to kill or be killed; in matters of lesser importance—as, for example, legal matters (Eulalia having been the first woman to take her law degree in course in the State of New York)—you might only hope to lose gracefully. That upon which she had set her mind she accomplished, won, or brought about. Aubrey had never known Eulalia to lose anything but her temper.

Kermit brought her out of her dueling posture by saying, "God-damn it, Grandmugger, I'd take you on myself but I wouldn't be in my right mind, as I certainly am, if I tried to stand up against the only revolver of cavalry to survive the Battle of the Little Big Horn!"

"Listen, Flintlock," Eulalia said, mixing humor and derision with practiced ease, "you couldn't stand to me with a Gatling gun."

"What's this about the Little Big Horn?" Uncle Peter asked, somewhat pompously.

"Eulalia was there. On the Indian side," Kermit said.

"Oh, Kermit!" Rexfordia said. "Why do you always make a joke of everything? Mother was *not* at the Little Big Horn."

"No joke," Kermit said, placing one hand over his heart. "No joke at all. Grandmugger was not only *at* the Little Big Horn, she *blew* it!" Then he broke into loud laughter, and did a little dance, and announced that he would honor the occasion with "four rootlely-toots on my bangalorum!" The which he did, then and without warning throughout the evening, the bangalorum consisting of a hand cupped over the mouth of an empty whisky bottle, and the rootlely-toots sounding like ships whistling, seals barking, and old soldiers dying after all. "The name of that song," he said, shaking his head and rolling his eyes demurely, "is 'Gone with My Wind, or When the Lightning Strikes the Shithouse Leave It Out.' And remember, friends, that nature abhors a vacuum, Rexfordia abhors whores, somebody should vacuum Uncle Numbnuts, and I am by nature hors de combat."

"Kermit!" Rexfordia said.

But Kermit was already disappearing, in hilarious collapse, behind his distant sofa.

"Hump, hump, hump," Eulalia said to Aubrey.

"Good evening, Eulalia," Uncle Peter said.

"Hump. You look ridiculous in those glasses, Peter."

Tengmalm's owl, Aubrey thought.

"And you, Julia, need a haircut," Eulalia said.

"Yes, ma'am," Julie said, smiling. Julie stood next to Eulalia, swaying slightly at the hips, looking at Aubrey as though she intended to swallow him up.

"And don't stand next to me like that, making me look older than I am."

"No, ma'am." Julie moved away, toward Aubrey.

"Hump. And where's that damned chucklehead of a painter?" And Eulalia went humping off toward the kitchen.

Julie looked across the room to where Uncle Peter and Rexfordia were in quiet conversation in front of the fireplace. Kermit was not seen, but was heard, humming softly, raising his voice now and again to sing: "In the evenin' by the moonlight, you can hear those darkies cussin'. They is madder than a bastard at every other colored pussin'!"

"My God," Julie said. "What this family needs is home movies!" She dropped, laughing softly, onto the sofa next to Aubrey and worked her rump forward and slouched down so that her head was beneath the level of the sofa's back. He looked away, but was aware of her gaze upon him, knew that it was steady and amused; and was acutely aware of how much of her thighs were exposed, and could almost measure her success in centimeters out of a sensual third eye when she made an indifferent effort to restore her skirt to the perimeter of her near kneecap. "Okay, step," she said softly, deep basso tones making her voice sound like an echo. "You can look now."

He turned back and looked down at her, holding the top of his eyes precisely on her eyes, yet saw, quite involuntarily, out of a vagrant lower hemisphere of vision, her knees and the four or five inches of leg and nylon above them (long, beautiful legs that fattened gently above the knee into graceful thighs, into marvelous thighs which, held and shaped by her stockings, and held just slightly apart and moving, damned near demanded that some part of his mind should imagine, or try to, what a voluptuously eager matrix lay above and between them; and some part of his mind, unbidden and unregulated, did begin this imagining until, suddenly, his memory of Julie naked, having found invitation, came flashing in upon him, brilliantly focused at her hips), and he blinked rapidly and groaned not quite silently before he was able to look away and up and fix his eyes on a wide-bottomed relative hanging in portrait vile over a false fireplace on the opposing wall, and lost his vision of Julie somewhere between the glower and the gleet of that female progenitor's hyperbolic strabismus. "Look at what?" he asked, somewhat belligerently.

"Not so loud," she whispered, peeking behind them over the top of the sofa. "I don't want the others to know I'm here."

"Why not?"

"That goddamned Uncle Peter. He keeps rubbing my back. I think he's trying to unfasten my bra."

Aubrey, having glanced at her furtively, snapped head and eyes away as if she had bit him. He tried to think of something to say to cover his blush, but could only manage a sort of goose hiss that launched and drowned the word: "Petesake. . . ."

"Oh, you blush beautifully, step," she said, near his ear.

"I'm not blushing."

"Oh, yes you are. *I* know all about blushing. And you look like you enjoy it, too." She giggled delightedly. "And I haven't even gotten to the really suggestive words yet. I mean, *bra* is practically a neuter nothing. How about panties! Or negligée! Or—or garter belt! Wow! Look at you, step! You're going to burst!"

He sat there, full of scarlet bile a moment, and told himself he was being ridiculous; that the only thing for it was a crisp, evenly fierce retort. He started to talk before he had it composed, but it fairly leaped to his tongue—he having taken spark, no doubt, from Eulalia and Kermit. "All right. So I'm blushing. So I also turn green just before I vomit!"

"Oops! Power brakes, touch of reverse. Easy, step. I'll be a good girl. I promise I won't get any juicier. Okay? If I feel any more nasty, blushable words coming on, I'll blow my siren. Right?" She reached out and patted him on the thigh; just two lightsome pats, but they ran down to his bowels in red alarm and heated all he sat on. She seemed to know, and moved her lips moistly around upon her grin, as if inviting him to read there something too close or intimate—or maybe too obscene—for words. He wound his eyes away from hers in slow widening circles and settled them again on the mandolin-bottomed relative. Julie sighed. "You know what, step? You're the return of the missing link. You're just what this holy family needed to complete itself. Sure as hell."

"That's nice."

"Now, don't be regressive. Listen. It's true. We've got St. Eulalia-Anne of the immaculate ballistics; St. Rexfordia-Mary of the Jersey cliffs, virgin mother of us all; St. Kermit the Josephite, patron of whiskers, movies, and mountains; St. Aline-Martha the fragile, busy about the Bronx, Westchester, and long silence; St. Arnie-Lazarus of Shelter Island, who hasn't quite yet risen from the dead; and St. Julie Magdalen of the sexy habits and the reversible wimple. Right?" She giggled toward him, leaned in very close, then sat back abruptly with a pouter smile and looked at him as if she held the mortgage on his head and shoulders. "Well?"

"Not right. Wrong. You haven't even got your genealogy straight."

"Don't be technical. And who the hell knows, anyway? All those dead people, two thousand years ago! Why, they even let the Romans take the census. And you know how those Romans are!" She laughed softly and brushed at her hair with one hand, her motions very positive. "Anybody could have been related to anybody for all those Romans knew. They were chasing blondes up and down the road to Damascus."

"I'm so glad to have an eyewitness report."

"Who isn't? But that's not the point, step. The point is, you are the mystic seventh. You make us complete. You've come to fulfill all the prophecies. Right?"

"Julie, I don't think you're funny. Not a damned bit."

"I'm not trying to be funny, Aubrey. Really I'm not. I'm just trying to explain, allegorically I will admit." She peered at him intently,

91

three fingers of one hand pressing her upper lip like a shade down over her smile. "I don't mean any offense, but look at it this way. Until you came home, we were half-dozened, half-brothered, half-sistered, half-realized, half-assed—oh, pardon me, step. No offense." She almost laughed. "Now, however! *Now* we are seven! Don't you see? The seven churches, the seven candlesticks, the seven stars, the seven trumpets, the seven vials, the seven seals, the seven spirits, the seven horns, the seven eyes of the Lamb, *and* the seven plagues!" She finished on a high-rise level that made her laughter sound nearly hysterical. "Not to mention," she cried, "the seven-headed monster!"

He sat looking at her. How the hell did she know so much about the Bible? And how the hell did she happen to be able to rattle off the apocalyptic sevens so glibly? He went eyes front after a moment, finding the motion of her soft laughter and the amused brilliance of her banjo-round eyes—all strung with silver mockery, and twanging—more than modesty or patience were ready to encounter. He said, only and loudly, "I wish I found you as hilarious as you do."

"Oh, step! Don't look so stern!" she said, laughing and touching at her mouth with her fingers. "You look like a constipated shrine!"

"Really, Julie," Rexfordia said, sharply, reproachfully, appearing suddenly *en passant*, her glare sweeping back and forth between them piercingly, like a beacon in a fog. And she was gone as suddenly, out the door and down the corridor before either could say her yea or nay.

"Oh Christ," Julie said, no longer laughing. "You think she heard me?" Aubrey shrugged. "Sure she did. What'd I say?"

"Something about a constipated shrine."

Julie grinned. "Well, you *did*. But I wish she hadn't heard me. I don't think she really approves of me, you know?"

"I don't know. But I wouldn't be surprised."

"Oh, you wouldn't? Okay, step. As the Christ, it's your duty to straighten her out, right? I mean, tell her to stop casting stones and all that jazz. No rush. Just so's you get to it before we crucify you." She started to giggle again.

"You're afraid of her, aren't you?" he asked, discovering confidence enough in the accusation to face her head on.

"Sorry, Master, but hell no," she said, grinning full watt. "I know it's the place of us loose women to fear the Lord and His hand-

92

maidens, but your dear sweet mother doesn't give me a twinge. I acknowledge, however, that I don't want to offend her."

"How come? I wouldn't have thought that offending people constituted one of the worries of your life."

"Very guilefully spoken, step. Oh, I'll bet you can be a son of a bitch when you want to be." She pouted happily. "But, I'll explain. You see, my own dear amoral mother taught me maybe five useful things before she left in quest of the Holy Grail. And one of them was, never offend a rich relative. Especially a rich female relative."

"Is that right?" He regarded her evenly, strongly tempted to unload on her: to see what those green eyes would do with a blast in reference to Karen Van Hatten, etc., stepmother extraordinary—something like "I thought rich *males* was your mother's specialty." But he held it, and said simply, "And rich males?"

"Oh, they were covered in the other four things. When it comes to rich males, you screw your way into their money, and then you screw them out of it." She seemed to know, again, what had been on his mind, and let him in on it when she said, "You haven't got the stomach for insult, have you, step? Your big problem is you want everybody to like you." She leaned to him and whispered breathfully, "But that's all right, doll. I'll like you anyway. And I'll teach you all about screwing as soon as my exams are over."

Aubrey grabbed his knees and stood up. "Look, Julie! I don't know what your problem is, but I have my suspicions. And gynecology isn't one of my fields of interest!"

"Oh, now," she said, also rising. "Of course not. I mean, I'm sure you're *interested*, but that's neither here nor there, is it? Not yet anyway." Still grinning, she took his arm. "Won't you, at least, escort me to the table, step? I'm so hungry I wouldn't even rape you on the way."

"Julie . . ." he started, but was interrupted by Rexfordia announcing dinner, and by Eulalia reannouncing it, and by Kermit shouting behind him.

"Oh holy Jesus Christ, yes! Let's eat dinner! Come on, Numbnuts! All hogs need to be slopped once a day! Aubie! By God, where've you been? Time to drink dinner! Louis Roederer, *brut*, fifty-three, by Christ! And I'll personally de-pancreas anybody who isn't drunk by nine-oh-finking-thirty!"

Aubrey followed Julie's lead to the door and as they passed into the hallway, she looked up at him round-eyed and wholesome and

93

said, "I shouldn't have mentioned screwing, step darling. But, you know, I'm just going to *love* breaking you in!" And she went off giggling ahead of him into the dining room.

All manner of business was discussed and all kinds of issues resolved at dinner, loudly; and Aubrey, still not recovered from Julie, and newly shocked and somewhat dismayed at the way his family generated spate and spite, and accepted both as the normal climate of living, was mostly silent—*entirely* silent, except for a few half-hearted attempts to defend Uncle Peter (who was a foursquare, bass-drum jackass, and no doubt of it) from Kermit's unrelenting, burp-gunning attack—but listened and made especial note of the following resolutions:

That, Tuesday being Mr. Jebb's day off, Aubrey should help Julie clean out her apartment and move her things Tuesday morning.

That Aubrey was somewhere between St. Francis of Assisi (Rexfordia's fancy) and a goddamned bandicoot (Eulalia's) for having left his worldly goods behind, and that Rexfordia and/or Kermit would, with the help of Abercrombie and/or Fitch, re-worldly-goods him first chance and thing.

That Aubrey looked peaked, underfed, sick, deprived, lonely, had become much too morose and close-mouthed, really ought to smile, laugh, talk, eat, drink, enter into the general discussion more, and should stop swapping his full champagne glass for Julie's empty so sneakily because Julie was already nearly as drunk as Kermit (which was pretty damned drunk).

That Eulalia definitely was related to the Father Murphy who stuffed his hat in the cannon's mouth to keep the British from firing on the Irish rebels. ("Stuffed his hat in the cannon's mouth!" Kermit roared. "He might as well've stuffed it up his . . ." Interruption by Rexfordia.)

That Arnie, his mental health permitting, would inevitably spend from Sunday noon to Friday morning with Rexfordia, because, after all, Kermit would have him for two weeks in Alaska, and God alone knew what that would do to the poor boy's soul and mind.

That there was nothing actionable about Solly's charge that a certain painter had descended from the bathrooms to the kitchen and was imposing upon Solly's hospitality to the point of drunkenness and had threatened to rape her in the freezer.

That the goddamned Greek had, without reasonable question, dyed a carp to look like a salmon.

That Father Murphy's heart had been cut out to grease the boots of the English captain. ("Well," Kermit pursued, "what they *should* have done was to grease his hat and shove it up his stupid . . ." Interruption—a short scream—by Rexfordia.)

That Uncle Peter was a certifiable blockheaded bastard (Eulalia's fancy) if he thought Eulalia's memoirs were to be distributed to the general public for money.

That Uncle Peter was a certifiable blockheaded bastard anyway.

That Julie should stop "ogling" (Rexfordia's word) Aubrey.

That the airplane that Kermit had recently financed for his guide (not named) was, according to Eulalia, a goddamned fool arrangement of turkey bones and canvas (she having a picture of it before her, submitted pridefully by Kermit), and that anybody who would presume to fly around in it over hilly country ought to be chained to a rock, and that *she* wouldn't fly in it, by God, if it came equipped with a skyhook dangling from the right hand of the Almighty. (To the which Kermit's reply was that when it came to ridiculous arrangements of canvas and turkey bones, Eulalia really ought to take a look in the mirror—Eulalia being dressed formally in one of her more formidable costumes, a sort of red bombazine half-shelter with matching ruby pendants at the grommets—to the which sally Eulalia, in her turn, took vigorous exception, informing Kermit that he had always been a burdensome ass but if he kept it up at his present rate of progress he would very shortly be a horse's ass, and opining that if his goddamned airplane ever managed to leave the ground she devoutly hoped that it would get just high enough so that when it came down, nozzle first, his injuries would not be trivial.)

That Kermit's soul was irrevocably damned to hell, barring the direct intervention of the Sacred Heart of Jesus.

That Julie should really wear two brassieres if that was all one brassiere did for her.

That Rexfordia's sister Georgia had purchased a red Stearns-Knight limousine in 1920, at a cost of fifty-five hundred dollars.

That the *Greenwich Village Follies* had definitely played Washington, D.C., in 1921.

That there were twenty-seven oak trees, two acres of ground, and seventeen rooms to the Tremont estate in the Bronx in 1917, and that the mortgage was one hundred and sixty thousand dollars, and that nobody had any money.

That Chauncey Olcott was a singer whose voice had a crack in it.

That rosewood pianos had far and away the best tone of all.

That Uncle Peter's story about the French intelligence officers castrating an Algerian rebel during forced sexual intercourse with a prostitute was a goddamned lie, and that Uncle Peter ought to be ashamed of himself for scheduling a book for publication with such a malignity in it. (This being Kermit's, Julie's, and Eulalia's resolution, objected to by Rexfordia who averred that Uncle Peter was only trying to let Aubrey know about the atrocities that were going on in North Africa. To the which Kermit replied that it was perfectly all right with everybody if she and Uncle Peter Breesvort Numbnuts wanted to have a sexy conversation, but that, after all, they *should* consider Aubrey, who was just then, as any reasonably intelligent casual observer would have noted, going through that most painful of experiences, the monastic menopause.)

That it would certainly do Kermit's soul a world of good if he took Aubrey to see Aline on Sunday.

That Uncle Peter should certainly be ready to bear the cost of a buckram-bound, private, two-hundred-copy edition of Eulalia's memoirs, and assure her of two-column reviews in all the major newspapers and magazines.

That Solly's report that the painter was still trying to rape her on the floor had small merit.

That Julie should wear *three* brassieres, of black bombazine.

That Uncle Peter could be called Uncle Numbnuts after all (passed by a show of hands, Kermit's two making up for the withholding of Rexfordia's, Aubrey's abstention being noted).

That Mr. Jebb was the most silent man in the world.

That the Greek had undoubtedly disguised an inner tube to look like a carp masquerading as a salmon.

That Kermit's soul was irrevocably damned to hell, barring the direct intervention of the Daughters of Mary Immaculate.

That what this country needed was a good five-cent monastic menopause.

That Julie should really wear *four* brassieres, if that's all three did for her.

That Uncle Numbnuts should be sent to Algeria in a vacuum cleaner full of ants, not including Eulalia, without *hors de combat*, or any other kind.

That it was far more likely that Solly would rape the painter.

That what really should have happened to Father Murphy was that the cannon's mouth should have been shoved up his . . . Interruption—a prolonged, piercing scream—by Rexfordia.

That Julie should, in addition to the four brassieres, procure and wear at all times a bulletproof vest.

That the Heart Fund should without delay set aside monies to buy Father Murphy a new hat. ("So that I can present it to him, in a very dignified manner," Kermit said. "And then take it and shove it . . ." Interruption—Rexfordia's chair falling backward to the floor as she rose from the table and ran for the stairs.)

That because Uncle Peter Breesvort Numbnuts had apparently gone home, and Eulalia had been led off to bed by her nurse, and Rexfordia had walked out, and Aubrey had refused to vote on any of the evening's resolutions, a committee ought to be appointed to determine if there was a quorum present.

That Solly—who entered during the quorum inquiry and staggered up to and fell against the table and put her hand in the mashed potatoes, and glared at the chairman and said, "Strycker, in the name of Jaysus, go home!"—was definitely out of order, but that she was bigger and drunker than anyone else present, and, therefore, was heard.

That the meeting was, with or without the consent of Father Murphy, irretrievably adjourned.

# · NINE ·

AND LATE AND ALONE he took a walk through the house, visiting all the public rooms and many of the private, moving in darkness with complete familiarity, going from memory to memory not quite eagerly but with interest, finding it necessary to convince himself that he had actually spent five years in other places, that he had actually left home, and that he would leave it again and probably not return. For it sometimes seemed to him, as he bumped along from doorway to sofa to knickknack to horrible looming portrait to abrasive drape, that the place still had a vital part of him captive; and that very part that sought its freedom most vigorously: his attachment, or sense of devotion, to whatever it was that constituted loyalty to family.

And just what the hell was that loyalty? What gave it birth and in what did it inhere? What could there possibly be about his embattled family—all gone their separate, positivistic, implacable ways—that could find a common ground in anything, and least of all in this house, this overstuffed heaping of remnants, this attic of shards? What could there be in the house—stacked with a mute history of discord and bitterness—that could inspire in him, or whomever, anything other than dreams of the non-claustrophobic, airy, disinherited liberty of the next world? And he walked and wondered, and found no answer.

The windows and most of the doors and walls were hung with full-length portieres, purple on one side and wine-red on the other, made of a type of mastiff-haired velour the which, when you touched it, you immediately wished you hadn't, and which, Aubrey was certain, was entirely impenetrable by light, heat, or large-caliber bullet. Where there were no drapes there were oil paintings, all of them full-figure portraits, a few being Warners or Masons, but most being Breesvorts, than which, Aubrey had long since concluded, there had obviously been no more facially ill-favored a dynasty since the Nibelungs, and all of them done in the heavy Dutch manner, blubber-lidded, scowling, jowlish, full of rheum and dark beer, and not one of them measuring less than two ax-handles across the nethers, looking, in fact, as if Protestant baroque had been run through the Hudson River school and left for dead (and these paintings were all over the house—one of an Aunt Hepzibah Breesvort had hung over Aubrey's bed until, it was determined, she started to give him nightmares with her cold mad eye and twisted lip and oddly misshapen head—even Rexfordia referred to her as the Young Woman With Water-Jug Head, a wild flight for Rexfordia—and Aubrey later discovered that Aunt Hepzibah was a double for *Malle Babbe*—all she needed was the owl on her shoulder). On the floors were Persian, Greek, Indian, Chinese, Russian, and God alone knew what other kinds of rugs, and enough of them to carpet the public square of Ulan Bator. They were not laid end to end or set down singly, but, there being an incredible excess of them, were piled one on top of the other, sometimes three or four deep with edges sticking out and up here and there, so that to walk across any floor in the house would have been hazardous if it had not been that the proliferation of furniture prevented one from taking two consecutive steps in any given direction. And the sensation of standing at certain vital junctures of the rugs was, Arnie once imagined, rather like that of treading the breasts of an expiring Amazon. The colors and designs of these rugs were Oriental jokes, as far as both boys were concerned, except for one design, on a rug that Eulalia said was no less than two hundred years old, the which Arnie maintained was an exact rendering of the line of march of the 1953 Eisenhower inaugural parade through Washington, D. C.: a nice job of prognostication for any rugmaker. And the furniture was all out of Victoria by Hieronymus Bosch, duplicable only if you had happened to purchase seventeen five-piece satin-upholstered living room sets at John Wanamaker's in 1896 and scattered them through a sixteen-room house, placing sofas back to back wherever possible. The knickknacks and less substantial, or occasional, or antique, furniture were squeezed among and under these more formidable pieces, a partial list of which had come into Aubrey's hands on a schedule of inventory of Fort Milligan he had received as a knowledgeable party during the contest of George Milligan's will, instituted by Aunt Ardiss Tyree in the late thirties against Eulalia (Aubrey's service, and Arnie's, having been a mistake by the court but kept by both of them out of simple boyish fondness for legal documents of any description): four rosewood stools with embroidered flowers in satin upholstery, two Martinique silver snuffboxes, a Louis XVI swan bed less casters, one Prussian bootjack, one Pier glass, two Empire style mahogany card tables with claw legs, one lyre-type clock of gilded mahogany with brass, four Creole slat-back chairs, one cherrywood candlestand chair, one Aaron Willard mahogany tall clock, one Behrens curly birch washstand, one Recamier-style rosewood sofa with gold leaf, one satinwood wine cooler, one William Hook sewing table, one Girandole mirror, one Randolph mahogany wing chair, one *kas* of tulip poplar painted in grisaille, one pine Bible box, one pinewood Spanish *trastero*, one pair of Spanish sconces with mirrors and candle brackets, one Sanderson beaker and porringer, one Sanderson tankard and one Sanderson caudle cup, one John Coney chocolate pot, one Timothy Dwight silver salver, one Cowell spout cup, one Willard banjo clock, one Peter Van Dyke mustard pot, one Syng baptismal basin, one John Coney inkstand, one Amelung flip glass, one Heyne communion service, one Paul Revere punch bowl, one Benjamin Burt teapot, two Cornelius Paulus punch bowls, one Amelung stenger bottle, one George Pullman buffet, one J. H. Belter settee, and one J. H. Belter rosewood whatnot. And add various tapestries, one astrolabe, a 1745 sextant guaranteed used by Captain Bligh, two Shaker icons which Shakers were not supposed to have, a bottle of 1795 Madeira wine which nobody ever had curiosity enough to open, two camel saddles, a pair of French dueling sabers, assorted muskets and flintlocks including an eight-foot Kentucky rifle, fourteen symbolic masks made by New Mexican Indians, an original Georges Rouault painting that hung in the downstairs bathroom, six blown-up Ansel Adams photographs of Death Valley mounted on cardboard and hung in the kitchen, and a moose head with its left antler and its right eye missing hung directly over the north end of the sixteen-foot dining room table (the moose not honorably taken, having been scragged and otherwise impaled by old Elijah Breesvort, Eulalia's bachelor brother, on the front bumper of his Hupmobile near Passadumkeag, Maine, one night in the late summer of 1923, but, being the only moose Elijah, a devoted hunter, had ever come near, to say nothing of done in by his own efforts, it was put into passable repair—which was more than you could say for the Hupmobile—and suitably mounted on polished teak, and left by Elijah to George Milligan in 1930, in which year Elijah went on to the happy hunting grounds), which, with its chairs, was supposed to have been designed by Norman Bel Geddes one evening in 1927, before dinner.

Then add a library of some seven thousand two hundred volumes, most of them in red or black leather bindings, spread throughout the house on built-in walnut bookshelves, or in other occasional bookcases, or simply stacked here and there, three volumes of Chateaubriand having been used for years to replace three inches of leg broken, by Arnie, from a Duncan Phyfe chair; most of the volumes of no conceivable use whatsoever, the majority of them having titles like: *The Pipkins of East Climax* or *Chronicles of Old Fort Orange*, or *The Dutch Reformed Church and the West India Company: The Formative Years*. So that Arnie had once said that whoever had bound such drivel in leather had no respect whatsoever for the trouble to which horses, pigs, cows, and naugas go to grow their hides.

And this was the house in which he had been raised from his second year, and never, in his almost five-year absence from it, had he felt the slightest desire to see it, or any of its artifacts, again.

And said, as he climbed to his room, Oh yes, one might think, looking at it from below, My, what a grand house, builded there for the ages, proudly high up with all that great gray rock for a doorstep and that gay red roof. Anyone might think that, and tell me how lucky I was to have been brought up in it. But I tell you, gentles all, this is a house of memories—all of its best moments gone. I, personally, wasn't here for any damned one of its best moments. A house of regret—all that lived in it and still live in it remind themselves and each other only of what might have been. A house of uglinesses, of money, of frustrated love, of exquisitely appointed crackings of the human heart. A house of afternoons, those interminable, locked-in afternoons that began to derange Arnie, all those solemn, dreadful, endless afternoons of boyhood, when we stood, looking out and down at the wide river and the dark city beyond, watching the water change color under the moods of the sky, watching it flow away, gone and out to the oceans, yet not changing outwardly ourselves, or going out, and regretting through all the long, hollow, torpid afternoons, through all those monstrous, unknowable, maddening afternoons of the child, that our gate was locked, that all we could do was stand at it, our faces pressed between its bars, and listen—listen—and all we heard were old noises, and behind them the lonely echoes of human weariness, sounding and re-sounding along the eavesdrops of the world.

And he got to his room telling himself not to be so damned dramatic. But he was thinking of Arnie. Of Arnie and of that time—that raw and blatant time—when Arnie would be standing in front of him, his great black eyes either mad or sane, one or the other without warning, so that Aubrey would have no time to prepare his reaction and, either way, Arnie would be way ahead of him, and spare him no embarrassment. And it might be "Shame, shame, Aubie babe. You thought I'd be nuts, didn't you?" Or it might be "Don't look at me like that, for Christ's sake! Haven't you ever seen a nut before?" Or it might be, oracularly, "I've been talking with angels, fallen angels, and I tell you, Aubie, they've just been waiting for me to fall, and I'm to take immediate command." Or it might be nothing; no discernible thing except the silent, black denial by those eyes of all kinship, history, or recognition—the utter, regressive, rejection of any object whatsoever, be it father, brother, or blue-tail fly.

He had seen Arnie just twice since his removal from the Titan Seminary. The first time just a month afterward, when Kermit had brought Arnie with him to Boston for the ceremony of Aubrey's pronouncement of simple vows, and Arnie had looked at him as Jesus might have looked at Judas, and said that he was, of course, perfectly sane but needed rest, yet needed above all Aubrey's loyalty, and why hadn't Aubrey left the Titan Order in protest? ("You have betrayed me! Betrayed all that we ever meant to each other! Betrayed the solemn promises of our fraternity!") The second time was at Easter, 1956, when Kermit and Arnie had dropped in at St. Titus' Hall without notice and Arnie, then in his demoniac period, had his eyes and face blazing with what was, at least, a good imitation of hellfire, assured Aubrey that everybody but the Neo-Manichees were on the wrong side of the contest for paradise, and that God and the Devil had recently commissioned Arnie and Jesus Christ II to found the New Church and lead the world out of its ignorance. And, at that time, Aubrey—foolishly not realizing how far the thing had gone—had reached both hands to his brother, and said, "Arnie, you know you don't really believe that. You'd be disgusted with me if I pretended to think you *did* believe it. I can't pretend with you, Arnie . . ." and had then seen the seal of insanity plainly in Arnie's eyes and had gone back to his knees with no heart for prayer, and a memory of Arnie, maniac, permanently lodged in the quick of his imagination.

And what would it be this time? There had been a clue in Aubrey's mail at Easter—a big, brown envelope addressed, as usual, in black crayon and block letters an inch high, to Master Aubrey Titanic Strycker, O. A. S. T., The Titan Rock Club, Mount Caucasus, Chelsea, New York. It contained a typewritten manuscript of twenty-one pages, being the first chapter, according to Arnie's accompanying note, of a work of great projected length to be entitled "Four and a Half Years of Struggle Against Lies, Stupidity, and Cowardice" (the which, according to Father Finnegan, was Adolf Hitler's original title for *Mein Kampf*—the Father Master having, of course, read the pages before Aubrey got them and having summoned him on Easter Monday for the latest in a series of little conferences concerning Arnie and the sanity of the Strycker family in general). And the manuscript was the strangest of all of Arnie's strange literary productions.

It began: "In that sweet Wagnerian September of 1934, just twenty months before I was born again to do what I am to do, we drove down in the black Horch from the Hotel Continental in Berlin, through our beloved Bayreuth, to Nüremberg. The road was crowded but way was made for our official cars, and the mood was joyous and the air mystic and charged with love, and we stood up in the car and greeted the people, and waved to the marching units and they waved back and cheered and saluted the *Führer*, and in their exultation, and ours, there was the pure, blinding light of truth and sanctity, and the overwhelming promise that at long last the ages would realize their fervent hope, that the Aryan peoples of the world were about to reclaim their birthright, and that what we would do in those following days at Nüremberg would determine the course of Germany, and of the world, for the next thousand years, and perhaps forever."

And it went on, in amazing detail, relating how "they" rode into

Nüremberg in triumph through the narrow streets lined with clamoring thousands; how they stayed at the Deutscher Hof with the Führer; how Hitler spoke that night at the Rathaus, and what he said, and how ecstatically he was cheered then and later; how the Führer strode like a Holy Roman Emperor into the Luitpold Hall the next morning to the tune of the Badenweiler March, and passed among his thirty attending thousands and received their salutes as one who is first among men; and so on: presenting it all as if he had been a participant, and in a crazy, fervor-ridden, bombastic prose that read like the Ring cycle put to words.

Aubrey knew, at least, where Arnie had gotten his visual knowledge of Nüremberg and the Nazi party rallies. At some time in the spring of their senior year at St. Titus' Academy, Kermit had arranged for them to see Leni Riefenstahl's *Triumph of the Will*, and Arnie had come out of it awed, dazzled, talking all through dinner about what the Church could learn from the film about pageantry, mob psychology, ceremonial music, and the use of the film as a propaganda weapon. Aubrey had been impatient with all of this. Christ did not found an army, He founded a Church. Certainly, He brought not peace but the sword, but He told Peter in the garden to put up his sword—Christ's sword was spirit, not steel. And so on. Their arguments had run on for days, with Arnie citing historical precedents about the Crusades, and the armies of the Popes, and the founding of the Swiss Guards, and the military basis of the Jesuit Order, and the fact that the First Reich had been the Holy Roman Empire, and with Aubrey replying that organization and the means didn't amount to a damn—one might be as effective as another—but that the end conditioned the means, the end was everything. The Church might seek world domination, but not at the expense of war; it might seek control of the minds of men through appeal to emotion by the use of gaudy vestments and processionals and massed choirs, but its end was to liberate, not enslave.

And Arnie had smiled throughout these arguments mockingly, as if to say that he was not really engaged, certainly not in the outcome, his mind having been made up from the outset as to where the truth resided. He was simply willing to be the whetstone upon which Aubrey might, if it pleased him, strike a few sparks. It was the old and galling business of Arnie the Argonaut condescending, Arnie the Spartan lending his broad shoulders, Arnie the sacred king taking time out from a busy schedule to prepare his foundering tanist for his six-month reign. And Aubrey had taken the Hitler business then as just another in a long series of odd enthusiasms, and had quite forgotten it until the twenty-one pages of manuscript had arrived at the novitiate.

"Is your whole family crazy?" Father Finnegan had asked.

"Only during Lent, Father," Aubrey had replied solemnly.

So, he thought, as he walked toward his bed, Arnie was a Nazi eight or ten weeks ago, and who the hell knows what he might be tomorrow? And gauging the distance precisely, as from long practice, he fell from his knees in a single concerted motion to the side of the bed, blessed himself, dropped forward, elbows to mattress, heels of hands to jaw, and said aloud, "Ah, dear Jesus, just please give Arnie back his mind."

He was awakened just after three by the sound of piano music, and went to his door to listen. There were a few final notes, then footsteps on the stairs, soft but urgent, and the sound of Rexfordia crying. She came quickly down the hall in her white robe and passed within three feet of him, but didn't see him, and was gone into darkness before he could speak.

He stood there for a long time, filled with the sight and sound of her, and with an old, nearly forgotten terror called up by the magnitude of her pain, and went back to his bed and knelt by it for what remained of the night.

And slept there on his knees, and dreamed of Arnie's eyes, gleaming hard as black agates, and of a time when they were twelve in a hot Hudson River August and playing in the meadow behind the tenant house upstate. Arnie was at bat and Aubrey was the outfield, and Arnie hit the ball so that it bounced once and disappeared over the side of the well house. Aubrey arrived in time to hear it splash into the water far below, and Arnie came running up saying that they would have to get it out because it was the ball Ted Williams had fouled into his lap some weeks before in Yankee Stadium. They tossed a coin to see who would go down. Aubrey lost. So they took the well rope and tied it around Aubrey's waist, and he took his shoes off and climbed over the wall of the well house and crouched down in the spidery coolness. And then lowered himself dreadfully into the well, his hands flat on the smooth slate stones that formed the collar of it, his feet tentative and cringing on the slime-slick rocks below, until his toes found a lodging, and then braced himself and gasped and ducked beneath the level of the ground.

And now that Aubrey was committed, his back pressed into one hemisphere of slippery stone, his knees, hands, and toes groping in the other, Arnie undertook to inform him all about Kaatskill County well-dwellers, including snakes of myriad wretched and poisonous descriptions, giant toads, alligators, and a variety of other reptiles up to and including something he identified darkly as a mulch dragon. So that Aubrey, forming individual and terrifying visions of each of the species, told him to shut up or else he wouldn't make the descent, and, perversely, Arnie shut up. And Aubrey made his way down, his toes dying a thousand deaths, his back pierced by fangs at every stony irregularity, and he was already down past the snake before he saw it, coiled on a ledge just at the level of his eyes, its huge black head as big as his two hands, its beetle-black eyes fixed and shining upon his not a foot away—a gigantic head, poised, ancient, monstrously malevolent—and Aubrey felt himself die and felt his soul about to leave his petrified body, when that awful head lifted slightly from the fat black rope of the body and moved perhaps an inch toward him and then withdrew again two or three inches, and Aubrey screamed and fell flailing and scraping to the bottom of the well.

And found himself ankle-deep in ice-cold muck, and almost knee-deep in water nearly as cold, and heart-deep in a terror beyond anything fearful or awful he had ever experienced. Then Arnie was shouting down at him, asking what had happened and if he had found the baseball. He told Arnie what had happened, and Arnie said to find the baseball, and that was too bad, and he would do what he could about the snake. Aubrey found the baseball and Arnie found, after a long search, a pole about ten feet long. He climbed into the well house, checked with Aubrey about the baseball, waited until his eyes were used to the darkness, and then said yes, he could see the snake. Then he began to poke at it, crouching way up there above Aubrey in safety, and reported to Aubrey once that the snake was stubborn and was striking at the pole, and said Christ, Aubie, it must be a monster. Aubrey assured him that it was a monster and told him to be careful or he might knock the snake down on top of him. And Arnie said to come on and climb out, he would hold the snake back with the pole, and Aubrey pointed out that the snake could strike around the pole very easily. Arnie considered this for a time and after suggesting that Aubrey might want to toss the baseball up to him, to relieve himself of the weight, of course, the which Aubrey refused to do, for fear the ball would come back down and hit him, Arnie said okay, wait a minute, he had an idea. And Arnie was gone another long time, but came back with a board about six inches wide and as long as the pole, and pushed it down in front of the snake, and told Aubrey that he had the snake blocked off, and come on now, and climb out.

Aubrey stood there in the cold muck, wanting to be anywhere else in the world than in that well, but unable to climb out; telling himself that there was simply no other way, but unable to begin climbing. And waited until he began to see snakes all around him, easing their flat, huge heads out of every parting of the rocks, and until Arnie began to protest that he was getting tired holding the board in place, and would Aubrey please have some guts and start climbing. Aubrey looked up toward his brother, toward the sweet sunshine of that lovely afternoon, and told himself that he must climb from that coldness to that warmth—he must do that or die of the coldness—and, at last, as Arnie was telling him that the snake was undoubtedly on his way down through the inner rocks to get him, Aubrey forced himself to touch the snake-headed rocks all around him, and started to select handholds, and finally found them and pulled his feet from the muck with horrible sucking noises, and began his agonized climb.

It was perhaps fifteen feet up to the snake's ledge. Arnie had put the rope through the well pulley again and was taking up the slack with one hand as Aubrey climbed. But as he got within three or four feet of the snake, Aubrey told Arnie to slack off on the rope. And Aubrey eased his way up and up, clinging to the far wall, and the snake was still there. It was backed up into the crevice, holding its head high and waving it gently, flicking its tongue. Aubrey almost fell again, but held himself, and told Arnie to adjust the board to cover the snake, and Arnie did. The board was not quite wide enough to block the ledge completely, but at least the snake was out of sight and Aubrey found the strength to begin to climb again. The snake struck the board twice, hard, as Aubrey went by, the sound of it like pistol shots in the twilit hole, and Aubrey swarmed all hands, feet, and terror up the last seven feet of dank rock, and was out of the well house before Arnie was. But Arnie came out fast behind him, pried the baseball out of his hip pocket, rubbed it, and said, "Oh well, Aubie babe. All's well that ends well."

But Aubrey went out into the middle of the country road and sat down there in the dirt; in the dirt where for eight or ten feet in all directions there were no rocks, and no grass, in which a snake might hide. And he sat there and trembled for an hour before he was able to bring himself to walk home. Because the snake was there waiting. Because the snake knew that, one day, Aubrey would be back. . . .

# · TEN ·

HE ASKED ROGER to let him out at Scribner's Book Store, and Roger did, shortly before twelve o'clock, and he went inside and walked up and down, touching very few books, but seeing about eleven thousand four hundred and ten that he wanted to read immediately. Then he went out into the sunshine and wandered, dallying, up Fifth Avenue, and almost got scragged in front of The Tailored Woman by a small tailored woman and a large tailored dog, and went on across the Plaza and into the side door of the hotel, and was seated at Kermit's table in the Edwardian Room, for all his time killing, by twelve-thirty.

And everything was exactly as he had hoped it would be. The old lady in the foyer who checked things thought she remembered him, and he certainly remembered her—or, if she wasn't the same old lady, she resembled the other remarkably, and what difference did it make, after all—and the maître d' also thought he remembered him, immediately after he had mentioned Kermit's name, and they had beamed and clucked at each other until the maître d' had escorted him to the table, and then had waited while Aubrey thought about inner fortification and finally ordered, as demurely as he could, a gin gimlet with a half jigger of Beefeater's.

"You mean, you want an *extra* half jigger, sir?"

"No. One, single, lonely half jigger, if you please."

The maître d' found that delightful, and Aubrey thought that perhaps it was. No use getting smashed my first day out and alone. Enough of that last night. Never mind last night. He looked around the room. It was not crowded. The table was perfect, being in the northeast corner on the east window, so that the view was of the Plaza and its birds and its Cadillacs and its bored chauffeurs and, across the street, the lineup of dowdy carriages and bony horses, one old buck, also a veteran of the sack of Acre, tossing his head and snuffling for the last elusive oat in his nose bag, and the Plaza fountain (according to Arnie, a fine centerpiece for a convention of bidet makers) putting its waters through gracious arcs high up in the sun-spangled air. In short, the most elegant and inexhaustible prospect in the whole city, and as he sat back and surveyed it with what he considered was remarkably incisive perception, he felt himself expand into very expansiveness, and his worries about Arnie drop away like Edwardian greatcoats in an early London spring.

Then his drink came, in the care of a waiter whose looks he did not really approve of—one of those narrow-headed people, gopherlike, long of ear and tooth, eyes like little canceled-out discs in a constant black-on-white slide from nose to corners and back again—but he took the drink and announced to his soul that he was about to indulge his body a mite but that it mustn't get alarmed. Then silently, with a scarcely perceptible inclination of the glass northward, he toasted Father Finnegan. He drank without choking, although he was, he freely admitted to himself, definitely startled. A real prime grade-A choice top-hole cut of Beefeater's is what we have here, Mr. Strycker. If that's a half jigger, I'm a half hitch. What we want, bartender, is a bit more restraint, to keep the clientele in harmony with the room, as it were. Lovely room, conducive in all respects to temperate indulgence, well-modulated conversation, and discreet laughter. What we need here, bartender, is sobriety above all things. Nothing loud or extreme or, to be sure, the beadle will appear and, tapping softly but firmly at the butt of the near ear, ask the offender please to leave. Just so.

He looked around the room and was glad to see that it had not been retouched, was being allowed to fade, as was distinctly proper, into genteel decrepitude; to fade until, one imagined, the shade of Edward VII would materialize some afternoon in the vicinity of the grand piano and, surveying the scene with a slightly, or regally, disdainful expression, would wave a ghostly hand, mercifully causing tables and chairs to splinter, dishes and glasses to crack, captains and waiters to pitch and topple (according to seniority, of course), and, finally, with one final epoch-ending gesture, cause the monstrous ceiling to come crashing down upon all. Clearly, it seemed to Aubrey, there could be no more eminently acceptable way to go (one having failed to assume flesh in time for the sinking of the *Titanic*).

Then the waiter was hovering over him, asking if he wouldn't like another drink, and Aubrey noted with astonishment that his first one was, as it were, consumed. He reflected for perhaps two seconds, then ordered another, repeating his admonition about the half jigger, and asked what time it was. It was twenty minutes to one. He nodded and smiled and went to work on the melba toast and butter because he could feel the first drink warm down there in his empty stomach. A resident of Fort Lee sets new record. Ex-monk found drunk in street within forty-eight hours of his departure from monastery. Hollywood interested in story.

"How fars zit to the ground?"

Aubrey stopped in mid-munch. A little girl's voice. Or my guardian angel's. He turned slowly. She was standing just behind him, on tiptoe, her chin resting on the edge of the window well. She was staring solemnly out when he turned, but then pivoted her head on her chin and put him to the test with two very direct and lovely hazel eyes.

"How far?"

"Well, ah . . ." Aubrey leaned into the window well and took a look. "I'd say it's about ten feet."

"Do you think that's high enough?"

"That's a very good question. Yes, indeed. High enough for what?"

"Huh?"

"I mean, are you expecting a flood or something?"

"A flood? How can I? It isn't even raining."

"Look, why do you want to know how far it is to the ground?"

"I don't."

"You don't.

"No."

"Then who does?"

"Tony Maroni."

"Oh. Anybody I know?"

"I don't think so."

She bent, reached under his chair, and brought up a doll about half her size raggedly dressed as an Italian organ grinder. She pushed it up onto the window well.

"No," Aubrey said, checking carefully, "I don't believe we've ever met."

"Well, we live in Tuxedo Park. With my mother."

"Oh, well, then. That would explain it. I almost never get to Tuxedo Park. Unless, of course, I need a new tuxedo."

"Daddy lives here."

"Oh."

"My name's Sarah."

"My name is Aubrey."

"Well, anyway, Tony Maroni wants to jump out the window."

"Why would he want to do that?"

" 'Cause that's what peoples do in New York when nobody loves 'em."

"Oh. Doesn't anybody love Tony Maroni?"

"No."

"Don't you love him?"

"Yes."

"Then why does he want to jump?"

"He wants—he wantsa knit suzyside."

"Well, I know, but if you love him . . ."

"He wants other peoples to love him, too."

"That's not unreasonable. I can't understand why anyone wouldn't love him. I mean, I love him, and I hardly know him."

"You do?"

"Sure. I'm wild about him."

"Daddy doesn't love him."

"Why not?"

" 'Cause, 'cause he says he's dirty, an' he's only got one eye, an' he wants me to leave him here from the ballet."

"Oh. Did you tell your daddy that Tony Maroni is going to commit suicide?"

"No."

"Well, maybe if you told him that, he'd change his mind about Tony."

She heaved a large sigh. "I don't think so."

"Is Tony Maroni fond of the ballet?"

"Yes."

"Well, if you got him some new clothes and a new eye, maybe your daddy would let him go with you."

"No. Daddy *hates* Tony Maroni."

There was a first hint of tears.

"Excuse me, sir," the waiter said. He put Aubrey's second drink down. "Her father asked me to bring her back to his table."

"Oh. Sure."

The waiter bustled around, took the little girl by the hand. She seemed to hesitate for a moment, then reached up for Tony Maroni and got him by one arm. She looked up at Aubrey, solemn-eyed, but didn't speak until she was a few steps on her way. Then she turned and said, "Are you sure you love him?"

"Absolutely. I'm mad about him."

"Okay." She received this as a solemn trust, and sealed it with a final flash of her eyes. Aubrey watched her out of sight behind the bandstand. Then he turned to his drink.

A moment later the waiter was excusing himself and informing Aubrey that the little girl's father, Mr. Lanio, had been on the telephone and had lost track of the girl, and wanted to thank Aubrey very much for "looking out for her," and Mr. Lanio had sent Aubrey a drink. The waiter wished to know if he wanted the drink half strength. Aubrey considered this for a moment. Then he asked, "How much will the drink cost Mr. Lanio?"

"Well, I don't think he cares about *that*, sir," the waiter said, his smile taking immediate leave of him and his eyes going flat-black.

"I care."

"Well, sir, I don't know, only half strength . . ." He turned and started thumbing through his checks.

"Never mind. You just tell Mr. Lanio . . ."

"Seventy-five cents, sir," the waiter said triumphantly, coldly.

"Oh, fine. Well, you tell that to Mr. Lanio. Tell him he just saved seventy-five cents, and that I would appreciate it very much if he would spend that seventy-five cents on an eye for Tony Maroni."

"On a *what*, sir?"

"Would you condescend to listen this time?"

"Of course, sir."

"An eye for Tony Maroni."

The waiter repeated it for him, nodded curtly, and moved away.

He glanced back once. Aubrey watched him until he went in behind the bandstand. And continued to watch until the waiter came out again, shaking his head and flashing his buck teeth. Then Aubrey went back to his drink.

Lord, you'll have to deal with those two, sooner or later. The waiter probably sooner, because I very well may seize him by his fat incisors and drop him out the window. But his particular judgment should be simple compared to that of Mr. Lanio. I shudder to think of the rapid epiphanies that will overtake him when he sees You face to face. He will very probably shed his scaly skin on the spot.

Then a certain troubling of the air, and on came Kermit, grinning through his beard, biting the back of his fist, the maître d' hopping to stay in front of him, and behind Kermit, well behind him, chin high and disdainful, hair floating as a crown of light, Arnie.

Arnie, looking right at him; the burning eyes first, then the tanned face and the heart shape of it, broadening from the narrow chin upward to the grand forehead, and upward again to the unkempt hair, bristling here and there on end like blond barbicans raised against his enemies; not a face with which one is merely born, but one that has got tortured into shape from within, etched painfully out by piety, grief, longing, disgust, love, shame, jealousy, hate, and all the other human acids; Arnie, carrying just the trace of a smile, his pace measured, moving with that imperial grace, that air of incredibly serene assurance that had always marked him out as an enemy of anything common, including the common man.

Kermit got to Aubrey first, clapped him on one shoulder, looked at him, but gave no sign, and stepped aside. And Arnie, his eyes hard blue and mocking, took Aubrey's hand in both of his, and held it tight, and smiled, and fixed his gaze with such calm, challenging confidence that Aubrey was aware at once that he was the one being tested, not Arnie.

"Aubie, I love your face. There's so much nobility in it."

Aubrey stuttered once before he was able to speak. "It's great to see you, Arnie." He could tell nothing from Arnie's eyes; clear, yet veiled; something vital withheld.

"Well, Aubie, that's good to hear. It's great to see you, too. You look downright spiritual." He grinned, a taut, thin showing of teeth. "But tell me, Aubie, what's the verdict?"

"The verdict?"

"Yes, yes, the verdict. Old Arnie would like to know how he is. Am I insane or sane today? You could always tell better than I could."

Aubrey almost groaned. "Aw, come on, Arnie. You look great."

"That so, Aubie? Then why do you look so ungodly petrified?"

And he shifted his gaze immediately and slipped their handshake and went to where the maître d' was holding his chair. And he sat down and looked out the window, his jaw up, his lips pressed hard together.

"And another of these," Kermit was saying as Aubrey sat down, pointing to Aubrey's glass.

"No, Kermit, I'd better not. This is my second."

"Your second! Jesus Christ! Any son of mine who stops after his second hasn't learned a goddamned thing from his father." He waved the maître d' away. He seemed to be in high spirits, though he refused to meet Aubrey's glances, and Aubrey told himself to relax, that Arnie was all right, that Kermit just didn't want Arnie to catch them exchanging signs and raising eyebrows.

Then Arnie was looking at him, his eyes impalpable and gone, looking at him eagerly and without affection, his wide mouth caressing his teeth and working around an obscene grin. "So they threw little Aubie out, too, did they? Why was that, little Aubie? You get caught playing four-finger ficky-fick?"

"Goddamn it!" Kermit said, half shouting. "What the hell kind of way is that to talk to your brother? I told you he quit!" Kermit worked his jowls but couldn't really manage to look indignant, those bellows already too much stretched.

Aubrey felt a radical falling of all that sustained him—a terrible collapse of high expectation—away and down into the bottom of his belly where it liquefied in pain and near anger. Only the moment itself survived the startled air, caught tingling and strange, and he could see every fiber of it, every degree of light in the room, every lineament of every object and face, every impulse of love and hate and disgust, and he knew that the moment would last and insist until he denied it.

He went at once to the attack, knowing of old that the shock of counterassault was the only thing to touch Arnie in his present mood, for better or for worse, and set his sentence in bitter-bold type along the quick of his mind before he spoke it. Then said, "Arnie, isn't madness indignity enough for you?"

And it worked. After a trembling moment of doubt, during which Arnie appeared to be hating and trying to remember simultaneously, and during which Kermit, gone pale, looked from one to the other of his sons, his mouth and eyes bugging back and forth between the reality and fantasy of it, Arnie began to chuckle, an ominous, threatening chuckle, like the firing of a submachine gun, with a thlot-thlot-thlot-thlot sound deep in his larnyx, and Aubrey knew the smile would come and smiled himself to meet it, and at the last possible moment Arnie did smile, his eyes up bright and winning and full of sanity, and said, "Masturbation? Why, Aubie, I know all about you and that dear old secret sin! All about it!"

"Sure you do!" Aubrey answered loudly.

"Four times! One for the money, two for the show, three to get ready, and four to go!" Then he threw back his head and laughed in that high, abandoned, cackling tenor, the exact pitch of which he and Aubrey had shared from boyhood, and with which they had been affrighting the spectators for all of their postpubertal years, and Aubrey joined in with it at once as if it were an old song, as if it were their peculiar property. Kermit sat there in dumb amaze, wondering, clearly, whether the trouble had gone or gotten worse; genuine, unbuttoned alarm preventing him from taking any part in their laughter.

And Aubrey loved Arnie then as he had always loved him, and studied him and saw in him then—just then, entirely taken as he was in laughter, pouring it out of him great and clean and untainted by delusion or malice, sounding it loud from the body like the shout of a pursuing satyr, yet sounding it also soft from the soul like the opening of a flower—all the fineness, all the strength, all the nobility that might have made his brother a great man, might still make him one if he could summon up his mind. And he could see Arnie gauging him, appreciating what Aubrey hoped and what he doubted, and there was a flitting mischief of self-doubt in Arnie's eyes, but he held it off and stayed with Aubrey and seemed surprised that he could, and when Kermit asked, in the silence after their laughter, what the hell the joke was, Arnie said, looking at Aubrey out of pure snapping-blue clarity, "Human laughter. That's the only joke."

After that there was no restraint, no inhibition, and very frequently all three were talking at once.

And Arnie said, "No, you see they tell me out there at the youth

116

hostile that no schizo is ever really sane. I mean, whole and entire. But I have them spooked. Ever since I got over a certain, well, Wagnerian phase a couple of months ago, I've been a model inmate. And yet, well, they don't know. The jobber—that is, my psychiatrist —says he'd feel very good about me if I didn't act so superior. Oh Jesus, I'm so anxious that that fink should feel good. Yes, indeed. And I am superior to him as a psychiatrist." He laughed and shook his head. "But, anyway, the jobber says if I keep up the good work he might be willing to unleash me on society by the end of June."

"Good!" Kermit said. "By God, I'll move up the Africa trip, or cancel it, and we'll go any damned place in the world you'd like to go, Arnie. All three of us, by God!"

Aubrey said, "You feel good now, don't you, Arnie?"

"Very good."

"And you look good. Why wait until June?"

Arnie became very serious. "Aubie, let me tell you something with as much objectivity as I can manage. Which, today, is a hell of a lot, probably as much as I've ever had at hand." He leaned forward earnestly. "They say—those finks who are supposed to know—the thinkjobbers—they say that on the day you know you're not quite sane— and I mean by sane the ability to cope with whatever might confront you in the course of, say, a month of normal living, or several months, or a year—they say that on the day you realize you are not able to cope, you are halfway toward a cure. Or part way, it all depends on the jobber. Well. I want you to know that I have been aware that I wasn't right since the very first day in the first grade. Please believe that I knew, I knew that I was not taking it as you were taking it, or as any of the others were. My whole idea was that the teacher was just waiting for the right moment so that she could run me through with the pointer. And that went on, Aubie, right on through high school. I always knew I had to play it close, and I did play it close, by sheer goddamned—to coin a phrase—willpower. Until we went to the seminary. And I've felt bad about that ever since, Aubie, because I did it—I went to the seminary—to put myself under the strictest available discipline. And maybe to remove myself from the way of harm. And I've always felt that, maybe, I influenced you too much. That maybe you went, at least partly, because I went, when, really, there was nothing like my need in you."

"You can forget about that, Arnie. You did me a favor, if anything.

I know I'm where I should be. Or I'm on my way to where I should be. And, somewhere along the line, to make it all right, or righter, I've grown me a vocation. An indestructible vocation, according to Father Finnegan."

"That's fine," Arnie said shortly, nearly sarcastically.

"Fine, my ass," Kermit said.

"Kermit told you about the Saharans, Arnie?"

"He told me."

"You don't approve?"

"I just don't want to talk about it, Aubie. Not yet."

Arnie was staring into his glass. Aubrey nodded. "Sure, Arnie. Please go on with what you were saying. I didn't mean to interrupt."

Arnie smiled. "Now there's a fault you haven't corrected. Apologizing for something you didn't do. But thank you, anyway, Aubie." He sipped his drink and smacked his lips. "All I wanted to say was that I've been aware I'm nuts since I can remember. And, it may be, the jobbers could have it right. Maybe I am halfway to a cure. And maybe I'll never get any closer. But for the last few months, Aubie, I've felt all there. Oh, it may break into pieces anytime. Anytime. But it may not. And if it doesn't, well, I'll be a free man. No. What I really wanted to say was that I will know if and when I'm all there long before the jobbers know it. And not only that, I will be the judge. I—and only I—can know when I'm in control. Then I'll just up and walk out."

And Aubrey was feeling his three drinks and knew it, but he was also feeling greater things, and he leaned toward Arnie and spoke, as he felt, with profound conviction. "Arnie, who knows you as well as I do? Maybe Kermit does, but no better." A glance at Kermit, and he was staring straight ahead. "And I tell you, you're in control right now. You are, Arnie. Don't even bother to go back to that place." Arnie looked more grateful than convinced. Aubrey turned to Kermit. "Don't you agree, Kermit?"

Kermit continued to stare straight ahead, but as the silence lengthened, he glanced once at Aubrey. And his eyes were split with anguish and reproach.

"Don't—don't put the old bastard on the spot like that," Arnie said, speaking slowly, his smile opening and closing with the strain of generosity. "He's been there and back with yours truly. With your dear brother in Christ. Haven't you, Kermit?"

"Isn't that at all," Kermit said, the greatest liar in the world except when it counted. "I just think you're right, Arnie. You will be the judge. You will know best."

"And besides, Aubie, I've got a month off. Why rush it? Why make predictions? In this business you just wait and see."

"But you may not have to go back," Kermit said, suddenly defiant.

"Ah, well. You're a good old man," Arnie said. He put one hand over one of Kermit's, then withdrew it and, quickly, said to Aubrey, "Have you noticed, Aubie? We've got a boat-tailed grackle for a waiter?"

"I have!" Aubrey cried. "A yellow-fanged jackdaw!"

"Who eats nothing but fiddler crabs!" Arnie shouted.

"I think he's *got* fiddler crabs!" Kermit added, howling gleefully.

When they went out, an hour or so later, the maître d', straining his comment through a rather grim smile, told Kermit that the Edwardian Room had seldom seen so merry a group.

And the first diminishment of Aubrey's high good humor was suffered when, in the absence of the checkroom lady, he reached for his hat, and there, belly down on the high metal shelves, with a claim check sticking from his collar and obscuring his grin, was Tony Maroni.

The second diminishment was something he shared with Arnie, who happened to be watching, as he was, an old lady feeding a flock of pigeons, as the three of them waited for Mr. Jebb to bring the car up to the door, and saw some of the pigeons venture toward some crumbs in the middle of the street, and saw a taxicab come in fast among the pigeons, and saw the pigeons rise, and saw one of them thump against the windshield of the cab and go skittering over the roof of it and fall to the street behind, a dead ball of feathers.

And Arnie looked at him and looked away, and, to the astonishment of Kermit after they were settled in the car, delivered the following monologue: "Death of a pigeon, Aubie, death of a pigeon. No more than that. Yet not a feather falls, they say. Don't they? Still, not a tragedy. A melodrama, at best, Aubie. Ah, but Aubie, does the old story of the earth, and of man walking up and down upon it, seeking good and finding evil, seeking love and finding hate, seeking to give love and finding that others have never learned to receive it, seeking faith and finding only a grim, half-bitter hope, seeking givers and finding only takers, seeking order and finding only a pathetically cruel and hilarious chaos—does that old story add up to a tragedy in any of its parts, Aubie? Sad though it be? Does it add up to anything that obeys the dramatic laws of cause and effect? Have man's noblest acts and emotions ever amounted to anything more than overblown sentiment or exaggerated passion? Of course not, Aubie. The whole damned history of the world, of nature, of the human race—oh, especially of the human race—is nothing more than the merest sort of bad melodrama. And the same goes for pigeons, Aubie. The same goes for pigeons."

# • ELEVEN •

Mr. Jebb, the world's most silent man, drove the car as if it were made of gingerbread, doing perhaps eight miles an hour up Fifth Avenue, and Aubrey sat on the park side of Kermit, who was doing most of the talking now, and felt the warmth of the sun and the best of slight breezes and tried to keep his eyes from resting upon the girls and women who seemed to be everywhere in their brightly clothed bodies. And he was disturbed that he had been drinking, but only slightly, and thought about entering the park and dancing upon the grass and taking the shade of a tall tree.

And Kermit was saying, "I don't think anybody really believes this, but I put two .300 Magnum slugs into that old bastard at no more than thirty yards, and he kept right on coming and ran me down, and kept right on going!"

"Who was that?" Aubrey asked.

"Big Ditmo."

"Big who?"

"Big Ditmo, the bear. The goddamned bear."

"Oh. But what's it mean, Big Ditmo? Is that what kind of bear he is?"

"Hell no, that's his name. Big Ditmo, for Christ's sake. The bear we're going hunting for."

"You mean we're going hunting for one special bear?"

"Well, Jesus Christ, haven't you been listening to me telling you?"

"I've been listening but this is the first I've heard of Big Ditmo. What kind of name is that for a bear?"

"Well, Jesus H. Christ, Aubie, how the hell do I know what kind of name it is? I didn't give it to him. Kunkel did. And what the hell difference does it make? A bear is a goddamned bear."

Aubrey hesitated, then took the plunge. "Who named him that?"

"Kunkel! What the hell difference does it make who!"

"Well, Kermit—I'm just trying to get it all straight. So don't explain, but don't expect me to know five minutes from now who Kunkel is."

"Who Kunkel is? Jesus Christ, you know Kunkel!"

"I do not know Kunkel. Arnie? Who's Kunkel? Kermit won't tell me."

"Kunkel is Kunkel, for Christ's sake!" Kermit howled.

"There. Does that clear things up?" Arnie asked.

"The Indian! Jesus Christ, Aubie, he used to be my chauffeur and drive you and Arnie all over!"

"Oh, Mr. Cranch."

"Yes! That's his name! Cranch! Kunkel Cranch!"

"Kermit, in the name of God, my eardrums," Arnie said.

Kermit glared at Arnie. Kermit's voice was a sonic wonder, a national resource, and the drunker he got the louder he got, and attempting to tone him down was like trying to clap a steam valve on Old Faithful. "Well, it's all these goddamned interruptions! I'm trying to tell a story, and now I can't even remember where I was."

"You were on the mountain on your ass," Arnie said.

"Well, goddamn it, if you don't want to hear the story . . ."

"I don't mind *hearing* it, Kermit. It's going deaf from it that bothers me."

"And *I* want to hear the story, Kermit, but I'm just trying to get the characters straight. I've been away four years. The last I saw of Mr. Cranch, nobody called him Kunkel."

"I've always called him Kunkel!"

"I never heard you call him Kunkel," Arnie said. "Not until you set him up as a guide."

"Ah! Arnie? He's a guide?" Arnie nodded. "In Alaska?" Arnie nodded and grinned. "Okay, just one more. Hold it, Kermit. Just one more . . ."

"Goddamn it! I did call him Kunkel!"

"Don't leave me hanging, Aubie."

"Is Ditmo Indian language for bear?"

"Oh, for Christ's sake! Ditmo is just a goddamned *name* he thought up! He probably got it off a wall somewhere! In the name of the scorched Jesus, can we forget about Ditmo!"

"Ditmo," Arnie said immediately, "could be either a Modoc or a Yurok word. Kunkel's father was a Modoc and his mother was a Yurok." He grinned at Kermit.

"Sweet blistered Christ!" Kermit howled. "Who *gives* a rat's ass? I don't care if his mother was *Sol Hurok!*"

"But, of course," Arnie continued, "Ditmo spelled backwards is omtid."

"Spelled backwards! Omtid! Arnie, for Christ's sake . . . !"

"And, of course, Kunkel isn't his real name."

"It is his real name!"

"His real name is Leknuk." Arnie, unable to hold it any longer, burst into laughter.

Kermit was not amused. "Listen, Aubrey, while your brother is having his jollies, Ditmo doesn't mean a goddamned thing except Ditmo, and Kunkel doesn't mean a goddamned thing except Kunkel! Backwards or forwards!" He glared at Arnie. "Now, can we forget . . ."

"Of course," Arnie said, "Kunkel is bad enough just as it stands . . ."

"I have the floor!"

"But he could have done much worse, being a Modoc."

"All right! All right! To hell with you! I won't tell the goddamned story!"

". . . actually had warriors in that tribe with names like One-Eyed Mose and Curly-Headed Doctor . . . !"

Kermit started to roar at the top of his voice to drown Arnie out. "Who the hell cares? Who gives a flannel fart!"

Arnie, unable to be heard over Kermit, had to wait for him to take a breath. "Hooker Jim! Mrs. Bagdough!"

"Red-assed bastards all, cried young Telemachus as he came forth from his tent passing air smartly in the direction of Carthage and crying *Carthago delenda est!*"

"Boston Charlie! Shacknasty Jim!"

"When the revolution comes and we have crossed the Rubicon

and have slain that jackass Cato, we shall enter the land of Hiawatha, rape all the women, smoke all the strawberries, and eat all the black cigars, crying, 'Down with venery, up your wickiup,' and we don't need the turd from that noble bird, you red-bollix son of a bitch!"

And through it all, the most silent man in the world, Mr. Jebb (who later told Aubrey, with no little pride, that Kermit himself, after riding a month or two with him, had demoted the former title-holder, Kunkel, to the rank of the *second* most silent man in the world), proceeded at eight miles an hour to Kermit's house, utterly unperturbed by the noise in the back seat, his proper British progress marked by just one peculiarity: whenever a following car—usually a taxicab (the drivers of which hate all Rolls-Royce automobiles, but especially high-backed huge ones like Kermit's)—tooted and started by, Mr. Jebb would put his gray-gloved hand out the window and—rather elegantly, Aubrey thought—lift one of the middle fingers on high. Just once, briefly, and although not a cabdriver went by who didn't give some kind of countersign with vocal accompaniment, Mr. Jebb saw none of it. Mr. Jebb had eyes only for the road ahead.

Kermit finally got to finish his story after dinner. The evening had gone cool, and Nelson, the man of all things domestic, had set a small fire in Kermit's office, or den. The fireplace didn't draw any too well, and they were getting more smoke than heat from it, but only Aubrey seemed to notice. Kermit had reached a certain plateau of inebriation upon which he was marvelously articulate, loud, and good-humored, and he had been so situated for several hours. Arnie had grown more and more snappish as the evening wore on, and seemed quite drunk, and had been staring morosely into the fire for over an hour, moving nothing but his drinking arm. Aubrey had not taken a drink since leaving the hotel, and was discovering that the soberer he became, the more exhausted he felt. His role as animated listener was getting very hard on the eyelid muscles and the grin and grunt centers.

"Now, if I'm anything, Aubie, I'm a good shot, and I stuck those two .300 slugs right down his thorax. Christ, I had no choice! He rose up out of pure blue ice, the lower end of the Mount Frosty glacier. And he wasn't fifty yards away, and he came right on in. Biggest goddamned head I've ever seen on a bear and fast as a tiger. Why the hell he didn't stop and chew on me, I don't know. Except that he's so goddamned smart. He saw Kunkel off to my left and just below me, and he figured he'd get the hell out of there before Kunkel could crank off."

"That was when, Kermit?"

"Two years ago this month. And I've been back twice, and this will be the third time, and this is going to be it. I'll nail his old ass if it takes all summer!"

"Have you seen him since that first time?"

"Well, hell yes, I've seen him. Everybody sees him. The old bastard comes out and does calisthenics for the troops! But just try and get a shot at the old son of a bitch! That's the trick." Kermit sat forward toward the fire and pounded both fists on the leather arms of his chair. "But all he's got to do is make just one more mistake, Aubie boy." He nodded at Aubrey vigorously, his eyes glowing, his anger quite sudden and genuine. "Just one more mistake, because I've got this new .500/465 double, specially made 480-grain bullet! And all I want that old bastard to do is exactly what he did last time. I don't give a rat's ass if he charges straight up out of the ground! Just so he comes right on in." Kermit got to his feet, balancing an airy double rifle, glaring across the room at a red, gold-bossed camel saddle. "And when he does, when Big Bastard Ditmo does, I'm going to wait him—and I'm going to *wait him!* And if he stays down, I'll drop it in his goddamned ear! And if he goes up, I'll run up and stick it down his goddamned throat! And we'll just see—we'll just see, by Christ! And if the Great Goddamned Ditmo doesn't go down, I guarantee you he'll do some mighty funny goddamned things standing up!" By now, Kermit appeared about ready to tear himself in two. It was clear that he wasn't quite rational on the subject of Big Ditmo. And, still glaring fiercely at the camel saddle, as if he'd fired and, by God, it *hadn't* gone down, he roared, "I'll go one better! If that old bastard can swallow two .500/465s, by Jesus Christ, I'll lie right down and let him skin me out!" And in the following, echoing, tumultuous silence, Aubrey fully expected to hear trumpets, bugles, and the roll of kettledrums, and see Jove himself come out of the fireplace in a fiery chariot and hang a medal on Kermit for creating the most vehemently warlike visage of the half century.

Instead there was a groan from Arnie. "Oh for Christ's sake, look at him. All he needs is a harpoon, a wooden leg, and Gregory Peck's stovepipe hat."

Kermit came out of his madding stare whirling and lunged, forefinger first, at Arnie's nose. Arnie moved not a pore, and continued to gaze into the fire. "Goddamn you, Arnie! This is one subject we don't joke about!"

"Oh balls. And they say I'm crazy."

"Goddamn it, that's enough!"

"Ahh, go shine your rifle."

"Arnie," Aubrey said. Kermit was standing over Arnie, finger still pointed, quivering violently.

"Look—oh, all right. I'll humor him." Arnie raised his head. "Well, Jesus Christ! Will you get your goddamned finger off my eyeball?"

Kermit dropped the finger and took a step backward, smartly. "By God, Arnie! If I were a violent man, I'd paddle your ass with a broken bottle!"

"If? Je-sus! Compared to you, the finking padded ward up at the Hostile is filled with Quaker pacifists! What the hell is the matter with you, anyway? It's just another goddamned shaggy-assed bear! I mean, you act like he's been pissing in your coffee or something! What the hell'd he ever do to you?"

"Do! I just told you what he did! He knocked me down and ran over me!"

"Well, Jesus Christ, Kermit! What the hell'd you expect him to do? You go squilching around up there firing shots up his nose and you figure he ought to erect a finking pavilion and serve lemonade?"

Kermit blinked, cast his eyes right and left, then found the throttle. "That isn't the point, goddamn it! I'm a hunter, and that goddamned bear humiliated me! I don't expect you to understand that!"

"You shouldn't, because I don't. Humiliated you, did he? Well, isn't that too goddamned bad. I suppose you would have liked it better if he had chewed on you awhile. Is that what you mean?"

"Don't play games with me, Arnie! And don't talk to me in that tone! What I mean is, I'm going to kill that goddamned bear—I, personally—if it's the last thing I do! Now you make any goddamned thing you want of it!"

Arnie held up both palms. "All right, all right. We've been through this before, and I want to tell you, Kermit, I think I have just seen the light." Arnie's face was, abruptly, a mask of sincerity. Kermit grunted. "I mean, I think I finally understand. Now. As I see it, you go out and hunt a bear, and it's kill or be killed, right?" Kermit nodded, dubiously. "Okay. I mean, both sides, man *and* bear, have to play it straight and true, according to the law of the jungle, right?" Kermit nodded again, even more dubiously. "Right. Now here you come, and here comes Big Ditmo, and you shoot your wad and he's still coming on like Union Pacific, right?" Kermit frowned. "Right. Here you are and here he comes. You've done your bit by the law of the jungle to the best of your ability and you failed. Junglegally, so to speak, you are dead. But what does that goddamned bear do? As he bears down on you, his finking duty is clear. He's supposed to act like a goddamned bear! He's supposed to rip you from your guggle to your zatch and generally just snort around there a while and act bearish! But what does the son of a bitch do? Why, he knocks you skidding on your ass, and *keeps right on going!* Why, the goddamned unjunglelike-ableness of it all! I'd be humiliated, too! Yes, indeed!"

"Arnie, Arnie! I warned you!"

"Wait, Kermit, one more thing. I agree with you! I think you *must* shoot Big Ditmo. But I've got one small suggestion. Obviously, since that bear has for two years refused to come out and fight like a man, there's something wrong with him. I mean, he's clearly deficient in some certain vital part, just as he was the day you were humiliated by him, and he's probably only getting worse! And I think—I mean, I *think*—I've put my finger on that deficiency. Yes, I do. I think what you've got to do before we leave is go downtown and buy a copy of *The Law of the Jungle*, and as soon as we get up there send Kunkel up under a white flag to read it to that goddamned Big Ditmo!"

Kermit was roaring before Arnie finished, and Aubrey thought he might strike him, but he didn't, and turned quite red and waved his arms and told Arnie he could not come to Alaska and that was that, and went stomping off to bed shouting about ingrates and mad bastards. Arnie didn't hear a word of it, being flat out in his chair in a seizure of hilarity.

Aubrey had been alarmed by the whole encounter. Kermit had gone far beyond anything he could ever have predicted of him. He had seen him drunk often, angry oftener, but never irrational. And there was no other word for it. In the middle of Kermit versus Big Ditmo, he had looked closely once and had felt his heart constrict and hold to see in Kermit's stare, unmistakably, Arnie's mad eye. And where did that leave the myth, so subtly fostered by Kermit over the years, that the madness came from the Milligan side of the house?

127

And what kind of irony was it to see Arnie, the schizophrenic patient, with the rationality all on his side, so cruelly exposing his father? And what the hell was Aubrey supposed to do on this mad bear hunt: referee?

He took these questions silently to bed with him and put them through his prayers, but not before a final shock: the discovery that Arnie, somewhere in the middle of his laughter, had lost the comic essence, and was now sprawled there, his eyes wide open and running over with tears, and as vacantly mad as Aubrey had ever seen them.

Sleep came and went, and he was awake when the chill just before dawn was on the house, and his darkness was all eyes: Julie's, Rexfordia's, Kermit's, Arnie's. And they were all streaming tears and lamenting a death, but whose he couldn't quite hear. And he prayed that the Saharans would summon him soon and flatly forbid him to go anywhere near Big Ditmo's mountain.

Then he went soundly to sleep, seeing at the very last a final single tear. And he thought, Ah, well, Tony, don't cry. God loves you, and that *is* a nice sane eye you've got there.

## • TWELVE •

Shortly after seven that red morning, all missal ribbons properly placed for Mass, he found Arnie in the garage, under the Rolls-Royce.

"I checked your room," Aubrey said softly, so as not to startle him. "Then I checked your bathroom. Then I checked the garage. And here you are."

"Oh by God!" Arnie's face appeared out of the tread of the right front tire. "You mean you didn't check my closet?"

"No, no. I can't say as I."

"Well, there you are. You see? There you ruddy are! I always spend an hour in my closet between the bathroom and the garage. Decompression and all that, you know?" He was on his back on a low-slung, little-wheeled dolly, but had cocked his head around so that his ice-blue eyes were mocking side up, traveling upon Aubrey from just beneath the front bumper. "So there he is, my Pollux, going to spend an alternate day with the gods. Black shoes, black suit, black book. And here I am, down here on my casters in Hades with my black heart. Oh twin! Look thou down with mercy. You can come to me, but I cannot come to you. If you care to join me down here, why, I'd be more than underwhelmed and less than overstood, recognizing always that my faery part may still be upstairs in my closet." Arnie blinked expectantly, as if he had made sense and was awaiting commensurate answer.

"It's the Sunday after Ascension," Aubrey began.

"Oh well, in that case," Arnie said quickly, "I simply must descend." And collapsing from the neck up so that his head struck the pad of the dolly with a thump and his eyes closed, he rolled out of sight under the car, making Chopinesque death march noises.

Aubrey sighed and sat down on an overturned bucket. He tied a shoelace and slapped some dust from one knee of his pants. He sighed again and looked toward the car. He had not really expected that Arnie would accompany him to Mass, but, having found Arnie up so unusually early, was encouraged to press further. "Arnie, it is not, as you know, Christian to work under English automobiles on Sunday."

"Of course not," Arnie acknowledged brightly.

"Then what are you doing under there?"

"Well, as a matter of fact, I'm looking for Mr. Jebb's first-line Dr. West toothbrush."

"Oh? Does he always keep it under the car?"

"Never! That's the tart in my crush, if I carry you. I had the misfortune to drop it while scumming the scruff from the chrome."

"The front chrome?"

"The very."

"But it fairly glistens. It's cleaner than my teeth ever were."

"Begging your reverend pardon, but the human os and its finking appurtenances are in no way or wise to be compared—but especially as to cleanliness—with the vehicle I am hereunder and to wit."

"My sincerest reverend apologies."

"Noted and marked for carbon content."

Aubrey shrugged, leaned forward into his hands. He peeked between his fingers, saw a June bug trotting down the middle of the concrete floor toward the car, and thought, There's a nice bug. Hurry now. Run right under there and bite Arnie on the brush. But the June bug veered off around a small pool of water, bounced off the left front tire, and ran in under a chamois cloth. Scratch Boris the Bug from the list of those up for the Areopagitic Order of the Antic Antennae. "Look, Arnie, there are only so many square inches under that car. If you haven't found the brush by now, it simply isn't there. It has, obviously, resolved itself into its atoms and taken the form of a June bug I just saw go by."

"For your information, I have given up on the brush. I have a new problem."

"Oh?"

"A loose housing. Exactly what this country needs more of, I always say, but not under the double-R."

"Can't you leave that to a garageman? Or the FHA?"

"No other choice, if I do say so. It needs a long-necked ratchet to reach the nuts. Ah, no offense, reverend."

"No offense, and, as a matter of fact, I just saw the last available long-necked ratchet running for its nest with a nut in its beak."

"Isn't that always the way?"

"Arnie, what do you need of that brush anyway? There are all kinds of brushes out here."

"I told you, I've given up on the brush."

"Yes, but you're lying, aren't you?"

"Of course. But, you see, Mr. Jebb places a very high value on his brushes, having gathered them, over the years, from every nook and cranny, you might say. If you will note, on that darkling burlap sack to your left, a marvelous variety has been gathered from all corners of the world." And Arnie, his voice muffled, if not mufflered, went on to describe each brush and its provenience. "There's your currying brush from the tack room at Calumet Farm, used very gently on the rugs to keep the pile perky. . . ." And so on, with your denture brush from Macy's basement, your wine-bottle brush from Bingen on the Rhine, your silver-backed military hairbrush from Abercrombie and Fitch, your wood-backed, no-nonsense scrub brush from the Fort Lee Hardware, a nearly new goosenecked toilet-bowl brush from Fuller, an electric razor brush from Ronson (". . . used for those tricky little places where Rolls is joined to Royce . . ."), and, of course, your missing Dr. West hard-tuft from Mr. Jebb himself, since it made his gums bleed anyway.

"Arnie, we'll buy Mr. Jebb a brand-new Dr. West hard-tuft."

"No need. I just found it." Arnie shot out from under the car on his rubber casters, waving the brush, and only a determined bit of heel-dragging navigation prevented him from bashing his head against the brick wall. He got up and came toward Aubrey, chuckling, shaking his head at the toothbrush. "Sneaky little rascal. Happened to glance down and there he was in the cuff of my pants. Knew just where to hide, didn't you, Dr. West? Oh, you should have heard him bristle and teethe when I apprehended him."

"I think we ought to take him to church with us."

131

Arnie smiled at Aubrey. "What're you, some kind of a nut or something? Taking toothbrushes to church?"

"I'll be happy to wait . . ."

"Aubie, babe, leave us leave off the proselyting, shall we? I know all the words and music better than you do."

"You don't go to church any more?"

"No." Arnie put one hand through his yellow hair, leaving a black smudge from his right eye to his hairline, and, still smiling, turned away toward the burlap sack. "God and I have a little nonaggression pact with a built-in trade agreement. When He gives me back my mind, I'll give Him back my soul."

"Well?"

"Well what?" Arnie had put the toothbrush with the other and was rolling up the burlap sack tightly, to enfold the brushes.

"Well, hasn't God given you back your mind?"

"Have to wait and see, right?"

"You seem pretty sane to me."

Arnie stood, holding the roll of brushes in both hands. "Aubie," he said, no longer smiling, "of this you can be sure. I'll never pretend to be nuts. If I act nuts, believe it."

"I wasn't accusing you of . . ."

"Besides," Arnie said, turning away. "I'm nuttier than a bastard or why would I be down here this early brushing the heap's teeth?" He threw the brushes in a locker, and shut it.

"You like cars."

"Well, Jesus Christ! I also like girls, but I don't go around . . . never mind." Arnie came toward him, wiping his hands on a white cloth, smiling easily, condescendingly. "I can see you're wearing your whitest armor this morning and far be it from me to cast the first smirch. Tell you what I'll do, Aubie, my Templar. I cannot, in good conscience, accompany you to the temple, but I should be glad to step out with you into the cathedral of nature, just across the street, and prance for a time in a holy manner upon the vernal grass." His smile was full now and his eyes shining delightedly. He tossed the white cloth aside, did a furious little goat dance in his engineer's boots, finishing with a slap-slapping of feet, a clicking of heels, and a British enlisted salute, palm out and vibrating. "Sir!" he shouted, then very rapidly in a poor to Midlands British clutter, "No time to dawdle, sir, with waxatoricals . . . get cracking, sir, 'cross the river

132

and into the wogs . . . keep the aspidistra flying . . . up the Queen and your tubers, sir! *Request* permission to wax wroth and keen and Sergeant York, *sir!* Pressure in all tanks . . . take her to six hundred . . . snorkers good-oh . . . up the drillmaster . . . Majesty's Own Darjeeling Tee-Shirts . . . this day ascend into heaven straight up the bucket, *sir!*" He took a step backward smartly, saluted again, brought an imaginary rifle to port and right shoulder arms, and stepped out whistling the "Colonel Bogey March."

"Arnie, I want to make eight o'clock Mass, if I can!" Aubrey called after him.

Arnie wheeled around, glared, twitched an imaginary mustache, appeared nearly to choke on his indignation. "I say, Major, that's ruddy bad show! Ruddy bad! Rather less of that, Major! Example to the men . . . Queen's own . . . smashing awful you ask me . . . fall in . . . knees high . . . one two, one two . . . no faltering now . . . good show . . . stiff upper . . . forty kilometers Rangoon. . . ." And so on, as he turned, marched to the side door, threw it open, and disappeared through it in the direction of Fifth Avenue.

Aubrey followed, walking and smiling reluctantly. As he cleared the alley, there was Arnie hup-hupping resolutely toward the side of a Fifth Avenue bus with the driver, held by a red light, staring down at him, mouth open. The light didn't change and neither did Arnie, and he thumped into the bus just behind the left front wheel. He fell back, shook his fist at the driver, howled in accent and almost incoherently about bloody wogs, and began to kick the bus energetically. The light changed as the astonished driver and one bug-eyed old lady passenger began to remonstrate with their attacker, and a cab behind the bus began to toot, and the driver gave up and put his vehicle in motion south. Arnie kicked as long as there was bus in front of him, took a final kick at the cab as it went by, then came to attention on the white line, ordered himself eyes right and pass in review, and, striking up his whistle, marched with elaborate choppings of hands across the street and into Central Park.

Aubrey found him stretched out with his feet in a small flower bed, his hands folded on his chest, staring up at the sky. Aubrey sat down in the dew next to him and started to pluck at the grass with his free hand. The day was bright and already warm, and somewhere behind him and over his head a woodpecker was angry at a tree. They were in a small plot of grass south of the museum, and he

133

watched the sun move on the gray stone walls of the building and thought of nature real and nature captured and, in a sudden stillness of air and the woodpecker, heard a horse whinny from the direction of the bridle path.

"Sweet Aubrey," Arnie said quietly, not looking at him, "since it doesn't seem likely that you'll be done in there before dark, I thought I'd describe the day to you."

"In where?"

"Why, in your brown study, of course."

"Oh yes. Well. Dreadfully decent of you to offer and all, but it wouldn't do for you to overdo, would it?"

"Tut-tut. All part of our pay-now-weep-later economy tour, Mr. S. Yes, indeed. We aim to abscond. Why, in just a minute, our seven-member all-girl orchestra—six cellos and a forty-inch glockenspiel, creating an enchantingly different sound, and choir, under the direction of three discalced Jesuits and their probation officer—will perform your choice of musical specialty numbers from the organ bar for your listening pleasure. We thought something like 'Those Hard-to-Lave Places' might go well—or wash well, if I may be permitted a pun, heh, heh."

"Have I a choice?"

"Why, your choice, Mr. S., of a certainty to be sure, and at no extra charge, naturally, except whatever supernatural honorarium you might wish to give to the girls, all of whom, I should add, depend largely, even grossly, upon the generosity of the listening audience, if I may be redundant. The girls receive no salary, God love 'em. Of course, all such offerings are deductible, and the Jesuits will be around in a moment with receipt forms acceptable to the IRS people."

"Horribly thoughtful of you."

"To be sure, Mr. S., and away we go, and a fine day it is! The sky is blue and full of people. There goes a load now, flying first-class into oblivion. Tinker Bell is serving breakfast martinis and everyone is smiling and lined up for the lavatories, and no one of them suspects that they are about to come to grief against a mountain. We never book airlines or craft, Mr. S. Flying, we feel, is always in the face of destiny. It is a madness, the peculiar madness of our age, the prevailing sentiment being that because we can, we ought to. We can also descend to the bottom of the sea, but there is no great demand, as yet, for tickets. It takes a bit of time for these things to catch on. A certain average threshold of sanity has to be overcome. Ah well, *ainsi soit-il* and farewell, good airborne, and many happy returns to your beneficiaries. Leave neat skid marks and make eighty-eight handsome corpses. Don't litter the jet stream, is all we ask. And you have my assurance that the next time I die suddenly it will be with Cocka-maimie Airlines. I shall, of course, arrive nude and bearded a half hour before flight time, or forty-five minutes if it's an international flight, and I shall stride up the first-class steps and calmly announce the second coming. Naturally, Tinker Bell will slug me with an empty champagne bottle and throw me back into tourist. But that's to be expected. For Tinker Bell knows, as do all the crew and the girls, that nude saints always travel tourist."

"May I point out that your feet are in the marigolds?"

"Bother the marigolds. They are inevitably dead anyway, my man. You put them in too deep." But Arnie looked down and moved his feet slightly, crushing two more flowers in the process. "While we are on the subject of gardening, Mr. S., I wonder if I might ask a personal question."

"Persons do virtually all of the questioning in this modern world."

"Isn't it the finking truth? Well? Might I?"

"Might, indeed, and might as well."

"And you can't find the farmer 'cause the farmer went to hell. But what I'd like to know is—is—do you or do you not use Vigoro on your hair?"

"Only after a tonsure."

"Honest goodfellow. And that's that best time, they say, the finks. New roots and all that ganglia."

"Funny you should ask that."

"Ask what?"

"About High Mass."

"Oh, well. I only asked because I can hear America singing, with Carl Sandburg conducting on his little cat feet. So that you'll understand that I'm not just lying here for my comfort."

"Oh?"

"Any shaped-up horticulturist could see at once that I'm actually pressing the grass."

"I'm caught out."

"You'll notice how it sticks up at all manner of odd angles where I haven't gotten to it?"

"I find it angularly stimulating."

135

"You would because you're a sex pervert. That's what makes this a thankless task. Perverts like you."

"The park's full of us."

"I mean, if someone should ask you how you spent your day and you say pressing the grass in Central Park . . . ?"

"Only your kind of patience, Arnie."

"Damned right. Why, I don't know how many body lengths there are in this lawn alone, and when you consider the whole thousand acres . . . !"

"The mind boggles."

"And the boggles mind, believe me. I'll need a bogglectomy before this is over."

"Still, the Lord's work is done little by little, and so few of us are qualified."

"Who else is there?"

"Few are called, but fewer are chosen."

Arnie glanced up at him for the first time, his eyes suddenly combative, his smile a holdover. "Chosen?"

"Why not?"

"The act of choosing implies free will."

"So? God chose you."

"You are exactly wrong."

"And you appear to be shifting gears without due notice."

"Any notice I might give is long overdue, so screw it."

"Conversation over?"

"Conversation *not* over. You have implied that God has free will."

"God does have free will."

"Oh, balls!" Arnie hung for a moment between anger and that derisive patience he had so often used on Aubrey as a substitute for anger. Aubrey watched his brother's face hesitate plastically, then assume the derisive expression. "Aubie, you dismay me. After all the years I put in trying to teach you to think, you present me with this patent asininity. I'm afraid they've stuffed you with philosophy beyond your capacity to cope. But then you always did have the *quid* and not the *quo*, the in but not the sight, the odd faculty of coming at the heart of a matter by way of the large intestine."

Aubrey had been too long away from Arnie's patronizing manner not to feel the affront, not to be angry. He told himself that he was

136

simply out of practice and that insult was good for his humility, yet he couldn't resist a gentle thrust, if only for the sake of tradition. "Lost as I am in the large intestine, it's very good to have this report by the honorable delegate from the spleen and to know that when, in my ass-backwards progress, I shall have arrived at that exalted junction to the far left, I might see him again, and all those other half-arrived students of Messrs. Spinoza and Schopenhauer."

Arnie shook his head and spoke through a long disgusted sigh. "You put me in mind of a firefly in the outer darkness."

"With my light showing you the way."

"With your light in your ass. What little there is of it." Arnie laughed hollowly, and rubbed at his eyes with one hand. "Aubie, why do you persist in arguing with me? You must be aware, that I have full possession of a reason so entirely superior to your own that the comparison beggars adjectives. Why do you keep resisting that fact? Why do you keep resisting me?"

Aubrey closed his eyes. The sight of Arnie's face was too much to endure, not merely because of the anger it inspired, but also because of the serenely deranged superiority reflected now, and ever more plainly, in the wandering eyes and the tight little smile. Arnie's present state of sanity was a tentative business, obviously, like a radio signal in an area of recurrent interference, fading in and out and attended always by a wracking-to-wraithy static, a constant threat of total loss of communication. After a moment of silence, Aubrey took in new air in quantity, popped his eyes open while holding the air and his true feelings captive, exhaled with the least of hisses over his lower teeth, and took a new grip on his missal. "Arnie, babe. I keep resisting you because if I didn't I would very shortly be as full of ferment and fertilizer as you incontrovertibly are."

Arnie set his jaw, to the diminishment of his smile, and darted his eyes once to his brother. Then he stared at the sky for a time and worked his nostrils in a way that suggested justifiable rage just narrowly contained. Aubrey rested easy, knowing that he had always been able to take Arnie in physical contest; rested so easily, in fact, that it occurred to him that a physical contest with Arnie was not only, perhaps, the least of his worries but the first of his hopes. And he put the thought down as he might his fists, slowly, the fingers of it still tensing and curled. Then Arnie was talking, softly and fast, as if Aubrey weren't present. ". . . most terrifying of all mental illnesses is schizophrenia, and is most terrifying because the so-called victims are often so very much more rational, so very much brighter, so much more incisive, intuitive, and independently brilliant than the so-called sane. Now the head jobbers tell me about heredity, although they can't pin down yet the precise genetic mechanism, and they tell me about a metabolic defect in amino acids and how this might lead to an underproduction of certain hormones, but they aren't sure. In fact, they're simply desperate to explain why they themselves, the self-styled intellectual elite, have nothing like my mental agility, my insight, my vision, my superlative ability to see relationships and make effective correlations. They are jealous, as all the world is, and as the world was jealous of Christ. They are jealous of my priesthood as they were jealous of Christ's high priesthood. Don't take the easy way here, Aubie. If I accuse you unjustly, I do apologize. But you always did take the easy way. Don't simply write me off as raving mad. That's the easy way. I expect better of you. I demand better. And maybe the best. Because, after all, you're my brother. You're bound to be remarkable in some respect. *Sursum corda*, all my brothers. Rise and meet the challenge. And what am I saying? Well, it's not very complicated. How does Fenichel have it? The schizophrenic has regressed to narcissism. Just like the Father and the Son. The schizophrenic has parted with reality. The schizophrenic has lost his objects. The schizophrenic's ego has broken down. The schizophrenic refuses to defend himself. The schizophrenic believes he has the task of saving the world. The schizophrenic thinks he hears voices and sees visions. The schizophrenic has delusions about his body being eaten by those closest to him—and what a last supper *I* would make! The schizophrenic requires to be loved unconditionally. The schizophrenic dares authority to judge and punish him. The schizophrenic—especially that first and greatest of all schizophrenics—thinks he is God!" Arnie sat up again suddenly and held his flatted hands out, palms up, to Aubrey. "Don't mistake me. I am only a priest in this exalted order of human beings. I freely resign myself to the fact that *I* am not the Christ." Arnie's tone was accusatory, and so were his close-hauled, nearly malevolent eyes.

Aubrey was caught looking at Arnie head on, eyes unlashed and wide for the wounding. And much as he wanted to turn away, he did not, and took Arnie's blinkless-blue ferocity with what intrepidity he could manage; and said quickly, "Well, I thank God, as do all of us greensward Christians, for minute and untoward favors."

"Meaning what?" Arnie said truculently.

"Meaning," Aubrey replied, as he got easily to his feet, "that I'm delighted to know you *don't* think you're Christ and that you *do* think you're only a priest. Because I'd hate to be tempted to vaticide *and* fratricide on the same Sunday morning, before Mass."

Arnie looked as if he had been drastically overreached, which was precisely the effect Aubrey had hoped to produce. "Oh now, wait a minute, Aubie, babe. That's a pretty extreme reaction from a Christian who's supposed to turn the other cheek."

Aubrey looked down firmly into Arnie's intensive offering of insincerity, and summoned all of the Strycker-Milligan mordacity just then at his command and ran it down his tongue. "Arnie, we're likely to be together for a few days and I want you to know, right now, that as far as I'm concerned you're sane, and I'm going to treat you as if you were, or are, or want to be, sane. So that when you start dealing me such a load of condescending horse turds as you just tried to do, be assured that this Christian will give you, as he is about to demonstrate, not merely one cheek but both of them."

Upon which Aubrey turned and walked briskly away, and felt that his effect was only slightly compromised by the sound of Arnie howling in laughter behind him.

# · THIRTEEN ·

WHEN HE GOT BACK from Mass, Kermit and Arnie were having breakfast together, both smiling eagerly up at him as he approached the
table, neither showing any least evidence of rancor left over from
the night before, Arnie showing no apparent memory of his argument with Aubrey two hours before. They greeted him as if he had
just returned from hazardous duty somewhere north of Point Barrow,
and both agreed boisterously with Nelson when he suggested that a
rare steak might be just the thing for Aubrey's breakfast. Aubrey
came nowhere near matching their free wheeling spirit of forgiveness
and charity. He attributed this partly to the commonplace that the
religious life does nothing to prepare one for spontaneity. The good
monk was grave, sober, reflective, an expert at pinching the little
jugulars of notions fay and sprightly. But his reticence had a deeper
root. Plainly, it seemed to him that the intelligent, honest thing for
Arnie and Kermit, and Arnie and himself, to do was to make a considered analysis of the reasons behind their mutual contentiousness,
allowing for drunkenness, family custom, simple propensity for argument, and sudden temper, but searching openly, ruthlessly, with
utter mutual candor to the hot core of whatever the hell it was that
could so completely frustrate their normal love for one another. He
refused to believe that as they sat there beaming at him, they were

140

either irrational or had forgotten. He acknowledged that he had never heard any member of the Strycker-Milligan complex reasoning out or attempting to arbitrate any personal or public dispute. But didn't it ever occur to them to try? Did they think that if they ignored something long enough it would go away? Or did they enjoy hurting one another, or need to hurt, or feel some compulsion to hurt? What was the answer? He had no idea. In that case, what was the question, as Miss Stein had it? He didn't know the question, either. So he couldn't very well ask it, and just sat there looking back at them, smiling.

"So, Aubie, what was the gospel for the day?" Arnie asked.

"Oh. Let's see. Oh yes. Jesus telling the apostles that he would send the Holy Ghost."

"Sure, it would have to be that one. Sunday after the Ascension. You know, when I was the Holy Ghost and Christ got back to the office and told me to go on down there and spit a little fire around, I took one look at those apostles—oh, they were a motley bunch of finks—and told Christ they'd just have to shift for themselves."

"Now Arnie," Kermit said. "Don't make fun of Aubrey's religious beliefs."

"Aubrey's? What the hell, does he hold the patent on them? I'm a Catholic, too, you know."

"Goddamn it, you know what I meant."

"No I don't, Kermit. Unless you meant that he's a nut, old Arnie is, and you can't be a Catholic if you're a nut."

"I just meant . . ."

"Isn't that what it sounded like to you, Aub?"

Aubrey blinked to a quick recovery. Arnie's sudden conversion and the sudden dissolution of the sweetness and light had caught him short. "Oh, no. Not at all, Arnie. I—ah—I think it was just a bit of wishful thinking on Kermit's part. I mean, he wishes they weren't your religious beliefs. Or mine."

"That's very good," Arnie said. "Kermit, did you hear Aubie snatch you back to shore? And don't spoil it by saying you were about to say the same thing. It takes lightning-fast mental reflexes to come up with something like that. And so beautifully diplomatic. Aubie, I've got to look to my laurels and laconics with you around. Since you got that university education, I'm turning into a counterpuncher."

Aubrey was dismayed to see Arnie straining as he said this, and to see him waiting for the complimentary protest. "Our intellectual pecking order has been established a long time, Arnie. I don't see as it's changed any, or that it's likely to."

"Gallantly spoken and truer than you know," Arnie said, grinning, then laughing. "Ho, by God! His humility passeth all understanding!" Then, almost without interval, he started to shake his head dolefully, his face drawn in sorrow. "No, no, no. Oh no. The overwhelming loss. If I'd been there—say I was John, who loved Jesus so, who wrote that gospel so radiant with love—and here is this most noble and gentle of men saying, 'Look, my dear and good friends. I love you all and my heart will die when I leave you, but they are waiting up on Morningside Heights to nail me to a cross, and I must go. I will, however, send a ghost to bless you and to assure you that I am who I say I am.' What could that have meant to the disciples? What could it have meant to me? Why, if he were going to die, would I give a damn about a ghost? If I'd been there, old Arnie would have said, 'No, Jesus! Don't go. I know where I can get three Bren guns and a case of Molotov cocktails. We'll blow the bastards up, Jesus! Don't let them nail you on a cross!' "

For a moment after this, it appeared that Arnie might cry, but he held on, and Kermit jumped in brightly. "Good steak, Aubie?" Arnie winced, but came up smiling. "I don't want to rush you, but they want us at the convent by eleven." Kermit sounded almost domestic.

"Oh yes, get there before eleven. That's when the eunuchs start playing stinkfinger."

"Arnie! For Christ's sake," Kermit said.

Arnie hung his head immediately, and appeared to be genuinely contrite. "I know. I know. And Aline's a sweet thing, and I love her. I want you both to know that. I do." Then, viciously, "But I wish to Christ she would stop treating me as if I were a goddamned *basket case!*"

Kermit appealed to Aubrey with a roll of his eyes. Aubrey had a mouth full of steak and no ideas. Kermit gave it his best. "Look, Arnie, she treats me the same goddamned way."

"Well, I'm delighted to hear it, for Christ's sake. But that doesn't help me any. How the hell can you say anything to pure, distilled, sweet-essence-of-lily-of-the-valley sympathy? I ask you. Every goddamned thing I say, she nods and bestows that mystic little smile, or that mystic little voice if the screen isn't open, as if to say, Oh my sweet lambchop Christ, yes, child. That's perfectly all right. You're a poor benighted idiotic fink, but all will be made clear to you in the next world."

"Arnie, that's not fair," Aubrey said.

"How the hell would you know? You haven't seen her since she entered that bomb shelter!"

"Aubrey, we have to get the hell out on the road."

"She was always that way, Arnie. I mean, sweet and wide-eyed. But she never meant to be condescending."

"She's condescending now. You'll see, old buddy. She's got Christ by the ring finger and she's squeezing till He says agape."

"Aubrey?"

"You're not going with us, Arnie?"

"Hell no. Oh, I might have, but Rexfordia called up. She wants me there by lunchtime. She sounds like the last rose of Boot Hill. What were you all drinking Friday night, formaldehyde?"

"So when will I see you?"

"Jesus, I don't know, Aubie. You know Rexfordia. Once I get within the walls of the Fort, it'll take a papal siege engine to get me out again." Arnie was a high school junior lamenting the trials of popularity, the hungry-eyed president of the senior class decrying, martyrlike, the awful demands made upon his devilishly variegated talents.

"Well, then, I'll probably see you tomorrow night. Over there," Aubrey said.

"Tuesday night," Kermit said. "How the hell do you figure you can spend a day with me at the office and buy all the goddamned gear you need by tomorrow night?"

"Oh, that's right."

"And didn't you promise Julie the other night you'd help her clean out her apartment Tuesday?"

"Did I?"

"Well, hell yes, you did. She told me on the way home."

"Aha!" Arnie said, gleaming falsely. "So the chaste Miss Chace has you in her orbit already? Oh, beware, step, beware. That young lady is majoring in pneumatics."

"Arnie, goddamn it. Watch your tongue," Kermit said.

"Why, Aubie, the virgin, is blushing!"

"Come on, Aubrey. We've got to go."

143

"Okay, old buddy. Don't look at me. You don't have to. I know all about how Miss Julie operates."

"Do you, Arnie?" Aubrey had not meant to sound quite as dubious as he did, but there was no help for it.

"Why the hell wouldn't I? Do you think I'm not good enough for her? Are you that much more attractive to her than I? Maybe she likes nuts. Oh, you bet your ass she does, and she'll grab you by them first chance she gets!"

Kermit started to speak, but then jerked his head at Aubrey, and marched out of the room.

"Well, I'll see you Tuesday night, then, Arnie."

"If you aren't getting laid, you mean."

"Arnie, for God's sake. Do we have to argue?"

"No, no, no." He was abruptly disconsolate again. "You be sure now and give my love to Aline. And you and he will have a long talk Tuesday night."

"He?"

"Old Arnie. You and old Arnie."

"Okay. Roger is coming to get you?"

"Well, I wish you wouldn't put it quite *that* way," Arnie said, slapping at one hand with the other. "I mean, Roger and I are good friends, but whether or not he's going to get me, well—that all depends."

"See you, Arnie."

Aubrey went out, taking with him a mental photograph of his final glimpse of Arnie, arms folded in front of him on the table, his face buried in them, one hand raised slightly, the fingers waving goodbye.

Mr. Jebb was waiting, impeccably attired, touching a tissue here and there to the already faultless sheen of the car. He touched his cap to Aubrey and Aubrey touched his hat to Mr. Jebb. Mr. Jebb held the door and bowed slightly as Aubrey walked in and sat down next to Kermit. Then Mr. Jebb took the wheel and rolled it, and the other four, imperturbably, at sixty-five miles an hour all the way to the Bronx. So that Mr. Jebb's middle finger didn't get an airing, but Aubrey noticed that it was ever in readiness.

Kermit talked about Arnie most of the way, but switched to Aline when he saw that Aubrey wasn't responding. And when Aubrey didn't warm to Kermit's ideas on Aline's incarceration, Kermit fell silent and stared out the window, and Aubrey had to hold himself from making any number of intricately worded and emotionally imbalanced proclamations, declarations, and appeals. And he had to hold himself also, from simply laying his head on his father's shoulder and saying, I love you best of all, Daddy. I love you better than anybody else does.

He remembered later that he hadn't gathered the slightest impression of what the outside of the convent looked like. It was on a street like other streets, and it was shaped and clothed with sunlight and shadow, and it had a front door that was the most irrevocable, sempiternal front door he had ever confronted. And it amazed him that it opened electrically, with a buzzering that came like needles out of a frozen, splintered silence. But once within, he remembered very well.

The silence was profound, and in it stood a white plaster statue of the patron saint of this particular division of Carmelites. "Look," Kermit said. "She looks like Honey Hohenlohe. All we need is a statue of Alec. With a British double, so we could hang rosaries on the barrels." They were in the parlor, or the speak room, and it was very clean and white, like the inside of a virgin's coffin. There were two straight chairs, also white, in the center of it. Kermit hung his hat on Honey Hohenlohe's head, and took one of the chairs. "You can't smoke," he said, returning a package of cigarettes to his pocket. Aubrey took the other chair. The room was about twelve-by-twelve. The walls were all white except the one in front of them, which was formed by a black curtain, under and around which iron grillwork could be seen. "Now we just sit on our duffs and wait until they are goddamned good and ready to make believe we're here." Aubrey smiled at this. It put the black and white of it down. And he was thinking, My God, never to run down a meadow again? Never to swim in the sea? Never to walk in a forest again? Never to lie on the earth? And Kermit was grumbling in short takes: how a pretty young girl—bury herself—down with life and babies—swamp between the principle and the act—goddamned if I can see—hell is paved with holy women—climb into her casket at seventeen years of age—four good men could convert them all overnight—got it from her mother —goddamned Milligan stubbornness—leave each one of you a million—and you're no goddamned better—might as well have had no children at all, for Christ's sake.

145

Then they heard shuffling footsteps on the enclosure side of the iron grille, and a sweet, unworldly voice greeted them with hello and told them they were welcome in God's holy name, and asked them who it was they wished to see. Kermit groaned and shook his head, but finally managed to growl, "Sister Margaret Michael Aline Strycker, my daughter, if you don't mind, and hurry"—and *sotto voce*—"before I light your candle at both ends." And a rustle of gathered skirts and the sweet voice thanked sweetly and moved off into the unglimpsable beyond, shooting bolts as it went, to fetch, they hoped, Aline. And Kermit went on grumbling and looking around as if he expected to see machine-gun snouts suddenly appear at all apertures.

Aline, when she came, came very quietly. They heard only one bolt shot, and that a misfire, and shrugged at one another, and were quite startled to hear, "Daddy? Are you there?"

"I'm here, Aline, sweetheart. How are you?"

"Oh, it's so good to hear your voice. How are you?"

"I'm fine, sweetheart, except that I miss you very much."

"And how is Mother?"

"I saw her just Friday, and she was beautiful as ever, and sent her love, and says she's going to visit you—on a—what the hell is that?"

"Never mind, Daddy. But she meant soon?"

"Oh, soon, soon. Yes. Very soon. Pentechrist! That's it!"

"Pentecost, Daddy. Oh, that's next Sunday. I don't know if Mother Prioress will allow it."

"You tell Mother Prioress to go bag her prior! Mother Rexfordia has rights a damned sight previous to Mother Prioress, by God!"

Aubrey tried to wave Kermit down, but Aline seemed used to it. "Now, Daddy. Please. I know that. And how is Arnie?"

"Just fine. We're leaving for Alaska next week. *This* week, by God."

"And Aubrey? Have you heard from Aubrey?"

"Well, not in quite a while, baby." Kermit winked at Aubrey. He could scarcely contain himself, and kept hunching his chair toward the grille, pulling at his beard and licking at his smile. "Nope, I'm afraid poor Aubrey is working too hard to pray us all into heaven."

"I'm so proud of him, Daddy. He will be a very holy priest. I'm so proud."

Kermit winked broadly at Aubrey. Kermit looked, at that moment, as though he, too, were proud, but there could have been all kinds

146

of reservations hidden behind that beard. Aubrey was tempted to speak to Aline, not having agreed to or even discussed Kermit's ground rules, but he held back, and listened, and found her voice like nothing he remembered. To Rexfordia's piano, Aline's voice was a harpsichord, distant, medieval, coming from afar through magic casements, and it enchanted and drew him, like a familiar song played on an ancient instrument.

"Listen, Aline, I have a surprise for you today. What's holding Mother What's-her-name up?"

"Oh, Daddy. She's not coming today."

"What the hell do you mean she's not coming, baby? I talked with her on the telephone. She said she'd open the damned blinds!"

"I don't know, Daddy. Sister Portress didn't say anything about it. And Mother Prioress did grant the privilege at Easter, when you visited the last time."

"So? Easter, for Christ's sake, was nine months ago!"

"No, Daddy. Just a few weeks ago."

"Well, goddamn it, Aline, I have a surprise, and I want to show it to you!"

"Well, Daddy, I could ask the Mother Prioress again, but I really don't think I should. Please, Daddy, I don't want to be an exception to the rules."

"Goddamn it, Aline, you were an exception to the rules the day you entered this miserable goddamned rabbit hutch!"

Aubrey tried to pull at Kermit's sleeve, but he tossed his hand away and got to his feet.

"Please, Daddy, I have to live as I have promised to live, as all the other sisters live. Or else I don't belong here!"

"That's right, by Christ! You *don't* belong here! Any more than Aubrey belongs where he is! Or where he's been." He flapped his arms distractedly at his sides, glanced at Aubrey, and moved closer to the grille.

"Please don't say that. I *do* belong here, Daddy."

"All right, so you belong here, you think. But you don't belong here, *I* think, and in any goddamned case, I want to see you! Now, today, and where the hell is the harm in that, I'd like to know?" He seized the grille in both hands and rattled it. He seemed alarmed at its fragility, and let go. "By God, I *could* tear this goddamned thing down, if you'd like to know!"

"I know you could, Daddy. But please don't. I'm not locked in. I can leave whenever I wish. And you are not locked out, Daddy. You can tear that grille down whenever you want to. But if I choose to be here, my choosing builds a wall that you can't tear down. Unless you want to hurt me very much. And even then . . ."

"I don't want to hurt you at all, for Christ's sake! I am just so goddamned sick of this whole hide, seek, and peephole horseshit that I could tear the front end out of the goddamned building!" And he rattled the grille drastically with one hand and kicked it, then walked away abruptly to the middle of the room and stood with his back to the screen.

"Daddy, I'm sure I can get permission to have the screen opened by midsummer."

"Midsummer! Jesus Christ! Who the hell will be alive in midsummer, for all anybody knows?" He stomped back to the grille. "Aline, goddamn it, I want this thing opened! And I want to know, right now, and without any goddamned pious equivocations, if you actually mean to stay in this hellhole the rest of your life. I really want to *know*, and I don't want any of your patent-leather, shocked-virgin crap! You know me, Aline, of old, and I know you! Now, just give me one goddamned straight answer! That's all I ask!"

There was a long, if not straitened, silence. Then Aline said, "I'm very happy here, Daddy."

Aubrey thought Kermit would explode into his component parts. He shook the grille until the whole wall vibrated, then went into a tight, short circuit of the speak room, stomping, gesticulating with both hands and his head, so absorbed in his anger that he seemed to forget he had Aubrey as an audience. And he shouted with all the sarcasm to which a shout is available, "Oh well, then, Jesus Christ! As long as you're happy, that's all that matters! To hell with your old man, and your mother, and all the plans they have made for you, and all the things they have set aside for you. To hell with making *them* happy. Let them go to hell. Let your old man live, die, and get buried alone, with no one to see it! Who the hell cares? He never did anything for anybody, and isn't worth remembering, and he won't get a Catholic funeral, and he will certainly go straight to hell! Oh, we'll pray for him. Oh my Christ, yes! We pray for everybody, we harpies do! Al Capone, Adolf Hitler, Senator McCarthy—and everybody can plainly see how much good it did *them!* We even

148

pray for the Devil himself, so why not pray for Kermit Strycker? It can't do any harm, and, after all, we harpies do belong to the Independent Prayer Mumblers and Shroud Menders' Union, and we don't want to lose our membership!"

Then, for a very long time, there was silence. Aubrey stared at the black screen, wondering how far Kermit would go, wondering if he really would tear the wall, grille, and Aline's peace down, and what in hell he could do to stop it, short of grabbing Kermit and trying to hold him. And wondering, finally, how it had happened that Kermit had not appeared in Boston and Chelsea with this house-wrecking act.

And Aline was saying, "I know I am selfish and inconsiderate and ungrateful, but I do love you and Mother very much, and I appreciate all you both have done for me. But there is only one thing I want to do with my life. And that is to be a good nun, here, in this convent." She paused, then started to say more but was interrupted by the rattle of the inner door opening. Kermit whirled around toward Aubrey, grinning broadly. He cocked an ear at the screen, behind which a whispered conversation was being conducted, then turned to Aubrey again, bent forward, nodding his wide grin, holding one index finger in the air near his nose, his eyes alight and crafty, chuckling delightedly—like a huge bearded elf who has just found the pot of gold—and he said, in his hoarse stage whisper, "That's the Chief Harpy."

"Kermit. She'll hear you."

A throat was cleared behind the screen. Kermit immediately ran for his chair in a knees-high tiptoe.

"You were just putting on an act, weren't you?" Aubrey whispered.

Kermit's expression was all surprise and outraged innocence, as if Aubrey had surely just asked the superfluous question of the year. "Well, hell yass, I was! It's the only goddamned way to get them to raise the portcullis!"

"Mr. Strycker?" This, clearly, the voice of authority.

Kermit snapped straight in his seat, composed his face instantly, selected a meek, put-upon tone, blinked his eyes as if he hoped teacher had not called upon him to recite, and said, "Yes, Mother Prioress?"

"I must apologize. I neglected to tell Sister Portress that the screen might be opened today."

"Oh, that's all right, Mother Prioress."

"Only because of the special circumstances, Mr. Strycker. I hope you understand that you must not stay too long."

"Of course, Mother Prioress."

"And, Mr. Strycker. In the future, will you please wait for at least three months between visits?"

"I certainly will, Mother Prioress."

A key was turned in a lock. "Oh, and one more thing. We do need a new screen, and if you'll donate the money for it, I think we could arrange to let you tear this one down."

"I'll take you up on that, by God," Kermit said, then put one hand over his mouth sheepishly.

Aubrey shook his head at him. "Down the pipe, Kermit. Zilch for the day."

Then the black-curtained screen was drawn aside and there, seated stiffly on a low stool, her hands hidden in the brown folds of her habit, was Aline. She stared at Aubrey, and her mouth opened slowly. "Aubrey. I can't *believe* it."

Then Kermit was on his feet, crowing and chortling and rubbing his hands together and looking from one to the other and back again in a perfect spasm of delight. And Aubrey was speaking automatically, expressing his pleasure and explaining his presence in something like an animated daze, because of his shock at this first sight of Aline in almost four years. For she had grown into the image of Rexfordia. Wide mouth, full lips, the white-parchment complexion, all of that wan, sweet, genteel, alas-I'm-dying beauty. My God, he thought, all she needs is that Packard Chummy to lean on. The eternal gamin takes the veil while all her wild friends stand around in the back of the chapel, taking surreptitious belts from their pocket flasks and asking one another, Why, oh why, is Sexy-Rexy doing it?

And, excited, her voice was a brilliant, earnest piping, and her eyes danced along, and she had to know everything and asked more questions than she left room for him to answer, but thought that Africa was a marvelous idea because it was so full of souls that needed saving, and thought that Aubrey was making a wonderful sacrifice for Our Lord, and thought that Kermit's beard made him look, the longer it got, like St. Joseph, and thought that Arnie would get well very soon, and thought that Aubrey looked so different, so spiritual,

150

that she might not have known him. "Oh, I think I would have, and I don't mean that you weren't spiritual-looking before . . ."

"You look so much like Mother, it's uncanny."

"That's what Daddy says."

"Well, it's true, goddamn it."

"Daddy, please don't swear. The sisters can hear you."

"They can hear him?" Aubrey asked.

"Yes. The walls are very thin." She nodded gravely. "Everybody knows when Daddy has visited me."

"Well, what the hell, I am what I am, and if they'd stop all this damned cloak-and-moat crap . . ."

"Yes, but, Kermit, you don't have to swear. You can't have any idea what it sounds like to a religious," Aubrey said. "It still makes me jump, after two days of it. These poor nuns must practically expire."

"Hell, it does 'em good to hear a man's voice now and then. Keeps 'em hoping." Kermit pointed a finger at Aline. "And, by God, I'm serious about wanting you out of here. Arnie's out of it. Aubrey's out. Now it's your turn."

"I'm not out of it. I'm going right back in."

"Well, we'll see about that."

"Aubrey? Will you take any of your training in this country?" Aline asked.

"I don't think so."

"Well . . ."

"But I get home every eight years, I think it is."

"Every eight years! Holy Jesus Christ! You're out of your god-damned mind, Aubrey! I'm beginning to think you're crazier than Arnie!"

"Kermit! Don't shout."

"Don't tell me don't shout!" Kermit's outrage now seemed quite genuine. "Eight years! You mean to sit there and tell me you're going to haul-ass for the Sahara Desert and we're not going to see you for eight years?"

"Well it may not be *eight* years. But they have this rotation estab—"

"Rotation! *I'll rotate* them, the bastards!" He pointed his finger at Aubrey. "Now, I'm telling you something. I've been pretty lenient with you about this goddamned Africa business, but you never said anything about eight years before this! And I'm not going to stand for it, by Christ! I've lost Aline, I've lost Arnie, and you're the last of the goddamned Mohawks! I *don't*—and I mean I *don't*—intend to lose you! Let's get that understood right now!"

Aubrey had his words all ready, but as he opened his mouth, he saw Aline shaking her head at him. Her eyes were great and hollow, and had returned to silence. The visit was over, even though it was another minute before the door opened at the rear of the enclosure and a nun, her face veiled, nodded to Aline and withdrew again. Aubrey held his words and sat and looked at her, and tried not to listen to Kermit, who was still orating behind him—all about how generous it was of the bastards to give him a day off every eight years and was he sure that the Saharans had a place in Southampton, because if they did he was going to make some subtle arrangements to blow it up by nightfall.

"I have to go," Aline said. "I'm sorry . . ."

"I'll come alone next time. Will they let me see you before I go?"

"Oh, I'm sure if Mother Prioress knows you're going to Africa, there will be special permission."

Aubrey started to say he was sorry about Kermit, but at that moment Kermit stopped roaring, and Aubrey shrugged and said, "I'll see you, then. In about a month, I figure. If they take me."

"They'll take you. I know it. And I'm so proud of you, Aubrey. I'll pray very hard for your intention."

Then she was on her feet and moving away, and Kermit was by the screen saying he was sorry about the noise, goddamn it, and then she was at the door, her eyes moving solemnly back and forth between them, and then she was, quite suddenly, gone.

Kermit stood and blew his nose a while and watched with great interest as Sister Portress closed the screen. "I'll get you a new one of those, Sister," he called out. There was no reply, just the soft closing of a door. Kermit turned and came toward Aubrey, his eyes down. "And I know where to get it, too. Just find out where they stored the sets for *Dracula Takes the Veil*." He snorted once, muttered something about the poor girl anyway for Christ's sake, took his hat from the head of the holy founder, said, "See you, Honey," and walked out.

And Kermit hummed "Nearer, My God, to Thee" all the way home.

152

# · FOURTEEN ·

AND FROM that first early moment when Kermit was standing in his room, parting the curtains to the day (the sun falling in dazzling pillars across the green rug), shouting for him to get the hell up because for Christ's sake there had been a great storm and Strycker Lines ships were sinking all over the world, and Uncle Jan Strycker (president of Strycker Lines, Inc.) was running up and down Sweden screwing all the Nordic blondes he could find, as he should have done years ago, God knows, and couldn't be found, and the lowly goddamned executive vice-president had to get the hell down to Hanover Square and make a few intelligent decisions before that bunch of jackasses his brother called employees had put the whole corporation down by the bow, and Aubrey had to come along because he would one day inherit the business entire unless Arnie shaped up, which didn't seem likely, or that goddamned Jan put a bun in somebody's oven and had to marry her and had a son or something similar, but that in any case he would inherit Kermit's share and it was about goddamned time he learned a binnacle from a barnacle because who the hell knew but that Aubrey might decide to let all those Africans go to hell without his ministrations, and hurry up, drop your cock and grab your socks, downstairs in three minutes, those in peril on the sea, and out the door saying they'd put off Abercrombie and Fitch until tomorrow, and down the hall singing "Many brave hearts lie asleep in the deep, beware, be-e-e-e-ware!"—from that spate of rapid-fire moments, the day belonged to Kermit, and Aubrey only tagged along to watch.

Twenty-five minutes after his feet hit the floor, they were turning south on F.D.R. Drive, and Mr. Jebb went at once to throttle, horn, and the head of the pack at seventy miles an hour, putting the fear of empire into all other competitors. Kermit was reading aloud newspaper accounts of the gale that had come in from the west over Britain at about the same speed Mr. Jebb was making, and had gone on across the Channel into France, Belgium, and Holland, and was still blowing over Germany, and, sometime during the night, Kermit read, as a note of special interest to Aubrey, the eight-foot iron cross atop St. Paul's in Hamburg had been torn off by the wind and sent crashing down through the roof of the church. Kermit closed the newspaper suggesting that the Church Militant ought to get a good lawyer and sue the Church Triumphant under an "Act of God" statute.

Then Kermit arranged his day, with a cup of coffee in one hand and the telephone in the other, enjoying himself immensely, winking at Aubrey, swearing in nautical phrases more often than usual, and taking a great interest in the traffic on the East River. Clearly, this was the return of the sea dog, and Aubrey enjoyed the show, and asked Kermit once if he was sure he wouldn't like salt instead of sugar in his coffee.

Kermit's first call was to Strycker Lines, telling them he was definitely on the way and to move the executive meeting up a half hour. Then he called Kaatskill Productions. He got Miss Taylor and didn't seem to have much more luck with her than Aubrey had had. "Look, goddamn it, it's very simple. When Miss Cowley gets in, tell her to tell Phil Cherry that I'll see him at eleven down at Hanover Square. Yes, Phil Cherry, *senior!* What the hell would I want to see that goddamned *Filcher* for?" He turned to Aubrey. "My goddamned secretary isn't in yet. By God, I'm going to follow that woman home some night. I think she's got a moonlighting job in Miami Beach." Then into the telephone, "No, that isn't all. I'm supposed to see my lawyers, about my will. They're coming to see me there—*there*, where you are, for Christ's sake!—yes!—at ten-thirty. Tell Miss Cowley to call them and have them come at the same time to Hanover Square. What? Miss Cowley's got the name—Wynken, Blynken, and Nod, or some goddamned thing!" He hung up, turned to Aubrey. "That poor girl needs her ears reamed. Or something reamed. Pretty little thing. I'll introduce you tomorrow." He laughed and poked Aubrey in the ribs. "When the beast charges, drop it on him. Hah! Those goddamned lawyers. They have been drawing and redrawing that goddamned will for—well, by Christ—it's almost two years! And the fees! I could have bought God off and taken it with me for what those bastards have cost." He laughed. "Yes, yes, great tragedy; the Pope fell down and broke his drinking elbow. Hah! Do you make the fist, gentlemen?" He took a swing at Aubrey, pulled the punch, and pressed his fist lightly against Aubrey's chin. "Hah! You're a great lad. Didn't even blink. I've got two fine sons." He nodded and pursed his lips. "Jesus, how I feel for poor Phil Cherry. There he is, brilliant mind, a goddamned financial genius—you know, he's vice-president of Strycker and Kaatskill—of course, get him off the floor of the Stock Exchange and I suspect he couldn't find his ass with both hands. But anyway he's got this son, Philip Cherry, junior—Filcher, I call him—and Filcher is the poorest goddamned excuse for twenty-some years of child raising I ever saw. The little son of a bitch is just a foul ball. He wears Italian clothes and goes mincing around, you know, in those tight-assed pants, walking like he's just been circumcised, and he fancies himself a big international sport. Well, he's just a heartbreak to poor Phil. Phil's got him in the investment department and he's always screwing things up. The last one was a sneaky little deal—some Italian or—Christ, I don't know, Greek, maybe—racing tire company—and Filcher went over there and saw all the races. Oh, cut a wide swath he did, all on company expense, and we took a loss on the investment—Phil caught it in time—and I told Filcher he got any more bright ideas about tires, of any kind, I'd seal off his ass with a blowout patch. So now Filcher is getting married—well, wait, goddamn it, you're going to the wedding, too—I owe that much to Phil, and, of course, Mrs. Cherry and your mother are great friends. . . ." He looked out the window and started to hum. "Almost there." He clapped his hands together and rubbed them. "Well, goddamn it, Aubrey, shall we go up and put the company back on its feet?"

Kermit went into the Strycker Building like a captain taking the quarter-deck, shaking hands and nodding to all kinds of people who recognized him, and claimed to recognize Aubrey, and talked all the way up in the elevator with Ace Hudgkins, who had been twenty years a bosun in the British Navy and thirty years on merchant ships after that, and who usually piped Jan and Kermit aboard his elevator, but was caught this morning without his pipe, for which he apologized profusely.

They made their way through more handshaking to Jan Strycker's office—a huge room papered with nautical charts—but there was no one at the conference table. Kermit scowled at his watch, saw that they were five minutes early, and led the way to his own private office.

Rexfordia had amused herself one summer decorating this office. Kermit had been away doing a picture and the office was to be Rexfordia's surprise. The which, Kermit said, it sure as hell was. Rexfordia's idea of what an office should be was J. P. Morgan's in the Morgan Library on 36th Street, and she had duplicated its ornate, classic Italian Renaissance décor, at staggering cost, to the best of her ability. So that Kermit had the exquisitely carved desk, the thronelike chair, bookcases full of unreadable, leather-bound books, a gilded false fireplace, gold candelabra, several expensive works of lesser Italian artists of the period, one illuminated manuscript, assorted incunabula placed cunningly here and there, great draperies tied back at the windows, and the windows themselves almost clerestoried and translucent and inset irregularly with stained-glass representations of various saints and popes.

Kermit's first reaction to the office had been to request that he be directed to the baptismal font so that he might vomit in it, and his second to have a little sign made reading LITTLE FORT MILLIGAN, and hang it on the door. And the office became the object of all kinds of jokes. Jan genuflected to Kermit when he was seated at the desk, and somebody was always sending him a monstrance or an incense pot. And once, when he was away on the West Coast, parties unknown had installed a full-size confessional box and put the water cooler in it. The monstrances, incense pots, and confessional box were all still there, and, as they came into the room, Kermit told Aubrey to help himself to any ecclesiastical supplies he felt he could use.

"Did you ever see such a goddamned business office? If I spent more than twelve hours a year in it, I'd be sucking doorknobs. Yes, indeed. Great spot for an exorcism." He put his hat on the desk. "Well, make your visit to the tabernacle and let's get the goddamned business done."

The goddamned business was done in less than half an hour. It appeared that very few Strycker ships had suffered damage or delay, that everything was under control, and that Kermit's presence had not really been required. Also, Jan Strycker had telephoned New York from Sweden a few minutes before and had made those two or three decisions that might have required Kermit's authority.

Kermit was definitely put out, and conducted the meeting in a series of barks. Aubrey sat at the far end of the room, near Jan's desk, and heard very little of what was said by most of the executives, who were subdued, soft-spoken, and came through only in occasional phrases: two antennas—Cherbourg—A.B. overboard—bow plates— goddamned dock at Bremerhaven—Liverpool harbor—salvage rig— Baltic—limey oil tanker—deck cargo—and so on. But he heard every word Kermit said, especially near the end when a loudmouthed man, smooth in looks, dress, and delivery, got up at the far end of the table and wondered if Kermit had any comment on the latest move of the Federal Maritime Board.

"What the hell was their latest move?" Kermit bellowed, apparently challenged by the questioner's loudness.

"They put out a letter Friday warning subsidized steamship lines that they must in future justify to the Board all wage increases and any other concessions made to the unions."

"What do they mean by *justify?* Isn't a negotiated labor contract good enough for them any more?"

"Guess not. The Marine Engineers Beneficial has already accused the F.M.B. of interfering with collective bargaining and called a meeting of all seafaring unions for next month."

"Didn't we just negotiate a new wage contract with the Marine Engineers?"

"Yes. It went into effect the first of this month."

"Well, what do you want me to comment on, Mr. Kuhn? Do you think we've been less than diligent in negotiating with the unions?"

"Oh no. I . . ."

"Do you think we'd have been a little tougher with the Marine Engineers if the cost of their wage increase came out of Strycker Shipping's pocket entirely?"

"Well, we're a little off the subject, I think, Mr. Strycker. What I wanted your comment on . . ."

"I don't really give a rat's ass *what* you wanted my comment on. Just answer my question."

"Well, you know that we have certain agreements with the union people. Give a little, take a little. These practices are well established for all . . ."

"You want my comment, Mr. Kuhn? Here it is. I'm going to recommend to my brother that we freeze the cost to the government on all separately negotiated contracts at that level of wages and costs which prevailed on, say, April first of this year, and continue the freeze for a period of a year."

"We couldn't possibly do that. The other lines . . ."

"Screw the other lines! They might even follow suit, for all you know! Sit down, Mr. Kuhn, before you fall down. By God, I know it's an awful shock for you to hear anybody talk about refusing money from the government! Practically an un-American activity. But let me tell you people something. This is supposed to be a free and private enterprise, not a goddamned branch of the Federal government, and as soon as we stop taking money from the government on a dole system, the better off—the freer and more private— we'll be! Are there any arguments?"

There were none. The meeting was quickly adjourned and the executives fairly trampled one another getting out of the room. And when they were gone, Kermit came toward Aubrey, shaking his head and laughing. "Did you hear that? Jan will never do it, of course. But I just thought I'd shake them up a little. But I'm right!" And a little later he was chuckling to himself, and said, "By God, they are priceless, devoted employees, and I probably ruined the lot of them forever."

They were standing at the window—Kermit pointing out the Old Slip and Coffee House Slip and imagining the time when the Baltimore packets used to tie up at the foot of Wall Street, and remembering the times when his father, and he, had walked the East River waterfront, seabags on their shoulders, bound for one pier or another, one ship or another, and all the ports of the western world (and Aubrey found his interest in it all far higher than ever before, higher than it had been years before when he had stood at this window as a boy and heard the same talk, and he found himself thinking that if, for any reason, he were not a priest ten years from that minute, he could be reasonably content to be the barking president of Strycker Lines, Inc.)—when the lawyers came, three of them, in single file, all with briefcases and narrowly cut conservative suits and extremely thin neckties, and all grinning modestly and legally and apparently over-joyed to see Kermit. They took chairs around Jan's desk, and Kermit sat behind it and immediately asked one of them to state the rule in Shelley's case. The man—probably the senior member of the firm there present, and certainly the oldest—started smoothly enough and then stumbled, and Kermit wouldn't let him start again, but asked a younger lawyer, who stated the rule without hesitation, so that the first lawyer kept glancing sourly at the second throughout the pro-ceedings. And Aubrey took it that one of the principles of Kermit's approach to the business world was the creation of controllable dis-sension and ill feeling.

Kermit's current will was read, and Aubrey heard his name several times but could not really determine who was to get what because, as he became gradually aware, most of the bequests were in trust funds, stocks, mineral holdings, oil and real estate, but he did hear, to his astonishment, that he alone and solely was to be left the two-hundred-and-fifty-year-old Strycker house, and the seven hundred acres around it, in Kaatskill County. He was very shortly imagining what a positively gaudy novitiate the Strycker mansion would make.

There was a long discussion over a bequest to Aline's order, it being so entailed that it could only be used for the improvement of the physical plant of whatever convent she might reside in. "But fix it so they can't be shipping her all over the goddamned place. In fact, fix it so she has to stay right where she is."

"Can they use the money to build a *new* convent?" one of the lawyers asked.

"They cannot," Kermit snapped. "Do you think I want to con-tribute to the spread of those lunatic asylums?"

The first indication Aubrey had that he was a main topic of con-versation came after a *sotto voce* consultation among the lawyers, when one of them addressed him directly.

"Excuse me, Mr. Strycker—er—I hope that's correct? I wonder, you are no longer bound by the vow of poverty?"

"No." (Aubrey caught himself on this occasion, as on many others thereafter, about to address the man as "Father.")

"And if you should go on to another congregation or order, will you be required to take the vow of poverty?"

"Not in the society I have in mind."

"Good. I wonder if I may ask you, just as a general thing, that if

159

you should ever take the vow of poverty again, you communicate directly and immediately with us?"

"Oh, for Christ's sake," Kermit said. "To hell with that. He isn't going to take any goddamned vows of poverty."

And that settled that. The lawyers went on for a time introducing other changes, and discussing insurance, taxes, the liquidation of corporate interests, the transfer of deeds, the settlement of liens, the limits of the discretion of the executors, and so on, and it only occurred to Aubrey, as the lawyers were leaving and Kermit had recited a bit from Sandburg about "The lawyers; tell me why a hearse horse snickers, hauling a lawyer's bones" (at which the lawyers all laughed nervously and dutifully), that Kermit might one day be dying of old age; if bears, lions, or an explosion from pure choler didn't kill him first. And he figured out that his father was fifty-nine, and watched him move to the door with the lawyers and thought, No, no. He can't be fifty-nine. He looks forty-nine, or younger. He'll live another fifty years and even then I can't imagine him dead. And as he watched Kermit coming back from the door, his love for his father was clearly and very suddenly defined in a split-second vision of Kermit dead, and of himself, in a blind, blasphemous rage, trying to lift the body from the coffin. And Kermit said, "Damned fools. Not a good trial lawyer in the lot."

Then came the Cherrys, father and son. "Filcher?" Kermit said into the telephone. "He's with you? Does he have to be? What? Oh Christ, Phil. All right." He put the telephone down and his palms to his forehead. "Filcher! I'll be seeing him Saturday, for Christ's sake. Well, Aubie, you must have peed on an icon somewhere long the line. The Lord has thrust Filcher upon us five days ahead of schedule."

Philip Cherry, Sr., was a dapper man in his middle sixties, tall, straight, light-footed, still handsome, hair and mustache in perfect gray order, his clothes London-cut from black mohair, shoes mirror-bright, and a white silk scarf around his neck, the ends hanging loose and fringed, this last giving his otherwise sartorially exact appearance a becoming air of gay or romantic abandon.

Philip Cherry, Jr., tender and wounded and brown of eye, must have resembled his mother, Aubrey concluded, because his father's brisk, clean-cut features were nowhere discernible in the boy's round face and yielding chin. The whiteness of his skin—alabaster and without blemish—made Aubrey think of field grubs. He was wearing an imported Brioni suit (Aubrey made discreet inquiry of Filcher, and he proudly displayed the label), the latest thing, with the padded shoulders, the short jacket, the cuffed coat sleeves, and the tapered, cuffless pants. Aubrey had to go some distance to shake Filcher's hand when introduced because he lurked, or sulked, in the vicinity of the conference table and eyed Kermit furtively and seemed constantly to be gauging the distance to the door. Aubrey classified him as a white creeper, and left him to his sulking.

But Kermit didn't. "Filcher!" he demanded. "Have you been robbing refugees again?"

Filcher gripped the conference table and rose to a half crouch and tried to make answer, but words wouldn't come. He kept looking behind him calculatingly as if seeking to fit his feet to the starting blocks.

The senior Cherry paused in mid-preamble, looked from Kermit to his son and back again, and asked what would give anyone that idea. "Why, Phil, that goddamned suit he's wearing! It looks like he stole if from a goddamned Helvetian homunculus!"

"Kermit, have you been listening to me?" the senior Cherry asked.

"Sure I have, Phil, but somebody's got to tell that boy. He keeps parading around looking like a bag man from the Mafia, he'll get deported! Jesus Christ! Why don't you get him Italian citizenship and rename him Maraschino!"

"You haven't heard a word I've said."

"Well, sure I have, Phil. But do you, for the sake of Christ Almighty and my aching ass, always have to start from the year nine and work your way out? I know you were born, that you're a citizen, that you're married, that you work for me, and that Filcher there is going to marry some unfortunate girl Saturday. He is going to marry a girl, isn't he?" The elder Cherry sighed. "Phil, I'm sorry, but I can't stand it any longer. Filcher! Just what in the name of poor patched Jesus is that goddamned garment you're wearing?"

Filcher took his mark. "Ah—ah—it's just a suit. Sir."

"New style is it, Filcher?"

"Ah—yes. Sir."

"Tell me, Filcher, did you see where the tailor got the cloth?"

"No—no, sir."

"Well, I'll tell you where he got it, Filcher. He got it off a pool table. A small pool table. Well, look, look at it, for Christ's sake!

Green felt, isn't it? Sure! I can see chalk marks from here! Fumble around in it a little, Filcher. I'll bet you'll find six goddamned leather pool-table pockets sewed right into it! Go ahead! Hah! You might even find a couple of balls! And, by God, Filcher, you could use 'em!" And Kermit laughed until he was wheezing for breath and wiping tears away, and Aubrey got laughing watching him. Neither Cherry was amused. In fact, Filcher, by virtue of some mysterious, unobservable motion, was halfway to the door. And at that point, perhaps because he figured he might just be able to run the ten remaining feet before Kermit could run fifty, he arranged his pointed-toe, buckle shoes, and took a stand.

"As—ah—as a matter of fact, Mr. Strycker . . ." Kermit's astonished gaze gave Filcher a bad moment, but he recovered. "As a matter of fact, the material in this suit is mohair."

"Oh, oh," Kermit said softly, even humbly. "Mohair. Well, I do beg your pardon, Filcher." Filcher straightened perceptibly. "Yes. I can see you're right, Filcher. I think it was the shape of the thing that threw me off. Yes, that's what it was, all right." Then, shifting into a snarling bellow, "What the hell difference does it make what *material* the goddamned thing is made of?"

Filcher took two insurance steps doorwise. "Well—ah—sir, I thought you . . ."

"You *thought!* That'll be the goddamned day. Listen, Filcher, as a matter that might interest you, the suit *I'm* wearing is made of mohair. The same goddamned material."

"Well, then, sir, why don't you like mine—same material?"

"Why? Listen, Filcher. Have you kissed your fiancée yet?"

This second apparent slur on Filcher's manhood brought him back strong—a quarter of a step, to be precise. "Well, certainly I have."

"And where do you kiss her, Filcher, on the lips?"

(And Aubrey could see it coming, the hoary siege gun creaking into position.)

"Yes, sir."

"Well, why don't you kiss her ass? It's made of the same material!"

Much later, after Kermit had made several snuffling circuits of the room and managed to bring himself under control, the elder Cherry presented Filcher's petition for a raise and a promotion. Kermit granted the raise, but averred that Filcher didn't deserve a promotion.

"I'll make a deal with you, Phil. Much as he doesn't deserve it, he can have the promotion on the day he comes to work in a new suit and a respectable haircut. I don't promote anybody who looks like the east end of a Venetian duck going west." Filcher, at his father's insistence, came forward and gave thanks, and said he would get a haircut and some other clothes, and even essayed a little joke and a chuckle about how he was going west day after tomorrow. Kermit smiled at the elder Cherry. "By God, Phil, he made a little joke. That shows promise. Now if we can only teach him to count. Yes, indeed. And, Filcher, that chuckle of yours needs work. Jesus, yes. Get somebody to check the tweeters on it."

When the Cherrys, plucked and pitted, had gone, Aubrey felt he should remonstrate with Kermit for being so hard on Filcher. And he thought of a couple of trenchant things to say, but, the propitious moment having arrived, he found he was too exhausted to say them. He had discovered, or rediscovered, that watching and listening to Kermit had the same effect upon him as might a half-mile run on a treadmill. Kermit's energy, the sound and the fury of him, forced the onlooker to compete, but to get nowhere, to accomplish nothing but his own enervation.

So that when Kermit announced that they would have lunch at Le Pavillon, and then rush right over to Abercrombie and Fitch and get a few thousand essentials for the hunt, Aubrey invented a toothache and pleaded it with immoral fervor. Kermit immediately called his dentist and got Aubrey "squeezed in" at four o'clock (the which squeeze Aubrey just as immediately canceled to his own satisfaction), and then called a certain Miss Balfour ("Diane"?) and asked her to meet him for lunch.

Aubrey went home, his conscience almost clear, in a taxicab, managed to restrain Nelson from giving him anything but a glass of milk, went up to his room, sat down on the edge of his bed, drank the milk, took up *pars verna*, telling himself that he would now read the office of the day, and was asleep before he finished the *Sacrosancte*.

## · FIFTEEN ·

THE NEXT MORNING at breakfast:

"How the hell do I know, Aubie? Her books, her clothes, her bags. Who the hell knows? Don't go if you don't want to. Goddamned city's full of moving men. Ho! Here's a letter for you. What the hell's that half-witted office messenger got all over it, hogshit? Christ! Nellie? Call Miss Cowley and tell her to fire that horse-faced bastard. Looks like Jeeter Lester and smells worse. Hup! Letter from my second mistake. Miss Gobbler Mailer. I mail it, she gobbles it. Jesus! Got to remember to divorce her next time I'm in Mexico. Hum, hum, balls! Who? I thought *that* son of a bitch died two years ago!"

And so on, while Aubrey read that Father Georges Bogart, S.O.S., Provincial of the American Province, having examined Mr. Aubrey Strycker's letter, would be happy to receive him for interview in Southampton at the address indicated at nine o'clock Thursday morning, fourteen Mai.

"Kermit? Can we go out to Southampton Wednesday night?"

"Hell yes. . . . Nellie, get Satchel-ass—what's his name?—you know, my agent, at MCA West. On the phone, the damned fool. . . . Hell yes, Aubie. Why not go in the morning? Get in a little shooting. I wonder if the Abercrombie's out there is open this early.

. . . Nellie? Where the hell'd Nellie go? Oh. You got him? Hello? Yes, hello, for Christ's sake! Well, put the son of a bitch on, missy! I'm paying a dollar a minute to talk to you? Hello? No, you god-damned cretin, this is Nancy Hanks! Who the hell did you *think* it was? Now listen, Satchel-ass, I got your letter and you have bitched things up as usual. Yes! What? Well, you damned fool, Hub's *left* the network! . . . Aubie, wait. . . . Shut up, Satchel-ass, I've got somebody important to talk to. . . . Look, Aubie, she called last night. At a delicate moment, I might add. I was just putting a soufflé in the oven. Anyway, she said she got out of the exam this morning—a male professor, no doubt—and wanted you over there as soon as you could make it. That's all I know. If it looks bad, call a moving man. . . . Hello? Now listen, Satchel-ass. I realize you think your first duty as an agent is to prostitute everything you touch, right?"

Less than an hour later, Aubrey was knocking at a big white door, saying a small prayer to Mary Immaculate for himself and for all those in danger on fourth floors. He waited, then heard shufflings within the apartment. He braced.

"Who is it?" The voice was querulous and female, but not Julie's. He told her who. "Oh yeah. Julie's expecting you?"

Aubrey allowed that he thought Julie was expecting him, and the voice allowed that it was nice to be expected, wasn't it, and that he had a nice voice, and that Julie was always promising to have the damned doorknob fixed, and that there was still lots of crap left around, and welcome. Then the door was opened by a plump, pretty girl with big made-up brown eyes and dirty blond hair. She was wearing a short nightgown and a white raincoat. Neither did much by way of concealing her fulsome person from the view of the most casual possible onlooker, of which category Aubrey was certainly a leader. She brushed some stray hairs out of her eyes and cocked her head. "Are you sure you're Aubrey Strycker?"

"No," Aubrey said, suddenly allowing a certain hellish abandon he'd been suppressing all morning to come to the surface, "I might very well be Ashurbanipal MacIver."

"Well, I wouldn't be overwhelmed either way, I'm sure. No offense, Ash. It's just that I was expecting you to be older."

"Well, if we just stand here long enough, I'm sure I can accommodate you."

She smiled. "You're cute, though. Come on in. Julie's in the shower. She overslept."

Aubrey braved five steps into the room. "What happened in here?"

"Yes, you are definitely cute, in that black suit and all. But don't worry, you're safe. I gave up sex before lunch."

Aubrey could think of no response to that one, Lent being long since over, and bent his attentions toward a place to sit. The room was a large, well-furnished shambles. Magazines, newspapers, milk bottles, whisky bottles, straw-covered Chianti bottles, two plates of nuts, articles of outdoor clothing including a rubber boot, a supply of overflowing ashtrays, several dozen dirty glasses, six vases of dead flowers, two odd high-heeled shoes, three brassieres, one ski pole, a miniature potted palm, three rolls of toilet paper neatly stacked, and sprinkled upon and more or less firmly clinging to all, the feathers from at least two, if not three or four, dozen anatine fowl.

The girl went to the sofa and tilted one of the seat cushions, dumping assorted debris to the floor. "Rest yourself, cousin. We had a little dinner party last night. To celebrate Julie's last exam." She picked up a half-eaten apple and took a bite.

"A *dinner* party? What'd you have to eat, live geese?"

"No, silly. Some of the boys had a pillow fight and some of the pillows broke. Some of the boys broke, too."

She stood in the center of the room, arms folded, both legs bare to the thighs, and watched him as he backed toward the sofa and sat down. Aubrey put his *custos oculorum* to the test, and it failed, fairly badly. "How are you called?" he said finally.

"I don't give my phone number to men in black suits, but you are an exception, and I'd give it to you, only I don't remember it at the moment. I just had it changed to something easier. However, Julie can tell you. She has a memory like nobody. You know, you're a humorous man. My name is Phoebe Rush and I'm 37-26-38. I'm trying to cut the last two down and build the other two up."

She tossed her shoulders and built them a little, and Aubrey looked away. "Aren't you going to tell me how *old* you are?" he asked.

"You didn't tell me how old you are."

"That's true. But then I didn't volunteer my measurements."

"A man's measurements do not make a *damned* bit of difference, if you'll pardon it. And, while we're on the subject, I would like to know if you think social security is any damned good."

166

"Well." Aubrey toyed with the idea of running. "I don't think it ever made anybody socially secure, if that's what you mean?"

"Exactly. That's what I'm going to tell the census taker next year."

"Yes. Well, he's the very man to tell."

"Certainly. He gets to meet everybody. Well, here comes Julie. I have to go feed the penguin, Ash." And, dropping the apple core in a chair, she walked out.

And Julie was right there to take Phoebe's place, wearing a pair of tight white pants and a red turtleneck sweater, her hair tossing behind her, her eyes and pouting lips at full power. And despite his resolution not to stare, he knew he was staring, amazed again at the beauty of her face, which, though not perfect or even regular in feature, had such a presence, such a nimiety of light, that it attacked the observing eye, and filled it, and peeled it, nearly as if she had the power to transfigure herself. Except that there was no goodness in her eyes, where, of course, the aural glow was centered; rather there was a sort of amused and unholy enjoyment of the effect she knew she was having, and, behind that, alive and pulsing, that desire that informed her whole person. There was, in those wide green eyes, something diabolic and raw and bestial. Yet not a something at all. It was, he acknowledged, pure, blatant, enthusiastic, and self-governing sexuality, and it struck him, as he watched her watching him, that there was nothing of the tease or the flirt about Julie. When it came to sex you were playing her game. There would be no diddling around in the lists. She came to joust, soldier, and if you didn't, then don't go around rattling your lance.

"Well," she said softly. "You met Phoebe?"

"Yes. She just left. She said she had to go feed the penguin. Does she have a penguin?"

Julie laughed. "No, Phoebe lives downstairs with her father. He's a waiter at the Algonquin. She calls him the penguin. I *love* Phoebe." Julie did not seat herself. She just stood there, swinging from the hips. "She's an art student."

"Does she always walk around dressed like that?"

"Oh well, there's a back stairway. Nobody sees her. I'm just lucky she was here to let you in. I'm sorry to have kept you waiting. We had a celebration last night."

Then she did seat herself, in the middle of the floor, in a sort of Indian squat. During this operation, Aubrey leaned back and looked

167

at the ceiling. A rubber prophylactic, inflated with air, and tied with a garter, was nestled against the chandelier. He looked down again. "Nice party?"

"Very. Phoebe brought her Negro boyfriend. He brought his tarot cards. Fascinating. He'd have made you nervous."

"Why? I've got nothing against Negroes. Or tarot cards."

"I didn't say you did, step. But this boy is very intuitive."

"So? I've got nothing against intuition, either."

"Oh yes you do. You know things about yourself you refuse to admit to yourself."

"You and I apparently have different ideas about the meaning of intuition."

"Oh, for Christ's sake, let's not get into defining terms. I just spent all one day reading Aristotle. Jesus!"

"I enjoy both."

"Both what?"

"Aristotle and Jesus."

"Oh come on, step!" She was grinning up at him, her remarkable eyes moving over his whole person, face, hands, even ankles, until Aubrey tried to sneak a look to see if he had forgotten to put socks on. Julie giggled. "I'll bet you've got hair on your chest."

"Now *there's* a piece of intuition."

"Step, you're just determined to go ponderous on me, aren't you?"

"*I* didn't bring up intuition."

"Screw intuition! Let's just have a nice, knock-down drag-out sexy argument without any goddamned intellectuality."

Aubrey was beginning to enjoy Julie, too. "Julie, you're the sort who goes around destroying language."

"I'll destroy your public image, step, if you don't cut that crap out!"

"No, no. I'm serious. Now, what you just said about having an argument without intellectuality . . ."

"You don't look serious. And I said *goddamned* intellectuality."

"Thank you."

"Don't mention it."

"It was a sloppy construction."

"Whose?"

"Yours. You can't have argument without *some* kind of intellectual process . . ."

"So my construction is sloppy?"

"I mean, you construed the . . ."

"Careful there, brother. What you don't know about my construction, and about how I construe . . ." Julie laughed as if she'd been taking lessons from Kermit.

"Ah, there was some moving to do?"

"Oh, don't be so damned prim! We haven't had our argument yet."

"We haven't? It seems to me we've had nothing but an argument since I—met you."

"Hey, that's right! You *do* know something about my construction!" She looked down at her breasts. "You mean to tell me you think these are sloppy?"

"Let's go back to intuition."

"*Large*, maybe. But *sloppy* . . ." She looked up at him brightly. "Maybe if I gave you another look." And still watching him, she seized her sweater by the bottom and started to pull it up.

"Julie, for God's sake!" He started to rise, but she reached up and pushed him back down.

"All right, step! All right!"

He watched her laugh (lips so red against her teeth, such full lips and her tongue moving between them, touching them lightly; the incredible beauty of the human face, and the force of it, and the joy; and the overwhelming single fact that he was alone with her, this incarnation of a hundred thousand hours of suppressed images; alone with her, and her laughter and eyes upon him; alone with her, with this girl—ah, *there* was the word, the shunned, unmentionable, unknowable word, that worst of all four-letter words, that secret, dark, unknowable sign for a secret, dark, unknowable thing: girl) . . .

"Step, you shouldn't get so antsy! I've got a brassiere on."

. . . and wondered if she had any notion how long, how persistently, that one instantaneous look at her naked breasts four days ago, with all of its attendant images, would be tracking up and down his mind, dropping pink-flesh reminders, leaping out at him, at the most solemn moments, bearing down ennippled upon him out of the reaches of his profoundest meditations, charging blatant, obscene, pointed and embossed like warheads, like the mammaries of the new Minerva, to poke out the eyes of his soul whenever he had begun to bring them open. And it seemed to him she could have no slightest notion of it because there didn't appear to be a damned or undamned thing, image, or idea available to the human condition that she did not, or was not ready, to allow herself. He doubted the thing could even be explained to her, and he wasn't tempted to try.

"Julie. Shouldn't we start cleaning this place up?"

"Step, just answer me one question. Do you think you could be seduced?"

"Julie, how come we talk about nothing but sex?"

"What do you mean, nothing but sex? We just wasted five or ten goddamned minutes on intuition!"

"Well, if we must talk, let's waste some more time on it. On intuition."

"Oh, you're a marvel, you are. You're right out of some goddamned medieval romance. Sir Lancelot with syllogisms."

"How do you know about syllogisms?"

"I know about all kinds of gisms, step. Now will you just please answer the question?"

"I don't know the answer. Let's talk about that Negro boy with the tarot cards. Why would he have made me nervous?"

"That's *exactly* what we are talking about! He'd have made you nervous because he'd have wanted to seduce you. Oh, hell yes. He'd have had you by the clyde within twenty minutes!"

"He's a homosexual?"

"Now we're getting somewhere! You know what that is?"

"Well, of course I know what it is. It's in the dictionary. But if he's a homosexual, what's Phoebe go out with him for? I didn't see anything homosexual about Phoebe."

"Oh, you're showing promise, step, *real* promise!"

"How about Phoebe?"

"You like Phoebe, huh?"

"I'd just like to know."

"I'll answer your question if you answer mine."

"I'm not sure I can."

"So I'll take a chance. He's Phoebe's favorite model. He's got a beautiful body. Hung like a bull."

"Hung?"

"Never mind. I wouldn't want to shock you."

"You mean you've had a sudden change of heart?"

"Hell no." She giggled. "But you might panic and dive for the door."

"Look, Julie, let's get something straight. And I'm saying this only because I don't want you to get wrong ideas about seminarians in general . . ."

"Of course."

"Don't be patronizing."

"Don't be dishonest."

"Will you let me finish?"

"I'll let you do any damned thing your hot little heart desires. Except run away."

"As I was saying, it's true that there are a lot of things that are not especially beneficial for a seminarian to know. Or anyone in the religious life. For example, I might know all about marijuana: its effects, its use, where to buy it, all the varieties of it, if there are varieties . . ."

"Only one kind. Indian hemp. As far as I know, of course, let me hasten to add, professor."

"But marijuana is forbidden to me as a seminarian. So what possible good can it do me to talk about it, or to think about it? Especially, say, with a dope pusher. No good at all. Hence, if I should happen to sit down next to a dope pusher on a train, and he should start talking about marijuana, I might pretend, the pretense being the lesser of two evils . . ."

"What's the other evil?"

"I'm glad you're listening. The other . . ."

"I always listen with my tongue."

"The other evil is temptation. If I talked with the dope pusher, and he showed me his marijuana, and described its joys, and offered me some for nothing, and just generally got me all excited about it . . . what are you laughing about now?"

"Nothing! Not a thing. Do please go on. I'm utterly rapt."

"Well, if he did—all that, I might—ah . . . be . . ."

"Seduced?"

"Sure, seduced is a good word. I might be seduced into trying it. Do you see? I mean, I know all about it, I could possibly even give the dope pusher lessons in how it's prepared, or cured, or . . ."

"Inserted?"

"What's that got to do with it?"

"Inserted in the cigarette."

"Oh. Oh, sure. Inserted. I might know very much more about it than the dope pusher. But I would not enter into a discussion of it

171

with him, I would not entertain the idea of what it might do for me to smoke it, I would not allow myself to be stimulated by the thought or the proximity of marijuana at all. Not because I'm ignorant of it, not because I'm afraid of it, not because I despise it, not because I despise out of hand those who smoke it, not because I'm prim, prissy, or prudish, but only because it would be a sin for me to smoke it, because it would be against the civil law, because it would be inconsistent with my vocation, and, in short and to repeat, because it is forbidden to me. What could be more pragmatically sensible—I mean, reasonable—than to refuse to torture myself, to refuse to contemplate that which I cannot have? Do you understand now?"

"So far."

"So far? That's all. I'm done."

"You're done? So all that was to tell me why you don't talk to dope pushers on trains? Christ, even I don't talk to dope pushers on trains. Airplanes, yes, but trains, never!" She waved her hands above her head. "I mean, on an airplane you're already high, so what the hell? Blow it all in, I always say!"

"Julie, for Pete's sake, is that all you got out of what I said?"

"Well, that's all you told me. I mean, Jesus Christ, is it my fault if you get the goddamned Good Samaritan halfway down the road and leave him there? If you're going to start a goddamned parable —especially such a windy goddamned parable—finish the finking thing!"

"I did finish."

"You did like hell."

"The application is obvious."

"Screw obvious! Here I am, a poor jackass of a maid of Galilee, squatting on my dirty alabaster box, waiting for the goddamned master to titillate my tale nerve, to demonstrate his feeling for construction, and he goes away and leaves it hanging! I say, Master, construe a little, and he says, Daughter, go construe yourself!"

Her laughter was a totality; it required all of her, or she required all of it; and again, not wanting to, he watched her tongue. It's like a clapper on a bell, he thought, attempting to mitigate his fascination with it. If you tied her tongue, she couldn't laugh. And the bell went on pealing until he tried to stand up again.

"Oh no, step! Not so fast. You haven't answered either question yet!"

He sat down, accusing himself of not really wanting to go. "Either question? Did you ask me two?"

"No! But you've got to finish the goddamned parable."

"Look, it's very simple. Wherever I said marijuana, just substitute —well, *girls*."

"Fine damned Christ substitute *you'll* make! An inspired preacher. My, yes. Folks, this week read *Tropic of Cancer*, and wherever he says 'screw' you substitute 'pray.' So we prayed against the wall for a while, then we got in the bathtub and prayed there until we damned near drowned!"

"Julie, that isn't what I said."

"All right, all right. I'll try it your way. I'm sorry, Mr. Pusher, but I've never smoked a girl in my life . . ."

"Wait, wait! Okay. I'll draw you a picture. All I was trying to say was that a seminarian, or any religious, might know as much about the physiology of sex, *and* the psychology, *and* the psychobiology, and yet not want to talk about it with a member of the opposite sex. You know as well as I do that there would be a vast difference between my reading a book on female physiology, and your giving me lessons in it with—with demonstrations."

"Oh, vast. More than vast. You'd learn a hell of a lot more from me."

"Julie, I'm done talking about it. No more."

"Okay. End of parable. All truth is your province, but the provincials are another matter. Right?"

"Maybe."

"Is one of the areas of truth your own person? Know thyself, and all that?"

"Of course."

"Good! That brings us to the big question again. Do you think you could be seduced? As you sit, right now, between seminaries, as it were."

"You said know thyself. That's what we're talking about, right?"

"Right . . ."

"So suppose I knew, right now, whether I could be seduced or not. What does it add to my knowledge of myself if I tell you?"

"Why, step, if you told me you thought you *could* be seduced, you'd be in the way of taking on just an amazing hell of a lot of knowledge in practically no time."

"And what if I said I thought I couldn't?"

"Well, then your enlightenment might take a little longer." She smiled sweetly.

"Julie, this is a wholly improper conversation. You ask a question that, one, I can't answer, that, two, I would not want to answer if I could, and that, three, serves no useful purpose asked or answered. And when I point this out, you get coy and start talking about my enlightenment. Now, if you want to have an honest conversation, let's have one. And start by telling me what possible interest the potentials of my seduction could have for you, my stepsister. I mean, do you want to see me seduced, even though you know it's the last thing in the world I want?"

Aubrey felt immediately that he'd gone too far. He hadn't called Julie's bluff, because at no point had she been bluffing. All he'd done was to challenge her to do what he had thought he didn't want her to do: to admit that she wanted, or intended, to seduce him. What the hell for? For the perverse pleasure of hearing her say it? Possibly, even probably. Because there were no feasible good motives he could claim. There was no pretendng that he didn't know, or hadn't already admitted to himself, that to attempt to seduce him was her clear intention. There was no pretending that he had sought to shame her. "I, your stepsister, would like to screw you." He could hear Julie saying that as blithely as she might ask for a match. Shame, where sex was concerned, wasn't in her, and he had known it. And he remembered that section of the Titan Rule about seeking the respect, the admiration, the eyes of women and provoking their desire and urging them to state their lusts frankly, all for the ostensible motive of rebuking them, but actually "for the gratification of the brother's own perverse cravings," and he knew that that was why he had challenged her, knew that he had taken that first classic step toward nonvirginity. And he sat waiting, his guilt rising already to meet and do combat with, and forbid his consent to, whatever pleasure might try to seize him at her words; sat there fighting with that antic piece of his mind that saw all of his spiritual crises as the most incongruous, belly-laughable little skits since Balaam went into Jerusalem on his ass; sat there, staring into her amused pout, certain that Julie, challenged to be indelicate, could invent indelicacy for the age.

But she saw his guilt coming, and snatched the pleasure from harm. Then she pinned her donkey to his tail. "How indelicate of you," she murmured, smiling. "I had thought you were more sensitive than that, step. You disappoint me."

Somewhere inside him a bottom fell out, the crowd was roaring with laughter, and there he was, onstage, on his ass. Great skit, Balaam. See you next year! And he came offstage angry. "*I'm indelicate! I'm insensitive!* How do you arrive at that, I'd like to know?"

"You were trying to force my hand, step, and don't deny it. You call for an honest conversation, and you begin it with a patent dishonesty." Then, her eyes glowing and rising on him from his throat to his forehead and back again, she said, "You ask me if I want to *see* you seduced. Ah, step, I'm too young for voyeurism. I was never a spectator at a seduction in my life . . ."

"I *heard* that!" said Phoebe, appearing suddenly at the front door. "And what a lie! Wow! Lying like that to a man of the cloth! Why, Ash, she's got a mirror on the ceiling over her bed *ten—feet—square!* And that's the only thing square that ever *happened* in that bedroom! Spectator! My God! In full, thrr-*robbing,* stereo-coital, flesh-colored, Venery-Vision!"

"Oh, Phoebe, turn it off. Have you been listening to us?"

"Damned right I have. Every pulsating word. I've got enough here to put old Ash between sheets for life. See?" She was dressed exactly as she had been before, and now began to pirouette her way across the living room toward them, showing her bikini-brief underpants as she came. "Note the firmness of the *rectus femoris,* Ash darling," she said throatily.

Aubrey thought, When the beast charges, drop it on her; and leaned to his haunches, twitched left beyond Julie's grasp, then crossbucked right, gave Phoebe a dazzling over-toe to the outside, spun out of the wings of an armchair, and broke free and into the clear just before he crashed into the fourth-floor banister. But it held and he gripped it like a long-last banister and was on the stairs before the pursuit had formed.

"Ash, darling, forgive me," Phoebe cried. "I had no *idea* you were a virgin!"

"See you tonight, Aubrey dear," Julie called. "I'd go with you—you coward!—but I have to wait for the moving man."

"Moving man hell! Don't you believe it, Ash darling. He's the representative from the Irish Marching and Sexual Society! *He is a* confessor nonvirgin!"

175

An old man, on his way up the stairs, grinned at Aubrey and managed to say, apparently with one of his last nineteen breaths, "Ah, Jesus. Just to be twenty-one again." He wasn't looking at Aubrey. He was looking up.

And Aubrey took a last look up, as he left the third floor, and there was Phoebe, astraddle the banister, most precariously and revealingly perched, waving at him. "Oh, Ash darling! I've lost you forever to a dirty old man! I saw you make that assignation! Don't do it, Ash darling! It dislocates the isthmus of Langerhans!"

"She means the islets," Julie said.

"I mean the center aisle! But if he hasn't got an isthmus, I just lost interest!"

And the last thing he heard of those two perpetrators of his abysmal defeat was the following intelligence from Phoebe: "We don't have a flush toilet, Ash darling, if the census taker should happen to ask you! No offense, of course!"

And he went home and—much later, but again quite early—went to bed with all kinds of things to worry and wonder about but first place for recurrence went to the thought of Julie naked under that ten-foot mirror.

# · SIXTEEN ·

HE WENT to confession the next morning at the big Jesuit church at 84th and Park. The confessor did not appear concerned with the details of Aubrey's visit to Julie's apartment (which Aubrey had to set forth at some length in order to make any sense at all) so much as he did appear genuinely intrigued. He asked Aubrey all manner of questions about Julie, Phoebe, the chattels he had been expected to move, and just why he thought his stepsister wanted to seduce him, and kept saying, disconcertingly enough to Aubrey, "And you're going to the Saharan Fathers?" his intonation suggesting that this might prove the most historically unlikely event since the defeat of the Spanish Armada.

Things did not improve. Aubrey got back to the house just in time to be seated at breakfast by Nelson, who did the introductions with a puckish sense of approval withheld, with Miss Diane Balfour, a tall, full-busted, multi-toothed young woman, whose clothing indicated that any air circulating before eight in the evening had a deleterious effect upon her whole social person.

Miss Balfour had just declared that she had had no idea that Kermit's son Aubrey was so . . . when Julie arrived, in a nightgown of length but of negligible depth or substance, to ask, "So what?"

Miss Balfour at once introduced three sections of grapefruit into her mouth and looked at Julie as a mongoose might look at a cobra, and said nothing.

Aubrey answered all of Julie's inquiries—which disclosed, among other things, that Julie intended to accompany Kermit, Mr. Jebb, and Aubrey to Southampton—in an excess of monosyllables, so that Julie, who seemed to be in short temper starting, was soon looking to Miss Balfour for controversy. Aubrey listened, without the slightest impulse toward comment, to the following exchange:

JULIE: Did you sleep well, Miss Balfour?

DIANE: Oh, of course. I just love the Stanhope. Just around the corner, you know. So convenient to Kermit's house.

JULIE: I know exactly what you mean, Miss Balfour. You'd think a first-class hotel like that would serve breakfast, wouldn't you?

DIANE: Oh, they do, of course. But so unimaginative.

JULIE: I agree. The man who invented grapefruit should have patented it. Sold it exclusively to Continental hotels.

DIANE: Have you ever stayed at the Stanhope?

JULIE: No more than you have, I'm sure.

DIANE: It's under new management, you know.

JULIE: Oh, were they the ones who built the tunnel?

DIANE: Tunnel? Oh, you must mean the new bar.

JULIE: Well, I suppose that's the impression you get.

DIANE: Kermit just *loves* it.

JULIE: Most men do.

DIANE: Oh, really?

JULIE: Of course, *love* is hardly a factor with Kermit and you, is it, Miss Balfour?

DIANE: Well, you'll have to ask Kermit about that.

JULIE: I will. I'm sure he never enters your *mind* in that respect.

DIANE: Well, a girl has to be pretty particular about who she lets—well, who . . .

JULIE: Lets enter her—ah, shall we say in your case—mind, Miss Ball-Four?

DIANE: Well, Julie, you'll understand better when you have reached my age. After all, I must be two or three years older than you are, and two or three years can make an awful lot of difference.

JULIE: Oh, an *awful* lot, if I may judge, Miss *Ball-Four*, from your —shall we say—maturity?

DIANE: Still, Julie, you are quite old for your years.

178

JULIE: You know, you may just have something there. I was older —I mean, from the standpoint of womanliness—at fourteen than most women are at, shall we charitably say, thirty-four?

DIANE: Oh, I think you're very precocious, Julie, but, after all, thirty-four—that's a rather advanced age . . .

JULIE: Well, I'm sure you know all about that, Miss Ball-Four, but are you sure you aren't confusing precocious with promiscuous?

DIANE: Of course not! Why would you say a thing like that, Julie?

JULIE: Well, it just seemed to me that years ago when you were my age, you might have decided that precocity and promiscuity were the same thing.

DIANE: I'm sure I don't know about that because neither word has ever applied to me. But it is quite possible, Julie, that in your case precocity and promiscuity are not mutually exclusive.

JULIE: And I, Miss Ball-Four, am quite sure that in your case, promiscuity doesn't exclude a goddamned thing!

DIANE: You are just a jealous little bitch!

JULIE: And you, Miss Ball-Four, are nothing of which I could be jealous! You're just a goddamned chippy-ass whore, and since your name is Ball-Four, I suggest you take a walk before I ruin your nose-bob!

Miss Balfour walked, out the front door, in a snit the size of a huff, and Julie buttered her toast as if it were an award for excellence in insult. Aubrey joined Mr. Jebb at the bumper as soon as he could, and they spent a long silence together. Kermit came out wreathed in shotguns, and Julie came out some twenty minutes later wreathed in maidenly smiles.

The view from the Queensboro Bridge, as they crossed it, was bleak. Wednesday had come dripping, gray, and anxious out of a hemisphere of rain clouds and looked as if its dawn were lurking out there somewhere but unwilling to come on in and get itself wet. The East River was running pewter-green and a cold wind from the south was scudding fits of rain in mottled patches across its broad surface. And they ran out to Southampton with the East River at the windows all the way, and with Kermit talking about death.

"He says it's a paternal aunt. Died of a seizure of the windpipe, or some goddamned thing. I wonder who seized it. Anyway, Phil Cherry the Elder has more goddamned living, about-to-die relatives than any man since Brigham Young. I swear, by Christ, he has a schedule all made out so that the goddamned funerals will be evenly spaced about a week apart. And I'll bet if you took the first six feet of topsoil off Tarrytown and parts thereto adjacent you'd find a goddamned solid layer of Phil Cherry's moldering ancestors. Unless he put the bastards in large piles in a vault somewhere, which would be very fitting, too, because they all should have been locked up years ago."

And Kermit laughed and put one hand on Julie's knee and the other on Aubrey's, and Aubrey thought, Careful, there, Kermit, we'll both get electrocuted.

"Well, it's a good day for a burial," Kermit went on. "But a man— a man—ought to be buried at sea on the day he dies. I won't speak for women. But a man. The sea is the only place. That's what my father believed, and, may the Lord have mercy on him, that's where I buried him. In the sea. On the day he died. Ah, there's a story."

And he told this story without theatrics, in a calm, muted voice, looking straight ahead, as if he were seeing it all again in vivid relief yet refusing to take himself back to it, refusing, as best he could, to be more than an observer of all that pain.

Of all that pain, and a night in August, 1918, in the Straits of Dover off Folkestone, when he had just been relieved from wheel watch and went forward to where his father was seated on the deck-load on the port side. (And this was Piet Strycker, then fifty-two and a ship's master since his twenty-eighth year.) Kermit had climbed up beside his father and Piet had patted him on the back and had pointed to where the Dover cliffs had begun to show their white faces across the quiet water. And they were inbound in convoy, having already lost two freighters to torpedoes and a full day's time to a freak, brutal storm in mid-Atlantic, and were making a straight run for the Thames estuary, and running scared and fast, aware that the U-boats out of Zeebrugge and Ostend were having their biggest month in the Straits since the previous September. And Piet was cursing the goddamned British—("Oh, he hated the British, but the Stryckers have always hated the British. My great-great-great-great— how many's that? My six-greats grandfather fought them under de Ruyter at the battle of Texel in 1673. And my three-greats grandfather died fighting the Tories at the Battle of Cobleskill in 1778. And my great-great grandfather fought them in the War of 1812. And my father fought them in any bar he could find one willing to fight. . . .")—they having just been joined by two escorts of the British Dover patrol, who had warned of loose mines off Margate and had taken a dim official view of the convoy's high-speed, unswerving course. And Piet had just said, "If the goddamned limey bastards would talk less and sink more submarines . . . !", when the first torpedo struck near the stern on the starboard side. Both were thrown to the deck, but were unhurt, and crossed to the starboard side and started to run aft, and were just amidships with Piet in the lead when the second torpedo struck directly beneath them. Kermit found his father, some minutes later, trying to struggle to his feet with blood spurting from the shoulder where his right arm had been. He carried Piet to the bow and laid him down and tried to staunch the flow of blood. Explosions continued to rock the ship, the port side lifeboats were in the water, and Piet was telling him, "Abandon, goddamn it, Kermit! Get off! I'm dead! Jesus Christ, can't you see that? Look at it flow. I didn't know a man *had* that much blood." Then two other ships were hit on either side of them, and the sky was bright with the roar and blast and fire, and Piet said, "Did they get one of those limey bastards?" Kermit told him no, and suddenly the bow of the ship started to lift. "She's putting her stern under, Kermit, and you'll have a goddamned high jump if you wait any longer! Get off! Get off!" Then Piet tried to stand up, but couldn't. "Goddamn it, she's burning her length. I don't want to burn. I'll be doing that soon enough. Put me over, Kermit. Put me in the sea." And he closed his eyes and seemed to be dead, but he came alive twice more. The first time he said, "But weight me first, Kermit. I wouldn't want to wash up on any goddamned British soil!" And the second time he almost sat up and said, in a normal voice as if he were bidding his son good-night, "And give my love to your mother."

Kermit buried his father with such ceremony as he could arrange. He tore some canvas and cables from a deckload, and wrapped the body with them, and weighted it further with turnbuckles and whatever loose metal he could find, and took the body in his arms and climbed with it into the bow; and now the bow was standing high and shuddering, and he stood for a moment, poised, setting himself to jump, seeing great clouds of steam down and away at the stern as the ship started quickly now to back down under the surface, and then he was ready, and told his father to rest in peace, and jumped as far out as he could toward the black water far below. And he managed to hold Piet's body after he struck the water, having thrust his arms among the cables he had wrapped around it, and he continued to hold onto it, and to go down with it, down and down in the dark cold, until his lungs could bear no more, and yet hung on for another split second, tempted perhaps to stay with his father in that peaceful, numbing blackness, knowing that he was suspended there between his own life and death, hesitating to leave his dead and rejoin his living. But released the body and felt it fall away, and then struck out, with pain like white fire behind his eyes, for the surface. "And many a time, in the Straits, I've thrown flowers on the water at the place where I buried him, and I only hope to Christ, so that I won't have to listen to him roar throughout a whole goddamned eternity, that his body is still there where I put it and didn't wash ashore on English soil."

And when Kermit was done, only Mr. Jebb, who was English, had anything to say, and what he said was "Aymen."

In Southampton they called Kermit's house Strycker's Ark, and swore it would float if the ocean ever engulfed it. And it was very like a ship, trim and graceful in all its parts, rounded at both ends, and long, with two broad, railed porches, one just above ground level and the other just beneath the roof, both porches girdling the house clear around. And since it was set at the very edge of the water—one of the few houses fronting the beach that did not have the protection of the high tidal dune—one could imagine, seeing it from the road across the broad expanse of perfect lawn, that it was a great white ship, moored temporarily to the beach and likely to put to sea again whenever the tide was right.

The house was just being opened for the summer, and Kermit's housekeeper—a fat-faced black-capped vireo with a harsh, alarmed voice—was not ready to feed them lunch because the steaks she had ordered hadn't come yet and why hadn't Kermit given her more notice, so that they went into the village to Herb McCarthy's and had clams with horseradish and rare steaks, except for Mr. Jebb, who had his steak well-done, a circumstance that outraged Kermit so much that he nearly banished Mr. Jebb to another table after all.

Then they went down to the beach with shotguns, clay birds, and a hand trap, down beyond the last houses, and stood on the high dune and sailed the birds on the wind off and down toward the surf, letting them travel as far as they would before blowing them into yellow bits. And when each had shot a box of shells, Aubrey had missed seven times, Julie had missed twice, and Kermit had missed not at all, except once after Mr. Jebb, who had come along as a volunteer, puttees and all, to throw the targets, had thrown one right at a man riding a horse along the water's edge and Kermit, using a long-barreled, ten-gauge duck gun, had hesitated a moment, wondering, as he had afterwards admitted, whether he would shoot the bastard out of the way with one barrel and then pot the bird with the other, then had decided to let the bastard live, and had waited, and had fired just as the bird hit the crest of an oncoming wave, and appeared to miss but insisted that he hadn't while Julie laughed and maintained that she could see the damned thing floating. The horse had taken off, passing from a walk to a full gallop in one leap, and Mr. Jebb quietly pointed this out and said that it was his opinion that the shot had to be scored as a probable bird, and a definite bastard's horse. And so it was resolved.

Aubrey was using a twenty-gauge, full-choke Breda automatic with three-inch Magnum shells and he admired it so much that Kermit gave it to him and suggested that he take it with him in the morning to his interview in case the provincial turned out to be a Berber chief. And the interview was very much on his mind; he had tried to think out what he would say, how he would explain himself to the Saharans, but hadn't gotten much beyond "I would like to join your Society because I think it is God's will for me." He'd have to do better than that—the Saharans might not accept him as an expert on the divination of God's will. So after firing a few rounds of his second box, he begged off. Kermit was annoyed, but he and Julie were firing in competition (the stakes being the third wheel of the Corvette Kermit was supposed to buy Julie if and when she won four wheels, and if and when she ever managed to get through a driver's test without telling off the state examiner), and Aubrey got away with small argument. He tried to lend his gun to Mr. Jebb, but Mr. Jebb fired one shot, at a lightbulb at three feet, give or take a couple of inches, and devastated it, and grinned infinitesimally, and announced that he was perfectly delighted with himself and would quit while he was ahead.

Aubrey walked slowly back to the house, through the windblown half-dusk of the sullen afternoon, and took his gun to Kermit's den and cleaned it and put it in the gun case, and sat down in an oversized black leather chair, and tried to think. The room distracted him, being his favorite room in the world. It was at the level of the beach, book-lined, with dark-beamed ceilings and black walnut walls, except for the seaward wall which was reinforced plate glass, against which the waves threw their spray at high tide. Through the window he could see two workmen loading a truck with sections of heavy steel plate that had been bolted into place along the seaward wall of the house during the winter months. Even these did not preserve the house from damage during hurricanes, but—despite repeated flooding, buckled floors, smashed bulkheads, undermining, collapsed foundations, and, once, the removal of the whole lower porch on the ocean side—Kermit wouldn't have things arranged any other way. He loved to sit in the lower den during a storm (and Aubrey had sat with him there during the first stages of a hurricane in 1954—until the water started to rise around the edges of the rug) and listen to the ocean come onto the land and batter the steel plates and try to push them through the big window. "What the hell," Kermit had said, "I can afford a few luxuries, and this is one of them." And that which could enrage Kermit more than perhaps anything else in life was a predicted hurricane failing to materialize or veering off out to sea. He would stump around the outside of the house, directing the workmen with happy roars—"Bolt 'em down, men! Batten all hatches! Dog 'em to the rims, boys! The son of a bitch is going to try us again!" —and he would glare at the sea and dare it to come on, and come very close to apoplexy when nothing happened.

Aubrey finally did force his thoughts to the business at hand by speaking them aloud. "To begin, then. My attitude is that the American Church no longer represents Jesus Christ as I would have Him represented, as I, personally, want to re-present Him. Since I have no notion of attempting to reform the American Church, I want to go where I can live as I think a priest ought to live, where I can serve Christ without having constantly to resist the temptation to relax into the lukewarmness and fat-cat corporation existence of nine-tenths of the American clergy, where I can be a positive force for good instead of a positive force for mediocrity. I'm running away, I suppose. Somebody ought to reform the American Church, but I haven't got the stomach, or the holiness, for it. I just want out. Jesus preached love, a positive, forgiving, apostolic love. Jesus went among the people, looked into their eyes, lived with them, taught them by His example. Charity was Jesus Christ's only law. If He ever

184

assigned a penance, I don't know of it. But the American Church? It preaches love, but doesn't practice it. What it practices is interdiction. It looks around now and then from its overstuffed chair, sees that maybe the faithful are about to run amuck, or aren't putting enough in the collection baskets, or are losing respect for the clergy, and it rises off its swollen buttocks long enough to deliver an anathema. To judge, proscribe, chastise, limit, ban, prohibit, condemn, and impute shame—these are what the American Church has taken as its functions. Does it go among the people, or look into their eyes, or live with them, or teach them by example? In the average American parish, for example? There will be a five-minute pause for general laughter. I've never met a pastor who wouldn't be shocked by the idea that his primary function wasn't browbeating the parishioners. The pastor is a businessman, a unit manager in the greatest corporation in the world. He has all sorts of good reasons for doing what he does and what he does not do. Does the pastor in most American parishes live far better than four-fifths of his people? Well, the priesthood must maintain a certain material dignity. Are most of his preachments about money? Well, God may take care of the birds, but I have to pay the coalman. Does he feel any love for his people, or even an obligation to love them, or make them feel that God loves them? Sure, I love them, as long as I don't have to look at them. All right. Is it the pastor's fault? Only partly. The main fault lies with the Church itself, the organization. If there are any saints among the American clergy, it is in spite of the Church, not because of it. The pressure is not toward sanctity. The pressure is toward efficiency, especially financial efficiency. Because money is power, and the Church in America has lots of power, but wants more. Or if it doesn't specifically want more, it is so geared and organized that it must naturally garner more. It is a capitalistic organization, its executives like any other executives. They seek promotion, rank, position, fame, power—and are trained to seek it, not in so many words, but as a simple corollary of the corporate structure. For the most part it is a subtle thing, an infection, a disease that has worked its way from the top down and the bottom up so many times that it's now a joke. The monk who wants to be prior, the pastor who wants to be bishop, the provincial who wants to be general. The ambition, the politicking, the ill feeling. But primarily the death blow to charity, to love, that is the real loss. The loss of the only thing Jesus came down here to establish. So that I have found it very difficult to imagine that if Jesus

185

Christ were to return to earth today, He would have anything to do with the American Church except perhaps to arm Himself with a whip and drive the executive money-changers out of His Father's temples."

He went on for some time and when he was all done he realized he was just beginning, yet had said nothing he could possibly repeat to a priest. It was all too brash, and not especially well reasoned. He had the resentment but not the rationale. And even if he had had the rationale, the Saharans wanted to hear positive reasons for his choice of their Society, not negations of what he was leaving behind. They wanted a bright-eyed, eager, this-is-the-greatest-outfit-in-the-world volunteer, not a backbiting deserter. "All right then, damn it!" he said, getting to his feet. "That's all I'll say. I'm here because I'm here because I'm here because I'm here! Now swear me in, give me my water wings, and point me toward the beach! Ashurbanipal MacIver will get the Prophet by the beard!"

He walked to the window and stared out at the surf, breaking low and yet heavily some sixty feet away. There was a big, ungainly sea gull at the water's edge trying to pluck something from the water. The gull would wait at the high-water line until the wash of a wave started to recede, then charge after the object, pecking fiercely and rapidly until the next wave came curling in, and the gull would retreat skipping and flapping out of the water's reach. He watched for a time, then nodded, and said very quietly, "There you go, MacIver. Just tell the Provincial that it isn't the scavenging that affrights you. It's the size of the American surf."

They went back to Herb McCarthy's for dinner, the housekeeper having announced that things in general were still too chaotic (her word) to prepare a meal properly. They had steaks again and Kermit and Julie got at least half smashed on three or four drinks and then finished the job on dinner wine. Aubrey had a bit of the wine, weathered two brief arguments about the impending interview and how he ought not to go to Africa, and braced himself for a long evening. A third argument arose, between Aubrey and Kermit, about how Aubrey, by God, was going to Alaska whether the Saharans liked it or not, but Kermit left the issue hanging in favor of a young lady across the room he thought he knew. She was dining alone, two tables from Mr. Jebb, who was also dining alone at Kermit's order, and Kermit apparently did know her, and sat right down with her, and never looked back.

186

"Oh, isn't he subtle," Julie said bitterly.

"I don't know if he's subtle, but he sure isn't bashful."

"Oh, wake up, for Christ's sake. She's from New York. I've seen her before. They just arranged to meet here, that's all. Make it look accidental. To spare your delicate sensibilities, step."

"I doubt that. Kermit's never worried about my sensibilities before. I think it's more likely he's worried about yours."

"Mine? Why the hell do you say that?"

"Well, you respond so vigorously to the sight of his girl friends."

"What do you mean by *that* little asininity?"

"I don't know what I mean. But why did you go after Miss Balfour this morning?"

"Because she's a goddamned whore, that's why! Call girl, hooker, and all-around bitch!"

"Apparently Kermit likes her."

"Oh, and I'll bet you liked her too, didn't you, step?"

"What's that got to do with anything? The point is, if Kermit had brought that girl over there along with us this morning, you'd possibly—quite possibly, I'd say—have argued with her all the way out here."

Julie suddenly smiled, an intense, unamused smile. "Why, you know, that *is* exactly what you want, isn't it, step? You want some bitch like Miss Balfour to grab you by the clyde and down you. That's exactly what you want. So you won't have any of the responsibility."

"Julie, for Pete's sake, how does that follow from anything we've said?"

"Never mind, step, how it follows. It's true. Isn't it?"

"No."

"Oh yes, it is. And it's good to know, step, because if that's what it takes, I've got it. I can outbitch, outwhore, and outscrew Miss Balfour with my pants on. But I'll tell you something new, step. I'm not sure I'm interested in screwing you." Her smile widened. "Nope. Not any more."

Aubrey blinked and tried to withhold all reaction beyond a blink. "I'm glad to hear it."

Julie laughed softly, evilly. "Aren't you interested in why I lost the urge?"

"No."

"The hell you aren't! You're practically undone with curiosity. So I'll tell you, since you aren't honest enough to ask. It's because I don't think you're capable of passion, step. Too many hooks in you. You're not only a virgin and a seminarian, you're a mama's boy."

"For Pete's sake, Julie, if you're trying your little reverse psychology just to start an argument, save yourself. And spare me. I don't intend to argue with you."

"How about construing? You like that better?"

"I'd like either to have a conversation with you, for once, that wasn't an argument and wasn't about sex, or else I'd like to go home."

"I only have conversations about sex. There's nothing else worth talking about."

"I've managed to find other things . . ."

"Well, you. You're so goddamned dull you don't exist. You know what I mean? You have no imagination. Or if you do, you filed it under mortal sin a long time ago and forgot about it."

"I hope I don't bore you, because if I do let's get . . ."

"That isn't what I said. I said you were dull. Left to your own devices, I mean. But you don't bore me. Because I can ask you embarrassing questions. I'm being very honest with you, step, which is more than I can say for you. For instance, you won't admit, even now, that you're titillated by my titillating questions. You won't admit that, will you?"

"Yes. I'll admit it." Julie's eyes rounded on her surprise, and she started to speak, but Aubrey interrupted.

He was feeling his wine a bit and was telling himself that it didn't matter a long damn in the scheme of Christendom whether he ever won an argument with Julie or not, yet he wasn't able to stand her accusation of dishonesty, especially since, as he acknowledged, it had come within an ace of being true. "Listen, Julie, step, or young lady, or what, I'm perfectly willing to admit that your little routine of using me as straight man to your Kinsey report is titillating. But I resist the titillation as best I can. I'm with you no more than I have to be. I'm not proud of feeling titillated, and I don't like to give you the opportunity of getting any more sex-centered than you already are. I'm also aware that you might give youself credit for having goaded me into this admission, by challenging my manhood, wit, passion, brains, and God knows what all. Don't credit yourself. You may really have *needed*, as a boost to your ego, to hear me say you titillate me with your questions, and if I'd known that, I'd have said it long ago. In fact, I thought I had."

"Well, I do appreciate your admitting it, even though it did take you a while to get it said. You know, you're long-winded, too. But you misjudge me. The only reason I ask you all these titillating questions is to get you ready for hearing confessions someday."

"Now who's being dishonest?"

"Swear to God, step. Just think how much you've learned about sex since you met me."

"I haven't learned anything from you. I knew it all long before I met you. And if you're just trying to prepare me to be a better confessor, forget it. I'll learn more in the confessional in one hour than I would from you in fifty years."

"Well, naturally, you have to complete my full course before you can fairly make that statement." Her smile grew wider, friendlier. "Because in the final hour of the course, I have what I call practical application. And in that one hour, step, I'll teach you more about sex and sin than you'll learn in fifty years in the confessional."

"How do you know anything about confession? Have you ever been to confession?"

"No. But I know about it. I know that most priests have no more idea about what sin is, have no more right to attempt to understand sin, than you do. It's all theory."

"Julie, can't you imagine what the brutal frankness of the confessional could do, in damned short order, to educate even the most innocent priest?"

"I can imagine, but that isn't the point. He doesn't *really* know. He's not involved, never has been involved, never intends to be involved."

"He *is* involved! He takes on the sins as Christ took on the sins of the world, and if he doesn't take them on—and I don't mean that he becomes personally responsible for them—but if he doesn't *enter into them* and assume them as if they were his, then he doesn't really administer absolution."

"Look, step, the priest may have all the compassion in the world, and all the sympathy and empathy and Christly sort of involvement, but he cannot really think of those sins as *his* sins. He isn't the man who committed those sins, and he takes pride in the fact that he isn't, and satisfaction, and smug refuge. He is *not* involved, no matter what you may say about no man being an island, and there but for the grace of God go I, and I am involved in the sins of every man who ever lived because Christ has gone to the cross, or all or any of that kind of mystic Christian garbage! In order for anybody to think of himself effectively as a sinner, he has to think of himself as actually about to go out, right *now*, to commit a sin! Murder, rape, or simple plain-ass fornication!"

"Wrong, wrong! It's a fallacy to say that I have to have committed a sin before I can appreciate the desolation of the sinner."

"Who the hell's talking about desolation? I'm talking about the sweet pleasure of it! That's what you're forgiving, isn't it, the pleasure? And what will you know about that pleasure? How will you be able to appreciate *why* or *how* a man can get infatuated with one woman, or a woman with one man? How will you ever be able to understand *anything* about sexual passion—and I mean the kind that drives men to murder, and women to break up homes, and other women to become whores, and men to become rapists, or housewives to practice birth control simply because they can't stand to stay away from their men until you get done tapping out the rhythm system —how are you going to understand any of that, and, on your own terms, how are you going to forgive any of that effectively if you have no idea what sexual passion is like?"

"I *do* have some idea . . ."

"How did you come by it?"

"Imagination. It's possible to imagine . . ."

"Sure it is, step! But *do* you?"

"Of course I do."

"You imagine that you're about to commit such sins?"

"Maybe not explicitly, but I certainly could . . ."

"We're not talking about could. Do you?"

"Yes . . ."

"You're a liar. And I'll give you proof. *Me*. If there was ever a time in your life when you have had a chance to appreciate, study, understand what it means to be seduced—I mean, in theory and imagination only, now—so that you might again on your feeble terms, forgive all those little girls and boys who will one day ask you for forgiveness for seducing or being seduced—if there ever was a time when you had the perfect opportunity to *involve* yourself intellectually in seduction, it's been since you met me. Will you admit that?"

"In Macy's basement at high noon."

"Okay. Now, what have you done with this opportunity? Have you actually sat down and thought about what it would be like to go to bed with me? *I mean imagine!* Imagine what a once-in-a-lifetime, Christ-be-to-Jesus, Walpurgis-Night, howling goddamned experience it might be! Here I sit, step! I mean, 38-25-36 and almost twenty-one, and I will be as indelicate as you wanted me to be the other day and come right out and say *I*, personally, am ready to go to bed with you any damned time you say! So! Step, my *boy!* You are faced with what is probably the first, and certainly the most attractive—if I do flatter myself—occasion of sin of your goddamned life. Right? I mean, real and earnest, solid, serious sex is what I'm talking about, step. Now, have you got the guts to sock your imagination into me? Just your imagination, step? For the good of penitents everywhere?"

She was regarding him with a sort of bland earnestness, her smile very thin, as if she had just announced that her mother was a nudist and would his family mind. And before he could stop working his jaw, Kermit was at the table, bending to whisper stagily, "You two can be heard all over the goddamned dining room."

"Well, isn't *that* too goddamned bad," Julie said loudly. "And who the hell asked you?"

"Listen, my girl," Kermit said, raising the flat of one hand just off the table. "You're still not so big I can't knock you flying into the next room!"

"You do that, Daddy. And I will get up and go over, and drag that goddamned whore of yours by her hair into the kitchen, and, by Jesus, stuff her full of curry powder." Julie spoke quietly, but with infinite threat, and turned at once, smiling sweetly, and raised her wine glass to the woman at Kermit's table, and nodded. The woman smiled, and nodded back, and, just when Kermit's expression had passed through incredulity and had arrived at pleasant surprise, Julie upped with her free hand, thumbed her nose hugely at the woman, stuck out her tongue, and fired a tongue-in-lips oral salute that must have been heard in Quogue. And then she called out, "Stuffed whore à la Kermit!"

Kermit whirled about and marched across the room and had the poor woman in transit toward the door in something less than thirty seconds. Mr. Jebb started to follow, but Kermit indicated Aubrey and Julie, and Mr. Jebb sat down again.

"Julie," Aubrey said softly, sensing that this situation could go away beyond the bounds of monastic acquaintance or ability to cope in just no time at all. "What did you do that for?"

Julie smiled gently, pouting her fondest pout. "I did it for my mother," she said quietly. "You know, you're a very sweet boy. I didn't mean all those things about your being dull, and not wanting to seduce you. I want to seduce you very much, darling."

And Aubrey was suddenly rendered speechless by a passing vision of her naked breasts. An exact and vivid vision, like stained glass with the sun behind it. And when that cleared, he was seeing himself as a person, just then, of enormous privilege, and saw long lines of eager-eyed, sorrowing young men ready to sell their birthrights to be seated just where he was seated and to be confronted as he was confronted, and to be propositioned as he had so baldly and publicly been propositioned. But he shook that fancy off, and kept shaking other fancies, until he was able to say to her, in his best Christ-to-Magdalen tone, "Please, Julie, let's not talk any more about that."

"All right, darling," she said sweetly, moving her hand under the table to his thigh and starting to tickle him there. "I just want you to know that I'm serious about it. Very serious, darling. I'm going to seduce you, even if you want me to."

He moved his leg. "Julie, I don't want to be seduced. You understand that by now, I hope."

"I know you don't mean that, darling. But it doesn't make a goddamned bit of difference, even if you think you meant it."

"I know what I think and what I mean. Those are my sovereign areas. Only I can know what I think or mean. If you want to know, ask me, don't tell me. I'll say it again. I don't want to be seduced, by you, Miss Balfour, or anybody. I've known you were serious about it all along, I think. I can't be sure. But even if you weren't serious about it, all along or now, and even if I didn't know, and even if I made four thousand Freudian slips, I don't want to be seduced."

"Jesus, what a mind," Julie said amiably. "Does it wind itself or do you stick a key in one ear?"

Aubrey snapped at her, not meaning to, but meaning to, "At least it's running! Which is more than I can say for yours!"

"I think I might cry, darling. This is the first time you've ever been angry with me." She continued to smile precisely as if she didn't give a damn. Then, abruptly, she said, "Wow! I've got it! Your mind is electric, and it isn't running at all! Nope, not at all. And do you know why, step?"

"Look, Julie . . ."

"Because you've never stuck your plug in a socket!" She seemed to realize that the whole dining room had certainly heard that one, and she looked around proudly, and would have risen and bowed, Aubrey felt certain, if there had been any applause. She beamed at him. "That may just be the profoundest thing I've ever said. And here I am, offering you what is, in all modesty, the best and most succulent socket this side of . . ."

"Modesty! My God, don't speak of modesty, Julie! There isn't a modest impulse in you. I don't think you've spoken two words in your life without some kind of sexual reference!"

"So? Is there something immodest about sexual reference?"

"Good God, if you don't know . . ."

"Step!" She raised both hands for silence. "Step, I've come to a decision. I want you to go home now. And don't say you won't go home, because if you don't, I'll make the goddamnedest scene since Oscar Wilde propositioned the Archbishop of Canterbury, right? Right. So get thee hence, with Mr. Jebb. He will take you home, and then he will return for me, in the fullness of time. Worry not. We have done it before, and I shan't think any more or less of you as a gentleman. But I want you to think more and not less of me. Oh yes. That's the whole purpose, step. I want you to writhe in your sheets, step, the whole night through. I want you to think about my soft, luscious, musky depths. I want you . . ."

"Good night, Julie," he said, getting to his feet as undramatically as he could manage it. "You have just made yourself a soft, musky bargain." He bowed to her, really not giving a damn at that moment whether this condescending, insufferable, stepling of a female got home safely or not.

"Grandly said, Aubie my boy. Only don't get too cocky. Especially don't get too cocky. Know what I mean? Or I might just sneak back to Strycker's Ark very late and barefooted and nude to the nubs, and creep up the stairs, and force your lock and mount you like a succubus. Climb right on, step. Draw you in like a popsicle."

She was still laughing and wagging her curls and raising her glass at him when he followed Mr. Jebb in tandem dignity out of the restaurant. And Mr. Jebb surprised him beyond measure by speaking, along about halfway home, a full-length declarative sentence in criticism of Julie's conduct.

Mr. Jebb said, "Miss Julie will want to apologize to you tomorrow, Mr. Aubrey."

There was a short silence as Aubrey neutralized the shock of it all. Then he leaned forward eagerly and peered into Mr. Jebb's capacious right ear. "Pardon me, Mr. Jebb? You *did* say something, didn't you?"

"Ace." (Mr. Jebb's yes was apparently out of Manchester, England, by way of Camden, Maine.)

"Well, I'm sorry but I didn't quite hear you. Could you repeat what you said?" Aubrey held tense until the marvel was accomplished before his very eyes. Mr. Jebb repeated himself with precision and with nearly imperceptible choppings of the jawbone that were definitely and cumulatively moral in effect. Mr. Jebb's disapproval of Julie's conduct was at least mandible-deep. Presented with such a prodigy (he'd have felt less surprise to have seen and heard the faces on Mount Rushmore fall into casual conversation about canasta) Aubrey had to overcome a certain paralysis of awe, and then a temptation to ask Mr. Jebb to say it again, before he could make comment. "I am very glad to hear you say that, Mr. Jebb," he said, in his best our-group-had-no-cavities tone. "I was afraid there for a time that it was all my fault."

Mr. Jebb said, "Ace."

Disconcerting, that. "Ah, do you think it *was* my fault, Mr. Jebb?"

"No."

"I mean, I'm not trying to blame it all on her. But I think she should definitely apologize to me. Don't you?"

"Ace."

Aubrey, squatting between front and back seats, held his ground for a time, working at the knees like a springboard, studying his companion in dialogue carefully, searching their exchange for some clue as to what might lure Mr. Jebb again out of monosyllables. The subject was touchy, from a chauffeur's point of view. In deference to this, Aubrey started slowly. "You think she'll want to apologize to me, Mr. Jebb?"

"Ace."

"Do you think she *will* apologize?"

"No."

"Do you think she'll apologize to my father?"

"Ace."

"Then why won't she apologize to me?"

Silence. Aubrey felt at once he'd gone too far. Mr. Jebb, wheeling into the driveway now at five miles an hour, was giving his all to motor safety. And continued to do so until the car was docked at the doorstep, until Aubrey had come out of his crouch, sat for a split second on the seat, and then stepped out as Mr. Jebb opened and held the rear door for him. Aubrey dared no more than a glance, and when he did Mr. Jebb smiled at him—a mere stretching of the lips that disclosed no tooth, but a smile for all that—and said, "Don't know why."

And that was that. Mr. Jebb was away, puttees and heels on gravel and hat down the stars before Aubrey had a question ready. Yet even as he watched the car roll slowly out the driveway, he felt a rush of gratitude toward Mr. Jebb, a vast satisfaction in the good man's vote of confidence, and a sense of privilege at having been on the receiving end of the first full-length Jebbian sentence in modern history. It buoyed him high and tall all the way up to his bed. He was even able not to think about Julie, and took his couch in a glow of good male fellowship, and imagined—whether before or after sleep came he never knew—that a uniformed flight of English angels—humming "Ace, We'll Gather at the River"—sang him sweetly to his rest.

# · SEVENTEEN ·

IT WAS an afflatus of pain, come upon him while he slept, a blast of that relentlessly obscene primal heat whose resistance had long since become a central fact of his life and the source of a variety of little home remedies that would have taken prominent space in any field manual for seminarians at large.

Do you feel a certain warming of the bowels? Then get thee hence to the playing field and run until you have no other thought but the inflation of your lungs. Double-time to the shower and never touch the hot water handle and stand under that salutary arctic stream until your red has turned to blue, until there is dead winter in your heart, until your rampant kernels have become the meekest of privates. And at dinner consume all the soup and gravy decency and digestion will permit, for the salt wherewith these are savored is pure saltpeter indeed.

He lay awake watching the first light come ankle-deep into the room, and wondered if there wasn't something to the saltpeter business after all. He'd asked a confessor about it once and had reduced the man to a snuffling fit of laughter. But he had left the confessional unable to dismiss saltpeter summarily. How could something so subtly and slyly and persistently of the very fabric of seminary life be just a big, potassium-flavored myth? And on this morning, he was more than ever convinced that his sudden withdrawal from a diet in which saltpeter was almost certainly a daily ingredient had had a pejorative effect upon his whole moral and physical tone.

For he had come awake more than a hour earlier fiercely erect and in pain from it, and had been praying all that time for deliverance. Or trying to pray. Actually, when he was not thinking about saltpeter, he was thinking about his appointment with the Saharans, and worrying about what he would do if the damned thing wouldn't go down. It was a judgment upon him, no doubt of it, for his hesitation about Julie and her foolish arguments.

Oh my God, I am heartily sorry, he thought, and I can't walk around like this. Maybe Kermit has an overcoat I could borrow. But I can't sit through the whole interview with an overcoat on. They might think I was just trying to show them that I needed to go to a warmer climate. All right. I've got to reduce the damned thing somehow. I'll try the cold water treatment.

But the shower didn't help, nor did a dozen deep knee bends, two dozen sit-ups, an extended session of free-arm swinging (since push-ups were not to be entertained), and three minutes of holding his breath while reciting the litany of the saints. At last, he decided, there was nothing for it but to try Father Finnegan's remedy, suggested by the Master in confession once when Aubrey had inquired about the control of ordinary matutinal erections. The remedy had seemed extreme at the time, but only because, he now concluded, he had never experienced before an erethism equal to it. And he took a long look at his defiant fellow traveler and, finding him not one whit diminished, decided to move resolutely to the ultimate sanction.

He stripped the belt out of his pants, doubled it buckle in hand, set his jaw, hardened his eyes, raised the belt on holy high, and brought it zealously down. And went at once into a screaming little two-handed mazurka that carried him over, under, around, and through most of the furniture in the room, and added a stubbed toe, a scraped shinbone, and a sprained knee to his peniscular abrasion. And he went forth to meet the day moving in a series of little spavined, crabbedy squats, left and right, and at forty-five-degree angles to his true course, his only consolation being the certainty that he would never be erect again.

197

Neither Julie nor Kermit was up—if indeed either was in—and he made no inquiry about them. He called the Saharan Fathers immediately after he'd downed some scrambled eggs reluctantly prepared by the housekeeper, whose house was still far from in order, by her own admission and by Aubrey's estimation of her eggs. A Father Paquette answered the telephone and greeted Aubrey with great cordiality.

"I'm so sorree we cannot meet you," he said, his accent forcefully French. "But there ees only a small walk."

"Oh, someone will drive me over there, thank you, Father."

"Ah, splendid. The Father Provincial is anxious to see you. Your father is a famous man, no?" And he laughed in a sort of a larruping hiccough for what seemed to Aubrey an inordinately long time. Easy there, Father, you'll score a piston.

Mr. Jebb found the house without difficulty, a small clapboard house on Job's Lane, in no way imposing. He told Mr. Jebb he would call him, or else walk back, and Mr. Jebb lost control sufficiently to grin just perceptibly and wish him good luck.

The front door opened as Aubrey reached for the knob. A small balding priest dressed in a flowing white soutane, a white capelike burnoose, and girdled at the middle by a broad black-leather cincture, stood within, grinning benignly.

"Brother Strycker?"

"Yes, Father."

"I am Father Paquette. Of the telephone."

He put out his hand and Aubrey took it as he stepped in. Father Paquette of the telephone had a rough, horny hand and a grip that had no business anywhere near his diminutive body. Easy there, Father. I'm severally wounded already. Why does he keep grinning like that? Looks much too happy. The world's a tragic place, mon père. Sober up there, now, before the deluge.

"Father Provincial is waiting to see you. Come, come."

Aubrey followed, walking now without difficulty. Step through this archway, a trapdoor opens, thirty-three feet straight down, everything artfully arranged so that you fall right into a legionnaire's uniform, cap and cape, bandoliers clapped on you from behind, and suddenly there is Victor McLaglen jamming a rusty rifle at you and bawling, "Fall in, ee-you bloody spindleshanks! The wogs are on the walls!"

But levity failed him as soon as he was standing in the presence of

198

Father Georges Bogart, the Provincial. Father Paquette of the telephone made the introductions almost solemnly, then went smiling and excusing himself out the door, and was gone before Aubrey had said a word, and he didn't say an intelligible word for long seconds thereafter. For Father Bogart was an awesome sight—a broad bull of a man, possibly six feet five, great of chest and arms and shoulders, hair white and close-cropped, his face dark brown from the sun and scarred and gashed like a well-used chopping block, but handsome for all that except at the mouth(which was thin-drawn and hard, yet not cruel, but as if dried and cured and stitched out of the hide of contrition)—and the sound of him also awesome, though he spoke softly, softly like low notes from a tuba, resonant and threatening the sudden blast, so that Aubrey thought him the only man he'd ever encountered who might stand to Kermit in a bellowing contest; the whole physical impression being that of a survivor of a grander and ruggeder time, a lost outrider of some vanished race of giants. Yet all this was only adjunct to the extraordinary look and presence of the man, a magnitude of spirit or soul, a sanctity as large as his body and felt by the onlooker in his every movement and glance, and his eyes like nothing Aubrey had ever seen before, being a nearly colorless gray and, though full of grace and compassion, yet distantly focused and taut with an immense sadness—the eyes of a man who has chosen his moment in time and holds it fixed before him, and attends its awful event, and is seeing, even as he speaks and listens to you, the passage of the nails and the flash of the blood.

The Provincial was aware of Aubrey's nervousness, and perhaps of his awe, and came to him and shook his hand gently and sat him in a chair, and went around behind his desk being ponderously pleasant about being glad to see him and how it looked like rain. And he began at once to ask the normal questions—about Aubrey's education, his father, his mother, his sister, his brother, his upbringing, his experience with the Titans, his knowledge of the Saharan Fathers and of the Sahara Desert, his knowledge of what a missionary priest was expected to be and do—and Aubrey had not given four answers before he knew that the interview was going wrong, that Father Bogart had sized him up already and had found him wanting, that he was not at all what the Saharans were looking for.

How do I know? I just know. He's looking at me as if I were a sty in the eye of general Christian vision. Yet he means me well. He wants me to know we're not talking about starry nights and harems. We're talking about trundling up and down Islam for the rest of your days, and about getting your throat cut for a Christian dog, or an American dog, or an anti-Algerian dog, or a whatever-the-hell dog. Father Bogart wants you to know that this is real and earnest mayhem you're getting into, and sudden death. If you think all of that stuff went out with Tancred and the conquest of Jerusalem, Father Bogart is only trying to suggest that you give it another think; and understand that you won't be armed, and that there won't be any bands playing, and that you won't even have the satisfaction of having fought a battle. Because you'll be there to do just one thing, and that is to love everybody. Charity will be your only weapon, Father Bogart says, and that leaves you damned short of weapons because you've been short on charity since the day you discovered there were other people besides Arnie, Kermit, Rexfordia, Aline, Solly, and Eulalia. Right? Right.

"Can you assure me, Aubrey, that a very substantial part of your motivation in applying here is a pure and positive desire to serve Jesus Christ in the Sahara Desert?"

Aubrey was all ready to make a positive affirmation, but something in Father Bogart's tone gave him pause. This was clearly a question to which the obvious answer would be only the beginning. How pure? How positive? How to serve Jesus Christ? And Aubrey was suddenly overwhelmed by the thought that only a stupid and vast presumption had brought him to apply here. This man is a saint. You can feel it in the room. Those eyes are the eyes of Christ, weeping over Jerusalem. He looks at you and thinks, Not a stone will be left upon a stone. He knows me like he shoveled the pile to make me. He knows what my answer should be. That I don't really know what in hell he's talking about. His eyes are saying he isn't kidding, that his Sahara is a special place for special and holy people, that his Sahara is full of heat and fleas, and those prop Arabs over there are carrying real daggers, and that from this quiet room you go to that hot place and from that hot place you go to that hotter place, and you thirst and go barefoot and scrape pus out of wounds and come to consider a locust a real delicacy when the hunger is upon you. Oh, your humble servant heareth, Father Bogart, and it curdles his whey. And how can he answer when he is almost never pure or positive, and has only the remotest acquaintance with Jesus Christ?

But he did answer, haltingly. "I feel, with all my heart, Father, that my vocation is to the Society of the Sahara."

There was a long silence. Father Bogart took in several huge drafts of air and sighed them out without raising his eyes. In the silence, Aubrey searched for an opening in the wall he seemed to be building around himself. He ran up and down desperately and asked himself in his panic if he had sealed up all the doors by accident. There had to be one door, one proper escape into this man's confidence. Even a narrow one, even a high leaping one would do. Father Bogart raised his face to him, and the gray eyes seemed to be wavering in pain. When he spoke, his voice was soft and hushed. "You didn't answer my question. Can you say yes or no to it?"

"Yes, Father," Aubrey said quickly.

The gray eyes flinched. The first of the nails. Aubrey looked away, to a toothless human skull at one corner of the Provincial's desk, and fixed his eyes on it, and held them there.

"You don't believe what you said, do you, Aubrey?" the priest asked.

"No, Father. I don't think I do. I'm not sure *why* I want to be a Saharan rather than, say, a Maryknoll, or a . . ."

"Can you tell me, at least, the things you tell yourself? Can you just make some attempt at it?"

Aubrey decided suddenly that there was no point in doing anything but letting it rip, saying exactly what came to him, just as he had done with Father Finnegan. If this man was a saint, as he seemed to be, there would be no fooling him in any case. "I can make some attempt at it, Father," Aubrey said. "But I doubt it will be what you would like to hear."

"Never mind what I would like to hear. Just go ahead."

And Aubrey did, at great length, recklessly, running on over his thoughts about the American Church, the shortcomings of the Titan Order, his antisocial upbringing, his intellectual pride, his difficulties with close community life, the influence of Rexfordia and her ideas about how he ought to be a secular, and his wish to get far away from American luxury, distractions, sophistications, and the hypersensitive American people; ran on through it all thinking that, what the hell, if he was going to go down, he might as well go down with all guns firing. And heard himself saying as he concluded; ". . . don't mean I've had any trouble with community life—I mean, nothing specific

—but that in anticipation of difficulty I became sort of the class clown. I wasn't able to be genuine because being what I genuinely am would have caused friction, resentment. I want to be somewhere where I can be genuine, where the contrasts are sharp and unmistakable, where the evil is clearly marked out, where the people are simple, where the subtleties and blandishments of civilization are minimal, where you are really forced to pursue the spiritual life and to love God not only because you wish to and wish to perfect your love of God, but also because you—well, you . . ."

"Can't find anything better to do?" the priest asked. And he lifted his eyes to Aubrey and again they flinched and widened and looked beyond him. The second nail. The palm of the right hand— the hand that raised Lazarus—cruelly pierced.

Aubrey stared at a bookcase, studying the titles, waiting for some sign or word from the priest. The silence was complete until it started to rain, and the drops struck the windowpanes heavily, fitfully, then stopped, and the stains of them were long on the glass. The sorrows of men running down the shingles of the universe, to no purpose and to no reservoir, unless there be a God. And, watching the raindrops glisten and begin to dry in the sudden sun, he understood that, whatever its outcome, this interview with this holy man had changed him, would leave its impress upon him.

See how he loves me. See how he neither judges nor condemns. And he comprehends, sees the bloodless cowardice of my soul, and enters into my terror as only a brave man can. And, in his goodness, he offers the quiet, familiar encouragement he gives to women, and to little girls, and to men who don't know where or what they are in the eyes of God. In his sanctity, he repeats the words of Christ. Just looking at him, I can see what it will be like when Christ comes like a divine wind to winnow the grain from the chaff. In his holiness, he shows me the cross and says, Do not stand there all of your days and ignore the bloody footprints He left upon the earth. In his innocence, he tells me that I know nothing of men as tender, gaping wounds, wounds that speak and gasp and cry out plaintively for someone, anyone, to come and give them comfort. But that much, at least, I do know. That much my mother taught me.

He tried to keep his eyes on the bookcase, but they came back to the skull, and he held them there, upon the hollow sockets, for a time, but moved them away finally and irresistibly toward Father

Bogart. And the priest asked, "Tell me, Aubrey, do you think often about the love you owe to God?"

Aubrey said to himself, once quickly, Be a man, be a man. "I don't think I do, Father."

"Do you meditate often upon the passion of our Lord?"

"No, Father."

"Do you make the Stations of the Cross daily?"

"No, Father."

"Do you try to pray constantly?"

"No, Father."

"Have you been to Mass and communion every morning since you left the Titan novitiate?"

"No, Father."

"Have you been faithful with your night and morning prayers?"

"No, Father."

"Do you say the rosary at least once a day?"

"No, Father."

And the questions went on, and there was the third nail, and the lance and the darkening of the sun, and finally Aubrey was looking away at the floor and answering in a whisper, and had retreated into a dark place and was hearing the Provincial as from a great and estranged distance. He almost hoped to hear the intonation of anger, but it didn't come. Father Bogart was calm, direct, succinct. And he said, at last, "I hope, Aubrey, that you didn't expect me to give you my answer today?"

"No, Father."

"In fact, you've mentioned your father's request that you accompany him on a hunting trip to Alaska. I see no reason why you should not, if you care to do so. I think it will be a matter of ten days or two weeks before I can possibly give your application proper consideration. If my decision is favorable, I will write immediately to the Father General in Rome, enclosing all of these records you have supplied. If my decision is favorable, the Father General would have to have grave reason not to concur. He is a very prompt and decisive man. If my decision is unfavorable, I will let you know as soon as I possibly can, although I will not try to communicate with you before you return from Alaska in any case."

He paused for a time, then turned in his chair toward a small fireplace and stared into it. And just as he started to speak again, he closed his eyes tightly, as if recoiling from the harshness of what he had to say. "In all fairness I should tell you that I find the reasons you have given me for wishing to join the Saharan Fathers the most immature and unacceptable I have ever heard. You speak of your desire to get away from America, your desire to remove yourself from temptation, your desire to escape the influence of your mother, your desire to leave civilization behind. All of these motives, Aubrey, are negative, selfish, the motives of a small boy. Not once did you speak of the desire to save souls—except your own, which is commendable but hardly apostolic—not once did you evince any zeal to bring Christ to those who have never heard of Him, not once did you speak of the simple love of your fellow men. These are difficult things to put into words, I know, but they manage to get themselves said, even during the silences, if they are truly felt. Yet you did not say them, nor did I feel them unsaid."

The Father Provincial's voice had dropped away to a whisper, and his head was bowed forward on his chest, his fists clenched tightly in his lap. The furrows around his closed eyes deepened, and he appeared to be suffering acutely. Barely audibly, he went on: "From your records and from what I have observed, you are a brilliant young man. In almost any sort of endeavor, your future would be assured. Except the priesthood. I must tell you that I feel very strongly that God is calling you to be a priest. It is a great blessing to have so strong a vocation, and it is very seldom seen. But your intellectual pride and selfishness still could destroy it. Watching you speak was like watching a potentially great actor acting in a foolish play he himself has written. Were he to turn to Racine or to Shakespeare, he would have no equal. But he prefers his own scribblings to Racine or Shakespeare, and, as long as he does, he will come to nothing.

"Jesus Christ has given you your lines, Aubrey. All you have to do is speak them, absorb them, make them part of your being. Silence your own prattlings, let it all go. It amounts to nothing. Hearing you, I could have wept for the waste that was there. And I tell you, very frankly, that if my decision in your case is favorable, it will be in spite of almost everything you now are. If I approve your candidacy, it will be because I see, or am given to see after long prayer, that God—for His own reasons—wants you to serve Him as a Saharan priest. And because it is apparent that the fine order of which you have been a member for the past five years has not really been able to touch you. That is, if I accept you, it will be in the hope that we, the Saharans, can touch you, that we by God's grace can bring out of you the man God sees hiding within, behind all of your foolish pride. I—I'm sorry if I have offended. I am truly sorry, but it is necessary to speak always the truth. It is necessary, in Christ, to be honest." And then the priest was getting to his feet and coming humbly, eyes down, his face contracted in pain, around his desk and, having touched Aubrey briefly on one shoulder, was backing away toward the door, murmuring his apologies abjectly. ". . . pray for me, for our Society . . . really very sorry . . . don't be discouraged by what I say . . . still a very good chance . . . certainly need priests . . . be hearing from me shortly . . . God to guide you . . . my decision may very well be favorable." And then, abruptly, nearly in tears, he was gone, saying at the last something about catching a train.

And before Aubrey could begin to think about what had taken place, Father Paquette, all smiles and cheerful phrases, was closing the door behind him, and he was walking among lawns and shrubbery, all fragrant from the rain, and trying to force himself to think. But did not even try to think so much as to contain himself, as his shock gave way to pain and the pain to its separate parts. Of which the first and weakest was indignation, that the Provincial had judged him so quickly, and apparently so accurately; had seen, with that saintly and forever doleful eye, something that Aubrey himself had only dimly suspected: that there was a secret and central place in his soul where was entrenched his desire to excel, to succeed, to gain ascendancy over Arnie, to do, after all and despite his countless denials, what Arnie had failed to do, precisely because Arnie had failed to do it. He could hear the voice of Father Bogart still, the exact words, and in them echoes of the words of a gaunt legion of prophets like him, who also came out of the desert to the houses and the palaces of the captains and the kings and the governors and the overseers to tell them that all pride pertained to God and that he who abused it or sought it for its own sake or used the proud name of God for his own petty ends was guilty of an unforgivable sin. And it seemed to Aubrey that those words, those ancient hoary voices, were pronouncing his end, had been reaching for him, threatening, like a hollow boom of outrage all across those angry

Christian ages, and that only now was it over because the last of the prophets had spoken. He had been brought awake, rudely, having heard the voices and the voice, and, listening, had seen the long-cherished dream, which had somehow survived his wakefulness and still had life and hope, brought to sudden and burning reassessment on the edge of the prophet's pain.

The death of the dream of the desert—and it was almost certainly dead, he thought—was the great blow. What would sustain him as this dream had sustained him? Unworthy and vain it may have been. But it had also been very effective in keeping him in hope, in line, in the seminary at all. What would sustain him? The Provincial had given him the answer: that which sustained every religious of pure purpose: love of God, and love of man. Faith, hope, charity—prayer, fasting, and mortification of the flesh. These would sustain him, and would keep the vain dream from rising up to haunt him.

So that he would have to start over again, start where he should have started five years before. And this thought was almost too much to bear. The waste of those years; his persistent, proud disregard of anything but his own will; his failure to take seriously the simple words: Thy will, not mine, be done.

He had walked aimlessly, and now stopped, realizing that he had no idea where he was. The sun was on the wet grass and leaves, and he blinked into the brightness and told himself that he could forget the Saharan Fathers. He would be perfectly truthful to Rexfordia about the New York archdiocese, tell her that he simply could not do it, and then select another society, another order, another congregation. The interview had humbled him. He would be damned glad to be accepted by almost anybody who would take him—except the New York archdiocese. And he said an act of contrition as sincerely as he could, and began to feel better, and walked on, deciding just to walk.

And he had walked perhaps a mile before he realized that he had left his hat with the Saharans. And he hesitated a minute, not thinking about the hat so much as a chance to speak to the Provincial again (if he could face the Provincial again), but then remembered about Father Bogart's train, and walked on and managed a small and miserable smile, and said aloud, "Oh, what the hell. They've got my head. They might as well have the hat that goes with it."

206

# · EIGHTEEN ·

HE CAME onto the beach about a half mile east of Kermit's house and walked toward it slowly, squinting into the bright sun to watch the sea birds come in on the wind from the south, close down over the gun-blue combers, superbly controlled and confident, lifting to the land and veering high above the barrier dune and curving back lazily toward the sea again. And watched the clouds, all white and fat and trudging on down the sky like polar voyagers not quite eager for the north. And was thinking of the rock monasteries of Cappadocia and how he could always simply disappear into one, when he saw Julie just ahead of him stretched out on her stomach on a white blanket, and peering intently through sunglasses and her blowing hair into an open book.

He slowed his pace and gave the thing two or three seconds of dynamic tension—tried to pretend that he might, just actually might, walk right on by her with only the curtest of nods if, indeed, he deigned to acknowledge her presence at all—saying that the last thing he wanted just then was an argument and that he might take advantage of her nastiness the night before, act grossly offended, and, in the interest of modesty and a true reformation of his life, break off diplomatic relations with her entirely. But he was kidding himself and knew it, and noticed that he was heading right for her with quickened step, that he was preparing his opening line and attitude as he went (casual, quietly witty, yet with that sort of knit-browed, myopic, jowlishly constipated aspect everybody expects of a man attempting nobly to conceal his secret pain), and that he wanted almost desperately to talk to her about Father Bogart, and about the interview, and about becoming a priest, and all the rest of it. Because, he assured himself, after all, she has a fine mind and just might be able to help me see things more clearly, or even if she does nothing but simply sit there and listen it will do me a lot of good. And was standing at her feet, contemplating the tawn-gold of her— she still unaware of him—before that other, camped somewhere off in the outback near his left ear, began to get through loud, clear, and mocking, and saying, Poor little Aubie wants to talk to a girl. Poor little fellow never had a girl of his own to talk to. Poor little Aubie admires Julie's mind very, very much. That's why he's standing here staring down at her rump. Poor little Aubie has lost his youth and doesn't know where to find it, but he *does* know where he'd like to look first. Oh yes. Everybody needs a little sympathy now and then, a little understanding, and poor Aubie's never got none of neither. And that ain't all poor little Aubie ain't never got none of. Well, if that's what poor little Aubie wants, he sure as hell came to the right place. God and wowser, yes! The answer to a virgin's prayer! What's a little venery between steps, I always say, as long as we're all climbing those golden stairs? Seize her by the riser there, Aubie old buddy, and spike her where she lies!

And then Julie was looking at him over her shoulder, grinning and talking. ". . . the hell are you *doing*, step? The flies after you or something?"

"Huh?"

"Well, you were glaring around up there something fierce."

"Was I?"

"You scared me half to death. It looked as if you were calling down the wrath, or putting a hex on me."

"I—I was just watching the sea gulls."

"Uh-huh." She was grinning full width and shaking her head. "So now you're a bird watcher."

"I've always been a bird watcher."

"Step, your versatility has no end, but you're a fog-job. I guess I'm lucky you didn't walk right up my back." She sat up and patted the blanket. "Won't you sit down? Let the birds and me watch you for a while."

He hesitated almost not at all, feeling abruptly quite relaxed and easy and warmed by her obvious pleasure at seeing him, and sat down on one edge of the blanket, holding his eyes to the surf. "I wouldn't have walked on you. I saw you from a distance, but just as I got up to you I—I got to thinking about something."

"Well, the next time you skulk up on a girl from behind, give her some warning at the last minute so she might at least roll over." He held eyes strictly front while she giggled at him. One quarter-glance at her very slightly harnessed bosom had made it clear that modesty lay only to seaward. "Okay. I see you're meditating. Or are you just hung?"

He grinned sparsely. "No. I feel fine."

"Smashing. And what are you thinking about?"

He cleared his throat, searched around for a lead-in, and surprised himself by uttering what seemed, at least at first, a total irrelevancy, and followed it with another. "Oh, I was thinking about how fast years go by. And how it seems like only a couple of years ago when Arnie and I were seven." He garnished these profundities with a wan, bittersweet smile that came and went quickly, like the years.

"Ah, how sad. Your lost boyhood." She sighed through her smile. "The dear dead boyhood. But, is it really dead?"

"Dead."

"Well, I can't tell you how sorry I am to hear it. Do you mind if I mourn with you? I mean, I'm all dressed for it, black bikini and all."

"No, no. Glad to have you. Sit on the family side."

"Poor little tyke. What'd he die of?"

"Hard to say at this distance. Claustrophobia is my best guess."

"Well, I wouldn't be a bit surprised. Boyhoods need air and a little space to hood around in. You just can't keep them trussed up all the time."

"Hum," Aubrey said, noting that it was almost time to change the subject and, therefore, time. "What are you reading?"

"All about the death of boyhoods."

"Am I mentioned?"

"Not yet, but I'm expecting to come across you anytime now. There are dozens of other interesting people mentioned, however."

"Anyone we know?"

"Oh yes. Freud, Jung, Marx. And Norman O. Brown. He's the author. It's called *Life Against Death*, and it's all about how their boyhoods died and they resurrected them."

"Fascinating."

"Only N. O. Brown doesn't like the way Freud went about it."

"How come you're reading a book like that? Isn't it, well—"

"Over my head? Shame on you, step. Girls actually do think from time to time. Even I. I enjoy thinking almost as much as I do screwing. And when I find a book like this one that makes me think about screwing in such a distinguished, well-documented way, why, I'm just the most devoted thinker you ever saw."

"I thought you said it's about lost boyhoods."

"It is! But lost girlhoods, too. And when you put the two together, it's about screwing, right?" She laughed softly.

"God, *I* don't know, Julie. Everything you touch is about—"

"In a religious way, of course."

"Oh, of course. I'm sure it's religious."

"Well, it *is*, you damned skeptic. Old Nob says—Old Nob is what I call Dr. Brown—well, he doesn't exactly put it in so many words, but he *proves*, to *my* satisfaction, that you can screw your way to heaven." He nodded, sardonically he thought. She was enjoying herself immensely. Out of the corner of his eye, she appeared all mammaries and moment. "All right, I'll explain. We are animals with repressions, right? We would be *happy* animals if we could rid ourselves of repressions, right? Like dolphins. Screw all day, over and over and never get tired of it. Repeat until you literally kill time. Old Nob says that eternity is the mode of unrepressed bodies." She spoke almost gleefully. "What it comes down to is the perfectibility of man and the gaining of eternity by means of screwing!"

"I don't see how you come to that conclusion," Aubrey said, shaking his head.

"You don't? Well, Jesus, step, he says we are compelled to repeat, right? Now, everybody knows that the animal, and the child, finds no antagonism between the pleasure principle and the repetition compulsion. Repression creates this antagonism. So, throw away your repressions, set about repeating the highest pleasure—what I mean, perpetual, solid, serious screwing—and bango! Nirvana! The Sabbath of Eternity! Paradise! The Absolute finking *Geist!*"

"Julie," he said, laughing with her. "That can't be what he means."

"It is! It is!"

"You can't have a society without repression."

"Who the hell says you can't? And how would you know until you tried it? And I know what your problem is. You think everybody is as evil-minded as you are! That's the essence of the good Christian's belief. And the good Freudian's."

"Wait, hold! How the hell do you figure *that*?"

"I thought you'd never ask," she said, fairly yelping. "Nob says that the doctrine of the universal neurosis of mankind is simply the psychoanalytical analogue of the doctrine of original sin. So! The Freudians and the Christians are piping the same little mealy-mouthed tune, right? Both pessimists. Better to be neurotic than chaotic. They even hate one another, as twins often do." She clamped her lips tight and frowned. "I—I meant no innuendo, or what the hell . . ."

"Well, Julie, for Pete's sake, I know you didn't. And what difference would it make if you did? Love, hate, and life, death—as you and Nob say, we've all got our share."

"So?" she said, all eager happiness again. "Are you converted, step?"

"To what?"

"Now, don't play dense. To the new religion I've been preaching, of course. Nob is the divinity and I'm his prophet, right? And, as Arnie would say—the fink—Nob spelled backwards is *bon*, which is French for 'screwing,' and what I want to know is are you ready to be introduced to the pursuit of perfection, the pursuit of the highest *bon*, which is the only kind I, personally, have to offer?"

"In the first place, I'm not ready to forget that I have a soul, and in the second place, it seems to me we've had this conversation before."

"Yes, but not on such a high, *bon*, religio-philosophico-psychoana-lytico-pyrofaxional level. I mean, here I am and there you are, with a big empty house full of beds—your choice of bedspreads—behind us, step, and we—you and ready I—could just play hob with Nobian abandon all afternoon! I mean, put your Nir with my Vana and throw in a little *kinesis*, and I mean wow! If we started right now, why, we could be in sempiternity by two-fifteen . . ."

"Julie," he said sharply, having managed to press his grin into

211

something he imagined was at least a stern smirk, "I prefer to get to heaven in a more orthodox manner. Though I do appreciate the offer."

"Well!" she said, pushing herself up on one elbow and pulling her glasses down from her eyes to give him a full measure of green amusement. "We are making progress. That's the first time you've expressed any appreciation of my efforts in your virginal behalf."

"Is that right?"

"Damned right it's right."

"I'm sorry. Maybe—maybe this is the first time I've felt grateful."

"Because of your lost boyhood?"

"I wasn't serious about that."

"The hell you weren't. You weren't maybe, but you were." She rolled over on her back—a voluptuous operation Aubrey had to close his eyes to avoid—and shaded her eyes with one hand against the sun. "You know, step, you are a very sweet person. You bring out the mother in me. And that's very funny, and I'd laugh except that I'm very serious. I want to carry you around and show you things—dogs, elephants, horses, Babar, and Lassie, and Black Beauty—and say, Look, darling, a naked woman. And then show you what to do about her. Which doesn't sound very motherly, perhaps, but"—she giggled—"after all, I'm your stepsister."

"Lovely day, isn't it?"

"Yes, you miserable, repressed, Christian prig. And what makes me very sad is the thought that you are convinced you ought to go to your grave a virgin. Do you really think you'll do that, step?"

"Yes."

"Gawd! Well, I guess the only hope for you is if the Church should decide to let priests marry." She turned her head to peek at him. "Step? What would you do if the Holy Roman Catholic Crutch should—say, next month or, even better, after you're a priest—pronounce clerical celibacy at an end?"

"I'll worry about that when it happens."

"What you're saying is you don't think it could happen. But it could."

"All right. I've nothing against marriage. I'm sort of used to the idea of celibacy, but I might get married if I were permitted to."

"*Might* get married?" she howled, grinning derisively. "Why, my dear brother step, you'd be tossed, laid, and wedded by the end of the first week of open season! You know what there would be? There'd be the goddamnedest stampede of panting, pantsless women the world has ever seen! Not only toward you—although you're succulent and first-prize grade-A prime—but toward every priest and brother under ninety able to walk! Can't you imagine it? The parish vestals, the pious young widows, the pious *old* widows, the housekeepers, maybe even the divorcees? Why, there'd be the damnedest shedding of virginal dignity since the nuns of Loudon got themselves possessed!"

Aubrey could imagine it and had to grin in spite of his reticence, thinking of all the priests he knew to whose hearts such a possibility would strike the ultimate horror. He could see them hiking up their habits and taking to the hills in great numbers, like foxes before the dogs. It would be hilarious, pathetic, absurd. And not very likely, after all. "Well, Julie, I can understand why a woman might want to seduce a celibate—I mean, from the psychological, forbidden-fruit angle—but what makes you think these women would want to marry a celibate?"

"Are you kidding?"

"Wait. What I mean is, why should there be any greater rush on priests than there is on ministers and rabbis?"

"Well, good God! There's no comparison! A rabbi or a minister could always get married, could always be approached and had. He knew it and so did women. No mystery. But the priest has been unapproachable, couldn't be had—at least, not without great and dangerous difficulty—and suddenly he *can* be had, legally! All that first-blush virginal potency, all that innocent eagerness, all that sweetness and light just waiting to be initiated into the pneumatic joys? The arts of love? By little old blushing me? Oh, the maidenly, matronly, holy joy of it all! And he'll be faithful, too, after all that training in it. And no fear of divorce. And he will be obedient, and thrifty, and easily influenced. And what a status symbol, girls! The hand that holds the cross this morning will be holding me by the crosstrees tonight! Why, the next-best thing to a Black Mass! And that's the whole secret of it, step. The power of the priesthood. No minister or rabbi brings Christ down on the altar, or if they claim to, nobody believes it. But everybody, damned near, believes in the awful power of the priesthood. The priest consecrates hosts, he drives out devils, he forgives sin. Oh dearies, the confessional! Talk

213

about a corner on neighborhood gossip! Wow! Just get the old man half shot and talking every Saturday night and the two-thousand-year-old seal on that institution will curl up and wither away! That's why confession never caught on among the Protestants. The women, who do most of the confessing anyway, knew that the minister's wife would have it out of the old man by bedtime, or shortly thereafter. And if priests are one day allowed to marry there will be a gross drop-off in Catholic confession, you can bet your cleanest shroud. And you can just imagine what a power the priest's wife would be in the neighborhood. Pretty soon she'd be assisting at deathbeds and performing the last rites and handing out holy water and religious medals and rosaries. And then slowly and subtly she'd take over the sodalities and the flower arranging and the choir loft and—oh, I tell you, dearie—there'd be no end to it until she was inside that altar rail correcting the old man's Latin and holding office hours in the rectory. Just no end to it, and if you make monsignor she'll move right into your new uniform. And the same if you make bishop or cardinal; and if you make pope, wow! Double wow! Imagine being the wife of the Pope! The Popess, first lady of Christendom, queen of all holy women, chief inspector of all other supposedly holy women, factotum in charge of closing up convents, condemning mother superiors, burning discredited virgins! Triple wow! Power! Sheer, maddening power! Those Sisters of the Loose Habits! Take them out and hang them all, the foul, fornicating bitches! In the name of the Father, and of the Son, and of the Holy Matron, of course! And there would soon be an outcry for a woman pope, and a great rush to canonize Pope Joan, and everybody, including Clare Boothe Luce—even Clare Boothe Luce! Oh! Wouldn't it gall her! —would have to bend down and kiss her holy ruddy ring finger! My God, the sweep and dimension of it boggles all! What a sweet, delicious mess! The vicar of Christ on earth, and the vicaress of the Virgin Mary. Christ's mother and the vicar's wife at one and the same time—mother and wife, how very American—and if they had a child, a son! Why, the vicaress would declare him divine on the spot, the undisputed heavyweight second coming of Christ, and kick the old vicar off the throne, install junior and then herself at his right hand, declare herself immaculately conceived, virgo intacta, and Mediatrix of all Graces and Taxes, and take to rising into heaven off the top of St. Peter's every August fifteenth just to show world society how a truly inspired social climber goes about it!"

And so on, Julie enjoying herself immensely and becoming more and more outrageously offensive to Catholic taste and acceptance yet always laughing so delightedly, and out of such a completely and finely satiric sense of the failures, and possible failures, of men to their God, that Aubrey couldn't and didn't resist her with anything like success and got to his feet and walked to the house with her—after Kermit had stood on the porch for two bellowing minutes, announcing the lateness of the hour, the distance to New York, the time of departure of their airplane in the morning, and calling upon Jesus Christ several times to witness how he had been conducting a search for them for over three hours—still laughing, with cramps in his stomach from suppressed hilarity, and accusing himself of being no kind of least defender of the faith.

Only much later, in the car, was the question of his interview raised, and then in the briefest possible way.

"Well, what did those goddamned dune-buggers have to say?" Kermit asked, as he served himself his second longish bourbon from the bar.

"Oh Christ, yes!" Julie said, leaning around Kermit with more apology than curiosity in her eyes. "I forgot all about your interview."

"They said they'll let me know."

Kermit snorted and bent away from his glass, smacking his lips. "Well, what did you want? Anything more than that?"

"No."

"Well, of course he did," Julie said, glaring at Kermit. "He wanted encouragement, anyway." Then, sympathetically, to Aubrey, "Were they encouraging?"

"I—I'd say they were noncommittal."

"Oh for Christ's sake, Aubie!" Kermit snapped. "They'll move the goddamned desert over here if you ask them to, and you know it! Now let's can the Modesty Blaine act and get down to the important question. Did they say anything against your going to Alaska?" Kermit frowned around at him darkly.

"No. In fact he said—the Provincial—if I remember his words correctly, that he saw no reason why I shouldn't go."

"Well, Jesus Christ! There's hope for him!" Kermit brought his glassless hand down smashingly on Aubrey's near knee. "Good! By God! I'll send that man a carton of U.S. currency!"

"Which reminds me, Kermit," Aubrey said. "I owe the Master at the Titan novitiate ten dollars."

"Well, goddamn it, I'll take care of that right now!"

And Kermit took up the telephone, called his secretary, directed the issuing of a check for five hundred dollars to Father Finnegan (getting the name and address from Aubrey with much beetling of brows and beard), and dictating a note to the Master saying that any man who provided Aubrey with money to clear the hell out of the religious life couldn't be all bad, and directing the good father to use the whole five hundred on hard cider or ambrosia or whatever it was that Titans drank, and have himself at least one lost weekend in his benighted, surcingled life.

While this was going on, Julie stretched herself out on Kermit's knees and fixed Aubrey with tender, empathy-saddened eyes and asked him if the interview had gone well—or, rather, she accused him, swolefully, of its near failure. Aubrey told her that it could have been better, Father Bogart having been a saint interviewing a self-revealed sinner, but that he hadn't given up hope. Julie sighed considerably more despairingly than Aubrey thought the situation or genuine concern called for; and closed her eyes and shook her head and batted her eyes at him, thrice—just the mite of the sorrowing widow, or worse—before she withdrew to port. And Aubrey watched her, and wasn't surprised at all to see her gloom turn to gleaming smile almost immediately as she looked out the car window at Shinnecock Bay, nor to see her lift her chin, run her tongue around her lips, and, utterly unconscious of his observation, begin to blink and bat her eyes happily, giving back the sun-touched waters green spangle for green spangle.

And Aubrey sat there—after Kermit had hung up, downed his drink, mixed a third, clapped Aubrey on the back, declaimed for a time about Alaska, bears, and the great outdoors, then announced a song called "Seated One Day With My Organ" and proceeded to sing it with nothing pulled but all stops—and watched Long Island go by, and told himself that his future lay not with Julie, Kermit, Arnie, Big Ditmo, money, whisky, safaris, Freud, Abercrombie and Fitch, or with any vested thing, but with Jesus Christ crucified and with his own vocation and redemption, and that he had better return to the fundamentals of Christian ascetics, return and relearn and rehearse them every minute of every day, or he would never see Father Bogart, or the Saharans, or his dream of the priesthood, or even his immortal soul again. And he made the resolve to correct the wrong he had done with Julie that afternoon as soon as he possibly could; to tell her, in no uncertain or beauty-tempered or smirk-compromised terms, that he was God's man and Christ's serf and would listen to no more of her derogation and blasphemy—resolved this firmly even as Kermit and Julie harmonized on the refrain: "And I struck one small obstruction, that twanged like a great hymen!"

Aubrey put his hand in his jacket pocket, found his rosary, pretended to fall asleep, and, feeling righteous and a bit desperate and calling upon the Blessed Mother to pray for him at the hour of his death, lost the pretense and the journey in sound sleep somewhere between Mastic and East Patchogue.

## • NINETEEN •

"IT'S A GODDAMNED GOOD THING," Kermit was saying, *sotto voce*, as he, Aubrey, Arnie, Mr. Jebb, and Roger got in one another's way loading, stuffing, and otherwise abusing an even dozen suitcases, hatboxes, and assorted other tucker bags into the already closely packed trunk of Rexfordia's Cadillac, "that your mother was not in charge of logistics during the war. Because there would have been just one boat for any and all operations, and those guns or troops that couldn't be jammed into that one goddamned boat, by Jesus, would have been left behind."

Kermit had reference to the fact that Rexfordia had insisted, with all of her wan, despairing power, that they all ride to the airport in one car. It didn't make any difference which car, but there could not be more than one. It had nothing to do with economy, of course, but very much to do with her private mystique of togetherness, demanding arm's-length contact between or among all familial parties in transit. Kermit laid it to a bad fright Rexfordia had experienced during a tour of Chinatown in 1936, when an unmistakably authentic white slaver had given her menacing eye-rolling indications—from the alarmingly intimate distance of only one hundred and nine feet with all the yellow lechery at his disposal—that he was about to drop her into a Mott Street manhole, directly under which, Rexfordia theorized, a Shanghai-bound junk was waiting to receive her. Ever since that day, Rexfordia had manifested the unwavering determination that expeditionary solidarity would obtain wherever the movement of two or more members of the Strycker-Milligan complex, for anything more than ten north-south New York City blocks (or, by Kermit's calculation, one hundred and sixty-two and a half rods), was involved. "By Jesus, you think I'm exaggerating, Arnie, but she thinks —she actually *thinks*, if you could unobtrusively remove the top of her head and take a reading—that all we'd have to do is get out of ball-scratching distance of one another, and the several regiments of white slavers stationed on yellow alert between here and Idlewild would clap us into burlap bags and ship us off to a Tsingtao whorehouse!"

"I believe it," Arnie said. "They're going to grab us on the way through Long Island City." Arnie was sitting on the curb with his head in his hands, suffering, he said, from the worst hangover God had ever vouchsafed to man. "I hope," he added, "that you are all done talking for the day, Kermit. I'm going to sit on the jump seat behind Roger, and if you say more than three consecutive words I will inevitably vomit all over him."

After Kermit had given Mr. Jebb final instructions about repelling all boarders and generally holding the fort, and Mr. Jebb had shaken hands solemnly all around, they were off. The pleasantries began at once.

"Arnold, you've got your foot on Van Buren's box," Rexfordia said.

"I wish it were up his ass," Arnie said.

"Christ Jaysus, look at his eyes!" Solly said, of Arnie.

"Oh God, the rhino speaks. Welcome to Noah's Ark."

"I'll rhino you!"

"Don't move, Solly, you'll tip us over."

"Well, Arnie, aren't you going to say hello to Julie? You haven't seen one another for quite a while." This from Rexfordia.

"Oh Jesus, is *she* here?"

"Screw you, Arnold."

"See? Everybody hear that? And *I'm* always being accused of starting it. I say good morning and she says screw you."

"You didn't say good morning."

"All right, for Christ's sake! Good morning!"

"You don't have to *look* at me. Christ! Turn around."

"Isn't she sweet? And to think that only yesterday she was the goddamnedest little lard-assed wisenheimish postpubertal pimply-faced bitch that ever was."

"Arnie!" This from Kermit, who had finally settled himself after pushing Aubrey over under the steering wheel with Roger. "Stop heckling Julie."

"And now, look! There isn't a pimple on her!"

"Kermit, are you sure you wouldn't like me to ride in the glove compartment?" Aubrey said.

"What the hell's the matter?"

"Don't argue with Elbows McFadden, Aubie. Just shut up and climb out there on the door handle with Roger."

"Well, Jesus Christ, if your mother would buy a car instead of a goddamned set of traveling fenders we'd *all* have room."

"This is the best car in the world," Rexfordia said.

"What you ought to do next time, Mother, is get two, see, and get them welded together. In the form of a cross. Then we could all ride in comfort, with cross ventilation, and all be buried in it together."

"Christ Jaysus, he's turnin' green!"

"Right. I'm getting ready."

"Ready to what?" Kermit said.

"Give the signal to the white slavers."

"Arnie, goddamn it, don't be telling tales," Kermit said.

"What did you say, Arnold?"

"I wouldn't incriminate you, Kermit. You know that." Then to Rexfordia, "Kermit says he's going to unobtrusively remove the top of your head to see if there are any white slavers in there."

"I did like hell!"

"White slavers?" Rexfordia asked, glancing at Solly.

"Yes, indeed, and they're lurking in Long Island City with five junks, and a tramp steamer for Solly, and when I give the signal by vomiting on Roger, they're going to jump out at us."

"I don't think that's amusing, Arnold. I see your *father* has been telling his stories again."

"I have not, goddamn it. All I said was a white slaver tried to capture you once in Chinatown."

"And he did. He was eying me all the time you were off running around somewhere."

"I was *not* off running around somewhere! I was taking a—I was passing water! Jesus Christ, did you want to go into the men's room with me?"

"Mother, you've got to stop this running around in men's rooms. White slavers just love to hide in the urinals and jump out at you."

"What in the name of Christ was he *drinkin'* last avenin', missus?"

"Scotch whisky."

"Ah, yes, Mother, but a very *special* Scotch whisky. You see, there's this guy out at the youth *hostile* who has been certain for years that he pees nothing but Chivas Regal. But he's never had guts enough to taste it. So I . . ."

"Arnold, must we always have nothing but vulgarity?"

"Mother, I agree. It's disgusting sometimes, to me, the way Kermit is always talking about passing water."

Kermit hit Aubrey in the right eye with his wristwatch and said, "Christ almighty, Roger, we're twenty-five minutes behind schedule! Don't stop here!"

Roger looked entirely distracted by this intelligence and raced the engine a couple of times, but since they were then at the zenith of the Queensboro Bridge and trapped behind a truck full of what appeared to be tombstones, there wasn't much to be done.

"Oh, Mother of God," Solly said. "We're suspended!"

"Now, it's all right, Solly," Rexfordia said.

" 'Tain't! 'Tisn't! Oh Jaysus, feel it shake! Goddamn bridges, missus, are always after lettin' you down!"

"She's right!" Arnie cried. "Everybody out! Out, I say! Every man for himself!" Arnie opened his door and jumped out.

"Arnie!" Kermit cried. But Arnie was already striding away toward the truck in front of them.

"Jaysus Christ, save us!" Solly said, in a sort of incipient shriek. Then she addressed herself to Roger. "Take me home! Turn this around and take me home, you Grake bastard! Don't just sit there!"

Roger worked the wheel and glanced back once at Solly and shrugged, and Solly broke into tears, and Kermit called upon Solly to shut up and upon Christ to help her do it, and Julie and Rexfordia reasoned with Solly about the superlative design and construction of the bridge—Julie saying that it had been carved all of a piece out of the finest County Waterford granite—and Solly was calming down from panic to mere distraction when Arnie came sauntering back from the truck and climbed into the car.

"It's all set," Arnie said. "He'll swap the tombstones for Solly and two hundred thousand dollars' flight insurance on her between here and San Francisco."

Solly returned directly to screeching panic, saying she had been dragooned into the flight, and didn't want to go, and the airplane would inevitably fall from the sky into the Harlem River, and so on until Kermit roared, "He's moving! Let's go!"

And Roger licked his lips and roared off at nine miles an hour.

"Well *I* think we're getting a flat tire," Rexfordia said. "I can feel the air going out of it."

"Oh, Jesus Christ," Kermit said softly. "But it would be no damned wonder with all the goddamned baggage you and Julie brought."

"Well, I don't know about that," Rexfordia said. "With all your guns and all. . . ."

"The Owl and the Pussy-cat went to sea in a beautiful pea-green Cadillac," Arnie said. "And they took some honey and plenty of money and about sixty-five hundred goddamned pounds of excess baggage. When they get done loading this baggage, they'll have to throw some people off."

"Really, Kermit," Rexfordia said. "How many pieces of my luggage were there, Roger?"

Roger, who drove hunched forward, eyes darting tensely, as if he were taking machine-gun fire from the white line, shrugged and then started to blink rapidly. Aubrey counted the blinks for the first eighteen but then lost track. After a long pause, during which Roger must have conjured up each piece of luggage in a separate image, he said, "Eleven, maybe, and Van Born."

"Oh Jesus, yes," Kermit said. "How's Van Buren?"

"He stinks," Julie said.

"Julie! That's the turpentine," Rexfordia said. "He rubbed against the wet paint in the bathroom and I had to use turpentine to get the paint off."

"Shouldn't let dogs go to the bathroom," Arnie said. "Let 'em use phone poles like the rest of us."

"It was green paint," Solly said solemnly.

"Jesus Christ," Kermit mumbled. "Van Buren's got a green bathroom and most people haven't got a green pot to piss in."

Rexfordia protested that it was her bathroom, Arnie said she shouldn't spoil the dog by letting it use her bathroom, Julie said Van Buren would look better green, and Kermit said shut up they were

222

almost there. But no one shut up, then or later, as the Van Buren argument ran right on into a dispute over reservations (only five had been made and first class was sold out), the which went on for forty minutes, each of its components deftly and concurrently and contrapuntally maintained by Kermit, Rexfordia, Arnie, and Julie against a triple quartet of airline employees, representing reservations, baggage, and seating, in the order of their appearance and defeat. Kermit took the bad news about the reservations as a personal insult, and opened hostilities by taking two paces back from the wicket, snatching off his hat, throwing it on the floor, and howling, "Je-sus Kurrrist! What the hell do you mean, only five!"

"I'm sorry, sir," said the clerk, who looked like the reconstituted corpse of the Artful Dodger. "Five is all I find."

"Find! You couldn't find your ass with both hands!"

"And another thing," Rexfordia piped. "I've got a dog!"

"And I," Arnie cried, "have two wombats with the measles!"

That did it for the Artful Dodger. He went slinking off down the counter after his despairing gaze and sent Fagin into the breach. A man in the line behind Kermit started to grumble and Kermit turned and roared, "And you shut the hell up!" The man shut up, and Fagin came on smiling. "What seems to be the trouble here?" he said amiably.

"What the hell do you mean what's the trouble? Can't that other moribund jackass talk?" Kermit pointed dramatically at the Artful Dodger. He dodged artfully out a back door.

"Well, yes. He told me. But I just wanted to be sure we had it right," Fagin said, the area between his eyebrows beginning to twitch.

"Right! Jesus Christ! You people haven't gotten anything right since Orville and Wilbur!"

"And up your bucket, too!" Arnie cried at another clerk, of obviously high rank, who now appeared at the back door, covering his purply bald head with an official cap. He scowled at Arnie and said, in a sort of backfiring whine, "Now, see here, sir."

"Kiss my trachea," Arnie said gleefully.

"Holy Christ!" Kermit howled, slapping his forehead. "Look at this vacant-eyed horse-faced bastard!"

"Sir, I'm Mr. Shotwell. What . . ."

"Are you the chief jackass?"

"Yes. No!"

"He's a zebra!" Arnie cried.

At about this point, Solly broke into tears and said she definitely wouldn't go, Aubrey offered to ride in tourist class (to Rexfordia's horror), and Van Buren snapped at a boy who was sticking his finger into his cage. It was all resolved when the man behind Kermit said *he* would ride in tourist class because he'd feel safer there anyway. He didn't elaborate, but the inference was clear, and Kermit glowered at him and said that it was very nice of the man, and how would he like a swift kick in the ass? The man mumbled about lack of gratitude, exchanged his ticket, and scurried away, thereby clearing the field for the second, or Van Buren, phase of the conflict, rapidly followed by the Solly phase, the excess baggage phase, and the Julie phase, the last being a grand finale with a supporting cast of airport cops brought on when an elderly gentleman complained to Julie about the delay and Julie told him to go shit in his homburg.

Solly was helped onto the airplane by a steward who, his eyes all tumwater and nerve ends, looked wholly uncertain that he was doing the right thing or, even if he were, that the right thing was in this case the right thing. For Solly appeared about to expire. Her eyes were swampy and rolling, her hands flailing, sowing liberally the grub-white beads of her ruptured rosary, and from between her rigid lips came the sound of a banshee. The steward engineered her toward the seat next to Arnie's.

"She's in your party, isn't she?" the steward asked mournfully, the undertaker to the next of kin.

"Never saw her before in my life," Arnie said.

"Oh, now, *look, please*," the steward said desperately. He stood there, swaying at the knees, eyes going a bit wild, one hand stabbing the air off to one side, grasping.

"There it goes," Arnie said, pointing at the overhead.

"What? What?" the steward said.

"The end of your tether," Arnie said.

"In the name of the Father and of the Son and of the Holy Ghost, so be it!" Solly said and, blessing herself elaborately, abandoned her person backward into the seat. She struck like the collapse of Jericho, and the first shock was immediately followed by a rendering of metals and meshes, as Solly saw it through to the horizontal, the seat shifting rapidly through all reverse gears. And there lay Solly, terrified, staring up into the eyes of the woman behind her, huffing like a beached whale, and calling upon the Mother of God to witness her plight and strike down her tormentors.

Restoring Solly to her feet required four men, a sedative, and solemn assurances that she could stand up all the way to Chicago (Solly had had to be told that there would be a stopover in Chicago, which was not true, and that she could get off there if she decided to). Arnie and Kermit agreed that the raising of Solly, in its complexity, compared favorably, by historical accounts, with the extraction of William Howard Taft from his bathtub. The seat, it developed, was still operational and a man in white coveralls came with a new sprocket, or whatever, and said the seat was okay just before Solly decided that her feet were tired and she would sit down after all. But the steward said a new seat might be more to her liking, and led her across the aisle, and winked spastically at Aubrey as he lowered her into the seat beside him and strapped her down. Then the steward started to edge away. But, just here, Solly began to sniff the air, and her nose to quiver. "Wait a goddamned minute," she said. "I smell kerosene!"

"No, no, ma'am," the steward said, too loudly, his face almost cracking right down the bridge of his nose. "That—that's, I mean, what you smell . . ." His head lolled and cracked the other way in a hideously hypocritical smile. "That's just *jet* fuel."

"Don't tell me, you goddamned blatherskite. I know kerosene when I smell it."

The steward edged over carefully, flicking one eye like the tongue of a short dog. "Madam, I assure you, it's jet-fuel."

Solly took a profoundly capacious sniff. "Kerosene!"

"But, madam," the steward said, imploring, tentative, very near to tears, "jet fuel is kerosene."

"Well, now, that's what I say. . . ." Then, the lost soul confronting the final horror, she achieved total comprehension. "Kerosene?" she screamed, and started to pitch and plunge in her seat, bringing more sounds of metal rending up from below. "You hear that? Sweet jingling Jaysus! They're going to feed the bastard kerosene!" The steward fled, crying, quite possibly, kerosene tears.

The seat was preserved from extraction, floor plates and all, only by the arrival of Rexfordia, who had been seeing Van Buren safely into the baggage compartment or wherever. Rexfordia got Solly to hold still and listen, and explained that jet fuel was a very special kind of kerosene, full of vitamins, minerals, and polyunsaturates, and guaranteed by *Good Housekeeping*. Solly noted that the airplane was already taxiing toward the runway, and swore for a time, then closed her eyes, and said it was all right as long as she could sit next to Rexfordia. So Aubrey gave up his seat and went over to Arnie, who was sitting, hard-eyed, in an aisle seat.

"Oh, Lord Christ," Arnie said. "I suppose the seer of the Sahara will want the window seat."

"Not if you do," Aubrey said, waiting in the aisle.

"No, no. Go ahead," Arnie said, moaning. "You need the exposure. Only, for Jesus' sake, don't tell me what you see."

Aubrey climbed over him, fell back, fastened himself in. "I never volunteer information."

"I know that. I know it well," Arnie groaned. "It's the misinformation that bothers me."

"I wish that were all that bothered me about you," Aubrey said easily.

"What the hell is *that* supposed to mean?" Arnie had cranked himself up and around to stare at Aubrey close range.

"It means your performance in the terminal, and your encouragement of Kermit and Julie, was as nice a tantrum as I've ever seen you throw. All you needed was short pants."

"Oh Christ," Arnie said, heaving himself back into his slouch. "I thought you had something serious on your mind." He blew out an exasperation of air, and closed his eyes.

"It's serious, Arnie. None of those people deserved what they got. It's just damned arrogant, snobbish . . ."

"Oh balls! It's survival of the fittest, and I'm tired, and for Christ's sake can the horseshit so I can sleep. Those people will never be the same, but any change in them had to be an improvement, right? So relax. It's a long way to Seward's Folly, and fighting and bickering all the way. I need my rest."

And he appeared to go promptly to sleep. Aubrey turned to the window and brooded through much of the takeoff, brooded until he was too scared to brood, what with both wings wagging, and with the airplane rolling on forever and then snapping its nose up with an awful thud amidships and screaming toward the vertical. He slumped in his seat, the fear rising in him, his closed eyes full of a vision of the four huge, vacuum-cleaner engines consuming kerosene at a marvelous rate and exhausting the supply and quitting just over the Triborough Bridge, until the airplane had gone straight out to sea for a time and hovered there, and then, its courage gathered, had banked and come about and taken on the continent. And somewhere between that time and the time—probably over Pennsylvania—when the pilot had begun to describe the route and weather conditions, he leaned forward and looked out and down.

And for most of the six hours it required to cross the continent he was looking down, seeing it all at once, all of a piece, for the first time. And what he couldn't see, he imagined he saw.

And in the East it was the shock of the city, the great Eastern city that began on the coast and spread like a gray blight, sprawling, smoky, dirty, and rotting always from the center outwards, stretching its endless corridors clear across the coastal plain and into the foothills of the great Appalachian Range and beyond it, losing ground and green grass in eastern Pennsylvania and Ohio, missing here and there a river so that it sparkled silver instead of dirty gray, gaining again in Cleveland and Toledo and all along the edge of the incorruptible lake, subsiding once more across the mottled top of Indiana and raising hope that it was over at last until Gary gave warning that there had merely been a respite before the worst shock of all, Chicago, the black, belching, cancerous, western extremity of the appalling Eastern city.

And the time of the East was the present, settled long ago and living for the future, yet preparing—like one gigantic, despairing, soot-filled engine of war—for none.

And in the Midwest it was the sweet, fat richness of the land, all the promise of the dreams of centuries fulfilled and surpassed and overflowing, six hundred and forty acres to the golden brown square, bursting with life out of the heart of the earth Mother, all across western Illinois, and Iowa, and Minnesota, and South Dakota, and Nebraska farther south, watered by the sky-blue roll of the wide Missouri and crawling, loam-filled, swole-belly fertility of the Mississippi, wandering pregnantly through the lush of this great northern land like a peaceful, fat blacksnake looking for a muddy delta in which to take its rest.

And the time of the Midwest was yesterday, settled yesterday and living in yesterday, in that hour of gentle, tender innocence before America learned that other nations, other peoples, had designs upon

227

its dream, before it discovered that the horn of plenty made a sound heard round the world; and it was the land of the black spring mud, and the tall corn in August and the fat hogs in the fall. And the land, too, of the November wind whispering winter through the broken cornstalks across the eternity of flat forgotten fields, sweeping unobstructed a thousand miles down across Saskatchewan and North Dakota, frigid winds just two hours out of Moose Jaw. The land of the wide summer evening, too, when the very sweetness of the air and the enormity of that vast tent of star-hung sky seemed to threaten—terrible much had been given and terrible much would be taken away—and the traveler outside Grand Island, for fear of the vortex and the dreadful pan flashes of heat lightning in the night sky over North Platte and beyond, took to early shelter.

And in the West, the Far West and especially the Northwest, it was the plain and splendid fact of the wilderness that still remained and the mountains that guard its approaches, rising in Montana out of the valley of the Yellowstone, and in Wyoming out of the Big Horns, standing higher westward in Idaho and Oregon and Washington, and standing even higher to the south in Colorado and Utah; rock-ribbed majesties dividing the continent; the Rockies, the Cascades, the Sierra Nevada, the Bitterroot Range, the Wasatch Range, the Grand Tetons, Mount Whitney, Mount Hood, Mount Rainier, and Sacajawea Peak, all snow-graced and bountiful, watersheds to the waiting lands beneath: the Missouri out of Three Forks, Montana; the Rio Grande out of Creede, Colorado; the Arkansas out of Leadville, Colorado; the Colorado out of Rocky Mountain National Park; the Snake out of Teton County, Wyoming; water down from the snowfields, running under the sun across the blue ice of the glaciers, taking channel before the wind in the fissures of the high, cold rock, gathering as it went, plunging into a thousand feet of startled air, its passage quiet and sublimely arched over the tree line, until it came to thunderous white in the boiling, foam-whitened fury of the gorge below; and then it was the seething, outraged, wildest force in all of nature, roaring downward, cutting its own steep banks, gouging, rending, washing away, growing ever darker, rushing with terrible power into the wide valleys and even into the plains and cutting there its own valleys a mile down deep and ten miles wide after two million years of fury; water down from the snowfields and the sky, sweetening the land, and every year delivering two million tons of that American soil to the oceans.

And the time of the West was the past, not yet settled and living for the past; not merely the past of the mountain men and the Indian wars and the covered wagons racing the snow to Oregon: but the remoter past when the wilderness was utterly unspoiled, and the buffalo ran in their herds of thousands, and the red men made the only human tracks for a thousand years; the same land that John Muir found when he walked the highest ridge of the Sierra Nevada and paused in a mountain snowfield and found himself in the Stone Age. And the land, too, of the vast salt wastes of Nevada and Utah and even Oregon, the Great Basin of bleak gray-white desert, pocked with gigantic heat bubbles that burst thousands of years before Christ; and here and there the salt lakes, shores empty, desolate, unvisited, forbidding; the gray roads running in their hundreds nowhere, blocked by drifted earth, gouged and ragged, like meteor tracks on the surface of the moon; the wet land, too, of the rain forest, and of the fog coming onto the beaches and scaling the cliffs to the moorlands and the mountains, and taking cover there under the evergreens and among the ferns in those redwood forests that have stood two thousand years; and of the foghorns calling tremulously each to each from Port Angeles to Coos Bay to the Golden Gate Bridge to Big Sur and beyond: the final land, the end of all the trails, where the pioneers had no choice but to turn about and set to work on the dream.

He watched until the airplane had banked south to its final approach over San Francisco Bay, then sat back in his chair to fasten his seat belt and rub his stiff neck, and found Arnie peeking at him out of one eye, smiling evilly.

"Well, Jesus Christ, Aubie. You got it all memorized?"

"What?"

"The country! The goddamned terrain! Every time I opened an eye, there you were like a refugee at a porthole. A couple of times there I damned near stood up and rendered 'America, the Beautiful.' "

"If I'd only known," Aubrey said, "I'd have made a formal request."

"Do! Do that! I can still render it."

"I meant a request for a parachute."

"Ah, Aubie. You get bugged so easily. I know I intruded upon your hour of ecstasy, ruined the sweet glow you'd generated by long and diligent contemplation of our nation's natural wonders. And all that bullshit. But! I had good reason. I've just thought up the official name for my personal philosophy, and my first thought—my first—

was that you should be the second man in the tide of times to know it." Arnie's grin was seraphic. "Generous of me? Aren't you ashamed of yourself? I should say."

"I don't like being second."

"Yes, well, you'll just have to live with it. Now! The word is—ready? Selfiscientism! Right? Selfiscientism! Ain't it a beaut? See what you can accomplish by sleeping?"

"It's a beaut. What's it mean?"

"How the hell do I know what it means? I'm not done living yet, for Christ's sake!"

And Arnie refused to discuss it further, and rendered "America, the Beautiful" all the way in to the hotel.

# · TWENTY ·

HE WAS STRETCHED on the bed, looking at two Mark Hopkins flies on the ceiling, when the telephone rang. It was Arnie.

"Aubie? Listen, I'm not about to go to that fink's bachelor dinner. How about joining me in a sneak to a good restaurant?"

"Great notion. Best news I've heard today."

"Good. I've been devoting my meditations to you and the African bit. I want to get it all straight in my lost mind before I tried to say anything definitive. I'm ready for you now."

"I've been hoping you'd have more to say."

"I *always* have more to say. I even wrote some of this down. I'll have a portfolio of selected prose for your reading enjoyment."

"I'm looking forward. When?"

"How's an hour? I'll hit the Kermit for some cash and meet you at the front desk."

"I'll be front."

Arnie hung up. The two flies were gone. Gone to the heart of an apple.

Minutes later, he thought he heard a knock at the door, and jumped up and brushed off the shanks of his pants and went across the room with a stalking step, as if he had just awakened from sleep. He pulled the door open. There was no one in the hall. He leaned out and peered left and right, down straight miles of grillwork baroque carpets of an off-vermilion shade rising at either end, he told himself, straight into Gimbel's basement. No one or thing of any mortality whatsoever. Then the knocking again, behind him. Well, what the hell? Poltergeists? He turned and went back into the room.

"Well, for Christ's sake, open up!"

It was Julie's voice, emanating, apparently, from a closet. He went to the door, pulled on it, found it locked, turned a thing for turning, pulled open the door, and there stood Julie, in the next room.

"What the hell," she said amiably. "Have I interrupted your twilight diddle?"

"I thought this was another closet," Aubrey said. "Is that your room?"

"No, it's just another closet. So it's almost that time, step." She was wearing a suit with a fur collar, and she ran her fingers in and out of the fur over either breast and smiled up at him as if she had just said something very clever.

"What time?" Aubrey asked, loosening his muscles to the rear in case Julie meant what he thought she meant.

"Arnie time. Didn't you talk to him just now?"

"No." He hadn't intended to lie.

"Sure you did. He told me he'd try you again as soon as I hung up. He got my room by mistake. Shook him up a little when I answered. And I heard your phone ring."

"Well, he didn't. It was a wrong number." Aubrey cleared his throat, annoyed with the high pitch of his voice, realizing that he was reacting to the beautiful length of her hair, floating about her shoulders in incredibly soft and intricate curls, and realizing that she knew—with her blatantly primitive assessment of all things pertaining to him—the thermal units to the nearest decimal he was just then striving not to put out. And he resented it, for both moral and personal reasons, and summoned up his horsepower, raced his motor, threw out his very best Thomistic clutch, skipped two gears and put his reaction into fifth gear forward. "And how in hell does it happen that you and I share a connecting door?"

"My affection for you dictated it, step," Julie said without hesitation. "I mean, when you start spreading your potent spirituality up and down the avenues of this ultimate city of the Western world, with your unkempt hair splaying out boyishly behind you in the Pacific breezes, why, I can just see some Peninsula jet-set redhead taking public pity upon you and leading you, as de Sade says, to her very own private barber. You know what I mean, step?"

"Look, Julie," Aubrey said, concentrating upon a white area just above the bridge of her nose, it being the most chaste neutral expanse of her person he could find, "I am perfectly capable of taking care of myself, thank you. And what's this about Arnie?"

"Why, I'm not sure, step, but Rexfordia told me at the beauty parlor that Arnie was going to make you see the error of your ways."

"What ways?"

"Don't you mean what error?" She seemed to come closer to him without really moving. "I don't know, step, but Rexie says Arnie's been writing things down all week and is going to read them to you, and after he does you won't want to go to Africa any more."

"Who's going to Africa?"

"Oh, Rexie thinks they'll accept you. At least she's afraid they will."

"I'm encouraged."

"You shouldn't be."

"I was kidding."

"I wasn't."

"Julie—you know, I almost never know what you're talking about," he said sarcastically.

"It's easy, step. I mean that no matter what your mother thinks or Arnie does, I've got plans for you."

Aubrey groaned and walked away to a window and stood there looking out at the half-finished spire of a large white stone church off a quarter of a mile to his left. "Julie, will you do me a big favor?"

"Not unless it's the favor I have in mind," she said, pouting a pout that seemed to gather everything of her to it from her lips to her pelvis. "You know what that is?"

"No, and I don't want to know."

"Of course you know. I can tell by the hitch in your chastity belt."

Aubrey turned on her, waving the palms of both hands. "All right, all right!" He glowered at her between his hands. "Listen, Julie. I'm sure you think this is very cute and amusing and all the rest, but I'm getting tired of it. Damned tired. I am not amused. In the first place, I'm your stepbrother. In the second place, I'm a Roman Catholic. In the third place, I intend to become a priest. Aren't those points clear to you yet? Isn't it clear to you that until you're ready to start acting toward me as a sister *should* act toward her brother, I don't give two toots in hell what plans you might have for me?" He wheeled sharply around and walked away toward a bureau, carrying with him a rare picture of Julie astonished. "Now, if you'll get back in your room and close the door, I've got to get dressed for dinner." He braced himself. But when she spoke, she sounded entirely in possession of her temper.

"Step, you're the last of the great self-deceivers. You are no more going to become a priest than I am St. Rita."

"Is that right?" Aubrey half turned to her. "Well, welcome to the club, Julie. Just get in line with the rest."

"Not because you're not capable of it. I believe you are," she said quietly. "I really believe you are."

Aubrey was flattered in spite of his will not to be. "I am overwhelmed. I do hope you'll pardon my stupidity, but if I'm determined to become a priest and I'm, as you say, capable of becoming a priest, why won't I become a priest?"

"Because you don't want to. Simple?"

"Oh, God!" He put one hand to his forehead. "So I'm being psychoanalyzed!" He shook his head. "Okay, Julie. I understand now. You want to play your little game, your little sex game, with me, so you can enjoy a little fringe titillation. Right? Hence you decide that I don't really want to become a priest so that you won't feel anything but righteousness in tempting me away from it. Right?"

"Wrong. Besides, I'm not playing any little game, and you know it."

"Oh, I beg your pardon! I didn't mean to intimate that should I suddenly turn aggressive, you would back off. Oh no. On the contrary, I'm certain you'd take incest in your stride like a trouper."

"I *told* you you could be a son of a bitch without half trying."

"You're a good judge of character."

"But I forgive you, step darling." She came toward him, her smile dazzling and annoyingly warm, her head cocked as if estimating him for mineral content, her jade eyes catlike and dancing. "This is the end of the line for you, Aubie. You just ran out of continence. Right here, in this ultimate city of the Western world, is where you, step, are going to meet your maker." She giggled, standing behind him, regarding him in the mirror hung over the bureau, and ran her hands up and down the fur collar of her suit.

Aubrey glanced at her several times in the mirror, then turned to face her. "Julie, would you please tell me something? Just tell me one thing? Why pick on me? There must be ten thousand men, young and old, who would be delighted to oblige you in your slightest whim. Why bother me?"

"Because, step," she said, wide-eyed, as if explaining something perfectly obvious, "I like virgins. Especially nice handsome succulent virgins who are stepbrothers and going to Alaska with me for a long secluded hunt. Does that narrow it down enough, or should I throw in the added attractions, like priest-seducing and incest and . . ."

Aubrey whirled to the bureau and with only slight awareness that he was making a dramatic gesture (and that awareness too late to be a motive) brought both doubled fists down on top of it, on the sides of his hands, causing an ashtray to go into a pittering dance that mocked the blow's proper echo. "Julie! Damn it, will you listen? I'm well aware that you go back to your privacy, if you've got any, after you've had your little sexy sessions with me and just giggle yourself into girlish fits over what an innocent jackass I am! And that's all right with me! The giggles, I mean! I don't give a tinker's torque how much you giggle, or what you think of me! Only arrange to get your giggling in from now on without my assistance, because I'm all done talking to you! I've given you every chance and opportunity to straighten up and treat me as if I were an intelligent, sincerely motivated, reasonably liberal individual, but you have insisted upon treating me as if I were some kind of Mongoloid idiot who hasn't even learned yet what he wants to do and why he wants to do it! You come waltzing in here rubbing your breasts at me and expect me, apparently, to roll over and start slavering!" He turned to her, not quite looking at her, and pointed a finger in her general direction. "Well, let me tell you something. You don't impress me a damned bit, except unfavorably, as a postpubertal, preadolescent, simpering stupe of a schoolgirl who's just discovered sex and thinks the world owes her a medal! You think you threaten me? By God, I could lead you forty miles through a wilderness of mattresses and perfume and you naked and oiled and pouting your damnedest, and I'd never be tempted, by my good Lord Christ, to so much as lift my visor and take a look! Now, to the rear march, little girl, and woggle your fat ass out of here before I throw you out!" And he turned around quickly—catching only a glimpse of her wide-angry eyes and her

235

lovely jaw set helmet-hard—and almost expected a blow in the back of his head, and waited, and braced, and sighed with relief as the connecting door was slammed with a report that must have sent seismologists for miles around rushing to their instruments.

Then, for no reason he could agree on, he found himself grinning at his reflection in the mirror, and abruptly felt more certain about his vocation than he had since Father Bogart's parting words. Then a knock. Arnie had sent up a dress suit.

He was informed at the desk that Arnie had gone on to the restaurant, and walked to it at the doorman's direction, and found Arnie behind a bottle of Dom Pérignon 1947, already well along in the sampling. He apologized for being late, but Arnie wouldn't hear an apology and, smiling benevolently, poured him champagne and toasted Aubrey's presence, his decision to go to Alaska, and his future, whatever that might be. Then Arnie explained that the restaurant was supposed to have something to do with Tangier. "And I did want you to feel that you are, Aubie, however westward your course, getting closer to Africa—if you're still set on it—all the swinging time." Aubrey only nodded and sipped and smiled. "Ah— I'm sorry, Aubie, I was too crocked to come to the telephone and talk Thursday night. Rexie gave me the best account she could of what you told her, but she'd been drinking double martinis all afternoon and wasn't too coherent."

"I noticed that. She wasn't even able to conceal her satisfaction that the Saharans hadn't welcomed me with cantatas."

"She's drinking too much these days. But, then again, who the hell isn't?" He signaled the waiter, ordered another bottle, and was silent for a time, regarding Aubrey with narrowed eyes, his fingers playing along the edges of an ashtray. Then he hunched forward to his elbows and looked into his glass. "Except, of course, Aubie. He's not drinking nearly enough, in view of his recent bitter experience with the saviors of the Sahara."

"I figure the champagne will do for me."

"Oh, it'll do, Aubie. It'll do. But it won't always do, you know."

"How so?"

"Why, have you ever thought about your alternatives in terms of alcohol? If you don't become a priest, well, if you're like me—and you are, Aubie, you are—but more of that later. If you're like me, it'll take a hell of a lot more than champagne with dinner to assuage your sorrows. And if you do become a priest, why, there's just no other consumer of alcoholic beverage in the world, collectively speaking, to compare with the Roman Catholic clergy."

"Oh, I don't know, Arnie. Most priests I know are reasonably sober people."

"But the altar wine, Aubie. Have you ever thought what the consumption of altar wine must be in the course of just one day?"

"Arnie, for Pete's sake . . ."

"Not a moment but that somewhere in the world a chalice is being raised on high, not a moment but that two or three scuppers of wine are being consumed by some priest . . ."

"Arnie, for God's sake . . ."

"Well, Aubie, it's alcohol, isn't it? The accidents of wine remain, don't they?"

Aubrey sighed and looked away. "Well, sure they do."

"So, if you'll pardon my callousness, you, as a priest, will all your life be two or three drinks up on the faithful every morning. Right?"

Aubrey's shoulders felt, suddenly, very heavy. He slipped down against the leather of the booth, his eyes batting, his voice just audible. He nodded grimly. "Arnie, I don't want to argue tonight. Yes, yes. I will surely be two or three drinks up on the faithful every morning. A fringe benefit of the priesthood, you might say."

"I don't want to argue either, Aubie. But it is, after all, wine."

"Okay," Aubrey said, barely heard. Then, after the briefest pause and more audibly, "But it is also, as you damned well know, after the consecration, the blood of Christ. I enter that for the record, Arnie. I wouldn't want you to think I'd forgotten."

Arnie sat silent and composed, turning his glass slowly, watching Aubrey, and the amusement left his eyes. Now they were troubled, in motionless search, exactly penetrating, as if Arnie were trying to read his brother's soul, his mind, his whole disposition, hoping either that he would not find Aubrey wanting, or else hoping that he would. And Aubrey was bothered by Arnie's eyes and didn't try to meet them. And he found himself thinking about a day on a picnic when he was small and sailing a new boat in some utterly still pond, and the boat was not moving, its tiny sail as calm and unruffled as the water, and his one terror that Solly would call and say that it was time to go home before a wind came. Then, suddenly, a raindrop and another, and he refused to believe it. Surely not raindrops. That would cut the day short. But that? Was that another? And in a moment there were thousands, and the storm. And Solly was calling. And in Arnie's eyes he had seen the first drop and then another and, watching him now, he felt certain of the storm.

"You look very secular in that suit. I think I ought to give it to you."

"Thanks for sending it over. That black one needed a cleaning."

"Good fit?"

"Perfect."

"Just another one of the ways in which we are alike."

"I think we're getting to look more alike."

"I'd noticed. The two eggs will grow back together, or I should say, will grow together for the first time."

"We might even end up in the Sahara together. On adjoining oases."

"You have just won the engraved cobweb for the most involuted thinking of the year."

"You put it beyond possibility?"

"I put it beyond conceptualization."

"I demur."

"I wouldn't believe you were awake if you weren't demurring to something, Aubie. Especially to something I had to say. That's the story of our lives. Arnie proposes, Aubie demurs." Arnie lowered his gaze and put his lower lip between his teeth. He smoothed his tie with one hand, and pulled himself up against the table. "You know, I remember one night up in Kaatskill County. . . . It was after dinner, and Eulalia was talking as usual, and you were out of the room for some reason, and Eulalia pointed her old chin at me in that crazy imperial messianic way of hers, and said, 'Arnie will be something remarkable. He will join those on the ramparts.' Whatever she meant I never asked her and never intend to. But I was embarrassed because it was an odd thing for her to say, almost as odd as my being embarrassed, and I excused myself and went out on the dock. It was September and we were about to go back to our sophomore year at the Academy, and I remember the smell of burnt leaves and the Hudson was calm and cold and reflecting the stars. And there was a train on the New York Central tracks across the river, blowing its bullhorn as it went through Stockport. I thought of autumn and the long winter, and there was a mist on the water, like the fog tonight, drifting and drifting like—like the souls of dead summers. I was fourteen and I think that that was the first time I ever really seriously thought that I might become a priest. And I got excited and went inside and told Eulalia and she said, 'Jesus Christ, you damned fool, what's remarkable about becoming a goddamned priest?' " Arnie smiled forlornly. "And from that moment I was determined to become the most remarkable goddamned priest who ever was. Oh, not just to show Eulalia, or to make Rexie happy. But because I'd suddenly realized, as Eulalia was speaking, that the priesthood was a pretty remarkable business. And I told you about it, and you fell right in with it, eagerly, so damned eagerly that it never really occurred to me that I might have influenced you far too much."

"I wish you'd forget about it, Arnie. If you did, it was the biggest favor you ever did me."

"Yes, yes, maybe. But suppose I'd decided to do you another favor. I was the prime mover. Let's not go through admitting that again. I had all the initiative. You were the contemplator. There was enough right there in the Fort Milligan compound to keep you occupied for years. But not me, Aubie. Not me. I got around. More than you've ever known. More than I've ever felt free, or objective, or sorry, enough to tell you. Suppose I'd decided to do you the favor of helping you to lose your virginity? Suppose I'd decided on *that* favor, Aubie? Do you think you'd ever have gotten near a seminary?"

Aubrey was not sure what he was hearing. "Did I miss a word somewhere, Arnie? How could you have helped me to lose my virginity?"

"A hell of a lot easier than you think."

He looked at Aubrey sharply as if he expected an objection, then looked away, his chin snapping, and ordered the wine poured. The waiter wondered when they would like to order and Arnie instructed him to bring them both lobster tails Baghdad when a third bottle of champagne became necessary. The waiter approved that arrangement, and went off to inform the chef.

"Arnie, don't you think three bottles is a little excessive, even for two potential drunken priests?"

"Aubie, please don't—please *don't*—kid me with that potential priest bit. I will blow my goddamned head off on the morning of my ordination if I am ever goddamned fool enough to con myself back into a seminary, and get through it. I promise you that. Blow my finking head off with the oil wet on my hands." He sipped his champagne, without a glance at Aubrey, then downed the glassful in several quick gulps. He reached out to the silver ice bucket, took the bottle from it, snatched the towel from the bottle, inspected the label, nodded, threw the towel on the floor, filled his glass and Aubrey's and put the bottle on the table between them. "Goddamned waiter let it get too cold."

Then a silence, and after it Arnie's most extraordinary performance since the night at Kermit's house.

"You remember Miss Conroy, don't you, Aubie? Sure you do. That pony-legged, soft-eyed little thing from Cliffside? How could you forget, after Rexfordia put us over the coals that day? Well, for a while it was all innocence. The only intelligent girl choir member and the only intelligent second tenors in the state of New Jersey. Oh, it was idyllic for a time. Wasn't it? Sweetness and light and long conversations about the lonely sentinel of the tabernacle and how we, you and I—brave, stalwart, pure-thighed, and bold—were going to go forth and defend His sacred honor. Oh, Jesus yes, the purity of some of those colloquies on the stone steps of the church on those long, star-sweet summer evenings must have been damned near orgiastic. The bowel-melting pleasure of it all. And then there came the summer when we were all seventeen, and she was graduating, and we were just entering our senior year. And you probably don't remember, but that was the summer of Miss Conroy's discontent. Her breasts were out, not far but far enough, and her hips were round and her eyes were full of that glorious I've-got-juices-of-all-conceivable-flavors-in-my-can girlishness. You didn't see it, I'm sure, but I saw it. And I saw, too, something that bothered me a hell of a lot more than her juices. And that was that she liked you far more than she did me. I mean, that she was titillated more by me, and more intrigued, and more basically drawn—like Eve to the snake, if I may plunge into rash originality—but she liked you better. Maybe, with that old-as-the-earth awareness that all little girls have, she simply knew that my intentions were not even slightly honorable. She knew that my only interest in her grand junction was to unload my boxcars and get to hell out. Oh, she knew, and she let me know that she knew. Not that she wasn't, like all ripe little girls, given to flirting with sudden deflowerment. It started with a few innuendoes on my part. Like 'Gee, don't boys have it lucky? They don't have to worry about—well, you know, things—things like having to wear a bra and all.' Let me point out here that I was still a virgin, too. But we'd talk around the erotic centers as seriously as if we were discussing the virgin birth, and she went so far once as to ask me how long a boy's penis was, and so on. And then I told her a few dirty jokes and once when she was sitting between us in a movie I took her hand and scratched her palm and she hooked her little finger in mine and squeezed. And I thought I would expire with anticipation on that and many an occasion, Aubie, but she always pulled back. And when she would pull back she would go to you, and ignore me, for days at a time, as if I were the foulest blemish on God's creation. You were the poet, the holy innocent, the shining knight who could fork his horse day after day and never become aware of his fork. And there were times, Aubie mine, when I was certain you were faking it, times when I was positive you were laying her in the back of the La Salle, times when I was sure that you were both ridiculing and laughing at me when, in my presence, you would go into those long goddamned disquisitions on chastity and the sweet rewards to those who went to heaven virgins. There were times, Aubie, when I could have slain you, bloodily, with a blunt tree limb, and never felt the slightest qualm. There were nights when I got out of bed and went over to your bed and stood over you and looked down at you sleeping and cursed you, and put curses upon you, and sought to make pacts with the Devil if he would only cause you to die of spinal meningitis or Scourby's Horror or something equally painful. There were times, Aubie, when I was so goddamned jealous of you, not only because of Miss Conroy's attraction to you, but also because of the very purity that attracted her, that I could have, by God, pushed you into that snake pit we saw in that Bengal lancer movie. You remember that, Aubie? I'll never forget it. There is no death I wouldn't prefer to that one. Yet I could have shoved you to the snakes, I hate you so much." He looked up, almost pleased in his surprise. "Hear that, Aubie? I used the present tense. What do you make of that, Aubie?" He shook his head sorrowfully. He smiled a brief smile that seemed to strengthen him, then he moved to the issue primary in a single short sentence. "I raped Miss Conroy one late August afternoon just before she went up to Ladycliff." He glanced at Aubrey once, his eyes immense with something mixed out of shame and male pride, and went on to his champagne with small sniffings and forced en-

241

joyment. Then he broke like a bubble and was, abruptly, humble and abject. "We were swimming out at the lake, and Roger came to get you early to take you to the dentist. And, if you remember, Miss Conroy was a tiger in the water. Christ, she could swim me into circles, although I think you could do a little better. Anyway, as soon as you were gone, she challenged me to a race to the raft, and by God I was still on my way out when she was on her way back, and I spent damned near an hour on the raft trying to coax my lungs out of their collapse, and I could see her watching me for a while, and then she went off to have a coke with Lambert—Eddie Lambert—you remember him. Tobacco Road with muscles. Well, I just stayed out on that raft, and sometimes I would get off and swim around it, until I was all rested, and until I figured I had maybe thirty minutes before Roger showed up. Then I swam very slowly back to shore, and I found Miss Conroy sitting in the shadows near the boathouse dock. And she was wearing this white bathing suit and there was almost no one else around, and she said that she'd waited for me because she was going off to college in two weeks and wanted to say goodbye, and especially wanted me to say goodbye to you for her. And then she got up and started to walk away, and I simply grabbed her by the arm and led her into the boathouse and said that there was something I wanted to show her. And she came along, Aubie, willingly. I mean, she was a fairly big girl and I couldn't have dragged her if she hadn't wanted to come. And she kept saying what, what, what do you want to show me? But I knew that she knew what I wanted to show her, and when I kissed her, she kissed me back, and when I stripped her bathing suit off her breasts she let me kiss them. But then she wanted to stop, and it didn't seem to be a good idea to me, and I didn't stop. And I raped her there, on a pile of boat cushions. She was a virgin, and she cried, and all that. But she wanted to know if she'd see me again when Roger started tooting the horn. And I told her I'd sneak out if she'd sneak out, and two nights later there she was at the fence behind the garage, and I let her in, and we screwed in the back seat of the La Salle every night until she went off to Ladycliff. We even screwed on our next swimming day, a week after the first time, when Rexfordia came with us, and you and Rexie were out on the raft and we went right into the boathouse in broad daylight and screwed for damned near an hour. And the night before she left she told me she loved me, and I told her I didn't love her, and she cried, but she went off to Ladycliff, and I never saw her again. But I saw in the Hackensack newspaper where she married some jackass from Paterson, and she's probably a good Catholic mother now, with four kids and a diaphragm."

Arnie held up one hand as Aubrey started to speak and permitted him to say no more than "Arnie, what's important is . . ."

"What's important is that I finish. Succinctly. One night I got to talking to her about you. We were in the La Salle and we'd already screwed twice, and I told her that I'd told you all about it, and that you had said that you'd love to screw her, too. That you had absolutely no scruples with reference to it, and that you'd only respect her the more if she'd let you. And she sat there, with her flower-print dress clutched around her legs, saying that oh no, you weren't that kind, you would never think of such a thing, so that I told her about all the girls who had offered themselves, naked of course, to us, and how you'd refused every one of them, as I had, but that she—Miss Conroy—was an exception. That there was something mystic among the three of us, that the friendship would be broken, or something, if she didn't at least talk to you about it, right there, in the back of the La Salle. And I must have laid on the greatest con job in the history of La Salle back seats because she finally agreed to talk to you about it. And I sneaked into the house, and clear up to our room, and woke you up, and you know what you said, Aubie? You sat straight up and stared at me and said, 'Arnie, we have to start getting in shape for cross-country tomorrow.' Then you laid your purity back down and weren't heard from again. Well, Miss Conroy was definitely disappointed, and though we screwed three or four nights after that, until she went away, she always asked for you. Even the night, the last night, when she told me she loved me. Even that night she wanted to know—oh, not in so many words, but she made it clear—if you'd changed your mind, after all, about screwing her . . ."

"Arnie, please, don't say any more."

"I won't. Except to say that I wanted you screwed because I'd been screwed. I didn't want you to have anything I didn't have. Not even virginity. Much as I was jealous of what she felt for you, I'd have willingly had you screw her, if I could only have waked you up." He sighed. "Ah, Christ, Arnie. Face it. Waking Aubie up has been one of the biggest problems of your life. And you probably

243

wouldn't have screwed her anyway. You'd probably have had another spiritual conversation." He shook his head, then ran one hand through his hair and rested it on the back of his neck. "Oh no, no. You'd have been screwed all right, Aubie. Miss Conroy was a tiger in the water, and Miss Conroy was a tiger in the back seat of that La Salle. Oh, she'd have screwed you. Maybe I knew that, too. Maybe that's what stopped me from dragging you downstairs to the garage. And suppose I'd done you that favor, Aubie? Suppose I'd done you the favor of dragging you right into Miss Conroy's favors? Do you think you'd have gotten anywhere near a seminary?"

"You did, Arnie."

"Very good. Extremely good. All right. I did get near a seminary. But you saw how long I lasted. How much of my departure—how much, for Christ's sake, of my psychosis—had its roots in my root? In Miss Conroy's fertile dust? Who the hell will ever know? I know this much, however. Once you've had it, Aubie, it's impossible to forget. Once a woman opens herself to you—once that's happened, Aubie, you're never the same. You are slightly more a man than you ever were before, and maybe much more a man. One thing is certain. You have no hope of being a *giant* of a man—a man who might rule the earth—*until* you have entered a woman. And let no one tell you any different."

"I don't want to be a giant, Arnie."

"Hah! I was just thinking. You may have no choice, Aubie, my son, if our sweet-bellied stepsister has her way. Oh, don't give me the blank eye, for Christ's sake! I can read the entrails as well as any ex-Templar. She's got you all racked and measured. And, my God, what a way to lose your virtue!"

"Arnie, I've had it all out with her. I mean, I've made it clear that—that I'm not interested in being introduced to any of her girl friends." Aubrey held his eyes as steady as he could, but Arnie was grinning right through his eyeballs and into his thoughts.

"Gallant, gallant. God, yes. I *told* you they'd revved up your uptake. So, you had it out with her? The question is did you *leave* it out?"

"Arnie! I don't think we ought to discuss it. Not in this context. You misunderstand too inferentially."

"Good, good. By God, you're becoming an opponent, Aubie! But let me be honest about our stepsister. I'd seen a picture of her long before I met her. Maybe you saw it. Je-sus! Miss Teen-Age Dental

Brace of North Hollywood. Then I met her a couple of times. They tell me. I mean, I wasn't too clear and I don't remember her from the watercress. But last year we all went up to Alaska together, and my Christ in heaven, Aubie, I couldn't believe my eyes! I've seen two surpassingly beautiful women in my life. One is Rexie, some years ago, when she was just perfectly fixed up. The other is Julie, the step-finking-sister we share in common, as it were. I mean the glow, the holy radiant glow, immeasurably beyond anything that brace-toothed picture could have become. But there she is. And the body, that incredible, luscious, air-foam, sponge-rubber, sugar-crotched body! Those long legs, heavy in the calves, but right, and that high, proud carriage of the head, so that she looks like she's about to say, 'Step aside, for Christ's sake, don't you recognize the Virgin Mary Cleopatra Magdalen when you see her?' And the pure white skin, without a fault, and the mouth and lips and cheekbones and those eyes so goddamned big that you figure she's wearing about ninety-five magnification contacts. But they're all hers—everything's all hers. And last year, Aubie, up in that thar great Alaskan boat-house, I tried to rape her, too. But she's a really big girl, Aubie, and she goddamned near unhung me forever. The details I will spare you. I will just say that if you have it among your, shall we say, mental reservations to mount her by surprise, by God, take along two Chinese eunuchs and a McClellan saddle!"

"Arnie, can we drop this subject?"

"Sure, Aubie. But, as usual, let me say one more thing about Julie. She is a girl, take my word for it—because even if you *have* noticed, you don't know what in hell it *is* that you've noticed—who needs her screwing regularly and in the grand manner. Now, for the first few days in Alaska, she'll be okay. I mean, she'll be in a mood of pleasant, outdoorsy withdrawal. And she'll don her knee socks and go stumping around the tundra, contemplatively aloof, playing Catherine to your Heathcliff, listening to your goddamned homilies as if she cared, measuring off those finking moorlands with her low boots solemnly, as though she were describing the dimensions of her grave. But then, suddenly, one day, passion will gather at the estuary and demand to know why she hasn't staged a flood lately. And on *that* day, Aubie, your virtue may well be in danger, you may become alluvial in her delta, you may walk thereafter as a giant upon the earth. And, oh Jesus God! How I will envy you *that* entrance into venereal frailty!"

Arnie blinked at him meanly. As he got drunker, Arnie's eyes seemed to recede far into their sockets, and the eyebrows seemed to droop and follow, until his eyes looked like two red, white, and blue flowers folding their petals for the night. Yet they were never quite folded, never quite asleep. All the good humor was gone from his manner now, and a certain somnolent condescension had taken its place. And his eyes were on Aubrey as the eyes of the fascinator are confident upon its victim.

"Arnie, tell them to bring the food. I can't drink any more of this without something to eat."

"Time enough for that, my boy. All night for that. So we leave the slowly undulating umbilicus of our dear stepsister, and move on to higher, less interesting things. What about that interview, Aubie, babe? What'd those sand-blasted bastards have to say?"

"They said don't call us, we'll call you."

"You know what they said to me? They said you look like a manic bastard to us. And I said, Oh shit no, I'm not manic, reverend Fathers, but my mother is. My mother taught me to be a cardinal, so I want to get out to your goddamned desert where the finking competition isn't so finking keen. I mean, she's interested in my holding sway, you understand, Fathers. Sway, indeed. And this guy who interviewed me, oh, he was big, Aubie, with huge, flabby jowls. I mean, he looked like the rear end of Laurel and Hardy. And he was French, and in his eyes were a thousand years of French maternal sentiment, a thousand years of Frenchmen who loved their mothers above all. Big, shaggy, sympathetic eyes, twin defenders of all mothers without exception. And he just couldn't understand why I would want to get the hell away from Rexfordia. . . ."

"You told them that?"

"Hell, yes. Didn't you?"

"Hell, no, Arnie. I mean, you have to be a little more subtle than that. Besides, it isn't just Rexfordia . . ."

"The hell it isn't! Don't tell me. I know your psyche like I wheeled the psyche to make it. Right? Right. So I says to this massive bastard, I says, Père? Listen. Have you ever been afraid of your mother? Yes, he says. Why, I says? Because she would punish me for doing something wrong. Right, I says. My mother, however, would punish me for doing anything at all. What do you mean, he says? I mean, I says, if I took a crap—until, by God, I was sixteen, right, Aubie?— without telling her time, place, and approximate displacement, she would punish me. How, he says? She'd beat me with her superego, I says. Oh, he says. So I try to explain. I say, Look, Father Huge, it's this way. She trades upon common decency in a way you would not believe. She contrives to make all of her intrusions appear to be founded solely in an overflowing concern for your welfare. So that to deny her—particularly at the beginning, which is the only time you really have a chance to make the slightest dent in her armor—is to put yourself in the role of the grossest kind of ingrate. She is, gross père, in fine, one of those women who would be saying the Mass if you so much as allowed them to arrange the flowers on the altar. Then he got it, or seemed to, and I went on. I says, by God, she'd climb onto the Pope's lap and wave at the populace if he so much as blessed her. He'd have to smite her with his miter to get her clear of the Vatican."

"Oh, come on, Arnie. You couldn't have said that. Or if you did, it's no damned wonder they rejected you."

"I did say it, and it was all the truth, and if they rejected me, by God, at least they knew precisely who and what it was they were rejecting. Right? Goddamned right! And I said worse. I said—and this was the truth, Aubie, as I cling by my foreskin to any sanity at all—I said, Father Huge, my nature is to bluster and to criticize and to pontificate and to seek to gain control over the minds of others. I know this as surely as I recognize the need in me to compensate for the control of my own destiny that my mother has sucked up. But I can laugh at my nature and my pretensions and my presumptions and all my thirst for power—I am certain I can—if you can just remove me to some goddamned God-forgotten place where my mother could never find me, never, not ever; if you can just promise me that the Society of the Sahara would refuse to tell my mother, ever, despite all tears, motherly protestations, and bribes, where I was hidden out. Guarantee me that, I said, and I guarantee you the humblest, most unassuming son of a bitch of a candidate you ever saw. And old Father Huge, he thought about that for a while and then he said, Well, my son, I'm sorry, but you look like a manic bastard to us."

"Do you want to know what I think?"

"Christ yes! At every finking waking moment!"

"I think, if you really told them anything like what you've said, you really didn't want to be accepted."

"Hah! You see? You, Aubie, are a goddamned ecclesiastical politician! Was anything I told them a lie?"

"Maybe not, but there are ways of . . . well, of phrasing . . ."

"Aubie, Aubie, you mean honesty, pure quill and human nature, *isn't* the best policy?"

"Sure it is, but there's such a thing as tact."

"Tact my ass! Where'd it get you, Aubie? You truckled your way right into Abraham's bosom, didn't you?"

"I'm beginning to think that maybe they couldn't see *me* for the good impression *you* left behind, Arnie!"

"I forgive you that," Arnie said very quickly, and he closed his eyes, stood up, and left the table.

Aubrey looked after him and would have cried out that he was sorry, that he hadn't meant to say such a thing, but Arnie turned when he had gone perhaps ten feet and came back to the table, smiling, nodding very slightly, drawing an envelope from his pocket as he came. He advanced until both legs were pressed against the outer edge of the table, then he tossed the envelope toward Aubrey. And he continued to smile; it went on without a quiver. It appeared fixed; a fluid thing gone solid. Then his lips moved. And very softly he spoke. "Aubie, you'll find various things in that envelope. All but one of them I wrote myself. The one I didn't write came from the office of a gentleman in Boston of whom I'm sure you've preserved some small memory. I want you to know that I had nothing to do with obtaining the Boston document. Our lovely mother, in her cups one night, telephoned him and had him send it to her special delivery. She wanted me to say that *I* had found it lying around the house. I couldn't do that to you, Aubie. And the only reason I give it to you at all is that, upon very careful reading, it worries me. Read this Boston document last, Aubie. Please. And, if you forget everything else I've said tonight, remember this: the Boston document describes a few dozen more of the ways in which you and I are very much alike . . ."

The captain of waiters arrived behind Arnie at this moment, saying, "Sir, your lobster tails."

Arnie turned to him at once. "Oh yes. Do me a favor, would you please?"

"Of course."

"Please glue the tails back on my lobsters and place them in the custody of the Sheriff of Baghdad." Arnie handed him a bill. "Keep the change." Arnie bowed to Aubrey.

"Sir, do *what* with your lobster?"

"Like I said, you and the chef play pin the tail on the lobster."

"But surely, sir, you must be joking. You don't mean . . ."

"Arnie, I'm sorry," Aubrey said. "Don't go."

"It's just as well I do, Aubie. You've got some reading to do." And Arnie patted the captain on the shoulder and sauntered out.

The captain turned and stared at Aubrey. "He's not coming back, sir?"

"I wouldn't hold my breath."

The captain looked at the one-hundred-dollar bill Arnie had given him and then at the check and back to Aubrey. "Sir, I hope you understand, I'll have to charge you for both orders of lobster?"

"That strikes me as eminently fair," Aubrey said, "in view of the fact that I intend to eat both orders. If you'll be so good as to serve them?"

"Oh? Oh, of course, sir."

The captain started to serve the lobster as Aubrey picked up Arnie's envelope, opened it, removed a sheaf of papers and began to read. And he read for more than half an hour and left the restaurant still reading. And left the lobsters untouched, and the captain of waiters damned near unstrung.

# · TWENTY-ONE ·

Arnie's envelope contained four documents.

The first was a newly typewritten carbon copy of what was apparently the first pages of Arnie's autobiography:

*As I rise now upon the dunghill of this world and point my tainted finger in the general direction of the Father, and stagger off into my two or fewer gutsy reams of travelogue, asking the while my single ancient hypostatic question about human misery, I think it only fair to admit first crack out of the bangalorum, as it were, that I am a white, non-Southern, apolitical, gentile, heterosexual schizophrenic, hence utterly without literary credentials, and that I will probably have nothing whatever to say about Buddhism, existentialism, miscegenation, communism, psychoanalysis, television, transvestitism, the Presidency, narcotics, atomic physics, segregation, the academic community, sea lions, or Jewish family life.*

*And the author wants the reader to understand at the onset that he will not be indulging in any damned self-pity. Arnie knows that self-pity is all humanism has to offer, and, ladies and gentles all, Arnie personally needs a hell of a lot more than self-pity to get him down to the end of this long ball-busting road. He doesn't know just what in the name of Christ it is that he needs, or even if it exists, but he god-*

damned sure needs it, and somebody had better come up with several thousand neatly packaged bales of it pretty finking soon or old Arnie is leaving the ship.

My credentials established, I want to say that there is nothing I intend to hide. For dear Christ Himself knows what it is like to be man alive, so what do I risk except, of course, my dignity in the eyes of all you good folks out there in no-dignity-land, to whom I would like to say, before I lose this golden opportunity, that Arnie doesn't give two toots in hell or a trumpeted goddamn what you think! Not old Arnie.

And the first thing I won't hide is that I love my brother Aubrey very much, and I want him to become a priest with all my heart because I want him to do what I didn't have guts enough to do. (And it takes guts, that's all, not to go out of your goddamned mind. Guts, and a very fat supply of dead nerve ends.) And the second thing I won't hide is that I hate my brother Aubrey even more than I love him, and I will probably shoot him if he decides to go back to the seminary. And I will certainly shoot him if he decides to go to Africa. I hope I don't love him too much to shoot him, because, really, that's the only thing for it.

The second document was similarly typewritten and bore the title "My Father Is the Greatest Man in the World, the Fink":

My nature, which holds that there is nothing more imprecise than the facts, leads me to imprecision. Given the choice between the shadow and the substance, I invariably choose the shadow. I am, therefore, one of God's worst observers and can almost certify in advance that no part of what follows will represent anything precisely as it was. Which, I agree, is a hell of a way to begin a literary enterprise in this day and age, but, to be exquisitely sincere about it, I don't give a big rat's ass.

We were at the foot of the mountain by four o'clock. My father said: "Good. We'll be above the snow line by dawn." Then the men talked and the other car came up with Aubie in it and it was determined that two of the men would stake out along the stream and the others would start driving down from the snow line at first light. One of the men said to my father: "Kermit, that's a long walk up there. Don't you think the boys'd better stake out with Bob and Rudy?" My father said yes and told us to be sure of the points before we fired.

My father's eyes were running and I could smell the whisky on his breath and he patted Aubie on the back but he didn't pat me anywhere. Then he went off with the other men, and Aubie went with Bob and I went with Rudy. And I sat down where Rudy told me to sit, and I waited, and answered when Rudy called to me from some birch trees along the stream to show me where he was, and where Bob and Aubie were. I had a sixteen-gauge with slugs and I thought about loading it, but didn't, and I listened to my ears sting inside my earlapper hat and finally closed my eyes. I opened them to the sunrise and the buck standing at the edge of the water, and there was only a moment, with the buck waiting in the sun, one front hoof so delicately lifted, his head held high and cocked, listening, hearing more than the dawn, hearing more than the lovely purity of the moving water, hearing more than the clear echoing of winter in the earth, hearing more than I heard, yet not hearing me whisper: "Run, run, run!" No, not hearing that, and probably not hearing the shot, or its own poor bleating as it threshed in the water, and not hearing Rudy say: "Nice shot, Kermit. I couldn't shoot because of the kid." And I was cold and afraid and didn't move, and I cried at the sight of the buck upon the waters. Then Kermit saw me and said: "My God, I didn't know you were there, Arnie! I could have shot you!" But old Arnie knew better. And I told Aubie. I said: "Oh, he missed that time, the fink, but he'll get me sooner or later."

The third document was written in ink on lined, legal-size, yellow paper:

The appearance of the Devil as an angel of light has always been considered, by those who have studied the matter, his most dangerous manifestation. The fear expressed is that in this disguise Lucifer is capable of deceiving even himself so that he actually believes that he is once again what he was before the Fall, the light-bearer. Lesser devils are also capable of this self-deception and, because they are less intelligent than the archfiend himself, continue in it longer, and often live among men for years, for the span of a human lifetime, doing untold harm.

Therefore let us ever be on our guard against the noonday devil among us, or within us, for the devils possess whom they will. Be vigilant against this devil in the robes of an angel, be bold in prayer, place yourself every hour under the protection of Our Lord Jesus Christ so that, with the Psalmist, "you will not be afraid because of alarms in the night or because of the arrow that flies in the day or because of the evil that walks to and fro in the darkness, or because of death, or the noonday devil."

And, under this, in an agitated, nearly illegible scrawl, was a commentary, or lesson, drawn from the first part:

I was born at high noon and Aubie at twelve-thirty. Thus, I am the perfectly balanced man, or the perfectly unbalanced man. The morning is potency, the afternoon is act. God tries to hold all men in potency, the Devil seeks to release them into act. Hence, I sit on the razor edge between the Eden of my potency and the Hell of my act. Perhaps I am more often devil than I am God. Perhaps I began as a devil and am, therefore, slightly overbalanced toward evil. Perhaps I am a noonday devil and will one day revert to the pure Hell of act. But if I am so constituted, where does that leave Aubie? He was born a half hour into Hell. He is a half-past-noonday devil. He is more self-deceived, more overbalanced toward evil, more committed to the Hell of his acts. And he doesn't know this, and one day I must tell him before he goes about the world seeking the ruin of souls, believing all the time—actually believing—that he is an angel of light! Men say I am Arnie, mad; he is Aubie, sane; I am Arnie, evil; he is Aubie, good; I am Arnie, weak; he is Aubie, strong! Oh, Aubie, do not judge your brother in this way! Arnie is far more often good, and far more intensely good, than you will ever be! What men call his madness is simply the result of the excruciating tension of his constant vision of the disparity between good and evil! Aubie is judged sane because it is more normal to be more evil than good! If you were perfectly unbalanced, as Arnie is, you would also be mad, you would also see the travesty men make of good! You would see the awful, revolting mediocrity of the best of the best of men, and the dreadful, terrifying blindness of those who set out to do what they call good! Oh, Aubie, child of the noon hour, come back to your Arnie, to the only person in this world who loves and knows you! Travel back those thirty minutes if it takes you fifty years, and rest with your Arnie, rest with me here on the golden edge of our noonday, and sit with me, Aubie, just sit with me, and shine!

253

The fourth document was a photostatic copy of a report made on Aubrey's mental health by a Boston psychiatrist almost four years before. It had apparently been addressed to Kermit and was in the form of a memorandum:

"I have completed my analysis of the psychological tests taken by your son, Master Aubrey Strycker, O.A.S.T., last Friday. The tests revealed no sign of pathology or gross, incapacitating personality defect. That is, his characteristic traits, motives, and behaviors are salient within his personality, and not so pronounced as to be considered unusual or abnormal. Or, to put it even more plainly, your son has no apparent need at this time for psychiatric treatment.

"The Rorschach test indicates that he is an intelligent, effective person with a wide range of interests, particularly in cultural areas. He is a very ambitious person and is striving for achievement in intellectual areas. He becomes less effective under stress and he is most susceptible to stress in those situations over which he feels he lacks complete control. Thus, when he feels he has not dominated a situation completely, he becomes constricted, less productive and less well-organized. In general, he has more than adequate ties with reality and has a realistic and accurate perception of situations and events. He does, however, perceive male authority figures as threatening and forbidding. This was suggested on the Rorschach and strongly supported by the TAT, where father figures were described as hypercritical and as somewhat nasty in their criticism of others. Although frightened and threatened by paternal authority, he does not hesitate to strike back. While he does not hesitate to challenge paternal authority, he is much more indecisive and submissive in the face of demands from women, even though he regards them as more sympathetic and less threatening. He also seems to become somewhat threatened and inhibited when confronted by sexual material, and possibly he feels awkward and uneasy around girls. The results also suggest a tendency to be passive and a desire to be taken care of by another person, especially a woman. This does not contradict the personality inventory indication that he is an active and dynamic person, but suggests that fear of this passivity and desire to be dependent acts as a motive and stimulus for this overt activity and independence. Perhaps this is also the underlying motivation for his lack of responsibility. By being somewhat irresponsible, by pretending to make decisions but not actually making them, by declining to finish what he has started and declining to consider any commitment as absolutely binding, he forces those around him, especially the women around him, to take charge of him.

"His extremely high self-acceptance score on the personality inventory may be something of a façade, employed to insulate himself from the fear that he is going to be criticized and attacked by father figures.

"A sidelight to the TAT and Rorschach results is that he likes to show off a bit, and often uses his intelligence and linguistic abilities to impress other people. Sort of flexing his intellectual muscles in front of others.

"I was rather surprised by certain aspects of his personality inventory. Taken alone, it would indicate strongly that he is a rebellious, iconoclastic person. He possesses self-confidence to a remarkable degree and is extremely sure of himself and of his own opinions, perhaps even to the point of excluding other points of view. He tends to emphasize social interaction and he functions quite smoothly in his relations with others. Indeed, I suspect him of being something of a potential con man, as the saying goes, not in an oily or dishonest way, but still, smooth, articulate, and somewhat opportunistic and manipulative.

"The extreme high deviation on the personality inventory in his case was in the area of self-acceptance. High scorers are: outspoken, sharp-witted, demanding, aggressive, and self-centered. The extreme low deviation was in the area of self-control. Low scorers are: impulsive, shrewd, excitable, irritable, self-centered, uninhibited, aggressive, assertive, and overemphasize personal pleasure and self-gain. He also scored very low in the area of responsibility. Low scorers are: moody, lazy, awkward, changeable, and disbelieving."

The doctor had handwritten a postscript:

I do, of course, hope to see you socially the next time you are in Boston. Until then, I remain, . . .

"And may he long remain," Aubrey said aloud as he finished reading the report for the second time. "May he long remain, indeed." He wasn't quite sure what he meant, but he meant it. He noted that a carbon copy of the report had been sent to Father Elihu Buzzey, O.A.S.T., Provincial at that time of the Eastern Province of the order. This, then, was the report Father Bogart had read. No damned wonder he arrived on me with both feet.

He had been reading for perhaps an hour, seated on a red-cushioned doughnut-shaped sofa in the middle of the hotel lobby—rereading until he had all four documents nearly memorized—when he heard himself being paged. He stood up, feeling not even slightly drunk any more, and went to the bell desk. The bell captain handed him the telephone. It was Arnie.

"Goddamn it, I'm sorry, Aubie. Why the hell aren't you in your room? Where are you, Aubie? Come up here! I've got to talk to you. Finking report was Rexie's idea. All hers. Now you know how bad she wants you in New York."

"Arnie, I'm the one who should be sorry. I'm grateful to you. It had nothing to do with you, the failure of my interview with the Saharans, I mean. I'm sorry I said that."

"Aubie, don't apologize to *me!* What about those other three things? I was drunk, Aubie, when I wrote them. Where are you? I've been telephoning all over the goddamned city!"

"I'm in the lobby."

"Well, come on up here. To my room. I've got to *talk* to you."

"Why don't we let it go until tomorrow, Arnie? I'm awful tired. There's nothing you've got to explain to . . ."

"No! Goddamn it, there's everything to explain! Everything! You wait right there, Aubie! Don't move! I'll be right down!"

Arnie hung up. Aubrey handed the receiver back to the bell captain. "If someone should ask if you have seen Mr. Aubrey Strycker, would you tell him that I decided to take a walk?" The bell captain took his name and Arnie's. Aubrey pushed his way through the front door. The doorman asked him if he wanted a cab, and that suddenly seemed like a good idea.

"Where's the nearest water?" Aubrey asked the driver.

"You want to drink, look, or jump in?" The driver was turned around, smiling at him.

"Well, a beach. Where there's surf."

"Ocean Beach. Nice bright night for it. But it's way the hell out."

"That's all right. As long as you bring me back."

"You mean you want me to wait?"

"Well, if you wouldn't mind. Besides, I've got no money. You'll have to bring me back if you want to get paid."

"By who?"

"My father. Or mother. Or hell, I don't know. The man at the desk has money, hasn't he?"

The driver laughed and shook his head and put the cab in motion down the narrow stone rampway. "Sure he has. The man at the desk has as much money as your daddy tells him to have, I'll lay ten to one on it. And your daddy's got enough money, I'll bet, to buy me, the cab company, the man at the desk, and the whole goddamned hotel. Am I right?"

"The cab company and the hotel, I'll agree to. How do you arrive at that?"

"Never mind, son. Never mind. I'm twenty-seven years a cabdriver in San Francisco. If I can't spot a rich man's son by this time, I ought to hang up my tag, right?"

"Do I strike you as a rich man's son?"

"What else? You said your father or mother would take care of the tariff, right? You didn't ask what the tariff would be, right? You figured if Daddy and Mommy were asleep, the man at the desk would take care of it, right? You're wearing a two-hundred-dollar suit, right? You don't give a thought from morning to night where the money's coming from or where it's going, right? What else? You're the son of a rich man. Am I right?"

"You happen to be right. But suppose I were just a man who wasn't used to handling money. I mean, suppose I were a mendicant monk, a wandering friar, who had no money and wasn't used to money, wasn't used to taking taxicabs, had no idea what it cost to take one in a big city. Suppose that. Would you have recognized me?"

"Hell yes! In a flash, son, in a flash. That's my business, right? Sizing people up. If I weren't good at it, I'd be out thousands of bucks after twenty-seven years. God, yes. Thousands. But, I tell you, I've only been taken twice. The first time was by a . . ."

"Excuse me, but what would have made you so sure I wasn't a poor monk? Other than my suit."

"Sure. Okay. First, no monk in my experience has ever asked me to go to Ocean Beach at ten-fifteen in the evening. Second, no monk, or priest, for that matter, has ever come out of the Mark Hopkins and

257

said, Take me to the nearest water. Right? I mean, I got the impression we could have been in the middle of Death Valley and you'd have said the same thing. You didn't give a damn *how* far it was to the nearest water. Right? And, besides that, you got that *tone*, you know? I mean, you're used to people doing what you say, right? You expect people to do what you tell them to do, even if you're only *asking* them to do it. Am I right?"

"You mean, I spoke to you as I might to a servant."

"No, no. Nothing like that, Mac. I mean, maybe I didn't make it clear. What I mean, you're just *used* to servants, I'm sure of that, but you didn't speak to *me* like a servant. You just spoke to me with that very nice, but, well I don't know, let's-pretend-we're-equal sort of tone."

"Did I?"

"*Well,* I don't express myself as well as I should. What I mean, you spoke to me as you probably speak to your old friend the chauffeur. You've got a chauffeur, right?"

"Yes."

"What's his name?"

"Mr. Jebb. Well, there's Roger, too. He's my mother's chauffeur."

"Hot damn! I love it. I *love* it!" The driver was shaking his head and laughing.

"You love what?"

"Ah, Christ, *I* don't know. I love the idea—I mean, I love the *fact* that there's rich people in this world. I mean they have so much class, you know? We've got *lots* of rich people here in San Francisco. Hell, yes! And I love every one of them. I mean, maybe they don't deserve their money, but they've got class, and they spend it with class. You'd get along here just fine, son. Just fine. You and your daddy and mommy . . ."

"My daddy and mommy are divorced, and I'm a Roman Catholic seminarian, and I haven't got a cent in the world."

"*Sure,* you are." The driver thought this over for a time. Then he said, "Son, I don't give a damn what you are, or what you told Daddy to do with his money, or what your religion *tells* you to tell Daddy to do with his money. Daddy has the money, and maybe Mommy has the money, too, and maybe you flushed all the money they gave you down the toilet. But money you were brought up on, and money you could have by snapping your fingers, and as a matter of fact, if you'll pardon my saying it, I never had a fare in my life who smelled more like money than you do, in twenty-seven years of driving a cab in a town *full* of people with money!" The driver laughed shortly.

"You aren't kidding me?"

"Hell no, I'm not kidding you, son! And I figure I'm not flattering you, either, if you are what you say. I can't help that. I tell the truth. I mean, if I started lying for tips, I'd become a waiter." He peeked at Aubrey in the rearview mirror, and saw Aubrey looking back at him, and set his head suddenly in the exact, slightly chin-up position Mr. Jebb employed. "Would you like to go by way of the park, sir?"

"Please call me son," Aubrey said quietly. "I like it better. And you go by just any route that takes your fancy."

"Yes, sir," the driver said. And he wasn't kidding.

On the beach, the moon was up and lighting white puffs of high cloud, and it appeared that he could see the surf for miles to the south. He could remember no night more luminous and no time, even at Southampton in midsummer, when the long white line of surf had seemed longer, or whiter, or more immediately touched with majesty.

He walked down to the edge of the wet sand and stood there, watching the waves, listening to their awesome collapse, and told himself some elementary things. That this land without this sea was diminished in point of beauty. That this sea without this land could never have come to so sonorous, so impressive, an end. That all earthly beauty was the result of comings together. That beauty was the happiest consequence of contrast, the true proceed of the meeting of things by nature disparate, or the meeting of persons by nature contrary.

He watched and listened, matching sight and pursuing sound, counting the interval between the waves—fourteen and sometimes fifteen counts when his cadence was right—and thought of the eternal curling of these waters. Yet not eternal, of course, partaking as they did more fully than anything else in nature of motion, the very essence of time; still, seeming to roll on rhythmically, relentlessly, powerfully, forever; if not eternal, then as close to it as nature, in all its variety, could come; if not eternal, then, perhaps, the pulse of eternity for mankind, the most apt imitation of timelessness in human experience; the most apt intimation of birth, death, and renewal again; the vision splendid itself, in which, if one looked and listened

259

divinely rapt, one might see and hear the gently timbreled stillness of all that lay beyond time.

The vision splendid. Hell yes. That's all's needed here.

And felt despair within him, sinking down the hollows of his body, sounding and echoing and coming to heavy rest in the pit of him like a great gray stone. Wounding him there, and tearing old scars, and the wounds all speaking at once about madness, and didn't he know he was mad, and did he think madness drew lots over twin eggs and only visited one of them, and didn't he realize that Father Finnegan and Father Bogart and only God knew how many others had read his madness like a red light in a snowfield, and did he actually think he'd been fooling anybody except that ass of a psychologist, and did he appreciate how deeply rooted and acute his insanity must be if he could so sincerely believe himself sane, and did he have any idea how galling his pose of sanity must have been and must be to his brother, and was he going to persist like a mad fool in his priestly studies, and hadn't he even considered what enormities he might perpetrate if he should become violent only after his ordination, only after he had deceived and conned some gullible religious group into presenting him for holy orders, only after he had received the power to call Christ out of heaven into small pieces of bread, only after he had gone out alone to some tiny desert parish and simple people to whom he was all that was good and all that was God—only then to run wild down his village street snarling like a mad dog, blaspheming, gesturing obscenely, pronouncing anathemas, all of it just as Arnie had done the day he lost control, that awful day Arnie had come into his inheritance?

Only his day, if he'd become a priest before it should have arrived, would be far worse than Arnie's. Intimations of what he might do had long been with him; in his fascination with exorcism, the raising of the dead, the bargaining of priestly powers to the Devil, the consecration of bakeries full of bread, Black Masses, witches' sabbats, and every other kind and form of perversion of religious usage? Madness freed one to one's fascinations. Could he do such things? However deranged? Hell yes, he could, and knew it pellucidly because he could see Arnie doing them, relishing them, boasting about them. He had to accept that what Arnie was he might well be; accept Arnie as a mirror of his possible future. And he did accept, and did shudder, and did resolve, at the last, to see a psychiatrist, or nineteen of them, before he left for Africa.

He waited then for the pain and clamor and despair to diminish, but they didn't; they, rather, waxed monstrous, hulking, blatant, and worked his soul like a cymbal. He turned abruptly toward the land and started for the highway. And had gone only two or three steps before he bent to the sand and wrote in it with his finger: God have mercy on me. He underlined each word, straightened slowly, looked down for a moment, then bent again, crossed out "me," wrote above it "us."

Then he went quickly up the winking beach toward the taxicab's headlights, and heard the sound of the ocean retreat behind him and heard the cab's meter click as he pulled open the door.

"See anything interesting?" the driver asked.

"No. Just the ass end of the vision splendid, going away."

The driver opened his mouth, shut it, and returned him silence, considerate silence; returned him silently eastward to his noise.

# · TWENTY-TWO ·

HOWEVER IT HAPPENED, he didn't see Arnie until they came together at the last moment in front of the church.

"What the hell happened to you?" Arnie asked fiercely.

"I'm sorry, Arnie. But I was so damned sick from that champagne I couldn't wait. I went for a walk."

"Don't give me that. The doorman told me you went off in a cab."

"Okay. So I went off in a cab. I—I wasn't going to tell you, but I went to a hospital to get pumped out. That's how bad it was."

Arnie was personified disbelief. "Bullshit. *What* hospital?"

"I don't know what hospital. I just told him the nearest Catholic hospital. But they didn't pump me out."

"That's nice. But I'm afraid the champagne was wasted anyway." Arnie walked into the church alone and sat on the bride's side, and told Rexfordia to go to hell when she tried to move him. And he smiled at the ceiling throughout the ceremony, a cruel, small smile that was meant to put asunder.

And the ceremony went on and on. The church was nearly full, the day warm, the minister unctuous, Prissy Cullenly fairly pretty, and Filcher Filcher. The only thing that made any of it bearable for Aubrey was the presence of the maid of honor. Julie was wearing a short, full-skirted dress of a soft rose color, her hair was piled on her head, and she was far and away the most spectacular object in sight. Even the minister kept glancing at her, or maybe glaring, because the minister did seem annoyed at the way Julie, with not much subtlety, was running the whole show—pointing and snapping her fingers, riding herd on bridesmaids, ushers, flower girls, the best man, and probably even the minister. For all Aubrey knew, this was the maid of honor's function, but he was quite sure Julie would have taken over if it were not. After all, she'd introduced the bride to Filcher, she had overseen the process of courtship, and now, by God, she was not going to tolerate any inefficiency in the driving of the last spike. It won't surprise me a damn bit if she goes along on the honeymoon. Old Filcher looks like he could use some instruction.

When it was over at last, and Julie had given the order to disperse, the guests were driven in hired cars to the home of the bride's parents. By some inscrutably fell mischance, Aubrey got seated in the same car with the bride's mother, and Rexfordia, and somebody's Aunt Rose, or Risen, as Aubrey preferred to think of her, who had a mouth on her that would not retrench, and after telling the bride's mother not to cry because marriage was a necessary evil, she pointed it like a hollow wind instrument right at Aubrey and, at close range, provided him with a history of the bride's family; a definitive account, back to the fifth generation preceding, with due notice of all blood relations in every degree of the direct line, and to the third inclusively of the collateral lines, not excepting fourth cousins twice removed. Or so it seemed, so that, when they had arrived at the bride's home, Aubrey fell out of the car and fairly sprinted away, pleading an unexpected hemorrhaging of his duodenal ulcer.

He tried to find Arnie on the enormous back lawn of the house where the reception was staged, but instead found himself shaking hands with a steady stream of people and explaining that no, he wasn't a minister and wasn't attached to any local church and that the suit was actually navy blue—a deep, sort of a sunken navy blue. And by now, and after Aunt Risen, he was suffering from a teeth and mouth fixation—a thing that had come upon him once or twice before during unlimited exposures to bared teeth, when the sight of the human smile filled him with the urge to run. And the open mouths seemed to be coming at him now in phalanx lots. He stood it as long as he could, then turned and walked swiftly toward a white wall at the end of the garden. He paused at a bar for a drink of some kind of whisky punch (the red-coated man said) and walked in under a jasmine bush.

And then he saw the man watching him. He looked to be an Indian swami, with a wrap on his head, and he was not so much coming toward Aubrey as hovering in his general area. He moved like a toy on a string, right fake, left fake, and turn yourself around, and he had his head cocked back, and his eyes rolling on and off target, and, of course, he was smiling. He appeared to be calculating just how many bites it would require to swallow Aubrey up before he moved in to accomplish same. Aubrey regarded him first with dismay, then with slight alarm, and finally with something close to loathing. He thought of running, or taking to the vines on the white wall, but restrained himself a moment too long.

The Indian closed rapidly, extended both hands, snatched Aubrey's hand out of its reticence, and gave it several purposeful wrenches, as if he intended to remove it at the wrist.

"I've been watching you," he said. "You're nervous, aren't you?"

Aubrey didn't answer, for at close quarters the man's appearance was appalling. His face was swarthy, sallow, hawk-beaked, downright scaly. His eyes were small and hard and the color of morion, and when they moved on you, you had to feel that Judas had just entered your garden and was about to give you the kiss. His jowls and throat hung down over his shirt collar, and his chin looked like a gallows—baleful, stenophyllously goateed. His hands were thin and olive-colored and the fingers seemed to be in unceasing motion, flexuous, prehensile, independently malevolent. But his voice was the worst of it, proceeding from behind a niggardly, condescending smile—the teeth long and almost tubular—and its tone suggested oil, ash, spittle, and venom. And Aubrey stood there transfixed, half expecting that the man's tongue was about to come slathering four feet out of his mouth, forked and fanged, and strike him, asplike and fatally, on the bridge of the nose.

"Well, don't be nervous," the Indian said. "Why are you wearing a black suit?"

"Because I vomited last night on the suit my brother loaned to me," Aubrey said quickly, deciding that in the next breath he would tell this creature that he couldn't stand the sight of him. And then take to the walls.

"Oh, very good! Very good, in fact, excellent!"

"What?"

"Oh, well, of course you would say 'What?' "

"I'm afraid I'm about to vomit again."

"Do you know, as I stand here, I am certain that you're a Roman Catholic. And yet you answered me in a perfect seventeen-syllable poem. Haiku of the highest order. Because I vomited last night on the suit my brother loaned to me! Why, it's a history of the human race! Do you see? But, of course, you see. You see all things. You are a very wise young man, aren't you?"

"Look, I'm not wise, I am Roman Catholic, and I am about to vomit. I think."

"So, you're not wise? Isn't it wisdom to bow to your mother's wishes and become a priest? Huh?"

Aubrey blinked at him. "Do you know my mother?"

"No."

"How do you know that I'm thinking of the priesthood, then? And what makes you think it's my mother's wish?"

"The priesthood was a guess. Your mother? Well, all Roman Catholic mothers want their sons, or at least a son, to be a priest."

"Look, I don't mean to be rude . . ."

"Don't you? It's obvious to me that you intend to be as rude as you can. Because I make you nervous. Do you know why I make you nervous?"

Aubrey set himself. "Yes. Because you look like you're about to bite me."

"Oh, now, that's a very interesting thing to say. Very interesting." The man smiled obscenely and worked his way closer. "And a very honest thing. You see, there's hope for you after all."

"Look, I'm a sick man. And when I'm sick, I vomit with incredible suddenness. Sometimes I vomit more than I've eaten." Play that on your fang hinges, you damned anhingidean.

"Oh, nothing that comes out of your mouth could defile me except, perhaps, your words. For you see you are prostituting your body of wisdom. And that is a great shame because you don't seem to realize that you are very close, very close. Even in this incarnation, it is possible for you to achieve everything. But, as you say, you are sick. You are sick in your soul, not in your body, although it is all one. All one."

He was so close now, having forced Aubrey to retreat flat up against the white wall, that his bad breath was all around them, and he was moving his mouth, held open and tilting from side to side, as if he were trying to envelop Aubrey's head in halitosis. "Sir, back off!" Aubrey said sharply. "Back, back!"

"Oh, of course, of course." He took one step backward, but kept moving his head, held his eyes on Aubrey, glinting and fixed. "I just wanted to get a close look at your earlobes, you see. Oh, you have so very little karma left. So very little. You are a man of destiny. Oh, you mustn't let your mother force you into the priesthood. It will retard you beyond measure."

"I'm not letting my mother force me into anything . . ."

"Oh, you are, yes, yes, you are! You aren't meant to be a priest. Not at all. Surely, you must see that. Surely, you must, because you are so obviously uncertain of yourself."

He was moving in again and Aubrey was sliding sidewise along the wall. Knock him down, for God's sake. Knock the bastard down! Or do vomit on him. Disgorge in quantity. Where's Arnie? For God's sake, where is Arnie? He searched among the people on the crowded lawn, blinking against the bright sunlight, wondering if he could possibly escape, if he could possibly make it across those dozen feet of lawn, across the abyss and into that forest of lovely laughing people, waving their drinks like tokens of normalcy. And the Indian was still talking.

"Oh, you must, you must come with me. We'll find a quiet place to talk." Then he took Aubrey by the elbow.

Aubrey wrenched free, spilling half of his cup of punch as he did. "Keep your hands off me, you damned creep!"

"Oh, please, please," said the Indian, not flinching even a little, reaching out again. "Mrs. Turns is one of my dearest friends. She will vouch for my . . ."

He touched Aubrey's elbow again, and without deciding that that was what he would do, Aubrey tossed the remainder of the whisky punch into the Indian's face. And all he saw as he walked resolutely away was the Indian bent almost double, rubbing at his eyes. The barman in the red coat stared at him as he went by and, quite solicitously, asked him if he wouldn't like another. Aubrey said no and handed him the empty cup and went at a half trot toward the house. He looked for Arnie, but was not seeing well, and jostled a few lovely people, gathered in their knots, smiling and laughing and begging Aubrey's pardon for standing where he clearly wanted to trot, and he saw Rexfordia and Julia standing in one gaggle of sylphs around the bride, and he heard Kermit shout, "Short taken, Aubie?" But he feared pursuit and somehow it seemed to him that only Arnie could deal with the Indian properly. And, having failed to espy Arnie, he made for the back door of the house.

A six-inch Japanese smile, just under five feet off the ground, met him a few yards beyond the door and led him directly to the library as the very best place in the house for nursing a headache, a place of "very peace and criet." The smile beamed, benign and effulgent, upon the perfect chair and illuminated an almost full "decranter" (try cruet, my dear and good friend) of "Nayporn cron-rock." Then the smile backed from the room and closed the door, having warmed Aubrey's day immeasurably, but leaving him in comparative darkness.

Aubrey hesitated for a time, but then went to brightening things up again with Nayporn and his cron-rock. And in a surprisingly short time, he was drunker than he had ever been in his life. He looked about the room, at all the black and red and green leather bindings, and all the gold lettering, and felt almost at home. Fort Milligan West, that was what this was. He was drinking from a heavy-bottomed water glass that was a duplicate of the one in the little brown rack (now green, of course, gorge-green, if that painter ever got to it) in his little old trundle bathroom. From time to time he had a coughing fit—the cognac wasn't even: sometimes there was much more cron than rock, or vice versa—and even those reminded him of the good old damp days along the Palisades. The chair was vintage Sloane's. The only deficiency was no footstool. He remedied that in the Fort Milligan manner. He leaned to a nearby shelf and removed two fat black volumes, the first *A Short History of Fort Point and Its Commanders*, and the other *The Roscoes of the Sunset*, and, un-intimidated, placed them at footstool distance, removed his shoes, and put one heel on *Roscoes* and the other on *Sunset*, sat back, and tried to think about nothing.

Then there was this girl. Not a girl, really, but a young lady, who, though he saw her only vaguely, was no doubt quite pretty because she said she was when he asked her.

"Well," he said. "I'm not allowed to talk to pretty girls. Or pretty young ladies. Although pretty young ladies are definitely more acceptable than pretty girls." She laughed and called him "Father" in a sweet, amused voice, and he corrected her on that, and she sat down opposite him and said that her name was Marcia Turns, and that she was a cousin of the bride. "Oh, *I* see," Aubrey said, with what he felt was enormous suavity. "Then this is the house of the bride's maternal grandparents?" She said that that was right, her voice touched with awe, as if he'd just solved Boxberger's Equation. Aubrey felt very good about his acuity in the matter, though he was vaguely bothered by the thought that Aunt Risen had already explained this to him. He offered to share his cognac with her, noticing that she was carrying some sort of thin-stemmed glass in her hand, and she accepted, and he poured with entire poise, especially in the vicinity of the wrist, he noticed.

"I'm a bit fleshed up around the ring finger," he said gaily, "but I pour good."

She laughed; a delicate tinkling. "I really shouldn't, you know. Not after champagne."

"Oh, but you should, you definitely should. After all, we don't want to leave any Turns unstoned around here, do we?" He laughed. Genially, he thought.

She groaned. "I've heard that before. It's a very old family, so don't feel bad. *Somebody* was bound to think of it."

"I suppose there's a history of the Turnses around here."

"Let's forget about the Turnses," she said.

"Well, really, I didn't mean . . . My God, the possibilities are endless, aren't they?"

"Endless."

"I promise to speak in straight lines from now on. Believe me. My promise is my bond."

"What we need is a new name in this conversation. What's yours?"

"Oh, I'm sorry. I thought I—Aubrey Strycker." He leaned forward and shook her hand. A very slim, warm hand. Like her face.

"Oh, I know. Your father's Kermit Strycker. With the beard?"

"Yes, yes, that's him, all right. The great white hunter himself."

"Oh, he's so handsome. I wish you'd introduce me."

"Be glad to, glad to. You just give me several days here to get my strength back, and I'll make it my personal business."

"And what do you do?"

"Do?"

"I mean, do you go to college? Or what?"

"Oh no, no. I—well, I, as a matter of fact, go about the country quitting a seminary here, getting rejected by an order there, you know how it is. In the holy orders business?"

"The what?"

"The holy orders business. My gracious, Miss Turns—ooops! missed a turn there! Straight lines, Strycker, straight lines are what's needed here. My gracious, Marcia—if I may presume—thank you. My gracious, Marcia! If you think salesmen have difficulties getting orders, you ought to go into my business. Not that you could, of course. Strictly male affair, these holy orders."

"What you mean is that you're studying to be a clergyman, don't you?"

"Why, the very thing! That's it, in a nutshell. How'd you figure that out? *Everybody* seems to be figuring that out today. Is it written on my forehead or something?"

"Well, you said seminary, so I just assumed . . ."

"So I did! Yes, indeed. I did say that."

"And you're in a seminary now?"

"No, no. As I say, I just *quit* one. Yes. There's no question now, according to informed sources, that that's just what I did. Long history of that in my family. Now, you take my brother Arnie. *He* quit one."

"Who else?"

"Who?"

"Yes, I mean, that's not a very long history. Just your brother."

"You know, you're *right?* Not long at all. When you come right down to the length of it." Aubrey was enjoying himself immensely. There was warmth, softness, an excess of wit. His day was a blessed, lucific, obtuse triangle, formed by lines of nepenthean force from her face to his face to the tall glass in his hand. Not that she was as pretty as Julie, or anywhere nearly as well constructed. K-cup spelled backwards is puck, he thought, and puck rhymes with ruck and several other unmentionables. Ho! Stand forth, Strycker! Strike like the Roman eagle you may become, with falchion gleaming at the nub of such thoughts! And nub spelled backwards puts me right back where I started, but boob spelled backwards leads nowhere. Therefore let us, and boob it is! What's his name? Bab? Bas? Bascomb! "Hah! I've got another!" he shouted.

The girl looked somewhat alarmed. "You have?"

"Yes, yes. Pray excuse my father's voice. He breathed it into me. But yes, indeed. Now, I will admit he's not a very available relative, genealogy-wise, but he *did* quit a seminary. Oh, did he ever. A legend in the order he is. In fact, Marcia, he quit the *same* seminary my brother and I quit! Now that must count for *something!*"

"Oh, it does. What seminary?"

"Why, the Titan! Titan, you know, of course. The Titans of St. Titus. He's one of your oldest anchorites."

"Of course. I'd somehow forgotten."

"Yes, well, it's hard to keep them *all* straight. Now, let me conjure this correctly, just so you know the relationship is extraordinarily well documented. Yes. Yes, I think I've got it, but you must not interrupt, if I may be so . . . Hum. His great-grandfather's sister married my mother's sister Ardiss's—hum, hum, hold, hold there—my mother's sister Ardiss's husband's grandfather—in 1865! And! At the very same local time, my aunt Ardiss's husband's grandfather's sister married Bascomb's great-grandfather!"

"Wow! I'm overwhelmed!"

"Wasn't that a peach?" Aubrey shed his pleasure upon her.

"God, yes! A regular fuzzy peach! Who's Bascomb?"

"Bascomb? Why he's my relative. My relative. The guy who also quit!" Aubrey looked at the girl, bending toward her a bit. She appeared to be very drunk, but still alert and only a little gone of eye. She was gazing at him with the precise expression he fancied he was directing toward her. "You're not drunk, are you?" he asked.

"Who, me? Jesus, no. If you'll forgive the invocation."

"*Ego te absolvo.* Now, Bascomb—I do forget his last name—Bascomb, I believe, is my cousin."

"Good God, really?"

"What do you think?"

"I just said what I think."

"I *think* we're fourth cousins about six times removed."

"I think you'd both better be removed before you screw the thing up any further."

"That—*that* is the cutest thing you've ever said. It's so incredibly cute I don't believe it."

"You're angry with me."

"No, no, Marcia. I mean it sincerely. Now, you see, Bascomb lost his faith. That's the difference. I didn't lose my faith."

"What did you lose?"

"Well, I think I've lost a mother, but I gained a quarter chance on the Sahara Desert. And you must admit, the thing has its equities."

"God, yes. I should say. You're not nuts, are you?"

"Oh no. It's been scientifically established. But that *is* what my brother, Arnie, lost."

"What? His nuts?"

"*Miss* Turns. I do believe you've been drinking."

Marcia looked embarrassed. "It just slipped out. I mean you said . . ."

"I meant to say—and do, please, excuse me—that my brother Arnie lost his *mind*. That's what I meant to imply. I'll try to imply more carefully from now on."

"I think we'd better start over. Bascomb left first."

"Oh, yes. Why, it was the most spectacular departure from the Titan Order since Linus the Heretic stole Frederick William's war horse and rode it out through the ninth general chapter of Brandenburg!"

"Oh! That sounds so—so, I don't know, war-horsy!"

"Well, Bascomb didn't use a war-horse, but it was almost as bad. He used a Cadillac convertible, they tell me. You see, Marcia, he was at our place on the Maine coast, where we go for six weeks in the summer, and he decided to leave and he sent to New York for his girl friend. And she came for him, in the dead of night, a beautiful blond girl, with her top down, and he walked right out in front of the whole community and got in, and off they went!"

"I'll *bet* they did! With her top down, too!"

"Miss—Marcia. Do I detect a note of, how shall I say, skepticism in your tone of voice?"

"No, no. Not at all. It's just that I don't know what in hell you're talking about!"

"Well, then, you'll just have to listen more carefully. I can't be expected to review this course forever. You will have to catch it while it's flying, Miss Turns, just like the rest of the gulls." He grinned broadly at her.

"You *are* crazier than a—a . . ."

"Loon?"

"Loon will do. But you're vastly amusing."

"Now *that's* the sort of hyperbole we need more of around here. Just for that, have some more Nayporn cron-rock."

"Oh, God, I don't know, Bascomb. I am swacked!"

"Please, the name's Ashurbanipal. Ashurbanipal MacIver."

At that convenient instant, the door was banged open, and there stood Arnie, between two brightly gowned girls, he with a bottle of champagne in each hand and some kind of long silver tube in his mouth. He spit the tube clattering to the floor, and cried, "Aubie, in the name of the sweet gibbeted Christ! Where've you been? I've been looking all over this goddamned charnelhouse for you! And why? Why did you throw acid in Swami Shikepoke's face?"

Aubrey snapped to his feet and saluted. "Sir! For the good of the corps, sir!"

"Well, Jesus Christ, Aubie, it's all right. But I do wish you'd told me! The son of a bitch has been following me around all day, peering in my ears! He apparently figured you'd gone right into a new reincarnation and bought a new suit of clothes at the corner Jim Clinton. I don't know. I finally told the little fink to get the hell away from me before I snapped his goddamned snorkel! I mean, Jesus Christ, I thought he was going to enter my third house right there on the spot!" Then, suddenly, he grinned radiantly. "But, Jesus God, Aubie, it's good to see you. I've been worried about you, boy! I was afraid Old Scrapple Balls there had grabbed you by the nirvana after all!" Then, to the girls, "Come in, come in, for Christ's sake, girls, and close the goddamned door. Yes. Use your bras to tie the handles, that's a good pair. Goddamned place is full of Bengal-finking-Lancers trying to ream poor old Aubie, there." He came across the room, rapidly but with several conflicting tendencies to reconcile, and ran up short against Miss Marcia Turns. "Ooops! What the hell was that?"

"Miss Marcia Turns. Marcia? I'd like you to meet my brother Arnie. Mr. Arnold Strycker."

"My God. You didn't say he was your twin brother. He looks just like you!"

"Well, Jesus Christ!" Arnie said. "For your goddamned information, you look just like all the other goddamned curveless, unbanked, underslung Turns I've been meeting all day! What the hell is your name? Up, down, right, left, in, over, buckle, key, pike, or screw?"

"Hup! Hup! Arnie! That's been ruled illegal. When it comes to Turns, this is the worm. No damned Turns jokes allowed, and besides, Marcia, here, and I have been having an extremely pleasant interlude."

"Oh, you have. By Turns, I'm sure. Now, Marcia, you can tell your cousin Arnie, has he been trying to assault you?"

"Not so's I've noticed."

"Really? Well, take him over there to the soundproof booth and give him another chance. He's a virgin, you know."

"He is?"

"Christ, yes. Never entered anything but a seminary in his life!"

"Arnie!"

"Yup, up, wheezus-whist! Call him the finking reverend, I do!"

Then Aubrey was accosted by one of the girls who had entered with Arnie. She had cruised to within four feet of his face, and was blinking myopically and moistly at the left flank of his nose. And the shock of recognition was only gathering when the girl curdled it with a cry out of prehistory.

"Ash, darling! They told me you'd entered the camel corps!"

Aubrey fell back into his chair just as Phoebe Rush rushed, and she went right on by, into the bar. Arnie said, "By God, Aubie, we tried to protect you, but Miss Roundheels had the scent. Phoebe, put your glasses on before you tip over the goddamned *Encyclopaedia Britannica*. Come over here and meet your adapter. Blind as a bastard, she is, but it helps develop the sense of smell."

"Ash, darling, where are you? Oh, there you are!"

"Phoebe, goddamn it, control yourself. Miss U-Turns here has dibsies."

"Well, what the hell do you think I've got here, Charlie?" Phoebe said indignantly. "Tangerines?"

"God, no, Phoebe. Honeydew melons, anyway. Aubie, I'd also like you to meet Miss Rosy-breasted—I mean, Miss Rosicrucian—honey, what in the hell *is* your name?"

"Rosie," the girl said quietly.

"Ash, darling! They told me you'd joined the camel corps! If I'd known you were here—I mean, I *never* would've had all that *other* social intercourse last night!"

"Phoebe, for Christ's sake, I did *not* say the camel corps! The Camaldolese! Goddamned hermits!"

"So, balls! I knew it was something with humps! Ash, darling, let me kiss your virgin right zygomatic bone!"

"You!" shouted Julie from the door. "You touch any part of his bone, you goddamned fizgigging Jezebel, and I'll slice off your mucronations with a tuning fork!"

273

"Oh Jesus, the Beast of Barnard," Phoebe whispered. "Quick, Ash darling! Into the hangings!"

"By God, Julie-Bitch! Magnums! Two magnums!" Arnie cried, popping one of his own corks as he went toward her. "Oh, by the great nexus! Sometimes, just sometimes, my little knocker-wurst, you do something right!"

Aubrey, hanging tense under Phoebe's hangings, suddenly slid to his haunches on the floor, said, "Hi, Marcia Turns!" and leaped toward what looked like a suit of armor. But it turned out to be a young man in a white jacket who, with amazing sinistral and dextral coordination, plucked both of Aubrey's hands out of their mid-amaze flutter, and started vigorously to shake them.

"My name's Thom Turns! Hello there!" He pronounced his Thom as if it were thumb, and that was about the size of him.

"Good Lord, I beg your pardon," Aubrey said. "I thought you were a short Norman."

"Oh no," the young man said, leading with his wispish forelock. "I'm Thom!"

And he didn't seem to want to let go of Aubrey's hands. "Arnie!" Aubrey cried. "Somebody you ought to meet!"

"What is it? Julie, push the sofa against it! That's a big strong Amazon."

"Arnie!" Aubrey said, quite loudly.

"Now what is it, my son?" At this instant, Arnie was struck by a flying volume just above the label. "For God's sake, Julie! You almost broke the bottle! Aim higher, girl, higher! Excelsior's what we want around here!" Then, to Aubie, "Well, what the hell, Aubie? Pig's knuckles don't go with champagne."

"He won't let go, Arnie."

"Why, I will, too," said Turns, letting go.

"Who the hell *is* he, Aubie?"

"Thom Thumb. I mean, Thom Thurns."

"My name's Thom Turns."

"Well, look here, my man, you grab Aubie again and I'll break your thumbs and Aubie'll break your thurns. You understand?"

"Oh, now, just a minute here . . ."

"Out, out, Thurns!"

"But he *lives* here," Marcia protested.

"All the more reason. He gets to see this room every day. Isn't that right, Thurns?"

274

"Turns!"

"Out, Thurns, before I kick you into straightaways! Out! Out! Julie-Bitch, hold the door! Mr. Thurns was just thath-thaying out."

And Arnie drove poor Turns, who was about half Arnie's size, ahead of him to the door, moved the sofa back, with Julie stretched out on it, opened the door, and put Turns into the hall.

"Arnie!" Aubrey said. "Maybe we ought . . ."

"No maybes, Aubie."

"I'm going to get Mr. Turns, senior!" Turns announced as the door closed.

"Fine, little Thurns. You thend thenior Thurns up here, the old thitheels, and I'll give him a thwift thwat on his thatchel-ath with a thwieback!"

Arnie slammed the door, pushed Julie and all against it, and Phoebe roared into laughter. And Julie joined her, and Rosie joined Julie, and Marcia came in late just before Aubrey found he could resist Phoebe's harking hawking no longer, and Arnie poured while the rest laughed, and then they all drank and laughed some more, for as long as perhaps eight and a half minutes, or thereabouts, when there came several loud raps at the door ("Who's that?" Arnie cried. "By God, I'll broach his brisket!") and into their midst, pushing the sofa before them, marched, not one or two, but six Turnses, including Aunt Risen.

Junior Turns said, pointing at Arnie, "There he is. He's the one who threw me out!"

Aubrey pushed his way back into his overstuffed chair, closed his eyes, and thought about how long it had been since he, personally, had been accused of taking part in a regularly scheduled, Strycker-Milligan, public disaster. I'm out of training, he thought. A little pep rally's what I need. Let me see. Fix the eye and stare at all present —all interlopers, that is—as if each had just raped the Queen Mother, had the crown jewels hidden in his or her haversack, and was speaking to you in this accusatory manner only to create a diversion. Yes, that's it. That's the very it. Second, make a noise like a growl now and then, and dart the head and eyes to and fro anticly—tic is the key syllable there—and make the fist and wave it recklessly, clutching now and again to make it appear you are grasping for flies. Third, when the scene begins to show definite signs of emotional or constabularish deterioration, put the head back and begin to shout—anything at all will serve, but the more scurrilous

275

and uniformly offensive to public morals and acceptance the better
—and if you can manage a little blue-faced, outraged dance at the
same time, it sometimes has a marvelously dispersive effect upon combatants and onlookers alike. Fourth, as the situation grows toward
the antepenultimatum, jab one or more fingers into the face or nearest convenient aperture of one or more combatants and shout that
you know who you are but suspect that *they* (or he or she or
both) are the miserable wretched habitually malefacting bastards
who just raped the Queen Mother and have swallowed the crown
jewels (or done *something* with them whose disproof will require at
least as collectively and enervating a probing process as would an
enema) and, if you can manage both simultaneously, begin to foam
patriotically at the mouth. Fifth, as the action falls away (rapidly
now as with your common ordinary run of public disaster) to the
penultimate stage turn *royal* or at least varicose blue, snatch off hats,
gloves, scarves, braces, belts, or surgical hammers (umbrellas,
canes, shoes, socks, hatpins, handbags, gunny sacks full of ball bearings, pocket flasks of quart size and above and children's ball bats
also make handsome knock-abouts), and have at the *combatants
only*, about the ears, eyes, nose, throat, and any other specialty area
that seizes your attention or of which you have made a study, main-
taining the while all the other optic, oral, guttural, and otherwise in-
timidating and diversionary actions that might conceivably affright
any part of the engaged or disengaged populace. And when, if it can
be clearly distinguished in what at this late stage promises to be—
scarcely has the least opportunity of being anything less than—a
public disaster of notable and virtually deafening dimension, the ultimate, or sixth, moment approaches, make the sincere fist, disclose
the purposeful truncheon, brandish the ax, or unlarrup the chain
and mace, but, by whatever means, reduce to the horizontal or supine
indiscriminately any nonmember of the Strycker-Milligan complex
who happens to be within convenient smashing distance, combatant
or onlooker (the business having long since exceeded the bounds of
nicety—although bashing more than one fellow member of the
Strycker-Milligan complex during a *public* disaster by accident or intention, no matter what the animosities involved, will automatically
result in that member's exclusion, for one month, from S-M-complex
*public* disasters of any description, except as an onlooker *if* the
S-M complex member wishes to do so, at his or her own risk,

of course). The seventh, or postultimate, phase will naturally take whatever form circumstances permit, be it an energetic—but dignified and any-of-you-other-bastards-want-a-thump-in-the-thorax-here's-my-card—sprint, or a face-off with officialdom, in which case the frustration, confusion, and profane denunciation of anyone, friend or foe, seeking to make answer, or organize a rational inquiry into the proceedings, especially if the general outcry and uproar show any least sign of flagging in volume or vituperativeness—shall be incumbent upon and mandatory for all S-M-complex disaster-area members. All of which took Aubrey just a few seconds to recall so that he felt, with respect to public disasters, that he'd hardly left home at all, and he was ready, if not quite eager, to do his part, when Arnie, rising in all of his disarming, elegant suavity, bowing to each Turns in turn, calling each by name and making small remarks about how the charm and tingling good-looks of each had come on astonishingly in just the last hour (or, in Thom Turns' case, eight and a half minutes), delivered them all, and especially Aubrey, from the exigencies of trial by public combat.

"Why, my land sakes, Mr. Turns, if I'd only known who young Thom here was! Why, I'm truly—truly—mortified. But, not to put too fine a head upon it, Mr. Turns, I thought, and you just ask your own sweet Marcia here if that isn't so, I thought I was defending your library from the intrusions of some audacious book thief! Oh, I can't tell you what a turn—what distress—it causes me to find out that, all the while, young Thumb—Thom—here was . . ."

"I told him! Didn't I, Marcia?"

"Well, yes. But, you must admit, you did look rather suspicious, Thom. Wrestling with Aubrey, and all," Marcia said, with extraordinary S-M-ish evenness.

"I didn't wrestle with him! I was just shaking hands!"

"Oh well, Thom, please let's not even discuss it," Arnie said. "Aubie's thumbs have always sprained easily, isn't that right, Aubie?"

Aubrey said, "Oh, yeth." And he held up both thumbs, palpably straining.

"Well, what about—well, what about . . ." Thom Turns said excitedly, his weakness like his eyes, rolling all over his face. "He called you an old—an old . . ."

"Thom, Thom," Arnie said. "Please don't, hm? I mean, Thom, it

277

was in the heat of the moment, and *I* thought you were quite another party, and, well—you understand, Thom, I was simply defending the honor of that household whose guest I have so very enjoyably been for the last several hours. Why I have never—and Mrs. Turns, believe me, I speak for my father, as well—I have *never* been made to feel so welcome. . . ."

And it went on for some time, lavishly, and what Aubrey got out of it all was that it is very nearly impossible to flatter the self-satisfied too much. The Turnses just stood there and received it like six wondrously plastic and capacious bladders until Arnie chose to seat them roundabout and pour them liberal quantities of their own champagne. And Arnie talked on until Aubrey began to get nervous again, because he knew that Arnie was in a dangerous mood, that the monsoon could come over the mountain at any time, and that there was nothing Arnie took greater delight in puncturing than something plump, overblown, swollen, and flushed. Aubrey waited and endured, wondering if perhaps Arnie had lost the killer instinct or his sense of timing, shrugging back at Julie's lifted eyebrows (amazing how that girl had mastered S-M tactics in only two or three years), and then sighed with something between relief and acute apprehension when Arnie unlimbered his bladder-bursters and moved to the attack.

"Oh, yes, I've seen and I've interviewed a lot of girls in Hollywood for this part in my picture—some of them pretty big stars, though I wouldn't want to mention any names, to protect *them*, you know— and I don't mind telling you that your very own little Marcia, here . . ."

"Oh, no!" Julie said. "Oh, Jesus, no!"

"Now, Julie, don't let your sympathy run away with you. I *know* it's a terribly difficult and demanding life—the life of an actress— and Julie certainly knows because her mother is an actress of some repute—but, well, if a girl has the beauty *and* the ability, I feel, I mean, I just sincerely believe, that, well, in a way, she owes it, not only to herself but to her generation—I mean, to give of herself, to make that demanding sacrifice." Arnie allowed his pause to become properly impregnated before he turned to Marcia. "How do you feel about that, Marcia?"

Marcia glanced at Aubrey and almost smiled, then did smile and allowed as to how Arnie had to be kidding. Arnie denied it, the Turnses raised a murmur of protest—and Aubrey could see that they were all uncomfortable, in no way taken in by Arnie yet constrained by polite-ness (and perhaps by the slightest of hopes, on the part of the women, that Arnie just might be speaking for his father, and em-powered so to speak) to stand and listen—and one of the Turnses, elder, said, "I'm afraid we have interrupted something here, but we told the young people—the bride and groom—that we would see them off from the library. You know, have our final toast here, since this always has been Prissy's favorite room." The speaker was an old man, cold of eye, a patriarch with built-in suspicion, disapproval, and a kind of wintry, falsely apologetic suavity. Aubrey knew at once that the issue was joined, that Arnie would find the old man's tone and condescension too much to ignore. Arnie's lips curled back, his eyes hardened, his ears appeared to extend, sharpen, and twitch, and he opened fire with a low, sweeping bow toward the patriarch.

"A most gracious apology, Mr. Turns, but entirely uncalled-for. You really haven't interrupted at all, and, to prove it, I shall proceed just as if you weren't here." Arnie paused to pluck up from a humidor and light a seven-inch cigar, and when he started to speak again—almost immediately—his voice and whole manner had drastically changed. "Now understand, I don't want to spend more than two million, right? The only way to get the flavor of a story like this is tell it with all the guts and juices built right in, right? I mean, we're all twenty-one, right? Now, I don't say this script doesn't need a little rewriting here and there. I admit it. The writer is a famous novelist, and he's also a dirty old man, right? So I have to go along with him. And I'm glad to. And Marcia will be glad to, I'm sure, if you know what I mean. I only want to point out that this here dirty-old-man writer is a little behind the times. What I mean, he isn't quite sexy enough for today's art picture. I mean, if this is 1942, it's a *very original* piece of work! But this is some later and the Italian groin school—great directors—Minestrone, Fettuccine—why, they just got there first, you know? They staked out the crotch as their province shortly after Lucrezia Borgia reached puberty, right? Right. Now! Here we come and we got the same ingredients. Eight parts crotch, one part good stinking earth, and one part v.d., right? And the v.d. is almost virgin territory. It's almost never been touched. So! Three shots for our side, right? Now the story. There's this Mexican hooker, see—and you will note the Mexican location which saves money, saves time, saves us from Sicilians and all that there kind of shit—

279

well, this here hooker comes in from the provinces with her pillow strapped to her ass, see, right into the big city, and she lays right down in the lobby of the Hilton and, in less than a month, screws her way right up into the penthouse, right?"

At this point, Julie and Phoebe begin to double over, the Turns men are exchanging glances, but the Turns women are willing to act as if they were all twenty-one, including Aunt Risen. Right?

"Now! In this here penthouse lives this here Mexican playboy by the name of Pancho Cajones. And he and Caja—that's the hooker's name—well, they get to balling it from morning to night, and pretty soon the earth moves for Pancho—and it's none of your goddamned Mexican earthquakes, either—and Pancho figures he's had it and the only thing is to give Caja a bath and marry her. So off they go to Acapulco in his shiny new Huff, and they check into Pancho's private swimming pool, and he scrubs her down good, and they're just getting down to some solid, serious screwing, see, when Pancho finds out he's got a dose! And I mean . . ."

"Arnie, Arnie," Aubrey said. "Don't you think . . . ?"

"Oh, come on, Aubie, we're all twenty-one here, right? A dose doesn't shock you ladies, does it?"

"It'd shock the hell out of me," Phoebe said.

"What does he *mean?*" Aunt Risen said. "Salts?"

"Mr. Strycker," said Patriarch Turns, "I don't think . . ."

"That's just it! Don't you see?" Arnie went on. Aubrey retired into the wings of his chair. Now let's see, he thought. Review of rules for S-M-complex public disasters. . . . "Nobody *thinks* in this here art film, Mr. Turns! That's the beauty of it, see? All they do is screw! Like I told you, it's the pure article! Well, anyway, Pancho has this dose, right? And I mean there is nothing like a dose to put the damper on love in bloom, right? And we got a sequence of who-gave-what-to-which the like I have not seen since Lassie bit Little Miss Marker and got the rabies! At the end of which Caja rises up with great dignity and says that she doesn't even know what a dose is and she hopes Pancho's balls drop off, and she stalks off into the hills . . . !"

"Mr. Strycker!" said a youngish Turns. "I've heard quite enough. This motion picture is definitely not for our Marcia!"

"Now, wait, wait, you got to hear me out, by God, because this here art film has a very, very *spiritual* ending. Yes, indeed. Now, I mean, you got to have contrast, right? Where would God be without the Devil? Where would virtue be without sin? Where would virgins be without screwing? Now! Miss Caja, the hooker, it turns out—no offense, Mr. Turns—is not far from her mountain home. See? I mean, things are getting bucolic already, right? I mean, there she goes up through the virgin-pure meadows full of flowers with her pillow strapped to her ass, and I mean, you got *contrast*, right? Beautiful! Now! She gets to her ancestral hovel, and it's Sunday morning and the church bells are ringing, and her old man, Juan More, grabs her, beats hell out of her, and, figuring that what with the church bells and all, what this picture needs is a little incest, he *downs* her! And when he's all done, she's laughing like hell, see, and she tells him about the dose and hopes *his* balls drop off! And that's the climax of the picture, right? Beautiful! And *then* there's this revolutionary in the confessional, right?"

"Mother Turns! We've heard enough!"

"Come, Marcia!"

"Out of my house, Strycker, get *out*, I say!"

Whereupon entered Prissy, Filcher, the Cullenlys, the Cherrys, Rexfordia, Kermit, and the six-inch smile.

"Jesus Kurr-*rist!*" roared Kermit, plunging into the room, halting suddenly, and rising out of a dangerous forward pitch with beard and smile beatifically lambent. And he bestowed them upon all alike, and said, "Jesus Christ, ladies and gentlemen and all you goddamned Turnses! Filcher—*Filcher*—is about to go *straight!*"

And, challenged by the master's voice, Arnie raised the pitch, losing none of the emotion in his voice and not moving his now tearful eyes from the ceiling. ". . . Caja, with head and bodice high, and with great dignity, walks down the center aisle, and there's this priest preaching against the revolution, and there's the revolutionary in the confessional about to make his move, and we pan slowly, and it's— it's beautiful, I tell you, and I'll scrag any bastard who says it isn't— and there's the congregation gasping to see such a hooker in church, and there's Caja with her pillow strapped high and proud to her ass, and then—*then!*—bang-bang!—dum-de-dum!—rootle-tat-tat! —the revolutionary turns her loose, hollers up the revolution, and stitches poor Caja right up the goose feathers! And slow fade, gentles, with the good people tromping the revolutionary, with the good priest solemnly announcing that Caja the Hooker died a martyr of the faith, and with a mariachi band in the pulpit, led by none other than Pancho Cajones, repentant in his cassock, playing that great Mexican national ballad 'Go Ye Forth Unfrightened by the Thunder, Daughter, It's Just Another Kind of Clap!' "

And the last things Aubrey heard, as he toed unevenly toward the door, were Prissy crying, Filcher blowing his nose, Phoebe laughing outrageously loud, Aunt Risen piping, "There's the man in the black suit who threw the acid on Swami!," and Kermit roaring, "Goddamn you, Turnses, take your hands off my Arnie before I hit you with Filcher!"

Then there was Julie, standing just without the door, cradling an untapped magnum in her arms, pouting a smile at him, and saying, "I shouldn't forgive you, step. But weddings always make me feel so full of sweetness, light, and sex." And as she took him by the arm and led him toward the front door, the recessional was announced by the Master of Public Disasters himself: "It's a fine song, goddamn it, and Arnie and I will now render it for you. Let's go, Arnie! You thunder, and I'll clap along!"

## · TWENTY-THREE ·

"It was all my fault," Aubrey said. "I don't know what happened, but I just got the idea that young Thom there wasn't going to let go of my hands."

Julie was hailing a cab, but she turned to him and touched his cheek with one white-gloved hand. "Now, Aubie darling. Let's not talk about it any more."

"Do I look drunk, Julie?"

"You look beautiful. Now come on, get in the cab."

She held the door and Aubrey took its measure for a time, then made his move, a touch high, and rapped his head smartly on the cab's roof. He ducked, without flinching, gave it the lowered shoulder with a hip snap, and came in straight up and legs crossed on the cab's back seat.

"Where you going?" the driver asked.

"What I don't understand is why he tried to shake both of my hands," Aubrey said. Then he saw that he was alone with the driver. "Where'd Julie go?" he asked.

"She went 'round t'other side, Mac," the driver said, staring at him. "Does she know where you're going?"

"If anybody knows where I'm going, I'm afraid, it's Julie. She ought to be here any minute." Julie opened the other door. "Here she comes now."

"You're such a gentleman, you damned oaf!" Julie said. "Don't you open doors for ladies?" She glared at the driver.

"Careful, Julie, don't bump your head," Aubrey said.

"Well, I'm sorry, lady, but I didn't think you were getting in."

"He's lying, Julie. He told me himself you were going around to the other side. Why do you lie about such a little thing, driver? Don't you know it's a sin?"

"Look," said the driver, who was dark, even swarthy, and small. "At least I'm sober!"

"This car has a very low roof, Julie."

"Yes, you're right about that, darling. And a very low form of operator. We're drunk, and we'll get over it, but he's a horse's ass and he'll never get over it."

"Look, lady . . ."

"Don't look lady me, you diminutive pissant!" She opened her purse quickly, removed a ten-dollar bill and tossed it up onto the front seat. "There! You're paid! Now, drive me where I tell you to drive me or I'll not only brain you with this bottle, but I'll have you prosecuted! Or else, climb right out of that seat and give me the pleasure of kicking you all over this intersection!"

Aubrey leaned back and closed his eyes. Public disaster was dogging his tracks. There were no two ways about it. Now here, here, he thought, sober up on the instant, MacIver, because you cannot allow Julie to do single combat with this poor diminutive teamster. She's got him outweighed, outgeneraled, and outmagnumed starting. All she's got to do is blow that cork and he'll starve to death sitting out the geyser. "Wait," Aubrey said. "Wait. I have a dishonorable compromise. We'll walk."

"We will like hell," Julie said. "If we walk, he walks, or I'll drag him!"

"Lady, lady, please. Okay, okay," the driver said. "We got off on the wrong foot here, that's all." Aubrey opened his eyes and the man was actually managing a smile. Not an amused smile, but a perfectly serviceable one. The world is full of cabdrivers, Aubrey thought. The world is full of people in taxicabs. Drivers and passengers are all at cross-purposes, and all either are really interested in is the fare. The world is one great taxicab, and we shall all run round and round in it until the franchise is revoked, and then we shall be buried in it, with the meter eternally running.

284

". . . learned some manners," Julie was saying. "Where are we now?"

"Lady, we are at the corner of Broadway and Scott."

"Julie, I need some air. Let's go to the beach. I've got some things to write in the sand."

"Oh, Aubie, darling, I don't want to go to the beach."

"I need a long walk, then, Julie. Let the nice man have his cab back, and let's take a nice long walk."

"Oh, I've got a perfectly wonderful idea!" Julie said. "We'll go back to the hotel and drink the champagne!"

"No, no, nope! Julie, please. I like champagne, and I think it's the nicest hotel ever built on the lot it occupies. But I need air. I've got to take out my soul and fly it in the breeze. Now, just look at those sailboats down there. What this cab needs is a jib."

"Did you ever walk across the Golden Gate Bridge, lady?" the driver asked tensely.

"That's it! By God, Aubie, that'll air your soul! And I just love those towers. They're so—so phallic, you know?"

"Oh yes," Aubrey said. "That's what we need more of around here. Tallic phowers."

"Boy, lady," said the driver, shaking his misshapen head and putting the cab in gear, "it must have been quite a party."

"No goddamned pleasantries, Shorty," Julie said. "I only took your suggestion so I could throw you off when we get there."

"Sure, lady. The Marin side?"

"Take your choice, Shorty. I don't give a damn where I drop you."

"You know, lady," said the driver softly, as he guided the car toward the bottom of the Scott Street cliff, "if I was six inches taller, I think you and I would get along just fine."

"If you was six inches taller," Aubrey said suddenly, hearing himself speak with some astonishment, "I'd have broken your nose five minutes ago! Now shut up and drive!"

And that did it for the driver, and Julie fairly melted at the eyes and pressed his hand and thanked him for protecting her, and Aubrey might have laughed except that he felt very bad about the poor diminutive teamster.

They wrestled with the cork in the champagne bottle until they were somewhere in mid-bridge, the cork being one of those bulbous businesses with enfolding wire, and Aubrey finally got it down on the floor between his feet, hooked his right thumb and forefinger around the bulb, and, while forcing the bottle down with his left hand, brought cork and bottle to a righteous partition. The explosion was signal, but the spray of wine was prodigious, striking Aubrey in the forelock and then, as he lifted it and bent it toward the front, washing down the roof of the cab and dousing the already cork-shocked driver from nape to dashboard. The driver yowled, Julie yowled and went into a paroxysm of laughter, and Aubrey stuck the neck of the bottle in his mouth and almost blew his tonsils out. Finally, he lowered his window—mouth still in place—pointed the bottle toward Alcatraz, fell back in his seat, felt the world begin to brighten, and, looking up, took the visionary gleam of the Marin hills full between the eyes.

They got out into a convention of highway fence sections, each painted yellow with black stripes—which color almost matched the blinked shadings of Shorty's eyes as he turned away from them, slapped his gearshift, and put the tires to spinning in the gravel and then squealing piteously as the cab lurched out onto the highway.

"I'm afraid our champagne fell upon deaf ears," Aubrey said solemnly, watching the cab disappear.

"It's the first bath he's had since they soldered him into that seat in 1936," Julie said, taking a sip from the gently fizzing bottle.

And Aubrey thought, Am I only drunk, or why does the air seem so clear?

The gate across the bridge's sidewalk was locked so that they had to run along the curb against the oncoming traffic, and they got over the low concrete wall and into the sidewalk just as a double-decker bus came roaring and rocking by, scattering cinders and blast in all directions. It was a Behemoth, and went by with the speed of rage and sudden death, and left the smell of brimstone in its wake.

And Aubrey was talking from the first, saying, Look, look, how the bridge is anchored in that mountain to the north, and look at all that strong water driving in from the west under the wind and meeting the water that is bound for the sea. Look where it all turns white and the currents form and swirl it, and, my God, Julie, look to where the southern end rises out of pine trees on that low hill. Oh yes, Julie, there were men here once and for some time, and they built themselves a *bridge*.

And he pointed out the high blue sky and the phantom black

clouds that came wispy and cautious, expecting night, out of the west; and coming down from the spines of the rugged north coast was a pewter fog, from the north and the west, in from the great water a thousand feet high, moving low into the trees. Look, Julie, he said and he thought, How it is enveloping the trees and possessing them silently, and what is it? Perhaps a malignant vapor out of the dank and charnel ocean, poisonous to life and to us; or perhaps a final ghosting out of the setting sun—a lightsome and noble thing, a soul, as beautifully free of vested things as are all the pristine things in nature, and yet always a pathetic and forlorn presence, short of life, frail in substance, trembling at the rebuke of the horns, the poor pariah soul of the failing day, showing itself, lingering, returning from the west, unwilling to leave this final land behind.

Julie said that that was all very poetic, but what the hell, it was only fog and have some more champagne before he got a chill. And he did have some more, and felt exhilarated to be alone with this beautiful girl, the only pedestrians on this greatest of bridges, two hundred fifty feet above the mighty gorge of darkling blue waters, the water moving in troubled swirls, torn by antagonistic currents out of God knew where, perhaps boiling up from below, up from the raw deeps of that savage place where the oceans from one side and the rivers from the other had cut down the mountains, cut through them and hundreds of feet below that, through rock and bedrock, and were still deepening this awesome breach of the land. And beyond the water the great city itself, seen in a light so pure and stilly clear that it was the whitest of cities, built to stand as a reproach to all the black and gray cities of America, built apparently from some neat stone so pristinely white that all other whiteness might take it as a standard.

He noted and pointed out to Julie how the roadway was suspended from the great main cables by steel ropes and giant clevises and several million of the most important rivets in the world, and told her that these rivets had been holding on for twenty-five years and were getting tired, so, for Pete's sake, don't jump up and down like that. Upon which Julie jumped up and down eight or ten times as recklessly as her high heels would permit.

Then they watched a freighter come out to them across the bay, from the time it cleared the passage between the city and Alcatraz, constantly forced northward by the currents, seeming to travel broadside as far as it did toward the Gate, finally skirting very close to the rocky Marin shore and fighting its way back toward mid-channel. And Julie said that it would pass directly under mid-bridge, and Aubrey said that it couldn't possibly unless it turned almost due south for a while, but they took their stand at mid-bridge, at lamppost 69, steel rope 127, and waited, and the ship did regain a little toward center, but they finally had to run back quite far so that they would be standing over the ship when it passed under. They arrived at lamppost 65 with the ship still a hundred yards out, and two men on the bow saw them and started to wave, and Aubrey waved but Julie didn't because her brassiere had broken while they were running, and she couldn't fasten it again, but then she took it out of the top of her dress and said that the hooks were broken, and then began to wave the brassiere, much to the agitation of the men on the bow and three or four other men on the stern, and she finally tossed the brassiere down toward the boat and the men on the stern started to cheer and jump up and down, but the wind took the brassiere, it floating sometimes in a sort of double-breasted salute to Twin Peaks, and it fell far astern of the ship. Julie was delighted with the whole episode and said she hoped Aubrey didn't mind but that she felt sorry for men on outbound ships, and Aubrey was generosity itself—the men of the *Kersten Miles* being irrevocably outbound—and went so far as to say that had he been the captain of the vessel, he would have put back and retrieved the brassiere. Julie thought that that was quite the most gallant thing she'd ever heard, and called for a drink of champagne to mark the occasion, and kissed him on the cheek, and said that she would do better by him later. Then she said that it was getting dark and they'd have to hurry because she'd noticed a sign at the other end of the bridge about how it was closed and locked at nightfall or thereabouts, and she set a brisk pace toward the other side. But it soon became apparent that Julie, without her brassiere, was a menace to Marin-bound traffic, her brisk pace causing her to jiggle at the breasts so hugely and compellingly that Aubrey thought one Volkswagen was going to come right up on the sidewalk to have a better look. In the interest of highway, and their own, safety, Aubrey removed his jacket and buttoned it around her, and Julie fairly purred as she stroked the black coat, saying that the Lord's burden was sweeter and lighter than any brassiere she'd ever owned, and that she felt so positively risqué wearing clerical black.

And now the city was red like the western sky, and they paused only to look at the oscillation meters, or whatever they were, in their little houses at intervals along the bridge, and one meter was showing alarmingly more oscillation than the other two, and Aubrey blamed this on Julie's too rapid stride as they approached it and told her that she was dangerous on bridges without a brassiere, he feeling quite gay and unrestrained and proud of humanity and human achievement, and pointing out the phallic towers as if he himself had just raised them to catch the wind for her and cause the wind to sing. They paused, too, to look at the old fort down under the south pier, all of brick and most monstrously forbidding, constructed around a paved central courtyard with three decks, all opening to balconies inward and to tunneled and tracked gun ports toward the sea, and with artillery mounts on the top deck at the seaward corners, all of it moss-grown and bleak and taking to the dusk like a corpse to its winding sheet, a place ruddled by the setting sun yet strangely unbrightened, a place where Melmoth the Wanderer himself might have ceased his wanderings and taken up his permanent abode.

And then they were off the bridge in the chill and sudden night, and called a taxi from a booth behind a round restaurant on the southern shore, and went down into a small park below the restaurant to wait for the cab, and saw there a statue of the man who had built the bridge and poured a little champagne at the foot of it and congratulated him on his thoroughly grand and animated suspension, and saw a huge section of one of the main cables of the bridge, and decided that it looked too much like the telephone company to be attractive, and then sat down on the pedestal to this display, and had some more champagne, and looked at the city, a terraced tiara of red and yellow stones, and at Alcatraz, a grim coronet, and at the bridge, the night-lights orange on fading purple, and the revolving red light on the north tower showing where the fog had surrendered early and was in ragged retreat out to and beyond the shouldering, unlit ramparts of the north coast.

They sat close and touching against the cold, and the cab was a very long time coming, and Julie talked about how Filcher and Prissy would soon be making love in Carmel, if Filcher hadn't died of divergent impulses before they cleared the San Francisco city limits (Filcher being a sexually ambivalent son of a bitch, according to Julie, she having been out with him once—a blind date arranged by the devious Kermit, he telling her later that he'd figured that if any girl in the world could straighten Filcher out it was Julie—no such thing having happened, however, Julie having been disgusted with him at first sight and Filcher having been scared to death of Julie and able to talk only, when he'd gotten very drunk near the end of the evening, of how he was an extremely wiry and gifted street fighter and enjoyed nothing more than beating up "big guys" and especially homosexuals, whom Filcher professed to hate, so that Julie had determined to fix him up with Prissy, who was in love with Julie and Phoebe and was about as lesbianic a virgin as Julie had ever encountered, Julie's hope being that Filcher and Prissy would cancel each other out, and would not argue all night about who had the right to do what, with which, and to whom). And she talked, too, about how much she loved to make love—she having admitted immediately, and rather superfluously, Aubrey thought, that she was not a virgin and hadn't been since her fourteenth summer—and what it was like for a woman to have a man caught, and leaping, and eager, and heavy upon her and yet tender (although she decried the dearth of tender lovers, most men being too frightened of being thought homosexual or effeminate to do anything more than charge into a woman as a cave man into his cave), and how the woman receiving a lover was, at once, in the most vulnerable of positions and the most powerful; vulnerable because the man was stronger (though not always in her case, Julie readily admitted) and could perform the act as brutally as he saw fit, and yet powerful because the woman, if she was expert enough and truly oriented toward the man's pleasure as well as her own, could tame him, mellow him, instruct him, and thus control his brawn and muscle and thrust as she could have done in no other situation; and if the man was already controlled and instructed and tender, even then, the woman could lift and titillate him to such a height of passion, as she herself rose to the same height, that any roughness or wildness he might be driven to would only increase her own pleasure, not merely because she would then be as prepared and eager to receive as he would be to give, but also because of the simple, elemental, inexpressible joy of having lifted a man—the lord of the world and the most powerful, driving, commanding, willful, indestructible, raw, irresistible force in all of nature—to his supreme mortal moment, and to feel him moving within her, and moving her also, toward that single incomprehensibly deathlike instant when selfless self and selfless self release into each other the essence of life and the power over death, the essence of human happiness and the power to give not an exhausted goddamn if you should die in the following instant.

And she spoke simply and without coquettishness, her eyes bright and intimate and close as a kitten's, as if this were something she really could keep secret no longer, some privileged information he really ought to have, some precious, brittle intelligence which she was confiding to him in so unadorned and direct a manner because she had known all along that he would certainly understand. And Aubrey received all of it in the precise spirit in which it appeared to be offered, and his mood was at first only expansive, but as Julie talked on and on, putting the most exquisitely delicate points into plain language as if she were reciting The Lay of the Last Minstrel to Norman Vincent Peale, his enthusiasm for her attitude of truth, free inquiry, and no-nonsense seized him, as he thought later, by his Freudian censors and lifted him clear of negation and inhibition, right out of all the text he'd ever conned, and had him at last so exaltingly liberated that, much later also, he remembered describing to her, with condescending amusement at his own former prudery, the extremely guilt-ridden and dubious pleasure he had derived from those four times in his life he had masturbated.

(And he really couldn't believe, remembering most of it the next day, that he had actually said such things to her; that it had not occurred to him that his exaltation might have been induced by a swelling of the glands or by the intake of champagne and not by influx of angelically visited intellectual enlightenment; that he had heard none of the myriad and frantic signals that must have been bombarding him from Central Celibacy, the Desert Fathers in combined chorus with dead Saharans, conducted perhaps by St. Augustine, and all singing, "Come, Leap Ardently Into the Thornbush, Brother, Before You Really Get Stung"; that he had completely forgotten Finnegan's Law of the Penetrability of the Sexes, which states that, other things being equal, unequal, or however blatantly improbable of fruition, no two bodies, one male, the other female, can long occupy the same space at the same time without penetration becoming not only imminent but inescapable.)

Nor did he realize then that his inspection of the million lights of that vast and splendid arena of lights was done only in glances between long, soulful, fascinated assignations with Julie's eyes, nor that his appreciation of the immediate and distant landscape was nothing more than a remote and fragmented part of his appreciation of Julie's several configurations, from her cleavage to her jointures, and her lovely, silk-stockinged legs, bare to a hand's length above the knee. And whose hand he wished could measure that length he should have known, but didn't, and the only justification he seemed to need for his topographical inventory of her person was that she was, far and away, the most beautiful natural object in sight.

And she was not only the center of his vision but as he began to talk—about everything from embarrassing erections to his simple country-boy awe about the thought of entering anything but holy orders—she also became his adoring and tactile audience (that is, small touchings here and there about his face, especially the lips, as if she were obliged to receive his words through the ends of her fingers —now officially part of the I'm-deaf-dumb-blind-and-whelmed-baby-but-I'm-reading-you school of seductive appliance). What she approved could not be less than holy, and he talked on, and recited in Latin, Greek, French, and Italian, and no one of his pontifications, no matter how asinine, was too egregious to elicit her round-eyed awe and amaze. And her transformation from self-confessed libertine to undefiled maiden went on without interference of rational process. In the course of the first ten minutes of his recitative, she went from scarlet lily to Rose of Sharon; within ten more minutes she was a virgin clothed with the sun; and within the half hour she had metamorphosed into the immaculate vestal of Venus, whose mount was unclimbable and whose thirty-eight-inch bosom was forever inviolate. Occasional Juliesque interjections, such as balls, screw, pecker, and worse, he easily excused as proceeding from her natural, inspired exuberance and were in no way taken as evidence of sexual initiation not to mention recidivism. Julie was, he told himself with a certain mature and tolerant jocosity, just trying to impress him with her dream-worldliness. There wasn't a membrane pertaining to her that wasn't as intact as the secret formula for Coca-Cola. And within that very same half hour, Aubrey of the Dunes was sweetly, erogenously, luxuriantly, and wholly innocently infatuated.

Julie knew it. Oh, of course, she knew it, he told himself later. She had calculated the business down to the last self-revelation, both physical and mental, down to the last admiring sigh, down to the last whisper of those fleece-battened malachite eyes, down to the last lubricious wetting of those plump, self-caressing lips, down to the last and most inflammatory stroking of the conchae of his ears and the flanks of his nose, down to final, surrendering, rose-petal show of tongue between those predator teeth, down to the ultimate, orgiastic, musky sigh of receptive capitulation—the soft motion of the mouth moistly suggesting that all labial apertures within his arm's length were ready and waiting to receive his envoys. In short, she had circled him round about with every contravallation available to the corps of females. She had raped his privates, seduced his sergeants, flattered his captains, and was now mounting his inner tower disguised as a nun. The seal of her empire was already upon him, and when she should ask him to kneel with her in prayer what reason could he have for refusing to do so, having no inkling whose victory it was they would be praying for, having, in his abysmal naïveté or asininity, no slightest notion that that wimpling lady did not intend to get to her feet again until she had introduced his most closely guarded weapon into the very tenderest reaches of her superlative natural armory.

She came close to making a mistake only once, and that just before the taxicab came when, Aubrey having paused to admire a Browning sonnet he had just arranged above her head, she started to explain why she had tossed her brassiere to the men on the ship—and she was rather more direct and quite a bit less demure than she had contrived to be in the previous half hour or so (perhaps feeling that things were—what with Elizabeth Barrett Browning and all—getting just too damned ethereal for operational efficiency), although she did not sacrifice one virginal palpitation to bluntness.

"As I said, I felt sad about them, as I do whenever I see a ship going out to sea. And I still feel sad."

"But they didn't seem to feel sad when we last saw them. They were doing little dances, and all," Aubrey said.

"But they'll feel sad tonight."

"Why?"

"Oh, Aubrey, darling. You're so innocent."

"Why do you say that?"

"May I speak without mincing words, Aubrey?"

"Well, of course, Julie. Isn't that understood between us by now?"

"I know. But I just don't want to offend you, darling. You see, what will happen tonight is that all those men—they're boys, really —all those boys who saw me today out there will be lying under their blankets and think of me in my maid-of-honor dress, and they'll think of my brassiere and how I threw it to them and of my breasts all bare without it, and they'll have erections, and think about—well—screwing me. And I won't be there to screw. Do you see what I mean?"

Aubrey needed a few gulps of enlightenment to shore up his composure, but they were available there in the charged air, and he was able to answer, "You mean, their disappointment is what makes you sad?"

"Yes, but only partly. In fact, not even very much. What makes me sad is the thought of all those wasted erections, if you'll forgive my frankness. I mean, a girl only finds so many erections in a lifetime, you know?"

"You mean, you're sad because you couldn't go to bed with all of them?"

"Oh no, that isn't quite what I said."

"Well, I don't think I understand."

"There's a difference between being sad about wasted erections and wanting to go to bed with a lot of men. It's the same as the difference between pure, womanly sympathy and desire for a man, and nymphomania. I like to screw and be screwed, Aubrey, but I'm not a nymphomaniac. Still, just from the standpoint of womanly sympathy —not so much, I mean, from the standpoint of my own desire—I feel sad about those men because it wouldn't be a great hardship to me to give them all, every one of them, a nice warm place to put their erections. Not all tonight, of course, but, say, in the course of the voyage. Do you see? Not for my pleasure, necessarily, but for theirs. Almost as a prostitute would do, but I would accept no money. Can you understand that?"

"Well, I don't know, Julie. If that's how you really feel about men —I mean, about all men wandering around the seas and streets—it doesn't make much difference, it seems to me, whether you accept money or not. If you give yourself indiscriminately, as a receptacle of frustrations, or a reliever of them, you're prostituting yourself. The sin of prostitution is not so much, as I see it, in the acceptance or nonacceptance of money. It's in the moral self-destruction involved. In—in—ah—having sexual relations with all of those men indiscriminately, Julie, you'd be destroying your own personality, all that it means to be a woman . . ."

Julie interrupted, sensing just here, probably, that she had gone too far, that she was treading the edge of serious error. "Aubrey, darling, I shouldn't have said what I said. I mean, I guess, to convey that I care very much—universally, you might say—for those who aren't able to enjoy sexual pleasure as deeply, and as willfully, as I think they ought to do. I couldn't be a paid or unpaid prostitute. I'm a one-man girl. In fact, I suffer from what I call Queen-Bee-itis."

"What?"

"Queen-Bee-itis. I mean, I'm a one-man woman *and*, for as long as I'm interested in that one man, I want him to be ready to give up every other woman in the world for me, because I know that before I'm done with him, he'll *want* to give up every other woman in the world. But I want to know that about him beforehand. If I sense that he's very firmly married, for instance, I don't want any part of him. If I sense that he's just interested in a one-night encampment, I'm not interested. I want to have time, and leisure, and I want to enter his bone and his marrow and his soul, and put him through a reformation of his whole sexual outlook. I want to leave my mark on him for life. Is that evil of me, Aubrey, darling? I mean, is it evil to want to teach a man what a woman is? Is it evil to want to tutor a man and educate him and show him how to make love to a woman so that his own pleasure will be multiplied beyond his wildest dreams?"

"Well, Julie, I—ah—I can't make an answer from a *moral* standpoint, but, speaking purely pragmatically, I don't see how there could be any imputation of intrinsic evil."

"Oh, darling, you put things so—so, I don't know, just that when you're done with them, they're so gorgeously *academe!*" She stroked his temple for a time, as if to relieve the strain his last academic cerebration must have caused him. "What I mean, really, darling, is that I want your honey, honey, but if you're just ejaculating between flowers, find yourself another she-bee. I want all of your honey, until you haven't got any more, until you can't even think of any more, until you can't do anything but lie there and gasp and think about dying. In fact, I could want you, darling, so much that I might want you dead. I might want you to give so much, and take so much, that I'd want you to die in my arms."

"Well, Julie, that's pretty extreme, you must admit."

"But flattering."

"Maybe, but killing a man, or wanting to, if you know what I

295

mean, would be worse than going to bed with those fifty or sixty men on that ship."

"Perhaps, but my interest is with one man. My war is with the *élan vital*."

"Your war?"

"A friendly combat, you might say. Because I'm not really going to kill anybody in bed. At least, I haven't yet."

"I'm sure you haven't, Julie."

"No. I want just one man, Aubrey, darling. You might even call him a victim. I want to see what he can stand, how he survives under constant demand, how he stands up in the long run, how long his honey holds out. I'm interested in people pressed to their limits, aren't you, Aubrey?"

"Oh yes. In fact, the Christian ideal of the monk . . ."

"What I mean," Julie said, interrupting briskly, "I want to find the man who could put *me* to the test, who could put *me* to sleep. You know, darling, I sometimes think I could have fifteen or twenty or fifty climaxes in one night, if I could find the man who is man enough to stay *with* me." She smiled at him sweetly and ran the fingers of one hand over his lips. "Do you understand what I mean, darling?"

"I—ah—I'm not sure, Julie. But it sounds to me like an awful lot of—climaxes. You—ah—you might wear something out that way."

"I've *already* worn a lot of things out that way, darling."

"You have?"

"But don't you worry, darling. Yours is going to have great longevity. Why, it isn't even *born* yet. That's what's so fascinating about you, darling. Here you are, twenty-three years old, and your manhood is still there in its little nest among the eggs. Oh, darling, we have to lift him out tonight and stroke his little wings and teach him how to fly, don't we?"

"Teach *who* how to fly, Julie?"

"Never mind, sweet. You just leave it to me."

He agreed to do that and had just started talking about St. Francis and the birds when the cab came. The driver was the third most silent man in the world, and had the heater in the cab on full blast. Aubrey rammed his head into the door as usual, and was delighted with the warmth of the car, and put his head back immediately and closed his eyes. And as soon as they were under way, Julie moved over against him, pressing her near leg against his, pulling his chin toward her with one forefinger, speaking softly with her face so close to his that he could feel her breath and, from time to time, the touch of her lips. He didn't open his eyes because he was very tired and because printed across the junctures of his optic nerves in undulating pink was the old admonition about not wishing to see what you cannot have. But he could smell her perfume, and he could feel her least touch, and he could hear her talking, whispering about how he bumped his poor head, and how handsome he was, and how she would put him to bed and put a hot compress on his bump. And he was thinking that she was a good and sweet girl, and a wonderful stepsister to him, and was perhaps the only friend he had in the world, and the only really true and loyal and warm friend he had ever had (because who else was there, and when had he ever felt so lonely and unwanted and forgotten in his life as he had today?) and she had talked to him and listened to him so honestly and maturely, and had taken him on that nice walk, and had never gotten annoyed because of his drinking, and hadn't gotten angry with him because he had started the public disaster at the Turns house, and was now rubbing his bump and was going to nurse him back to health, and was, well, just really so good and true and beautiful and admired him so much that he had never before been so thrilled just to be with someone, he had never before understood or experienced the joys of true friendship.

And she went on talking in that incredibly smooth, low-pitched, reluctant-honey voice, telling him to rest, telling him to sleep, and actually putting him to sleep, paralyzing him into it. And just before he slept, he felt a strange, warm, sweetness spreading through the bottom of his loins and wondered if it might be internal bleeding from the bump on his head; and he heard, or thought he heard her say, ". . . my dear sweet untapped stepbrother, Julie's going to tap you tonight before the moon is high."

And it happened very quickly.

Julie was propriety itself. She assisted him to his door, seemed to understand perfectly when he said that the thing he needed most in the world was a long night's sleep, and gave him a very demure little speech about how wonderful and charming a date he'd been, and, with exquisite chasteness, kissed him on the point of his chin and fled away in maidenly confusion to her own room.

No more than ninety seconds later there was a knock at the connecting door. Aubrey, it happened, was sitting on the bed pointed right at the connecting door, and after an inspection of his shoes, which were still on despite his ardent intention that they should not be, he pushed off the bed and caught the door open as he went three feet by it. Julie fairly blushed her way into the room, still fully dressed, a glass of water in one hand and displaying a yellow pill between the thumb and forefinger of the other. This pill would, she said, make him feel better and would prevent a hangover. He downed it without question. Julie then guided him back to the bed and helped him off with his shoes and tie, and, he modestly preventing her further assistance, she went trippingly about other little errands of mercy, such as locking his front door and putting on the chain latch, turning on his bathroom light, turning off his bedroom light, calling the operator and instructing her that absolutely no calls were to be put through to his room, and finding his pajamas and laying them out for him on the foot of the bed. Then, after a final, Nightingale-ish fluff of his pillows, she blushed her way out again, closing the door softly behind her. Aubrey managed to arrive at nudity and to negotiate his pajamas, and then stretched out on the bed, dragged one blanket half over him, and fell asleep thinking that, really, Julie was a saint and he would certainly talk to her tomorrow about joining the medical missionary sisters.

Within the half hour, he was lying on his back, eyes wide open, staring at the ceiling, more fully and brilliantly awake than he had ever been in his life. He knew that he was still drunk, but his body felt lightsome, completely in his control, his senses supercharged, his mind racing and darting and touching all shadows with dazzling light, his perception outrunning his comprehension, his inward eye transfigured and dancing with eager, flashing visions of all he was and all he would be and all he would accomplish in just no damned time at all. And these sensations seemed to be getting stronger and more vivid, and he felt that he really shouldn't be lying there but up and doing and seeing and running and jumping; but he also felt an enormous pleasure just lying there, felt his power growing and informing every nerve in his body, felt such an intensity of sensual ravishment that he wondered if he might not be having a spiritual seizure.

Then, suddenly and without a knock, the door was opened and closed and Julie was in the room, turning from the door and coming toward him, barefooted, smiling, her hair soft about her shoulders, dressed only in a short, white nightgown, and, hesitating not at all, but coming to him simply and silently, the high magnificence of her breasts just perceptibly moving, the motion of her stomach and hips and thighs, and the cuneus of darkness centered between them—the motion of the whole incredibly golden suit of her flesh—almost audible to him, a whisper heard but not quite understood, a murmuring out of a world whose existence he had acknowledged but whose voice he had never expected to hear, an almost sound that had been haunting him for all his lonely days.

Before she had reached the bed, he knew he could not withstand her. Time had come to a drumming stop and all of the sensate wildness that was visiting him had become, at first sight of her, erotic. She was his only reality, brilliantly lighted, brilliantly voluptuous, brilliantly seen. He saw all of her surfaces with intense clarity, and it seemed to him that he could also see her essence, the within and the being, the heart and its history; could see all that was Julie—all that was girl, all that was woman—coming to offer herself, to open herself to him, and he would go into her because, just now, he willed to know her more than he willed to live, more than he willed to know God, and as she knelt on the edge of the bed and bent to kiss him, he thought, I will go into my stepsister Julie because I can no longer deny myself the knowledge of what is there.

The touch of her hair on his face as she bent to him made him gasp, but the following shocks, as she kissed him open-mouthed and moved her tongue into his mouth and moved the tips of her breasts on his chest and then broke the kiss and suddenly straightened and stripped the nightgown up over her head—the arch of her body giving her breast and her stomach full, rounded, blatant size and beauty—these shocks of sight and touch moved him to a single response and she said one word as he took off his pajamas, and that was "Hurry!" and he did. And she led him to her and within, and then she was gasping and moving against him, but he held himself in the first few seconds of penetration, and raised his head and shoulders, and reached out one hand and seized the headboard of the bed, and tightened his grip on it and shook it with all his strength and tried to ignore for a few seconds the motion and grip of her thighs. But wasn't able to ignore her, and all he managed to say was My God, this is a mortal sin! And no damned wonder!

# · TWENTY-FOUR ·

THE DREAM that brought him awake was not the worst of them, but it had its moments. He was nailed alive in a rough box coffin, the hard wood of the lid pressed down firmly against his face, on his way to hell in it and in the jaws of a prodigious maelstrom, a clear vision of which was the central horror of the whole business: a cyclonic funnel of white water as broad as the great southern sea, entire islands swirling in it, along with whales, trees, coconuts, ships, assorted natives, but no other coffins, all of it going around and around with him in that vast perimeter with the speed of comets, and all sinking with him slowly and inevitably down from the crest of the cataract, down and down into the pulsing eye of hell, now obscured by ash and steam, then exposed, with the damned leaping and screaming in the flames, screams that came up to him so fiercely and loud that they shut out even the Krakatoan roar of the waters, screams that finally included his own name and accused him of causing the cataclysm, accused him of tearing the tree of knowledge— and it screaming like a monstrous mandrake—out of the heart of the earth.

And then there was an hour of pure agony when he fought his way out of sleep into full possession of his hangover, and then, to the tune of church bells, fought off enough of the hangover to come into an even fuller possession of his shame. And it was a thorough and scalding shame that reached him in all his parts, told him that it was Sunday and that Christ was in His churches, waiting on His cross for him to rise out of his self-disgust and take his pitiful soul in both hands and return it humbly to Him who loaned it; that enormous shame of the new nonvirgin, ramified beyond endurance, or very nearly, by thoughts of all he had betrayed in that single act and by the knowledge that if he should yet be ordained a priest, he could never speak or preach to anyone about chastity without feeling the guilt of the hypocrite; that shame from which doleful voices proceed, accusing in sad cadence and saying, Here we have all been watching for two thousand years, and did you desert us in the night?

And he groaned and asked himself why for most of the hour, and paced his room, using all of it, from the toilet to the front window and back again. He finally summoned enough courage to look at himself in the bathroom mirror. He still felt drunk, and now saw that he looked drunk. Only after a cold shower and a shave did he begin to look or feel sober.

The doorman directed him to Old St. Mary's Church in Chinatown, and he went down the steep slope of California Street angry and disgusted, throwing his feet into step as if he hoped they would come loose at the ankles. He allowed himself to observe the new sun on the Berkeley hills and the early blue and cloudless sky of Pentecost Sunday, but took no pleasure in either, and moved toward the ordeal of confession with almost masochistic eagerness.

Confessions were not being heard, but he went to the sacristy and found a young, tender-eyed Paulist priest in front of the vesting table, just reaching for the alb. After the briefest of estimatory pauses, as he inspected Aubrey's by now rather disreputable-looking black suit, he met Aubrey halfway across the room, nodded at once when he heard Aubrey's request, and went quickly, humbly, to get his stole.

He heard Aubrey's confession through a small portable screen, and Aubrey watched him the while, overwhelmed with compassion for this young priest who should not have been exposed to such sordidness as incest (whether it was or not Aubrey wasn't sure, but confessed it as such) so early in the morning. Yet he told all in considerable detail, sparing the priest nothing, wishing to miss or conceal no least part of his guilt. And the young priest did appear to be distressed, and even closed his eyes during the recital of the sexual specifics, but rallied vigorously when it came time for direct examination.

"You were a virgin prior to last night?"

"You are quite certain you are no longer in vows?"

"You were completely aware that you were committing mortal sin?"

"She is a stepsister through your father's second marriage?"

"You actively participated in the intercourse the first two times, and more or less passively participated in the third instance, is that correct?"

"She is three years your junior?"

"Are you confident that you and she will not be thrown together alone during this hunting trip you speak of?"

And so on, his questions incisive, impersonal, merciful, and his penance so light that Aubrey asked him to repeat it when he had finished the absolution. The priest repeated it, the sorrowful mysteries of the rosary, and then said, "I will remember your intention in my Mass this morning. Please remember that no penance could possibly be equal to the offense. Would it serve any purpose to give you a more severe penance? I think not. Besides, I want you to be able to finish your penance in time to participate in the consecration, to give all of your attention to it, in my Mass this morning, and to prepare yourself for an entirely devoted reception of Our Lord into your soul. You say you are going on to another seminary. I hope you are, and that you do become a priest. And in view of that intention, I can imagine no greater penance than the thought that must be yours at this moment, and will be yours when you approach the Communion rail this morning: that Our Lord and Savior Jesus Christ died upon the cross to buy you forgiveness for the sensual indulgence you allowed yourself last night, for the terrible injury you did to the soul of your stepsister." The young priest put one hand over his eyes and shook his head very slightly. "I will remember her intention, also. And you pray for her, and dedicate your Communion this morning to her salvation, to her repentance. As God loves us in proportion to our love for others, so does He forgive us in proportion to the forgiveness we seek to obtain for others. God loves you very much, or He would not have called you to the priesthood. But think of this: How could even God repay you if you, by your prayers and example, managed to bring your stepsister to repentance?"

Which was so stupefying a thought that it distracted Aubrey throughout his penance and Communion. Julie repentant—Julie inhibited by anything more than her own shortness of breath—was, in the cold and holy light of that good morning, something damned near inconceivable to him. The fancy of Julie professing allegiance to anything beyond that which she could feel with her hands and test with her body took on no verisimilitude whatsoever. Julie was so essentially and substantially of the natural order that he could find no place at all upon her image for a supernatural mark.

But he did his best, and prayed for the long life of the young and holy priest, and prayed for Julie's conversion to some form of godliness, and prayed for everybody involved in the public disaster the day before. And then knelt there until the eight o'clock Mass was well under way, praying for the preservation of his own vocation, able to be reasonably objective now about his sexual initiation, able to consider it without drastic emotionalism, and yet still profoundly puzzled as to how and why it had happened. His prayers gave him no answers—he had allowed himself to get superdrunk and supersusceptible and supersensitized and supernaturally disoriented, and that was that—and he climbed back up the hill to the hotel wondering if the Alaska trip would not be a mistake after all.

Kermit was standing in the center of the hotel lobby surrounded by Rexfordia, Solly, Arnie, and baggage, and two or three restive bellmen. An argument was in progress, the first issue being where in hell was Aubrey, and the second being what was all this crap about Rexfordia wanting Arnie to forgo the Alaska trip. As Aubrey came up, Arnie was insisting, loudly, that, goddamn it, he had never thought or hinted that he wouldn't go to Alaska, and it was just some damned figment of Rexfordia's imagination. Then Arnie saw Aubrey and gave the alarm.

"Well, Jesus Christ! The finking reverend! We thought the white slavers got you!"

"Christ Jesus, Aubrey! Where the hell have you been? Goddamned airplane leaves in an hour!" Kermit said.

"I've been to Mass. It'll only take me a minute to pack."

"I already packed you," Kermit said. "What the hell did you do in that bed of yours last night, run foot races?"

"I didn't sleep too well."

"Aubrey, that suit looks *awful*," Rexfordia said. "You can't go to Alaska in *that*."

"Oh Jesus, now she's going to start on Aubie," Arnie said.

"Why the hell can't he go in that?" Kermit said. "You can go to Alaska, by Christ, in your bare ass and a jockstrap if you want to!"

"Kermit, please, the people," Rexfordia said. "Oh, Aubrey, I do wish you'd come back with me. Solly and I have reservations on a very nice train, and . . ."

"No more, no more!" Kermit cried. "Goddamn it, Rexie, they are both going with me! You had Arnie all last week and you can have Aubrey when we get back! Jesus Christ, if you must be irrational, at least be fair about it!"

"Don't be roarin' at her like that," Solly said. "Sure Arnold spent the last week with us, but we didn't see him for more than a god-damned hour put together in the whole time, so occupied he was in his goddamned writin' or whatever the hell it is he's doin'. A lot of goddamned foolishness, that's sartin, instead of passin' the time with his poor mother."

"Who the hell made you town crier?" Arnie said.

"Where the hell is Julie?" Kermit said.

"I'm just tellin' you what's right," Solly said.

"What the hell do I care what's right?" Arnie said.

"And would you tell us in the name of Jaysus and the mercy you might even show a jackass in a manhole what in the name of Christ crucified it is you're writin'?"

"A book, a book! Jesus Christ, Aubie, would you knock her down when you get a minute? Goddamned old harridan's been after me all morning."

"A book! That's what I thought!" Solly cried triumphantly. "Here, for Jaysus sake, we got every goddamned cubbyhole in the house stuffed full of books already! I even found one in the oven the other day! Haven't you got enough damned books without your havin' to write another, for Christ's sake?"

And it went on with Rexfordia saying that it was all right with her if Arnie wanted to be a writer, and with Kermit saying Arnie was going to be an actor after yesterday's performance at the Turns residence, and Solly saying something like this: "An actor my bun-yock! The whole lot of 'em's nothin' but nitwits, pimps, and whoors, up there thinkin' of nothin' but showin' their parts to the public, and sayin' things they don't mean, and kissin' people they don't know at all! Jaysus Christ, a bigger bunch of Sligo pissants was never rounded up under any callin' . . ."

Kermit interrupted to announce Julie, who had just stepped off the elevator, and the confusion started at once with Kermit shouting at the bellmen, and with Rexfordia starting to cry immediately and twist her rings and look from Arnie to Aubrey and make little desperate lunges from one to the other to kiss them wherever she happened to strike, and with Solly telling Julie to for Christ sake get a move on, and with an assistant manager of the hotel telling Kermit that there was a long-distance call for him from his agent, and with Kermit telling the assistant manager to please tell his agent to go piss up a rope, and with Julie—very simply dressed and her hair piled up on her head—giving Aubrey a smile of teeth and eyes and complicity and asking him if he had slept well, and with Arnie shouting (as he struggled toward the door with Rexfordia pulling at his coat), "Mother, I don't need an electric blanket!" and with Kermit kicking at a dog some lady had on a leash because the dog had barked at him, and with Solly telling the lady that the dog was foaming at the mouth (which it wasn't), and with Julie shouting to Aubrey to come get in the cab with her as he went firmly over and got in the other cab, and with Rexfordia kissing Aubrey goodbye and telling him to pray constantly for a vocation to the New York archdiocese because obviously the Saharan Fathers didn't want him, and with Solly kissing him and saying almost exactly the same thing with due notice of the futility of trying to salvage blackamoors, and with Aubrey hearing one of the bellmen say to another, "Jesus, Jonsie, I don't know. They must be all nuts!" and with Arnie crying as he escaped into the cab with Aubrey, "Jesus blistered Christ, Mother! If you want my goddamned coat, take it! But I'm going! I'm going! In the name of God, have you no mercy?" and with Julie shouting at Aubrey through the window, "So little tillie-ass went to church and got his bollix welded? Well, screw you, step!" and with the whole scene in the Mark Hopkins courtyard resembling, finally, the start of the Sebring race, with all kinds of spectators, people rushing back and forth, Kermit shouting loading directions, and then standing dramatically at the door of the front cab, shouting back at the other driver, his arm upraised, "You! Wake up, you goddamned smog-eyed bastard! Follow this cab to the airport and don't lose us or I'll be back and deal with you!" causing both drivers to race their engines as Kermit jumped in beside Julie. The doorman slammed the door behind him, Solly waved both arms as if she were experiencing great pain in both from the shoulders out and shouted, "Oh, Jaysus, the

Narth Pole!" over and over again, Rexfordia had her right arm crooked around the neck of a short bellman who was supposed to be preserving her from a fainting fall to the pavement but who looked devoid of air and ready to join her there whenever she took the notion, and the last voice heard was Rexfordia's as the cabs shot away at thirteen miles an hour, "Oh my sons! My two darling sons! He's taking them from me! The vulgar man!"

When they were about a mile down the road, Arnie, who had been stretched out limp with his feet on a leather gun case, apparently exhausted, if not emotionally disintegrated, opened his eyes and said, "Say I'm weary, say I'm sad, say that Freud and Zen have missed me. Say I'm Rexie's boy, but add, Camus spelled backwards is sumac. Right, babe? Right. Now, what's all this shit about the Turnses?"

"I didn't say anything about them. But what happened?"

"What happened? You don't deserve to be told, you goddamned deserter. What happened to you? They say you went home sick, but Phoebe told me you went off with Julie, and if I know that piece of epidermis, you went home screwed! Right?"

"Wrong. I returned to the hotel unscrewed and unsung."

"Well spoken! Just for that, I'll tell you what transpired. Actually, not much. Old Turns decided, after long debate with Kermit—you know—Turns said, 'Sir?' and Kermit said, 'Shut your goddamned mouth!' End of debate. So Kermit and I left, went downtown and worked our way up Nob Hill, bar by bar. Had a grand time, except that Kermit fell in love with a stripper and there was some difficulty about a bass drum."

"A bass drum?"

"Oh, Kermit got out of it all right. He just told them that he had intended to kick the drummer."

"Sounds like a lovely evening."

"Oh yes. Finest kind of relaxation." Arnie scratched and sighed and lit a cigarette. "Hum, hum, Aubie. I don't know, and who the hell ever did?" He smiled up at his brother. "You're looking good, kid, but a little siphoned off or something. You sure Julie-bitch didn't get to you? Ooops! Forgot it was Sunday. Well, guess who I met in the lobby last night about four this morning, as a matter? Old Phoebe the Philter! Yes, indeed. And she said she had her filter ready and how was my blend, and we sort of micronited a few times before breakfast. Say, Aubie, is this a champagne flight? I need some encouragement." Aubrey had no idea. Arnie slipped even farther down in the seat and peeked up at him between his fingers. "There are people all over the world, Aubie, with their asses nailed to invisible walls. Right? Hum, hum. Yes, indeed. So what did you think of your psychiatric report, my lad, hm?"

"Very interesting."

"Change your thinking any?"

"About what?"

"Christ, I don't know about what! About joining the camel corps!"

"You mean the Saharans?"

"All right, goddamn it! Yes, I mean the Saharans!"

"No. If they take me, I'll go. The report said I was all there— that my defects were salient within my personality—didn't it?"

"Oh Christ, yes. Salient. Me too. Both of us. We bulge here and there, but our defects are salient. Until, of course, they aren't. Well! I can see you're very impressed. So I will now address the American Society of Psychiatric Jobbers. Gentlemen. You all know my mother, Oedipus Rexie. Hold, hold! Hold back your drooling army with Viennese banners, while I rise in my simple humanistic magnificence and say, No, no, I am sorry, gentlemen, but you are wrong. For you see, in the first place, I am a perfectly executed genital character. In the second place, after long and incredibly mature consideration, I feel free to state that while my mother may well be in love with me, I am definitely not in love with my mother. I thank you, gentlemen. Now truck on home, like the good pre-oral monsters that you are."

It was a champagne flight, and Arnie sat next to Aubrey and drank off goblets of it as fast as the stewardesses could pour it, drinking Aubrey's first in a gulp and then nursing his own until he could grab one of the girls by the bottle. So that by the time they were halfway across Oregon, and Aubrey had gotten tired of looking at all those evergreens and red mud, Arnie was extremely well lubricated and discovered that he had a small lecture to deliver.

"You see, Aubie, it's this way. You're going up narth here to the Pole to shoot bear because you need violence. Why did Christ drive the money-changers from the temple? Why did He choose to be crucified? Because He knew the value of violence, knew the exultation of it. That is: I can kill. And he knew the pride of it: I have killed. And He knew the attraction of it for men as a thing to repeat: I can kill again. So He got a little violence into His life, knowing that

307

it had the power to attract men. Certain men. But those it doesn't especially attract, like you, Aubie, are worried about the violence in Christ's life. You figure you ought to have a little of it in your life, too. Right? Sure. That's why you're going hunting with us. Oh, not to test your courage. But to see if you can endure to kill—if you can take life—if you can live with the remorse of it. Like all Christians, you long to be crucified, but you can't arrange that too easily in this day and age. You can't get near death any legitimate way, short of a war, except by hunting, and so you hunt. And you get near death that way again and again, not only learning to take life and live with the remorse of taking it, but also, like a good Christian, hoping that what you are hunting will rise up and take your life, crucify you. Like all Christians, you want to be a Jew, and you can't really ever forgive Christ for doing such a disgustingly brave thing as allowing Himself to be crucified. But! Cheer up, Aubie, I understand some of those brown bears can drive nails with the best of them."

Aubrey found this virtually incomprehensible, but Arnie wasn't in the mood for questions, and fell asleep shortly thereafter. But just before they got to Seattle, Arnie woke up and delivered another instruction. "I wonder if you are aware, Aubie, that the desire for power is very strong in you. If you need evidence, simply consider how doggedly you have always fought me for the ascendancy between us. You've never considered my desire for that same ascendancy amusing or frivolous. You would have so considered it if you really hadn't given a damn for power yourself. But you do desire power over men, over me. Oh yes. You may even have entered the priesthood to stay with me, as it were, in respect to that desire. And you may be going to Africa, to do what I failed to do, just so that you can prove, with precise specificity, how superior you are to me. And, of course, there's another side of the coin: your very fear of gaining that ascendancy over me. There's a will to fail in you, Aubie. I was thinking the other night about you and Julie-Bitch. I don't see, really, how you can avoid screwing that girl. No, sir. Because, you see, it will satisfy both your will to succeed and your will to fail. If you screw her thinking, There, that's something I did that Arnie couldn't do, that she wouldn't let him do, you satisfy your will to succeed, to beat me. And if you screw her thinking, Oh Christ, now I can't be a priest because I've lost my virginity, you satisfy your will to fail. And I just don't know how to advise you, Aubie, because I don't know yet whether I want you to fail or succeed. But what worries me most is, I don't think you know yet whether you want to fail or succeed. Oh, it's a fierce problem, Aubie, and I don't think we really ought to seek a solution with any energy until we get a few drinks in us at the Seattle airport. I figure we have an hour and a half between planes, and that ought to be just right for mapping out your future. Right, Aubie? Right, babe. And do try to stop staring at that one stewardess. Old Julie-Bitch is glaring at you so dreadful jealous that I do believe she might short out our radar."

But they were twenty-eight minutes late getting into Seattle, and the bar at the airport was crowded—apparently by local people who liked it—and Kermit and Julie and Arnie managed to get only two drinks apiece consumed before the Anchorage flight was announced for the second time. Aubrey had resolved to drink no more, and sat the whole time staring at some kind of mobile, apparently left over from Christmas, rotating dismally over the heads of the customers at the bar, while Kermit and Arnie argued about the ability of Kermit's racehorse to avoid being trampled in the course of the coming season, and Julie alternately glowered at Aubrey and studied a volume entitled *Scorpio: the Year Ahead.*

The flight from Seattle to Anchorage was an unmitigated horror. The aircraft climbed into a black, driving rain as it left Seattle, and stayed in that rain in its attendant thunderstorm for nearly seven hours. The craft flopped and shuddered and rolled and wobbled and bent, and rose and fell immeasurably drastic distances, so that Aubrey was at first afraid the damned thing was going down, and then afraid that it wasn't—that it would simply go on rising up and up and right on out into the outer darkness.

There was a procession of the sick and dying in the aisle from early on, in defiance of the seat-belt sign, most of the lurchers looking entirely ready to lurch all over anyone who displayed an empty pocket—a circumstance that put Arnie in great and indignant apprehension ("Get on with you, goddamn it!" he kept saying to innocent passersby. "Do I look like a goddamned flight surgeon?") —most of the ambulants carrying their little bagfuls of regurgitation and waving them menacingly about as they clutched for handholds, their miserable parade something Dante might have described as that punishment reserved for those who refused to believe that God, had He wanted humans to fly, would have equipped them with wings.

Arnie finally engaged the stewardess in single combat. She had just stopped one of the walking wounded next to Arnie's seat and warned him that if he didn't stay fastened, he might get hurt and the airline couldn't be responsible.

"Responsible?" Arnie howled. "You're about the most irresponsible goddamned responsible outfit I've ever seen!"

"Sir?"

"This goddamned storm, missy!"

"We didn't cause the stor-um, sir," the stewardess whined.

"No, but you didn't avoid it, either, did you, Fatchops?"

"Sir, this airplane is equipped with radar . . ."

"Radar! Don't give me *that* crap. You know what radar spelled backwards is? Hah! I didn't think you knew! We're heading for a mountain, aren't we, missy? Yes, indeed. And all you can do about it is smile. Well, let me tell you something. If my Bristol barrel full of rattlesnakes breaks back there in the baggage car, you'll wish to Christ you had radar in your snood!"

"Sir, the pilot . . ."

"The pilot! Jesus Christ, you mean there's actually somebody trying to *guide* this shitbox?"

The stewardess, a homely, sturdy girl, now squatting in the aisle, bringing her face to a level with Arnie's and apparently feeling called upon to quell this outbreak before it spread, informed Arnie that the storm was an act of God, and, having noticed Aubrey's black suit, called upon him to confirm this sentiment. Aubrey received a thumping elbow from Arnie in the left breast, but he had already formed a dislike for her bovine presumption, and said no, he didn't think storms were acts of God because, as a matter of fact, he was a Manichee and he believed that the forces of evil were responsible for all storms, and that, clearly, this airline was in league with the Devil because it was so expertly exposing its passengers to the tortures of the damned. And Aubrey was taking his time explaining this when he noticed the poor little man in the aisle, the one whose arrest had started the whole altercation and who had been trying to get around the stewardess ever since; a living cipher of defeat, Kafka's bewilderment incarnate, holding one hand to his mouth and trying not to drop the bag he held in the other. As he came up against the stewardess whose aisle squat was preventing his progress toward the men's room, he turned his great, sad, nauseated eyes toward Aubrey, attentively, without anger, as if he would wait forever if Aubrey should decide to talk that long. Aubrey pointed and cried to the stewardess to clear the runway, the stewardess looked around and straightened and yelped forward into Arnie's capable arms, the little man shot down the aisle on the crest of a sudden nose dive by the airplane, and Arnie put the stewardess through a course in manual dexterity before he restored her, blushing, shocked, and no vital unvisited, to the vertical some few swift seconds later. She stood there in the aisle and blinked a few times before Arnie put her to rout entirely by saying, "Well, dear Christ, Miss Skagway, if you want me to do any better than that you'll have to go take that goddamned corset off!"

And Arnie alternated between near and utter collapse due to laughing fits from that moment until they were on the ground in Anchorage. And Aubrey tried to ignore him, and read the Divine Office for Pentecost Sunday, and snapped his eyes shut whenever an image of Julie naked came dancing onto the page. And she didn't miss a psalm.

It was after midnight when they stepped from the airplane and there was a gray twilight still in the sky and the wet smell of the land was strong; and all around him, as he walked toward the terminal, there was a strangeness in the air, a threat of sudden change, an almost palpable animosity in the thin and gentle drizzle. And with these a hum, as of great and elemental activity somewhere far beyond human ken and influence; a whispering, as of massive and resentful movement of ice and waters and the earth itself far out in the wildernesses of mountains and sea; a murmur that told him at once, without the least forethought or preparation, that this vast and raw country bore him a grudge because he was of the race of men and that it wanted him, by whatever means, gone.

And he found himself looking over his shoulder at the lowering sky and thinking of dying violently and without warning; and found himself checking his resources, examining his readiness to die, and at one point standing in the middle of the brightly lit terminal, staring absently at the floor, wishing with all his heart and power—for perhaps the forty-thousandth time that day—that he had his virginity back and that he had never set out for Alaska.

# · TWENTY-FIVE ·

KERMIT was at his door before seven the next morning, hammering industriously and shouting, "Hah! Up! Up! For Christ's sake, Kunkel's here with the new airplane!"

Aubrey pushed himself up on one elbow and shouted, "*Deo gratias!*" Although, after four hours' sleep, he couldn't have sincerely given a damn if Kunkel had grown personal wings.

Ten minutes later he had showered and was shaving and marveling at the modern conveniences, the almost East Ohio grandeur of the appointments of the Anchorage Westward Hotel, he having expected something one notch above a lean-to, and was remembering the drive in from the airport through streets that had looked exactly like the outlying areas of Poughkeepsie, New York, when there came a second pounding on his door, and he charged out impatiently with lather in one eye and ran into the coffee table (made of some sort of adamantine substance of the size and shape of a petrified dinosaur's kidney), and got to the door with his right shin in one hand and violence in his heart.

But it was Julie, in her bright red robe and her hair combed out into a sort of cobra's hood, and as he opened the door, she was pointing at a newspaper somebody had left on the floor outside the door, and saying, "That old fart, de Gaulle."

Then she bent over and picked up the newspaper, letting the

312

robe fall away from her breasts as she did, so that he had, before he could avert his eyes, a clear view of them, and she glanced up quickly as she straightened and caught his embarrassment and smiled and said, "How are your shower handles this morning, step darling?" And while Aubrey scanned the adjoining wall for an answer, she pushed the newspaper into his stomach, eased by him, kissing him on the shoulder as she passed, and said, all at once, "My, you look nice in a lather. The towel's nice, too. Especially the legs. I broke the hot handle on mine, so I'll have to use yours. You go right ahead with your shaving." And before he had the door closed, she was moving across the room in her bare feet, shedding her robe as she got to the bathroom door, and, poised there, completely nude, her robe in a pile behind her, one hand flat on her postern, and the tips of her breasts only in the bathroom, she said, "Care to join me, step? Or have you been washed in the blood of the lamb?" And almost immediately he could hear her splashing and yelping in the shower.

He knew what had to be done—a lengthy sprint in no particular direction—but found himself wobbling around the room, wiping the lather from his face, fingering his suitcase, staring at the Anchorage telephone directory on the desk, climbing without dispatch into a pair of drawers, some socks, his shoes, pants, a T shirt, and, while buttoning his dress shirt, standing for a time looking out at the clamshell, wind-gray coffin of Anchorage, Alaska, and was only moved to real and present action by Julie's whooping invitation: "Won't you join me, step? You must have worked up a sweat by this time."

He fled from the room, swooping up tie, jacket, and hat as he went, and really didn't stop until he was in the elevator where he donned his tie, absorbing the startled inspection of a Klondike matron who obviously had not seen the like of him since her last visit to an undertaking parlor, and who seemed to give special attention to his feet, the reason for which Aubrey did not discover until he started to step forth into the lobby and found that his right foot was in his straw hat.

And there was Kermit, in the middle of the lobby and shouting as usual, but this time in great good humor and at a listener who seemed perfectly capable of withstanding the blast: a red boulder of a man, with close-cut hair, flat face, classic American Indian features, a permanent dubious squint, an equally permanent dubious smile, and the damnedest hugest pairs of hands and shoulders since Mighty Joe Young. And this was Kunkel Cranch, unchanged, except for his clothes, in the almost six years since Aubrey had last seen him, and he turned toward Aubrey at once, and said gently, "There's Mister Aubrey!"

Kunkel's greeting was quiet but contusive, and Aubrey, when he thought about it, was very glad to see him. Solid, solemn, and silent, he might have the effect of sobering up the whole expedition. He already seemed to be having this effect upon Kermit. In his fringed buckskin jacket, Kermit was dressed for the hunt, but he was also putting on his hunting personality, his outdoor aspect, his bearslayer's brow. Just now, under Kunkel's influence, he was in the this-is-a-very-serious-undertaking phase, the voice loud but gravely modulated, the manner intrepid but denoting immense and professionally masculine respect for all wild beasts, the eye fierce but wary, the head high but never still, always cocked or half cocked over one shoulder, or in passage between left and right, never tarrying long, always keeping the stealthy enemy in sight. (Other more or less inevitable phases still to come were: the gay, aren't-we-a-grand-bunch-of-brave lads phase; the sentimental, just-before-the-battle-Mother phase; the dramatic, we-who-are-about-to-die-salute-you phase; and the outraged, what-the-hell-is-holding-up-the-goddamned-hunt-for-Christ's-sake phase. This last phase, the most frequently repeated, could be brought on by practically anything—bad weather, a flat tire, the scarcity of game, a broken leg—or simply arrive for no apparent or revealed reason. And there would be Kermit pacing up and down, fists doubled, muttering apocalyptically, roaring in intermittent and thunderous barks, glaring darkly about, as if he were a medieval baron, newly caparisoned for battle, angrily addressing his troops, perhaps saying, "Here we're up in the middle of the night, gear polished, blood up, sinews summoned, and now that pusillanimous son of a bitch of a king has called the battle off!")

In short, Kermit's greatest acting was done during the hunt, and Aubrey had always thought it a damned shame that his performances could not be captured on film for public release. As far as Kermit was concerned, of course, those performances were being recorded. Somewhere, somehow, the Great Cameraman was on the job, His ubiquitous Zoomar lens capturing all of the gaudy flamboyance of it, and Kermit's eternity would consist in watching this greatest of late-late shows run over and over again on the wide screen in the Vahalla Music Hall.

(And Arnie maintained that what Kermit was really after in all of this hunting was the perfect ending: glorious death in combat. Arnie had told Aubrey about going out with Kermit, during the last Alaskan trip, to hunt beluga whale, and Kermit kept the party out two days hunting for a white one, but finally settled for a ratty brown one, into which, Arnie swore, Kermit drove his harpoon hard and true, turned to Kunkel, and cried, "Cut!" Then fell on his ass when the whale took off, and roared, "Goddamn it, stop that whale!" What he really meant to say, according to Arnie, was "Doesn't that goddamn whale know he's supposed to charge the boat and bite my leg off?")

Arnie came down in a sour mood, looking odd and uncomfortable in his hunting clothes, and greeted Kunkel with typical reserve. "Hello, you goddamned red Indian. You raped any white women lately?"

Kunkel grinned, called Arnie by name, clapped him once on the back (slipping four discs, Arnie reported), and said to Kermit, "Ready?"

And after that, in rapid succession: Aubrey and Arnie had what Arnie called "breakfast interruptus," with Kermit poking his head into the dining room every fifty seconds or so to demand that they hurry; Julie arrived for breakfast and refused to sit at their table, and when Arnie hit her on the jaw with a soft roll, hit Aubrey in the mouth with a hard one; Kermit arranged for all nonessential baggage to be stored in the hotel and got in an argument with a man who said he wouldn't be liable for damage or theft, and Kermit said the hell he wouldn't, and the man said the hell he would, and Kermit won the field if not the argument by saying that, as a matter of fact, he might be in error because the man did look like the most unreliable son of a bitch he'd ever laid eyes on; Aubrey was outfitted for the hunt at a place called Van's Sporting Goods and left his black suit with a nice man there who said that he just might keep it to get buried in; everybody but Kunkel got properly licensed and tagged, or whatever, and Arnie asked for a special license to shoot Kermit in the ass if he tried to keep them out at Cold Bay for more than ten days; two cabs were commandeered and loaded to drive them out to the airport, and the great Big Ditmo hunt was almost under way.

The day was overcast and the city of Anchorage looked dismal and woebegone, which impression was not helped by the fact that the driver of the taxicab (and, Aubrey wondered, where in the name of God will I ever be free of taxicab drivers if not in Alaska?) was a great, fat-mouthed slattern of a woman who insisted upon delivering a running, gap-toothed commentary on the local sights, her vulgarity emphasized by some kind of dust-bowl, outback accent through which one could distinctly hear the grapes of wrath being trod, until Arnie said, "For Christ's sake, lady, we only speak English." She got indignant, and Arnie told her to kiss his guitar pick, and that ended that.

But the truth about the place would have been hard for Aubrey to come by in the best of circumstances. It puzzled him, and annoyed him. He looked out into the gray, soundless rain to the mountains, and smelled the strong odor of the earth, and felt that this country did not yet belong to man and never really would. And it was something more than the knowledge that this was an immense and northern and largely unpeopled country. It was a clear apprehension that man was here trespassing on the outer limits of that region in which pure nature had chosen to take its final stand, and had set limits, and had gathered itself, and was saying to its adversary, This far and no farther. And, as a consequence, everything man-made seemed tenuous and most presumptuously set down, and one moved beneath that veiled sky tentatively, and started at the turning of a leaf, and told oneself that nature would not be forever patient, would not forever endure the multiple affronts of the race of men.

And the affronts of Anchorage were many, and bald, and it was no comfort to Aubrey to think that Chicago, and Toledo, and New York had once offered the same affronts to the wilderness in which they had begun. Because man should have learned by now how to build a city without affronting the wilderness around it. But here it all was, all over again; and Arnie said, "Jesus Christ, just look at it! By Christ, I'd like to make them a speech. I'd say, Don't talk to me about city planning, and prospective improvements, and FHA and all that crap. Just look around at your city. If this is all you came here to do, if this mess is what you remain here to extend and to variegate, in the name of pure nature, or Emerson's oversoul or Jesus Christ or whatever it might be that strikes a response in your shitpot hearts, go back to Grand Rapids, or Rockland, or Oklahoma City, or DeWitt, Iowa, or Yakima, Washington, or Novato, California and add your excrement to those great piles where it won't be noticed. Let this land, at least and at last, stand pristine and untrammeled, so that, on the day of doom, we can stand before the throne of the Great Artificer and say, Sire, behold one small corner of your dear magnificent earth which we restrained ourselves from beshitting! Aubie, I tell you, it might be our only claim to salvation."

And Aubrey said that maybe he was right, and looked out at the shabbiness row on row, and the neon, and the unkempt streets and imagined that he understood now the easy tendency of newly settled cities to spread out in all directions. It wasn't because the settlers had bravely beaten the wilderness back. On the contrary, the wilderness had taken one look and fallen back by itself in horror, had withdrawn its gentle boundaries into safety from contamination. And here it was happening again, and, seeing it—remembering, as he did, looking from the hotel window that morning north across Cook Inlet to where Mount McKinley rose mighty and sun-spangled and alone twenty thousand feet imperially up from the plain below and comparing its high majesty with the jackdaw, jerry-built city that confronted it—he wished that nature would set pathetic fallacy aside, take stock of its retreat before the depredations of humankind, note how little of the good earth was left untrampled and unfouled, and determine to hold the line; steel itself and shake this city a few times to give it fair warning, then raise a volcano under it and blast it, and, finally, in the fullness of time, come marching back in over the city limits and sow wild strawberries on the barroom floors.

Kunkel's new airplane had one engine, three wheels, six seats, and a capricious look about it. Arnie announced that the goddamned thing looked like it had been used to dig the Erie Canal. And it sounded no better than it should have and wheezed and worried until Kermit, who had insisted upon flying, started to roar at Kunkel as they taxied toward the runway, saying what the hell was the matter with it and that it was only eight months old and why the hell didn't Kunkel have the engine tuned when he came to Anchorage. And Kunkel grinned and said it sounded much better when it got off the ground and that the engine still had the guarantee on it.

"Oh well, Jesus Christ!" Arnie shouted. "As long as there's a guarantee on the finking engine what the hell are we worrying about? I mean, even if the finking wings drop off, that guaranteed engine will keep us up there, right?"

"Shut up, Arnie! I can't hear the skip!" Kermit said. "By God, it *is* skipping!" Kermit glared about fiercely and Kunkel lost his grin and started to shake his head.

"No skip. Propeller bent," Kunkel said, his tone slightly aggrieved.

"Propeller bent! Christ stabs Pilate!" Kermit bellowed. "You can't fly around with a bent prop!"

Kunkel explained that the propeller's pitch exaggerated the vibration of the engine when the airplane was on the ground, Kermit said that was ridiculous, Arnie said would Kermit mind stopping because he wanted to get out, Julie (curled up in the two rear seats, almost hidden among guns and bags) said that it stank like a monkey cage back there, Kermit said the tower said either to take off or get to hell out of the way (and Kermit told the tower, after several tense exchanges, to go bag its ass), and Aubrey said nothing but wondered what the old airplane could have been like if this was the new one.

They sat out on the end of the runway for a time while Kermit revved the engine, cursed the manufacturer, blamed Kunkel and the unreliability of red Indians everywhere, damned the perversity of inanimate objects, swore that he'd sooner take off in a Volkswagen bus, but finally, announcing that he'd be goddamned if he'd miss a day's hunting, released the brakes, shoved the throttle forward, and put the expedition into tentative motion. Aubrey closed his eyes and prayed, Arnie delivered a running commentary on various objects and parts he claimed had dropped off on the runway—"Stop, stop! We just lost the goddamned differential calculus!"—and Julie said that if she died in the crash and Aubrey survived she wanted him to have her Maidenform bra and her copy of Jung's treatise on the Book of Job. Aubrey opened his eyes, smiled obligingly, and closed his eyes again; he did not like going into the air under the best of circumstances, and just then the circumstances seemed parlous indeed. The little airplane shuddered and wobbled and actually took off twice—its first flight about eight inches high and twenty feet long —then bounced off whining at an angle with Arnie shouting that they were overloaded, that the airplane was some kind of an Apache and only flew well in box canyons, and that if Kunkel had any decency at all he would jump overboard to lighten the load.

Which was not a comforting way to begin, and damned little comfort from that point on as far as Aubrey was concerned. They seemed to pick every air pocket available for the first hour, and to stand still for a time or even lose ground in the face of a powerful headwind as they cleared Cook Inlet and went inland along the eastern slope of the Aleutian Range. The airplane continued to rattle and bang and just generally to perform with dogged reluctance, but when Arnie ceased to predict that the bottom was about to fall out and laid his head back and went to sleep, Aubrey began to relax and to look at the country—the mountaintops and high country that lifted above the low overcast—and to think of its vastness, the incredible reach of the northern snowcap, its whiteness, its loneliness, its billion years and more of silence or of cataclysmic sound unheard before the coming of eared creatures; where the sun never stood directly overhead, where, above the Arctic Circle, the direct rays of the sun could not often reach at all, where the Ice Age had not retreated, and where man was made to understand how tenuous was his purchase on the surface of the earth. And, pondering it, he felt better about Anchorage and the other marks men had made upon this immensity, so insignificant those marks after all, so bound to be obliterated, so nearly pathetic under the regard of those mountains.

The ground was occasionally visible, especially after they were down over the Alaska Peninsula. Then the rain and the clouds broke up a little to give them a clear view of almost every active volcano they passed over. Aubrey counted eleven of them, from Mount Redoubt in the east to Pavlov in the west, and he took it as boding nothing to their good that nature should combine to give them so clear a view of her furnaces. They had an especially good look into the Valley of Ten Thousand Smokes, where Mount Katmai was situated, and where in 1912, it blew its vast innards twelve miles into the air and sent its dust visiting around the world several times. And Aubrey peered down into the crater and recalled reading about Father Hubbard, the Glacier Priest, pacing around down there inside it and almost getting done in by the poison vapors, and he gave and cited this fact to Arnie as the only documented instance of a Jesuit having gotten out of hell alive.

Kermit handled the travelogue in a loud and enthusiastic voice, but Aubrey took nothing from it except the place names, because Kermit saw it all as a hunting ground, and Aubrey saw it all as the nearest thing to a God-damned region he had ever observed. For this land belonged to itself and to no thing else, and even its self-possession was precarious. It had to do constant battle against the sea, against the weather, against fire. It looked to him like the place where Vulcan dumped his ashes long ago, and also the very place for God to send the Devil if the Devil should ever die. A place where the continent, taking fire from below, had thrust itself out most improbably and had gotten itself all torn to hell for its trouble. Plainly, the sea didn't want land where this land was, and the sea had set about removing it in its monstrously efficient way, and had worn it away, and gouged it out, and besieged it until there was almost nothing left but mountaintops; mountaintops filled with fire, and agitated air filled with violent motion, and an atmosphere filled with such an incredible abundance of snow, rain, sleet, and water of all descriptions that Aubrey decided that this place, and this place only, truly deserved designation as the Urinal of the Planets.

After they had passed a place called Port Moller, Kermit announced that they were damned near there, and it appeared that the peninsula had really begun to break up. The ocean had made inroads from the north and only the ridges of the Aleutian Range held the Bering bays from joining the North Pacific as little as eight or ten miles away. But as they came up on Mount Dana and Pavlov Volcano, the land began to rise and widen out again, and they had to bank around Pavlov because it stuck up over eight thousand feet and was spewing smoke and brimstone out of its ulcerous crater on the northeast face, and they could see where the lava had flowed down the sides and melted the glacier and turned it pot-black for hundreds of feet below the rim. And then they were over Cold Bay and Morzhovoi Bay, two horseshoe-shaped bays opening to the south, each bay about five miles across with perhaps ten miles of land between them; and in the middle of this dividing land was Mount Frosty, the six-thousand-foot, broad-shouldered home of Big Ditmo.

Aubrey was supposed to have his first sight of the Lodge from the air, and Kermit swooped down over it, but it was drizzling and the visibility was maybe nineteen feet in all directions by that time, and Cold Bay radio was telling Kermit to get back on course and approach the place in the proper manner. They broke out of the overcast just in time, it seemed to Aubrey, to avoid running smack into the whited side of Mount Frosty, and Kermit edged around it to the north and there was Shishaldin, the Torch of the Aleutians, on Unimak, the first of the Aleutian Islands; Shishaldin, ninety-four hundred feet up, perfectly conical like Fujiyama, belching a single mass of black smoke just as Aubrey described it—ominously, he thought, like a smoke signal telling him to clear the hell out—and yet one of the most beautiful mountains of the Western world. And then they were banking down over the airbase, on the upper western shore of Cold Bay, and it appeared to be the most woebegone governmental installation since Andersonville. The general impression was of mud, and huge mud puddles in the mud-track roads, these roads circling all about shacks and Quonset huts of various bleak descriptions set down in the mud, and other mud tracks circling nothing and continuing to circle nothing right on out to nowhere, with a few muddy tracks straightening out into further dismal nowheres among the burnt-sponge hills. And Aubrey was thinking that if he was ever asked to establish a penal colony for insolvent frogmen, this was the very place.

The landing was a masterpiece of suspense. Kermit flew the airplane the way Francis X. Bushman drove a chariot: shoulders hunched competitively forward, wheel seized as if there were some dispute over it, eyes flashing, nostrils distended, brow furrowed suspiciously, rearward glances frequent and sulphurous, as if he suspected that somebody was out back sawing the tail off. Anyway, he came into the landing strip about two hundred feet upwind of it, and for a moment it appeared that he was going to put the thing down on a parked fire truck (and Arnie shouted, "Forty trumpets and the drum roll, please, for after all I am Shelter Island's premier firebug!"), but the wind blew the airplane sidewise so fast that they were almost off the runway on the downwind side before they stopped bouncing and got three wheels firmly on the ground.

Then they were on the parapet and there were a few men walking toward them in the drizzle, and then more men, and Kunkel went off at a sprint to get the jeep, and Kermit greeted a couple of the men and shook hands all around, and the men stared at Julie, and one older man came running up and greeted Kermit as if the Old Man of the Mountain had just arrived to grant a general amnesty, and Kunkel drove up with a bright new red jeep with trailer and the men all joined in with the unloading of the airplane, and Julie got into the back of the jeep immediately, after speaking to no one, and Aubrey stood there and watched the proceedings, lending a hand here and there, but mostly watching the other men, the Cold Bay men.

And he said to himself, Do you see? There are people who live in

this place the year around. Employees of the government, or whoever, they live here. In this Godforsaken outback. And you think you
are in the way of doing such a marvelously heroic thing for Christ in
going to the Sahara Desert. These people have no motive but money,
yet look what they are willing to endure. And you, whose motives
are supposed to be of the highest, could you live here if there were
a monastery to receive you? Why, you'd probably bitch until the day
you died about how nobody could stand such a place except maybe
water sprites and skin divers.

He learned later that there were approximately one hundred people at Cold Bay as permanent residents, employed by the Federal
Aviation Agency (which controlled the whole reservation around
the airstrip), the Weather Bureau, the International Flight Service,
the Post Office, the Alaska Communications System, Reeve Aleutian
Airways, and the Flying Tiger Airline; that in 1958 the Air Force had
spent eight million dollars installing one of the dome-shaped Distant Early Warning stations about ten miles north of the airstrip on
the Bering Sea; that within the next three years there would be a new
fire station, powerhouse, central administration building, and new
houses for men and families, complete with lawns; that most of the
men who came out to Cold Bay looked upon it as a sportsman's paradise; and that the forlorn buildings he had seen from the air were all
that were left of the former military installation, Fort Randall (later
known as Thornbrough Air Force Base), established in 1942 and
abandoned in 1955. But all of this really made him feel no better
about the place. He would take the Sahara Desert, unseen, to Cold
Bay, seen, forty-nine out of fifty, and that with or without air condi-
tioning.

# · TWENTY-SIX ·

AND AS THEY DROVE out beyond the limits of the newer, central buildings of the base—it was discovered now to be in a great construction
and raising-the-roof-poles turmoil—they passed through the community of the old buildings: scabrous huts, infinitely mottled and
patched, each with its tumor of rusted oil drums and its network of
broken duckboards, most windowless, many of clapboard and torn
tar paper, but the majority metal-roofed Quonset buildings, all deserted, beetled, wind-scarred, smutched, and, with few exceptions
buried to the wattles in the brackish tundra and the mud. And
Aubrey wondered what in God's name manner of moles could ever
have inhabited such places, and began to look half seriously for their
screaming ghosts, and to feel a serious apprehension, a first stirring
of real fear in his civilized bowels; for it was one thing to fly over
this wild and blasted country, but quite another to put your feet
down upon it and to move out into it, only human, leaving behind
other men, riding four wheels brashly out over its water-blackened
moorlands to its snow-covered, fire-bellied mountains, to its several
ready deaths: by fire, by water, and by beast.

And they went out and out, toward the south, toward Thin Point,
right along the edge of the bay, through a country of moribund little
lakes and sunken meadows of rot-black tundra, until, at one point,

Kunkel had the jeep shifted full down and crawling at fifteen miles an hour along the ruts of a strip of mud he said was a road, and until the road came to an end and they were out on the stringy brown-black furze of the tundra itself and all around them to the right were miles and miles of curly dead moss, and Kunkel had the jeep doing perhaps eight miles an hour and was talking about how the trailer was pretty heavily loaded and they might have to leave it and come back. And Aubrey, right then, was ready to resign his commission in the Big Ditmo Avengers Association, and take any means available of getting back to the high civilization around the airstrip. Then they cleared a rise and were out on a high, wind-ripped plateau above the bay where the tundra was fairly firm, and they picked up speed, and the first hard rain smashed against the windshield of the jeep, and even Julie looked around at Aubrey and raised her eyebrows as if to say that they might get blown away but at least they were not going to sink into the earth and out of sight. And here the tundra looked healthier, and there was another form of vegetation: tangles of thin-shanked, stunted trees, none more than three feet high, beaten flat by the wind, running plagiotropically and gnarled along the ground as if seeking a place to hide, and in that dump of rain Aubrey could easily imagine that this was just a large form of sea-weed, and that the bay was about to rise up and overwhelm them with its leaden, malevolent waters. And the air itself was so washed with gray-black gloom and rainwater that the difference between sky and water seemed very slight indeed, as slight, Aubrey told himself, as the difference, in this doom-wedded place of horrors, between life and death.

Then, abruptly, they were in another sunken meadow, all gears grinding, and climbing up a long, low hill toward what appeared to Aubrey to be a derelict ship, hull over and dead, at the top. "There she is!" Kunkel cried. And there, apparently, she was. The Lodge; all but buried in thick tundra, it was, without a doubt as far as Aubrey was concerned, the most forlorn structure in the Northern Hemisphere, in good repair, but discolored, pocked, and leprous, and squashed down into the black fester of dead weed like a great gray beetle settling into its grave. Aubrey decided at once that if Kermit had paid the government more than fifty cents for it, he had been unscrupulously victimized.

A surprise came falling and flailing out of the front door immediately they pulled up, waving wildly, shouting all the way up the thirty feet of duckboards, a remarkable-looking personage—bald, gaunt, long, and loose-socketed, with a walk like a crow in flight—who yanked open the canvas door on Kermit's side and howled, "Lord God be praised, you're here, Mr. Kermit! And I seen him! I seen him, I tell you, just *this* afternoon comin' back from fishin'!"

"Seen who? Big Ditmo?"

"Yes, sir! Like Leviathan on the hills, he was! Why, I just naturally fell to both knees at the sight, I don't mind sayin', for as the Great Book says . . ."

"Damn it, McGeorge, never mind the goddamned Great Book! Where was he?"

McGeorge took two steps backward. "Now, Mr. Kermit, there's no call to go cussin' the Great Book. No, indeed not. I don't hold with it, and I don't mind allowin' as to how that's a mighty poor way to commence this enterprise. . . ."

And so on, with Kermit and Kunkel climbing out of the jeep, and Kermit doing an agitated jig while the old man, swaddled to the throat in his sick-green waterproof overclothes and hip-high rubber boots, went through a longish quotation from the Book of Job instructive as to blasphemy and Leviathan, so that they were all out of the jeep into the cold wind and rain, and Julie and Arnie had gone on down the duckboards and into the Lodge, before McGeorge was ready to say that he had seen Big Ditmo laboring haunches-deep in snow on the lesser slopes of Mount Frosty, about three miles due west of the Lodge, and heading up the mountain toward a place called B-17 Ridge.

"Well, it's too late to try him *that* far," Kunkel said, pointing his Mount Rushmore face west and winding his nose in a professional circle.

"Hell, Kunkel," Kermit said from the trailer, where he was already rummaging among the gun cases, "we got plenty of daylight yet."

"I know, but he'd be up on that ridge by now. His favorite place. And that's a good climb, Kermit, and there's lots of water between here and there. We'd be two, three hours just getting up there and back. If we *didn't* stick the jeep." Kunkel shook his head and leaned on the trailer. He looked exhausted. It had been a very long speech for Kunkel.

"Oh, he'll keep, Mr. Kermit, he'll keep," McGeorge said. "Why,

I'll surmise he ain't even actually awake yet, way he was staggerin' around. 'Course, I *could* be wrong."

McGeorge said this in a manner that indicated that on the day McGeorge was wrong, why, you could look for the opening of the seven seas and the coming of the last agonies of the earth. And he kept right on talking as the four of them unloaded the jeep and the trailer into the front foyer of the Lodge (a pleasant surprise to Aubrey, it being lined with new plywood and heated by a big modern kerosene stove), and his voice was a split-reed tenor, the tone ministerial and nostril-crushed, and the accent out of western Iowa by way of, maybe, Texarkana, so that when he said, all in a rush, "Got three Dolly Varden today, may the good Lord Lazarene be praised," Aubrey couldn't be sure if it was a weather report or another chunk of the King James version.

He was interrupted once, by Kermit, who demanded, "Now, god-damn it, McGeorge, you're sure it was Big Ditmo?"

"I'm sure, Mr. Kermit, I'm sure," McGeorge intoned happily. "Sure as God's judgment is upon us!"

"Well, he never came that far down before, far as I know."

"Can't help that, Mr. Kermit! Can't help that at all!" Then Mc-George posed on one leg and raised his eyes joyfully toward the dark sky. "And I call upon you to remember that the great Lord Lazarene only came this far down once Hisself!" And he held his pose and blinked his left eye heavenward—an ecstatic nictitation, a tic so majestic you almost expected to hear a tock—until it appeared he was having a vision, until, in fact, Kunkel brought him out of it with a slap on the back of the head.

And the man McGeorge fascinated Aubrey from the first, and before the evening was over he had talked to him, or rather, listened to him, for perhaps an hour, and in that time had learned most of the pertinent facts of McGeorge's seventy-four years; all of it delivered smack-out, twanging, and double-barreled through the nostrils, which might have been hard to take except that after he'd gotten warmed up a bit and had had a couple of straight shots of Old Fitzgerald, McGeorge's intonation took on the quality of Gregorian chant as Mahalia Jackson might render it—a unique, gospel-loving, hallelujah singsong—and his whole face took part, his left eye blinking and his right eye whisky-bright and rolling, his thin lips lolling around an idiot and holy grin, so that all things proceeding from him had the import of good news and prophecy, and Aubrey felt at times that he might just be in the presence of an exalted man who got most of his information pure quill from a fiery cloud. The only variation of this delivery occurred when McGeorge was saddened by some incident in his life, by something said or contemplated, and then his voice would become a mournful plaint, a Cro-Magnon lament to a god unknown, still incantated but without hope, fearful, profoundly redolent of the suspicion that the powers of darkness had risen up at last and taken control of the totems. And it was in this tone and mood that he most often took off into one or more of his solemn high, antiliteral, freewheeling quotations from the Book of Job, somehow injecting just a note of Christian acceptance, but still the voice of a man protesting the divinely sanctioned intrusions of Satan into the affairs of earth, and announcing above all the indignation of all humanity at the fact that the sufferings of men were a necessary part of the divine scheme. McGeorge had grasped the problem of evil by the forelock and dragged it around with him like a black gonfalon, and, since his final reverence for the master plan of the Almighty was apparently never impaired by even his most prolonged outbursts, one might have believed that the spirit of Luther had taken a new stand in one of McGeorge's hip boots and that of Job hisself in the other.

Aubrey asked him early on, quite sure of the accuracy of his guess, when and where and at what happier time McGeorge had been a preacher. McGeorge blinked back the question for nearly a minute before—reluctantly, and assuring Aubrey that he'd never been worthy of the honor—he admitted that he was an ordained minister of something called the Reformed Open Bible Church of the Unexpurgated Enlightenment of Bellingham, Washington. (And shortly after this, Arnie broke in over Aubrey's protest and informed McGeorge that Aubrey was a seminarian and on his way to the African missions, so that McGeorge almost collapsed from an influx of respect and deference, and started to call Aubrey "the young reverent," and regarded Aubrey from that moment with a sort of wary awe, as if he expected him to rise in flames anytime and start pronouncing particular judgments.) It was while in the service of this church that McGeorge had come to Kermit's notice. Sent as a missionary to Los Angeles to evangelize the Jews of Beverly Hills (no slightest exaggeration here), he had labored manfully for a year with no success, then, deciding that neither he nor God liked Jews any-way, had sat down and written a long letter to Ben-Gurion respect-fully requesting that he order all his coreligionists back to Israel to do penance in the desert. Ben-Gurion's failure to do this caused Mc-George to conclude that Ben-Gurion didn't like Jews either, and McGeorge went down to Central Casting and got himself hired at once as a frontier preacher in one of Kermit's movies. After several years of this, he told Kermit that the set lights bothered his eyes, and Kermit hired him as a part-time cook and full-time assistant to Kunkel, and he had been with Kunkel ever since. He had two ambi-tions: to convert Kunkel (to whom he referred, on the sly, as "that heathen red man"), and to be buried in the nicest graveyard in the town of his birth, Clinton, Iowa. He loved to cook, fish, build furni-ture, and polish old wood to a mirroring glow. These last two pench-ants had resulted in the wholly untoward and improbable beauty of the interior of the Lodge.

For, beyond the plywood foyer, the Quonset hut (in fact, two fifty-foot huts joined end to end) was a ruddy shining marvel. The plywood walls and ceilings had been stained deep brown and then waxed and polished until they looked like solid walnut. The floor was of some kind of knotty wide boards that had been scrubbed smooth and nearly white. Just beyond the foyer were the bedrooms, four of equal size and two larger ones, all with large built-in double beds. Beyond these were, on one side, the bathroom (with a toilet and shower, both of which performed admirably when the water tanks were full—and, in that country, there was never a period of more than minutes when they weren't) and on the other side a stor-age room, pantry, and freezer (electric power supplied by a gasoline-engine generator that was situated about a hundred feet from the Lodge and had the sound, hour after hour, of a Hudson River tug-boat). And beyond these was the mess hall—living room, dining room, and kitchen all in one—which surpassed everything else in im-probability and splendor. The whole far end of the building was formed by a huge, raised-hearth, stone fireplace within which *Romeo and Juliet* might have been performed with the mantelpiece serving as the balcony; the furniture was all handmade and massive, the chairs like medieval thrones, a dining table twenty feet long and sur-rounded by thick-timbered, high-backed refectory benches, and every piece rubbed, oiled, and shining. This room was McGeorge's masterwork, and his delight at Aubrey's delight, when he first inspected it, was downright transporting. He chortled and danced and clapped his hands, but, in the end, gave Aubrey to understand that the credit all belonged to the Lord, and that He had even caused the Russians to serve His holy ends, because McGeorge had gotten all the timber from a deserted Russian officers' club, some miles distant in what was called the Russian area, where ten thousand Soviet troops had been stationed during World War II.

So that, after McGeorge had explained that his last name was M'Naghten and that it was one of his relatives who gave the name to the M'Naghten Rule pertaining to insanity in criminal jurisprudence, and then had gone into the freezer to get the meat for dinner, Aubrey went to his room, unpacked his new clothes and gear, spent some time pulling off price tags and taking out pins, inspected his built-in, Brobdingnagian bed, and then, feeling better about the expedition than he had to date, feeling that perhaps with the Lodge to return to in the evenings he might survive the hunt after all, he knelt down and said a prayer of thanksgiving for their safe journey, another prayer for their continued safety, and a final prayer for strength against impurity—this last the beautiful prayer beginning "Hail, Holy Queen, Mother of mercy, our life, our sweetness, and our hope. . . ."

But in those several hours that brought on a howling Bering snowstorm just before they retired for the night, there was certainly life, but damned little sweetness or hope. He walked from his room directly into an argument between Kermit and Julie about Aubrey's indoctrination into the care and feeding of big-game firearms. He was met by Kermit who was waving a large-bore British double-barreled rifle and saying, "For Christ's sake, baby, I don't give a damn what you think you can do with a .300! Aubrey's going to carry the new .378. And he's got to learn how to use a big weapon. Hah! Aubie, come here!"

"He already knows how to use a big weapon, don't you, Aubie dear?"

Julie was wearing close-fitting, nearly-transparent black tights with a matching top, high-heeled shoes, and a red scarf at her throat, and was so startling a sight—her breasts out straight and pointed like armament, her hips, her crotch, her whole body so fulsomely and roundly revealed—that Aubrey moved his mouth but said nothing.

329

She came directly to him, tinkled her drink under his nose, pouted her most salacious smile at him, then turned and walked slowly away—the black material so voluptuously clung to her marvelous back and buttocks and legs that he couldn't take his eyes away—and eased herself down (smiling back at him now with her tongue) upon a fur rug on the floor, and stretched out and arched her back and touched the vaulting peak of one breast with her free hand and, looking at him with slow rolls of her eyes, said, "Oh yes, to be sure. The young reverent knows all about using his weapon."

Kermit, who had been engaged in removing a single-barreled rifle from its case, said, "He does not know how to use this weapon, for Christ's sake! I taught both these boys all they know about hunting, right, Aubie? Now, this is a brand-new Weatherby Mark Five .378 Magnum bolt-goddamned-action rifle, right? And you and I will now go outside and fire a few rounds."

"You mean," Julie said with languorous hauteur, "you're going out there and fire that weapon now?"

"Well, hell yes, now! You know of some reason why not?" Kermit was as drunk as bourbon straight could make him, which was reasonably to quite.

Julie, her sex suit temporarily parted at midriff, scratched her bare stomach and winked at Aubrey. "Why, no reason in the world why not, Great Gray Hunter. Just that you'll scare every goddamned bear between here and Kodiak back into hibernation."

Kermit was in the middle of an heroic pull at his drink and choked on it and stared at Julie for a fine moment of bug-eyed outrage, and then went into a string of goddamns and worse that sought to instruct Julie that what she knew about bears, if it were panther piss, would not suffice to drown a nit on a gnat's nut. And he was red-faced and quite near, it appeared, to a spasmodic seizure, when Arnie walked in.

And Arnie spotted Julie at once and went right toward her saying, "Well, Jesus aching Christ! Look at her!" And he went into an off-balance, frenetic single-footed war dance around her, beating his mouth with one hand and making lewd but uncompleted passes at her with the other.

Julie struck at him several times, and then lay back and closed her eyes. Kermit roared, "Goddamn it, Arnie! Cut that out!"

Arnie stopped, grinned at Kermit, said, "Party-pooper's what you are, Big K. And screw you, Julie-Bitch. I've got some nice fishy lady friends over at the King Cove cannery." He walked over and fell into a chair and continued to stare at her. "Yes, sir. These Aleutian maidens swim all the way over here just to get serviced by old Arnie."

"You know, Kermit," Julie said, with soft, cruel calculation. "I think you'd better find a new madhouse for old Arnie. He's getting crazier every year."

"Julie!" Kermit said, the shock of it seeming to sober him a little.

"It's okay, Kermit, it's okay," Arnie said. And he spoke easily, but his eyes were tight and close upon her. "She's right. I am getting crazier every year. And she's getting nothing but tittier. And, Christ, is she proud of them, sticking them up there like that at us. One for Aubie and one for me, right, Julie-Bitch?"

"Arnie, leave your sister alone," Kermit said.

"She ain't my sister, Kermit. Nohow. Or is it both of them for Aubie, Julie-Bitch? I mean, I don't see why one should be for me. You never showed me a thing."

"And I still won't," Julie said.

"Now, no goddamned arguments tonight!" Kermit said, coming to stand between them. "You shut up, Arnie, and you shut up, too, Julie, or by God I'll put you both out in the snow!"

"Oh, a coolie!" Arnie shouted. "A quickie in the snow!"

Julie had her right arm thrust straight up, glass in hand, and shook it now at Kermit. "Daddy dear, why don't you put the nice bolt-action phallus away and get me another drink?"

"Why, God bless you, Miss Julie," McGeorge said, coming forth out of the prodigious flames in the fireplace behind him. "I'll be happy to get you a drink." He was wearing an ankle-length white duster with drawstrings, demonstrating to all exactly how he would look in his shroud. He billowed over to Julie, employed a daring right backhand to snatch the glass from her hand, smiled down in a paternally cadaverous way, and said, "Scotch whisky, ain't it?" Julie nodded vaguely, and McGeorge turned immediately toward Aubrey and put on display for the first time a large dead fish he had been holding by the gills in his left hand. "Just look at that, reverent!" he cried, waving it enthusiastically. "Think you could handle some of that Dolly Varden along with your steak?" He leaned to Aubrey conspiratorially. "Even Jesus ate fish," he said, with sudden emotion.

331

"Never ate anything but fish." He stepped back with a dramatic flourish of the trout.

"Oh, for Christ's sake," Arnie said.

"Goddamn it, McGeorge, don't drip it on me," Julie said, slapping at the fish.

McGeorge took an agile leap sidewise, clutched Dolly Varden to his bosom, and murmured his apologies. Then he peered timidly at Arnie, whose face was in shadow in the wings of his chair. "Ho, there, Mr. Arnie. Didn't hardly see you when you come in. Heard you're feelin' better."

"Ho to you, you old bastard. I heard you'd died of the Eskimo crud."

"What? What's that?"

"I said!" Arnie shouted. "I heard you'd died of palpitations of the right vascular hornspoon!"

"No, no! Not me," McGeorge said, backing away into the dining table, then edging around it, his eyes surprised and fading—matching exactly the look of the visible eye of the dead fish—his fear apparent, his face anciently aquiver. It was plain that Arnie was a thing of mystery, darkness, and mortal threat as far as McGeorge was concerned. "Ain't nothin' the matter with my hornspoon," he muttered, and exited briskly, center stage, fish couchant, into his leaping flames.

"We could go out and snap in a little," Kermit said. He was standing now in front of Aubrey with the rifle at parade rest staring at some kind of battle horn that was suspended by a string from the ceiling. Kermit blew at it once, causing it to turn slightly, then gave Aubrey an inquiring eyes-right.

"Yeah, yeah. Go snap in," Arnie said sourly. "Snap and snap. And why don't you crackle and pop while you're at it?"

Julie giggled. Kermit glared at her and then at Arnie. Arnie was grinning down at Julie, looking not at her face but at her breasts—obviously and intently—which stood up sharply and moved when she laughed. Kermit snorted and walked to the gunrack and stood the rifle in its place. "You are a pair of goddamned ingrates," he said sadly. "I've done all I could for both of you, and all you give me in return is the worst you can lay your tongues to." Aubrey stared at Kermit, not believing what he heard, yet having to believe it as Kermit went on. "I'll say this, and I'll say it just once. You, Julie, and you, Arnie, have cut my heart up goddamned near as much as it can be cut. I love you both with what's left of it, and I ask you—I ask you, just as a goddamned small favor—please!" And he caught himself, and lowered his voice again. "Please, don't ruin this—this hunt for me as you did the last one."

The only sounds in the following silence were the crackling of the fire and the growl of the generator engine. Aubrey looked to Julie and Arnie, and both had their eyes closed, and Arnie was rubbing at his forehead with one hand, and the silence went on for some time. Then Kermit turned and glanced at Aubrey, embarrassed, utterly vulnerable, and tried to smile—a dismal, shattered smile—then gave it up, doubled both fists, hammered one down on top of the gunrack as he furrowed his whole face angrily, and shouted, "Where the hell is Kunkel?"

Julie and Arnie opened their eyes and appeared to be breathing again. McGeorge, just arriving with Julie's drink, gave Arnie a wide swath and kept his eyes on him furtively as he held the glass out toward Julie, actually putting it into a tight orbit just out of her reach. "Oh, Kunkel," he said. "I think he's feeding Sordini."

"Sordini!" Arnie said. "Is that goddamned Sordini still alive?"

"Oh, my Lord, yes, Mr. Arnie. Oh, he's just fine, long's we keep him away from the females at the airstrip."

"Jesus," Julie said. "This must be Down-With-Females Week in the Aleutians." She sat up and plucked her drink out of McGeorge's hand. She raised the glass very slightly to Aubrey and winked.

"Well, we all get horny," Arnie said.

"You just don't know, Mr. Arnie," McGeorge said eagerly, "how much trouble it gets to be. He comes back all broke out with somethin' different ever time!" McGeorge, in a moment of reckless warmth, had approached to within ten feet of Arnie.

"Well, you know how it is, McJesus. That goddamned Sordini just can't let his dork go undocked. I mean, he is the official daisy of the Aleutian chain, and that's that."

"Now, Mr. Arnie, I wish you wouldn't call me that. Indeed, I do."

"What? I was talking about Sordini, for Christ's sake, McJesus!"

"That there! What you just said."

"Well, goddamn, McJesus, what in hell else would I call you? Christ, you know I'm a finking nut! Like Kermit says! You want I should suddenly start acting sane?" And Arnie barked the last word and half-rose from his chair, and put McGeorge into disorderly, duster-dancing withdrawal. "And bring me an old-fashioned, for Christ's sake, McJesus. Before I occupy your goddamned metaphysical person and spirit you off into outer finking *darkness!*" He got to his feet and slapped Aubrey on the shoulder as he started for the hallway. "I'll be out with Sordini. I'd better give the son of a bitch a bath if he's going to sleep with me tonight."

Aubrey looked after him, blinking. Who in hell was Sordini? Nobody had explained him, one way or the other, and Aubrey had assumed, up to the moment Arnie had mentioned sleeping arrangements, that he was some kind of subservant, perhaps the chance product of an Italian sailor and an Aleut fish packer. He felt that it was a mistake to ask Julie, but Kermit was near the fireplace instructing McGeorge in a loud voice not to trim *all* of the fat off the steaks, for Christ's sake. And so Aubrey said to Julie, bracing himself for nothing like a straight answer, "Who is Sordini?"

Julie looked startled, but recovered smartly, taking a long drag on her cigarette, exhaling elaborately, rolling her hair-wrapped head toward him, pouting, eyes widening with entire deceit, and said, "Oh, yes. You haven't met Sordini, have you?"

"No."

"What makes you so curious, darling?"

"Well—don't call me that, Julie—well, because Arnie said he's going to sleep with him, if you have to know."

She seemed to suppress a burst of laughter, then leaned toward him, and spoke confidentially, just above a whisper. "He and Arnie were fags together in the madhouse."

"Oh come on, Julie. That's a fine thing to say about Arnie."

"Screw Arnie. What about poor Sordini? He gave up everything for love." She shook her head dolorously. "He was Arnie's psychiatrist, and he gave up *everything*."

"Julie . . . ?"

"His wife, his five children, his castle overlooking the Strait of Messina . . ."

"His castle?"

"Of course. He's Grand Duke of Messina, pretender to the Italian throne. And that isn't all." She was nodding solemnly, but her lips were beginning to take liberties.

"Julie, will you for once give me a straight and honest answer?"

"He was Palermo's leading alchemist!" she cried, then, bursting

334

into laughter, "and the Mafia's leading witness *and* second tenor! He and Arnie sang Sicilian vespers in duet!"

"What's she shouting about?" Kermit said, grinning, barely heard over Julie's scream of glee.

"Sordini!" Aubrey shouted back.

"*That* goddamned beast," Kermit said. Then, to Julie, "Will you stop the noise? You'll scare the bears away." He turned and nodded, to indicate a score, to Aubrey.

"And—and," Julie gasped, "the castle fell into the Strait, and Sordini was in straits, and Arnie was in a strait jacket. . . !"

And she went on and on until Aubrey walked out to the fireplace and stood in the lee of a cabinet in deference to McGeorge's fire, and talked with McGeorge until dinner was served, learning, at last, upon McGeorge's solemn assurance, that Sordini was a "lattimore receiver water dog."

Kunkel and Arnie joined them for dinner, and the steak and fish were slightly burned but delicious, and Aubrey had never been so hungry, and things were peaceful and munching until Kermit fixed Aubrey with his white-hunter eye and announced portentously that Aubrey would do all right. Aubrey was not sure what Kermit had in mind until his father glanced toward the gunrack and worked his trigger finger a couple of times along the near side of his wine goblet.

"Oh, yes," Aubrey said, nodding. "I'm sure I will. But we're not likely, are we," he heard himself adding, for no accountable reason, "to see a bear the first day?"

"What makes you say *that?*" Kermit demanded, hunching toward him and taking Aubrey's occult measure with narrowed eyes.

"Oh, he picks up bear signals from the Vatican with his left ear," Julie said.

"And *bull* signals, too," Arnie said. "Christ, Kermit, you've heard of *Osservatore Romano,* haven't you? Where the hell do you think they get all the poop for those papal bulls?"

McGeorge appeared and insinuated a fresh bottle of wine between Arnie and Kunkel. Arnie seized and tilted it so quickly that poor McGeorge's fingers were still working in bottle-clutching postures as he backed away. Kermit was continuing to glower at Aubrey, his eyes moving in judgment of base motives and glancing in censure of the levity from the left. "What the hell kind of a thing is *that* to say?" Kermit said. "What the hell do you *mean*, we won't see a bear the first day?"

And there Aubrey sat with his foul canard hanging, quite visibly, in the air in front of him, having grossly offended against decency and the creed of the bearslayer. And his only thought was to right his flagrant wrong. "Oh, I'm sure we'll *see* a bear, Kermit," he said, feeling in every respect compromised. "I only meant that I'm not likely to be"—he hesitated, wishing to select just the right word, and he came up with what he felt was an extremely fortunate choice— "*afforded* a shot at a bear the first day."

"Hum," Kermit said, regarding him with patroonish asperity, and there was a moment of distinctly tense, eyeballing calculation, during which Aubrey felt his *Zeit* irretrievably separated from his *Geist*.

Julie said, "Raise your right earlobe and repeat after me. I, the young reverent, do solemnly swear, by my unruffled pubic hair, and at the risk of my diplostemonous immunity, that I have no secret papish information about the unavailability of bear on this here cold peninsula tomorrow or any other day, and . . ."

"Goddamn it," Arnie said, "if you're going to administer the oath, do it properly. He's got to hold one hand on the orifice of the fundament and the other on an acknowledged relic of the peter of Paul the Apostle, the while being liberally daubed with Kodiak bear grease of the 1912, which, as you will note, was the year of the Katmai, which was manifestly of the good, and profoundly affirm that nothing has intentionally passed his lips which might be construed as anti-there-goes-the-bear-ism, *and* that he has peed on no icons of the family *Ursidae*, whether plantigrade, carnivorous, or omnivorous, within the last three—or four—months, the time limit depending upon the strictness of the interpretation hereunto applicable."

"Shut up, Arnie," Kermit said. He hummed at Aubrey. "Well," he said judiciously, his absolution clearly conditional, "you'd better come with Kunkel and me tomorrow."

"Oh, Christ!" Julie said. "I put up with the gospel according to Mc-George for six goddamned days last year!"

"Look, Julie, just for the first day, until I get Aubrey broken in."

"No, damn it! Pair him off with old Arnie, here. They can compare visions, or something."

"I ain't going tomorrow, Miss Julie, Bitch of the North. I only came for the mineral waters. Those bears, they don't *like* me on the first day, and I never go where I'm not wanted."

"That must limit your movements pretty damned severely," Julie said quietly, glancing at Kermit.

Kermit held up one hand to Arnie. "Quiet, goddamn it! Arnie isn't going tomorrow. He's going to do some fishing first. So, just for tomorrow, baby? For your old man?"

"Oh, shit!" Julie said. "If I've got to put up with *that* goddamned old maundering Monophysite all day, I'd better get fortified. *Good night all!*" She rose immediately and walked from the room, her buttocks pinching extravagantly. Arnie watched her out of sight, then looked at Aubrey and shook his head.

"C'mon," Kermit said gruffly. "Kunkel says Pavlov's running over."

Kunkel, staring into his wine, neither confirmed nor denied.

"You go ahead, Kermit," Arnie said. "I've promised to give Sordini a finger wave."

Aubrey followed Kermit out and they stood by the jeep in the cool night and looked toward Pavlov, thirty-five miles to the northeast. The sky was overcast and they could make out only a faint red glow on the clouds east of the peak. There was a growing wind from the direction of the mountain, driving a few snowflakes before it, and at times the wind became almost hot and carried the smell and taste of ashes upon it.

"It must be sending it up pretty high to carry it this far," Aubrey said.

"It's up pretty goddamned high starting," Kermit said softly. "I'd like to be here with a camera when that big bastard really blows its top." He thought about that for a minute. "Well, maybe not. Pisser Duffy—he's the local hermit—says that the last time, Cold Bay was knee-deep in ash from it. I think that was 1942, and they had a little one in 1948. But there will be a big blast one of these days. Take the top right off her."

"I like her better with the top on."

Kermit suddenly changed the subject. "Look, Aubie, I should have explained about Arnie. He's bad now, but he's going to get worse. He always does when we go hunting. He—well, he has an idea . . ." Kermit chopped at the air with the side of one hand and turned half away. He stood there for a time, shaking his famous head very slightly, his lips pressed hard together. Then he said, his tone even and precise, "He thinks I only bring him along so, sometime when things are just right, I can shoot him."

Kermit stood there in silence and Aubrey wondered what he could

337

possibly say. He felt certain that Kermit didn't want him to say anything, but the thing was too monstrous for no comment at all, and he tried to speak and produced several half-born mutterings which only caused Kermit to wince, and to move away from him, and down the duckboards to the door. He paused there, waiting until Aubrey caught up with him, and braced himself on the doorjamb, his wide shoulders stiff, the heels of both hands pushed hard into the wood, his head turned enough so that Aubrey could hear him. "Do you know," he said gently but with piercing crispness, "I'd fall down on my knees and stay there forever—more, by God!—I'd not only let you go to Africa, I'd go with you, if Arnie could pull out of this, if he could get his sanity back. Oh, Jesus, Aubie, I know what they say about the prodigal son—that you worry about him more, that you secretly love him more." And Kermit waited, and hauled in his eyes, as if he knew that Aubrey would be waiting to hear the rest of it with great interest. And, finally, he nodded his head quickly, and said, "And it's true. Do you see, Aubie? You—you—I'm sure of. I know that you'll be okay, that you'll make your way, that you'll never really hurt yourself too badly. If you know what I mean. But Arnie. Arnie is my cross, my crucifixion, and I worry about him, Aubie, I worry about him and I—I love him so goddamned much!" He turned, abruptly, roughly, to Aubrey, and, without really looking at him, put his right arm around him and hugged him. "Oh, Aubie, I know, I know. But, I love you, too, so goddamned much. You know that. You see it, don't you? It's just that you're no worry to me, that way. Oh, you worry me, with this Africa business, but I figure I can fight that one way or the other. And you can take it, Aubie, you can take it. I've always known that about you. You don't need me so much. You're stronger. But Arnie—oh Christ, Arnie. . . ." And he brought up his right arm, swinging it like a punch over Aubrey's head, and held it in front of him and studied it for several seconds, and surveyed it, and moved it, and worked his trigger finger, and suddenly made a fist and slammed it into the front door. "Yes! By Christ! I'd cut off this right arm and mail it to the Pope, if Arnie could get his mind back!" Then he suddenly backed away from the door and stared at his bruised fist. "No!" he roared. "No, I wouldn't! That's the whole goddamned trouble! Shoot him? Jesus Christ! I've shot him every day of his life!" He started to swing at the door again, but caught himself in mid-punch, and let his fist drift in softly against the wood. "I'm sorry,

Aubie. I'm sorry." Then he grabbed the doorknob violently and shouted, "Oh, sweet blistered Jesus, yes! *I am sorry!*" And he charged through the door, leaving it open behind him, and went to his room without looking back.

Aubrey went in slowly and closed the door, and went to his room and knelt fully clothed by the bed and started to pray. And he knew that he was praying without attention, that his mind had no notion of what his lips were doing, but he couldn't force his mind to attend or to take part in his prayers. And at the center of his distraction, speaking to him out of a very old place, was a puzzlement about the fact that Arnie was the favorite son. It wasn't, as Kermit had tried to describe it, a sympathetic affection born in Arnie's mental troubles. The preferment had started long before Arnie's problem had become apparent to anybody. It had started even before Kermit had returned from the wars, and had only been made more obvious when Kermit had taken Arnie out from under Rexfordia's wing and made his first-born son his very own, and Aubrey had turned to his mother as the default candidate for her affections; and had never been elected.

He knelt there and wondered how there could be so much choice between brothers born thirty minutes apart. What was his failing? What did his parents find in Arnie, what *had* his parents found in him, that they had not found in their second-born? What it was Aubrey thought he knew—a certain flamboyance, a certain fickle ability to charm people into opposition with one another and yet maintain the confidence of both opposed, a certain dreadful cynicism founded in the abiding belief that humans were happiest when provided with apparently valid motives for hate—yet he could not allow himself to accept this estimate of his brother, however obviously demonstrated, however frequently demonstrated, Arnie's duplicity had been. Aubrey called himself, as he always had done, a resentment-filled, jealous jackass, a Christless Christian; and climbed into his bed and stared at the darkness until his self-disgust drove him into sleep.

# · TWENTY-SEVEN ·

THERE CAME A TIME in almost any manic undertaking when Aubrey began to anticipate the climax and lose interest, or began to foresee the consequences and lose heart. His mind always danced ahead and looked the thing over from all angles and had its several laughs or purgations, or whatever it was the undertaking was supposed to produce, in advance, and then went beyond that and bugled down all the possible dark alleys of aftermath and came back pale and shaken with reports of phantom calamities and all four horsemen ready to ride. And, if alone, he immediately turned back, satisfaction accomplished, and, if with others, he might issue one false final laugh and say something like "Oh yes, won't it be a riot when the prior picks up his soup plate and finds the cockroach? But, you know, I've been thinking, he *does* have that heart condition. . . ." Enter conscience, *exeunt omnes alii*, smiles fading, manic undertaking abandoned. Which explained, Aubrey supposed, why he had gotten invited along on damned few manic undertakings in his lifetime.

And the next morning, when he came to with Kermit swinging on his cowlick as if it were a subway strap and thunderously announcing the hunt, Aubrey fervently wished that his invitation to this particular manic undertaking had been lost in the mails. And he lay there, after Kermit had gone muttering out leaving the light on and the door open, and said to himself (and to a raffinose-eyed caribou head affixed to the wall over the foot of his bed), Fellow Alaskans, the great blond and bearded hunter has been telling us true, and he really does mean to shoulder his assorted barrels and go out poking among those fifteen-hundred-pound carnivores with intent to kill or be killed, and he really does mean that we should walk at his right hand and take the good with the bad, the ram with the rod, and the swash with the buckle. Once out the front door, we will have to kill or be killed, by the bear. Or be maimed by the bear. And even if we should kill the bear, we will undoubtedly have to do a little chortling dance to show how pleased we are (having vomited as unobtrusively as possible), and then help skin the bear, and then help carry the bear in triumph home. The which, if the bear be as foul-smelling as we would be after hibernating all winter, and if the bear be, as we would certainly be, all foully dight with dung, ought to be good for at least four more vomits and a fortnight of the dry heaves. However, fellow Alaskans, we see no other course but to go forth after the bear, because Kermit will undoubtedly break our collective polar ass if we do not.

He got his prayers said, noting that above mid-snout the caribou looked remarkably like Father Finnegan, and went out, boots in hand, to the mess hall. McGeorge was there, stoking, and Kunkel was there, sharpening a knife, and Kermit was there, in his new white ermine hat, waving a gun.

"How'd you sleep, young reverent?" McGeorge asked, with an eager frown, as if Aubrey had only to say that he hadn't slept too well and McGeorge would go in and stomp hell out of the mattress.

"Very well, thanks."

"Didn't feel the earthquake?" Kunkel asked, peering at him down the edge of his knife.

"Earthquake? Was there an earthquake?"

"Wasn't much, reverent. Two small ones, matter of fact." McGeorge brightened and grinned broadly. "But, the Lord be praised, we'll be getting a bigger one. Or a big one. That's always the way. Coffee?"

Aubrey nodded, and ducked under Kermit's barrels toward the fire, cautiously, because, as usual, it appeared to have been built of an even dozen New York Central, or maybe Siberian, railroad ties (and Aubrey did suspect McGeorge of having attended firebug school somewhere and of having taken a degree in Comprehensive Conflagration), and Kermit shot a rifle bolt in his right ear, and said, "Aubie! I've decided, and this is final, that you should use the .378 Weatherby instead of the Westley Richards double, and I'll tell you why."

And he did tell him why, holding a new, bescoped and bestrapped and very beautifully shaped rifle at high port about two inches from Aubrey's nose, and tightly, as if he wished to forestall until the last possible moment its relinquishment into Aubrey's obviously unreliable possession (and when talking to Aubrey about guns, Kermit always had the eye of a constable lecturing the village idiot who has just fired the township cannon into the left hip pocket of the circuit court judge), and Aubrey retained none of the details, but it all had to do with how the barrels of a British double were set so that the bullets converged after ninety-five yards (which Aubrey conceded *did* seem like a reasonable distance) and that, patently, Aubrey should not be allowed to get within ninety-five yards of a brown bear until he became a more experienced shooter (Kermit pointing out that the brown bear could run forty miles an hour or thereabouts, so that the issue, as far as Aubrey was concerned, became that a brown bear should not be allowed to get that close to *him*), and how the Weatherby was a rugged piece of rifle with a much greater range and would certainly knock Aubrey on his *tokus* if he weren't properly braced when he fired it (whereupon ensued some lessons in bracing, during which Aubrey decided he would not fire the damned thing unless he were braced, haunches and hocks, against a small mountain), and how, finally, Aubrey should bend his first efforts toward a throat or a heart shot because neither would damage the skull and Kermit did want to register all skulls with Boone and Crockett (and they seemed like the very people to register skulls with, Aubrey silently acknowledged).

And Aubrey nodded at all things as if he understood just what Kermit was talking about, and Kermit seemed somewhat pleased and said that Aubrey should snap in a little before they got under way, and left the rifle in Aubrey's hands, cuffing him behind the head and smiling indulgently as he did so, as if to say, "Well, yes, you can take the car tonight, son, as long as you don't point it at anybody." And Aubrey read the look in Kermit's eyes, and he thought, Well, very few of us can love what we don't understand, but Kermit is making the effort, manfully. He doesn't understand me or my purposes even a little, and has no idea why anyone would want to go to Africa unless for a safari, cannot comprehend the forswearing of women and all the other soft things any more than he can comprehend the forswearing of hunting, gambling, shooting, and all the other hard things. He keeps searching my face for an answer, and I must keep searching his face for a place to put one, because all he wants in the world is for me to emulate him, to act as he acts, and to like what he likes, and to walk as he walks, and to swagger as he swaggers, so that —well, maybe, so that—he might know that he hasn't lived in vain.

And immediately he realized this, Aubrey tried to act enthusiastic about the Weatherby, and threw it up to his shoulder repeatedly and even smartly; and peered through the scope with spastic little cluckings as if, through it, he could see clear into the next world; and drew and shot the bolt so often and with such abandon that Kermit, who was both surprised and delighted at Aubrey's verve, told him gently to be careful about shooting the bolt or he might break it off.

Then Julie, smartly draped in about nine yards of yellow rain gear with matching boots and a sort of off-the-ears hood, and smoking a cigarette through a long holder because, as she subsequently explained, she hated the smell of burning rubber, came into the mess hall crying, "Short live Big Ditmo, and all those other bears in mind!" And she came crinkling right up to Aubrey, kissed him on the end of the nose, and whispered, "Don't use anything, darling, I've got a cordite filter." And she blew smoke in his face and smiled at him—and she seemed radiant, and glowing, and perfectly happy at being so early awake—and said, "Don't lock your bolt on my account, young reverent. I just *love* to hear it sliding back and forth." She moved away to Kermit, who was seriously engaged with one of the thick black steaks from McGeorge's blast furnace, and kissed him on the forehead and came back to Aubrey at once. "Go ahead, don't let me inhibit you. Slide your bolt. After all, *I* was there for your debut." She took some coffee from McGeorge and stood there sipping it and smiling at Aubrey as he, deciding well to hell with you missy, worked his bolt with what vigor he could muster eight or ten times.

"Well," she said. "You're improving. No two ways. How do you feel about the hunt, young reverent?"

"Don't call me that."

"You didn't answer my question."

Aubrey lowered his voice. "Listen, I have no intention whatsoever of firing this rifle unless its barrel and my head happen to be down a bear's throat simultaneously. Does that answer your question?"

343

Julie rolled her green eyes as if to reprove him. "You'd be surprised how fast you'll fire that rifle, young reverent, when you suddenly discover the zoo is out. Yes, yes, yes. You'd be surprised. And I hope you are. It might serve to quicken your reaction to certain other animal stimuli, if you take my meaning. And if you don't, darling, let me just tell you, without embroidery, that the bears around here are the least of your worries. Don't you worry about Big Ditmo, bear. Just you worry about old Julie, bare. In fact, I dreamt you and I were bare together again last night. Yes, yes. Bare, and together as hell."

McGeorge came over to fill Aubrey's coffee cup. "Bet you're excited about your first big bear hunt, right, young reverent?"

"Oh yes. Yes, I am, McGeorge. I just hope I don't make any mistakes, that's all."

"You won't," said Kunkel from the far end of the dining table, giving Aubrey a chewing, Indian death smile. "Don't make none, Mr. Aubrey, because they'll likely be your last if you do." And his expression was exactly that of an Indian scout announcing to his white employers—with understandably mixed emotions—the massacre of the whole Seventh Cavalry at the hands of the outlaw segment (every tribe had one, headed up by Chief Left Wing) of his very own people. Not that Aubrey felt that Kunkel wished him any ill. Just that Kunkel took some small and innocent amusement in the natural deficiencies of white men. Aubrey smiled back at Kunkel with what intrepidity he could manage, which wasn't much, because he had never felt more downright trepid than when standing face to face with this ex-chauffeur. Aubrey was quite sure that after one unobstructed look at Kunkel, grinning at him a hundred years ago across the wide Missouri, the westward course of empire would have suffered an immediate and decidedly eastward turn.

McGeorge then caused Aubrey to confront and attack a steak about the size, color, and texture of the Black Book of Solomon, refusing to hear any protests about Aubrey's monastic stomach and its being conditioned to a breakfast of coffee and a piece of toast, and standing over Aubrey and quoting from Job or somewhere about the merits of starting each day with a side of beef. And Aubrey was about to get snide and ask what the Bible had to say about eating charcoal (the outer half-inch of the steak being pure carbonaceous ash), when Kermit rose up with a trumpeting belch—something he managed every morning in place, apparently, of a hunting horn—

clapped both hands down on the table, snatched up his gun, rattled it, grinned murderously, and bellowed, "Lay on, Kunkel! That goddamned Big Ditmo has seen his last sunrise!"

When they were outside, with Kunkel laying on and the rest of them laying after, all boots, barrels, and bogproof, Aubrey took one look upward and wondered if poor Big Ditmo had yet seen his first sunrise. The sky had died and gangrene had set in. It was the color of mustard gas, with all the mustard (Dijon, with horseradish) intact and roiling, and it seemed to gather and start right at them as soon as they moved toward the jeep. Aubrey called for a gas mask and Kermit seemed to take inspiration from this and ordered Mc-George to ride in the trailer, with the other impedimenta. Aubrey and Julie got into the back seat, Julie promptly gripped him under one knee and wouldn't let go, and Kunkel roared west through an inch of new snow as if he knew precisely where the potholes were. And he did, and didn't miss a one.

They forded several small streams and one rather dashing one, and then were climbing through deeper snow and shallow mud along the back of a gently rising ridge into the foothills of Mount Frosty, all but the lowest reaches of which mountain were hidden in the overcast. Kermit said that the B-17 Ridge was the most prominent promontory on the eastern slope, and that it was named in honor of an airplane crash on it a few years back. As they moved upward, the muskeg and brush willow became sparser, the snow deeper, the sky more hostile. A wind full of thin rain came up, and stayed up. Aubrey looked out at it all and thought that Thomas Hardy should have seen Cold Bay and environs before he tried to scare anybody with the natural malevolence of Egdon Heath. Next to Cold Bay, Malebolge itself was a shady nook.

They had ground to a halt in deep snow just under B-17 Ridge, and Kermit and Aubrey were back at the trailer with McGeorge just beginning to unlimber rifles and food packs, when the earthquake came crumping in over the hills like a battery of siege guns. Aubrey was standing there, looking up, wondering what in God's name the noise could be, expecting to receive a large avalanche in the left intermaxillary area, or a tidal wave between the eyes, or a full complement of volcanic ash and mountaintop in the sideburns, or a dunghill in the crotch (Job having dropped in on a whirlwind to see his old friend, McGeorge), when it struck and lifted the trailer just high enough to thump Aubrey lightly under the armpits and knocked him backwards full length into a trench full of rotten snow.

And the rotten snow was thick and soupy, of the color and consistency of marshmallow ice-cream topping, and he settled softly into it, almost floating but not quite in his bogproof suit, until he hit bottom, being then almost out of sight, managing to hold his head free, wondering if his disappearance into the very bowels wasn't imminent, feeling the snow sloshing over him and the ground grinding under him, seeing the jeep and trailer doing a one-two, wheel-to-wheel dance with Julie swinging fetchingly on the end of a canvas door, wondering again if these weren't his last sensations of mortality and telling himself to treasure them as such, and doing so, and yet, as the thing went on, thinking, Pliocene and Pleistocene are having it out down there below and I hope they come to an accommodation soon. Who's to save me as I lie here gelidifying, and who's to know that I've gone to another epoch, fissurewise, to join the primordia? For God's sake, Earth, you had plenty of time to settle your squabbles and innards before I came along. You don't want me down there anyway. I'd never make it. I'm constitutionally Cenozoic. Why, the closest I've come even to Tertiary is the Third Order of St. Francis. I like lobster but I'd not care to live with them, or with trilobites or nautiloids either. I'm strictly mammal-oriented, as my old friend Rift Epicenter here will be glad to affirm. . . .

And then, suddenly, it was over, and McGeorge said, "And behold the great Jehovah shook the earth!" And Kermit said, "Jesus Christ, that ought to wake the old bastard up, Kunkel!" And Kunkel said, "Don't like it. Don't like it at all. Loosens up snow all around the mountain." And Julie said, "Whee! Hah! Hup! I lost three pounds!" And Aubrey, struggling to rise from the snow and it sucking at him diabolically, finally had to call out for assistance, and McGeorge and Kunkel extracted him like a giant sloth out of quicksand or, with liquid squelchings, like a yellow tooth out of a soggy white gum.

And after that Aubrey was doubly apprehensive about Big Ditmo. It was his first earthquake, and it had severely shaken, among other things and as only one's first earthquake can, his confidence in the reliability of the earth as a firm surface for running upon. Having been the premier quarter-miler of St. Titus' Academy and Greater Fort Lee during his junior and senior years, he had been nourishing and counting rather heavily upon his conviction that when it came to a wind sprint between Big Ditmo and him, he would leave the bear at the blocks. But if the damned track were in violent agitation, where would that leave him? As so much potential bear grease, no question. With the result that he took up his rifle with renewed, or revised, interest and shot his bolt in such a determined manner several times that Julie said, "Easy there, young reverent, or you'll snap a cap," and Kermit, with a certain paternal benevolence, said, "Careful, Aubie. You'll break it off."

After a conference among Kermit, Kunkel, and Julie, which Julie clearly won, the troops were unevenly deployed; Kermit and McGeorge in one direction, and Julie, Kunkel, and Aubrey in the other, in a sort of great-circle route, the intent being that each party would trudge around and ever upward until they came together again, hopefully without potting one another, somewhere on B-17 Ridge. Kermit was self-designated first (and, in fact, only) rifle of his detachment, it having been agreed by all responsible members of the hunt the year before that it was safe, under certain very strictly controlled conditions, to permit McGeorge to fire straight up into the air, or straight down into the ground, but in no other direction whatsoever. (It appeared a little later that the weapon McGeorge carried was a .410 shotgun with shells loaded with rock salt, and when Aubrey protested to Kermit about this, saying that it left poor McGeorge at the mercy of large beavers, to say nothing of bears, Kermit's only reply was "Better him than me.") Julie, armed with a .300 Magnum, was appointed first rifle of the other party, and Aubrey second rifle. Kunkel would fire only to protect their proper persons from bearish assault. And, looking at Kunkel's monumentally stoic features, Aubrey took heart and left his safety on, for certainly anything Kunkel fired at would be stricken, if not struck.

Julie led off looking distinctly huntressesque, with weapon held high, sling engaged, butt (of rifle) to hip, and her pretty green eyes—following the lead of her belligerent chin—sweeping the terrain before them precisely as if she would recognize an enemy if she saw one. And as he followed her, Aubrey was caught up in the spirit or the mystique of the thing, and found himself practicing encomiums such as "That's the way to shoot, Julie, babe!" or "Let him come, Julie, babe, I'm right behind you!" or "Stick it up his nose, Julie, babe!"

And yet, for Aubrey, it was one of those awful times in life when what is being done is thoroughly frivolous (like Kermit driving the 300 SL Mercedes-Benz roadster he used to have—before he wrapped it around a stanchion on Twelfth Avenue, Christmas, 1955—a hundred and thirty miles an hour down the Northern State Parkway with Arnie and Aubrey strapped into the single seat beside him, Arnie screaming out of mixed joy and fright, and Aubrey screamless, joyless, and staring at the moon)—and likely to end in sudden death at any moment. And, for that reason, he felt very happy that Arnie was not along, was off somewhere relatively safe fishing with Pisser Duffy, because, as he remembered now, his greatest fear on those awful night rides with Kermit had been that the car would crash and that he, Aubrey, would be thrown clear and by some miracle survive, and have to walk along the highway picking up bits and pieces of Arnie and Kermit; this fear seizing him to such an extent that he had invented a special prayer against it—an orison in roundelay that had consisted of the single petition: "Dear God, take me before Arnie and Kermit, and do not take them without me"—so that he never said any prayer, morning, noon, night, Latin, English, public, or private, in which his prayer was not included at least once. And there was something else, something not yet—and perhaps not likely to be—clearly defined, that put the hunt preclusively beyond his sympathy and acceptance, and that was that Arnie, who had never seemed to him really frightened of anything before, had appeared to be (and this the purest kind of intuitive divination on Aubrey's part) at least extremely apprehensive, if not fearful, about taking any part in it, and would take part in it only to please Kermit. The hunt, this particular hunt, was, then, not merely frivolous, but oppressive. It had, Aubrey decided (especially in view of the earthquake that launched it), a darkness upon it. He did not try to define it less primitively than that; what was primitive in its essence did not deserve predicamentals of any greater refinement. No good would come of this hunt, and that was that, and Aubrey put one foot in front of the other in the aboriginal, eye-shooting, ear-bent, soul-shriveling dread that each footprint he left behind him might just possibly be his last.

But the day came almost to nothing except sore feet; a long day's journey into chilblains. Before it was over, Aubrey would have welcomed another earthquake for the simple diversion of it. In the first two hours, he bent knees and reached booted feet upward through rain, snow, sleet, and constant wind, and through a landscape that tor pure, tabescent desolation had to rival the nether side of the moon. There was tundra, muskeg, willow scrub, snow (fresh, rotten, and falling), and deeper snow, impenetrable willow thickets, crevasses, abysses, cliffs, and ten thousand large to huge fire-blasted boulders strewn all about, evidence that Mount Frosty, now classified a *caldera*, might become what it had obviously once been, a rock-blowing caldron, any old time at all. When they arrived on B-17 Ridge, there were Kermit and McGeorge, looking like two snow-bound Tibetan monks with their parka hoods up over their heads and their breaths like white death rattles in front of them, sitting on what looked like what remained of the wing of a dead airplane.

"See anything?" Kermit asked.

"Not even a track," Kunkel replied.

"Well, we'll work a little higher. That's where he usually is," Kermit said.

And in those three sentences was contained the remainder of the day. Except that it was mercifully decided, after a second rendezvous on a still-higher ridge, that McGeorge and Aubrey should return to B-17 Ridge while Kermit, Kunkel, and Julie (who was one of the strong saying nothing) would be deployed as skirmishers, three abreast, and work straight up to the foot of the glacier on the east face (and Mount Frosty did have at least two glaciers, much to Aubrey's amaze, each of them all blue ice and creeping still), and then take separate, great-circle routes down again, the hope being that they would either see Big Ditmo on the way up or else bypass him and, if the latter, flush him out on the way down (Big Ditmo being an exceeding tricky bear, having—after long pursuit, apparently—learned the great-circle route from Kermit) and drive him into the waiting arms of Aubrey and McGeorge. Aubrey took a dim view of the whole plan, and put his view into verbals, but Kunkel told him that this was the way Kermit wanted it, and that, in such bad weather when the airplane could not be used to spot or to drive, it might as well be Kermit's way as any other. Aubrey acquiesced, deferring to Kunkel's patience almost as much as to his own disinclination to provoke Kermit's impatience, and rallied McGeorge out of what looked to be a permanent squat, and rallied himself so far as to push the safety off his rifle, and made a regular Retreat from Moscow out of their descent, with McGeorge following him so closely that, if his .410's barrel hadn't been dragging in the snow, it would certainly have been in Aubrey's right ear, or worse, and with McGeorge essaying no other reply to Aubrey's frequent halting, and full-stop inquiries, as to what McGeorge might have seen or heard, than a sneeze (which, McGeorge explained, was due to hay fever), and with Aubrey praying in short takes all the way down, telling himself that the good Lord did not want His bears to catch hay fever and would therefore keep them out of McGeorge's sphere of influence. And telling himself, too, that there hadn't been so seriocomic, so petrifying and yet so ridiculous a situation since Vassily Popoff rode his borzoi hound into battle against Murat and the Grand Army.

But they made it down to B-17 Ridge without incident and sat down on the fragmented wing, and McGeorge told Aubrey the story of the crash of the B-17; unintelligible, most of it, so that all Aubrey really got by way of fact was that it had happened in 1947 or 1948, that eight men—all aboard—had died in the crash, and that there hadn't been enough of any of them left to fill eight flowerpots. McGeorge had gotten the story from Pisser Duffy, who had been in the Cold Bay area since 1931 or thereabouts and had seen quite a few airplanes come and go and clobber in. And McGeorge's reconstruction of Pisser Duffy's account was not startling for its repertorial exhaustiveness. A sample: "Well, reverent, as you know, people are supposed to stay on the ground, and we have right here the holocaustic evidence of what happens when they don't. If you'll notice, Jesus Lazarene never went up in an air-a-plane. Most He ever went up in was a boat, and He let Peter do the steering, without a doubt. Now, old Pisser will tell you that the pilot of this here air-a-plane wouldn't trust to the people on the ground in the cyclometer who was tryin' to tell him where to light. There was a great and windy storm at the time. But I tell you, young reverent, and I think you will agree without fail, that what he didn't trust to was the good Lord Hisself, and stay on the ground in the first place. That's what I'm always tryin' to tell that heathen red man. And Mr. Kermit, too. Like the Prophet says in the Book of Job, 'He hath fenced up my way that I cannot pass, and He hath set darkness in my paths.' "

And so on. Yet for all of its circumlocution and bombast, Aubrey found in McGeorge's statement something of sense, and more of sadness, and he sat there on the shattered wing and looked down that tragic meadow of snow to where one engine and a bent propeller appeared to be stuck into the side of the mountain, and he thought of the eight young lives that had come so quickly and shockingly to a violent end in that forgotten damp, and he suddenly decided that if he fired his damned Weatherby Magnum in no other cause for the remainder of the hunt, he would fire it now—however ambivalently and even ambiguously—in honor of those eight men, there so sorrowfully and so remotely dead. He proposed this to McGeorge, suggesting that the old man might even care to contribute a little rock salt to the salute.

"Oh no, young reverent," McGeorge said, shaking his narrow head soulfully. "Mr. Kermit would be awful, awful mad if you did that. It'd scare the bear away just as sure as the great Lord Lazarene rose from the dead."

"That," Aubrey said, "is what I would call a fringe benefit, Mc-George." The old man seemed unmoved and Aubrey bent to him and fixed his gaze as intensely as the watering of both his eyes would permit. "Do you want to see Big Ditmo today, or any day, Mc-George?" The old man blinked away snowflakes and appeared to be about to say something relevant, but then subsided. "I mean, Mc-George, do you want them to drive that bear down here upon us, and then trust to my marksmanship? I who haven't fired a shot since Concord Bridge?" (Such special pleading, Aubrey felt, allowed a certain Jesuitical latitude with reference to literal fact.)

McGeorge was given definite pause by this. In fact, so profound was it that he appeared for a time to have died. But then he started to hum, and he went on humming for a while, then he hawed for a while, and finally he hawked for a while, and then he pulled at his nose, eyebrows, and the trigger guard of his .410. But in the end, to Aubrey's relief, he squinted from beneath his snow-covered eyelashes, issued a wink that summoned all the duplicity Iowa had ever contained from Clinton to the river, and said, "Reverent. If you say you saw a bear, what I mean, if you say you saw Big Ditmo and took a shot at him, why, I sure would be the last one to say you didn't see him."

From that moment, Aubrey and McGeorge were in it together, and, hesitating for only an instant to beam effulgently upon the newly ordained member of the Ancient Society of Devout and Cowardly Dissimulators, Aubrey raised his .378 Magnum (the official rifle of the Society from that time forward), pointed it generally at the side of the mountain, then picked out a peculiarly bear-shaped willow branch in his four-power scope, roundly dedicated the round to the memory of those thereinbefore departed, and, while beginning to remember Kermit's admonition about the weapon's kick and seeking to set his feet, accidentally touched off the damnedest rocketing explosion he had even remotely been party to since Arnie had used cherry bombs to blow the right front headlight out of Solly's Volkswagen.

He couldn't believe the force of the recoil. After the noise, there was at first a pleasant drifting sensation, but the drift turned very shortly to drag, and after that he realized that he was on his back and that his collar was filling with snow, and that there was a pain in his gun shoulder which he would have thought could only have proceeded from his right arm being amputated in the vicinity of the near wisdom tooth.

He was not long off the ground, and still brushing snow out of his smallclothes, when the three skirmishers arrived, all in a heat and more or less simultaneously, rifles and tongues at the ready, all fierce-eyed and safeties off, inquiring stridently as to the whereabouts of the bear. McGeorge was deep in exegesis concerning the destruction of Jerusalem and the certainty that Christ would have given the disciples gunpowder if He had meant men to fire shots, and Aubrey, in his concussive shock, was not able to make a good job of his lie that Big Ditmo had appeared suddenly in the vicinity of the B-17 engine making noises commensurate thereto. Not one of the skirmishers believed him, and Kermit was all but unhinged to find Aubrey's rifle buried in the snow some twelve feet from Aubrey's nearest skid mark.

But it made no essential difference. The hunt was incontrovertibly over for the day, and they were in the jeep—except McGeorge, who was, as usual, precarious among the impedimenta in the trailer—and halfway back to the Lodge before any serious question was raised. And this by Kermit, who turned from the front seat, his eyes fulvous and without any trace of the indulgent amusement evident in the expressions of Julie and Kunkel, and said, "So, you thought you saw Big Ditmo, and McGeorge thought that you thought that you saw him. Is that it?" Aubrey nodded, making the several mental reservations pertinent thereto as he did so. "Well, let me tell you what you do next time," Kermit said harshly. "If there is a next time, you take a good long second look. And if you still think you see a bear, and if McGeorge still thinks you see a bear, you shoot McGeorge."

352

So that the first day of the hunt ended with Aubrey more or less in disgrace, with Julie giggling and slapping him from time to time on the knee, with Kunkel biting at what was certainly one of the few Modoc grins since the defeat of Captain Jack, and with Kermit shaking his head and beard all the way home as if he had taken Aubrey's salute square in the Achilles' tendon.

# · TWENTY-EIGHT ·

Somewhere in the long shank of that interminable evening, Aubrey
was propped up, comatose, on one of McGeorge's medieval thrones
near the far end of the dining table, his right eye open. His left eye,
his whole left side, had long since gone to sleep. Fifteen feet away,
or thereabouts, Kermit was talking. Kermit had been talking for upwards of an hour already and was enjoying himself hugely, enjoying the sound of his marvelously resonant voice, and showing no
sign of flagging.

Arnie was seated at Kermit's right hand, bright-eyed, eager, grinning, his chin thrust out toward Kermit, a most avid and energetic
listener. Every time Kermit had shown any inclination to stop talking, or any hesitation about what to say next, Arnie had jumped into
the silence with suggestions. "Tell us about the war, Kermit," or tell
us about Paris, or Berlin, or Wall Street, or Clark Gable. Aubrey had
dismissed the idea that Arnie was being sarcastic, or playing some
other kind of game. There was something very odd, even for Arnie,
in his whole mood and manner. His eyes, his voice, his gestures were
those of a boy of twelve. Every now and then, when Kermit had
come to a particularly dramatic or sonorous conclusion, Arnie would
clap his hands vigorously and give out little yelps of delight. Aubrey
had sat there watching, in dull, sleepy amazement, wondering how
long it was going to take Kermit to notice that Arnie was not simply

in good spirits, that Arnie had, in fact, left for the past some time ago.

McGeorge, seated across from Aubrey, also clapped from time to time although he was plainly just following Arnie's lead, his automatic politeness in no way hindering the conversation he had been having with himself—and perhaps with an unseen party or parties—since he had finished his dessert. He paused from time to time for a sip of wine, but then put his lips right back into fulsome motion. It occurred to Aubrey that he was having a debate with Job over some point of doctrine. If so, Aubrey's money was on McGeorge all the way because it was obvious that Job hadn't gotten a word in yet, and wasn't likely to.

Kunkel, whose capacity for motionless repose was legend, had maintained an utter stillness, indulging not twitch nor twiddle, for about a half hour, since, in fact, a passage of air of such Ripuarian magnificence and authority that Aubrey had thought the man's vitals had come undone. Even then, Kunkel's composure would have shamed Buster Keaton, and he had continued in it, graven, dipped in bronze, the mighty reddleman already in the bosom of his fathers.

It had been shortly after the salutation by Kunkel that Julie had gone off to bed, stopping long enough to whisper to Aubrey that she would see him later, if he survived. Aubrey had risen to leave shortly thereafter, but Arnie had raised such a strident protest, saying that Aubrey had to stay and hear the stories too or it wasn't any fun, that Aubrey had subsided.

On the floor in front of the fireplace was Sordini, surely the sloe-est-eyed, mournfulest-looking hound in Alaska and the Northwest Territories. Sordini mostly slept for exercise, that is, he ran and yipped only when asleep, and did it on a regular ten-minutes-on, ten-minutes-off schedule. McGeorge had wondered to Aubrey what could possibly be after Sordini, and Aubrey had suggested it was the Hound of Heaven, which conceit had pleased McGeorge very much. But whatever was after him, Aubrey was betting on Sordini to win going away.

Outside the wind was high and kept him in apprehension of the roof's being snatched off. Kunkel had driven up to the airstrip in the late afternoon to tie the airplane down more securely, and had come back with reports of gusts up to sixty miles an hour. Aubrey had helped Kunkel tie the jeep and the trailer down, and Kunkel had told him that he never much worried about the wind until it got over eighty miles an hour, which it fairly often did, and that he once had seen the wind gauge in the Cold Bay weather station climb to a hundred and forty-five miles an hour and stay there for almost six minutes. Kunkel had said there might be such another wind anytime— had said it almost gaily, as if he could scarcely wait—and Aubrey had decided, upon Kunkel's dinner salute, that wind and the big Indian had an undeniable attraction for each other.

But Kermit's wind had the floor, and in fact he was now telling a story about wind; about a lawyer he claimed to have known who always managed, somewhere in every case he ever tried, to quote the immortal words of Patrick Henry about liberty and death. But when this same lawyer took on a case defending a farmer accused of knowingly selling a colicky horse to another farmer, Kermit and his friends went to court to see how the lawyer could possibly work in the immortal words. "And the son of a bitch!" Kermit cried, bringing one fist down on the table, looking around at each of his listeners with his eyes shining, the light from the fire moving on his face, his smile wide and genuine and including them in his great self-confidence and delight. "The son of a bitch, what does he do but, in his summation, he defines the colic. 'And what, ladies and gentlemen of the jury, *is* the colic? Well, let me tell you. The colic is nothing more or less than an impaction of wind, trapped within the animal under great pressure, and in constant motion from the front of the horse to the back, and from the back to the front, gathering speed and force and combustion, and crying out the while, in the immortal words of Patrick Henry, 'Give me liberty or give me death!' "

Arnie went into a perfect frenzy of delight. He clapped his hands, bounced in his chair, pounded the table, pulled at his hair, and laughed and mugged so fiercely that Aubrey didn't understand how he kept from tearing his mouth at the corners. Arnie was back at about age ten by this time, and getting younger by the minute.

My God, Aubrey thought, McGeorge will have to break out the Pablum if this keeps up.

McGeorge was clapping perfunctorily, his mouth and left eye winking in unison. Job was apparently not an easy man to convince.

Give it to him, McGeorge. Don't let him give you any dunghill.

Kunkel's expression had changed slightly. His lower lip was thrust out a bit farther, and his heavy black eyebrows were hauled down like twin storm clouds.

Bad news in the tribal council. Chief Left Wing and his boys have taken over the long house. They've nailed up the doors and windows from the inside, and the word is they're boiling three loons and a dingo in oil. Next thing you know, they'll have a serious impaction running around in there. Smoke the bastards out, Kunkel. Give 'em the immortal words before they blow the long house all to hell.

Now Kermit was talking about Kunkel just as though Kunkel were not there, which, Aubrey conceded, was truer than not. ". . . Kunkel and I, we'd been shipping two or three years together by then, and one night we're up around Greenland in a tar-barrel fog, and Kunkel, who's got eyes like a tall eagle, and who, by God, can *feel* an iceberg coming up just by the change in the temperature or the smell of things or some goddamned thing, he was with me on the bridge and we were taking turns at the wheel and at going outside to peer around and blow horns and whistles and things, and holler at the guys on ice watch. The captain, his name was Moore, he drank straight grain alcohol—carried it around in a hot-water bottle, and always needed a new one because that stuff ate holes in the rubber— anyway, it was this trip that the stuff finally got to him and I was sort of in command by default and trying to get Moore to Halifax before he died. And I was getting impatient about poking along, and I was about to ring down for more speed when old Kunkel came diving through the hatch, rang full astern, grabbed the wheel from me, put it hard over, and said, 'Ice.' And then I saw the iceberg. A small one, about the size of St. Patrick's Cathedral, or the box it came in, standing high, with a sort of steeple on its one end, and sitting broadside to, dead ahead. As I say, Kunkel had us full astern, but it didn't take in time and we were going right on in. And it was all up to Kunkel, and I said to him, 'Kunkel, if you fix it so that son of a bitch doesn't dump us, you can be best man at my wedding.' Now, who the hell would expect he'd hear me say that, let alone that he'd remember it later? But, but, by God, he did hear it, and he did remember it, and he held me to it later, by Christ, when it came time to get married! Right, Kunkel?"

Kunkel stared straight ahead, still frowning, then took a long drink of his whisky. Kermit accepted this as an answer.

Good Lord, Kunkel, don't take this sitting down. Can't you hear that impaction whistling around the long house?

"But, but!" Arnie cried. "What about the iceberg, Dad?"

"Oh, well, old Kunkel picked his spot right and put us into it, broadside and easy, right under a big overhang where the ice sloped in and away. He said it was luck, but it wasn't. Best goddamned helmsman I ever saw. We ground up some superstructure, and we were a while getting away from the damned thing, but didn't hurt the hull much at all."

"But what about the captain, Dad?"

"Old Augie? Oh, poor old Augie died. Put old Augie ashore dead and full of preservative. I think he'd have kept for months with all that alcohol in him."

"And Kunkel was your best man?"

"Sure he was, Arnie. You know that."

"And what about the wedding, Dad?"

Kermit looked at Arnie almost angrily. "Well, good Christ, Arnie. You know all about the wedding. I've told you a dozen times." And he reached suddenly for the whisky bottle at Kunkel's elbow. "Hey, you goddamned stone-faced redman!" Kunkel didn't move. "Look at him. Shittier than a caribou. And no goddamned wonder! Put away almost this whole jug all by himself. I keep telling him that the goddamned red Indian isn't allowed to drink whisky, but he won't be advised. It's right in the goddamned Articles of Confederation. Have to find them someday and read them to him. Yes, by God."

Kunkel's chin was down on his chest, his fists were clenched, and he was staring at his thumbs as if he were contemplating biting them off.

"Hey!" Kermit shouted at him good-humoredly.

Kunkel jumped about eight inches off his chair and came down again, staring wildly.

Hup! Charge, Kunkel! That damned impaction just blew both ends out of the long house.

"Son of a bitch!" Kunkel roared, staring at McGeorge.

McGeorge's colloquy with Job got abruptly suspended somewhere between his upper and lower plates. He flinched and jumped backward, from which vantage point he began to gather himself at once, and when he did rise, he was on the top step of his pulpit, winking fire. "The red heathen speaks! The viper's tongue spits with the gall of asps! Wickedness is sweet in his red mouth! But, behold, the triumphing of the wicked is short!"

"Oh, shut up!" Arnie said.

Kunkel continued to stare at McGeorge, but he seemed puzzled. Clearly this was not Left Wing; not unless he had gotten severely damaged in the explosion.

Deal with him firmly either way, Kunkel. He's the kind who goes around starting impactions, no doubt about it. You can tell by the click of his teeth.

But Kunkel looked away from McGeorge, reached up his glass and drained about four fingers in a long neat swallow. His shoulders and chin fell about four fingers beneath the tribal yoke, and the council apparently went back to higher things.

I give you greeting, Kunkel. The quality of your mercy is admirable. And to hell with the long house. It was too long anyway.

McGeorge was looking from Arnie to Kunkel to Kermit and back again. He was patently angry with someone, but he wasn't sure with whom. He appeared to consult for a moment with Job, then lifted one hand, knocking over his wine glass as he did, and admonished the whole congregation. "The heathen shall perish forever like his own dung! They which have seen him shall say, where *is* he? He shall fly away as a dream, and shall not be found! Yea! He shall be chased away as a vision of the night! Amen!"

"Goddamn you," Arnie said, in a girlish tenor screech. "Get out, get out!"

McGeorge was not perturbed in the least. He bowed to Aubrey with courtly grace from the hips, raised two fingers in a sort of a forkball benison, and said, "The peace of Jesus to you tonight, young reverent." Upon which, he took Job by the elbow, gave Aubrey a final series of winks, wheeled left smartly, and went out waving one hand, his prophetic grandeur only mildly marred by the cyclonic motion of his mouth.

Goodnight, McGeorge M'Naghten, and flights of angels sing thee to thy rest. And don't apologize to Job, even if you did quote that old fink, Zophar.

"You get annoyed at McGeorge for something, Kunkel?" Kermit asked.

"Oh, to hell with them, Dad. They're both psychotic," Arnie said, with no trace of self-consciousness. "What about the wedding, Dad?"

Kermit looked at Arnie as if he had just begun to realize that his son had relocated. Then Kermit drained his glass, fumbled in the semidarkness on the floor behind him, knocked over some empty bottles, cursed vaguely, and finally extracted a new bottle from the cardboard carton. He opened the bottle with lugubrious care, filled his glass, Arnie's, and Kunkel's, glanced at Aubrey, shrugged, and resumed the hunched-forward pose of the prose minstrel, hands cupped around his glass, with a gentle, amused smile as if tasting impending hilarities.

"What about the wedding, Dad?"

At this point, Aubrey fell asleep. When he came back for a brief stay, Kermit was saying, ". . . goddamnedest noise I've heard since Horses Aspromonte slipped the winch and dropped that Bentley automobile through the foc'sle of the old *Shenstone!*" Laughter.

When Aubrey returned for the second time, Kermit was saying, ". . . Ritz bar in Paris. This guy comes in and orders champagne and orange juice, half and half. This hits Kunkel as very funny, and one thing leads to another, and this guy steps back and kicks Kunkel under the chin, and Kunkel goes ass first through the doors of that bar, across the hall, and right into the other bar. So I knock the Frenchman down, Kunkel gets up, shouts, 'You clean that one, I'll clean this one!' And he turns around and belts a perfect stranger. We were still separately engaged when the gendarmes arrived, I with my fists, and Kunkel—who had cleaned his bar easily—with a woman who said she was an apache dancer and old Kunkel was kind of figuring he saw a chance for a little tribal crossbreeding!" More laughter.

When Aubrey returned for the third time, it was to a sound in the room that had the high shrill of steam escaping from a valve. He opened his eyes. Arnie was seated across the table from him, playing a flute. Kermit and Kunkel were gone. Sordini was still there, enjoying just then one of his rest periods.

Arnie stopped fluting. "Did you enjoy that?" he asked.

"Oh, very much, Arnie," Aubrey said. "What tune is it?"

"I composed it for you. Especially. It's based on 'Tan-trum Ergo.' " He smiled at his little joke. "I call it 'Somewhere the Blowfish Are Blowing.' "

And Aubrey realized at once that he was now confronted with yet another Arnie. He was almost debonair, his age not readily calculable, his speech and mannerisms somewhat mincing and foppish. He looked at the wall over Aubrey's head, lifting his chin slightly, pivoting his head slowly, as if someone had asked to see his profile. His lips were pressed fat together and his jowls puffed and heavy.

360

"Oh no, no," Arnie said. "Too much light." And he got up and walked around turning lights off, leaving just one burning. Then he returned to his chair, placed a glass in front of Aubrey, and nodded to it. Aubrey shook his head. Sordini started to run as Arnie shrugged and poured himself a long drink. He raised the glass to Aubrey. "You have the face of a saint, Aubie," he said with reverence. He held his eyes, large and limpid, on Aubrey as he drank. Aubrey was embarrassed by Arnie's gaze, and looked away. "No, no, don't be nervous," Arnie said. His eyes continued to move on Aubrey like little blueblack moons. "Yes, yes, that's it," Arnie said. "St. Bernard of Clairvaux."

"The others have all gone to bed?" Aubrey asked.

"What, what? The *others?*" He looked at Aubrey with an exaggerated pout of disappointment. "What do *we* care about the others?"

"I care a lot about the others," Aubrey said with just a touch of harshness.

Arnie appeared surprised by this, glanced suddenly around him, blinked for a time at Sordini, cleared his throat, took a fast sip from his drink, raised his eyes to Aubrey, smiled. "Why, God bless me, the others are no better than they should be, I'm afraid." And Aubrey could see in Arnie's eyes that something, whatever it had been, had just ended, and that Aubrey had obviously been included among the others, for better or worse.

And, abruptly, Arnie was talking loudly, his tone grating and slurred, and he appeared to be denouncing something, and presently was waving his arms and beating on the table. Nothing he said was clearly pronounced. The words were English, but strangely accented, drawn out, stretched, hung, and quartered. He might have been reciting the Sibylline Books in Old English for all it meant to Aubrey. His manner was oracular, yet at times he spoke with intense sincerity. At other times he would be silent for as long as five seconds, staring at Aubrey in apparent anger, or grief, or with head cocked as if he expected applause. He posed his head at every possible angle for emphasis, and worked his mouth, even when he wasn't talking, puffing his cheeks and pouching his lips so that they seemed to go in and out of a recurrent pucker. And he pulled at his eyebrows, and finally started to issue little squealing noises, like a pig. And he brought the performance to a fitting conclusion by throwing his head back and screaming with his whole lung power—a scream that went on for thirty seconds and more, until Aubrey thought he might well split himself from crotch to crown if he kept it up, until, in fact, Aubrey was certain he was witnessing the final turbinations of a mind.

But when the screaming ended, there was a new Arnie onstage. He was breathing heavily and sweating a bit, and he kept his head back, his Adam's apple bobbing in his taut throat, and only brought his chin down when Aubrey asked him if he was all right. First, a panoramic display of teeth. Then his eyes, flat and hard. "Of course, I'm all right," he said. "How about you?" His eyes glittered on Aubrey. "A gentleman must from time to time clear his throat, don't you agree?" He picked up his flute and shook it across the table. "I call it Touchhole. Cute?" Then he turned his head and gave Aubrey the left eye with raised eyebrow. "Did you enjoy my pre-clearance recital?"

"You mean the flute?"

"Of course not, stupid. I mean what followed."

"I couldn't understand a word you said."

"That's to be expected," he said, wagging his smile indulgently. "Certainly you wouldn't understand, brother mine. One would have to be as profound a student of human cybernetics as I am, and much, much more, I'm afraid, to understand. You see, brother, I speak with tongues. With *tongues*." He stared at Aubrey, then licked his lips, and, in the same soft, even polite, tone, and with an entire formality of language, and with much winking and cocking of eyes and head and cunning little turns of the nose, he started to talk again. "I'll translate some of it for you, however, as a gesture of fraternal charity. Catholicism," he said portentously, "is the communism of the cowardly conservative." A pause and a wink. "We are all victims of the virgin birth, even if we don't believe it." A touch of wrist to chin. "I was an extremely good archer until I became interested in Zen."

This went on for some time. He seemed delighted with his little aphorisms and almost laughed once or twice. He asked questions, sometimes ten or more in rapid-fire strings, but never allowed Aubrey time to answer even the first one. He covered all kinds of subjects, mentioned all kinds of unconnected things and persons. Capital punishment, Socrates, Eva Perón, applejack, telesis, *Gammer Gurton's Needle*, shock treatment, injection fuel systems, the Falcidian law, Wobblies, sea anchors, incubi, bullfighting on horseback, Guernica, the grandissimus, the Lame Duck Amendment, and ithyphallic ritual. His final statement of the series was "I am ardently—oh ardently—in favor of contraceptive pills for Roman Catholic nuns."

Aubrey considered this for a moment, as Arnie sat there looking down his nose at the table, grinning with his lips only, challenging his brother to make some comment. Aubrey knew that he had been challenged, but hesitated to enter into it with Arnie. It could lead nowhere but to bitterness. Yet we might as well be in bitterness, he thought, as in madness. Might a hell of a lot better be in bitterness. So Aubrey said, "I suppose you want to argue about that, Arnie, don't you?"

"Why, no." Utterly superior innocence, even disdain.

"All right. I suppose, then, you think it's funny."

"That's a *right* suppose. You're batting fifty-fifty, two-point-oh, as usual, brother mine. I do indeed think it's funny, but you'll be amazed to know, I'm quite sure, that the Vatican doesn't think it's funny at all." He looked up at Aubrey with something like scorn in his expression. "You reveal your ignorance, brother mine, because, you see, the Vatican has given this matter very serious consideration."

"I doubt it."

"Unfortunately, I haven't the documents here to dispel your doubt, documents that were only brought to my attention because a certain sweet-natured young priest was admitted just before Christmas last year to our Shelter Island retreat. A brilliant young man, of quite wealthy family. But enough of that. Just picture, if you can, the enemy poised on the hill. The troops, to a man, are in an ugly, rapacious, sex-starved condition. Their growls can be heard all the way down into the little valley, and into the little white convent, and into the little white chapel, where the little white nuns are cowering around their little white mother superior. What is the little white mother superior to do? Obviously, she issues her little white nuns little white contraceptive pills, with instructions to her little white nuns not to take the little white pills until they see the great black eyeballs or the little white eye-whites of the great black troops!"

"No doubt I owe you an apology, Arnie. It does sound reasonable."

"But of course! Is the holy Roman Catholic and Apostolic Church ever anything but reasonable?" He stared at Aubrey in self-consumed triumph.

Aubrey felt like punching him on his little white nose. But he said, "I'm sorry, Arnie. I didn't know about it."

"Of course, you didn't know about it! Dear brother, you haven't yet grasped the simple fact that even though I haven't had the advantage of a college education, as you purportedly have, I know many,

many things that you have never heard of. You wouldn't want to dispute with me over general knowledge or intelligence quotients, would you, brother mine?"

Aubrey decided to let it all go. Nor was he sure at all that he did want to dispute with Arnie in any intellectual area. Aubrey said, "We both know you have the better mind, Arnie."

"Very gallant of you. But it *is* true that I've read all the classics." He smiled toward humility, but missed rather badly. "Oh, the Harvard Classics, of course, and the Great Books, and the *Encyclopaedia Britannica*. Just lately, I finished reading the entire Modern Library." He seemed to startle himself with his last statement, but recovered, and curled his lower lip at Aubrey with more contempt than one would have thought a lower lip could convey. "Naturally, you don't believe that."

"I do, Arnie. Of course I do. If you say so."

"If you say so," he said, mimickingly. "Well, brother mine, just to prove it to you, I will first name for you every title in the Modern Library, beginning with the Giants, and when I'm done, I'll be glad to give you a summary or outline of any volume you care to name."

And before Aubrey could protest effectively, Arnie was off and running, and Aubrey could only sit there while he spat out the titles venomously, with incredible rapidity, so that Aubrey somehow felt accused of each title, as if he had either not read, or else had written, each one of them, the latter only with the diabolical intent of forcing Arnie to read them. And Aubrey was by now, he confessed to himself, something more than a little afraid of Arnie, afraid that his brother had slipped all cogs at last and would not be recoverable until returned to Shelter Island, if then. Aubrey was also very tired, even desperately tired, and he began to be afraid that he would fall asleep again and that Arnie would become angered and strike him with a bottle, or worse. So that he started to think about escaping, and determined that he would make his break for the hallway during the pause between the Giants and the regular size. And he waited for the pause eagerly, perhaps too eagerly, because Arnie seemed to notice him setting himself, poised and ready to sprint. And Arnie fooled him, and ran *The Wisdom of Catholicism* right into *The Grapes of Wrath* with no pause at all, and went whidding off down the regular-size list with a tight little smile, singing out the titles complacently, even viciously: "*Vanity Fair, The Golden Treasury, Walden and Other Works* . . . !"

"Arnie, for God's sake! I believe you! I believe . . ."

". . . The Compleat Angler, The Life of Jesus, The Oregon Trail, Of Mice and Men, What Cheer, or an Anthology of Humorous and Witty Verse . . . !"

Aubrey decided that there was no use in trying to get away without offending against courtesy.

Just get the hell out of here as quickly and stealthily as you can. Arnie is no longer with it. Gird up thy grit and hominy, take on the aspect of a very Cooper Indian, and make for the exit.

He considered for a moment slipping unobtrusively under the table and duckwalking out. But Arnie, hawk-eyed, noted his pre-est preliminary slouch. Aubrey told himself, again, to hell with it, and began to ease his chair, with what casualness he could manage, back from the table. Arnie noted this too, and raised his voice, but didn't pause to throw anything or remonstrate. And then Aubrey began to wonder if Arnie hadn't actually mesmerized himself, if he had been noting Aubrey's movements consciously or had been, as it were, merely reacting to shiftings of light and shadow. Still, wishing to get out of it without an uproar if possible, Aubrey proceeded with almost yogilike patience and subtlety, so that by the time he was on his feet, noting with pride that the tingling in his spine was due to numbness, not nervousness, Arnie was slowing slightly and his eyes were taking on an unmistakable glaze of uncertainty. Aubrey perceived at once that Arnie had lost his place, was not really sure whether or not he had named all of the Modern Library regular size, and Aubrey, seizing the advantage as he noted Arnie's expression essaying the shift from retreat to attack, from confusion to protest over Aubrey's having risen, fixed Arnie with the sternest, most atrabilious eye he could summon—as if to assure Arnie that one misstep, one lacuna of even a split second's duration, would result in Arnie's having to go back and start all over again—and began to edge toward the head of the table. Arnie appeared daunted for a few seconds, but then, just as he seemed certain to commit the interstitial sin, he came upon a veritable covey of unannounced titles; and his satisfaction, as he pounced and shook them through his teeth at Aubrey, was almost obscene.

"Progress and Poverty, Dead Souls, Moll Flanders, Rebecca . . . !"

Aubrey concluded instantly that it was time for impavid decision. If Arnie was going to go violent on him, he might just as well do it sooner than later.

Take destiny's bit by the snaffle, MacIver. Take the measure of the distance, and leap for the nearest opening. Cry him good-night, and the rest of the angels, but get out of here.

Yet he stood for another moment, looking down at his brother, at this man who was sometimes his brother, and asked himself what kind of beast he was to desert him in this manner. Could he not watch with Arnie an hour? Could he not watch in the hope that Arnie would return and reoccupy this babble of a body? Could he not try at least to coax his brother to bed, and not just leave him here to go ranting on, perhaps all night? But the charity for it, the energy for it, was not in him, and he knew it, and turned suddenly, knocked over a chair, kicked the case of whisky into an horrendous clatter of empties, took the business end of the mobile battle horn pinging between the eyes, vaulted around Kermit's chair, and ran across the room and into the hallway. There he paused and looked back, pavidly. There was no pursuit. Arnie was still at full gallop, and so was Sordini. And the last he heard from Arnie was "The Turn of the Screw!"

Then, praying that God would do something about unscrewing the inscrutable Arnie, he went into his room, closed the door, stood by it, hanging onto the knob, stripped off his clothes, and knelt down among them and went on praying there, in the cool darkness, for charity and chastity, and forgiveness for failing his only brother.

He was awakened some time later by the clouting of the wind across the roof, and found that his arm had gone to sleep, the hand still clutched to the doorknob, and he staggered to his feet, stuck his arm out in front of him and followed it to bed.

366

# · TWENTY-NINE ·

HE GOT INTO the mess hall in time to hear Arnie, who was apparently much recovered and standing by the fire in his bright red long johns with a white towel wrapped at his waist, declaiming as follows: "Why, McJesus, you goddamned facinorous old cockalorum! If you ever tell me another lie like that, I'll pack you up in ptarmigan turds and ship you off to the Serbonian bog!"

"It's true, it's true!" McGeorge said, shaking his head back and forth, addressing himself to Kermit—who was clipping his toenails and paying McGeorge no attention whatsoever—and keeping a wary eye on Arnie. The poor old man looked like Jonas, poised in his white duster at the gates of Nineveh, his pipey forefinger extended, getting ready to shout a few damnations in at the King before running like hell for the nearest camel. "It's true, Mr. Arnie, I swear it in the name of the great Lord Lazarene Hisself! And when I find that book, why, I'll just purely prove it to you."

"The book's in the john on the shelf," Kermit muttered.

McGeorge delivered himself of a joyous exclamation, appeared to rise eight or ten inches straight up, floated there a minute ecstatically, then took off toward the john like a cumulus cloud in a downdraft. Aubrey watched him go, then bade Kermit and Arnie the best of the morning, and asked what it was all about. "Oh, old McJesus is trying

367

to tell me that there was a wave a year ago in Lituya Bay seventeen hundred and twenty feet high."

"What's he trying to tell you that for?"

Arnie shrugged happily. "Who the hell knows? I think he wants to insinuate that the Lord Lazarene was after me, with giant waves yet."

"He could've made it more believable. I mean, a hundred-foot wave would do the job."

"Now, Aubie, don't go slighting the Lord Lazarene. He isn't one to waste water. If He sent seventeen hundred and twenty feet of water, He must have figured, by God, He needed seventeen hundred and twenty feet." Arnie cocked his head amiably. "Too bad I wasn't in Lituya Bay at the time. From what I read, it must have been quite a sight."

"From what you read?"

"Yeah. What I read. In the pamphlet old McJesus went after. You shouldn't have told him where it was, Kermit. I'm only trying to drive the old bastard schizoid so I'll have some company."

"That's all we need around here," Kermit said. "A schizoid, half-witted preacher."

"What makes you think he's half-witted?" Aubrey said. "I think he's okay. And pretty intelligent."

"You do?" Kermit said. "Christ."

"You think old McJesus is *sane*?" Arnie said.

"He seems all right to me."

"Holy Jesus! You mean I'm crazy and McJesus isn't?" Arnie was still grinning, but he'd lost a little candle power.

"I didn't say you were crazy."

"Oh, come on now, Aubie, let's not beat around the finking bush."

"Look, I don't know whether he's sane or not, but I think if you keep telling a person he's crazy, pretty soon he begins to think he is, and pretty soon he begins to act like he is."

"You think that's what happened to me, Aubie?"

"No. I told you, I didn't say you were crazy."

"And I told you, don't con me."

"I'm not trying to con you."

"Okay, let's put it this way. Do you think I'm crazy or don't you? Yes or no."

"Goddamn it," Kermit said, "we're *all* crazy, and any goddamned fool can see it." He shook his head and went to pulling on his boots.

368

"Christ. We'd have to be crazy to get within one thousand god-damned miles of one another."

"What's that supposed to mean?" Arnie said.

"It means I'm getting goddamned sick and tired of all the arguing and bickering around here! For Christ's sake, can't we ever have any peace?"

"Well, may the sweet risen Jesus have mercy on your hypocritical soul," Arnie said. "Old Mouth Almighty himself wants us to turn in our irasciphones!"

"Now, Arnie, watch your goddamned mouth, that's all."

Arnie was grinning widely again and he raised his eyebrows gleefully at Aubrey as he went on: "Why, dear God, next thing a sweet-smelling, thornless rosebush will sprout in his spleen and come popping right out through his belly button in full bloom!"

Kermit started to smile in spite of his best efforts to resist. "I'll sprout you a swift kick in the crupper . . ."

Arnie danced away, laughing, from Kermit's halfhearted charge. "Ah, see, see how he loves us! Oh, the ruddy roaring *charity* of the man! Stand back, gentles, back! There, just now, he firms up to belch! And when he does! Ah, when he does! Cakewalking down his rosy tongue right out of his fat mouth will come the turtle dove of peace and the bluebird of happiness singing their tender duet, 'Don't Talk While I'm Contradicting, Moishe, or I'll Crump Your Craw With a Crux!' "

"Get out! Out!" Julie shouted from the direction of the bathroom. "Lurking in the shadows, you dirty old man!"

Poor McGeorge came backing into the room, bowing humbly and apologizing in the name of the Lazarene to Julie, who stood at the bathroom door shaking a hairbrush at him. But she was smiling, looking beyond McGeorge to Aubrey; then she nodded and wished all a good morning and, with a flounce of white dressing gown, disappeared into the bathroom.

"McJesus, you old lecher!" Arnie cried. "Were you hiding out in the water closet again?"

"No, no, Mr. Arnie. I was just trying to find . . ."

"Oh, where's my Holy Bible! I must read to this lecherous old man the story of Susannah and the elders!"

"No, Mr. Arnie, look! Don't you remember?" McGeorge waved the government pamphlet. "The giant wave!"

"What? What's that?" Arnie snatched the pamphlet from Mc-

369

George's hand, riffled quickly through it, slapped his forehead, and rolled maidenly eyes toward heaven. "Oh! Oh, God save us! Pornographic pictures of naked women!"

McGeorge staggered backward, clutching at his duster. "No, no. Waves, waves," he murmured, his eyes great and round and lustrous with shock.

"Waves! Oh, I should say! Every wave in the U.S. Navy, from the looks! And a few Wacs, too! Nekkid! Nekkid every one! Oh, McJesus, I beseech you, eschew venery! Oh, eschew it, my son!"

This went on for some time, until Arnie's preachments and posturings had Aubrey and Kermit helpless with laughter, until McGeorge was looking from one to the other of the three Stryckers as if, indeed, he were the only sane man in the lot. Then Arnie almost ruined the whole business by throwing the pamphlet into the fire—delivering as he did so the finale of a long speech about the fallacy of the phallus in fellatio (mixing all liberally in several combinations), while posed in his long red underwear on the hearthstone, feet wide apart and arms raised, so that he had the form of a large red X, and, with the fire blazing behind him, the appearance of Satan in his flames defying heaven—but McGeorge got the tongs and fished the pamphlet out, and Arnie was so exhausted by his efforts that he sat quietly while the old man read about how an earthquake on the Fairweather fault on July 9, 1958 had caused forty million cubic yards of rock to fall three thousand feet into about seven hundred feet of water, raising a gravity wave that traveled between ninety-seven and one hundred thirty miles an hour out of Lituya Bay and reached a height of seventeen hundred and twenty feet, and so on, until Kermit said, "Oh, for Christ's sake, McGeorge, we've all read it. Where's my steak?"

"But he . . ." McGeorge said, pointing to Arnie.

"It's all a goddamned lie," Arnie said. "A clever forgery, is all. The old bastard printed that pamphlet up while he was hiding in the water closet."

And McGeorge went back to his cooking, a sadder and older man, muttering to himself about the United States Government Printing Office and how Arnie was all wrong about the water closet.

Then Kunkel came trundling into the room, wreathed in about one-eighth of a smile, with the intelligence that it just might be a clear day and the sun might even come out, and that Pisser Duffy had just gone by on his way to the freshwater lake and said that he had seen three bears mating about a half hour before, just off the road.

"By God, that must have been quite a sight!" Arnie cried. "Three of them. Hot damn! They don't call this the Aleutian Chain for nothing!"

And Arnie went on about this, lubriciously, until Julie came out, and Kermit told Arnie to get the hell in and get some clothes on, and Arnie went to his room loudly complaining that if Julie could wear her tights right out in plain sight of everybody he didn't see why he couldn't wear *his*. And the good mood of the morning had even touched Julie, and she apologized sweetly to McGeorge and said that she knew he hadn't meant to lurk, and kissed Kermit and hoped he'd slept well, and greeted Kunkel demurely and complimented him upon how nice and red he looked (Kunkel liked to look as red as possible), and then sat down next to Aubrey and, with unprecedented, eye-batting, honey-throated femininity, inquired as to his health, his opinion of Cold Bay, his thoughts as to the prospects for the day's hunt, and how late he had gotten to bed the night before. And all of this blandly, guilelessly, after the manner of Little Dorrit asking about the welfare of the Marshalsea inmates. Aubrey was wary at first, but then said to himself, Who the hell am I to be wary, and received Julie on her own terms, and found himself completely charmed and even flattered by her improbable sweetness.

And the day itself was improbable and sweet. The night's winds had apparently swept the sky clear for a hundred miles, and they were just fording the brook that marked the halfway point between the Lodge and the first of the foothills—the air already warm and lightsome and the brook running soundless and pretty in its tundra-bound course—when the sun came suddenly shining in from behind them. And even Arnie fell silent as they drove slowly toward the mountain, seeing it now for the first time in the sun; seeing it with the sunlight splendid all across its broad shoulders and its several lesser peaks, and as they began to climb, seeing the main peak itself at the top of the windshield of the jeep, proud, remote, topping its broad, graceful snowfields and a final length of spine-sharp ridge, the beautiful and absolute and worthy monarch of this westernmost point of American mainland. And Aubrey watched the mountain until his neck ached; watched the slight streamer of snow, pink and then brilliant white against the rich blue sky, standing south off the peak; watched the light and shadow move across the great blue-white saddle of the glacier, the refractions of light seeming to cause the air itself to dance and to run the ridges; watched as the wind blew from time to time across the whole eastern flank of the mountain, with a light touch but enough to lift the topmost snowflakes before it from the lower reaches to the fluted summit, lifting and turning and carrying them upward and beyond, so that the wind could almost be seen, transfiguring itself in countless diamond-points of light, a passage of quicksilver, a dazzlement out of the essence of light itself; watched this first great mountain he had ever so closely and boldly approached and walked about upon, and made it his own, adapting his eye to its every lineament, expanding his memory to receive it whole and undiminished and without loss of majesty, taking it unto himself and his memory as something of extraordinary value, a certain grandeur he would always have with him, a mystic height, secret and towering in his soul, whereon he could try himself again and again, knowing that the peak was unattainable, but knowing, too, that should he ever attain it, and stand upon it, and have ears to hear, there would be a sound gentle in the wind: and that that sound would be the beating of the heart of God.

When they got up on the lower ridge, Kermit and Kunkel were talking about how they wouldn't see another day like this probably for years and perhaps they ought to take advantage of it and do a little air reconnaissance. They agreed that Big Ditmo had very likely shifted his center of operations and that the best way to search it out was from the air. Arnie seconded this motion loudly and conditionally, the condition being that he be allowed to fly the airplane "a little more than the eight and a half goddamned seconds I got in last time." Kermit said he'd be happy to let Arnie fly longer than eight and a half seconds if he thought, for Christ's sake, he could arrange to point the airplane in some other direction than right at the side of the mountain, as he had done last time. And so on, the debate taking upwards of five minutes, with poor old McGeorge standing outside in the snow (having dismounted from the trailer), peering in through the isinglass, wondering probably if they had all taken leave of their senses or were somehow stuck, looking like the lone survivor of a shoot-out at the Sanhedrin.

The issue decided in favor of flying around a while, Kermit signaled McGeorge to mount up, Julie suggested that she and Aubrey and McGeorge could walk back to the Lodge from the old landing strip (about halfway between the new airstrip and the Lodge) if that would make things easier (Julie getting sunnier, if anything, as the sun climbed, and Aubrey having declared that he wished to do no more flying than was absolutely required of him, and McGeorge having been, automatically, as it were, disqualified from air reconnaissance because of his tendency to pull any available lever to see, as McGeorge put it, "what the good Lord Lazarene had in mind when He ordained this handle"), and Kunkel and Kermit came back in harmony and on key to say that that would make things a damned sight easier, and only Arnie, squatting on a first-aid kit in front of Aubrey and Julie, had anything untoward to say about the arrangement, turning to look long at his stepsister, then saying, "Okay, Julie-Bitch, but I'm going to instruct McJesus to consider that .410 the rod of Aaron, and you'll have two half-moons full of rock salt if you try to do any climbing around on the finking reverent, here. Right, babe?"

Julie smiled sweetly and leaned toward Arnie as if to confide a singularly precious intimacy, and, at a range of no more than eight or nine inches, spat in Arnie's face. The jeep was rocking for some time thereafter, with Kermit holding Arnie, and Aubrey holding Julie, and all four shouting about foulmouths, one moment's peace for Christ's sake, spittle, and who was descended from what bitches. The arrival at the old airstrip was speeded by a little reckless driving on Kunkel's part, and the party divided in twain rapidly, with nothing like affection marking their respective farewells.

And then they were out on the open road, Julie and Aubrey walking side by side, McGeorge shambling on in front of them with his .410 on one shoulder and Julie's .300 on the other (Julie having insisted, with rare girlish reserve, that Aubrey should be the one and only rifle of the detachment, and expressing, too, the most sublime and abandoned faith in Aubrey's ability to handle his weapon superlatively in any and all contingencies) so that Aubrey would be unencumbered and free to distribute projectiles in all directions if necessary, and McGeorge in a black mood because the others were going up in the air where they had no business going (and he had muttered to Aubrey for a time darkly about gravity, boils, and whirlwinds before he had noted that Aubrey's mood in no way matched

373

his own, and had gone out by himself fifty feet ahead to ride point, herd, and the winds of prophecy).

And Aubrey's mood was indeed in no way dark. It was, rather, buoyant and more than buoyant. With his mountain in sight, his all-protecting rifle in hand, his stout boots treading scorn into the mud of the road, his nostrils and eyes drinking in the air and the intoxicating, sun-stricken, warmth-startled effusiveness of this incredibly clear and pellucid northern day—so abruptly and arrantly springlike, so vagrantly full of southern promise—his mood was one of sudden and swollen joy, of acute, tingling sensuality. Yet he felt no slightest erotic inclination; he had thought, and was thinking, about it, and it seemed to him that he was blessed by and enjoying a marvelous innocence of imagination. Not a moral innocence, necessarily—he conceded that readily, because morality pertained to the will, and he acknowledged that if his will alone had had to be pitted against the agglutinantly sexual willpower of his stepsister and her severally ramified physical potencies, his will wouldn't serve to keep his lip zipped, to say nothing of his pants—but, exactly, an imaginative innocence. His imagination was free of all but the purest and most exalted images, and he fancied he was safe because of this; it seemed to him that the simple, snow-driven, sun-blasted cleanness of his imagination would do all on earth, on that strange and vernal day, as it was done in heaven.

He knew that he was as aware of every striding motion of Julie's body as if he had wiped the wondrously intimate joints to make her. Yet because his imagination called up nothing remotely obscene as a result, he assured himself that his awareness was one with the equinoctial surge. He was an extension of all nature; nature's impulses were his impulses, and all of them, by eternal decree, were ineluctably good. The sweet stirring to life, this very and rare Aleutian madness of sunshine, were his own and proper body and blood. And that column of smoke, lifting pure and white out of the black mouth of Shishaldin and standing straight and tall as a virgin in the unbelievable calm, that—ah, *that*—was his soul. He was a giant upon the earth, a lord of the world, a child of northern light grown great in the eyes of God and man. The Aghileen Pinnacles, twenty-five miles to the east northeast, colossal white spires raised nearly five thousand feet against the utter blue sky—those soaring Gothic pinnacles bristling like battlements of God's final and mightiest fortress—why, those pinnacles formed no more than an adequate cathedral for the intumescent and impatient reach of his faith. The Bering Sea and the North Pacific flowed neither as silent nor as deep nor as broad as did his hope. And his charity! Why, its fire had such intensity and compass that not all the volcanoes of the world, stacked one upon the other, could have approached its holy heat. Shishaldin, move aside. Here strides the new Torch of the Aleutians.

And his conversation with Julie went on swimmingly, and once he recited a little Shakespeare, and Julie showered breathless gold all over his remarkable memory. And once he fancied that all that spadiceous, puce-sponge tundra would, one day, in the words of Winfield Townley Scott, all come green again, and Julie regarded him with angelic awe as if he were the pure, reconstituted essence of chlorophyll. And once he got all bollixed up in a poetic amaze about how volcanoes had their guts in hell and their mouths in heaven, and he said, "And, you know, Julie, for all their destructive power, they bring fire, one of the essentials of life on earth. It's almost as if they were shooting forth life itself, like the—the . . ."

"The male organ," Julie said, with just that perfect touch of virginal withdrawal that assured all spectators that she was certainly not familiar with such things except through her biology courses.

They were walking now where the road ran along the edge of the cliff seventy or eighty feet above the water and were looking south out of the mouth of the bay and McGeorge turned to shout a commentary on the local topography from time to time, pointing out Deer Island and Fox Island five miles out to sea, and Lenard Harbor, and Mount Dutton fifteen miles to the east, its lower slopes rising abruptly like the walls of a fiord right up a thousand feet out of the bay's far shore, then went on backing and building for ten miles to the forty-eight-hundred-foot peak of the mountain. And suddenly Aubrey saw, at the top of one of these rugged cliffs, what looked to be a huge mountain house, and he was astounded and excited and starting to point it out to Julie, when McGeorge shouted, "Look, look! Mr. Kermit's castle! Clearest I ever see it!"

"Christ," Julie said softly. "Doesn't it look great? It looks better than it did in the movie, don't you think, Aubie?"

"What movie? I don't know, I mean, *what* movie?" Aubrey said, fairly dancing with curiosity.

"Baronov. You mean you never saw *Baronov?*"

"One of Kermit's movies!" McGeorge said, coming up to him, waving his arms and rolling his eyes happily. "Oh, sweet Lordy, yes! Great movie it was!"

"It was a bomb," Julie said. "The castle was the best part about it."

And, gradually, Aubrey got the facts. The mountain house was the main set—Baronov's Castle—built at Cold Bay by Kermit after inspecting the real castle at Sitka and deciding that it wouldn't do; Kermit's version being mostly a "front" with no real building behind it, but appearing to be a full-sized structure of two high stories, built of massive logs with a sort of blockhouse on top, square and windowed, and with what appeared to be a grand staircase spread across the whole middle third of the front. McGeorge, who had been with Kermit at the time, was telling about how it wasn't really made of logs at all but of some kind of curved and stained light metal, and how long it had taken to build, and how awful the weather had been, and how Kermit had been almost four months getting just forty-seven minutes of film out of the whole operation, what with having to pack in cameras and lights and generators and crew and actors overland around the head of the bay, and what with the studio howling about the budget, and with the script not finished and the writers drunk most of the time so that Kermit had had to write several of the scenes himself, and on and on, until Aubrey had begun to understand what it was that challenged Kermit in the producing and directing of motion pictures: it was the sheer adventure and power and responsibility of it all. Here at Cold Bay he had been captain of industry, general of armies, mentor of artists, conqueror of elements, architect of a grand concept, king of a mighty hill. And no matter what might be said about the foolish pretensions of movie makers, and about the frivolity and inaccuracy and even dishonesty of the final product (why in hell hadn't he shot the film at Sitka?), and about the profit motive and the delusions of grandeur suffered by every movie producer without exception, still it had taken a man of not inconsiderable courage and other parts to do what Kermit had done here—if only because it was just here that he had done it—and Aubrey felt proud of his father, and stepped out to the rim of the cliff with Julie, and studied his father's castle with some pride.

And now the sky was clear and wide and calm. Only far out to the south, beyond the islands and lying low on the blue-white North Pacific, was there a cloud, flat and squared and as deeply whited as a polar cliff. The sky awed and then defeated the eye. The ocean discouraged it, until it followed to where the water's blue came white and finite all around the edges of the bay. And he looked at Kermit's castle and wondered how it had stood and withstood so long as it had, it being most audaciously set down at the brink of a precipice, and remembered, or tried to remember, another building, another precipice, that had so impressed him. And he did remember, just as Julie was suggesting that perhaps they ought to go, and he told her about it, drawing it out of a back closet of his memory, out of those lonely and remote days at Fort Milligan during the war when, every now and again, Eulalia would swoop up Rexfordia and the children and take them over to have their minds broadened at one of those funny little upstairs halls along 57th Street in New York across from Carnegie Hall where somebody or other was always showing educational and travel films, and where, one rainy afternoon, they had seen a film, in color and with wretched, screechy music, about the construction of Timberline Lodge on Mount Hood, in Oregon; told her how it was certainly the finest, ruggedest building in the world, mounted grandly just below the summit, so magnificently, so incontrovertibly ensconced that Eulalia had averred that it couldn't possibly have been a WPA project, as the film's narrator had claimed, and had further averred that if it was a WPA project, it was clearly F. D. Roosevelt's greatest work; how it had seemed to him, quite simply, that the heart of a towering forest had been cut out and carted in state to that promontory and laid down there end to end and side by side with such success and reverence that one could say that, for once, God's trees had really suffered no diminution at having been felled; how it was the one building he knew of in all the world that, erected in a place of great natural beauty, stood worthy of the view it commanded; how the view from Timberline Lodge was to the south over a hundred and fifty miles of the white ramparts of the Cascade and Sierra Nevada Ranges, and to the southwest across several hundred miles and seven distinct ridges to the sea; and how, in the final shots of the film, standing down in front of the Lodge and looking up at it from the snow-banked road, seeing it broad and trunk-ribbed against the white of the majestic peak behind it, and the dark blue of the nightening sky beyond the peak, he had

377

thought of himself right there, standing in that long-since-faded twilight, when all the world to him, and perhaps to everybody, had seemed to be dreadfully old and lost and in its last days, and had thanked God that at least once before the disappearance of humanity from the earth, man and nature had come together to produce a graceful mutual expression, had builded at least one monument, in an ancient and splendid place, to the ideal that man, as lord of the world, might indeed use and rearrange nature without outraging it; and how, finally, he had substituted other music for that of the film in the last lingering shot of the vast Lodge—remembering the performance of the Ring cycle he had heard at the Metropolitan Opera House in 1943, with Arnie asleep on one side of him throughout all but the first twenty minutes of all four operas, and with Rexfordia rattling librettos on the other side of him, and with the gods and Siegfried and Erich Leinsdorf doing fifteen hours of battle all told —and had heard the soft start of the flügelhorns and had hoped to see, as Wagner gave tender, incredibly evocative notes to the woodwinds, Janssen himself as Wotan lead the gods across the whited Oregon highlands into Valhalla.

And Julie, who, he thought, looked unmistakably underwhelmed if not bored by all of this, was straining to say something kind, when McGeorge gave a shout and pointed his .410 due north, and there came, McGeorge informed them, Mr. Martin Newton Small of Belkofski and King Cove, captain of his own vessel and general, all-around Aleut extraordinary.

And Mr. Martin Newton Small did, indeed, come on like the last of the great Aleuts. For despite the fact that he appeared to be molting, if not quite shedding his skin—his outer garment slung over his shoulder with his rifle, his undergarments appearing to peel off and to cling most precariously and to take advantage of whatever breeze to get as far away from him as possible, so that a raggeder, more crusty, more unsanitary-looking gathering of smallclothes could scarcely have been imagined—he had a certain dignity of carriage and presence, and wore, with entire confidence and as if to give the lie to the rest of his costume, an only very slightly mildewed black bowler hat.

McGeorge went whooping out to greet Mr. Small, as he might a long-lost friend, and Mr. Small returned the greeting with enthusiasm and came down to meet Julie and Aubrey with his adumbrated, two-toothed smile firmly and unself-consciously in place. He remembered Julie from the year before and shook her hand eagerly, yet timidly, and his eyes were also eager and yet timid when he looked at her, as if he couldn't allow himself too much exposure to such unexpected pleasure. And he was happy-eyed, and rubber-booted, and old, and spoke English with facility, and shook Aubrey's hand with hard bony fingers, and Aubrey studied his face and found it smooth and almost unwrinkled and gray, like ironwood, or like the gnarled joint of a dead apple tree, polished by winter.

Mr. Small wanted to know where his old friend Duffy the hermit was, and McGeorge told him, and then he and McGeorge got into a charming little argument about certain recipes McGeorge had given Mr. Small some time ago. And Aubrey listened with the feeling that he was being put on by Mr. Gallagher and Mr. Sheen.

"Now, that caribou *tereyaki*," said Mr. Small. "I used the garlic, the onion, the sugar, the soy sauce, and a bit of nutmeg to make up for the ginger."

"Oh no, Mr. Small! Got to have that ginger!"

"Didn't have it, McGeorge, didn't have it. And in the caribou tamale pie, didn't have no three-oh-three can of creamed corn!"

"Well, you can substitute *there*."

"Didn't have no red peppers, either."

"Oh well, that's the trouble! Tell you what I'll do. I got some extra red peppers over to the Lodge. You come over with Mr. Duffy tomorrow, I'll loan you some."

"Used paprika."

"No, no. *Got* to have those red peppers!"

"And the Stroganoff—the caribou Stroganoff—I don't know. . . ." And Mr. Small shook his head as if to indicate that McGeorge had plucked that particular recipe out of *Captain Billy's Whiz-Bang*, or worse.

And McGeorge admitted that the recipe actually was for moose Stroganoff, but that he couldn't see why caribou couldn't be substituted without any trouble, and went on to assure Aubrey, almost indignantly—Aubrey having made a grinning and not quite deferential inquiry—that McGeorge had gotten all of those recipes by mail and kitchen-tested from the University of Alaska. He had, it was true, developed certain variations for each, and said that, in fact, if Mr. Small wanted to substitute bear or caribou meat in the recipe for Reindeer Spanish Rice (one-half pound of ground reindeer), why, he could practically guarantee the results.

Their culinary conversation had gotten around to fish when Julie whispered to Aubrey that perhaps they ought to make their own way back to the Lodge, McGeorge being engaged in a home economics refresher that would obviously take all semester. To the which Mc-George agreed when Aubrey had made Julie's decision known, and Mr. Small bowed formally and tipped his hat and shook Aubrey's hand, and McGeorge said that he would accompany Mr. Small down to the freshwater lake to where Pisser Duffy was fishing, and that he would certainly be back at the Lodge in time to prepare dinner.

And as he walked away west across the tundra with Julie, Aubrey watched Mr. Small and McGeorge talking their way along the road, two old men arguing about food; two old men on the way to their separate graves, talking about that which would, however nourishing, not long sustain their lives; two men, like Famine and Death, ambling down the land, twin figures of all that was mortal, and of all that was magnificent, in human hope and endurance. For it seemed to him just then that, whatever humanity was all about, it might never have a greater symbol of its defiance of the defeat of death than two old men, striding upon a barren landscape, talking about how their food might most temptingly be prepared.

And then he was alone with Julie on the wet tundra, and extremely conscious of it, conscious of it rather more physically than imaginatively—or rather more acutely in *both* respects—so that it suddenly occurred to him that there were two great mysteries for human rationality, of its unaided self, to encounter and resolve, or not resolve depending upon the intellect engaged: that man *may* enter a woman, and that man *must* enter the earth. Human reason alone had no two greater involvements; and human reason and imagination, however aided by divine intervention or grace, had no two greater confrontations. And the more he thought of this, the more conscious he became of Julie, so delightfully forking along beside him, and he told himself to take care, to recognize that she was the fork and he the knife, that she was the fee and he the male, that she was the musk and he the ox.

# · THIRTY ·

So THAT when they got to the Lodge, he was on his guard and opened the door for her and smiled and said that he thought he would remain outside for a time and observe the air reconnaissance of the mountain, and keep an eye out for marauding beasts. And she was a veritable paragon of womanly submission and deference to male superiority, and smiled at him so admiringly and yet so wistfully and yet so enticingly as she announced her headache and her intention of taking a short nap, that Aubrey could just marginally resist reaching out to pat her upon her lambent, enparkaed head. But he did resist, even when she caressed his cheek briefly, her eyes toying with the finest, most aristocratic of tears, as if she were a nobler Scarlett O'Hara, with one foot on the last train from Atlanta, bidding an ungabled and charismatic Rhett Butler farewell and telling him, telesthetically, to preserve the great city at all costs, even at the cost of their unlikely future together. And then she was gone, wind and all, and Aubrey turned to face his secondary enemies.

He paced for a time up and down the duckboards, carefully inspecting the muck on either side for invaders, and scanning the sky and the mountain for his own pleasure, not really expecting to be called upon to lay down life or barrage, his rifle slung debonairly, as he thought, over his shoulder, thumb in sling, his eyes upon the furze-fat hills mostly in an epistemological attempt to convince himself that he was really, really in Alaska, and only very occasionally feeling that delicious apprehension that Big Ditmo might appear at any moment and charge. And yet, for all his euphoria and dismissal of danger, and ebullient good humor, and almost mystical identification of himself with the entire nature of things, a certain loneliness began to move upon him; a tenebrific invasion of his bright-souled complacence; an uneasy awareness that perhaps he was being watched, that there were enemies about to enshroud him, nameless, unknowable, nontellurian, even invisible, and that the very beauty and salubriousness of the day were a snare, that there were monstrous, nontectonic presences just beyond the duckboards about to swoop down upon him, suck him up into unspeakable vortices, carry him off to outer darkness and the void.

And much as he fought this apprehension, telling himself that it was ridiculous, that it was a perfectly natural agoraphobic reaction for him to have, having been so long enclosed behind seminary walls, he couldn't beat it off, and after another look at his mountain (which also seemed to threaten now) and a lecture to himself about bravery when alone and the nobility and wild grandeur of the human condition even if there were only one human around to exhibit those qualities, he went into the Lodge, telling himself that he would have just a touch of Old Fitzgerald to warm his cockles and then, manfully and without fail, return to his appointed post. Through all of this, his afflatus suffered no appreciable diminution: he'd decided upon a drink and that was that, and the lords of this world did not have to excuse their decisions with petty ratiocinations.

Before he was done, he had had three touches of Old Fitzgerald over snow, about two and a half fingers each in a squat tumbler. In the middle of the third one, seated as he was out on the end of the duckboards, with the fat glass in one hand, his rifle held upright in the other, the bottle between his legs, and his eyes closed, he determined that, however bullish he was feeling about bears, what he really needed was a nap. After all, it was a sturdy front door, and had all kinds of lox and bagels, and would certainly withstand Big Ditmo until, at least, he was able to mount a proper ballistic defense.

So he took the glass to his lips, drained it while taking a last, sweeping, fat-glassedly exaggerated survey of the countryside through the bottom of the tumbler, rose, tossed the glass toward the east, plucked up the bottle, palmed the rifle nicely just forward of the trigger guard, and bounded, staggers and elbows, down the duckboards, into and through the front door. He worked the locks without setting the bottle or gun down, then made his way with circumspection and on tiptoe into his room.

And he had removed all of his outer clothing, all but socks, pants, and shirt, when he saw that his bed was occupied; that Julie, dressed in a short, black, transparent nightgown, in no way sufficient to modesty, was stretched out on her back, sound asleep, in the middle of his patchwork quilt.

And then the issue was clear and harshly lighted, and there was no least shadow upon it; and as he snapped around to face the door, he told himself that the real test had arrived, that it was time to let go of one horn or the other, that his moment in the great decision area had come upon him; and he went on multiplying such phrases without thought, not being either sober or over his initial shock, yet perfectly aware somewhere in the top of his heated brain that aphorisms weren't going to serve him, that there was room for no more damned comic opera, that the choice was *not* between God and mammaries—that he would want to become a priest no matter what he did in the next hour—but that it was between himself man and himself boy, and that his future as giant or dwarf was out there waiting in the matrix of the next few minutes, embryonic, livid as an exposed nerve, primate and adaptable matter, waiting for him to arrive and to impose upon it whatever substantial form he might then require.

And he stood there, staring at the door, tracing the grain of the wood with his eyes, trying not to see Julie there but seeing her there, her tanned skin almost the color of the wood, her nightgown hiked above her stomach, the light from the small curtained window full enough and fair, her breasts veiled by the nightgown but in no way concealed by it, her hair spread out above and around her head, her lips pouted almost belligerently; seeing her there until he closed his eyes, and seeing her there, too; seeing her until he began to sweat, until he began to think that he might faint and that he might not even have the strength to open the door.

He came back strong once, his shoulders squared, his fists clenched, his eyes darting so as to accept no images whatsoever, and worked himself into a state of nonstop admonition.

Do not turn around, do not take another look, do not try to think of any excuses why you should. If the others come and find her there, let them. Don't pretend that you're not sure who it is. It is Julie, and she is alive, well, and absolutely all there. And to look at her again would be a mortal sin. You have already looked at her, too long, like the foul, stinking, hot-eyed hypocrite that you are, but you were surprised perhaps, and puzzled, and you might even conceivably have been concerned, and, hence, you might have gotten away with it so far without committing a foursquare, first-class mortal sin. But if you look at her once more there can be no equivocation, and you will have offended God grievously. And if offending God isn't enough to prevent you, just remember that there are no priests out here, no chance to confess, everybody will be firing shots, bears will be jumping out on all sides, and even if you survive all that, you will have to fly back to Anchorage with Kermit Ben Strycker at the controls, and if he doesn't kill you, or a volcano doesn't shoot the airplane down, there will probably be an earthquake just as you land and you'll die in the crash and go straight to hell after all.

And this persuaded him so far as to reach his hand to the doorknob, but there he hesitated, knowing that the issue might have been perfectly clear but that the motion hadn't been carried, feeling an incredibly powerful inclination to turn around and take just one more look at her, despite everything mortal and immortal he could summon to prevent himself; and he was hanging there, refusing to focus his mind on the fact that he had already made his decision to look at her—just as he had refused, a moment earlier, to focus his eyes upon any particular part of her anatomy—when Julie spoke to him, spoke softly and huskily and fresh from sleep, spoke in a voice that traveled from his atlas to his sacrum to his coccyx with the speed of evil and left only liquid desire in its wake.

"Oh, Aubrey, where have you been, darling? I've been so *sick*."

He clung to the doorknob, and every grained wave of the wood seemed to describe her, to portray her most intimately, to represent her anfractuously and pulsingly, as if she were an odalisque heating her naked body over an open flame, and as if she would possess and ingest him, even *in distans*, as soon as she should determine that their ardor was mutually extreme. And he spoke to her out of a fervently dry mouth. "I—I just walked in from outside and found you here. I—why—what are you doing in my room?"

"Oh, Aubie, darling. I'm so sick. I thought you'd be in here, and I knocked, and then I thought you might be asleep so I opened the door and looked in, and your bed looked so close and soft that I just lay down for a minute. I guess I fell asleep."

"You feel sick?"

"Oh, I feel just awful."

"Where?"

"Well, I think you'd call it a fever."

"Can you make it back to your own room?"

"If you help me, I think I could. But I feel fine, here."

"Well, Julie, you know, the others will be back, and they might, you know, draw the conclusion that . . ."

"I understand."

"Well, look, I'll go into your room and get you a robe or something . . ."

"Oh, but Aubie, darling, I'm so hot. I don't want a robe."

"I mean, just until you get into your room, you know?"

"Oh, I see." There was a three-second silence. "Well, suppose I wrap your quilt around me. Would that be all right? I mean, it would save you a trip and all."

"Oh, I don't mind the trip . . ."

"Please. I'll just wrap it around me and I'll look just like a Navajo squaw." The sound of the quilt being snatched, briskly, from the bed did not reassure his higher processes. She didn't sound sick, and she didn't snatch quilts from beds as if she were sick. But his lower processes were ascendant and in sympathy. If Julie said she was sick, the least he could do was to help her in any way consistent with modesty. The higher processes were not permitted a rebuttal. "I didn't realize that this nightgown was so—so revealing. I just felt so ill, you know?" There was a final rustling of quilts and things. "All right, Aubie. I think you can turn around now."

"You've—ah—you have the quilt around you?"

"Yes, darling."

He let go of the doorknob and turned slowly. Julie was standing near the bed, facing him, wrapped head to toe in the patchwork quilt. She had her eyes cast down and she did, as a matter of fact, look somewhat debilitated. He started toward her, suppressing as best he could an impudent wish that she had tricked him and not donned the quilt at all, and was within five feet of her when she threw the quilt wide open and let it drop to the floor, and stood there, minus even the nightgown, smiling at him, somehow purring, swaying and swelling, reaching her hands behind her head and fluffing her hair out and forward until it touched and moved upon the prodigal motion of her breasts. And in the instant before he closed his eyes, he saw that there was no tiniest reticence or trace of shame in her bold green gaze.

And he thought, Lord, it is too much. I have fought the good fight, I have fired and reloaded and stood to my guns. But, Lord, your servant wilteth. His grape is exhausted, his barrels are melting, and he is fresh out of musket balls. Look you, Lord, to your infinite mercy, for your servant is down by the bow.

And within three minutes, down by the bow described his position exactly.

And once he heard an airplane come down and down and then roar in quickly from the direction of the bay, holding straight at the Lodge, coming on and on until he tensed and almost stopped, thinking to run, then thinking that if he was going to die it was fitting he should die right in the act, and lifting his face from Julie's hair and turning his head slightly to look at her, he saw that she was in pain, or appeared to be, and that her pain was gathering and gathering as the airplane came on and did not seem to break and subside until, with a terrifying lifting screech, the airplane cleared the rooftop and went howling on up the valley toward the mountain. . . .

And once Julie was above him, moving gently, leaning slightly forward, her hands gripped to his waist, her head thrown back so that her hair hung free until it touched and moved in the small of her back, her eyes closed and her lips pouted and smiling and pursing out a small secret song, her breasts standing pendantly out and down to him so fully and gracefully formed that he had not thought flesh could assume such symmetry, her abdomen roseate and delicately bowed to him, her hips and thighs so voluptuously grown yet so lightly and expertly restive; and, for the first time, he was able to strip his eyes wide and look at her, inspect her in that magic light from the high tender curve of her throat to where he was so exquisitely caught, and it seemed to him that this inspection of her was somehow the most brash and flagrantly irretrievable thing he had done, that it was the blatant and final abandonment, for now she would be with him as long as he lived, for as long as there was any passion or poetry within him, for as long as there was blood in him to make memory poignant, and he knew that however vehement and intense the pleasure she had given him, or was now giving him, the mind would retain the image long after the flesh had forgotten the ecstasy; he knew that it was this image of her, arched and exultant upon him, that would haunt his priesthood, that would visit his most solemn hours, that would drive him madding from ten thousand meditations. And yet he couldn't look away, and held his eyes upon the jeweled stroke of her pure and savage body, and began to know in those moments of watching what an infinitely ramified sacrifice celibacy would thenceforth be for him.

And once he reached his hands to her breasts, and felt their tips rise and swell against his palms, and saw her head toss perfervidly and hungrily, and saw her stiffen and lift to reach for and thrust against the press of his hands; and it seemed to him then that this—not the image—was the unforgettable and final abandonment.

And once, when they were lying side by side, he placed his hand flat on her stomach and moved it slowly down over her navel, down and down to where all that was physical in her and all that was spiritual were joined and found expression, and, though she appeared to be sleeping, at his touch she came awake, there first, and then in her eyes, and she smiled and moved against him and spoke his name, and the dark, plumping, luxuriantly lipped response of her mouth and body put the issue beyond issue: this was the final and ultimate abandonment.

And once she was kissing him on the eyes, closing them with her lips, and he fell asleep, listening to the sound of the generator engine and thinking of tugboats.

And he dreamed of the Hudson River, and of walking down a dark forest corridor through a stand of hundred-foot pines toward brilliant sunshine and the sounding beach, where someone was calling his name. And he knew that he would wake up long before he did wake up, and he tried to hold on, feeling there in his dream all of the sweet and summery innocence he had ever known and would never know again; but he couldn't hold himself within it, and it faded, and he came out of sleep slowly into a searching, raw regret, knowing that that holy time was forever gone, and knowing and remembering, with a vividness that even recalled the fragrance of the pines, how young and pure and great of heart he had been on that darkling path.

# · THIRTY-ONE ·

AND THERE, by the bed, calling his name, was Arnie. Aubrey sat up quickly, saw that Julie was gone, and said, "What?"

"What? What the hell do you mean, what? You know goddamned well *what!*"

"Arnie, what do you want?"

"I see one thing I want." And Arnie reached suddenly across him and snatched Julie's black nightgown from a tangle of sheeting. "Well, what have we here?" He spoke softly and stepped back from the bed with a false, demure smile, and fitted the nightgown to his shoulders. "Oh yes, a perfect fit," he said, making an anemonetic circle of his lips, and producing little sucking noises as he looked from the nightgown to Aubrey and back again. And his eyes were baleful and drawn in and mad-bright.

Aubrey closed his eyes and turned his face toward the window. "Arnie, will you stop making that damned disgusting noise!"

"What's the matter, young reverent? Does it remind you of something?"

"Arnie, I don't feel well. Could you just—leave me alone?"

"You don't feel well? A little run down, Aubie?" He was continuing to make the sucking noise between sentences, and was peering through the nightgown at Aubrey. "Oh, sheer, *sheer.* Oh, yes indeed. She must be quite a sight in this."

Aubrey lay back down and pulled the sheet over him. "I don't know what you're talking about."

"You see, you see? How sins multiply once you leave the state of grace? First you're fornicating, then you're lying."

"Arnie, for God's sake, can't you just leave me alone?"

"You don't deny it, do you, Aubie?"

"Deny what?"

"That you screwed her!" He shook the nightgown at Aubrey. "That you screwed Julie-Bitch, our stepsister! That she got to you, and gave you your finking jollies all afternoon! You screwed her, and don't try to deny it!" His voice shrilled high and his eyes were wild and sliding behind a film of tears, but he was trying to hold himself, and even tried to smile—a grotesque flexing of teeth. "Oh, I knew she'd get to you, Aubie babe. Oh, I just knew it. And I knew you wanted her to, and that you'd let her because that would be something else you'd done that I couldn't do. Isn't that right, Aubie? You had yourself a nice rutting little victory over old Arnie today, didn't you? And so did she. Oh yes. So did she. Did you laugh about that, Aubie? Did you laugh about old Arnie together while you were putting the blocks to her?"

"Arnie, get out of here!"

"Do you deny it, goddamn you?"

"Yes, I deny it!"

"Then where'd *this* come from? Or do you always wear black shortie nightgowns to bed?"

"I deny it. That's that. Now get out." Aubrey closed his eyes.

"Oh, Aubie, old young reverent, please don't try to lie to your old artificer. To me! I, who hammered you into gold out of bourgeois shit!" Aubrey looked up at him coldly. Arnie touched the rolled nightgown to his forehead and attempted a smile. "I'm sorry. I shouldn't have said that. But, Aubie, we—we have always told each other the truth. Please don't lie to me. Because I *know* she screwed you this afternoon. *Didn't* she?"

Aubrey looked away from him, looked the mounted caribou straight in its glassy eyes. He found he could lie to the caribou with ease, despite its resemblance to Father Finnegan. "No, Arnie. Not that it would be any of your business if she did. But no, she didn't. And I didn't."

"I just love your righteous indignation, Aubie. I just love your holy, apostolic protest. For Christ's own sweet gibbeted sake, don't

389

you know—don't you remember—that I *always* know when you're lying to me?"

"For the last time, I'm not lying!"

Then Kermit was standing in the door. "What the hell's all the shouting about?" he said gruffly.

Arnie stuffed the nightgown into the front of his shirt. "Ah—Aubie, here, says he's sick."

"That right, Aubie?"

"I—I feel a little better now."

"You don't look good," Kermit said. "Julie doesn't feel so hot either. I hope you two aren't coming down with something."

"Oh, I think Aubie will be all right," Arnie said. "He just got his bowels a little screwed up today, didn't you, Aubie babe?"

"Well, the water sometimes does it," Kermit said.

"Yeah, and the heat, too," Arnie said, and he turned quickly and left the room.

"I wondered why you didn't come out when we buzzed you. Damned Arnie almost ran us into the mountain again. Arnie tell you about the bears?"

"No."

"Saw four of them. I think one of them was Big Ditmo. He rose up on his hind legs and clawed at us. I had the glasses on him but I couldn't be sure. He was big enough, and mean enough, and if we only had skis on that goddamned airplane we'd have set down right up there on the snowfield and gone after him. Hell of a lot of glare up there today. Even Kunkel wasn't seeing too well." He walked to the bureau and filled his glass from the bottle Aubrey had brought in with him. "Glad to see you've got your own bottle these days." He grinned at Aubrey. "Have one?"

"No, thanks. I think I'll skip dinner, too."

"Is it that bad?"

"Oh no. I just don't feel hungry."

"Well, just don't crap out on me tomorrow. If that was Big D, he'll be right down on the Ridge tomorrow, and we'll need all six of us to keep him there. We drove the four of them damned near to the bottom. Well, we didn't really drive them—they were headed down anyway—but we speeded their progress a little. Christ, I don't know. I wanted to get right out there this afternoon but Arnie, by God, he just *had* to get back here to talk to you about something. And I said okay, we'd drop Arnie off, but then Kunkel set up the bagpipes. He said those four bears would still be there tomorrow—although I don't know what's to prevent them from climbing right back up there tonight, or right now—and he said it hadn't looked like Big Ditmo to him. But I don't know about Kunkel any more."

"You don't?"

"I mean, one goddamned minute he's saying let's shoot any bear that'd make a good trophy, to hell with Big Ditmo, and the next he's saying that big one today wasn't Big Ditmo, so let's not bother going out. It's as if he's just losing interest. We hadn't been out a half hour in the Cessna before he was saying, Oh well, this is the third year, nobody's seen Big Ditmo but McGeorge, and maybe he laid down somewhere and died, or fell off a cliff, or I don't know what the hell. Jesus Christ, Aubie, if I wanted to shoot just *any* goddamned bear, I'd go to Kodiak."

And Kermit talked on and on, and filled his glass again and insisted upon putting the bottle near the bed where Aubrey could reach it, and tried to say something about how happy he was to have his two sons with him hunting and to have them getting along so well, and tried to say something else about how much Arnie was being steadied by Aubrey's presence, and concluded by trying to say something very hesitantly about how he *did* think Arnie was a little bit jealous of Aubrey's friendship with Julie and maybe if Aubrey could arrange to be a little less friendly with Julie, just during the hunt, there might be less trouble from Arnie, and he said none of this well or comfortably, and got embarrassed and stood through a long silence pulling at his beard, then turned suddenly, picked up Aubrey's rifle, shook it at him, said he would give it a good cleaning for him, and went out. Then he put his head back in again and said he would send McGeorge in later to see if he needed anything.

But if McGeorge came, Aubrey didn't see him. He saw only the devils of memory, dragging a naked Julie, writhing lasciviously, back and forth across the backs of his closed eyes until he escaped into sleep, into a dreamless oblivion.

He was awakened hours later by the sound of knocking. Not at his door. Very soft. Four taps and a long pause. Then he could hear a voice whispering tensely, but couldn't make out the words. The next time, the whisper was louder.

"Julie? It's me, Aubrey. I've brought your nightgown."

Then, Julie's voice: "Who is it?"

"It's Aubrey."

"I can't hear you."

"It's Aubrey. The door is locked. I've brought your nightgown."

"It is like hell Aubrey!" Julie shouted. "Get away from my door, you goddamned mad creep!"

"You bitch! You goddamned bitch! I know about you and Aubie, and I'll tell Kermit!" Arnie was still whispering, but the sound was harsh, rasping.

Then Julie spoke much more softly. "Oh, poor Arnie. Does poor Arnie want to get laid?"

A hesitation, an inarticulate choking, then a clear, abject "Yes."

"Well, swim to King Cove, you goddamned fink!"

And the sound of Julie's laughter, dark and cruel, and the sound of Arnie cursing her, and the sound of a door opening and Kermit saying, "What the hell's going on out here?"

"Oh, for Christ's sake," Arnie said hollowly. Then, achieving full volume, "Can't you see I'm on the transatlantic wire?"

"You all right, Arnie?"

"Sure I'm all right! In view of the fact that my father is a mono-maniac, my brother a hypocrite, my stepsister a goddamned whore, and I a goddamned finking *madman*, why, you'd have to say God has been very good to me!"

"Ah, Arnie, you shouldn't say things like that."

"Why not, goddamn it? They're true! Truth is a madman's privi-lege! His *only* finking privilege! That bitch in there screwed my brother Aubie this afternoon! Here, you see? Here's her nightgown! I found it in Aubie's bed!"

"I know, Arnie. I know all about it. Now come to bed."

"You *don't* know all about it, you goddamned old bastard! And don't patronize me like a goddamned O.T.!"

And the sound of this for a time, and finally the sound of Kermit leading Arnie off to his bed, agreeing with all he had to say, murmur-ing to him about Julie's offenses, and Aubie's hypocrisy, and all the evils in the world, until, at last, Kermit's door closed and all was silence.

Alone then. And reaching for the bottle, and finding it and drink-ing from it again and again until he had drunk it all. Then he lay taut and whiskied and scorched at the eyes, and saw his eyes reflected

392

in those of the caribou, the small light from the window lighting them each by each and making them, flickering, brilliant. The only lights in an otherwise opaque darkness. And the silence. Not even the sound of the generator. And he thought he heard the thump of the surf but wasn't sure, drowned out as it was by the silence. But from time to time he strained to listen, for it was gently measuring out his life, ebbing and running down toward the moment of his death, and he was not ready to die.

And what did it mean to live? To live meant to balance fearfully between life and death, love and hate, knowledge and ignorance, faith and doubt, truth and falsehood, and a hundred other mutually nonexclusive coexistents. To be alive meant to be in a constant state of awareness that nothing was ever quite enough, that there was always more potency than act, that there was always more need than generosity, that there was always more guilt than forgiveness. And so on, to the end of irreconcilable opposites, to the end of God-damned opposites, God could not approve them, their inextricable mixture; therefore, He must damn them. And if He damns them He must damn life. God is the truth and the life, but He is not *life*.

And here I lie, he thought, in the midst of life, in the slough-belly of my guilt. Today I have lived, ecstatically, and yet I wish I had died instead. Now, isn't that a sweet commentary on being alive?

He essayed a hollow laugh but produced only the hollow, and lost his defiance in it, and rolled to one side and drew his knees to his chest and gasped; keened under an overwhelming spasm of regret and contrition and abject shame, and asked God to forgive him this second time too, asked Christ not to turn His back upon him, asked all of heaven to pray for him and yet to look away until he should have done penance.

And said, "Oh my God, I am heartily sorry for having offended Thee . . . ," and asked himself how he could have done it, yet did not ask himself, afraid of his answer, knowing that he had intended to do it—to go back to Julie and that secret, awful, incomprehensibly sweet pleasure, that damned and delightful crucible—even at the instant he had promised God to amend his life; had intended to go back in full consciousness and in the clear light of mind and sense, aware that his guilt would be the more but aware also that his pleasure would be the more; aware that the dim memory he had harbored of her body, of the touch and fragrance and yielding deeps of her, of

393

the luxurious slide and grip of her thighs—this memory would be confirmed, must be confirmed, whatever the consequences. And it was. Dear God, yes, it was. And what did he know now? That he would not go back to her again? He swore that he wouldn't and rammed his forehead against his knees as he protested it, but heard the mockery anyway, like laughter, far down the valleys of his mind, telling him he was a bigger God-damned hypocrite than ever; telling him that he intended to go back.

He went to sleep saying that he would not go back; chanting it, driving images of Julie before him as he marched into sleep, saying that he would not go back to her, or to any woman, or to any sin whatever. He would go back only to that time of innocence, to where it had begun, to where his purity had returned to await him. He would go back, all the weary way back, to innocence. To the greenness. To all the tall green trees. To all the good green grass. The weary way back to that holy green time. . . .

And came awake some time later staring into the darkness around him, out of no dream, but out of a horrible, humming, chambered sounding of Julie screaming that she was damned and that he had damned her; heard her screams, even awake, like echoes walking down the darkness away from him, heard them fading into piteous whimpers out to the borders of time, down to the anterooms of hell. And he almost called to her, and did say, aloud, "No, no. I won't—you won't. I'll do penance! I'll dedicate my life to expiation . . . !"

Then groaned and lay back down and pretended he could not hear the nearly inaudible throb of her screams as the flames took her; and seized a handful of his hair and pulled at it until he thought his scalp might peel; and said that he was a madman and a lecher and a fraud and had no business aspiring to the priesthood. No business and no right and no vocation. And closed his eyes and saw Julie in the flames, in a raging vortex which filled his whole inner vision, filling all of him until he felt the nausea rising in his throat, and thought, Dear God, I have lost my mind as well as my soul. Dear God, help me! And saw Arnie in the flames accusing him of committing incest with Julie, of debauching his own sister, of seeking not only his own pleasure but also seeking to humiliate Arnie, to take petty revenge, to impugn Arnie's manhood.

And saw Kermit and Julie in intimate embrace, and Arnie and

394

Aline in intimate embrace, and Rexfordia standing to one side weeping as she watched the four lovers. And Aubrey screamed to his mother to watch him as, just behind her, he was being crucified. But Rexfordia could not or would not hear.

And leaped from the bed to his knees and started a dozen prayers, but felt his sin alive and moving within him and beginning to possess him again—lascivious, dancing images in brilliant color of Julie naked above him and introducing him into her body moved in the darkness of his closed eyes or in the chill black of the room—and finally was saying aloud the exorcism from the rite of the baptism of an infant, and repeated it again and again until the images were gone, until he was beginning again to sleep.

"I exorcize you, every unclean spirit, in the name of God the Father almighty, and in the name of Jesus Christ, His Son, our Lord and judge, and in the power of the Holy Spirit. Depart from this creature of God, Aubrey, whom our Lord has called to his holy temple, so that he may become the temple of the living God and the Holy Spirit may live in him. Through the same Jesus Christ our Lord, who is to come to judge the living and the dead and the world by fire, Amen. Ephphatha, 'Be opened,' so that you may perceive the fragrance of God's sweetness. But you, O Devil, depart; for the judgment of God has come."

And returned to his bed and began to be asleep, still praying; yet saw oblivion coming to embrace him, hulking and vast, and clothed in ten thousand centuries of darkness. . . .

# THE SECOND PART

## · THIRTY-TWO ·

Morning again, and he had been lying awake for hours watching the shadows leave the walls, watching them grow toward the light and disappear in it, and he was remembering a time when one of those who had quit St. Titus' Hall after two years had come back a year later to visit, and had brought his pretty young new wife with him and introduced her to some of the boys, including Aubrey; remembering how he had stood at an upstairs window and watched them walk away hand in hand in the early spring evening, laughing and kissing lightly as they went, and how he had felt something like disgust, a monastic revulsion, to see them, to see him who had been among the elect touching a woman, kissing her, and worse, and the word "unclean" had come to him and stayed with him long after he had watched them out of sight. And he had turned away wondering how the defector could have done it after only a year away. And now he knew. After only two weeks away, he knew.

Lying there, then, when the door was eased open and Arnie, in his hunting clothes, flute in hand, came in, sat down on a three-legged stool facing Aubrey, and began to play the Kyrie from the Mass for the Dead; and played it well, with total absorption, never lifting his eyes, negotiating even the difficult final phrases with precision and grace.

So that when he was done, Aubrey nodded to him and smiled. "I didn't know you played so well, Arnie."

Arnie looked at him sorrowfully, his eyes slouch-lidded and pained. "I tried to get into her room last night. I tried to tell her I was you."

"I know. I heard it all."

"I figured that if she screwed you, she ought to screw me. Or, if she didn't, I'd kill her, the bitch."

"Arnie, she didn't have anything to do with me. And don't talk about killing, for God's sake."

"Why do you say that, Aubie? Why do you say that she didn't screw you? Goddamn it! I was your brother before she was our step-sister. We came out of the same womb at the same time. We lived in the same womb nine months together. I've known you since you were a goddamned egg. Why do you lie to me to protect her?"

And Aubrey looked at him in surprise and something of shock, because Arnie looked and spoke tired, like a man condemned, his voice coming out of a weariness and defeat and utter lack of hope that Aubrey had never imagined could mark Arnie's least impulse. "Arnie, I'm not lying to you."

"You are, Aubie. You are." He pointed a finger, then curled it back and rolled it around his flute. "Oh, *I* know, Aubie babe, I *know*, just as I've always known, even when we were hundreds of miles apart, just when you were sad, just when you were happy, just when you were victorious, just when you were experiencing any kind of very high or low emotion. I *knew!* And I knew yesterday, and I know now that you are no longer a virgin *intactus*, and I wish—oh Christ, Aubie, I *wish*—you wouldn't try to tell me any different!"

"Arnie, for Pete's sake, it's none of your business if I am a virgin, or if I am not a virgin. What has it got to do with you?"

"Oh! Oh. Oh. I see," he said, rubbing one hand across his forehead and into his hair, nodding, letting the tears form and flow from the corners of his eyes. "What have I to do with thee? Is that it, Aubie? Have we come that far, you and I?"

"If we have, you've driven us there, Arnie."

"I've driven us there! I didn't screw her! You did!"

"That's more than you know, Arnie."

"I *know* it! I know it as surely as I know I'm sitting here with you lying to me!"

"Look, Arnie, if I were to marry Julie within the next fifteen min-

400

utes, I don't see what it would have to do with our fraternal affection. I assume that that's what you're talking about."

"You don't see? You really don't see what that would have to do with us, you and me?" He looked at Aubrey intently, and his hurt and surprise seemed quite genuine. Then he shook his head and rolled his eyes and took in breath between tight, thinly stretched lips. "Don't you know yet, Aubie, what my hopes are for you? Don't you know—wait, wait!" He interrupted himself and held up one hand dramatically and took a deep breath. "No. Wait. We'll never make it this way. Look. Let's start over again. Okay? Let's forget all about that bitch . . . !" Aubrey started to protest, but Arnie waved him silent, insistently, with the flats of both hands. "I'm sorry, I'm sorry! I'm really not sorry, but it slipped out! Now!" He pursed his lips and nodded several times. "Now. Okay. Yes." He fixed his eyes on Aubrey without the slightest effort to shield himself, committing those eyes unreservedly, openly, to Aubrey's inspection. "Take a good look, Aubie. You may not believe it, but I'm with you this morning. I'm with *it*. I mean, I'm really *with* your goddamned sick reality. I'm in tune. My left nut knows what my right nut is doing, you see? My bollix are salient within my personality! You understand, Aubie? It's a horrible, horrible state of mind, sanity, but this morning *I am sane!*" He stared at Aubrey, wild-eyed, but utterly clear-eyed, and went on staring until Aubrey nodded, then laughed bitterly and smiled and shook his head. "You probably like me better when I'm nuts. But I have to take it as it comes. And as it goes."

And his tone, as he finished, was so purely and honestly straight out of misery that Aubrey quickly said, "I'm sorry, Arnie, but I've never told you a lie that I didn't feel I absolutely had to tell you."

"So you admit you're lying about . . ."

"Arnie, goddamn it, that's not rules!"

"I know, I know, Aubie. Okay, okay. The Rules. The Fort Lee Rules to the death, babe, yes, indeed. I subscribe. You wouldn't believe how I subscribe, how I *have* subscribed, how I've gone over our first eighteen years minute by minute, hour by hour, loving them, Aubie. Loving them." He looked at his feet. "And loving you, Aubie. Loving you for your generosity. Loving you for when you'd come over to my bed at night, after I'd been a son of a bitch to you, and say, I'm sorry, Arnie, and touch my shoulder and find my hand and take it and squeeze it in both of yours, and the tears running down your face, until I had to forgive you, Aubie, I *had* to forgive you, and pull you to me and hug you because I knew if I didn't you'd lie awake all night looking at me, praying for me, praying for yourself, asking God not to take either one of us until the sweet Jesus had seen us friends again and laughing together again—I *had* to forgive you, Aubie, I had to forgive you time and time again and all of my life since I can remember. I had to forgive you for being such a good and sweet brother while I was being such a miserable son of a bitch to you hour after hour and day after day. Oh yes. I had to forgive you, Aubie, because if I hadn't, how in the name of Christ could I ever have forgiven myself?"

"Arnie, please, don't tell me I was always in the right. I know better than that. Don't tell me what you suffered because you had a brother who had none of your guts, none of your free will, none of your spirit . . ."

"Aubie, don't tell me that! What I had was nothing so sane! And if you think now that I did, you're wrong. Flat ass wrong! What I had, as I've told you, was an awareness from, by God, the age of reason, that I wasn't quite rational, that I wanted to do things that, when I'd tell you about them, would make your eyes grow round and, very sensibly, you'd ask me why, and I'd blow up and say what the hell do you mean, why, for Christ's sake? I'm Arnie Strycker, ain't I? What the hell do *I* need of why? You remember that, Aubie? Sure you do. I can see it in your face. Sure you remember all those goddamned things I dragged you into by accusing you of having no guts, or no brains, or no imagination. Sure you remember. How we fired on the Fort Lee police car with the twenty-two, and how we started up the town road-grader and ran it into the side of the town garage, and how we damned near killed Roger when we wired his bathtub. You knew, you knew. But you went along with me because you loved me, Aubie. And did I love you? No, no. No, Aubie, I hated your guts, because I was always putting myself in the position of your having to forgive me. Everybody knows what a hellish goddamned thing it is to have to accept forgiveness, especially when the ostensible forgiver is the one receiving it! And that's how it always was with us. And that's how it is now, Aubie. And that's why, although I tell you with all my heart that I love you with all my heart, I *still* hate your guts. Do you see? I know it isn't any of my business what you did with Julie. How the hell is it any of my business, except that I'd give both arms to screw her myself. That's the only reason it's any of my business, and it's a bad reason. And I know that you're right, by common decency and the Rules, not to admit that you screwed her. But I hate your guts for being right, and for having been screwed, at the same time! Do you see, Aubie? Isn't that how it always was with us? You were always right, and yet you were always screwed!"

And Arnie dropped the flute to the floor and put his face in both of his hands and groaned, and there wasn't a thing Aubrey could say, short of attempting a rebuttal that he knew would begin and end nowhere. But he did say, "Arnie?" And he said it again and again, as Arnie went on sorrowing. And then he said something else, something that brought Arnie out of his hands. "Arnie, look. This time I'm not right, and we both know it. This time I'm asking your forgiveness, and we both know that I should, and we both know why."

Arnie looked up at him, his eyes wet-wide and piercing. "Sure, Aubie. Sure. We both know that to be true, and we both know why. Don't we? I have to forgive you—now, now listen close and keep it all juggled straight—*I have to forgive you* because you have done something I wasn't able to do! Isn't that it? You screwed her! More than that, *she* screwed *you!* Don't you see, Aubie? It's the same old shit! Are my motives for requiring you to accept my forgiveness honorable? For Christ's sake, Aubie, no! I'm just jealous! That's all! Blind ass jealous! No, wait, Aubie! Don't interrupt, because we have finally come to the point. Yes, yes. . . . You see, I'm also jealous of the fact that you are actually going to become a priest. I'm especially jealous of the fact that you're going to go to Africa and become a Saharan priest. But! I *want* you to become a priest! I do, Aubie! I do want you to become a priest, *and* a Saharan priest. Don't you see? I want you to become a priest, just as I am glad that you screwed Julie. And I am glad, somewhere down inside, and don't ask me to reconcile the sin with the ambition, I'm glad you have had that pleasure, because I wanted you to have it. And I wanted you to have it, not only because of any twisted little motives of reducing you to my level—those same motives that made me plot to have you screw that bitch in the back of the La Salle—not only because of those motives, but also because *I* had had that great pleasure, and I wanted you to have it too before you died. And let me go on, straight on, as straight as I can go with this. In the same way, I want

403

you to have the priesthood, because I know what it once meant to me to have it. More! I want you to have it—and I'm trying to stay with you now, Aubie, oh Christ how I'm trying—I want you to have it precisely and exactly because I couldn't and *can't* ever have it! I want you to succeed where I failed, Aubie, because we are part of one another, we are involved with one another. And I, the failure, undoubtedly am more aware of that than you are. I know it more truly because it *burns* me, it scorches me, it crucifies me to have failed. And if I should tell you five minutes from now that I don't want you to make it as a priest, knock me on my ass because I'll be lying! If you *don't* make it, Aubie, if you don't make it, do you know what it will prove? It will prove only that all of the resentment, all of the jealousy, all of the hate, all of the bitterness that I've felt toward you since we were little have won out! Have beaten you down! Have defeated you—you in whom I live and move and have my only claim to rationality! And if you can see me exulting at your failure, you are probably right. I might well exult, like a mad bastard. But can you imagine taking the thought that I have succeeded in making you fail to my grave? Christ Jesus, Aubie! Can you imagine *that*?" He shook his head violently from side to side, and pushed the tears on his cheeks away with his hands, and seized his hair hard in ten fingers and pulled his head down almost to his knees and was silent. And before Aubrey could say he knew not what, Arnie was up again, facing him, his eyes driving on him like two sparking electrodes. "And after all of this, Aubie, you'd better make it! You'd better do it! Or, by God, I'll haunt you with it until the goddamned day you die! If you don't understand *now* . . . ! Do you understand? Do you understand that because I knew I was nuts, and because I wanted you to make it, I wanted to get to a different seminary? Do you understand that that was why I did it? I *knew* I might crap out anytime! I *knew* it. I wasn't going to tell you about the Saharans at all, but I had to, finally, because you'd have spent your life hating me if I hadn't. But, Jesus God, I didn't want you to become interested in the Saharans. I was only trying to get away before I disgraced you, and, by Jesus, I almost made it, didn't I? You're goddamned right I did. And I think I *would* have made it, at least as far as the boat, if there hadn't been that mixture in me, that mixture of love for you on the one hand and hate for you on the other. The Sahara Desert! Jesus Christ! Why would *I* want to go to the Sahara

Desert? Just to save your ass from disgrace? Screw you! But I tried, Aubie, I tried, and I damned near made it, and I tried only for your sake, believe me, and I tell you that now only—only, Aubie—so that you'll know how much I have always wanted—how much I *now* want—you to become a priest! *Any* kind of priest! And I tell you that now only—*only* again, Aubie—so that you'll understand *why,* aside from any goddamned horniness on my part, I am so goddamned pissed off at that goddamned bitch across the hall for getting into your pants! *She* doesn't give a sweet goddamn whether you become a priest or not! But *I* do! And don't try to write my anger off any other way, Aubie! *Please* don't." He extended both hands toward Aubrey, palms up, neither his face nor his eyes betraying any awareness that he had done so, that he was conscious of any gesture whatsoever. "Aubie, we both know enough scholastic philosophy to be able to reason syllogistically. Right? Right. Now, listen, and hear. That which is defective is evil. Arnie is defective. Therefore, Arnie is evil . . ."

"Arnie, I won't accept . . ."

"Then *don't* accept, Aubie! Just understand that this morning, for once in his goddamned life, Arnie wasn't defective! And that, therefore, he wasn't evil! He was speaking truth, from the heart, from the balls, from the goddamned untainted finking hot-lined viscera! Just remember that, and remember too that God makes use of defect and evil, when it suits His purpose! God takes His revenge by making an evil defective like me come suddenly sane for a few minutes and serve His purpose! And if you don't believe that, if you don't believe that it is sound theology or what the hell, I want you to read a couple of things I've written out for you! Written out from my memory of the French—they're both by Frenchmen—and in my own free and miserable translations. But accurate, Aubie. Oh Christ, so accurate. And you just read them, and you remember what I said, and you put what I've written out here and what I've said here together, and you think about it. And I know you, Aubie; I mean, I know how bright you are—Christ, I ought to—and I know you'll come up with the right answer. And when you do, you accept that as my answer, my statement, my word to you, now and forever. And if I, by Jesus Christ, should die today telling you something different, don't you believe it, Aubie, because it will be a goddamned lie!"

And Arnie plunged from the stool, turning away at once, tossing

405

an envelope on the bed as he turned, and was out the door, slamming it behind him, before Aubrey could make any protest, and certainly before he could think of any protest to make.

He found the envelope, tore it open almost ceremoniously, and took out a single sheet of white paper. On it, in pencil, were two quotations. The first was identified as being from *Le Milieu Divin* by Pierre Teilhard de Chardin, S.J.; the second from a letter of Paul Valéry to Pierre Louÿs about 1900.

The first read as follows: "By virtue of His perfections, God cannot stipulate that elements of a growing world—or of a fallen world in the process of rising once more—should avoid alarums and diminishments, even in the moral order, for *necessarium est ut scandala eveniant*. But God makes it good, He takes His revenge, if one may employ such a phrase, by making evil itself serve the greater good of His faithful ones, that very evil that the current status of creation does not permit Him to put down (crush) immediately. As an artist makes use of a fault or an impurity in the rock he is sculpting or in the bronze he is casting in order to effect more perfect lines or a more beautiful surface, so does God, without sparing man the partial deaths nor the ultimate death, which constitute an essential part of our lives, transfigure them by integrating them in a greater scheme— as long as we trust in Him with purest love."

The second read as follows: "Briefly, I believe—and this is my whole metaphysical and moral credo—God exists and so does the Devil, but within us. The worship we owe to this indwelling divinity is nothing more than the respect that we owe to ourselves, and I mean the search for a better self by means of our intelligence and as directed by its innate potential. Here is my formulation: God is our individual ideal; the Devil is all that tends to deflect us from it. . . ."

And, beneath these, was written: "Aubie, my partial death will transfigure you if, and only if, you do not permit me, and your own Devil, to deflect you from that transfiguration."

# · THIRTY-THREE ·

THE DAY was angry and intermittently wet as they drove out toward
the mountain; now a smash of wind, now a blast of rain, now both
at once, and always the gray Aleutian fog that appeared to be rising
straight up out of the ground. And it was just after dawn, but warm,
so warm that they were all loosening buttons and pulling zippers—
the quarters closer than usual because McGeorge had caught a chill,
he said, and was riding inside—and Arnie, in the worst of moods,
early on had told Julie that Arrid didn't do a thing for her, and Julie,
in reply, had suggested a stick deodorant for Arnie and had further
suggested where he might stick it.

After the sun of the preceding day, the tundra had gone very soft
on top and what road there occasionally was had a three-inch coat-
ing of mud, like frosting on a very hard cake, so that the jeep traveled
in a fairly consistent series of lateral skids, Kunkel driving fast, sometimes reaching thirty miles an hour, with a great show of elbows and
iron-mask fortitude.

McGeorge, crouched on the floor amidships next to Arnie, was
holding the hood of his military parka tightly around his head and
muttering something that sounded like "to the back of the bus" but
turned out to be, when a particularly bad bump had trebled his
volume, "eternal rest to us." Aubrey solemnly seconded the motion.

They arrived under B-17 Ridge with the headlights on against near darkness, falling snow filling the headlight beams for fifty yards, or however far the light penetrated that sudden storm, and Kermit held up one hand like the major of Seventh Cavalry he had so often portrayed and the troops held firm to their billets, boots, and saddles. Kunkel turned off the engine and the lights. Whatever it was that had made the air warm abruptly deserted the atmosphere. The Japanese had shut off the Current. They all began rebuttoning and rezipping with the wind howling around them, and Aubrey thought of the souls of eight dead men wandering about out there, peering in at the isinglass, wondering what in God's name would bring six free-willed civilians to that place of wrath and tears.

And Aubrey was thinking about Arnie's visit, and the priesthood, but mostly about dying: thinking about it in the awful, utterly black-and-white way that the Roman Catholic must think about it, especially that Roman Catholic who does not happen to be in the state of grace, especially that Roman Catholic who, through long innocence, has come to regard the state of grace as a principality to which he holds an unrestricted passport. And he felt himself pulling away from all contact with Julie—so firmly and palpably squeezed into the narrow seat beside him—and felt himself accept, as one who could do no other, the simple polarities: Julie must go, or his vocation must go; and, even more fundamentally, Julie must go, or any least pretension on his part of a firm purpose of amendment—any least pretension on his part of a claim to salvation—must, until Anchorage (and he yearned to revisit that used coffin of a city), be forgone. A Catholic in mortal sin might still be saved without confession if, with the firmest sort of firm purpose of amendment, he was able to pronounce a so-called perfect act of contrition—that is, to aver with entire honesty a contrition that proceeded pure and simple from sorrow at having offended God—but Aubrey had no hope of making such a perfect appeal to divine mercy, considering it, as he did, impossible for anyone in real and present fear of damnation to be so divinely unselfish about remorse. If, as Aubrey also believed, there was no such thing as the unselfish human act in any circumstances, how could there be such an unselfish act of contrition where the circumstances intimately involved one's eternity? So he didn't try to make a perfect act of contrition, but he made an imperfect one—one that merely begged divine mercy for mercy's sake—over and over again, and withdrew from Julie until that hip that was pressed against the raised rear fender of the jeep was numb and metallic and moribundly in need of a small, private salvation of its own. And Julie noticed, or had long since noticed, and during the Japanese snow storm she, with typical boldness, went to the feminine offensive.

"Well, Jesus Christ, young reverent, is there a recession in heaven this morning? You act as if God has called in all mortgages."

And she smiled sweetly at him, with more than a little genuine, clear-eyed fondness and understanding. So that he undertook at once to respond to her challenge, knowing that it was toward a dishonest end—that is, toward creating the impression among all those present, especially Arnie (and, dear God, he thought, how I wish I knew how to reassure and pacify Arnie—with emphasis upon pacify) that nothing whatever had happened between them yesterday, or at any time —and said, "I guess there's a mortgage on everybody's soul at one time or another."

Julie winked at him and leaned against him, reaching her right arm under her left to tickle his abdomen, and smiling at him with eyes, teeth, and pout, and with an unrestricted metaphysical bravado that reached Aubrey for the first time, and said, "Sure, reverent, but what does God need of the interest?"

"God takes an interest!" Arnie said suddenly, loudly.

"What the hell would you know about it?" Julie said.

"At least I won't be judged as a priest spoiler!" Arnie said.

"Oh, won't you, you pissant?"

"Watch your tongue, Julie-Bitch, or I'll rip it out of your fat mouth!" Arnie managed his viciousness without moving, without even raising his head.

"I don't think you will, you pretentious horse's ass. And you will be judged as a priest spoiler long before I will, and don't allow yourself the luxury of thinking any differently, because, at least, my motive would be healthy and natural!"

"Hah! There! Did you hear that, Kermit? Did you hear this diabolical bitch admit that she screwed Aubie?"

"Goddamn it!" Kermit said. "Can't we ever have any peace? Anywhere, anytime?"

"Peace! Jesus Christ! Didn't you hear her?"

"That isn't what I said at all, you damned liar!"

"Jesus Christ!" Kermit roared. "Shut up, all of you! Dismount!

Out! By God, I'd sooner go hunting with a bunch of goddamned nanny goats!"

They dismounted, grumbling, and disported themselves around the trailer while McGeorge, like Dante distributing penances, handed down the guns and packs. Julie looked at Aubrey once, almost contemptuously, and whispered, "Thanks for defending my honor." Aubrey had no reply; he was too astonished to speak. Since when did Julie need any help defending anything, and wasn't it his own honor that had been at issue?

Kermit then surveyed the group with what looked like incipient amazement, as if he'd never seen any member of it before—or as if he had chosen to forget that he had—and divided the six into three pairs of marauders. He did this with what he must have considered acute psychological insight, if the shrewd constrictions of his snow-filled eyebrows could be taken as a fair index. He assigned Julie to Kunkel (no possible chemistry there), he took McGeorge unto himself, and wedded Aubrey to Arnie with a series of firm, no-nonsense nods (nothing like a little combat to bring brothers closer together). They synchronized their watches and agreed to regroup at the jeep for Phase Two. Julie stood next to Aubrey throughout this first briefing, and looked straight ahead, into nothing, her eyes angry and brooding. Aubrey thought to speak to her, to explain what contrition meant to him, but he felt slightly ridiculous there, suddenly, on that desolate and snow-shot and wind-ridden and God-forgotten hillside, and let it go, and looked to his bolt action and found that he had no bolt action, that he had been dealt a double-barreled rifle.

Abruptly, they were tripartite, and he went squilching off after Arnie, complaining that he had a double-barreled rifle by some mysterious miscalculation.

"What?" Arnie said wiffishly, not turning around.

"My rifle is double-barreled. I mean, I've got the wrong rifle."

"So? Didn't you pack your own rifle?"

"No. McGeorge said he'd pack it for me."

"Well, he packed one for you, didn't he?"

"Yes, but not the right one."

"So?"

"So, I'd rather have one with a single barrel."

"So? Throw one of those barrels away."

Aubrey considered potting Arnie in the back of the head with a snowball, but refrained, Arnie being by then somewhat out of range.

He inspected his rifle. It was not loaded. He dug around in the musette bag McGeorge had given him, and down among crusts of bread, jackknives, railroad flares, a wad of cotton, a mascara brush, a tiny can of linseed oil, and a snarl of fishhooks, lines, and sinkers, there were about a dozen of the largest damned cartridges Aubrey had ever seen. Anything they would fit, he decided, ought to come equipped with wheels. But the bullets fitted his rifle perfectly, and he mogged off after Arnie, loaded for bear, thinking that, yes, this rifle really ought to have a caisson as an accessory for use in carting home the body of anyone damned fool enough to fire it.

By that time, Arnie had great-circled his way clean out of sight, but had left tracks and assorted spoor, including two Tootsie Roll wrappers, a cigarette butt, and a right-handed leather glove. Aubrey picked up the leather glove, and straightway went to toying with a cleverness for when he should return it. But he had lighted upon nothing clever when, in a small fatness of fog, he came upon Arnie, spinning the wheel of his cigarette lighter. Arnie glared at him despairingly.

"Have you been lost?"

"No."

"Then where the hell have you been?"

"Fifty paces right flank rear. Here's your glove."

"Shove it up your ass. Have you got any lighter fluid?"

"No." Then, remembering, and very brightly, "But I've got a small can of linseed oil." Aubrey started digging for it in the musette bag.

"Linseed oil! Jesus Christ!"

"Maybe it burns."

"You think so?"

"Most oil does."

"That's fine. So when you find it, light it and shove it up your ass with the glove." Arnie turned, threw his cigarette lighter far down the mountain, and walked away.

"What are you mad at me for?" Aubrey called after him.

Arnie stopped and turned around, frowning. "I'm not mad at you, Aubie. I'm just *mad*. Remember?"

Aubrey watched him turn away with a scornful toss of his hooded head, and watched him hunch his shoulders up under his jaundice-yellow rain suit as he moved off into the saturated grayness.

And he thought, My God, there goes my brother, alive in his time and in his space, and here am I, alive in my time and in my

411

space. But we are alive at the same time, at this moment, that is, we are contemporaries, and it is within my power to close the time and the space between us—to run to him and put my arms around him and to tell him that we are together—but there is far more than time and space to overcome. And all of that "far more" is Your province, my God. All of that which is beyond energy, beyond mass and gravity, is Your province. Or, at least, I believe it to be. You alone are the entelechial force; You alone can cause growth, can cause physical and intellectual and spiritual evolution, can effect polymerization in the physical and supra-physical, can suspend the second law of thermodynamics so that energy does not suffer diminishment but grows and dimidiates and ramifies and reproduces itself anti-entropically, until nerve becomes simple apprehension, until simple apprehension becomes syllogism, until syllogism becomes selection, until selection becomes affection, until, in short, heat becomes love—You who do these things are my God, and, I, standing here on this wet mountain in my sin, ask You with all my heart to suspend just one more of Your usages, and give my brother Arnie, now instead of waiting until the hereafter, his full quotas of energy, nerve, apprehension, rationality, so that his energy may become affection, so that his heat may become love. Amen.

And then, Arnie being almost out of sight, he set off at a trot after him, taking advantage of Arnie's tracks.

The sky was infernal. The sun had managed to rise perhaps two yards above the horizon before it had lost itself in black clouds, and was hanging somewhere behind them, blood-heavy and dismal, radiating in baleful gore-splattered fingers all across the eastern quadrant. Aubrey thought he could smell Pavlov's brimstone, and found that his teeth were gritty with its ash, and felt the air growing colder as the blue metallic cold of the rifle came through his gloves and touched deeply into his fingers. And he ran on, and was in and out of a furious rain squall within twenty-five steps, and saw Arnie ahead of him as he came out the other side. And he wiped the rain out of his face, and looked at the scarlet and brack of the roiling sky, and thought, Well, Lord, you can't tell what might happen between now and three o'clock but it does promise to be a great day for a crucifixion.

They were at first on a broad terrace that ran like a roadway south, and gradually up, to the level of B-17 Ridge, and on higher. The terrace was, at its mid-point, about thirteen hundred feet high on the eastern slope, and was, very ominously, he thought, covered with boulders that had come rolling down the mountain God alone knew when. Maybe yesterday. Most were half buried, but some sat in relatively slight depressions, the biggest of them about six feet round, blast-white, and certainly separated from their parents by violent means. He was glad to see these boulders just where they were, inert, their rolling days more or less over, and he kept an eye cocked high and to the right, up the mist-shrouded and impossibly steep reaches of gray and white toward the summit whence all that fat stone had come. He called to Arnie, saying hello and observing that they were obviously right in the middle of Frosty's favorite bowling alley, but Arnie only snorted and shook his head and asked him why he didn't keep his mouth shut. Arnie apparently thought that somebody had called a moratorium on rolling stones.

Then they were in a sort of catch basin of a meadow, hip-deep in rotten snow, trying to find the high rim of the basin but unable to, and it seemed to Aubrey that there was something directly beneath him that desperately wanted his boots because, even when he was standing perfectly still, the suction went on quite actively. It occurred to him that he was standing in some kind of vomican *caldera*, and he plunged on, knees driving, and almost caught up with Arnie.

At last they were going straight up, or very near it, on a long, wind-beaten ridge, shaped like a scimitar, with a pure white, sensibly sloped field of snow on one side, and a sheer drop of probably two hundred and fifty feet on the other. Arnie was putting his tracks, as Aubrey expected he would, right out on the brink of disaster, so that Aubrey flaked off to his right about five feet and broke his own path, praying that Arnie would keep his balance. He remembered, for the hundredth time, that he was no longer in the state of grace and that, therefore, his prayers would not be heard, and he failed and died a little, but went on praying anyway. The wind now had an excellent shot at them, and took it, rising into blast time and time again from its steady and watered position in the northeast. And it was cold, and then very cold, and after a time, at the handle of the scimitar, Arnie stopped and waited, and asked for his glove.

"Sure," Aubrey said, and reached around behind him to where the musette bag was riding the small of his back.

As he brought it forward, Arnie wheezed and said, "By Christ, that's a relief!"

"What is?"

"The musette bag. For a minute there, I thought you *had* shoved the glove up your ass!"

They both laughed, and when they were through laughing, Arnie smiled at Aubrey and nodded once, a forgiving nod, and Aubrey nodded back, feeling that he was absolved of whatever he had been guilty of in Arnie's eyes. And Arnie went on smiling, and took Aubrey's rifle and showed him how to work the safety, and they trudged on and upward.

Almost at the top of the ridge, Arnie stopped again and checked his watch and said that they had been out over an hour and ought to head back. And just as they turned, they saw a bear, away to the depths and gone down near the foot of the mountain, and on the far side of the deep ravine. Arnie put the glasses on him and said that he was young and small. Aubrey took a look, adjusting the binoculars to his weaker eyes, and thought the bear certainly smaller and whiter than King Kong, maybe, but still much too large to be running around without collar or tag. And the bear was running, and Aubrey was alarmed by its quickness and energy, and while he watched, the bear, for no good or apparent reason, stopped, reared to its hind legs, pawed at the sky for a time, then fell to all fours and took off down a gulley at a sturdy commuter's trot. Aubrey gave the glasses back to Arnie and said that the bear was big enough for any purposes he personally had in mind—that is, to run like hell from—and Arnie grinned and said that Big Ditmo was at least three times as big and twice as fast as the white one, and that old Big D was probably watching both of them at that moment. Aubrey looked to his safety at once, disengaging it, and stayed much closer to Arnie on the way down.

It began when they moved high—the visibility being now somewhat better—to avoid the basin full of rotten snow, and Arnie had gotten about twenty feet ahead of and slightly above Aubrey. The snow was deep, but powdery, and Aubrey paused to put his hood up because the wind was blowing the snow down his neck. And as he worked at tying the strings of the hood at his chin, his eyes caught a movement high up to his left. There was a snow-filled draw running from the basin perhaps five hundred yards up the mountain. About halfway up, the draw passed through and divided a large thicket of short, bone-gray and black willow scrub. It was in the near half of this thicket, on their side of the draw, that something large and

414

dark had moved. He called to Arnie, who was about to cross the draw, and he was almost dismayed when Arnie did not tell him that, for Christ's sake, he was seeing things, but quickly turned, unlimbered the binoculars, and put them on the thicket. Aubrey was suddenly frightened or excited, or both, and hurried toward Arnie, whose grin was wide and calm, and who was talking to himself as Aubrey came up.

"Ah, you see. Ah, you see. The old bastard can't stay away from me. I knew he'd have to say hello. I knew he'd have to have his jollies with old Arnie."

"What? What'd you say, Arnie?"

Arnie just went on grinning, moving the glasses slowly back and forth, and asked Aubrey once if he was sure he had seen something move. Aubrey said no. Arnie said, "So, so. You're not sure. But *I* am sure." He moved the glasses higher, studying every inch of ground. And he was at it for some time, patience personified, until Aubrey began to shift from foot to foot and mutter that it had just been his imagination. The clouds had cleared slightly, but the sky was still sleet-gray and the light like old silver tarnishing.

"Arnie, you can't see anything clearly, can you?"

"Hell yes. I can see tracks into the willows. Everybody isn't blind, like you."

"Look, Arnie, I was seeing things."

"That's what Rommel's lieutenants told him, in the desert. But he knew better."

"But it could have been a shadow. Or snow blowing. Anything!"

"But it wasn't *anything*. It was Big D, Aubie."

"How do you know? I was the one . . ."

"It's just the kind of place the old bastard would hide in. I noticed it coming out. Besides, Aubie, Big Ditmo and I are good friends. There's a vision beyond eyes."

Aubrey looked at Arnie closely; observed the set grin, the high cock of the chin, the thrust of his brother's whole body. Arnie appeared to be taking his breath, his life, on a higher plane, to be communing silently with presences, or a presence, that were beyond Aubrey's apprehension or address. And Aubrey was suddenly hesitant about making any new objections, feeling certain that a door was closing against him and his words, word by word, objection by objection. So that he only said, "You do see something, Arnie?"

"No. But I hear him talking. He talks to me, Aubie. Oh yes. He's a loquacious old bastard, Big Ditmo is. And he's looking right at me, right down the tubes of these binoculars." Arnie shook his head admiringly. "Well, Aubie, we've got two choices if we want to flush him out and get a look. We can circle around and up and come in on the thicket on the downwind side and a little above it." He lowered the glasses and turned to grin at Aubrey. "I figure about a mile's mog, through deep snow and mostly straight up. How's that grab you?"

"I am ungrabbed."

"Thought so. Second choice. Risk the wrath of Zeus the Pater, and fire a shot into the rocks above the thicket."

"Third choice. Get the hell out of here and on back to the jeep."

"Now, now, Aubie. You wouldn't begrudge me the face-to-face confrontation with my good friend, Big Ditmo, would you? Besides, I have to give him his annual agitation."

"His what?"

"You'll see." Arnie was fitting the glasses back into their leather case. Then, quickly, he snapped his rifle forward by its sling from his right shoulder, put his left arm into the sling, wrapped the sling with expert swiftness, brought the butt to his right shoulder, and peered into the scope as he aimed toward the willows.

"Arnie, wait . . ."

"I knew you'd say wait," Arnie said, grinning again. And, at once, he fired.

Aubrey rocked back from the report, still looking at Arnie, who was working the bolt of his rifle with his lips working rapidly over and around his grin, and Aubrey managed to say, "Arnie, for God's sake . . ." before Arnie shouted him down.

"Hah! Hah! Hah! I told you, Aubie babe! There's your genus Big Ditmo!"

And then Aubrey turned and looked up, and saw. The bear was up on its hind legs, huge forepaws framing a monstrous shag of a head and a barbarous cavern of an ivory-studded mouth, and it was making a great noise that sounded like a bark, a woof, and a growl all at once, but with a volume out of another time, and it stood there, two hundred yards above them but still towering and beyond anything Aubrey had expected of the animal kingdom (and he thought, Sweet Jesus and dear God, the zoo is really really out!) and the bear stood up there, high and mighty and brindle-brown, for ten seconds or more before he fell to all fours again and started moving toward the draw. And Aubrey heard himself shouting to Arnie to shoot. But Arnie was standing stock-still, his rifle butt to hip, watching and grinning. And then saying, "Take it easy, Aubie. Take it slow and very easy." And Arnie's voice was low and flat and preternaturally controlled, as if he were commenting upon the passage of a fly through a hairbrush. "We can't go around shooting Big Ditmo without a clear and unobstructed field of vision. After all, we don't want to hurt the old bastard seriously."

"What the hell do you mean, we don't? We want to kill him, don't we?"

"Why, Aubie, how very unfinking-Christian of you. Why should we want to kill him?"

"Well, good God, Arnie! What the hell did we come up here for?"

"I came up to get away from the routine of being a nut. How about you, Aubie?"

"But, Arnie. You mean, you're going to just let him walk away?"

"Practically. That's what I did last year. Oh, I'll nick him a little, just to keep him happy. Look at him! Isn't he a grand old son of a bitch of a field marshal of a bear?"

"Arnie, for God's sake! Will you stop all of that crap and shoot? Or I will!"

"No you won't, Aubie. First, because that goddamned double rifle isn't accurate over a hundred yards and the distance is well over two hundred. And, second, because we don't go around potting old field marshals. We just nick them a little, Aubie, to make them feel important and dreadnaughty, you know what I mean?"

"No, I don't, Arnie! You mean that that bear is Big Ditmo, and that we've traveled four thousand damned miles to shoot him, and that now you're not going to shoot him?"

"I'm going to shoot him, Aubie. A little. I mean, the poor old bastard, what's he got in life but the idea that he's sought after, that he's still king of the mountain, and all that jazz? I mean, you can't let him walk away without a little nick to let him lick and think about what a fire-balled old bastard he is and how he foiled the old bipeds for another season, by God."

Aubrey could not believe what he was hearing. "Nick him a bit . . . !"

"Sure, Aubie. Soon's he gets to that draw, a little more into the open, I'll nick him a bit."

"Arnie! He's big as a house! You start nicking him, he'll charge!"

"Oh, he wouldn't do that," Arnie said indulgently. "Not Big Ditmo. Not on old Arnie."

"How the hell do you know he won't?"

"Because he told me. What the hell do you think he was talking about a while ago? He was saying, Good to see you, Arnie, babe, and how'd you make out during the past year? And he was saying, Now I'd like it this year just over the right shoulder, so's I can show it to that old bitch of a wife of mine and say, See, you old bitch, they came halfway around the goddamned world again this year to try me and I beat them! Now, get the hell out to the den-kitchen and fix me sixty-four steelless steelhead or, by Christ and Ursa Major, I'll snatch you bald."

"Arnie, will you just listen to me? That is a wild animal! He doesn't hear what you're saying! It's all in your own mind!" Aubrey was on his toes, speaking, shouting, directly into Arnie's near ear. But Arnie just went on grinning and nodding and watching. "Arnie! For God's sake! If you aren't going to shoot to kill, don't shoot at all!"

"You just don't understand, do you, Aubie? No, no. You just don't understand how it is with old field marshals. Well, there he goes toward the top of the draw." The bear was just visible, now his back, now his head, among the stunted willows, and he was moving, by fits and starts, toward the draw, and approaching it cautiously, as if he knew what Arnie had in mind. "When he's in the open, I'll nick him!"

"Arnie, just answer me this. If he *does* charge, what will you do?"

"Why, Aubie, animals aren't like people. They don't tell you one thing and then do another. He won't charge, because he told me he wouldn't."

"But suppose he just goes berserk, Arnie . . . ?" And Aubrey caught himself by the mouth, and tasting the leather of his glove, looked away into the wind.

"That's okay, Aubie. Don't you feel bad. I do love you, Aubie. Just like I told you. And old Big Ditmo, why, he loves me, just like he told me. Oh no. He wouldn't charge, not after telling me he wouldn't. And he *wants* me to nick him, Aubie. Hell yes. What's an old soldier got to show if not his scars? Right, Aubie?"

And then the bear was on the lip of the draw, poised, and Arnie had moved over and down into the draw a yard or two so that his line of fire was straight up and clear. "Arnie, listen. Let him go this year. Okay? Tell him you'll be back next year. Okay?"

Arnie turned upon Aubrey suddenly, viciously, his words snapping like icicles off the edges of his teeth. "What the hell do you mean, *tell* him? He talks to me! I don't talk to him! Don't—just *don't*—give me that patronizing baby talk, Aubie, or I might shoot me more than a bear!"

Aubrey had bent back, as he had done from the report of Arnie's rifle, and he stayed back, as Arnie drilled his eyes at him one final and flashing time, and then turned to his surveillance of the bear. And Aubrey could, then, only wait and watch, or, at least, that was what he told himself to do. Arnie was down on one knee, peering intently up the draw. The bear was half out of the willows now, pawing at the snow beneath him, turning his head exactly as if he knew how and why he was being watched. And the bear held in just that position for perhaps a full minute, then took a final look down at them, and plunged out into the open, into the deep snow, and began to wallow and claw desperately toward the far bank. There was just a split second, as Arnie took aim, and Aubrey thought he was still holding himself and watching only, but saw himself, as if he were watching the whole business from ten feet in the air, striking at Arnie's rifle and shouting at him to hold his fire just as the rifle leaped in Arnie's hands and the roar of it thundered up and down the mountain. And, immediately, Arnie struck at him, with a sweeping backhand, and knocked him, knees over, five feet down the hillside, and stood over him shouting, "Goddamn you! You made me gut-shoot!" And Aubrey lay perfectly still in the snow, and watched Arnie, watched his brother through the next incredible moment. Arnie turned back toward the bear—and Aubrey raised himself sufficiently to see that the bear, had not, or was not, turned toward them, but was lunging belly-deep through the snow, and was then struggling up the far side of the draw and disappearing into the willows—and Arnie shouted, "It wasn't my fault! He hit my arm! That finking, goddamned, stupid brother of mine hit my arm!" And then Arnie raised his rifle on high and slammed it down into the snow and without a glance at Aubrey marched down into the draw.

Aubrey got to his feet slowly, retrieved his rifle from the snow behind him, struggled up ten feet and plucked Arnie's rifle from the bottom of its neat silhouette, slung one rifle over each shoulder, and put himself in motion in Arnie's tracks. And all he could think of, as he pursued his brother down through the knee-deep snow and in among the great boulders and all that long way back down to the jeep, was that, once upon a time, St. Francis maintained that birds talked to him and everybody had called him a madman.

# · THIRTY-FOUR ·

KERMIT came down the mountain in full howl, brandishing his rifle like a war club, plowing his own path through the knee-deep snow, and sending his goddamns cracking on ahead of him through the wind like mortar fire.

Arnie, leaning casually on the leeward side of the jeep next to Aubrey, with his arms folded and his first-line sardonic grin in place, said, "Jesus Christ, Aubie, look at him come. Attila the Fink will now address the Beverly Hills Bear Grease and Penis Club on the evils of entering before breaking."

"Do you suppose he's all that angry about those two shots you fired?"

"Who the hell knows? It could be anything. I think, maybe, that goddamned fur hat of his finally grew into his beard and he can't get it off."

"Yeah, but he's hollering at us."

"Sure, he is. There's no doubt but that you were right the first time. He heard two shots and he expects we should each be wearing a bear for a watch fob. It's the little things that piss him off, you know?"

"There comes McGeorge."

"Of course, McJesus may have shot him in the ass with the fourten. Careful there, McJesus! Goddamn. You'll fall down and break the mountain."

"Kermit's closing fast."

"Let him close. Ignore him. You know what McJesus told me last year? He wants to climb Frosty."

"McGeorge does?"

"That's what he said. I told him I'd go with him when he was ready. You have to feel sorry for the old fart. I mean, he hasn't reached a peak in years." Arnie chuckled softly. "Goddamn, Aubie, I'm hungry."

"Kermit's in the last two-twenty."

"Ignore him, for Christ's sake. Jesus! He already requires more attention than a passive sodomist with the piles!" Arnie screwed his handsome face in a kind of self-chastisement. "I mean, he's a good old bastard, and all that, but I refuse to squat and strain whenever he says guano."

And then Kermit was upon them, still goddamning, and almost out of breath. He addressed himself mostly to Arnie, and about all he could get out that was intelligible besides goddamn for the first few seconds was that he had seen it all and what the hell was Arnie trying to do, for Christ's sake.

"Take it easy, Kermit," Aubrey said. "You'll have a heart attack."

"Easy my ass! And you're no better! I saw it all!"

"How the hell could you have seen anything?" Arnie said.

"Hah!" Kermit cried, waving his free arm and bending to within a few inches of Arnie's face, his eyes blazing, beard bristling. "You'd deny it if I hadn't seen it, wouldn' you?"

"I deny it anyway!" Arnie said. "And will you get your damned beard out of my mouth! Jesus! Bacteriological warfare!"

"You deny it!"

"Kermit, either keep your goddamned distance, or else send those teeth back to U.S. Steel and get them cleaned!"

"That's enough, by God! Now, you start giving me some answers or I'll start kicking your ass!"

"Sure, Kermit. What would you like to know?"

"What? Why, goddamn it, I want to know why you gut-shot Big Ditmo like that!"

"I didn't."

"Don't tell me you didn't! I had the binoculars right on you both, and I saw it all! I was right up on the ledge at the foot of the glacier!"

"Nice view from there?" Arnie said.

"Arnie, I'm warning you!"

"Kermit," Aubrey said. "Will you control yourself. It's only a damned bear."

"Only a damned bear! Je-sus Christ!"

"Wrong approach there, Aubie. Zilch in psychology. Tilt, tilt."

"What? What was that?" Kermit roared.

"I was just saying that if you saw it all and you're so damned full of information, what the hell are you asking us about it for?"

"You know damned well! Why did you do it?"

"Why did I do what?"

"Gut-shoot Big Ditmo, goddamn it!"

"I didn't."

"You did! I saw him moving away, dragging ass!"

"So, maybe I shot him in the ass."

It appeared for a moment that Kermit would hit Arnie. He doubled his free fist, drew it out behind him, and held it there. His mouth was working and so were his eyes, pantomimic studies in exasperation. Then he threw back his head and howled, "Arnie! Will you in the name of sweet garnished Christ give me one straight answer? Just one!"

Arnie was gazing impassively off toward the far end of the meadow, picking genteelly at his nose with a little finger. "Sure."

"Why in hell didn't you take him when he was up on his hind legs all that time?"

"How could I hit him in the ass at that angle?" Arnie said easily. And just as Kermit appeared about to pop his eyeballs, Arnie added, "All right, you want a straight answer?"

"Yes! In the name of . . ."

"All right! But don't start handing me a rasher of moose turd about how I'm lying, right?" Kermit nodded in splenetic, red-faced eagerness. "Right. I nicked Big Ditmo because he asked me to."

"Who? Aubie?"

"No, Big Ditmo asked me to. Aren't you listening?"

Kermit did a fast double-take, bulge-eyed, from Arnie to Aubrey and back again, opened his mouth to roar, held himself, peered in at Arnie's eyes, started to shake his head, raised his eyes to heaven, and groaned. "Oh Jesus God, deliver us!" Then he frowned at Aubrey, blinked, gathered his scattered parts, and made a ludicrous attempt to sound calm and reasonable. "Now, Arnie, if nothing else, even if the bear got down on his knees and asked you to nick him, simple goddamned humanity, simple honorable hunting conduct would . . ."

"Oh holy Christ! Listen to him, Aubie! Jesus God! I am now getting the goddamned code of the pissant hunter!" Arnie slapped his forehead. "Please, spare me! I don't give a rhomboid *crap* about the code of the hunter! I don't subscribe to it! Shove it up your wreathed horn!"

"Oh, so you don't subscribe to it! After all . . ."

"Oh, *now* he's happy! Look at him gleam, Aubie! He's going to by God liquefy for sheer joy! He's found me out!"

"So you *did* gut-shoot him!" Kermit cried triumphantly.

"How the hell does *that* follow?"

"I knew it all along!"

"Oh lovely, lovely! Hear that, Aubie? Precognition!" Arnie laughed evilly. "Precognition! I wish I had it!"

"I wish you'd both shut up a minute," Aubrey said.

"You haven't got a goddamned word to say!" Kermit shouted. "You caused him to shoot low!"

"So he caused me to shoot low. So what?"

"So you gut-shot him, that's what! That's the whole . . ."

"I don't give a big rat's ass *where* I shot him!"

"I don't believe that!" Kermit said, staring closely at Arnie, shaking a finger in his face. "I've taught you better than that. I've tried to teach you respect for animals, Arnie, and you go and pull a goddamned fool stunt like this. Why?"

"You know anybody who's more qualified for goddamned fool stunts than I am? I mean, if us goddamned fools don't pull them, who will?" Arnie laughed softly.

"Arnie, there's a wounded animal walking around out there bleeding his guts out! I don't think that's funny!"

"Oh, don't give me that crap! He's been walking around for years with two of your bullets in his head!"

"That's different!"

"How is it different?"

"I tried to kill him!"

"Jesus! And they say *I'm* crazy!"

"The difference, goddamn it, is obvious! A dead bear is better off than a wounded one!"

"What if the wounded bear recovers?"

"He won't! He'll bleed to death!"

"He didn't bleed to death when you shot him in the head! Unless, of course, you missed! Twice!"

"I didn't miss!"

"So, how was your shooting him different from mine?"

"I told you! I tried . . ."

"To *kill* him! And I only tried to *wound* him. That makes you a hero scoutmaster, and me a schmuck, right?"

"Oh for God's sake," Aubrey said. "You're not even sure you hit the bear, Arnie."

"Sure I'm sure."

"In the gut!" Kermit cried.

"All right, Kermit!" Aubrey said loudly. "So suppose he *is* shot in the gut. What then?"

"You admit it!"

"I *don't* admit it, Kermit. How the hell do *I* know where he was shot?"

"Jesus Christ, you *ought* to! You helped Arnie aim!"

"Just answer his question," Arnie said calmly.

"Goddamn it, *I'll* ask the questions!"

"So ask, and up yours with a runcible spoon."

"What did you say?" Kermit howled, advancing with flat of hand poised.

"I said, gentle knight, how would you like to . . ."

"Arnie!" Aubrey said. "Look, Kermit, I'm ignorant of all of this. Just tell me, will you *please?* So I'll know. If he *is* shot in the gut, then what?"

"Then what *shit!* It's a goddamn shame, and we've got to get out there and . . ."

"*Why* is it a goddamned shame?" Arnie shouted.

"Why? Because a bear is suffering out there, that's why!"

"Oh! So it's the bear's suffering that bothers you?"

"Yes! For Christ's sake, Arnie, what the hell do you think I've been trying to *tell* you for the last twenty-three years of your goddamned . . . your . . ."

"My goddamned worthless, idiotic, lunatic, expensive—take your choice, Kermit. And I've got more if those won't do."

"Don't start playing on my sympathy, Arnie! This is a serious matter!"

"Your sympathy? Where did you develop *that*, for Christ's sake? Watching whores at christenings?"

"Arnie! I'm warning you for the last time!"

"So, I'm warned. Sane or insane, I'm warned, right? So why don't you rear back there and shoot me both barrels and get it over with?"

"Arnie, will you listen? I've spent a lot of money coming up here for three years running . . ."

"Oh, well, money! You should have mentioned money sooner!"

"Arnie," Aubrey said. "Kermit doesn't deserve that . . ."

"Well, he said money, didn't he? What the hell do *I* care about his goddamned money!"

"I only meant . . ."

"I know what you meant! You meant that money—your precious stinking money—is what keeps me out of state hospitals and asylums, right? That's what you meant! And if your goddamned money means that much to you, put me in Matteawan, goddamn it! Put me there, and see if *I* give a goddamn!"

"That isn't what I meant at all!" Kermit cried, his eyes now tight and distressed and wandering, like little distracted knots of muscle looking for a limb to flex on.

"Screw you!" Arnie said. "You think because of your goddamned money you can stand here on the side of a goddamned waterlogged mountain, to which you paid our fare, and tell your two sons off, and threaten them, while you wave your big fat fists and your rifle at them! Well, screw you! You fink! I'll walk back! Or I'll swim! Or I'll crawl! Or I won't go back at all! And you can shove your goddamned money up your tokus in doubloon lots!"

And Aubrey, unjust as the charge was, yet felt a strange empathic accord with Arnie's emotion—the emotion only, because the thing wasn't susceptible to a reasoned analysis—and heard a voice that inhabited his mind and his body at the dark corners speaking to him through and with Arnie; a voice that was almost never heard from or dared to be heard, a voice that whined without honor or timbre or conviction, a voice that said, Daddy, get me hoe, rake, and shovel, you miserly fink, a voice that was out of childhood and out of infantile resentment and fed upon the adult heart, the parental heart, the enemy heart, knowing precisely how far the seven-year-old beak might be thrust therein before adult pain became adult retaliation. And still, Aubrey felt the voice taking the measure of his lips, felt it possessing his mouth from corner to corner, felt it drawing his whole face into a sneer, and felt it surging and leaping in all of his oral muscles to form words—bitter, excoriating words—with or without the consent of his mind. And he struggled with the voice, as red and white sheets of light came and went like heat lightning across the surfaces of his eyes, while he told himself that he loved his father, and, therefore, to regulate his tongue, and to say nothing, and to lie down in the snow and speak into it with that stranger voice if that was what had to be done. But he bit the voice out of his tongue and looked away.

And Kermit made no direct answer, but stared at Arnie, and blinked, and moved his mouth but said nothing—while Arnie looked away, unconcerned and entirely composed. And, watching his father —watching that monumental temper being held against the most adverse and aggravating of circumstances—Aubrey suddenly understood how entirely this father had involved himself in the insanity of this son; how completely this father accused himself, how utterly he was consumed by the pain and shame and indignity of it; how he suffered in and with Arnie in his madness, in and with his son in that most disgraceful of disgraces that can visit man alive. And Aubrey almost reached out and touched Kermit, to comfort him, but just as he did, Kermit turned to him; turned to him the saddest, most pitiful compound of disappointment and fear and old dreadful grief that Aubrey had ever seen on that face, on screen or off. But Kermit was speaking to Arnie, even as he turned. "You go and do whatever the hell you like, Arnie! I've had enough of helping a man who hates my guts!"

Arnie turned without a word and walked away, around the trailer to the other side of the jeep and climbed into it, behind the wheel, and sat there, laughing so loudly that it came through the canvas on the wind almost without diminishment. Aubrey happened to look at McGeorge, who was standing—his old shoulders bowed, his lips working—about twenty feet from the jeep, in the teeth of the wind, staring hard at Aubrey as if he expected that the young reverent would deliver them all from imminent disaster. And Aubrey tried. "Kermit, listen. Arnie doesn't understand what you're talking about."

"The hell he doesn't! He understands a hell of a lot better than you do!" Kermit's gesture included his rifle and almost delivered the butt of it into Aubrey's throat.

"Fine! Maybe he does. But I understand it in a different way! A more explicable way!"

"Bullshit!"

"Kermit! Will you put the goddamned gun down before you blow out a tire with it, or one of my eyes?"

"Don't tell me how to use a gun! You, by Jesus, you don't have the belly for hunting, do you? You got scared, didn't you? You panicked, and said, Oh Christ, Arnie, don't shoot him, and you hit Arnie's arm just as he fired!"

Aubrey's time had an abrupt, stunning, wholly unexpected stop. For, in his father's eyes and tone were the elements of an old and unresolved and heretofore mysterious issue, an issue about which Aubrey felt he had suddenly received the whole truth. And he received it badly, in the center of his stomach, and he left it to settle there, in the bile that gathered around it. He said only, "That must be a great pair of binoculars you have there, Kermit, if they enable you to see right into my fortitude, or lack of it."

"Aubie, I'm sorry I said that . . ."

"Sure you are, Kermit. But it's what you believe, isn't it?"

"No! No, it isn't! I'm just trying to get to the bottom of this! Why *did* you hit Arnie's arm?"

"I don't remember why, except that I didn't think Arnie ought to shoot the bear just to wound it."

"Well, goddamn it, that's what *I* think!"

"For a slightly different reason, however."

"What the hell do you mean? What different reason?"

"Well, you don't believe that Arnie shot to wound because Big Ditmo asked him to."

"Hell no, I don't! Do you?"

"Sure I do."

"Aubie, Jesus Christ! One nut in this family is enough! Don't you start telling me that Arnie talks with bears!"

"I believe Arnie when he says he talks with bears, and so should you."

"I don't, and don't you tell me what I so should!"

"Okay, if you don't believe what Arnie says, why in hell do you think Arnie shot to wound?"

"That's what I'm trying to find out, for Christ's sake!"

"Well, you're never going to find out standing there shouting, are you?" Aubrey's voice came out of him diaphragmatically and with all the force of five years of sermons behind it. Kermit looked startled, and even a little pleased.

"All right, Aubie, you tell me," Kermit said, just slightly below a roar.

"Arnie says that Big Ditmo talks to him, but he doesn't talk back to Big Ditmo."

"Holy Jesus Christ! That's a switch! That I'd have to see!"

"And Big Ditmo asked Arnie to wound him a little so that he could show the wound to Mrs. Ditmo." Aubrey felt a smile coming on, and pushed it back, or tried to, but Kermit's expression—out of incredulity by Bearslayers Amalgamated—was too much to withstand, and he did smile slightly.

"Goddamn you, Aubie, don't put me on!" Kermit howled. "I have had enough!" And he blinked fiercely, then turned to blink with Aubrey, as Aubrey pointed to the rear fender of the jeep where stood Arnie with a jack handle in his hand. "Well, what the hell, Arnie," Kermit said. "You want to hit me?"

"No," Arnie said immediately. "I thought Aubie was going to try to fight you." Then, looking at Aubrey, Arnie said, an entreatingly intense quaver in his voice as he balanced the jack handle delicately in his hand, "Don't hit my father, or I'll break your head in."

Aubrey started to speak, tried to speak, but found that all that pertained to speech within him was limp and gone to inaction. So that he simply stared as Kermit gave him one last, excoriating sweep of paternal eyes and went to Arnie, clucking softly, stepping with elaborate formality, and put his arm around Arnie's shoulder and led him, talking in gentle syllables that the wind carried away, back toward the front of the jeep. And even as he watched, Aubrey was thinking, Be careful, Kermit, and take the jack handle away from him. And he was vastly relieved when Kermit was careful, and did take the jack handle and threw it, with rich man's abandon, far out toward the inscrutable east.

Then Aubrey turned around, unable to watch Kermit's and Arnie's quiet communion any longer, and saw Julie and Kunkel coming down the long snowfield from the north, and he could see Julie waving at three hundred yards and waved back to her, and jumped in the air and waved with both hands. He wanted to walk to her, to be with her, suddenly, with all within him that was capable of—and newly freed—to want, and was astonished when McGeorge came up beside him, as if by telekinesis, fixing him with his old and wise and prophetic eyes, and saying, "You mustn't take it too hard, young reverent. Those who are of the Lord are of the Lord. He didn't explain His holy ways to men, and He doesn't ask us to be in the favor of men. Not any men, reverent. Be they father or mother or sister or brother." And then, abruptly, he wiped the raindrops out of his ancient eyebrows and looked toward Kunkel and Julie, and the prophet gave way to McGeorge. " 'Sides, reverent, Mr. Arnie didn't mean what he said. Just all wrought up about the bear, is all."

Aubrey had gotten the message, but the message he had had always with him. What he needed at the moment was mutual need, and Julie came to him, with facefuls of it.

"Aubie, darling. We heard the shots." She came directly to him and kissed him wetly on his cheek. McGeorge stood to one side and looked toward the sky. Kunkel kept walking.

"Arnie fired two shots at Big Ditmo. He missed. I think."

"You think?"

"Well, he said he gut-shot him—I assume that's a shot in the guts —but it didn't look like it to me."

Julie was smiling and standing close, her eyes wide and her pout wider and her whole face as moist with affection as with rain. He realized that he was taking far less than she was offering. He was glad to see her, even to have her kiss him, because, just then, he needed to feel wanted—was amazed, in his rational appraisal of it, at how suddenly and desperately he had felt that need—but was allowing himself no suspension of awareness that Julie, considered as anything other than loving stepsister, was a prime occasion of mortal sin. He backed away from her, smiling and nodding, hoping she wouldn't notice that his withdrawal was more than physical, but she did and smiled at him with her eyes, blinking them as if against the wind, but with cynicism, and with a force beyond the wind's.

"I swear," she said softly, as McGeorge—who had been hovering like a guardian angel just off Aubrey's port quarter—approached, "you are the most fickle, Christ-ridden, off-again on-again—and I mean that sincerely—lover it has ever been my confusion to seduce."

And before Aubrey could attempt an answer, McGeorge said, "Storm comin' right along, young reverent. Comin' right along, like as I told your father. I said to him, I said, it don't make no difference whether you shoot that bear dead in his tracks, or if he bleeds to death from the belly. He'll still be dead in the mornin'."

"I'll bet that endeared you to him," Julie said gaily.

"I think he's ready to call the hunt off for the day," Aubrey said, as he turned away toward the jeep.

"Don't think so, young reverent, don't think so! He's bount and determint to get that bear today. He told me, Mr. Kermit did, to mind my own business."

"Whatever that is," Julie said.

And they walked toward the jeep in the first galing winds of the storm, and Kermit came around from the front bumper with Arnie by the arm, and Kermit's mouth was dilated for roaring and his lips moving and his free hand gesticulating, but for once—and, as Aubrey thought, blessedly—there was a greater wind blowing than his father's and none of them could hear a damned word Kermit said.

# · THIRTY-FIVE ·

"ALL RIGHT," Julie said. "Since you insist upon talking about Arnie, tell me. What do you think is going on?"

Aubrey and Julie were alone in the back of the jeep, Julie on the rear seat with a blanket around her, and Aubrey on a folded half-shelter on the floor in front of her. Aubrey had been wrong, and Mc-George right. The day's hunting was far from over, and a big storm —or a big storm by non-Aleutian standards—had come roaring in shortly before they had finished eating their midmorning sandwiches and coffee. But Kermit had refused to accept the weather as sufficient excuse for the suspension of the code of honorable conduct for hunters, and had roared and shamed Kunkel into accepting his decision, and had sent three sets of skirmishers out to track and kill Big Ditmo; and Kermit had taken Arnie with him south toward the draw where Arnie had shot at the bear, and had sent Kunkel and McGeorge south also, but with instructions to circle three to four hundred feet below the draw and then climb up toward it, and had directed Julie and Aubrey, offhandedly, to go straight up and keep an eye out. Julie and Aubrey had gone straight up until the others were well out of sight in the driving rain-sleet-snow ventosity, then had crouched down for a time behind a wind-hardened lip of old snow, watching the water run down each other's noses, until they had decided they could

432

risk returning to the jeep. And they had returned with great difficulty, because, even going downhill as they were, the wind, and its incredibly dense burden of water in its various forms, had driven them very nearly to a standstill, their loose rain suits billowing like sails and the deep snow catching at their boots, until Aubrey had had to take the lead and pull Julie down the last seventy feet of ridge by pure dint of arm muscle, and leg muscle, and his mid-descent determination that, by God and all that stood him six-feet-two, no damned wind was going to prevent him. But even now, within the jeep, as the wind rose and the smash of water against the plastic windows made it appear that they were parked in a heavy surf, Aubrey was apprehensive the wind might win after all, and at least half of his attention was constantly upon the little snap-fixings that held the canvas top to the body of the jeep. And his mind was upon these when he said, in answer to Julie's question, "Things fall apart. The center cannot hold. And neither can the guards nor the tackles."

"What the hell is that all about, young reverent Yeats?"

Aubrey smiled at her. She was forced to shout, as he was, to be heard over the storm, and shouting gave her an intensely committed aspect, as if she were truly involved in her question and his answer. "All I said was that Arnie did not deserve a drenching because he loves Kermit."

She grinned and shook her head. "That's all you said, but that isn't all you meant. And don't tease me."

"I tease you? Why, how that does reverse our roles!"

"What's with you, darling? Bering water in your bearings?"

"I'm worried about Arnie. Somebody has got to tell Kermit. Somebody he'll listen to. Like you."

"He doesn't listen to me. That's an illusion. When you see him nodding at me, he's just approving my figure."

"Well, it's a start. It's more approval than I've got from him."

"You mean he doesn't like your figure?" She patted him on the shoulder. "I do."

"Listen, Julie, I think this bear-hunting business with Arnie along has gone far enough. Arnie could get killed."

"So could I."

"Be serious."

"I am." She smiled at him, then nodded. "Okay, so what's going on with Arnie and the bear?"

433

"*And* Kermit. That's the whole point. Arnie has identified the bear with Kermit."

"Well, Jesus, Aubie darling. Is that so farfetched?"

"I mean, a full-blown, psychotic transference, or whatever. Up on the mountain today, while *I* was seeing a bear, Arnie was seeing Kermit."

"Are you sure it *wasn't* Kermit?" She put one hand over her grin. "All right, all right. I'll do better."

"Much better, I hope. You were about to flunk the course."

"May I ask an intelligent question?"

"Yes. You're allowed one a semester."

"If Arnie thought the bear was Kermit, why did he shoot it?"

"Arnie says the bear asked him to."

"Oh *well*, then. . . ."

"Look, Julie. Arnie doesn't shoot to kill because he loves Kermit, and also because he knows that Kermit himself wants to kill the bear. There's no contradiction in that for Arnie. He has always defended suicide. But Arnie does shoot to wound. Obviously, he doesn't want Kermit to kill himself, so he tries to drive the bear away. He did it last year, too. Yet, for all of that, he resents Kermit a little and wants to nick him here and there."

"Or maybe he thinks he's doing Kermit a favor. Kermit does love his wounds. Christ, he can't even take a bath without being sorely disappointed if he hasn't got some kind of a wound to show for it."

"That sounds reasonable."

"Are you kidding? There have been only *two* reasonable things done on this whole mad-ass expedition so far and you and I did both of them, darling. And we mustn't stop there, you know."

She started to bend to him, lips first, and he pulled away. "Look, Julie, this is serious."

"Damned right it is."

"I mean about Arnie."

"Arnie isn't anywhere near as serious as I am."

"Julie, just one favor?"

"Then what?"

"What? What do you mean, then what? Then, nothing."

"Oh Christ!" She sat back and gazed up at the roof. "You are a study, darling! A here-I-come, there-I-go study." She took a deep breath. "Well! What I mean, what I have in mind, I sure as hell don't want to do here. I mean, not with all those dead people peeking in the windows at us, right? But I thought we *might* warm one another up a little while we're waiting."

"If you're cold I can start the engine and turn on the heater."

"Oh great! Wow and wowser! Just the thing! And *then* maybe we can play mah-jongg?"

He shook his head and tried not to watch her, but as always, did watch her, and thought about saying goodbye to her. Despite his contrition, it would not be easy; forgetting her would not be easy. He said, "You don't care about Arnie."

"Frankly, no," she said, shifting down to a giggle. "The bear that bites Arnie will die four minutes later of galloping pustules."

"All right, forget it." Aubrey spoke snappishly and stared away between the front seats at the gearshift knob.

Julie leaned forward and examined his face. He pulled back, glared at her, and looked away at the right-hand windshield wiper. Julie nodded and sat back. "Yup. Clear as a wart on the Pope's nose. The St. Jerome syndrome."

"What's that supposed to mean?"

"Well! I'm glad you asked. I thought I'd been cut off without a word."

"That'll be the day."

"Right. Now, the St. Jerome syndrome gathers unto it everything that proceeds from the statement: *nihil non in utero.* Need I translate?" She smiled engagingly.

"No need." Aubrey still didn't look at her. How, he asked himself, does this odd girl know about St. Jerome?

"Clearly, you have decided that I'm a stupid, unreliable, passionate, deceiving bitch, right? And that I'm so unfeeling I won't even save Arnie from bears."

"It's a simple request."

"You're the simple around here," Julie said lightly. "You're so damned simple you're unbelievable."

"Look, I told you to forget it, so forget it! Just quit while you're ahead, okay?" He glared at her. He knew he was displaying more anger than the dispute over Arnie called for, but thought it justified anyway.

"Depends on what you want me to forget. If you mean yesterday afternoon, I'm afraid I can't oblige." Her voice and eyes had abruptly

435

gone to soft fur. "I had too much fun yesterday afternoon to forget it. Didn't you?"

His anger flashed brilliantly, and he let it thunder. "No, I didn't have *fun!* I had a few minutes of mixed pleasure, well aware the whole time that I was committing a mortal sin!"

She looked at him for perhaps a full second, then slowly lowered her eyes. And he was startled into silence by this first display of humility or shame or whatever it was. Without looking at him, she eased herself back, pulled her knees up, tucked the blanket in around her as she turned sideways on the seat, and looked out the back window. Then she spoke very softly. "Well, mortal sin. Okay. I'd hoped we were gaining on one another, but at this point it doesn't look good. I mean, you must know, darling, that I don't believe in mortal sin, I don't believe in your being a priest, I don't believe in your Church, I don't believe in God. I like them all, especially mortal sin, but I don't believe in them. Now, the issue becomes, should I let my knowledge that you *do* believe in all of them prevent me from getting my jollies? And I'm afraid I resolved that issue in my own favor. But I was far less bitchy about it than I usually am. I mean, I didn't torture you, darling. I took you as soon as you could be made ready. Also, I wasn't unscrupulous. Believe it or not, I thought about what a hell of a nice hunk of man you were and how awful it would be if you became a priest only to discover that you were horny, that you *shouldn't* have become a priest. I explained all that to you, more or less directly, I think. If your God exists and wants you, am *I* a match for your God? Not if He's worth a damn as a God, I'm not. So what was there to prevent me? If God wanted you He'd have you after all. You'd be a better priest for having screwed a little, for having suffered in sin a little, for having screwed your own sister—although that incest jazz misses me completely, darling—which is to say, as I've said before, that you'd understand the sinner better and you wouldn't march around so proud and arrogant and virginal. You'll always have cause for humility, step darling, and that may just be one of the best things that's ever happened to you."

"You have my undying gratitude."

"Don't be assy, step. I only wish you meant it. And I'm sure you do mean it, somewhere down in that marvelously equipped center of venery you own. And I'm sure, priest or no, someday you'll be grateful to me on all levels. So I'm not at all sorry for what happened, and I did have fun, and I couldn't dream of apologizing to you—sincerely, I mean. I've never apologized to a man before for seducing him. I don't think it's good public relations, not to mention sexual relations. But. And however! If an apology is what you want, since I do admit I was the prime mover, I'll do the best I can. Is that what you want, step?"

"No . . ."

"Didn't think so. Not really. An apology from me would not go to the crux, would it? I mean, apologies have no place in your system. Apologetics, apologias, yes, but apologies, no. You hold yourself entirely responsible, don't you? Forgiveness from God is all you give a damn about. I know the drill. So, I won't apologize. Which relieves me. Much as I like to keep my lovers happy, I do hate to lie. And I *did* give you fair warning, step. You can't say I sneaked up on you. Tricky I was, but sneaky I wasn't. That dexedrine I gave you in San Francisco that lovely night was as tricky as I ever got. I'm sure you knew it wasn't Alka-Seltzer, even before you took it. Well, that's all intercourse gone forever, alas."

"Julie, I'd rather not talk about it."

"Asininity received and noted. If you'd like to stand out in the rain, you can avoid the address I'm about to make. Otherwise, poor darling, I'm afraid you're for it." She loosed the strings of her rain suit at the chin, pushed the hood back, and freed her hair in a rush of perfume, tossing her head and curls and the proudest of her pouts as she did. But she didn't look at him and returned the glowing green of her eyes to the window and stared out for a time in silence. Aubrey worked his thumb along the stock of his rifle, spreading a little oil he had found in the trigger guard along the drying stock; and watched the streaks and thought of Father Finnegan's desk and the finger marks he had once made upon it during another silence a hundred years ago. Julie sighed. "You see, step, what I told you in San Francisco that sweet night was all true. I have no joy in life except in a good screwing. It's the simple truth. The delightful truth. I'm not, by your standards, a good girl, step. I've never pretended to be, since I was old enough to know there was a difference between good and bad. I lost my maidenhead at fourteen, in bed with my mother and one of her lovers. He was a hairdresser or a clothes designer or something. My mother used to let me hide in the closet, from the time I was twelve, and watch her get screwed. She always told me ahead of time

437

and got rid of the baby-sitter and left the lights on in the bedroom. I'd get in the closet and crouch down and watch. It wasn't long before I knew all there was to know, voyeuristically speaking, because what Mother doesn't know about screwing is of no interest. But she made me wait until I was fourteen before she let me join the parties. I was a big hit and just enjoyed hell out of it. My mother always had handsome men and she never got jealous of me. Christ no. Although, after that first time, she never remained in the room. She explained later that she didn't want to inhibit me with her there watching. Big kick, my mother. That was before she met Kermit, of course. No. Not 'of course.' Just before. She's a nymphomaniac, I suppose, but happy —one of the happiest people in the world. She just purely loves to screw. That's her life story, and she can't understand—just simply cannot comprehend—why everybody doesn't love to screw as much as she does, nor why they don't go at it as energetically, as unashamedly. I've only seen her unhappy once in my life, and that was the time in Las Vegas when she slashed her wrists. I don't know what you've heard about that, and don't tell me, and I'll tell you the truth. She'd lost—in less than two days—sixty-three thousand dollars of Kermit's money, and she felt awful about it. And I'll tell you something. She was faithful to Kermit until that little episode. As irrational as it seemed to her, she was faithful to him. She told me about it once as if it were some kind of a damned oddball quirk of Kermit's—his asking her not to screw anybody else, not even good friends—like expecting a flower to accept honey from only one bee. She loves Kermit very much. They fought all the time, but it's a shame they separated."

"Why *did* they separate?"

"You don't know?"

"How would I know? Kermit doesn't discuss such things. He doesn't even talk about Rexfordia."

"But it was in the newspapers. In the columns. Not the truth, really, but enough so's you could guess."

"It wasn't in the Boston *Pilot* or *Our Sunday Visitor*."

"The what and what?"

"What I mean is, we weren't allowed to read secular newspapers."

"Not even *The New York Times?*"

"Not even the *Christian Science Monitor*. Although I'd read the front page of the *Monitor* now and then over in the college library."

"Jesus! You were a daring one, weren't you, step?" She giggled. "If

I'd only known, I'd have sent you a gift subscription to *Escapade*, or one of those."

"A newspaper?"

She laughed and bent toward him, shaking her head slightly from side to side. "Oh, you're just so goddamned innocent I could sing you a bawdy song." She sat back again. "And how are things back there in the sixteenth century?"

"The thirteenth," Aubrey said, relaxing his defenses somewhat; wanting to hear her talk some more. She reached an index finger and touched him on the point of the chin. He pulled back and lowered his eyes.

"Whoops!" she said softly. "Welcome to the twentieth century. God, how I'd love to live with you for a year or so, step darling. Just to watch the opening of the bud."

"I—I thought we'd already taken care of that," he said sourly.

She shook her head. "Oh no. We just planted a little seed. It takes a while for the root to find itself. Oh no. You're not even above ground yet."

"Well, wherever I am, I'm going to stay there."

"Are you telling me or asking me?"

"I'm telling you," he said stiffly.

"Well, there you go, challenging me again." She sighed deeply, unzipped her rain suit top, folded her arms beneath her breasts, and peered down at him. "Getting hot in here." He looked away from her smile, went back to his trigger guard. "You know, darling, I envy you in a way. I really do. Just as I've envied most of the best men I've known. Men are, apparently, able to dissociate more easily than women. From body, from sex, from parenting. That's why there are so many more great reputations among men than women. And yet, in another way, I don't envy you at all. Because I believe in this life. I don't believe in an afterlife, certainly. And I don't even believe in the value of greatness in so far as it makes for fame after death. If you're great, well, you're great, and I suppose that's that. There's really not much you can do about it. But there are those who sacrifice all else and, not being great and knowing it, do still manage to acquire a small measure of fame. You see this especially in women. Maybe there are no great women. And exactly because what St. Jerome said is true to a hell of an extent. I have a private theory that women only become great when they can combine, pervert, sublimate, put to work, their sex drives into whatever the hell greatness interests them. Edna St. Vincent Millay is my favorite example." Julie pouted her lips and put her tongue just visibly between them, and blinked down at him twice, hugely. Yet she didn't seem to be looking at him so much as she was enjoying an entirely private fancy. "Howsomever! What I meant to say, or have said, I'm not sure, is that I don't feel I've injured you because whoever's got you by the scruff up there has really got you. As you said, once, I don't actually offer you trouble. I don't like to admit that, step. But it's so. I think I *could* offer you trouble, given a little time, but—well, let's not open *that* can of spikes. I've never met anyone like you before. Have I? Well, maybe one other. But men are usually men, as my wisdomic mother used to say, and she was right. But you! A saint you are not, but otherworldly you definitely are. Wow and Christ and God, yes! Even at those moments of—how shall I put it delicately enough—of *supreme* passion?—okay?—fine, fine!—even at those moments I felt you were offering up your guilt and pleasure to—well, to mortal sin, as you say, but more than that—to the relief of the pain of somebody, somewhere, hanging on a cross. I—I don't know. Oh, your body wants me, all right. I'm not finding fault with your—your commitment to the business at hand—is that delicate enough? Your body wants me and probably a bit of your will, too, so bad that even now, right now, I think I could down you without much effort. But your *whole* will doesn't approve, and wouldn't approve or join, and it wouldn't, I swear, if it were only promised to the Young Republicans, or something worse. You're loyal, step, loyal. Forgive me if that sounds as if I'm saying I don't see much of God or Christ in you. But, to be perfectly frank, I don't. I'm no expert on God or Christ or what they stand for or what effects devotion to them is supposed to produce. But what I see in you is nothing more or less than iron willpower— the ability to withhold yourself—your essence or whatever it is that your willpower works on and worries about—to withhold yourself from those lesser things that your will condescends to allow your body to do. You enter into nothing wholly, step darling. Not even into a woman." She smiled very gently, perhaps seeing that she had offended him, which she had, most comprehensively. "You remind me of a ballet dancer I was once in love with. The other man I said was like you. A great lover, like you, but he withheld love. His inner sanctum was reserved, strictly, for ballet, and I've no doubt he'll be great at it someday. That's how you impress me, step. If you stick with it and drive yourself into the priesthood, there's no question but that you'll be great at Jesus someday." She laid her head back, arching her throat and smiling, her eyes on the window as a gust of wind and rain shook the jeep and bowed the windward side of the canvas alarmingly. Julie waited until the gust had passed and talked quietly into the following lull. "But, as I've told you, I don't think you should be a priest, I don't think you really want to be a priest, so I have no conflict with Jesus, or God, over you. Your conflict is between your body and your will to have or find a soul. Nob and I—you remember my friend Nob?—we explained to you about the non-existence of the soul, but you wouldn't accept our explanation. Okay. That's your problem, your conflict. My conflict is much simpler. There are ten or eleven potentially screwless days between now and the end of bear season, and you're the only stud on the range. As Lovelace said to Lucasta, I could not love you, step, so much, loved I not screwing more. Right? I'm sorry. I don't mean to use the word love lightly. I do love you, step, quite a surprising bit. I'm sure that doesn't flatter you, or, if it does, you don't admit it. But it's true, and I think I ought to let you know it's true, just as I think I ought to let men know when they're good or great or piss-poor lovers. Who the hell else will ever tell them if I don't? Okay, so you're the only stud, the only potentially errant knight on the turf. So beware." She turned and smiled almost maternally. "I do hope you didn't think I was going to be merciful about this, step? Or in any way honorable. Not a damned bit of it, Galahad. So screw down your visor, point up your lance—oh, by all means, point up your lance—raise your drawbridge, call the chaplain, lock on your chastity belt, and do whatever the hell else you think you need to do to defend your finking turret, because Lady Julie is going to mount her an assault just like in the good old days before ladies were invented. For ten, eleven nights running. Or standing still! Or en passant! However Sir finking Aubrey, step darling, wants it!" And she laughed, her Kermitian laugh, giving it birth from deep inside and sending it out early to drown out a new wind. Aubrey tried to hold stiff, tried not to smile, but did, yet held his hand over his mouth and looked away so that she would not interpret his smile as assent in any tiniest way. "Don't hide those pearls, step! Go ahead, be a daredevil! Grin at me! Oh, step, you'll get ulcers that way! Repressed laughter is very high in ulcer content!" She went on

441

laughing. Aubrey managed to scowl his lips into submission, and sat trying to narrow his eyes and think about the Sacred Heart of Jesus. And almost succeeded until he was interrupted again by Julie, having flagged herself down to a chuckle, saying, "So, you're still going to go out for the camel corps, right, step?"

"The Saharan Fathers. If they'll have me."

"Well, they'll have to take what's left over."

"Julie, let's get this understood! I'm not going to have anything more to do with you! I'd like to be your friend, but I can see now that that's impossible! So let's drop it!"

"Okay, okay," she said, smirking, rolling her eyes at the roof and patting her hair. "Hell yes. Why not? As my mother always says, The fish is full of sea. I used to correct her until I figured out what she meant."

Aubrey held his question until a certain respectable interval of silence had been observed, then, finding, after close inspection, that the subject matter was neutral enough so that it would involve no compromise on his part, he asked it. "Why did they separate?"

"Oh. Well, she was pregnant. Five months. When she slashed her wrists. You know Kermit wanted another son, after you and Arnie went celibate on him. So, unfortunately, she had a miscarriage. While she was still in the hospital with the wrists. Two days after she cut herself, I think. Anyway, that was the end of it. Kermit—well, he paid her off. He's still paying her off. He's got a good heart. I don't blame him, actually. But—well, he's a man. . . ."

"Kermit blamed her, you mean, for the miscarriage?" He felt like a tourist asking if that was the Statue of Liberty, but gave his face to her bravely.

She giggled slightly. "She slashed her wrists over nothing, right?" She held her lips wide around her teeth, but noiselessly, as if daring him to say the obvious. And then she hurried on, as though she'd seen something in his gaze and was afraid he might say it. "Kermit doesn't condition his reactions by what might have been, any more than he does by what might be. The money might have bothered him if she hadn't slashed her wrists and caused all that bad publicity. And the publicity might have bothered him if she hadn't lost the baby. Kermit is a man of the hour, isn't he? I mean, he's a wonderful man if you happen to catch him at the right hour and if you prevent that hour from going by so that he notices it. Right?" Julie took the edge from her smile and added it to her voice. "I love him, but I also hate him at times. Just as you do. That makes us normal. Whatever *that* means."

"Are you telling me or asking me?"

"Tie score, right? And now that we're even, answer me one foolish question."

"Foolish or loaded?"

"Both."

"I'll have to hear it first."

"Jesus! If you ever open a bank, let me know. Okay? All I want to know is, at the risk of incriminating myself, can a stepbrother and a stepsister marry in the Catholic Church?"

His reaction was close to stupefaction, but he prevented it from reaching his face, or felt that he did. "I *should* know, but I don't."

Julie was smiling, perhaps a little tensely. "Don't go into shock, darling. I was just wondering if I could marry Arnie."

Aubrey decided to play it straight. "Well, since you aren't related by blood but only marriage," he said, as if he were quoting, his voice semiofficial and in refuge, "I think a dispensation . . ."

"Oh, for Christ's shoeless sake!" she said sharply, and he took some vagrant satisfaction in seeing her jaw go angry for the first time in their conversation. Took this satisfaction, that is, until she continued. "A damned fool is born every minute. Kindly cut your umbilicus and join the others in the incubator." And he thought she was referring to him, but she didn't look at him, and decided she must be referring—because, it seemed to him, she was the fool, if any—to herself. And a yard of silence stood between them for minutes.

"Julie," he said, finally, tentatively. "This thing about Arnie. If he isn't going to shoot to kill, he shouldn't hunt."

"So? Why should *I* speak to Kermit? Are you serious, or just artfully changing the subject? Never mind. You're callous enough to be serious. You know what Kermit would say if I went up to him and said, Listen, old sock, no offense, but Arnie thinks you're a bear? He'd say, That's fine, and I think Arnie's a jackass. And even if he didn't —I mean, even if Kermit should look down at me out of that magnificent scraggle of his and say, And *why* does he think I'm a bear?— why, I'd die laughing on the spot!" And she laughed, and was still laughing when the door of the jeep was pulled open and there was Kermit, looking in, the water pouring off him, a cigar caught in his

443

teeth (bedraggled, the far end of its parabolic, water-bent length stuck deep in the lower reaches of his beard), and roared, "Well, Jesus Christ! You two are about as much use as tits on a mule!"

"My God, he *does* look like Big Ditmo!" Julie shouted, and went off again after her glee.

"For Christ's sake, you old bastard!" Arnie cried, pushing at Kermit from behind. "Will you either get in, or get your lard ass out of the way so somebody else can!"

"Stop pushing!"

"Well, get the hell out of the way, then!"

"Well, damn you, give me room!"

Arnie stepped back with a dramatic gesture. "Room? Sweet blistered Christ!" Arnie swept his hand through the driving rain toward the bottom of the mountain. "You fat-assed old fool, you want room there's the whole shitbox state of Alaska! With running water! Go run in it, and roll in it, and snuffle it in your shitface beard! I give you all of it! I don't want one finking Italian centimeter of it! All *I* want is a couple of goddamned underslung square feet of shelter!"

It was now apparent that Kermit had gotten one of the laces of his rain suit somehow caught on the door. He was trying to back away, and turn toward Arnie, roaring curses the while. "Son of a bitch! He tied me to the door!"

"Holy Jesus!" Arnie howled, bending in to observe Kermit's fumbling and wrenching. "What the hell are you doing? Counting your money? Jesus Christ! He's going to charge admission!"

"I'll charge you, you goddamned pup! I'll kick your ass up into your eyebrows!" And at that instant, Kermit came free of entanglements, turned, and lunged toward Arnie. Arnie jumped aside, dodged around Kermit, dived for the door, and came tumbling into the back of the jeep as Kermit took a kick at him. Kermit missed Arnie, but hit the bottom of the door with his toe, uttered a deafening cry of pain, and went hopping and swearing about in a small circle with his booted toe clutched in both hands. And Julie went laughing on.

"Serves you right!" Arnie cried. "I hope it's nothing trivial, you dry-balled old miser!"

"Jesus Christ!" Kermit howled. "I think I broke it! My big toe!"

"Too bad it wasn't your goddamned leg!"

At that moment, Kunkel opened the door on the driver's side and started to climb in. "Kunkel!" Kermit roared.

444

"That's right, Kunkel!" Arnie shouted into the startled Indian's face. "No sneaking in the back door! Get the hell around the other side and pass through the finking turnstile like everybody else!"

"What, what?" Kunkel said.

"I broke my goddamned toe!" Kermit roared.

"Go on! Pay the old fink his fare before he, by Christ, makes us all buy Blue Cross!"

Kunkel did close the door and went around the other side to where Kermit was stripping off his boot, and there followed an examination of the toe, there in the rain, and Kermit and Arnie went on exchanging threats and imprecations until Aubrey decided to intervene.

"Arnie, for Pete's sake. Can't you see he's hurt?"

"What!" Arnie said, and he turned for the first time to look at Aubrey. And Arnie's face had nothing of amusement, or sympathy, or sanity about it; his eyes blue-black, the pupils tight and hard and ringed with defiance, their essence long since departed for the past. He seemed to have trouble recognizing Aubrey, then said, "Well, if it isn't Aubie the Audacious. Aubie the Auriferous. Aubie the Aulic Owl." Then he looked around at Julie and blinked. "And there's Julie the Jade!"

"Don't hand me any of your crap," Julie said with abrupt force and anger. "You just remember, Funk-Eye, that you're no damned relation of mine, and I'd just as soon shoot you as ignore you!"

"Hum, hum," Arnie said, studying the floor of the jeep. "So Aubie au Naturel and Julie Jiggle managed it right here. By God, you two ought to get a citation from Willys Overland."

McGeorge entered from the driver's side, saying, "Think it'll rain, young reverent?"

"Goddamn you, McJesus!" Arnie said. "I told you about saying that! Once more! Just once more, and, by Jesus, McJesus, I'll crucify you with icicles!"

"Well, now, no offense, Mr. Arnie."

"There was offense! I was offended! And I'll bet you didn't pay your fare, did you?"

McGeorge, who looked as if he had spent the last ten years touring the engine room of the Titanic, peered at Arnie bug-eyed. "Why no, no, I . . ."

"Jesus Christ! Goddamned inefficiency! People climbing in at all the apertures without paying their fare. Old fart of a conductor with

445

a broken toe! How the hell do you think we're going to make this facility pay? I mean, if you goddamned people want the Mount Frost-Your-Balls Division of the Delay, Linger, and Wait Trunk Line, of the Cold Bay, Conch, and Shitbox Railroad to keep on operating in four-wheel drive between here and the Shelter Island hostile, you better start paying the old fart his goddamned admission fee!"

"Now, Arnie!" Kermit said, turning from the front seat as Kunkel started the engine. "I've had enough of your mouth for one day! If you'd like to walk back, just keep it up!"

"Is the toe broken?" Julie asked.

"Is the toe broken?" Arnie said, mimicking her.

"Kunkel says it's just sprained bad, no thanks to Arnie."

"No thanks to me? Jesus Christ! I'm awful, awful sorry for removing my ass from in front of your finking foot!"

"I warned you, Arnie!"

"Ho! Stop! Hold it!" Arnie cried. "We forgot the goddamned turnstile!"

Kermit started to turn around again, but held himself, and bowed his head and said nothing.

"Well, did anybody see anything?" McGeorge asked brightly.

"See anything!" Arnie said. "For Christ's sake, McJesus, yes! I saw steelhead, Dolly Varden, a porpoise, two whales, and an octopus riding a World War One torpedo with Visit Our Fallopian Tubes painted on the side!"

"You go fishin', Mr. Arnie?"

"Hell no! That superannuated old hammertoed fink up there led me right into a saltwater lake! Didn't even know we were underwater until we came to the sunken ship."

"Oh now, Mr. Arnie . . ."

"No, no, it's the plain truth, McJesus! We went right up the gangplank, see, and at the top was this turnstile. And on it was a sign, see, and it read: Butt Disposal. Admission fee one cigar butt, or fifty cents. Well, the old fink started to go right on through, and I said, Now wait a minute here. Either put in your cigar butt or fifty cents. I mean, there are rules. But you know what a goddamned old miser he is, and he wouldn't be advised, and he wouldn't put butt or money in the turnstile, and just charged right on through." Arnie paused and eyed McGeorge, who was quite curious.

"Well, what happened, Mr. Arnie?"

446

"Oh, nothing much. The turnstile chopped his ass off."

And so they rode back, the six of them, forced together, touching, and therefore connected, under that one small canvas roof like the components of a bomb. And Arnie went right on talking, quietly, viciously, calmly winding an engine of resentment and hate the like of which Aubrey had not imagined possible in his brother. And there was no defense, no sanction. There was only the brutality of Arnie's voice, only the tick-tock out of his mad limbo, and the tense hope that he would go on ticking more or less quietly until he could be returned to where he could have his explosion among enemies.

## · THIRTY-SIX ·

EVERYONE but Kermit slept all afternoon. Kermit was heard by all, sleeping or trying to sleep, pacing up and down the corridor and the mess hall, from the front door to the fireplace and back again, in what sounded like iron boots, in an effort to keep, as he said, "the toe from stiffening up." He carried an open bottle of Old Fitzgerald with him the whole time, so that by dinner, although Kermit's toe may not have been stiff, Kermit proper—which is to say, all of him above the right metatarsal arch, and excepting only his tongue—was at least temulentively taut. Arnie had also been drinking and appeared to be somewhat restored, although his eyes were still parlous with enmity, and he was still trenchantly and bitterly in pursuit of Kermit's good temper. It was Arnie who, after a general silence, broken only by compliments to McGeorge on his rare roast beef and Yorkshire pudding, and by the scraping of knives and forks, and by the sound of Kermit's jowlish, labial appreciation of the Beaujolais, put the company with a single remark back on war footing. He addressed Kunkel, McGeorge being at the fireplace, rapt in his ashes and duster.

"You see any snow bunnies today, Leknuk?"

Kunkel bared his teeth, red with beef blood. "Can't say."

"Why? In the name of diddlers the world over, why can't you say?"

"Don't know, and don't give a damn," Kunkel said, with entire openness. "Don't like rabbit."

"Okay, Leknuk, score one for the Modoc nation. Even I, with my limitless patience, haven't got what it requires. In other words, Leknuk, you are off limits. Modoc spelled backwards lacks one letter of being a variant of prophylactic, which describes you perfectly, and my compliments to Captain Jack." Kunkel nodded seraphically and returned to the long house. "But *I* saw a snow bunny today; a fairy snow bunny, which it isn't every day, you see, if you follow me. And this fairy snow bunny gave Kermit and me three wishes. And I, generous to a faulty companion, gave Kermit the first wish. But he, being faultier than I had thought, declined. So I, continuing in my generosity, took the first wish. I said, I wish I had a rattlebox for Aubie. And Kermit, apparently enraged that I should waste a wish on something so slight, shouted, I wish it was up his ass! So that we *had* to use the third wish to get it out again." Arnie smiled at Aubrey. "And what I want to know is, Aubie babe, where the hell is my rattlebox?"

"I could answer *that* one," Kermit said shortly. "But I won't."

Arnie surrendered a bit of his composure irretrievably, but obviously without regret, having accomplished his primary purpose. "By God, he's alive! He lives! Strike the timbrels smartly! Old Strycker the Strychnic lives!" Arnie raised his wine goblet in toast, but didn't drink. "We salute you! We had thought you had died of the big toady trots!"

"Arnie!" Aubrey said wearily, weary as one becomes of an old refrain. "Why don't you and I argue for a while and let old Pater the Zeus nourish his injured member?"

"I am the only injured member at this board," Arnie said quickly. "And the only defective one, as well. I will choose my opponent, if you don't mind."

"I don't mind, but . . ."

"But at least he's *got* a mind," Kermit said quickly.

And Aubrey thought, in the silence that ensued—with Arnie staring in disbelief at Kermit, and with Kermit fighting an immediate patency of remorse—Deal with us kindly, oh Christ, because our anger is not really with one another.

And suddenly and loudly, from the vicinity of the hearth, McGeorge said, "And the first shall be last, and the last shall be first, and, oh my Jesus God, the confusion!"

Arnie looked away from Kermit and shouted, "Shut up! Shut up, McJesus, and tend to your goddamned carbons!" Then Arnie gathered himself, pulling in his elbows, and said, "Now! About that no-good goddamned finking bastard of a suffering bear! Tell me, Pater the Zeus, do you really give a rat's ass?"

Kermit blinked. "By God, I do! Ruining a great trophy!"

"Oh! Oh now! *Now* we're getting down to where it itches, aren't we, Kermit? It isn't at *all* that he's out there suffering and dying. It's that he's suffering and dying without the high priest. It's your revenge you're worried about. You want to add him to your dead-head collection where you can gloat over him."

"No! That's got nothing . . . ! Don't you understand anything about hunting? I do *not* gloat over my trophies! I *honor* them!"

"Oh, I *see!* You think mounting an animal's head on a board and hanging it on a wall does that animal honor?"

"Of course!"

"That's very good to know, Kermit. Don't worry about a thing. I'll handle all the details myself."

"Now what in hell are you talking about?"

"Why, your funeral arrangements, Kermit, when, if ever, you should pass on to your reward." Arnie affected a very good imitation of Kermit's own best funebrial tone. "Fear not. We, the bereaved, will not falter. We'll mount your head on a platter of finest worm-wood . . ."

"I never thought," Kermit said, in a tone of reproach, "I'd ever hear one of my sons talking about my funeral."

"Gets you where you live, doesn't it?" Arnie said brightly. "Yes, yes, in those fell moments it's nice to know that your moldering clay will be molded by one of your own. Why, I'll even trim your god-damned beard. *I,* who won the O.T. barbering and clay contests!"

"Arnie, shut up!" Aubrey said.

"Or maybe some nice beaverboard. Or *bear* board, if they make it, and we'll hang you—let's see, now—yes! The very place! Between the wild boar hog and the African dik-dik!"

"Goddamn you, Arnie!" Kermit was plunging around trying to get to his feet, but had a bottle in each hand and couldn't manage it. He gave up in a howl of pain, having apparently struck his injured foot on something below the table. He closed his eyes and began to curse vehemently, addressing no one, but shaking the bottle nearest Arnie rhythmically, as a priest might a thurible.

Arnie was already moving away from the table, grinning and chuckling, his lips and whole face and the very sound of him mad and demoniac. He glanced away from Kermit to Aubrey once or twice as if he expected to find or gain Aubrey's approval of his success, and, not finding it in his brother's dismayed and grim stare, gave his hard black eyes balefully to all as his declared enemies. And, nothing daunted by his hostile audience or by Kermit's pain, shouted, "Or maybe, you old fart, we'll cut you off at the belly button and mount you up like a centaur! That is, if we can find a well-preserved horse's ass to tack you to!"

And under Arnie's delighted, stridently eager laughter, Aubrey almost smiled, and even Kermit shook a near grin around until it died. And Arnie, feeling that he had put his enemies to rout, went cackling off down the corridor to his bedroom and slammed the door thunderously behind him.

Then Aubrey saw that Julie was laughing, bent over her plate with both hands up, striving valiantly to conceal her seizure, but did peek up once to see Aubrey looking at her and surrendered it in volleys over the table; and got to her feet with her head back, and cried, "Oh, Jesus!" and went staggering off down the corridor to her room.

Kermit had found his smile again, or it had found him, and he put the neck of one whisky bottle into it and drank long and patiently. Sordini suddenly started to bark, jumped to his feet, and ran howling down the corridor and started to scratch at Arnie's door. Aubrey listened, heard the door open and Arnie greet the dog as his only friend in all the finking world, and then heard the door slam almost gently.

"Aubie!" Kermit said loudly.

Kermit was blinking at him, tearfully, drunkenly. "Yes, Kermit."

"Aubie, I'm disinheriting him! I am, by God! Tonight! You get it all! All!" Kermit brought the two whisky bottles in from right and left fields and just missed a hundred-proof collision behind second base. He unscissored his arms and slammed the bottles down on the table with a will that half lifted Kermit from his chair. And when the silverware had stopped rattling and McGeorge had righted the overturned glasses and Kunkel had returned his gaze straight front from the half-degree turn with which he had honored the occasion, Kermit said, "All! Yours, Aubie! Unconditionally!" He parted the bottles again and left them out there in the right- and left-field corners, indicating thereby (and with portentous nods of eyes and spaghetti-shag of brow) the scarcely-to-be-credited expanse and largesse and nearly obscene prodigality of the legacy he was, in fee simple, bestowing, and roared, "Well, goddamn it, haven't you got anything to say?"

Aubrey had something, but didn't say it, his love for his father sober overcoming his detestation of his father's theatrics when drunk; and he smiled brightly out of a sudden thought, and said, "Oh yes. Thank you. The men will be very thankful indeed."

Kermit blinked. "The *men!* What men, for Christ's sake? What the hell *men?*"

"Why the members of the camel corps. Now I can buy all of them new bugles."

"Bugles! Jesus Christ! Have you lost your mind?"

"Not at all. Best buglers in the world are Berbers."

Kermit stared. "What did you say? Camel flops? What the hell is the matter with you, Aubie? Don't you understand? I'm giving you *all! All!*" Kermit brought the bottles back together with a smashing clank, but both held together.

"No, no," Aubrey said, getting to his feet. "Camel corps. The First Albigensian Eremetical Arab and Camel Corps Marching and Humping Society. Which reminds me. Thanks to your generosity, I can now also buy all of those nice deserving camels new humps."

And, feeling another smile, or worse, coming on, he nodded goodnight to Kermit, Kunkel, and McGeorge, strode to his room, found that he no longer felt prompted to laugh, and got immediately to his knees. And prayed for all those taken in madness, in whole or in part, himself not excluded, and prayed for purity, and for Julie's salvation, and, last and most fervently, for the alleviation of Arnie's insanity.

Yet smiled when, as he got into bed, he heard Kermit roaring, "Kunkel, did you hear him? Did you *hear* him? Humps! Jesus Christ! Humps and bugles!" And fell asleep to the tune of an impromptu lullaby from the corridor as Kermit stumped up and down singing, "Oh, I was humping with a camel and my bugle in my teeth!" But by the time Aubrey was passing into sleep, Kermit had given over song in favor of rootlely-toots on his bangalorum, interspersed irregularly with corrosive blasts on the mobile battle horn, distressed howls from Sordini, triumphant belches (that, Kermit averred before and after, would have stripped a lesser man of his tonsils), and at least four trips to the front door to fire double-barreled .50-caliber salvos at what Kermit claimed was a whooping crane that kept crapping down the chimney and putting the fire out. "And I wouldn't mind so much," Kermit roared, as he went clumping and cackling with laughter past Aubrey's door after one of these sorties, "if the son of a bitch didn't have to beller 'Whoops!' every time he does it!"

452

# · THIRTY-SEVEN ·

AUBREY came awake to a sound like the bark of a fox. It was repeated several times before he got his eyes open, and repeated several more times after he had blinked his eyes into accommodation with the bright light in his room and saw Arnie, not three feet away, bending over him, yelping.

"Arnie, in the name of God! Go to bed!"

"Bed! Jesus Christ! I've been in bed! It's four o'clock in the morning, and high time all good eremites were out on their knees praying for St. Michael the Archangel to smite devils across the ass with his broadsword as they prowl about the earth seeking the ruin of souls." Arnie grinned as he came out of his rhetorical flight, and frowned immediately as he put on denunciation. "Where is Sordini, you goddamned dognaper? You stole him, didn't you? You spirited him away!"

"Arnie, Arnie," Aubrey said, not looking at his brother. "Please leave me alone. I haven't seen Sordini, and I don't give a damn if I never see him again, and I sure as hell did not nap him! Now, will you get out? Out!"

"Aubie, babe," Arnie said quietly, his voice thin and sinister. "That dog may not mean much to you, but he means more to me, just now, than you do. Do I make myself quite clear?"

453

"I didn't steal him or spirit him, Arnie. Have you looked in the bathroom?"

"Do you deny that he's been in your room time and time again, and that you've encouraged him to lie down and to sleep here, and that you've even fed him in here?"

Aubrey opened his eyes and took a good look at Arnie. Things were closing in around Arnie's pupils until now they were as small as beads in a small rosary; nearly as small as they had been the day Arnie had been dragged away from the seminary. And Aubrey decided to take caution into his mouth and leave it there until Sordini had been either located or forgotten. "I don't deny anything, Arnie. I just say that I haven't seen him."

"Hah! You admit you stole him from me, then?"

"No, I don't."

"He slept outside your door last night!"

"Can I help that? What can I do?"

"You can return him to me."

"All right, Arnie. I return him. Formally. He's yours."

"Dog spelled backwards is God. No man should attempt to steal either a man's dog or his God. Right?"

"Absolutely right."

"Is your God *my* God?"

"Well, that depends, Arnie. If you come back to the Church . . ."

"I'll come back to the Church! When I have reformed it to suit me!"

"Well, then, your God will be my God."

"But—ah, but! Until that time there can be no compromise! When, in fact, my God is your God, *then* my dog will also be your dog! But not until!"

"Of course, Arnie."

"I mean, I feel that this is merely fair."

"I quite agree."

"I don't say that you can't pat him from time to time. After all, I'm not a beast."

"I appreciate it, Arnie."

"I'd hoped you would."

"Arnie, now that we've settled this matter between us, I wonder if I could persuade you to turn off the light."

"Of course! Indeed. Why not, now that we're speaking as gentleman to gentleman?"

And Arnie went immediately to the light switch, turned off the lights, closed the door—from the inside, to Aubrey's dismay—and came back, with the three-legged stool in hand, set it close to the bed, sat down upon it, and produced his flute from the hip pocket of his red-and-black-checked hunting pants. "We will now begin the celebration," Arnie said portentously, his voice out of one of Kermit's B movies, "of the twenty-fifth anniversary of the *Führer's* appearance in Nüremberg in September of 1934. Yes. We start this celebration some months ahead of time so that it will attain a fitting solemnity by the time those very sacred anniversary days have come round to mark precisely the quarter-century."

Aubrey groaned and closed his eyes as Arnie went into a soulful, lingering rendition of *Deutschland über Alles* on his flute. And Aubrey was preparing himself for several hours of this—and wondering why in the name of God his brother hadn't taken up a sensible and pleasant-sounding instrument, and one he couldn't carry around with him, like maybe the pipe organ—when Arnie stopped, let the echoes die away, and said with unction, "That was for the *Führer*, the fink." Aubrey opened his eyes and looked at Arnie, but in the near darkness Arnie's expression was hidden, and he was already off into a slow, singsong, nonstop recitation about one night in Nüremberg, so that Aubrey was left to wonder for a time how the *Führer* had gone from hero to fink since Arnie's last sojourn in Nazi Germany.

And Arnie was talking about how he wandered clear of the city and went up a dirt road skirting a huge meadow—the Zeppelin Wiese —and, remaining concealed behind a row of short trees, approached a campfire, one of hundreds lighting the night sky above the great field, and saw that there were perhaps twenty men gathered around the fire, many of them polishing what appeared at first to be broadblade battle axes. He stared at these, watching them glint balefully in the firelight, until one of the men held his blade high over his head to inspect it and Arnie could see that it was a shovel. These men, Arnie explained, were members of Hitler's Labor Service Corps, the *Arbeitsdienst*, and there were fifty thousand of them camped outside of Nüremberg that night. Now they were singing, and they sang *Lili Marlene* and *Erika* and others, and he was suddenly seeing them all as corpses—trim, muscled, proud, but dead—and he watched sadly as, fitfully seen through a thin early mist that now began to drift in over the grass, they began to stand, one by one, until all were standing and all singing with intense emotion *Deutschland über Alles*.

And their voices, clean and powerful, charged the night and filled it with the pathetic noise of the idealistic young who, in their purity and innocence and stupidity, always fought the wars of the world.

"And I tell you, Aubie, I didn't know then how the war would turn out, but I knew that every one of those young men would die, as young men have always died, led forth by some ringing myth or other, a myth promising to turn putrid death into a shining, ever-lasting life, promising with terrible cynicism something better—as though there could be something better—than sweet, glistening youth. And just as I turned to go back to the hotel, one of the men began to wave his shovel and chop the air with it in time to the music. He was younger than the others, and shirtless and muscled and tanned, and I looked at him closely and saw that it was Arnie. And I watched him, swinging his shovel like a battle ax, and I whispered to him and tried to make him hear. I said, Arnie, listen to me. Do you remember when you were Siegfried that night in the opera house in New York and how I warned you that a guy named Hagen would spear you in the back? And he did, and they played your funeral march. Very pretty music it was, and sadder than death, and they carried you up a hill in the moonlight and into a mist. And I asked you then and I ask you now how in hell they ever taught you that anything was really worth dying for. Can you answer me that one? I guess you can't, Arnie. They've told you you'll live forever, and you believe them. You believe them. You've got it conned by rote. The word. The song. The shovel. That's what you're singing, Arnie, the song of the shovel. Look at the shovel, Arnie. Don't you see? Don't you see that they've got you hypnotized, and that you will go, full of courage and the hot sap of your body, from this field to another field, where you will be struck down by another spear, on another gentle evening, and your blood will leak out through the hole onto the ground and you'll put your hand over the hole and cry because you'll know it's your only life leaking out, and you'll smell the night flowers and hear the night birds and you'll remember how it was to see sunlight in a girl's hair, and you'll know at last that there is nothing, or nearly nothing, worth dying young for? You'll learn that they actually only gave you that shovel, Arnie, so that you could dig your own grave. And in the end, because you have been so well trained, you will take that shiny shovel and do just that, and tumble into it, and die with tears in your eyes for all the life you didn't get to live. Ah, Arnie, sleep tonight, and when you wake up in the morning, breathe the air and lie in the sun and smell the fat earth and listen to the wind in the trees and kiss a girl and make love to her if you can, because it's September already and the leaves are beginning to tremble and turn, and your shovel is as bright as your eyes but won't always be, and your time to die is coming, Arnie, and, out in the pit, if you listen, you can hear them playing your song."

There was a silence, and Aubrey lay dumb in it, searching for something to say, or, rather, seeking to pick a first thing out of the thousand things he wanted to say, but unable to do it, unable to get beyond the near panic induced in him by the sound of utter despair in Arnie's voice.

Arnie was on his feet, backing toward the door, before he started to speak again. "The last clear view I had of him, as the mist swirled up between us, his head was thrown back and he was laughing wildly and holding his shovel at arm's length in front of him with both hands. And there was a thin jet of blood shooting from his throat, arching and splattering against the shovel's blade. And then a funny thing happened. Suddenly I became Arnie, laughing and bleeding, and I looked out beyond the campfire and there was Aubrey, standing behind some short trees, watching me. And I thought, well, that's how it's always been, all our lives. Aubrey watching me from afar. But I did wish, just that once, that he'd come to me. But he didn't, and the mist kept rising up between us, and then he was gone. And I watched for a long time, hoping the mist would clear, and finally it did, just a little, but Aubrey was gone. There was another man standing there who looked like Aubrey. But Aubrey was gone. I called to him, called him Aubrey, to make sure, but he didn't answer. And I lay down then to die and I cried for a while because I wouldn't see Aubrey again, couldn't tell him that I was sorry, and that I loved him very much, and—and just tell him goodbye and thank him for being good to me. And then the *Führer* came, with his beard all full of blood from where he'd bit me, and reminded me about digging my grave, and I dug it, and got in, and covered myself with the cold dirt. And then I died."

He was standing by the door and began to grope behind him for the doorknob, then hesitated. "Oh, I almost forgot." He walked to the bed, his eyes down, his face shadowed and grimly composed, and placed the flute at Aubrey's feet. "I'd like you to hang onto Touchhole for me while I'm gone."

"But—where are you going?"

457

"Oh, I thought I'd take a walk. Or maybe a ride in the jeep."

"Where?"

"Just around. Up and down."

"Out on the mountain?"

"Why would I go out on the mountain? Nobody's going hunting today. Kermit's foot is too bad. He's been groaning all night." Arnie was backing away toward the door, and now opened it and stood silhouetted in the light from the corridor, his handsome face very young and kind, his eyes wistful and sorrow-wide and straining as if he intended to see Aubrey very clearly and take his seeing with him. "I didn't mean what I said about Sordini. I think he likes you better anyway." And he held there in the doorway for another second, peering, until Aubrey could see tears in his eyes. Then he said, "Goodbye, Aubie. I'll—I'll see you later. And thanks." And he closed the door softly.

Aubrey was immobile for one terrified second—his mouth open to speak, the beat of his heart sounding in his pillowed ear like cannonading—before he leaped from the bed toward his clothes, shouting, "My God! Arnie! Wait!"

He was at the door, boots in hand, when he heard the jeep engine turn over. He turned first toward the mess hall, thinking to get a rifle, but then, hearing the jeep roar into motion, pulled on the boots and ran for the front door, shouting to Kunkel and Kermit and beating on their doors as he passed. He saw the jeep when he was about halfway up the duckboards. Arnie had it in a tight turn, circling back toward the front of the Lodge from where Kunkel had parked it on the lee side, and it came on jouncing and throwing mud, the engine screeching high as one or the other of the four driving tires bounced free of traction, the open trailer bucking along behind, and the headlights waving their beams drunkenly in the cold gray light of the reluctant dawn; and still came on as Aubrey cleared the duckboards and stood in the middle of the trail, waving his arms, expecting Arnie to stop, looking right at Arnie, looking at him as the jeep bore down on him, and stood there until it was clear that Arnie had no intention of stopping. He leaped to one side just as Arnie turned hard over in the other direction, and landed on his right knee and elbow and felt the rear wheel of the trailer brush his leg as it went by and went bounding after the jeep off the trail and out onto the tundra toward the mountain. And there was only an instant to de-

458

cide, with the jeep slowed in the soft-sponge tundra and Arnie work-ing the gears, and Aubrey took the instant when it was perhaps half over, jumped to his feet and sprinted for the trailer. Arnie was already shifting to high and gathering speed when Aubrey arrived at the tail-gate and seized it with both hands. He ran several steps, gathered himself, jumped, and took the top of the tailgate in the pit of the stomach; but hung there precariously balanced, the jouncing getting nothing but worse as Arnie got back onto the trail and gunned the jeep, and was able to pull himself into the body of the trailer only because one of the tarpaulin ropes had come free and fell across his arms. He lay flat on his back, a tie rope in each hand, his feet wedged against the tailgate, and tried to cushion himself against the leaps and falls of the trailer, but took a severe pounding as Arnie roared up the road at maximum possible speed, taking bumps, stream beds, snowbanks, willow scrub, hillocks, rocks, and all else—including the edge of a small lake he happened to skid into—as if he had not noticed them. So that they were on the mountain in some-thing like half the normal driving time, and Arnie drove higher than Kunkel had ever done, taking a different route along a wind-packed ridge of snow that dropped away fifty feet along its leading edge, a route that brought them out on a broad terrace of softer snow just below the boulders south of B-17 Ridge. Arnie skidded to a stop in the middle of this terrace and was out of the jeep and running, rifle in hand, away and up toward the boulders before Aubrey could straighten up and raise a shout; and went on running as Aubrey con-tinued to shout, and climbed rapidly toward the big gray rocks perched above him, never turning, his head bare, his rain suit loose and billowing about him in the soft, mournful wind.

Aubrey sat down to lace his boots, glancing up from time to time to keep Arnie in sight, and was in the middle of the second boot when he saw another movement off to the right of Arnie and studied it, and made out one bear and then another directly behind the first, moving slowly, cautiously, up from B-17 Ridge toward the boulders.

And at first he couldn't believe his eyes, couldn't believe that two bears could appear just there, as if by appointment, as if they knew that Arnie had plans for them. But he looked from the boulders to the bears and back again, and the color was the same but the bears moved and the rocks didn't, and he called himself a jackass and vaulted from the trailer, shouting and running as he struck, and was halfway across the terrace before he realized that Arnie couldn't hear him and wouldn't pay any attention if he could and that Arnie and the bears would be face to face before he could get anywhere near the top of the ridge. He ran back to the jeep and leaned on the horn with one hand while he rummaged through the glove compartment for some kind of weapon, and was about to settle for a small hatchet attached to the fire wall when, in the well under the right front seat, he found a flare pistol and three flares. The pistol was new and partially wrapped in a sheet of instructions and he had to consult these before he could determine how the pistol was loaded. He put the extra flares in his zipper pocket, tooted the horn a final time, and, pistol in one hand and hatchet in the other, took off running for the mountain.

When it began to happen, he was standing in Arnie's tracks among the first of the boulders, puffing heavily, vastly relieved to see Arnie about two hundred fifty feet to his left, close to the bottom of the draw where they had seen Big Ditmo. Arnie was half turned toward Aubrey, binoculars to his eyes, watching the two bears Aubrey had seen, now traveling almost straight up Frosty, tending back whence they had come, proceeding independently and far apart now and moving very quickly by means of a rhythm of bounds and plunges as they broke through the crust of the high snow at every step, their color somewhere between dirty gray and ocher, their flight somehow aristocratic and indignant, suggesting to Aubrey two society dames fleeing a lawn party which had just been invaded by a skunk.

Aubrey started toward Arnie without hailing him, deciding to get as close as he could before making his presence known, and walked in Arnie's tracks, feeling somewhat ridiculous now with his hatchet and flare gun, and was within a hundred feet of Arnie—who still was holding the binoculars high on the mountain—when he saw a third bear, a huge great-headed Big Ditmo of a bear, on the far side of Arnie, lumbering in, head lolling, at a sort of happy-idiot, pigeon-toed trot, directly for Arnie's back.

And though he started forward at once, the horror of inevitability had already taken him at the belly, and though he opened his mouth and worked it toward a scream, there was a strong instinct in him that wanted no sound, no voice; that wanted nothing but a place to hide. But he did scream and run toward Arnie, staggering in the deep snow, driving his ankles through the thick crust as he failed to

460

lift his feet clear of it (and, strangely, hearing that sound of the snow crust tearing against his boots—a sound like a saw in wet wood—and hearing it as from a great distance), and saw Arnie turned, looking at him, the binoculars just slightly lowered, his rifle still slung at his right shoulder, and saw the bear coming eagerly on, and felt the flare pistol cold in his hand, and yet could believe none of it. And the bear was almost upon him as Arnie whirled around to face it, and had time to swing the rifle once as a club before the bear, bounding like a cat on a ball, smashed him to the ground. And Aubrey went in at a dead run from fifty feet out, screaming, terrified to see the great size of the beast, to see Arnie small beneath it, to see the huge spile-nailed claws raking Arnie's shoulders and back and trying to turn him belly up, but most terrified to see, as he closed ground and started to slow, the massive, brutish, shag-patched face of the bear, lifted by then from the vicinity of Arnie's neck and pointed right at Aubrey: one ear up, the other down, snuffling and watering from its black-nubbed nostrils (stuck like a punctured rubber ball at the end of its fat gray cylinder of a snout), its mouth slack open and full of broken yellow teeth, its brown-yellow eyes running and tired and only mildly fierce, all of it gathering into an almost human expression of surprise as Aubrey lifted the gun and fired the first flare straight into that expression at a range of six feet.

The bear screamed once and went backing away, growling, chuffing, tossing its head and slapping at its face with its forepaws, not in full retreat but back from Arnie. Enough so that Aubrey could go to him, reloading as he did; and touched Arnie's back and felt the blood there and shook him and shouted at him until Arnie peeked up and came out of his huddle to his knees and scrambled backward to his feet, watching the bear, crying, "It's Big Ditmo! What did you do to him?" And snatching his rifle out of Aubrey's reach as Aubrey grabbed for it, saying, "No! It's Big Ditmo! I didn't gut-shoot him! He's all right! Look! I don't have to kill him! Or anybody!"

Now Big Ditmo had gone to his hind legs and stood monstrously over them, roaring down from twelve feet in the air, still flailing at his burns with his forepaws, yet looking at them, measuring them, his eyes raw and red and wild-wide with pain. Aubrey heard himself screaming at Arnie to shoot and tried again to take the rifle but didn't dare move his eyes from Big Ditmo and tried then to push Arnie back and to pull him back but couldn't do either, with Arnie screaming, "What'd you do to him? Goddamn you, why didn't you stay away! Everything would have been all right! He loves me! He's pure! He doesn't want to kill me! He saw you!" And there were perhaps three seconds of this as they faced Big Ditmo across twenty feet of snow, three seconds of the certainty for Aubrey that he would die here because he couldn't leave his brother to die alone, three seconds that ended as Arnie started to walk toward the bear and Aubrey shoved him aside so that he fell to one knee, and, light as a kitten, Big Ditmo came to all fours and charged.

Aubrey had time to set his rear foot and extend his arm. And, stock-still, with the flare pistol steady, wrist and elbow locked, he watched the bear come on, and, in the first of the two seconds it took Big Ditmo to reach him, drew his bead on the right eye and— actually, incredibly—thought, When the beast charges, drop it on him. He fired directly into the eye, saw Big Ditmo's head snap away to the left toward Arnie, then took the bear's right shoulder and the full force of its charge in the center of his chest.

He came up spitting snow, gasping for breath, with a scorching pain in his chest. Everything behind his breastbone was raw and abrasive, but the bone itself felt whole. He wondered if a lung might have been collapsed, and checked his collarbones and his legs, and sat up, and only then did he hear Arnie screaming.

Fifteen feet away Big Ditmo was astraddle Arnie, head bent and tearing savagely, huge forepaws raking and clouting, roars high-pitched and like a scream and intermitted as he socked his jaws again and again into the middle of Arnie's body. Blood was everywhere. Aubrey cried out and got to his feet, still gasping, struggling to stand, and started for Big Ditmo. And for an instant, when he looked at his hands and saw that he had neither flare pistol nor ax, all of whatever constitutes courage left him, left him hanging in air like a wet rope, so that he had no idea how he could be moving at all, moving toward the bear as he was doing; had no idea what he would do when he got there except probably cause Big Ditmo to kill him, and yet heard Arnie's screams and was vaguely conscious of his own, and knew that he could do nothing but what he was doing.

He came at the bear from behind, thinking to kick it or leap on its back, but saw the rifle before he did either. It was lying near Arnie's head. Arnie had his arms and hands up over his face and his knees drawn high, but his clothes and flesh were shredded and pulpy

462

with blood. Aubrey eased up alongside Big Ditmo, smelling him—the rotten, dead-dog, penetrating stench of him—and brushed against him and reached the rifle out of a snow rut full of blood just as the bear tossed his head high and turned toward Aubrey, full around to present his left eye, his right eye being now little more than a burned-out socket. Aubrey stepped away, hoping the bear would leave Arnie, but Big Ditmo stood fast, his one eye hauled tight, blood dripping from his jowls. The rifle was broken just behind the trigger guard but was hanging together. Aubrey bent it as straight as he could, heard it crack but set it to his shoulder anyway, walked in until his range was perhaps ten feet, tried to aim at the bear's good eye, held on it for a split second but then felt the stock break nearly free, and fired quickly as Big Ditmo started a barking roar and lunged toward him.

And again went spinning and slipping backwards, with a lacerating pain in his right arm and hand, but fell this time uphill; came abruptly up against a high bank of snow and lay there at a forty-five-degree-angle tilt on his back, and watched Big Ditmo as he, having apparently come to a sudden stop at the noise of the rifle, now took two or three fast trotting steps toward him, then veered off and went by within a yard of Aubrey's feet—barrel-gaited, rolling, wall-eyed, and making small chastened whimpering noises as he went—and disappeared into the head of the draw and went crashing and sounding far up and into it, leaving great red paw prints in the snow behind him.

And leaving Aubrey, who had been poised for death, staring and petrified behind him. And leaving Arnie pitifully clutched and inert in the bloodied snow behind him.

Aubrey went to his brother and knelt beside him. And Arnie was torn beyond belief, and Aubrey was over him for some time before he realized that Arnie was still screaming.

Aubrey stood up and stripped himself nude to his boots. Then he put his rubber rain suit back on, tore his underclothes into strips, and bent again to Arnie. He was bleeding from deep claw gashes on his scalp and face and neck and from chewing wounds all across his shoulders and chest and from lesser claw and teeth wounds from his throat to his right thigh and knee, where the flesh was shredded to the bone. Aubrey could see most of these before he forced Arnie, as gently as he could, to his back and stretched out his legs. He didn't look down at the lower body at first but gave his attention to a large flap of Arnie's left shoulder hanging loose from the bone. He stripped the clothing away from it, wiped one clear stream of blood out of the wound along the white bone, and folded the flap back into place. And tapped it, and saw the blood ooze out around the three sides of the flap, and looked at the blood on his numb right hand, and screamed once so loudly that Arnie stopped screaming. Then he forced his eyes down, slowly down, toward the middle of Arnie's body. Another flap of flesh had been torn downward exposing half of the rib cage on the left side; there was a shallow hole about the size of an apple in the pit of the stomach; the right thigh appeared to be laid open its whole length very nearly to the bone; and the left leg appeared devoid of calf muscle.

And Aubrey saw all of this as from a high remote place, a remove toward which he had been tending since that first sight of Arnie writhing beneath the bear. And began to pray that Arnie would lose consciousness; yet saw that Arnie's eyes were now wide open and that he was regarding Aubrey solemnly and moving his lips to speak, but producing no words or sound, producing only more blood. Aubrey wiped his lips and face and tried to tell him he'd be all right, but Arnie's eyes registered nothing, and Aubrey saw that he was conscious of nothing but his pain.

He wrapped the worst of the wounds, except the one in the stomach which was deep enough but not bleeding badly, and swathed Arnie in what clothing remained, and, slipping his arms beneath him, lifted him from the ground. Arnie screamed once, grabbed at Aubrey's arm, went limp, and appeared to die.

Aubrey felt his knees flutter and begin to go. He called to Arnie, looked down at the lolling head in the crook of his elbow, and almost set him down again. But told himself there was nothing to be done even if Arnie were dead; then told himself that Arnie was not dead but would be if his weak-kneed brother didn't get him out of there. And he ordered himself to walk, to find the guts to walk. And found them, and started off the mountain.

And it seemed to him that he fell most of the way, or slid on his back, holding Arnie high in front of him, cradled, his arms locked in a desperate numb embrace. But however it was done, he moved down and down, feeling blood running into his rain suit and down his legs, seeing it pump from the hole in the stomach and drip and run away into the snow, seeing Arnie's head bobbing limp and apparently lifeless and his blood-heavy hair floating out on the rising wind, hearing himself saying the Act of Contrition a thousand times in Arnie's stead, and hearing himself crying and seeing most of what little he saw through a wash of tears. Yet walked, and fell, and got up again, and tobogganed on his back down most of the final slope, and delivered Arnie at last into the trailer and wrapped him in the tarpaulin and took off his boots and put his socks over Arnie's hands and arms, slipped his boots back on and climbed into the jeep. He drove the long hard ridge slowly at first, picked up speed as he thought of the loss of blood and of Arnie's not feeling the bumps now anyway, and was doing thirty miles an hour by the time he had to make the turn onto the main trail; and went into six or seven long skids trying it, and missed the turn but kept going out onto a tundra-tufted snowfield, fought the wheel and brought the jeep out straight and running. He looked back at Arnie and saw that he was still on his back against one side of the trailer, still out cold. Then looked ahead again and saw Kunkel trotting on the trail some fifty feet to his right, and put the jeep into a slow arc and stopped it at Kunkel's side.

Kunkel went immediately to Arnie, threw his parka over him while Aubrey made an unheeded report as to what had happened, then helped Aubrey into the trailer and told him to cradle Arnie in his arms. They had not gone another half mile before Kunkel came to an easy stop, and there was Kermit at the side of the trailer, staring and cursing softly and finally roaring as he took Arnie in his arms, demanding to know how it had happened and why Aubrey hadn't shot the bear, but not waiting for answers from Kunkel (Aubrey kneeling dumbly in the trailer, not speaking, not really seeing or hearing), Aubrey not hearing, refusing to hear until Kermit started to limp away toward the jeep saying quietly, intensely, "Oh God, spare this one, this son of my heart."

That Aubrey heard.

Kunkel held Arnie while Kermit got into the back of the jeep, then handed Arnie in to him, and came back to Aubrey explaining about the heater in the jeep and asked Aubrey to help him unhitch the trailer so that they could make better time to the airstrip. Aubrey got down but Kunkel already had the trailer free and dropped the tongue in the soft mud and straightened slowly to look at Aubrey, the Indian's hunter eyes great with the first sorrow Aubrey had ever seen in them.

"You must not blame your father. Or yourself," Kunkel said. Then he gripped him by the muscle of one arm—the numb arm. "You aren't hurt?"

"No." The question surprised him and he said no again.

"I am very sorry about Arnie." Kunkel turned quickly and started away. "Come."

"Kunkel?" The Indian turned, his broad, flat face dreading the question before it was asked. "Is he dead?"

Kunkel hesitated, glanced toward Kermit, then nodded once and held his eyes vacant of focus. Then Kermit was roaring and asking did they goddamn it want Arnie to bleed to death, and Aubrey told Kunkel to go ahead, told him that he didn't want to go, and Kunkel protested as Kermit went on roaring, then reached into the jeep and handed Aubrey out Kermit's double rifle and musette bag. Then Aubrey was alone in the road, watching Kermit, framed as he was in the rear window, holding Arnie's corpse; watching Kermit and the blood coming in long streaming drops from under the tailboard of the jeep and falling to the ground below; watching Kermit and saying goodbye to Arnie until his view of both was obscured by the rooster tail of mud rising five feet in the air behind the speeding jeep.

# THE THIRD PART

## · THIRTY-EIGHT ·

HE SAT on the tongue of the trailer, the rifle standing between his knees, and listened to the wind; the wind coming on, blowing southwest, down from Pavlov and Pavlov Sister, down from Veniaminof and Aniakchak, down from Chiginagak and Katmai, down smoky and full of ash from all the black-mouthed mountains, down six hundred miles of peninsula bringing black clouds and a cold rain and the taste of bad fires burning. And he knew that Arnie was dead, yet kept telling himself that Kunkel could have been wrong, and started all the prayers he knew but lost them all, lost them in pain and in guilt, and lost them, too, some of them, in the simple brilliant knowing that Big Ditmo was out there, high above in the wind, watching until he should come.

He was up there on his mountain, wounded and perhaps dying, but certainly not dead; and watching, not with any particular malice, or any malice at all, but watching as he had always watched, as he had been watching that morning, guarding himself against the enemies who were always there, and against those who had traveled four thousand miles to make him an enemy, to chase and wound him year after year, to seek him out even though he, as if he were aware that his size and courage would always affront men, had retreated as far as possible from men, had withdrawn out and ever out, until his back was to the sea, until the western land had found its end, until there

469

was only that final mountain in that final fire-gutted wilderness; and there he had taken his stand. He could not have done more to avoid the sight of men, yet they had sought him out, had found him with their bullets and their flares. And he had found and killed one of them. And if he did not know any of these things as a human would know them, yet he remembered; remembered not least the taste of flesh and blood and man's sweet quick, and now in his pain would know where to taste them again.

He refused to allow himself to think that he might not go up. Nor did he permit himself to analyze why he would. Or, if he did, his analysis was extremely brief. Kermit would go up. Arnie would go up. End of analysis. Both would go out and up and search out Big Ditmo and kill him if he, Aubrey, had been mauled. Kermit would certainly do it if Aubrey didn't. So Big Ditmo was doomed in any case, and who better than a hermit-elect to give a hermit-suffering into the blessed company of the hermits-triumphant?

But, having so determined, he still sat there in the rain, nearly numb with cold in his rubber suit and aware of it, but even more numb with the thought of Arnie dead. He had not permitted his grief; had held it at the gate of consciousness, where it crouched, a black presence patient against its certain coming hour. But, even unadmitted, it had its effect. And so did another presence, his fear, bright and winking under his heart, or under his soul; but down there somewhere moving around and agitating and throwing baleful light in dark places. It lit up his mortal sin most energetically; a surgical light on an operable cancer. If he should die unclean, he would go to hell. God's mercy failed before God's justice. By the rules of the game, he would go straight to hell.

Then the trick here, he thought, is not to get killed. Come in, one time, intrepidity . . . and all you other nostrums. And may God have mercy after all.

He unbent to his feet painfully. Where he wasn't bruised, he was stiff. The cold was wet and incisive, though he guessed that the temperature was not much below freezing. The day was now extremely dark, the clouds thick but disparate, roiling about like pieces of doom trying to fit the last day together.

His right arm was senseless from the armpit to the end of his index-finger. But he was able to bend it slightly at the elbow, and, with shooting pains that he felt proper to a trigger finger, was able to curl the forefinger into an incipient hook. Then he lifted the gun with his left hand, set it against his right shoulder, ordered the right arm to rise, which it very slowly did, and managed to grasp the thing and aim it. The process was painful but possible, and that was all he needed to know. He had no doubt that, faced with Big Ditmo, the eye of the hunter would restore the arm of the hunter instanter to pristine efficiency. Then, having checked the rifle to make sure where the safety was on and where it was off, he dug into the musette bag for the bullets; and these were beyond anything seen before or since —enormous .500/465 480-grain missiles—and he loaded the rifle thinking of the pain, his own and Big Ditmo's, potential in those two bullets.

He moved out knee-stiff and stumping, his feet and boots all one, fused skin to skin and sole to sole. Yet not quite dead, for after the first two or three steps little messages began to arrive tingling at nerve endings around his shinbones. He gave them welcome and asked if the feet or the boots had come alive.

He hadn't looked directly at the trailer but something hanging over the tailgate drew a backward glance when he was already past it. And there was Kunkel's big green military parka, the hood filling with the wind and flopping upside down, halfway to the ground and straining toward it, like a ghost, he thought, anxious for its grave. And he suddenly was acutely aware of how cold he was, with the rain suit wet with water and blood inside and out and the wind and his motion pressing it to him here and there and here again in recurrent dank shocks; so cold that he felt no warmth in his belly or his crotch, and marveled that his breath should steam even slightly white in front of him. Cold, God yes, but he hesitated, staring at the trailer; yet finally went to it, eyes down.

The parka was only a little less bloody than his rain suit, the gray fleece lining matted with it, but he knew it would be a hell of a lot warmer once his body had heated it up. He took off the top of his rain suit, peeled it off like adhesive from a wound, and was appalled to see that his entire front torso was running with blood, and watched as the cold raindrops struck and caused it to run faster, and groaned aloud and wiped at it with his rain suit and seized the parka and put it on without hesitation; and found himself as he pulled the drawstrings of the hood tight at his chin, saying the prayers he used to say when donning his Titan habit.

471

One of his wool socks had come out of the trailer with the parka. He took a fast look over the tailgate to see if the other sock was within but the trailer was empty. He found a Swiss army knife in Kermit's musette bag and used it to cut the sock in two at the ankle. Then he sat down again on the trailer tongue, rubbed his hands together until he could deal with his bootlaces—one boot was still only half laced, but he raced grimly past the memory of what had interrupted him— and opened the boots and took his feet out and wiped them from blood-red to white, and then rubbed them from white into an agonized pinkness, ankleted one, wrapped the other, and strapped them back in their boots.

A pair of gloves found in the parka pockets completed his dress, and he gave it final arrangement by tucking the skirt of the parka into his rain pants and, after inspecting it to see which side was the bloodiest, by putting the top of the rain suit on over the parka, inside out. And, feeling bulked and battened, and already much warmer, and with pains of rudely awakened nerves reporting in from all of his parts, he took up his bag and his gun and set out for the mountain.

The wind was strong at his back until he came to the turnoff to the ridge trail, and then the wind grew abruptly to a blast, smashing at him as he stepped out onto the first hard snow, forcing him sideways, making him drive his stinging feet down hard to get and hold a footing, pushing at him as it came on and sucking at him as it went away. His progress slowed; he rested frequently, his back to the wind, finding that he was able to lean on it comfortably. During one of these rests, there was a sudden douse of rain, a total air-filling downpour, the emptying of a cloud on his head. It went on for a minute or two and left him on his knees, head down, searching for air. When it was over, he raised his head cautiously, started to rise, then stayed on his knees and said a prayer that he would survive the day and its deaths, whether by clawing, freezing, volcanic explosion, or drowning. He got up and went on, the wind down to a softness now, but still ominous, blowing generally cold but containing now and again a pocket of warm, ash-fat, brimstoned air—much warmer than he had felt before and much more redolent of cremated rock. It snowed for a few minutes, and he nodded at it, and was about to ask where the fog was—it being the only climatic abomination that hadn't yet visited him except hailstones—when the first finger of it came sinuously in over a round-top foothill far down to his left; a forefinger, as it turned out, riding point for a great gray hand of fog that groped in from the direction of Littlejohn Lagoon over the southern saddle of the mountain, and palmed the lowlands and laid a fast, ragged thumb diagonally across the eastern face. It closed on Aubrey just as he got to the place where Arnie had turned the jeep south along the high ridge. The tire tracks were fresh and it was the short way to Big Ditmo's draw, but he thought of the sheer drop off one side of the new trail, and saw his visibility dwindling from the fog, and took the old trail to the north. As he started, he was in a neat little eye in the fog bank, a tiny, gray-china cup, and he almost stopped, feeling strangely protected and close and warm, and he looked up quickly as if he expected to see there something familiar; but saw the black clouds still gathering their doom around the rim of his cup, and called himself a jackass and went on climbing, up and up between the tire ruts in the hard snow, up to the wall of fog and through it into near darkness.

He reckoned the time at no later than nine, figuring that it couldn't have been much after six when he and Arnie had arrived on the mountain, but it might as well have been night. The visibility was about seventy-five feet in all directions, and he kept all directions visible much of the time, doing a complete turnabout every ten paces or so, pausing sometimes for some seconds to see if a certain rock or snow mound would not turn into a bear under diligent scrutiny. The wind was gone now and the silence entire except for the crunch and squeal of the snow underfoot. And he began to understand what the man had meant when he spoke of praying constantly.

He cleared the fog as he started up the face of B-17 Ridge and there was a wadded cigarette package in the footpath just as he came out of the dark. He picked it up, pocketed it, grateful for anything that made that nowhere look like part of the somewhere; oddly cheered to find any evidence of other men in that particular wetwashed corner of the earth. And he climbed to B-17 Ridge and moved upon it tensely, suddenly aware that he was truly in bear country, not apprehensive that he was being watched, but *knowing* that he was being watched, and he went as a skirmisher, rifle up and ready to fire. By the time he was at the beginning of the boulders, he was not so much afraid as he was immobilized very nearly by his fear

—having to throw one leg out in front of him as if he intended to shuck it off before he could manage to take a step, and then starting at the sound of his foot crunching in the snow—and not so much wary as he was spastic, putting his five or six senses through such a frantic combined maneuver that he knew they would never really be the same again, would never again assume their separate roles or independence of one another. But he also felt impatient, and abruptly his mood was to get the damned business over with as quickly as possible. And his mood was also touched with the fatalistic, macabre humor of the condemned. To die was the worst that could happen to him, if God showed mercy. And he felt almost chipper for a time; even when he came to the still red and rutted place where Arnie had done half of his dying. He stood over it and after saying a prayer for Arnie's recovery said aloud, "Well, Arnie, here I am. I with you. And if you've gone on to where you can actually hear me, I may even join you there, shortly. Only one thing. If he starts eating a hole in my belly, kindly strike him with a thunderbolt."

Then he turned at once and started up the draw, up toward the divided patch of willow scrub. And he checked the safety on his rifle every fourth step, walking with an awareness of each step, his eyes dancing as if to fast music, his heart close and high and familiar in its protest, only his hands quiet and perhaps even sure on the hard and cold metal of the rifle, his finger on the trigger light and calm, young but intimate with the power beneath it—intimate not by experience, but by utter reliance upon the power that the finger could release. And he thought, Come on, Mr. Ditmo. I know you're up there. Let's both face to our business this morning, and get it forever over.

And, suddenly, there was Mr. Ditmo, down on his belly in the snow, facing Aubrey, apparently asleep, or perhaps dead, a seepage of blood on the snow all around him and in front of him, his right eye great with swelling or a blister, the eye itself either sunken into the socket or fallen out of it, his whole face scorched and blackened. Yet there appeared to be no blood issuing from face or head, and Aubrey thought that it might just be what had dripped off the bear after his saturation in Arnie's blood. He approached with rifle butt to shoulder, with elaborately planned movements and placements of each foot, with two inspections within the first ten feet of the breech of his rifle to make sure two of his very best and most healthy-looking

474

bullets were engaged, laughing at himself a bit as he went, yet genuinely terrified at the sight of the bear in his gore, and assuring himself with nods of his head that his world might just come to an artery-spurting end any old time Big Ditmo decided to wake up and trundle down the draw.

He advanced in this manner steadily, up the sluicelike tile-smooth draw, to within sixty feet of the great brown hulk before it stirred. And that first stirring of Big Ditmo in that funeral moment left no other stirring to be desired. Without a sound, he rose, coming up and forward as if on hinges, rocked a bit front and back, side to side, staggered slightly in the first two or three quick-trot steps, then, all four legs located, came right on in, head high and tossing.

For Aubrey there was a long second of hesitation, a visiting of pure awe at the sight of the beast, and such a beast, with its charge in progress down that snow-packed chute-the-chute against Aubrey Strycker, personally. And his thought was: Here I am, and my move. And maybe my last. Both barrels, real and earnest.

And although it seemed to him he moved very slowly, too slowly, he got the rifle up, rammed it painfully hard into his shoulder, found Big Ditmo's skull top at a range of about thirty-five feet, held and raised to the bear's shoulder, held again and fired. And staggered back into a half turn as the cordite flame—a flat sheet of fire that seemed a yard long or longer—startled him and as the rifle's recoil clubbed his whole right side into new pain, but forced his shoulder back and the rifle barrel down from where it had kicked high toward the mountaintop, found the bear at perhaps twelve feet and put his second shot right in on top of the first. Then let the rifle fall away, turned to run up the side of the draw, and had taken two or three steps when he was hit at the left hip and plucked clean out of his lateral motion, and was aware at the last that he was in the air moving at high velocity.

He was conscious next of an entire silence and the smell of wet dogs. He was flat on his back, head downhill. His neck had gone utterly stiff. He lay there still and cold, remembering he'd once been told by a doctor that his neck had apparently been injured at birth and would break easily. But he finally did turn his head and found it and his neck in fair condition and uncracked. Next he considered a warm flowing all up one leg, perhaps some old blood flowing out of his boot, but rather more of it than seemed possible. He told himself he might have a compound fracture with the skin punctured. If so, it hadn't begun to hurt yet. He lifted himself to one elbow and, expecting to see nothing above him but his legs—having assumed that the bear had run him down and gone on as he had done with Kermit—was astounded to see Big Ditmo spread-eagled belly down in the draw, his bushel-size head a yard beyond Aubrey's toes. His good eye was wide open and staring; and it was a good eye now, and benignly glazed, and Aubrey thought of the good eye of Tony Maroni.

There was blood coming from Big Ditmo's head and mouth, slowly now, but a pool of it had formed at his snout and out of this pool a small stream was running down a long heel mark into the torn right leg of Aubrey's rain suit. He lifted the leg, found it whole, set it alongside the other—discovering as he did so that Big Ditmo's last charge had done his left hip an injury that creaked as well as pained—spun himself slowly around and climbed to his feet.

He checked his physical person over, flexed his left arm, found he could not lift his right arm (and had a new bruise on his collarbone, apparently from the recoil of the rifle), did one shallow knee bend, and then rechecked himself, very nearly unable to believe that he was unfractured. He breathed deeply several times. No new pain had been added to the old one in his chest, but the fulsome inhalations of the smell of Big Ditmo limited his satisfaction at this discovery.

He walked upwind of the bear, stepping around the carcass delicately, inspecting it as he went; only beginning then to comprehend what he had chanced and what an incredible extravagance of good luck or divine grace had attended the outcome. He noted that his two shots had entered within five inches of each other just behind the right shoulder, apparently striking something vital, but gave himself no credit for skill. At the range offered, he could scarcely have missed. He remembered thinking, just before he fired, that he would not try the skull because the bullets might bounce off. Now he remembered the boom of the gun, and the leap of it (how he had to bring it down quickly after firing the first barrel), and the sheet of pure flame each bullet had taken with it three or four feet out of the barrel, and decided that the gun might safely be used to kill express trains if Kermit should ever find that necessary.

He found the rifle half buried in the snow at a point just below the place he had departed the ground. He knocked the barrels free of snow. The gun seemed undamaged. He paced off the distance he had flown through the air and made it eleven paces, give or take a pace. After striking him, Big Ditmo had gone into a sort of staggering wallow-step, had fallen once, gotten up, and had fallen the second time and died with his left paw stretched toward Aubrey. There were still shreds of flesh and cloth in both front claws and in the snarl of yellow fangs along the sides of the mouth. And he thought about Arnie's remark to Kermit in New York: "What the hell'd you expect him to do . . . erect a finking pavilion and serve lemonade?" And he gave Big Ditmo, his remains, to know that he was sorry, and gave him goodbye as one hermit to another, and was about to go when he saw another wound, a third and freshly made bullet hole, just at the base of the skull on the left side; obviously his earlier shot with Arnie's broken rifle. He hadn't missed, and it gave him some undefined comfort to know that his last shots had merely saved the bear from a slow death—that the first shot, fired in self-defense, was the fatal shot.

He turned then and hobbled down to the musette bag, which had somehow gotten thrown ten feet farther than he had, dug two more bullets out of it, reloaded the rifle, and hung the musette bag by its strap over his left shoulder. He tried aiming the gun but his right arm was numb beyond function. Then he just stood there for a time, thinking of the long road back, wondering idly if a limp in each leg might not properly be called a blimp, and saying finally, in an exhausted sighing whisper, "Lord, Lord, send me no more bears this day. The effects of original sin are upon me, and I am no match for any more of Your animals." And he went down the draw thanking God that it was over, but came out of the draw, in sight of that ruddled gash in the side of the snow-white mountain, and knew that nothing was over, that the grief of it had only begun.

And turned away to white, untracked snow, and, heading straight down east, carrying his grief more painfully than he carried his body, he walked off Big Ditmo's mountain.

477

# · THIRTY-NINE ·

HE EXPLAINED IT ALL to Julie and McGeorge as best he could, but made a bad job of it, too exhausted to be coherent, too deep in his own shock to deal adequately with words or descriptions. They asked him if Arnie had died and he said he wasn't sure. But they knew. And Julie didn't cry but whimpered, and McGeorge didn't whimper but cried; and they helped him out of his clothes and washed him off and wrapped him in a blanket and rubbed him with liniments and bandaged his bruises and filled him with soup and set him in front of the fire. And then sat and stared at him until he could stand it no longer, until, murmuring excuses, he escaped to his room, tore the tags off some new clothes, dressed himself, got some extra boots from Arnie's room, and went out on the duckboards and stood there, eyes and mind closed, through the noon hour. When McGeorge called him for lunch, he went in reluctantly, amazed that it was only one o'clock, and sat with them, again in silence, until the fish grew cold. No one ate. Aubrey sat bowed, his hands clasped and moving in an arc slowly up and down between the tabletop and his forehead, fingers touching each gently in turn, as if that flesh and that wood had things to communicate to each other—and kept this up until he was staring at the brightly polished board and seeing deeply into it, and suddenly sat up, snatched his arms back folded

478

against his chest, having seen, in the baleful gleam of the tabletop, out of its thick deeps, Arnie's eyes, dead and startled-wide, gazing up at him. He looked away to Julie seated across from him, composed, her lips pressed together grimly, her breathing scarcely discernible, her eyes moving upon him in sympathy and in sadness, and he wondered at all her golden, auburn beauty, and remembered her, calmly and without guilt, as he had last seen her that mystic afternoon: naked and lying on her back, her knees slightly pulled up, her hair tumbling upon and flowing over her rose-white breasts, her huge green eyes savagely alive, and her lips full of blood yet amused and murmuring that she loved him—a vision of all that was woman, indelible, lucid down to the last clinging shadow, one of a thousand images of her that would be with him as long as he lived—and he could not imagine that she would ever grow old, could not imagine her body or her face changed by age in any particular, could not believe that she would ever die. And he looked at McGeorge, yellow in the light from the lamps, yellow with lamplight, age, and dust, a dust still gathering upon him, his eyes like old window glass, yellow with the light and with the years and with much service in a place of prolonged winter, and Aubrey could easily imagine McGeorge already dead, could see death in his desiccated glance, yet knew that the old man was younger than were his ancient yellow eyes.

Then McGeorge began to talk to himself, reciting from Job a passage that might have been written as a fit description of Big Ditmo. Or of Kermit. And Aubrey listened, grieving. ". . . the glory of his nostrils is terrible. He paweth in the valley and rejoiceth in his strength. He goeth on to meet the armed men. He mocketh at fear, and is not affrighted; neither turneth he back from the sword. The quiver rattleth against him, the glittering spear and the shield. He swalloweth the ground with fierceness and rage, neither believeth he that it is the sound of the trumpet. He saith among the trumpets, Ha, ha; and he smelleth the battle afar off, the thunder of the captains, and the shouting. . . ."

Here Aubrey got quickly to his feet and walked from the room, choosing not to acknowledge Julie's protest, and went out to the end of the duckboards again and stood there in the early bleak afternoon with the snow like floating feathers around him, and the wind down, and the sky coldly lighted at the center of its gray dome: a somber high redness, a curiously mottled, wine-dark afternoon not much different from night, so that he almost expected a passage of owls, a settling of owls upon the joist of the lowering day, a gripping of horny claws around the blood-black roof pole of the world, and a single derisive hoot as an instruction to men upon the meaning of death. And, waiting for the hoot, he heard the sound of the jeep's engine far down the storm toward the bay, and thought it hoot enough, and waited again, hearing the motor come on, finding in it as right a symbol of Arnie's death as any offering of owls.

Kermit was alone and angry. He came out of the jeep bounding and strode purposefully toward Aubrey as if he intended to strike him. Yet he held his face down until it appeared that he would walk right on by, then stopped at Aubrey's shoulder, lifted his eyes for one bare, tortured, accusatory blink, and said, "He's dead." Then he brushed past his son and stumped heavily down the duckboards and into the Lodge.

And there was new grief in the certainty of Arnie's death, a moment when the owls did come and did hoot and left behind them the echo and the sound of black wings rushing; but this was replaced by a greater pain, a no that never got said, when he understood that Kermit was blaming him, blaming him so utterly and bitterly that he would, or could, say no more than he had, that he had given Aubrey no smallest sign of affection, had made it clear that no explanation would be heard or believed, had rendered his judgment with two words and a single blink of his eyes.

But Aubrey had to hold himself from going to his father and trying to explain anyway. He turned and paced away toward the jeep, and around it, ordering himself to walk, ordering himself to accept the fact that Kermit did not want, would not listen to, an explanation of what had happened. And asking himself, too, why he should bother to explain, or why he should have to. If Kermit was so ready to blame him, was so ready to conclude that Aubrey had caused Arnie's death by some deficiency of conduct or courage, the knife was home and twisted. Nothing Kermit could say could remove that knife. It was there, after long hovering, and there it would stay. He realized then that he had possibly invited, even dared, Kermit to put that knife up, or to put it in, by not offering an explanation earlier. He had not even protested that it wasn't his fault, although he remembered that, as Kermit had carried Arnie away to the jeep, it had occurred to him to do so. A reflex perhaps, born of old blame, and he had resisted it, had told himself that it should not be necessary for him to say it. He had not even explained to Julie, out of the same pride. So that he had invited the judgments of everyone concerned, and he took small comfort in the thought that, thus far, only Kermit's had been a condemnation. And he was wondering if he could really have it right, if he might not have misread Kermit's grief as accusation, and asking himself if it were possible that Kermit could believe him such a coward that he could stand by and watch Arnie die, when Kermit suddenly was standing before him and put the issue beyond doubt.

"Take this," Kermit said, thrusting a rifle toward Aubrey. He had his own big double rifle and a bottle of whisky in his free hand. He spoke roughly, and his eye was hard and glowering. Aubrey took the rifle and the musette bag that went with it. "You and I are going up on the mountain. And we are going to stay on the mountain until we kill that goddamned bear."

"But, Kermit, I . . ."

"Shut up and get in the jeep!"

"I already *killed* the bear!"

Kermit had half turned toward the jeep, but now turned back, his eyes spitting anger. "Don't tell *me* you killed it! I already got that goddamned lie from McGeorge!"

"I didn't tell McGeorge."

"Well, if you *did* kill the bear, why in hell *didn't* you tell him?"

"I—I don't know . . ."

"You don't *know?* Well, *I* know! Because you're a goddamned clever little sneak, that's why! You take my gun, fire a few shots and then come back and say nothing and expect everybody to believe that you were a big brave boy and too modest to brag about shooting the bear! Well, you can expect a goddamned half-witted old man like McGeorge to fall for it, but not me! You haven't got guts enough, by God, to save your own brother from being mauled! Let alone go out and take on that bear by yourself!"

"Did Arnie tell you that?"

"Tell me *what?*"

"That I didn't save him?"

"No, he didn't tell me that! Arnie was a man!"

Aubrey was taken at the middle as if by a broadsword and wished that Kermit had delivered the sword instead of the words; for, just then, there was not love, human or divine, he wanted more than Kermit's; even in his anger he could not pretend that Kermit's love wasn't greater to him than any other possible love, proffered or promised. And he tried to put this into his eyes, but received back from Kermit, in those first few following instants, all of the contempt, scorn, bitterness, indignation, and disappointment that befitted a father whose beloved son had died because of the cowardice of the merely tolerated.

Aubrey snapped himself away and walked to the jeep, shouting, "All right! I'll show you the corpse!"

Kermit turned from the door, one leg already into the jeep. "Don't try to bluff me, you sanctimonious liar! Get in! I've already seen a corpse!"

They rode out to the mountain in silence. Kermit gave half of his attention to the road and the other half to his bottle, and he had put most of the fifth inside him by the time they came to a stop, yet appeared to be entirely sober as he turned to get his rifle and bag from the back and said, "You are about to become a man. I'm taking this along just to protect myself. When that bear—that corpse—charges, you do the shooting."

Aubrey was already out of the jeep and had a second or two to prepare his response as he walked around to the other side to confront Kermit. And his response was not calculated to keep the tentative peace. The evidence was within two thousand yards, and he intended to show it to Kermit if he had to drag him to it unconscious. "You mean," he said, walking up close to Kermit as his father closed his door, "that you think I won't run away, as I did when the bear mauled Arnie?"

Kermit put his full spinning weight into a backhand slap to the side of Aubrey's head that, as the follow-through force of it pushed him more than hurt him, sent Aubrey staggering sideways until he fell to his knees in the snow. And Kermit came at once to stand over him, finger pointed between his eyes, looking right down at him, not with any immediate or following compunction but with righteousness, as if, by God, it was Aubrey's own doing and what was he going to do about it. And Kermit held the finger, quivering, for a time before he shouted, "Don't you dare speak to me like that again or, by Christ, I'll slap your gutless face all around this goddamned mountain!"

Aubrey had had all he could take. He lifted easily backwards from his knees to his feet, and let that dark face and that dark voice take immediate snarling possession. "You want to fight? Is that it?"

Kermit stared, and his face appeared to split into three parts, cut lividly and neatly across the eyes and the mouth, and he roared unintelligibly, out of pure astonishment and rage, threw his rifle aside into the snow and brought his hands up, not in fists but palms huge and flat, and held them wide on either side of Aubrey's head, as if he were about to pronounce a *Dominus vobiscum*. And he roared, "Goddamn you! I'll give you the licking of your life! You impudent pup!"

Aubrey moved quickly back two steps, lifting his boots carefully free of the snow, removed his gloves, threw his rifle off one shoulder and musette bag off the other, now hearing his other voice, his dark face and voice, talking loud and clear. "All right! If you're ready to start slapping me around this mountain, go right to it! But you'd better be ready to go all around the mountain! Because if you hit me again, I'll clean your goddamned bearded clock!"

Aubrey held himself openhanded and ready. And there was a moment when he knew that Kermit would hit him, when he was thinking, That's all, then. I'll kill my father on this mountain because I can't let him know the horror of having killed me. Kermit was looking at him as if he had never seen him before. And Aubrey, still dreadfully ready, was wondering if he ought to strike first, when Kermit took a step toward him, right fist doubled and poised a yard off his hip, but hesitated, then held himself and stared at Aubrey for an intensely surprised and resentful moment, and went on staring and brought his eyes back into close focus, and forced his lips together until his mouth was closed. Then forced his lips apart again in a hard, muttering smile. "Turn the other cheek. Forbear meekly as a lamb. Forgive those who kick you in the crosstrees." He smiled thus, grimly, then let his right arm drop and its hand fall out of fist, his smile fall into a sarcastic slack. "All right. Maybe you *do* have guts enough to have killed that bear. Show me."

He took up his gun, and Aubrey took up his, and Aubrey led him up the mountain, and showed him.

Kermit stood at the snout of the great dead carcass, bending now to inspect it at peering distance, reaching now to touch it at the wounds, putting a finger forth again and again to poke into and rim the socket of the gone right eye, and went on standing there, and bending there, never quite straightening to his former height, until Aubrey thought he would cry out in sympathy for the exquisite and ramified pain that his father was enduring. And just as he was lifting one foot from the snow to start toward Kermit, his father turned to him, turned a face to him that he had never seen nor expected to see, a face refined in agony to the last decibel of human tolerance; and came to him, and wrapped his arms around him, and said, "Oh God, God, God! I'm sorry, Aubie, I'm sorry!"

And there was something in Aubrey that refused to give over its stiffness, something deep and permanently frozen, but it was nothing that Kermit noticed, and nothing that Aubrey brought to his notice. He only said, "I shot him with your rifle, Kermit."

After that, when Kermit, in the grip of a frightening humility—abject, whispering, guilt-haunted—questioned him for the how and the why, Aubrey led him down to the bottom of the draw, to where the patch of Arnie's blood was only then being transformed from bright red to dull pink in the blithe and drifting snow, and started from the beginning, and ran this way and that and demonstrated and shouted and aimed and took his several positions in his very footprints, and ended the first act leaning where he had leaned to fire the broken rifle; and went right into the second act, afraid to pause for fear he would catch humility from Kermit, and led his father up the draw and pointed to where he had placed his feet as he had come up the draw, his barely visible footprints unbelievably close together like plaster casts in approach-avoidance, and then ran ahead sixty feet past the carcass to point out where the bear had been lying before his charge, and then ran back down to Kermit and pointed out where he had taken his stand and waited the bear as he charged and fired, and then had taken to the side of the draw, and where the bear had struck him and knocked him into the air.

When Aubrey was done, father and son stood there in the fetid wind and spoke to one another in chastened and, for Aubrey, sweet respect. Kermit's pride was inordinate. He walked around and around the bear chortling and cursing; and ran his fingers in at the bullet holes Aubrey had put in him; and ran his fingers over the grooves left by the two richocheted bullets that Kermit had glanced off the bear's skull, just behind the left ear, two years before; and announced several times that there was no doubt that this was indeed

Big Ditmo; and posed in Aubrey's tracks and announced that he couldn't have placed the shots better himself; and inspected Aubrey's two shoulder shots and said that there weren't four inches between them; and measured Big Ditmo's skull with a six-inch cigar, and announced that it was better than thirteen inches in width and better than nineteen inches in length, both of which measurements he announced triumphantly, saying that the brown bear competition only took a twenty-seven inch skull and that Big Ditmo might go thirty-four and win the Boone and Crockett competition for the year; and, finally, although decrying the fact, good-humoredly, that Aubrey's goddamned heroics with the Very pistol had ruined the head for trophy purposes (the bear's head, upon close and calm inspection, being burned badly over half of its surface), still he would like to bring it back for official measurement at Harry Swank's, and took out his big hunting knife and went about severing the huge head from the carcass, and did sever it after Aubrey had found the hatchet to break the skull from the spine and hooked his belt by the prong of the buckle into one of Big Ditmo's ears, and gave his rifle to Aubrey, and dragged the head, gushing blood, with great effort and stiff-chinned pride, down the draw behind him. He paused only once, and that was over Arnie's blood. He stood hunch-shouldered, his parka hood back, his fur hat off and in one hand, and spoke a little monologue about his feelings in the matter. Aubrey listened without objection, it being clear that Kermit in no way blamed him for Arnie's death. Kermit blamed God, wondered what God, looking down, could approve the irony of it all; that Arnie should have died because, in his mental muddle, he had confused Kermit's worst enemy with Kermit himself. What good God could have so cunningly arranged this ending for a quarter of a century of his son's life? What good God? His outrage brought tears to his eyes, yet he said that he was not crying his own tears, but Arnie's; not feeling his own pain, but Arnie's; not indulging his own sense of loss, but protesting Arnie's own very real and brutal loss of years; that all that had survived Arnie was their mutual love for him, son and brother, and that they must never lose it, must preserve it inviolate, not taint it by any association with divine mercy or any of that goddamned claptrap, not prostitute it to any aspiration or faith in a higher love or benevolence. For Kermit there could be no higher love. The thought of it was an indignity, just as was the thought that there could be in man any guilt equal or comparable to the monstrous pain God inflicted upon the best of men. Under the burden of such a gratuitous, overpowering, pain-condemned guilt, there could be no dignity, and therefore Kermit rejected that guilt; just as he rejected the love, the divine love, that that guilt was supposed to imply.

And, delivered in Kermit's sonorous, powerful, lyrical voice, this sermon of sorts, this declaration of the lordship and sovereignty and defiance of man, was so persuasive that Aubrey offered no protest or amendment, and simply turned, in humble deference to a greater human force than his own, and, after a last look at the very lightly pink scuffling of snow where Arnie had passed his final moments, followed Kermit and the gory head of Big Ditmo down the mountain.

On the way back, they stopped for the trailer and hooked it to the jeep without looking back at its blood-spattered interior. Then Kermit suddenly seemed to be drunk, and asked Aubrey to drive, and sat and talked the rest of the way into the Lodge; said that Arnie had been pronounced dead shortly after noon; that he had tried to call Rexfordia but had been unable to get through, and had sent her a message explaining it all as best he could; and that Kunkel was flying on Reeve Aleutian to Anchorage with the body. And he turned once, just before they got to the Lodge, looked back at the head of Big Ditmo, nodded, and said yes, that certainly did *look* like Big Ditmo, and it almost certainly *was* Big Ditmo, but that he really wouldn't feel right about it until, after a few months, Kunkel made his report about whether or not Big Ditmo had been seen on the mountain. And Aubrey almost protested this, but let it go, seeing that it seemed to make a great deal of difference to Kermit, seeing that Kermit's inspection of this new dead head was very nearly rueful.

Aubrey packed nothing but his journal, his books, his toothbrush, his razor, what he wore on his back, and Touchhole, Arnie's flute. He helped Julie with her bags, and found that she was entirely and genuinely subdued, and received his help with a simple gratitude that affected him almost as much as had any of her earlier self-assertiveness. He found himself wholly in command of his voice and intentions in her presence. Virtue was his and Julie seemed to see that it was, and she made no attempt to slight it, or to pretend, as usual, that it had a relativity in inverse proportion to his reaction to her physical facts. He was conscious of her physically but for the first time he was able to place his metaphysicals against her physicals and find not only that he was still in control but that she, willingly and not falsely, was granting his ascendancy. He was even able to conquer an initial feeling of loss—that she actually was ready, if he could trust appearances, to relinquish him to his own willpower—and he emerged from her room, bags in hand, feeling that he had trussed up and locked one hundred and twenty pounds of temptation that would not threaten him again.

When they were ready to leave, McGeorge came to him with a tremor in his voice and hands, his heart in his eyes, and said, "Young reverent, I'm an old man. And I'm not likely to see you in this life again, less Mr. Kermit asks me to go to Africa with him, which ain't likely at all. So I just want to say, the Lord Lazarene watch over . . ."

"McGeorge, would you give me your blessing?"

McGeorge stood in front of him, his left eye stunned into a fixed open position, tears filling it as rapidly as they did the right, yet his jaw and face held sternly, prophetically high and certain. And he said, "I'd be proud to give you my blessing."

And Aubrey then saw the old man arrayed at last in the grandeur and nobility and holiness that was truly his, and, knowing that Kermit and Julie were looking on from the jeep, knelt down on the duckboards and bowed his head, and felt McGeorge's hands come to rest softly in his hair, and was not really surprised to hear a voice young and full of power and as clear as clarion trumpets prevail over the storm and pronounce the benediction like a battle cry.

"May the sweet Lord Lazarene watch over you, and walk with you all of your days, and gather you at last into His blessed arms, and give you peace."

Aubrey got to his feet slowly and took the old man's hands in both of his and looked into the rutted, tear-ridden face, and, feeling in those ancient fingers the whole sadness of the death of men, said, "I thank you, Reverend M'Naghten." Then he turned quickly and walked up to the jeep.

He glanced at Julie as he got in, half expecting to see her mock-eyed, but she said only, "That was very sweet of you."

He turned to watch McGeorge as they drove away, the old man standing at the top of the duckboards making small, pathetic gestures with his right hand until the mist moved in upon him and took him out of sight. And so shall he die, Aubrey thought. And so shall he die, and may the good Lord Lazarene gather him at last into His blessed arms and give him peace.

## · FORTY ·

THEY FLEW EAST into darkness with Kermit, clearly a far better pilot drunk than he was sober, talking the whole way about Arnie, and crying a little, and pretending to search out and add up all the ways in which he was personally responsible for Arnie's death. Aubrey made a dialogue of it when it seemed like the thing to do, but most of the time watched the peninsula go by, and the mainland and the night come on—watched the long gaunt shadows of night take the summits of the mountains, and watched ragged gray clouds move down those shadows on a mile-high wind, like skeletons chasing their bodies of light west to the far east—and thought about his own guilt, his own part in Arnie's despair. And he questioned all over again his motives for departing the Titans and, after departing them, insisting upon the Saharans. Did he really feel that strongly about the Sahara Desert? Couldn't he have chosen a thousand other places to hide out? Couldn't his real motive have been to make Arnie's defeat as specific as possible? And Julie? Not so much the first time, because he'd been taken by surprise and without opportunity for calculation, but the second time? Hadn't he known it would be virtually impossible for Arnie *not* to suspect that he and Julie had been in bed together that afternoon? Had he taken any precautions against falling asleep? Wasn't it due only to Julie's wakefulness that they hadn't been found in bed together by Arnie?

And so on, his self-interrogation exhaustive but not productive of conclusions. If he had stayed in the Titans, Arnie might not have felt his failure so acutely, might not have become so jealous of Kermit's affection. If he had knocked Julie down whenever she approached, Arnie might not have felt so challenged, or threatened by his brother, and might not have so radically regressed. But it was all "might," and who the hell knew, and the closest he could come to a conclusion was that his mortal sins certainly hadn't done the situation any good. He stared down into a few volcanoes as they became available and gave himself lectures on hellfire—sincere, imaginative lectures —and tried to get deeper into the problem, but, somehow, his mind would not function, would not make connections, would not allow the evidence before the court. The heart had its guilt but the mind had its rationalizations, and he let it all go at last and listened to Kermit argue with a man over King Salmon radio about his assigned altitude. Kermit wanted to go higher; the man said Kermit was high enough. The man did not know the half of it.

Yet Kermit made a perfect landing in Anchorage, on a glistening, Christmas-lit runway, and though he taxied somewhat erratically, narrowly avoiding a collision with a bright yellow pickup truck, brought them safely to port on the ramp. Julie had slept most of the way and seemed genuinely surprised to find they had made it. She talked all the way in to the hotel about a hot bath and getting dressed up for dinner, and invited both of them to join her in the dining room at nine. Kermit said he would be in the bar with Kunkel after he had checked with the undertaker. Aubrey said he'd try to make it but that he was going to go to church before anything else. Kermit, thinking that Aubrey had in mind only praying for Arnie, said piously that that was very thoughtful of Aubrey. Julie shook her head at him and said; "Step, be sure to tell the priest that I'm a good girl at heart. It's just that I'm a better girl at screwing." Kermit didn't think that was funny, Julie said who the hell asked him, and Aubrey looked out at Anchorage's streets and decided that it was one of the garden spots of the world.

The priest, caught at the shag end of a long day, looked, sounded, and moved tired, but came from the rectory to the church with good grace and appeared to brace himself under his stole, possibly sensing an ordeal; and proved to be a holy and honest confessor, almost passionately concerned with the qualification of facts, the nuances of motive. Aubrey, with the deliberation of one who has waited for his hour, laid the whole business out on the screen between them like pieces on a chessboard. He started with the day he left the novitiate and worked his way out. He confessed the old sins and the new in equal detail; having no trouble at all describing the sins with Julie, but floundering as he had done before in attempting to accuse himself (with historical footnotes) with reference to Arnie. And the priest, who had the habit of saying "Huh?" at the end of almost every sentence (which gave his utterance a curiously boyish and naïve inflection), found the strength to engage it all, and had the mind to comprehend it; and when Aubrey was done and had answered several questions, the priest delivered himself of an incisive and excoriating instruction. He dealt first with Julie, speaking rapidly but without anger, and made the penitent feel he had never understood chastity before, had had no idea of what it was he had surrendered, had had no least notion of how gravely he had retarded the likelihood of Julie's reformation. "You came to her an unknown quantity. Would her seminarian stepbrother be just like all the other men she had known, or would he be a saint, huh? She waited and she watched and perhaps she even hoped with all her heart—her secret heart where resides the purity that makes any woman beautiful—that you would be able to resist her. Sure, she had to try you, if she is the sort of girl you describe—I mean, if you haven't misjudged her, although I don't think you have, except in this particular—but she hoped, I feel certain, just as she hopes there is a God for her, too, and you failed her, you failed that secret hope, my son, and how can that damage ever really be repaired, huh? Only through the grace bought by the blood of Our Lord. You must pray for that grace for her, obtain it for her, and you must always remember that if, God willing, you persevere to the priesthood, every woman you will ever meet will be searching you, searching your eyes and your heart —as Mary Magdalen may well have searched the eyes and heart of Jesus—looking to see if you are a man of God or just a man, ready to tempt you—even the purest of women out of their simple, natural, forgivable vanity—some just to see if you will make a pass, others, like your stepsister, who will take a certain satisfaction in seducing you. Women are like that, my son. You should not forget, ever, for one minute, that they are all temptresses because it is their nature— God made them that way—temptresses from Eve on down, but, I tell you, women judge a man of God only by how chaste he is, *only* by this, and they can *smell* your unchastity, your weakness, like a stench to high heaven. It attracts some, it repels others, but it intrigues them *all*. Yet in the end it disgusts them all. Every woman in the world is looking for the man who can resist her advances, that holy man, and him will she trust, him will she allow to lead her to God. Whether you know it or not—whether *she* knows it yet or not —you are, you will be, a stench in the nostrils of your stepsister until that day you prove that you can resist her. . . ."

Having done with chastity, having reduced Aubrey to such an intensity of remorse that he could scarcely kneel upright, the priest slowed the tempo of his voice and emotion, and went to lesser matters for a time: to drunkenness, to the respect due one's father, to the importance of strictly regular daily prayer, and finished this interlude with a reprimand about receiving the blessings of Protestant ministers or the minister of any other persuasion or sect than the Roman Catholic.

And then, clearing his throat, pushing himself back straight in the box, bending his weather-beaten face down and forward to the screen so that he presented the dappled near-baldness of his skull to his listener, the priest spoke of "the heinous sin of pride," and of Aubrey's offenses to his brother. He asked Aubrey to understand that no priest would presume to judge definitively of such a complex matter, and one of such a tragic issue, from the confines of the confessional box. All of the facts—the contributing and, if any, mitigating circumstances—were simply not available to the priest. Still, he must judge as best he could; and his judgment was that Aubrey's pride, his attitude, his lack of compassion, his defensiveness, his resentment of his brother's pathetic attempts at domination, his fiercely competitive nature ("I can hear it in your tone, my son. I can feel it through this barrier in the timbre and texture of your voice. I, anyone, could discern it in your phrasing, your choice of words, your almost arrogant verbal facility, huh?")—all of these had, in the priest's opinion, amounted to what anybody might have taken, but Arnie very likely took, as a spirit of revenge. It was, therefore, the priest's judgment that Aubrey's attitude and actions had almost certainly contributed to his brother's desperation, to his eventual despair, and that Aubrey was not at all amiss in accusing himself except in so far as he did not accuse himself harshly enough. The only apparent mitigating circumstance was that Aubrey's self-ignorance had held him innocent of willful intention to do harm, though not innocent really but only because God, in His infinite mercy and contrary to the dispensations of even the civil law, did hold ignorance an excuse. That such self-ignorance should exist in a man who had just completed five years of religious life astounded the priest and would, he felt, astound any reasonable man. Certainly, admittedly, only Aubrey could know how and to what extent he might have sought revenge upon his brother, even hated his brother—and even Aubrey could only come to this knowledge after long meditation—and, therefore, only Aubrey, and God Himself, could properly estimate his guilt; only Aubrey could know among all men how his fornication with Julie might have served that hate. But, in the judgment of a provincial priest, who held himself neither saint nor seer nor even an adequate confessor—whose only qualification (he said) that might distinguish his judgment in this case was a history of his own failure to conquer petty pride—Aubrey should hold himself culpable as, at least, an efficient cause of his brother's death, of what was in effect ("in my best estimate—my deduction—from the facts you presented") his brother's suicide. The priest's absolution and penance were based upon, conditioned by, that conclusion; and he pronounced that absolution and assigned that penance (the Stations of the Cross every day for six months, for the intentions of the repose of Arnie's soul and the salvation of Julie's) in the most awesomely solemn and humble and Christlike manner, and begged Aubrey to remember, as he turned away, whispering in a suddenly abject and woebegone entreaty, that confessors were not inspired, were liable to error, were not psychiatrists, not psychologists, seldom saints, and that Aubrey must pray constantly for all priests without exception.

Aubrey nodded and staggered blindly from the box, and marched the Stations of the Cross as though hung on rubber ropes. He felt his way along, his mind all blank shock, his face a wet mask, his every motion jerky, automated. And he was done and out on the street in the twilit darkness, in the smell of the waking earth, before he understood that Arnie was dead, and that he, Aubrey, had killed him. And the thought stopped him short and brought him around staring into the dark street behind him, into a dark clapboard coffin of a street, and he stood there, his head harked high, listening, daring and dreading that voice to speak again, to lie again. He could feel the rain colding deep into the bones of his face. Which was the dream, this or the other? Had he not just been talking to Arnie that same morning? As he had always talked to him? As he had talked to him the night before he took his vows, and those nights before he took exams, and those thousand nights he had lain awake thinking of Africa, talking all those things over with Arnie, picturing him in his own cell in his own place, his own sweet sad place of confinement? He said aloud, "Dear Christ, no!" And two fat Indian girls swaddled in mackinaws came at him giggling and divided their paths around him and went off up the night chirping laughter. No! Two fat girls walk the streets, sounding their empty heads, flaunting the dumb life that fills them, while somewhere in this damned charnel city lies Arnie with no life in him at all. Again he said, "No!" And repeated it, and walked in a stunned half circle until his nose was against a lighted plate-glass storefront, and there was a small bald man inside staring out at him through steel-rimmed glasses. And life in *him!* Life in that scrobiculate little hairless wretch and no life in Arnie! How can that be? How can such an outrage occur? And he stared at the enemy, at the outrage, until the little man found something to do among his dry goods, yet kept a nervous, glassed-in, glinting eye on the crying man at the window, the wild man with the wild eye, talking to himself at the window.

And he felt the tears on his face with the rain, but continued to stare at the outrageous man within, and heard himself begin nearly to sob, and felt a thick, fat flowing within him, a bile-black pain, part agony, part anger, taking him at the gorge, choking him, welling full and hot out of some strange and dark and furious place far down in the secret snake-folds of his belly, an awful, ulcerous place not reached or tapped in memory, but burst now and bleeding in spurts and terrible flashings, flowing in sorrow and ebbing in an enraged grief that shook and racked him his entire length.

And he cried out; "What, what, what! Didn't I know? Didn't he die in my arms, and didn't I know? Did I think I had nothing to do with it? No guilt? Ah, dear sweet and stumbled Jesus Christ! I knew I murdered my brother! Why did I pretend he had suffered no change but good? That I would see him and hear him and touch him again?"

"Sir! Sir!" said the little man from his doorway, his narrow head in a narrow crack and his voice a piping like Arnie's flute. "Please don't pound on the glass!"

493

Aubrey was using the sides of his fists. His consciousness was made up of little islands, and on one of them the little man was seated, or rather the head of the little man, long and narrow and silver, in the shape of Arnie's flute. All the other islands were being inundated; the island of sweetness, the island of light, the island of sense of consequence, and even the island of grace. He had no idea what was happening to him, and made no effort to prevent it, made no effort until even that corner of his consciousness that normally stood by as observer had joined him in his protest of Arnie's death.

"Sir! I'll have to call the police!"

And in those words Aubrey suddenly found the reason why he had not yielded to this grief before. "That's it!" he cried, advancing on the little man. "Do you see? I couldn't let anything, not even grief for my brother, come between me and my confession! I had to be safe in a state of grace before I could acknowledge my guilt! Do you see, Mr. Touchhole? Do you see? I'm nothing but a goddamned hypocrite! Plenty of time for guilt after you're on the right side of God! Oh yes! Don't think about Arnie dead before you are shrived, because then you might be so appalled at the thought that you might not presume to ask to be shrived. Do you understand, Mr. Touchhole, what a miserable, safety-first, pride-ridden son of a bitch I am?"

"My name is not Mr. Touchhole," the little man said, closing the door to within an inch of his nose.

"Oh yes, it is! Yes!" Aubrey shouted, and he heard himself shouting, the observer not quite gone after all, and he called at himself, called himself back and asked what it was all about, and told himself that people had died before, that he had not betrayed Arnie, that this response, the extremity of it, was irrational, but washed all of that away with the single thought that he would hear Arnie's voice no more upon this earth. "You see?" he said to the little man, who was down to the very tip of his nose, and it quivering. "Do you understand that my only brother, my twin brother, my sweet and good and holy brother died, became dead, early this morning, in my arms, and only now—only now!"

The little man blinked and advanced a half inch of nose. "Oh, I see," he said, in B-flat major, using his larnyx for the first time. "I'm sorry to hear that."

And Aubrey stood there, heaving from the lungs, his eyes burning, biting at his lips, feeling himself coming back on a countertide, growing gradually aware of sidewalk, and storefront, and the face of the little man; so aware, so nearly self-conscious that he was able to modulate his voice. "I believe you are, Mr. Touchhole, I believe you are sorry. You're a good man and I'm sorry if I've frightened you."

"Oh, that's all right, son. You just get hold of yourself, is all. You haven't been drinking, have you?"

"No, no. I just—listen. I want to see my brother. Where is the funeral parlor? Where?"

"Well, well . . ." He hesitated. He examined Aubrey top to bottom and back again, then made his decision and backed into the store, pulling the door open after him. "Look, son. You'd better come in while I telephone and find out just where your brother is. Might be any one of three or four places. The hospital, the morgue. . . ."

And assuring Aubrey that he could be trusted not to call the police, he led him by the elbow to the back of the store, wrote down the information on a pad, then read it back to Aubrey before he started phoning. "That's right," Aubrey said. "Arnold Strycker. Died— Died—pronounced dead at Cold Bay this morning . . . Kunkel Cranch. . . ."

Aubrey was coming back now, seeing, hearing the little man, feeling as if he were recovering from a faint, or as he had felt upon returning to consciousness after being knocked out one afternoon when he and Arnie had made parachute jumps, using pillow cases, from the roof of the porte-cochere at Fort Milligan. Time was making a humming noise in his inner ears and he could almost control its return, could regulate its descent upon him. And he chose to retard it, and to let his tears go on running unwiped, to hold himself at a median level for fear he would lose it all and run back to the confessional.

The little man was saying, Yes, yes, and writing on his pad, then hanging up the receiver and turning new and eager eyes to Aubrey as he handed him the slip of paper. "Here you are, Mr. Strycker. Isn't your father . . . ?"

"Oh yes, yes, he is!" Aubrey cried, backing away quickly. "Oh yes, indeed, he is, my father is!" And went on backing with the little man coming on, all unction and oil and oddly genuine sympathy, and offering to call a cab, and to advance Aubrey some money if he needed it, until Aubrey ran into a rack of shooting coats, whirled off and leaped for the door and through it with a last and final and booming "Thank you!" And then was running on the broad wet sidewalk, running easily, the light somehow greater than before, the rain thinner and not nearly abundant enough on his tongue, the night lifting and midnight hours away. But he was running, snapping out the backs of his knees, riding the toes and front arches of his hunting boots, running toward Arnie, and Arnie waiting there, waiting there to take the baton for the Anchorage leg.

He stopped for directions once, presenting the slip of paper palm-flat in at the jowl of a lady cabdriver, seated in her front seat, picking at one ear. "Where?" he said.

She held the finger in her ear for a startled time, her blowzy eyes darting. Then, apparently without looking at the slip of paper, she took the finger from her ear and pointed across the street diagonally. "There!" she shrilled.

"Thank you! And good luck with the waxworks."

And it was there, and so was the man who did the sewing, expecting him, averring that he'd have recognized Aubrey anywhere as Arnie's twin brother, and leading Aubrey in, apologizing as he went, saying that he'd scarcely begun, that he'd be working all night to make the eight o'clock plane to Seattle, that he'd seen them come and he'd seen them clawed but that Arnie was the worst and what kind of an animal was that bear anyway, half of a lion? And this stitchman was old, older than his craft, his face rubescent and epispastically scarred, his voice a moan from a pox-stricken sail loft, his eyes like those of the needles through which no man might pass or be passed, and his body like coarse thread, wound and wound on no spine at all, so that he was a circlet without a spool, a fleshy cycle without a cylinder, a spinning without a spindle, and he seemed to unravel as he walked.

His voice warmed to death talk as they went deeper and deeper into the place, as the smell became more and more defeating. And the stitchman rattled on and on until Aubrey, gagging, could answer him no longer. And his eyes flashed on Aubrey with the true pride of the unsqueamish as, swiftly, he turned from closing a final door, plucked up nimbly the edges of a tabled and mounded sheet, and, deliberately but quickly, drew it down to the belly pit of all that remained of Arnie.

Aubrey went back from the sight like a spitting cat, drawing all the air his lungs could contain up and in through his open mouth in one horrified gasp. And he clawed for the doorknob behind him with one hand and covered his eyes almost at once with the other. But too late: for he had seen the gape-mouthed, slug-white, nail-hackled horror that was there—the canescent, dreadfully torn, naked trunk of his brother—all cross-stitched clumsily in blue like a cartographer's marks for an antic railroad all up and down a whited desert; had seen, too, the cold blue flaps of flesh as yet unsewed; had seen what looked like a wad of white fish-paper stuffed in the hole in the pit of the stomach; had seen, most horribly, Arnie's face, the head lolled toward him, the jaw ghastly slack, the teeth slightly bared in a grin of last, indescribable agony, and the near eye, the left eye, wide open and staring—a living, surprised, pleading eye, fixed upon Aubrey leperlike, asking only not to be loathed.

And heard then, in the silence—a silence that obtained only because Aubrey was unable to reverse the gasping intake of his breath and scream—was the stitchman, saying, "That's him, isn't it? That your brother?"

"No, no, no! You butcher!" Aubrey screeched, turned away now, releasing his swollen lungs, grappling with the doorknob with both hands, the valves of his heart sucking at and welcoming a sudden, engulfing tidal surge of that black blood that his will had so recently turned back. "You stinking, foul, bastard of a butcher! May God damn you to hell!"

And he wrenched open that door and left it banging and echoing behind him, and tore at the next door and the next of that carrion place, and went howling and cursing down its decayed corridors, and screamed piercingly when some hag, some decomposing, friable, grave-haired victim of zoothapsis, suddenly appeared in his way, grinning hideously. He charged her desperately, still shouting, and knocked her back into a wall, and felt that arm and shoulder which had brushed against her immediately die and grow rigid, but went on and out and out, and flew into the street, dancing for his life, too terrified and stark of lung to scream any more, and ran again, taking on the driving rain as an engine takes on water, and revived enough to begin to see his way, to remember and retrace the startled streets back to the hotel—other pedestrians turning at ten feet hearing the clump of him, and then at thirty and more feet (as he revived enough

497

to shout and howl Arnie's name again) hearing the anguished voice of him, and scattering before his onrush like seals to their rocks— and came down the last fifty yards and into the hotel lobby in full sprint, came up short in front of the newsstand against the immovable bulk of Kunkel, bounced away, stood speechless for a moment, then put all that remained between the bare survival and utter collapse of his lungs into one despairing howl of summation: "Kunkel, Kunkel, Jesus Christ! You took him to a goddamned taxidermist!"

# · FORTY-ONE ·

KUNKEL supported him into the bar and coaxed him into a double old-fashioned. The good red man also had an old-fashioned, and said nothing until he had ordered them both a second. Then he said, "The son of a bitch said he was an undertaker." He spoke quietly and Aubrey was vaguely cognizant that Kunkel was trying to comfort him, that the man was an undertaker and probably the best in town, but that Kunkel would be the last to offer this information if Aubrey chose to think him a taxidermist. And so they sat, side by side, silently putting their drinks to deep and warm rest, until they had each had four, until the piano player came on—a lady of respectable years and parts, in a gown rather too flashily spangled—and Kunkel, who could not abide pianos, excused himself, escorted Aubrey and his fifth drink to a table in the dining room, and left saying that he would see about that goddamned taxidermist.

Aubrey drank his fifth drink before Kunkel had done bowing formally at the cheekbones, and set about flagging down the waitress, using finally, as all other ruses failed, the waitress being highly defensive, both napkins and one corner of the tablecloth. He shouted his order as she came alongside.

The waitress glared at him. "Really, sir. There are more appropriate ways to attract my attention than white napkins flying all over."

499

"I'm sure that's true," Aubrey said. "But I've been trying for five minutes and I waved all I could locate. I'd have waved a scarlet letter if I could have found one."

"Look, sir!" she said nastily. "I know your father's a big shot and all that, but don't you think it's a little early for you to be getting so fresh?"

"Fresh? Fresh? My God! Don't you think it's a little late for you to be taking on airs of offended virtue?"

The waitress retreated, nether quarters atwitch. Aubrey shook his head. He was already drunk and knew it. But he certainly had not intended to be fresh. He had only intended to get another drink before any least necrotic cell in his present general numbness had begun to show signs of revival. The problem was that this waitress seemed to have more male friends in the dining room, singly seated, who apparently required lengthy whispered consultation, than might Jim Farley at a Roosevelt family gathering. She fairly shot about the room, propelled by pelvic thrust, but got nowhere near a discharge of her proper duties. What's needed here, Aubrey decided, is a nose cone on her intake, or a stabilizer on her afterburner, or maybe a gerrymander on her cherry picker. Any of those would do the job. Yes, indeed.

Then, he noticed, there was a very definite sound of cocked eyeballs off to his right. He held steady for a moment, then let the corners of his eyes point ever so slightly to starboard and got the picture in a single blip. At the next table was one of the waitress' most ardent and arch props. Not a very young man—Aubrey's guess was anywhere between twenty-five and forty—but a handsome, prepossessing, unwholesomely familiar-looking man, sitting alone, clacking his ice, and regarding Aubrey with the calmest, most unwavering, boldest stare since, he fancied, Lot's wife went saline. Aubrey looked about in the other direction to see if Julie or Kermit might not be approaching, then decided it was time, after his next drink, to get to his room, bolt the door, and draw upon room service. But he continued to observe the young man in glances and saw that he was impeccably attired in evening clothes, with black tie, black jacket, and a bristling of the best sort of glass studs. There were two incongruities, however. The young man was wearing a pair of black horn-rimmed glasses from which one lens (the left) was missing, and he appeared to be teething on the handle of a dark shepherd-staff walking stick held upright between his legs and braced against the edge of his table. Aubrey's drink arrived, swinging and slopping, just as he decided that the young man looked at least dangerous, if not immoral, and he swooped up the drink and started to quaff it off without benefit of tonsil interference, when the young man got to his feet, smiling affably, and started toward Aubrey's table.

And Aubrey was thinking, Ah, Christ, a duel, and here I sit with my breadsticks. Yet, young teether, don't tread on me, for, by God, tonight I am equal to all comers. And goers, too, for that matter. My brother lies yonder dead and cabineted with Dr. Yukon Caligari, and tonight I am living in and for that only brother. I have received his soul and his heart and his tongue, and have made them mine, and have added my very own labefactionally angelic refinements. And if you think, young Funk-Eye, that you have met with vitriol, violence, and vituperation heretofore, you are about to be slathered by a finking expert.

"I don't think you remember me, do you?" the young man said slowly, as if it caused him great effort to speak. He stood over Aubrey, his drink in one hand, his cane in the other, peering down half-glassedly over a thin smile.

"Well, of course I do!" Aubrey said with a certain loud, genial iciness, not moving, holding his eyes down as he swallowed at his drink. "You're Funk-Eye!"

"Heh, heh," said the young man. "I didn't think you'd remember my name."

"What, what? Of course I do, Funk-Eye! Let's see, now. Tell you where we met in a minute. That's right! The Cyclops Convention in East Islip!"

"The name's Morton . . ."

"That's right! Funk-Eye Morton!"

"*Peter* Morton. I think you've got me confused . . ."

"What's this, what's this?" Aubrey looked up at him challengingly. "You mean you're *not* Funk-Eye Morton?"

"No . . ."

"And you *don't* sell horn-rimmed monocles to one-eyed giants?"

"Listen," the young man said, the first traces of alarm troubling his gaze. "I'm Pete Morton, and I met . . ."

"Now *you* listen," Aubrey said sternly. "If you're not Funk-Eye Morton, and I can see now that you're certainly not Funk-Eye Morton, although there *is* a certain funky resemblance around the conjunctiva—I say, if you're *not* Funk-Eye Morton, I must demand that you cease going around representing yourself as Funk-Eye Morton! Good God, sir, have you no honor?"

"Well, this is just ridiculous," Pete Morton said, beginning to glance about, as were other diners, and to edge away from the table.

"Oh, indeed it is! Indeed! Going around with one windowlight missing from your bifocals trying to disguise yourself as Funk-Eye Morton! Shame, sir, shame! And I tell you, sir, that you'd better give over this masquerade before Funk-Eye himself hears of it! He'll have none of it, sir!"

"Is there some trouble here?" the waitress said, coming up to lean one hand on the table, snapping gum, hips, and eyes, all managing to imply clearly that if there was any trouble its origin in Aubrey was a foregone conclusion.

Aubrey contrived to appear happy to see her and hunched his shoulders forward and leaned to her confidentially and modulated his tone to a most reasonable, sincerely hesitant pitch. "Ah," he said, and batted his eyes at her. She stopped snapping immediately on all fronts, and bent to him, eyes wide and concerned, completely won over by his first syllable. And he thought, Arnie, babe, I'm going to make you look like an amateur before this evening's over. But easy, Aubie. She's measuring you for her launching pad right now. "Ah, yes. Yes, there is a bit of trouble here, Mrs. Prynne. You see, Mrs. Prynne, this gentleman here . . ."

"My name isn't Mrs. Prynne," she said, almost quietly, adjusting her yaw and pitch just slightly and beginning to reshield her eyes. "My name is . . ."

"That's what he did to *me!*" Pete Morton said.

"You're out of order, sir! Control yourself! Now, Mrs. Prynne, please! You just said that you're *not* Mrs. Prynne?" Aubrey gave her Arnie's best have-you-taken-leave-of-your-senses aspect.

"Look, *sir*, I don't know what's going on here, but my name is Selda . . ."

"You mean you're *not* Mrs. Hester Prynne, mistress to the good Reverend Arthur Dimmesdale, and mother of Pearl?"

Selda was now backing away. "You some kind of a brownie or something? Who's this Hester? What is it with him, Pete?"

Aubrey rose a foot off his leather and, not too loudly, shouted,

"Captain, captain, front, please! The dining room is full of imposters!"

By now the whole custom was alert and staring. Aubrey held his elevation for a moment, glaring about indignantly, then suddenly assumed a most benign smile and bestowed it, with a slight bow of the head, at each aghast face, and slowly subsided into his silo. And he sat there, smiling upon his ice cubes and thinking. Now, Arnie. Don't you dare tell me you could have done any better, or I'll cut you off without any protoplasm. Arnie's wild laughter, sounding out there sweetly, was seal enough. But now there was a consultation among Selda and Pete and, after much shooting of nervous lash and lid, Pete made bold to take three giant steps forward.

"I'm sorry," Pete said. "I mistook you for my friend Arnold Strycker."

And what followed seemed to Aubrey to proceed with great, time-defying rapidity, events rushing on and superseded by other events with magic swiftness, none of them apparently connected until it was too late to part cause and effect, none related—even upon mature reflection—but all working cumulatively for and against, in and around, over and under him, until he was receiving Arnie's signals very weakly (yet achieving Arnie's purposes and effects in all quarters), until he was as drunk with sensual image and the sound of his own voice (or whosever voice) as he was on bourbon, until it all ran together in a grand, smoky, ecstatic, laughing, crying, vuluptuous, and despairing continuum the particulars of which would patently have required a lifetime of withdrawn meditation to identify and interpret. Or longer than a lifetime.

There was Pete, who made physical exercise out of simple speech; his head in constant motion, his mouth working in and out of a compulsive pucker, his eyelids rising and falling like those of a sleepy-time doll; his sentences coming out of him with a strange slurring inflection, as if he were angry at words and the language, as if he were straining phrases through a mouthful of cockleburs, until it was a damned wonder to Aubrey that he could talk at all. All of this compounded into a felony upon the human face by the most appallingly intense repertoire of mugs, grimaces, stretchings, and mouthings Aubrey had ever encountered. And none of this explained until Pete, who talked constantly and in heat but let his light find its own way from under his bushel of teeth and lip, and who had an awful time getting past the first person singular pronoun, as if it were something to pause and suck over until the sweet marrow was extracted, and who had set his plumpish visage no more than two-and-a-half pug-septim lengths from Aubrey's, as if he thought that cheek-by-jowl were vis-à-vis, who, in short, had the mannerisms, bray, and jawbone of an ass, finally got it munched out of him that he was an early Method actor (the "early" had nothing to do with Alaska time, being some hours ahead of California time, he, upon inquiry, solemnly gave Aubrey to know), that he was even now garbed to play Mark Antony (having spent the afternoon rehearsing) in his little local theater group's modern-dress production of *Julius Caesar* (of which group he was organizer and director), that he had tried to meet Kermit the year before but had gone to Arnie's room by mistake, upon which Arnie ("Heh, heh") had passed himself off as Kermit and talked with him for ten minutes (the long and short of their total acquaintance) and hired Pete on the spot to play Pancho Cajones in his forthcoming production of *Montezuma's Revenge* at seven thousand a week ("Heh, heh, that Arnie's quite a card"), that he had only discovered that Arnie wasn't Kermit when he happened by the hotel as they were leaving for the bush and had gone up to Arnie and spoken to him and Arnie pretended he had never seen Pete before in his life and said he was not Kermit Strycker but was in fact the subabbot and cellarer of the Abbey of Our Lady of Giblets near Paradiso, Alabama, and that he would be happy to receive Pete's application for postulancy through regular channels with Pete's check for one thousand dollars to cover mailing and wrapping of the complimentary ton of Southern fried giblets Pete would positively receive if his application were dated not later than 1969 and if Pete's postmark bore all of the numbers in sequence already stamped on the hinder parts of the lucky winning guinea hen, that Pete had then tried to address Kermit, recognizing him from his pictures, but Kermit had seemed angry starting and had informed Pete that there was indeed a certain equity among actors but that Pete's face would unbalance the whole goddamned industry, that Pete still thought Kermit a great man and felt that he could prove himself if Aubrey would only accept several dozen complimentary tickets to that evening's production (and tickets began to pop out of Pete's several apertures like offspring out of a seahorse), that it was fatelike that Pete should be there in the dining room and he only was because a girl Pete knew was an airline stewardess and a knockout and was due in tonight and very bright and Pete was certain he could talk her into playing Calpurnia because she spoke perfect English like you and me, and she wanted to be an actress in the worst way, and, she had claimed, had once, two years ago when she was only sixteen, danced nude in the Folies Bergère, and, finally (Pete being then on his third drink and slowing somewhat around the smalls of his sprightly mandible) that Pete didn't always carry a cane and go around with one pane out of his glasses, but had gotten into an argument with his last Calpurnia during dress rehearsal—another mishmash about Cassius and the old soothsayer peeking in her dressing-room keyhole and then telling her they'd seen the Ides of March plain as hell—and had fallen down and twisted his ankle, and broken his glasses, and, really, hadn't been in "top voice form" ever since.

Aubrey had, by this time, sacrificed, in the interest of keeping a straight face, most of the scar tissue built up during five years of suppressing laughter in the seminary. He had also consumed two more double old-fashioneds of the good, had received tacit permission from his conscience to get away from Pete by whatever means (despite the sad-edged sympathy and wondering sorrow the poor fellow's recital had elicited from him) and had made his excuses, saying that he was suffering from a severe attack of the Fundy flux, and was receiving Pete's sincerest sympathy through his flatted mouth and out of his obviously crushed early Method ego, when he happened to glance toward the cash register and espied Julie, imperiously surveying the dining room. Aubrey whirled about, put his hands up flat like blinders on either side of his face, fixed Pete with such true-blue-eyeism as he could muster, and, striving not to, spoke with ghastly suggestiveness. "Listen, Pete. How would you like to have a date with my stepsister?"

Pete recoiled from him, eyes wide and pulsing like two archery targets on a hot day. "I've got a date," he said, St. Anthony replying to the pimp of the desert.

"No, no, Pete, you don't. . . . Oh, well." Aubrey peeked around and there came Julie, lovely in a white woolen dress that held *supra* and *aedificatis* together in a spectacularly fluid manner.

"Is she . . . ?" Pete said, his eyes out to do tribute and staying out.

"Too late, Pete. You've got a date."

"Yes, but she might not show up," Pete said eagerly.

"Mightn't she?"

"Well, you know airlines."

"Oh, indeed. Yes, yes. I *do!* Well, I'll just introduce you two interesting people and see—see what develops." He dreaded what might develop, but left that to higher powers. The trick now was, remembering his confessor's strictures, to show Julie that he could resist her. And then resist her.

"Are you all right, darling?" Julie said, bending to him, her breasts touching her wrists as she reached in to take his hands, her eyes instinct-green and warm, her lips and mouth swimming in his vision— the erotic adytum of all his desires. "Kunkel called my room and said you weren't feeling well."

Aubrey told her he was fine, lifted himself until the table prevented him, greeted her in a squeak but rallied supplely and dropped into a tentative baritone and introduced Pete to her (referring to Pete inadvertently as Funk Pete Morton, and Pete had never looked so funk-eyed in his funking life), and went on handsomely to describe Pete's exalted estate on the last frontier, but got stopped, mid-estate, as she sat down and slipped her bottom and hips along his leather to him and placed her near knee hard against his thigh; and he let it go over to Pete, who was grunting, and put his hands over his face and thought about how he might escape. Pete, bug-eyed as an ant in labor, was grunting around the middle of his first sentence and Julie was grinning at him, and Aubrey knew right away that his plan wouldn't work. Escape was the only course.

"Well, what do you know?" Julie said sweetly to Aubrey, Pete having managed to explain that he was wearing a tuxedo. "Pete here is wearing a tuxedo. I'll bet *I* know what Pete's regular job is."

"Oh what?" Pete said, like a delighted idiot.

"I'll just bet Pete here is a retired Grand Master of the Teut-Aleut Chapter of the Germanic Protective and Benevolent Order of Peninsular Caribou. Right, Pete?"

Pete's jaw fell away to a loll, then snapped to as Julie reached over and touched his hand. Pete issued a small, benevolently intended, but victim-type laugh, and Aubrey immediately began to feel protective toward him. After all, he had introduced Pete into this fanning mill and it would be his responsibility to get Pete out unfanned, if possible. Julie was smiling sweetly as Pete started to announce himself as Mark Antony; then Julie interrupted to ask if he were suffering from hyperthyroidism, and Pete asked, Who, Mark Antony? And Aubrey began to say prayers in short little takes for the single-piece emergence of Pete the Funk. And prayers, too, for himself, and thought about going back to the church and saying the Stations of the Cross again, and thought about his confession and yet refused to think about it, and put his hands to his face to cover his tears and his drunkenness and his shame, and was about to stand up and dive across the table if he must to escape, when he was required to stand up, partially, to greet a Miss Denise Revere, Pete's erstwhile date.

Denise was a short-haired pretty blonde with long off-black eyes, longer legs, and the longest streamers—on a knee-length, short, green gown—seen, Aubrey thought, since Maude Adams had wed the jolly green giant. Denise was arriving, gownwise, long after she had greeted Pete, inspected his lapel, told Aubrey that he looked nice in hunting clothes, and asked Julie if she was from Anchorage. Thus, Denise's fate was sealed before her rump had hit Aubrey's leather. She made an effort to reel in her flowing green aftermaths, but didn't extend herself at it and let the strays settle where they might. Even Selda seemed awed by so improbable an abundance of fabric, and spent most of her serving time thereafter stepping around such greensward as still occupied the floor.

Denise appeared frightened of Julie from the first moment, and, therefore, started a nonstop flight into inanity by means of a rapid-fire monologue that threatened to separate her lower lip from her dimples. She looked like a stewardess trying very hard not to treat the rest of them as passengers, but there was something permanently altitudinal about her eyes, Aubrey decided. A certain hardness of the eyeball that was more than pupil but considerably less than teacher: the fixed resignation of the schooled victim strapped as the aircraft plunges straight down toward bedrock. Julie smiled at her once and said that she, Denise, must be one of those French girls (Denise had already announced, loudly, that she was born in Rouen, like Sand Joan) who used a bidet instead of a toothbrush because she had such a nice jet-streamy delivery. Somehow, Denise took this as a compliment and worked less cautiously with reference to Julie from that point, running her inquiries about Aubrey's vital statistics together almost gaily, blithely (made easier by the fact that she got nothing but a bathetic gaze from Aubrey, he certain that her comeuppance was even then on its way up) with laughing notations about how Aubrey was cute but quite drunk, wasn't he (her speech now incredibly rapid, and accompanied by such a wanton display of tonsil, teeth, and red inner mouth as seemed to defy probability; but she put probability to rout and even managed to introduce traces of an entirely charming accent now and again, when the verve or emotion of a passage seemed to call for it—so that she reminded him of Julie, and yet reminded him of Julie not at all: where Julie was magnificently arrived, Denise was intensely on the make; where Julie was unafraid and almost serene, Denise was vulnerable, fawn-eyed, on the fringe of the forest of this world, her tongue at the salt lick, her eyes feardarted and desperate, her body held tense, ready to take to the trees and darkness at the first snapping of a branch, a guilty thing, but fast. And he knew all of this about Denise without giving it conscious thought, knew it was an intuition out of his own long-ago wonders that he had been born to wealth. And he felt profoundly sorry for her, as he did for Pete, faced as they were with the privileged, moneyed, luxuriant-flesh-on-liberal-bone extravagance that was Julie, and tried to define what it was that made the Strycker-Milligan complex so formidable in battle and in the forums, peaceful or angry, of men: not simply money, but the hauteur of money), and how she couldn't possibly play Calpurnia, and how Pete needed a haircut, and how she needed a manicure, and how Pete should switch to an electric razor, and how Aubrey's eyes seemed strained and was he ashamed to wear his glasses, and how he shouldn't be, especially if they were heavy brown-turquoise rims in which he would look darling, and how Julie's teeth certainly appeared to be her own, but were they, and if not where had she gotten the capping done because Denise had a couple of teeth that needed capping herself.

The which teeth she was pointing out with the aid of a lip-hooked finger, when Julie said, almost mercifully Aubrey thought, that Denise certainly did need some capping, at oral and other apertures, and while Julie didn't feel free to give out the name of her dentist, she could recommend a blacksmith in Keokuk who would be more than sufficient to Denise's needs.

And, after a petrified moment, during which Aubrey was speechless and Pete petrified (and during which Aubrey was shouting soundlessly to Denise to get up and run), Denise struck back. "Did I hear you correctly, Miss Chaste?" (And now Denise's eyes were

508

somewhere out in the hedge schools and her teeth bared so that it was obvious they didn't need capping so much as they needed scraping or honing or melting down, and her fingernails were nervous on her fingers and striking little defects into the tabletop.)

"You heard me correctly, I trust, if your ears are in better shape than your teeth," Julie said, smiling evilly.

"Monsieur Morton!" Denise said grandly.

Pete gave it the old Rotary left-right-triple-take-who-me routine, genuinely flabbergasted, then shot a pavid glance at Aubrey as if he feared he was about to be presented with matched dueling sabers. "What—what's?" Pete said, succinctly.

"Julie," Aubrey said, trying not to sound thick-tongued, but failing, "I protest your damned hauteur. This girl—this very nice young couple—have, by God, done nothing to deserve such treatment from you."

Julie smiled sweetly. "I'm simply trying to instruct the ignorant, step darling. You take him on and I'll take her on. What's this hauteur crap?"

"I would slap your face," cried Denise helpfully, "if you didn't outweigh me by so much!"

"Oh, I'm sure you could go a couple," Julie purred with utter equanimity. "You look to me like you eat Spanish flyweights for breakfast."

And that did it. Denise was on her feet demanding that Monsieur Morton get to his feet; Monsieur Morton was looking from Denise to Julie, apparently trying to make up his mind between the short sure and the long shot; Julie was smiling up at her adversary and advising her to clear to hell out before Julie rolled her up in her goddamned gown and dribbled her out like an Irish football; Aubrey was wondering how it could have come to this again so quickly; Pete was then on his feet, extending his cane to Aubrey with a shrug of a smile; Aubrey shook the cane genially; Denise said that some people had no breeding; Julie said that it was manifest that breeding was Denise's destiny, if one cared for mongrels; Aubrey said that there was no reason why they couldn't all be friends; Julie said that if Aubrey liked Denise she (Julie) was quite confident that Denise would oblige him, on the front steps of the Federal Building if he liked, couchant gules; Denise screamed briefly; Aubrey was suddenly standing in a sort of abbreviated squat (because of the damned table) telling Julie that such remarks were uncalled-for and out of order, and was fattening into a sermon on the wealth of beauty and youth and the worthlessness of human position and the vanity of mortal power and how all things pass away, and other such Biblical apothegms, when Pete and Denise passed away, heads high, like Antony and Cleopatra, Denise leading the way in her many spinnakered barge down the center of things, with Pete, like a rowboat after a great green dreadnought, foundering along in her waggish wake. And Aubrey thought, Good reasons have perforce given way to better.

I am dying, Egypt, dying. Or about to. It's now or never. Still on his feet, he waved for his check, but Selda appeared to be experiencing a ripple-breasted regressive episode two tables away, being engaged in argument with a single gentleman of decayed aspect. Aubrey decided to go to her, took a well-calculated parabolic leap around the curvature of the booth, crying Julie good night and scattering little funky theater tickets like stuffing as he went, struck the apogee of the table with one hip, bounded off his leather with the other, hooked one foot in the metal underslingings of the table, and fell forward, flank and flange, on the floor beneath the booth. He was very drunk, he told himself, and as the hue and cry rose above and around, he instructed himself to crouch cunningly until they thought him immobile and then sprint for the exit. By fair means or foul, he had to get away from Julie; get away before he started to cry or die or both. And then Julie was peering down at him telling him to take it easy and asking him if he were sick, and he began to bounce up and down and wave that section of the tablecloth he had taken below with him and howl for his check, and Selda squatted in maidenly fashion in front of him saying that she had the check but that he'd have to get up first, and he reached out and snatched the check and signed it just there, using the floor as his backing, adding ten dollars as a tip to Selda, thinking, Dear Christ without shoes, forgive me. Then Julie was helping him to his feet, and Selda, smiling ambivalently, lent a hand, and Aubrey began to lunge away but Julie hung on, swearing at him, telling him to stop making a spectacle of himself, and he was lunging about trying to run but Julie was dragging on his arm, and he was shouting to her please just to steer him out to the lobby where he would explain all and do penance on his knees. And then Selda was waving the check in at his nostrils saying that he'd signed a phony name, and he cried, "Well, that's all your fault, Mrs. Prynne, all your fault!"

"Listen!" Selda invited, ear-splittingly. "My name isn't Mrs. Prynne and your name isn't MacIver!"

"My name is MacIver! That's how much you know! Ashurbanipal MacIver! Subabbot and co-cellarer of the Abbey of Our Lady of Giblets, Paradiso, Alabama!"

"You're not!" Selda shouted. "Your name is . . ."

"And you're not Hester Prynne, mother of Pearl! You're an impostor. Help, I say! The room is full of finking impostors! The Great Deceiver is upon us! She! Her! That woman is Adles, wife to the Great Deceiver!" And Aubrey had little control now over his panic—his panic at all the people around him, all the open mouths, all the noise, all the eyes staring, and wanted only to run and hide— and did run as Julie turned to sign the check, down the Nile against the stares, the headwinds, the cross seas, and all conceivable odds. He brushed a bit of butter from one table as he passed, but dipped his jib (as he fancied), bowed from his poop, and shot away again toward the delta, down the main channel between the white banks, all crowded with impostors, all staring up astounded, knives and forks in midair, mouths pendulous in mid-chew, and Aubrey got through them all without taking any direct hits. He shot out into the lobby, gave it left full rudder, and ran down a perfect scow of a bellman with his red eye on the starboard side. Aubrey instructed him briefly in the rules of the road, raised the Strycker ensign (a twenty-dollar bill Kermit had given him for cab fare), thrust it upon the bellman, mentioned Old Fitzgerald, gave out his room number, and watched the bellman scuttle off full ahead, all knots and no knowledge. Aubrey shook his head and ran off toward the elevator, clumping in his boots, watering sorrowfully at the eyes, and scratching his navel.

He went directly to his room, taking the corridors in a zigzag course, groaning all the way, not able to believe that he could be so drunk, yet afraid not to be drunk and as drunk as possible, vowing to be drunk forever rather than think of Arnie's dying, of how he had obviously willed and contributed to his brother's death. And he came up to his door, his key at trail arms, saying, "Do you see, in the name of God, do you see how the world is? I have no idea what I'm doing from one minute to the next! One minute I am crushed with my guilt, and the next minute I am prancing through my role in a foolish morality skit. *I—I—I!* Who am guilty of my brother's death! I! Oh dear God, dear Christ! I'm an oligarchy of emotions. As the world is! I must hide, dear God. Oh please, let me hide. Hide deep in the *splendor ordinis.* Where each emotion has its order and its splendor and must await its turn. I cannot deal with this other, dear God. Not sober. Not even a little sober. Dear God, God, my Maker, forgive me my hate of Arnie, for Arnie will tell You that I loved him next myself, and often more."

"Are you all right, sir?"

The speaker was a large lady who it seemed to him, had been turned and shaped on the genuine Primo Carnera lasts and who stood at thumping distance, right arm raised to thump. He discovered that he was standing, hunched over, his forehead pressed against the door of his room. He gave a diversionary smile as he put his key in the lock, averred that he was just a bit delirious due to the longitude, turned his key, leaped within with the door, slammed and locked it behind him, and fell away sharply to the bed.

At first he sat. His face was a rubber mask, all sounds were echoes, all movement was lurch and lunge, and there was a rectangular hum in his head, a pulsing in four bars of unequal duration that fitted together to suggest everything from near-perfect squares to parallelograms that lay almost flat on the floor of his brain. In the middle of one of these latter, he stretched out on the bed and gave his stomach, head, and consciousness to God; but the Almighty didn't choose to accept. And growing in the center of that semester's succession of geometric figures was a red light, a pinpoint at first, but pulsing a thousand straight lines out from its center like a sunburst, the lines growing longer and longer, the heart of it plumping larger and larger; and he told himself that it had nothing to do with his drunkenness—his swimming, awful, nauseating drunkenness—but that it was, that red light, quite simply, madness coming upon him.

Then a knock at the door, his stertorous command to enter, and enter the bellman, yellow-coated now, gap-toothed, tansylike, carrying two bottles of Old Fitzgerald on a tray, and, behind him, Julie: straight up, dual-powered, her smile upon him like a third Cyclopean eye (focused, he imagined, exactly between the horns of his dilemma), her progress majestic and measured, her top gallants set for collision, her grappling hooks clutching wind.

He gestured toward the bellman to have a seat and sample the goods, but that idiot took it as a wave off, bowed once, smiling hideously like a sunflower and went out, flopping at the pistil. Aubrey heaved a great and victimized sigh as the first step in a rather elaborately developed scheme, just five seconds old. The bellman had, damned helianthic petal-ass that he was, put the tray down on the television set. This was situated halfway between the front and the bathroom doors. Julie was, just then, on screen. He would wait, there on the bed, feigning faints and other frenzies, until she was over by the window. Then he would make his move.

"Step, darling," she said tensely. "What in hell is the matter with you? You are acting like a psychopath."

"That's telling me."

"I know you're playing a little game, Aubie, darling," she said coldly. "You're going through a little infantile phase, or, rather, you're forcing yourself through it. I wouldn't mind if it were genuine, but it's all an act. You think you're supposed to feel sorry about Arnie's death —far more sorry than you actually *do* feel—so you're going to toddle back to when you and your brother were little golden animals full of uncritical, narcissistic love for one another. You can't really get back there, but you're doing your best to act like Arnie anyway." She had paused near the window. He could tell by the sound of her voice. He peeped out from between his fingers. She had her back to him, adjusting the blinds. He put his knees on notice of imminent flex, turned until both feet had fallen in a controlled slide to the floor, then suddenly threw himself upward to a standing start, failed to start, fell away sharply right, but kept his head and let his left knee go and came to an upright kneel with his nose an inch away from the seventeen-inch screen. He hadn't made a heard sound. Julie was still tinkering with the blinds. He regarded his reflection on the screen for a second or two, then reached up, seized both fifths by their green necks, and charged, kneeling like a Lough Derg pilgrim, for the bathroom. Julie heard him, turned, shouted, but he was within, bottles down, hands to knob before she could get in motion. He snapped the lock as she struck the outside of the door.

Then ensued a long siege, during which Aubrey ran himself a bath, opened himself a bottle, got snug inside the bath and snug outside about half the bottle, and began his reply to Julie's long soliloquy on his madness and other shortcomings by saying, "Julie, be a sport."

"Step, listen. I'm not pursuing you. I'm just worried about you.

Down there in the dining room you were an entirely different person."

"Don't you understand, Julie? I'm a schizophrenic, just like Arnie. I'm the other half, the half whose madness is currently more acceptable to society. Not much more, but more. You understand? Neither do I. However, Julie, you deserve better than that at my hands. And I'll do my best. I think you honestly believe, and believed, you were doing me a favor when you seduced me. Didn't you?"

"Thanks for giving me all the credit," she said, sounding less stridulous, more like her confident self. "What the hell are you doing, step?"

"Taking a bath."

"I'd behave myself if you'd let me scrub your back."

"No, you wouldn't. All women are temptresses, and you won't behave yourself. Besides, you won't respect—you won't respect me," he said, repeating himself as he took all the banter out of his voice, "until you discover that I can resist you. I am resisting you, right now."

"Resisting me? Christ! You're resisting consciousness. I feel like I'm talking to a whisky-soaked catechism."

But he had only begun, and went on, and told her what the priest had said about women, and chastity. She laughed and argued and hammered on the door and went out once and got a key but couldn't poke the key he'd left on the inside out of the keyhole. And when she began to sound angry, and when he began to be so drunk he pulled the plug and covered himself with all the towels and mats within reach so that he wouldn't drown or freeze, he told her about seeing Arnie's corpse and what the priest had said about his guilt with reference to Arnie's death. Julie fairly howled with indignation and said the goddamned priest didn't know what he was talking about and how could he possibly judge, and wasn't Aubrey able to exercise individual, personal, objective judgment that, biased—even wildly biased—as it might be, would be five hundred per cent more accurate than the priest's could ever be? Aubrey said he could not. And changed the subject abruptly, and successfully, because the new subject interested her far more. He simply said, "Julie, listen. About our love affair, as they say in the movies, it's all over. I'm really, really, really going away. To be a chaplain in the camel corps. But even if I weren't, it's all over. Not only because it's a sin. And not only because you're my stepsister." He paused. He was very drunk now,

514

barely able to talk, seeing nothing but whitenesses in circular motion, and this with his eyes wide open. "Are you listening?"

"I'm listening, step, my drunken beauty."

"No, no. Don't write it off as me drunk. Take my word. I'll tell you why. Even if I were as free as—as old Eben Flood—I couldn't have an affair with you now. Or marry you. Arnie died—and I believe this, *know* it, so don't bother trying to talk me out of it—Arnie died partly because he loved you, or lusted after you, or what the hell, and couldn't have you . . ."

"If he hadn't tried to rape me . . ."

"Never mind that. It doesn't make a riddlely damn now. I could never so much as kiss you without thinking of Arnie. Sounds very dramatic, doesn't it? Can't live in this house, Thurston. Not after what's happened. Too many memories. . . ." He belched loudly and took a long drink of whisky.

"Do you really believe that, step?"

"No faith necessary. It's a simple bloody fact. I've been a proud, miserable, conniving, God-damned wretch! Please don't quote me until I've cleared it with the foreign office."

"You don't really believe that, Aubie darling."

"Oh, yes I do. Yes, I indeed do. Because it's far more so than unso. It answers too many questions about why I've done what I've."

"So? Arnie hated you, too. Everybody hates everybody."

"That doesn't help me much."

A silence. Then "Well, what's the consequence? Won't they drum you out of the regiment?"

"Oh no. All kinds of blackguards reform and become priests. Even good priests. Even saints. That's why you shouldn't view the whole episode too causatively. Even without Arnie's death, I'd have gone on to Africa. Or somewhere. I mean, be objective about it. You saw me downstairs tonight. Believe me, toward the end there I wasn't seeing, hearing, or feeling Arnie. It was all me. Trying to cope with the modern world. I can't cope, Julie. Arnie told me that once. I just can't cope. People don't mean what they want to mean. It's that bad. Got to go to a desert, I do. I'll find one. If not the Sahara then the Tasmanian or the Australian or the Gobi or the ruddy Painted."

This speech exhausted him, and, as Aubrey later remembered, it marked the beginning of a long series of comforting, contraposing, cajoling addresses by Julie—she providing all the stimuli (other than alcoholic) and he providing all the reactions—these last more and more like sleep as she talked on, seldom more than a grunt proceeding out of his towel-swathed nest in the bathtub; and he began to see things: banks of white clouds passing near the shower nozzle; visions of hell; sudden bursts of white apple blossoms; eucharistic pageants, full of ciboria and pyxes big as automobiles; all of the hues brilliant and unforgettable, all of the sensations intense and splendidly varied and extensive, all of the sounds sharp, high-pitched, screaming; yet all of the sense of any of it lost, only certain words taking fire at each letter and burning into the sod of his memory and remaining, ash-black and smoking, deeply scored there until, perhaps, some spring of sanity should lift the green of grasses through and around them and the fragrance of the quickened soil should overcome the odor of fire. And the rectangular hum, with its sonor parallelograms, began again and got louder and louder, and the red light surged into a giant pinwheel of rockets and flame, raw and violent and filling the sky of his whole consciousness; yet he discovered the fire was present to him only when he closed his eyes, as was his whole uncertainty about his sanity, so that he kept his eyes open as long as he could, and, aware that he was defeating something that sought to possess him, began to feel a certain pride of self-dominion, a joy of conquest over occult forces, and finally an exultation of triumph in the knowledge that, as Arnie had once put it, all it takes to conquer madness is guts. He thought, I can keep my eyes open forever! I can! Let the damned thing hum and spin! I'll never close my eyes again!

But came awake in silence—Julie gone, or no longer speaking— and realized that he had slept for some time, but was drunker, if anything, than before he'd slept. And stared at the ceiling in the bright light of the room and almost screamed, seeing there plainly the vision of hell he had dreamed about, seeing Arnie there, Arnie's vein-blue corpse, wrapped in flames. All right, Arnie. If this is the price, if this is my penance, to see this vision forever, I accept it. But he was wrong, Arnie. You know I loved you, and I know it. But Arnie stood like a great red figure X in the flames and said nothing and laughed wildly, until his wounds were all bleeding, until there was a final spurt of blood from Arnie's throat, until the four humming lines became a huge flaming square and only Arnie's maniacal laugh could be heard above the blast-sucking roar of the flames.

And after that a time of sleep and awful bedlamic dreams, and a doctor, and Kermit shaking his beard.

516

And after that the time of returning, of going down and across the great land, four thousand miles to that hole in the ground where they would put Arnie down at last. They carried him with them, and Aubrey was aware of this in every fiber of him, in every fiber and moment he was aware that Arnie was with them, back there in his pitiless wood. And he looked down at the earth from thirty-five thousand feet and thought of just six feet more, and poured his liquor into his grief and dreamed that the airplane and Arnie's coffin would never, never descend.

And there was a time of waking and of morning, and a time when he could hear the secret sounds of the river as he came out of sleep, out of a clinging narcotic blackness, out of a rude memory of sitting beside the coffin until the guttering hours, until the candles had burned down and gone out and light had died, until black and final dead of night. Then Solly was in the room, in the morning light, and he remembered he had promised her he would call Father Donovan at St. Titus' and ask to serve the funeral Mass, but hadn't called and was glad now that he hadn't, for the thought of walking upon the altar of God that morning, in whatever cause, appalled him.

Solly went snuffling in her black rummage to the window, opened the curtains to the sun and the shining river, returned to the tray she had set on the bedside table, rattled a little silver coffeepot at him, and filled a cup. Then she looked dolefully down at him, and said, "There's only an hour . . . the undertaker'll be after comin'."

"Thank you, Solly."

She blinked out a new tear from either eye, sniffed as she glanced at the whisky bottle half empty beside the tray, turned quickly and went out, her great broad bottom rolling dolorously in rhythm with her sobs. She paused at the door. "Drink that coffee, mind."

He nodded, waited until she had closed the door, and reached for the bottle. The door opened suddenly and there was Solly looking.

"Oh Jaysus, a whisky priest!" she wailed, and slammed the door.

He went to the window and stood in his shame, his sickness; watched the sun, lifted well now over the mountains, pouring a golden track across the flat steaming calm of the splendid river; thought, The year's at spring, the tide's at flood, God's in His heaven, and Aubie is drunk; and drank from the bottle, as he thought of other mornings when he had knelt to this window, this scene, this holy water, and prayed for the grace of a vocation, had prayed so fervently in that holy green time, his eyes dancing to a pure vision of

517

all that holy greenness. And he thought, I fled Him down the nights and down the days, and it took me only three weeks to get away from Him. Tomorrow is Corpus Christi. Tomorrow the Body of Christ. But today the body of Arnie. Then he knelt down at the window and tried to pray for Arnie and himself, to pray that his vocation was not lost, tried to remember when and where he had begun to lose his will to persevere. Since Anchorage certainly, since that confession, since that fantasy of an evening, but just when, just where, had he realized that the moral force of his indestructible vocation was dying? A cedar of Lebanon dying within him; that fine bark-fat green-great tree, sap-swollen, grown tall and fragrant against the sky, dying within him; whisky-sodden, purulent in shame and doubt, a crapulous abomination, fallen across his soul, tumefact and bloating until it should die at last and choke the spirit and life from him. Dying within him, and down without a sound, because he hadn't been there to hear it fall. Ah Christ, to find the roots, to find the green sprouts of it, and to raise it again, to raise himself again upon that holy tree.

And he searched those three days but found nothing. For it seemed to him that he had passed them in a flying madhouse, full of people who looked like Kermit constantly shaking their shaggy heads, and people who looked like Rexfordia insisting upon seeing the bodies of their dead children and then screeching to find them torn and stitched with blue, and people who looked like Eulalia pointing fingers at the shaggy people and issuing endless declamations and affixing blame, and people who looked like Solly wagging their woe-begone tear-puffed faces at him and brogueing out homilies on how Jaysus overcame His sorrows and did His Father's will, and people who looked like the hundred relatives or whatever who had filed past the coffin the day before (while he sat, defender, at the head of it, dead-hearted, dead-centered, dead-drunk, making bitter comments from time to time about their phony piety, and going into hysterical laughter at least once, and waving them all on and away with fierce and threatening gestures—and remaining just there, holding his position against all opposition, offering, at various embattled moments, when they tried to unseat him, Eulalia, Kermit, Rexfordia, a priest, and the undertaker, violence by bashing with a standing candlestick, until they all left him alone, alone with Arnie in his massive, scrolled-metal, sealed box); his only friends Julie and his bottle, and his brother's frightened voice (frightened, for Arnie didn't want to go

down, because the box could not keep the worms away forever—
"Can it keep the cold away, Aubie? Can it keep the cold away and
the rain?"—frightened at how they had removed his guts and stuffed
him full of white butcher's paper and stretched him out in stiff purple velvet velour like mastiff hair, like Eulalia's drapes, so that he said,
"Oh Jesus, Aubie, I don't want to go down! Where the roots of a
tree will come knocking one night, and knock and knock, and gouge,
and break through the box, and come creeping to me like a snake,
flicking, touching, pushing, sticking into my goddamned wax body,
and thrusting right through me and out the other side, and growing
fat and thick and bursting me open! Ah Christ, Aubie! When they've
all gone to bed, pry the lid off, and take me out, and keep me, keep
me anywhere, but keep me from going down!"); going down, diving
for three days in that flying madhouse, diving down from high heaven
to hell, through awful dark and blinding brightness, down and always down through a smoky black sky, exploding now and then horribly, its rockets made of the limbs of the damned, down and ever
down to the fiery bowels; his only hope a long drink from his bottle
and Arnie's assurance that one of the rockets would strike them and
that Aubrey would be caught in air by a wild angel and deposited in
a mountain limbo, a sweet gathering of quiet shade beneath an over-
hanging peak, a place where a man, if he looked assiduously to his
bottle, might approach his final end without heard challenge, and be
received among the dead as unharked as a shadow when it passes
into night.

He got up and went to a desk and took up a letter, and removed
it from its envelope and read it for perhaps the fiftieth time. The
Saharan Fathers were pleased to accept Mr. Aubrey Strycker as a
candidate for the holy priesthood in their Society. It would be necessary for him to repeat whatever he had already done of his novitiate
year, this at the Saharan Novitiate near Mostaganem, Algeria. The
novitiate year normally commenced on April 30 each year, the feast
of Our Lady of Africa, but special arrangements would be made for
Mr. Strycker to make his novitiate with the group now in process
with an extension after April 30th next for as many days as necessary
until the full year-and-a-day requirement had been completed. However, Mr. Strycker should report to the house in Southampton as soon
as possible, prepared to leave for Africa, for a final consultation with
Father Provincial, traveling instructions, and a general orientation.

Certain lists of fees, expenses, requisite clothing and other impedimenta were enclosed. Aubrey scanned these last with his lips bitten together, stuffed the papers back in the envelope, threw it on the desk, and, bottle in hand, marched into the bathroom.

The drive to the church was clamorous. Aubrey was in Kermit's car—Mr. Jebb driving—with Kermit and Rexfordia and Eulalia. There had been some dispute about the gravediggers. Kermit, who had yielded under great pressure to permitting the burial in the Breesvort family lot instead of in the Strycker lot far out at the western end of Kaatskill County, was now saying that he should have stuck to his original plans, a grave having already been dug in the Strycker lot in a place of great honor (Kermit's words). Eulalia fought back, saying that both Arnie and Aubrey were Breesvort-Milligans, and that anybody with half an eye could see it just by looking at them as early as their second year, and that Kermit's damned relatives had been hillbillies and apple knockers (as a matter of fact, Kermit's ancestors had arrived in the county before 1700, in the same shipment the Breesvorts came in), and ought to be honored to have someone bearing the Strycker name buried in Breesvort ground. Rexfordia was weeping softly and didn't enter into the discussion. The climax came when Kermit averred that Arnie's grave had better be only six feet deep, and not twelve, or all bets were off. This was a reference to the fact that Eulalia had had her husband, George, buried twelve feet down so that she could be buried over the top of him. Eulalia waxed exceeding wroth over this and allowed as how it was none of Kermit's goddamned business, and that he, Kermit, would have to be buried twelve feet down because six feet wouldn't be deep enough to preserve the county from an all-pervading stench. At this point, Aubrey intervened to say that if they didn't all shut up, at once, he would knock the undertaker down as soon as he could find him, and then start to work on relatives and friends. All shut up, at once, and Aubrey sat back in the silence thinking that a reputation as a dangerous drunk had certain advantages, at least on days of ceremony.

He took his place in a rear pew, much to Rexfordia's discomfort, and finally did have to offer to knock the undertaker down because the latter kept tapping him on the shoulder and asking him to move up. He wished to be no closer to the ceremony than he had to be, for reasons he could not, or would not, fathom; and the ceremony was only barely under way when the humming, the awful brain-searing rectangular humming, began with the soft organ music and continued as the Mass began. And it brought on a new phenomenon, to accommodate his wide-open eyes: a prism or crystal, lodged in the forefront of his vision, slowly revolving, through which he saw all that he saw, and which gave the Mass and all things in that damp stone church an almost unbearable clarity and shine. The air itself, at first laden with the burned, malefactious, yet desiccated odors of almost any church without exception, began to be cleansed, took on a brilliant purity like the crisp and rarefied air of mountain country, and though he approved the cleansing, he was chilled by this new atmosphere, and by the lucidity it lent to his seeing.

For it seemed to him that he could see through solid objects: through the marble floor into the church basement and the dark earth beneath; through the stone of the main altar and into the sacristy behind where the black cope hung on a standing rack like an angel of death crouched in wait; and through the solid metal thicknesses of the casket, where Arnie lay, waxed and wan and postured forever stiff, yet, as Aubrey saw him, his dead eyes filled with tears, unmoving but seared with desperate intensity, still entreating Aubrey to prevent them from stuffing him into the earth. Yet, for the first time, Arnie did not speak. As if he were angry at Aubrey for letting the business go that far—down an aisle to an altar Arnie held alien—Arnie spoke to him no more. And Aubrey, expecting to hear the voice again at any moment, could not keep his gaze from the casket, from looking within, then looking away in horror; but slowly began to stifle doubt, to remind himself of the resurrection of the body. That anguished, insistently echoing voice and that beloved form were not really still forever. Arnie would rise.

And found himself listening closely to the Mass, translating the Latin from the altar and the choir. He had always been highly critical of, and distinctly repelled by, all of it; by the exquisitely emotional direction and drain and torture of it. Mournfully measured by the choir (dreadful in its every member, but nice of them to be out and willing to keen on this Wednesday morning), this Mass of the Dead, this Black Mass, this Mass of the Defunct had always come to him like a cry of pain, a wail of the lost out of a grief-blasted bewilderness of black night and blacker snow. Was there any single note of hope in it? What had it been designed to accomplish? The more pro-

521

found resting of the dead? The lamentations of the choir, the lowing of the organ, the dread intonations of the priest—did any of these serve a valid purpose? He had always thought that they served only to torment the living, to induce in them an emotional response to death that really could have no salutary or lasting effect.

But now, hearing this Mass, this lamentation for the first time as a memorial to someone he loved, he was finding himself not only more involved in it (when he slowed his mind and his eye, and listened), but learning from it. And his fierce eye was seeing down the past to a beginning, to boyhood, to Arnie alive running down the years toward death, mind darting, soul caught, heart hammered out by insanity, poised precariously in life, his golden head turned to smile, or turned in agony as he finished a race, or turned with lips smirking to say, "Jesus God, Aubie! I can't break all these streetlights by myself!" Began to understand what this Mass had to say to the living. Do not forget this dead, but remember him in the sweetness of the life God gave him; remember that although life is indeed sweet, it is often sweetest in memory, and that this present life will be sweetest in eternity; remember that the present goes into the past before it can be apprehended, but that God has prepared eternity for the full apprehension of what and who you have here come to love; so that, as you have seen your brother smiling and the toss of his head and the flounce of his hair in some long-extinguished sunlight, you will see him again in eternity, in that time beyond time. Take this dead in good and inevitable part, and take your anger in good and inevitable part, and persevere in this hope of resurrection until your own day of anger has come upon you, until there is no more need of hope, and you see him, and Him, face to face.

All of this he extracted from the Latin and came into knowledge under its insistent, heavy pall. He would see Arnie whole and living again; and, suddenly, did see him. Arnie walking slowly, disdainfully, walking in his own particular beauty, floating as he thought, like an angel of golden light striding down a summer blue sky. And he moved to meet him, as in a fantastic ballet, and Arnie spoke and shook his hand and told him he should stand straighter and noted that it had been fifty years since the hunting of Big Ditmo. An imagining, but as clear to him as actually seen; a vision of reincarnation in which all of the holy, glittering things that his sleeping (nearly dying) fancy had tried to bring to life from the cold facts of religion—but had failed, had left to wanded fairies in boy dreams long years before, technicolor productions out of a private land of Oz—had passed into act, flesh was given to the ages, Arnie restored and Aubrey, as they had been when happiest, to grace and green innocence, to that only temporal reality which has anything to do with joy, to the same innocence that human love imposes or can impose upon the apparency of things, in a magnificently sweeping solipsism, transforming the dried timber of bodies into lithe saplings, transforming the drab and rotting shingles of this world into the tender, vivid petals of a better, untempted Eden.

And when this imagining was gone, he found that all his hallucinations had gone with it. His vision was flat and cold and pierced nothing. His head was heavy with hangover but free of hum and hellfire, and he heard no voices. He was, abruptly, there in the gray of the country church, on his knees, in that position that had become so natural to him, in that setting of altar and sacrifice that had become so natural to him, in that aloneness-apartness that had become so natural to him, the only significant differences (yet how significant, and significant of what?) that he was wearing one of Arnie's suits instead of his habit, or a habit, that his fingernails were dirty, that he smelled of whisky new and old, that he could use a shave, that he was hungry enough to eat hamburgers right now in the center aisle if anyone cared to serve them, that up front were his grandmother (seated and glaring about defiantly, a little black-bonneted cormorant with red-pepper eyes) and his father, mother, stepsister and three-quarters of a hundred aliens who claimed relationship—these instead of his classmates or underclassmen—and that his brother Arnie was dead-dead in that coffin-island in the aisle instead of alive-dead on that other island in the Atlantic.

He drummed his fingers on the back of the pew—the old, body-shined wood of the pew—and thought about who he was. And it seemed to him plain that, for all his sins of the past three weeks, against God, man, Arnie, or Julie, he was still the same God-committed, Christ-drawn, unworldly church-creature. No matter what he had done, no matter what he might be guilty of, nothing made any sense to him except that Christ was divine, Christ promised heaven, Christ died on the cross. Believing this, as he did—as he believed, or knew, that there was incense in the air—as he believed that there was wood just then under his knees and hands—as he believed in any reality whatsoever—he could conceive of no other life, no other manner of living out his hours and days and maybe years, than in the service of the church and faith Christ had founded. A simple damned-human-life-anyway set of facts. He was in the world but not of it, and hadn't been of it since he'd learned to tell time.

Nor had Arnie; which was his bulwark against the guilt the priest in Anchorage had, he felt, justly pointed out. His only, just-arrived bulwark. He had injured Arnie in that place where Arnie could least stand to be injured: his identity. Such as it was. In a constant losing warfare against the specter of total insanity, Arnie had sought to identify himself, first, as the renegade prophet-mystic, who had built his own close just out the monastery gate, who was loved and revered by all the fathers and young monks, who saw visions and wonders undreamed of by others because God had chosen him as victim to bear the special burden of the seer, who was amused (or pretended to be, nobly) by the judgment of the generality of men that he was insane, and who, like an undercover agent in a foreign country, had the fascinating task of conversing and consorting often with the Devil. And, second, Arnie had tried to identify himself as Aubrey's mentor, the mastermind behind his career in the Titan Order, the crotchety, often heretical (but only to test his charge's readiness to define and refute error), never benign, and always merciless devil's advocate. And, third and not quite as probably, Arnie had sought identity as the free spirit who thought the world mad, God's hammer and goad to the race of men, who chose to live among madmen freely just to demonstrate that (he being of course perfectly sane) what society thought madness wasn't necessarily mad at all, who found irresistible delight in coming out of his seclusion, his self-imposed exile from social intercourse, from time to time to challenge the usages of the normal as merely the less sophisticated analogues of the usages (utterly uninhibited, and therefore infinitely more valid) of the so-called abnormal. All of these attempts at self-identification had been harmless, innocent, pitiful, pathetic—certainly nothing a sane man would resent, nothing a sane man, and a Christian, would seek to expose, nothing in any of it, even in the worst excesses of Arnie's mannerisms, language, or pretensions, that should have affronted Aubrey in any way, that should have come anywhere near overcoming the deep love he had always felt for his brother—and yet Aubrey *had* been affronted, even before he had left the novitiate; had, in fact, left the novitiate partly (or largely, or only, or who the hell would ever know?) because Arnie affronted him, in some way Aubrey had not yet defined and might never define beyond the phrase "sibling rivalry" (the which phrase made gorge and gonads ache because, in saying everything, it said nothing); and had met his brother on each of those three desperate plateaus and had struck him down: had denied Arnie the pleasure and the security of theological debate by getting angry and walking away; had simply rejected Arnie's attempts, however ludicrous or late, to warn him against sexual involvement with Julie; had told Arnie that he (Arnie) had no stake in his brother's priesthood, his decisions, his life (knowing, even at the moment he said it, that poor Arnie had no other stake he gave a damn about except in Aubrey's priesthood, knowing that Arnie would only attain the priesthood through Aubrey's priesthood, and that by the same pathetic association, a purely symbolic priesthood, but *everything* to Arnie); had, if only by his stupid and needless and self-indulgent presence, been the instrument (had he once called himself the "referee"?) of all the quarrels between Kermit and Arnie, had been the sanctimonious catalyst, had been "that other," culpably unaware of the tension he was causing for the most part, yet seeking favor, seeking preferment, seeking love (and thought, You didn't know? Why, you arrant jackass. Have you been born yet?). And so on, and on, remorselessly, angrily, until it seemed to him that he had relived every moment of his three-week inter-regularity. And he acknowledged his guilt in every instance, and yet, when all the accusations were in and weighed, he could say, Yes, yes, but Arnie didn't like the world any more than I do. I'm sorry for what I did, I'm sad that I won't be seeing Arnie for a while, and I'm sorry his death was so grisly and painful. But, good conscience, peer about a little at the world. Who the hell would *want* to live in it if he could be sure of going straight to heaven? My missionary zeal to the contrary, if I could be a suicide at this moment and be assured of purgatory or heaven, I would, by my faith, pay out my guts like a clothesline, if necessary. And Prince Hamlet and a lot of other nice people would line up to join the exodus. And if I feel this way—and why would I not?—that we have here no lasting home, that this is a vale of tears, that we are born in sweat, sin, and guilt, these have been dinned into me since I was dinnable—what of Arnie? He's free now of the terrible apprehension, the crushing indignity of insanity. He's enjoying a perfection of the intellect, eternal in duration. Good conscience, I tell you, if I had cleaved my brother from brow to buttocks with a dull stone ax, I could only say now, He is far better off where he is. . . .

And then Kermit was shaking him by one shoulder and frowning, informing him that it was time to act like a pallbearer and would he please start acting right and stop crucifying his poor mother. Aubrey climbed to his feet, bore his share of the pall, put his arm around Rexfordia during the ride out to the grave, bore the pall again and, despite his matter-of-fact orientation, was dismayed to see the open earth; and retired at once from the graveside, veering off as the gaggle of grandames, aunts, and assorted others who had followed the coffin threatened to engulf (or speak to) him, and climbed a low hill backed up in jack pines to the very edge of the river, and sat down on the lead-pipe fence, and watched the sky—watched the puff-belly white-clouds travel busily, like fat farmers, southbound to market along the wind-driven Hudson—until he could hear the final Latin, and looked then, and prayed with the priest, and went on looking as the mourners started to move away, as Uncle Cletus helped Rexfordia away, as Julie (a frightful, lovely beauty in black) paused to look and let him know she saw him up there and that she was sorry after all, as Kermit came halfway up the hill and peered at him and asked him if he were all right and if so what the hell was the matter with him, as the priest walked away slapping his book shut and nodding to the undertaker and his men, and as two undertaking gnomes crept to the bands beneath the coffin and loosed them and lowered the massive gilded box into the ground. He watched as Arnie went down, and let his eyes cry since they seemed determined to, and thought of how he would hear Arnie's voice no more on earth, how he would never again see him (as he once had—oh, more than once) running among these tombstones and through them and over the fence and stopping on the road with the sun in his yellow hair and waving for him to come on, how that half of him that was his brother was really gone and was now being covered with earth by two gnomes in shirt-sleeves. But held himself to the lead pipe on which he was seated, held himself hard with fists clamped on pipe, held himself as if he were clinging to the outboard railings of the world; and endured the gnomes until they were done and gone (out the gate to a gnome of a double-ended car, glancing up at him, but talking about taking a swim, and cleaned they their shovels before whirring away on their bobbin-tiny wheels); and endured a short sun shower in the small of the afternoon; and endured a dog that trotted in the newly cut stubble of timothy hay around Arnie's grave as though he'd buried a bone there and someone had played him a monstrous joke; and endured his own pain, and clamor of loss—endured on that piping through the whole sweetness of the late spring day, endured the smell of apple blossoms and the rumble of a Lake Erie grain boat and the scolding of a kingbird who apparently thought he owned the fence—and only left, stiff at the legs, stiff at the heart, when the sun had gone out of the sky.

He stopped at the gate of the cemetery and looked back at the mound of new earth. He could smell the earth on the air, rich with the promise of worms, and shuddered. And leaned there on the gate for a long time before he spoke. Then said, "Ah, Arnie, our trouble was we never grew up. We never gave a damn about growing up, as children never, ultimately, give a damn. We brought our clouds of glory with us, and kept them with us, like daydreams, and got lost in them. So? So, good night, Arnie. Though you may come with me if you like."

He turned away and walked quickly, wondering what it was he had said, wondering what he might say that would finish what Arnie and he had tried to say to each other from the time they could talk, and before that; but could think of nothing, and told himself it didn't make a damn because it was foolish and too late to be talking to Arnie anyway, and went slowly out to the county road, out to the murmurous evening, and turned toward Eulalia's house. And had gone only a few steps along it before he stopped and looked back at the grave and studied it, marked its position with reference to the trees and the larger tombstones, so that he knew exactly where it was, so that he could see it in its piped-in meadow when he closed his eyes, and then went on, having taken his picture, and looked to the bit of moon then rising and said to himself, Lightly. Lightly through this world. Keep a solemn eye, but remember, for the funerals of children the bells, if used, should not be rung with a sorrowful sound but rather festively.

# THE EPILOGUE

# · FORTY-TWO ·

In that straitened silence, that quaint solemnity, he sat as with an old and familiar friend. He noted that Kermit had bought the nuns a new screen—a handsome barricade with long clean vertical lines and made of a stuff like white tile—and that the speak room had been painted to match. There was still a strong odor of paint in the room. Even the holy founder had been painted. He sat wrapped around in whiteness, in the eye and odor of it, and just sitting there was a ceremony, his return to the heart of the apple.

She was permitted outside the enclosure and came to him quickly, fawn-eager, smiling as she came and crying as she arrived. She looked thinner, her face drawn fine and pale, her eyes huge, burning, straining darkly toward him out of their fever of silence. And her beauty, the glow and grace of her, was even more incredible to him than it had been three weeks before. He touched her at the shoulders as he kissed her and could feel the delicate bones underneath the thick habit, and lifted the weight of his hands and kissed her very gently on the cheek, as if afraid that, like a rare and fragile doll, she might break.

They talked for nearly an hour. It was Corpus Christi, and there had been a death in her family, and her brother was off to the African missions—clearly a day for special permissions and indulgence. And she said she wanted to hear about Arnie's death, but cried so bitterly, covering her face with the wide sleeves of her habit, that he gave up before he was well under way. And she said she wanted to hear about Africa and the Saharans and where he would go first and for how long, and she watched him with such intense pride as he told her what little he knew that he felt like the grossest of hypocrites, like a damned impostor, and told himself he would never come anywhere near the purity of intention, the holy simplicity, she had already achieved. She talked very little and then only in answer to his questions; about her vows, her duties (she was currently a laundress), her health, and about Kermit's and Rexfordia's visit the day before. (Mother Prioress had suggested that Aubrey come alone so that he might stay longer.) Aline tried to fake a description of the visit as pleasant and uneventful, but she was a poor liar and had to admit, under questioning, that the visit had been a parental running argument, ending with Kermit roaring, Rexfordia crying, and Van Buren barking. They had agreed on one thing, however: that Aline should do her very best to talk Aubrey out of going to Africa, because Africa was an awful place full of bugs and snakes and Algerian rebels, and because it was so far way and now with Arnie gone it was very selfish of Aubrey to leave his poor mother, because Rexfordia was not at all well—she had been collecting the symptoms of angina pectoris together for years and felt she had the project nearly completed—and Aubrey might never see her again; because Kermit was not feeling so well himself; because America needed priests and the American Church needed administrators; and because Rexfordia felt that she and Aubrey together, if he would only stay close to home, might very well be able to convert Eulalia to the faith before she died. This last was a new twist, and Aline admitted that it had been Kermit's fit of laughter over the thought of Eulalia's conversion that had started the fight.

"I told them I couldn't try to influence you and that they should understand—try to understand—that the Saharan Fathers is God's choice for you." She looked at him solemnly, sweetly, utterly confident that he was as sure of that simple fact as she was. And he felt surer of it just looking at her.

"Well, you know Mother. She's got a fixed idea about me administrating the New York archdiocese."

"I'm sure she means well. She loves you so much."

"Yes, well, she'll get used to the idea of Africa. I've arranged for her to meet the Provincial, Father Bogart, in Southampton. I think he'll charm her into it. Or scare her." He described Father Bogart to her. "Kermit mumbled something about how he might just go along himself. If Kermit goes, *I'll* have to be there because that's one meeting I wouldn't want to miss." Aline laughed with him, a nun's tinkle of a laugh, her eyes glittering on him, her expression happy but already wistful.

"How long will you be in Southampton?"

"I can't seem to find out exactly. But at least a week. The Fathers can't ship me unoriented."

She smiled. "You won't stay at Daddy's house?"

"No. I move right in with—I was going to say the community, but it'll just be Father Bogart, Father Paquette, and me. Anyway, I move in tonight. Kermit will be out on weekends until I leave. Mother will stay there the whole time, with Solly."

"And Julie?"

He glanced at her quickly. The question had been innocently put. Her eyes were on him unblinking, guileless. He called himself a jackass. How could she know? And he tried to answer without stammering, but did stammer, and blush, and put his feet into a little shuffle as he stared down at them attentively. "Oh, Julie, she—we— I said goodbye to her this morning. I mean, she decided to go someplace—Nantucket, I think, a girl friend of hers has a place—for a while, you know. To rest."

"Oh."

"I—I think she was more upset than anyone had thought over Arnie's death." He lied gratuitously, without purpose, wondering why as he spoke the words.

Then Aline wanted to know if he thought Kermit and Rexfordia might reconcile, and Aubrey, remembering nothing but unrelenting dogfight between them for the two days since Arnie's burial said no, he didn't think so. And he found her studying his face as if to memorize it, and realized that she was beginning to say goodbye; and she told him how proud she was of him, and how hard she would pray for him, and how hard he must pray for her, and how time went very quickly and if she didn't see him again for four or five years—until he was ordained—why, that would be all right because the joy of seeing him a priest would be so great. And she was fairly gasping

533

when she finished, her mouth formed in a small oh-ing, her eyes preternaturally brilliant and selfish; and he stared at her thinking, My God, my God, she is really going to stay in this little blockhouse for the rest of her life (and I think I'm making a sacrifice), and she is really going to wait here patiently until I come to her a priest, and look at me just as she's looking at me now, never having doubted I would make it, accepting my priesthood now and always as God's certain will and therefore inevitably ordained; and he began to remember when he had looked upon his priesthood as inevitable, just a month or so ago, and wondered if he could ever return to that attitude, and began to return to it even as he wondered, even as he took on surety from the serene excess of it in Aline's gaze.

When the Portress called from behind the screen, she got immediately to her feet, put both hands to his face, kissed him softly on both cheeks, told him to be careful, to pray always, to write often, to love God, Our Lord and His Blessed Mother, and to pray for her as she would pray for him. And her eyes magnified under her tears and gave their great size to her sorrow, and he took her in his arms and said goodbye and held her until the Portress had called again, and let her go reluctantly and watched her look at him a last time, then turn and go in modest quick-step—her slight body bent forward, her hands out of sight in her choir sleeves, the whole figure of her pathetic and yet strangely powerful, suggesting—or, rather, projecting —irrevocable choice, absolute commitment, and happiness—and disappear behind the screen; and listened and heard the heavy inner door click shut behind her.

He went out and rode downtown with Mr. Jebb and thought about Aline, and said to himself at one point, Yes, well, you see what a vast amount of spiritual insight you have. You grew up with a saint and all the time you thought she was a wood nymph.

There was a taxicab parked in front of Kermit's house, the driver slumped back, cap over eyes, his meter running. Aubrey went in, hoping it wasn't Kermit home so early because he still had about three hundred and ten pounds of miscellany to pack, a small part of the fifteen hundred pounds (Aubrey's estimate) of clothing, shoes, boots, camp equipment, rain gear, pith helmets, suntan oil, bug nets, snake traps, firearms, bullets, knives, haversacks, and God alone knew what all (including a portable toilet with collapsible seat) that Rexfordia the Shopper and Kermit, working in tandem and at cross-

534

purposes, had the day before purchased from Abercrombie and Fitch and others in order to outfit him properly for the great African adventure (Aubrey's only comment had been "What? No bugle?") just in case they were not successful in browbeating him out of going with the Saharans, or browbeating the Saharans out of taking him after all. Kermit was not so much interested in preventing the journey to Africa as long as it was clearly understood that a safari would be the first order of business (Kermit being a firm believer in the long stall). Aubrey had said nothing about the safari to Father Bogart and was fervently hoping that he might be present when Kermit broached the subject to Father Huge.

He put his new black hat on the hall table and started for the elevator, and there, standing in the doorway of the office, pouting a sad, easy smile, stood Julie. Dressed in a closely fitted white dress, hung here and there with deep green scarves, she was a sight to arrest all motion. And she arrested his. He stood dumb for a few seconds, but she waited him out.

At last he managed to say only "Julie?" He was asking her.

"I hate you in black. Especially ill-fitting black."

"But you're—you went to—I mean, why didn't you go to Nantucket?"

"It's one of Arnie's old ones, isn't it?"

"Yes. I got it yesterday on the way through Fort Milligan. But . . ."

"I'm sorry," she said, lowering her voice. "I'm sorry, Aubrey darling. I came all the way back here from Idlewild to say something important to you and start by criticizing your hand-me-down clothes."

She was far more subdued than Aubrey had ever seen her, and this worried him. What could subdue Julie? He took a couple of steps toward her and, as he did, she backed away into the office and sat down on a hard bench in front of Kermit's desk. He followed and stood in front of her. She smiled up at him, a foul-weather-brave-girl smile, but supremely genuine, and pointed across the room to a chair. "Is there anything wrong, Julie?"

"Over there," she said, guide to tourist. "Over in the nice big fat deep easy awful chair. I've got a little going-away message."

He went to the chair after slight hesitation, looking into her eyes, seeing the beauty there and the same ever-present threat of storm; seeing also two needlepoints of pain, silver on green, dead-center in either eye, giving her a defensive, distinctly vulnerable look. She was watching him, almost smiling, and tilted her chin up another quarter notch as she started to speak.

"That's my cab out front, and I'm going to run for it when I'm through, and I don't want you to follow. Right?"

He stared, completely bewildered. "Does that mean . . . ?"

"That means please don't try to catch me. Just sit there." He nodded tentatively. "Okay. First, about our goodbye this morning. I'm sorry, Aubrey. I was trying to be cute because I didn't know what else to be. It all came on so fast. Friday night you locked me out of the bathroom. Saturday through Monday we were traveling and you were too drunk all the time to talk anyway. Tuesday the funeral. Yesterday on the road and I couldn't get you alone to talk to. Then you went shopping all afternoon. I didn't really believe you were going to go to Africa until you went shopping. Or rather, I've believed since I've known you that you'd go sometime, but not now. Does that make sense?"

"I—guess so. But look, Julie, I'm sorry I . . ."

"Don't be sorry. It doesn't help a damned thing." She looked down at her hands, then set her chin high again. "So, you're going. And last night I got mad and said I was going too, to Nantucket, which I'm not, and this morning I was still mad and wanted to hurt you. And I tried, by being so disgustingly blithe about saying goodbye. You looked hurt and confused, and I knew you were standing at the front door when I got in the cab but I wouldn't look at you."

"Julie, you don't have to . . ."

"I do. I want to. I was at the airport having breakfast before the bitch calmed down enough to think about it. And you know what ailed me as well as I do. Not merely the woman scorned. I was even more angry about the fact that I couldn't screw you any more. You were depriving me arbitrarily of a long happy summer. But at the airport I realized how ridiculously I was behaving. My mad act wouldn't bring you back, and you'd told me forty times a day since we met that you definitely were going. And, improbable as it sounds, I realized then, too, for the first time that you *did* want to be a priest —although I was sincere when I told you in San Francisco that you really didn't want to. You wanted to be a priest, you had said so, and now you were leaving for the seminary. Where or how did I decide I had some claim on you? Well, I knew the answer to that one, and that's what I came back to tell you, Aubie. Face to face, as I think it should be told, so you can know I mean it. My claim was, and is, simply that I love you, Aubie. Very much. I think it's important you know it because it's probable no other girl will ever have occasion to say it to you, and you may find it nice to know, when you're alone in some damned desert, that you are loved, and were and will be, by a girl, by the only girl you ever went to bed with. I love you, Aubie, so that I'd marry you in a minute, and will, if you ever decide to return from the thirteenth century and if Kermit ever gets around to divorcing my mother, and if I haven't already married some second-best. I mean, Aubie, please remember me, and if you should give it up"—and she got slowly to her feet as she continued to talk, and collected her purse and gloves, finding them and his face in short quick glances through the first quiet tears he had ever seen in her eyes, yet betraying nothing in her voice and thrusting her chin high again as she finished speaking—"though I don't expect you will give it up, but if you do, please let me know first chance? Because, dear Aubie, a good woman—or even a bad one if she loves you—is almost as hard to find as a good man. Goodbye, darling. Forgive the drama and all, but this way you'll remember. And so will I. . . ."

He opened his mouth to speak and his knees to rise, but she was gone, high heels clack-clacking on the marble floor of the foyer, and the iron gate clanged to and the front door slammed before he'd cleared the office door. He leaped to the gate in two bounds and to the door in one, and charged front and staring onto the sidewalk just as her cab came out of a U-turn squealing slightly at the tires and shot a red light south down Fifth Avenue. And his only and last sight of Julie was her auburn hair floating gently out behind her, as she appeared to be leaning forward, hands to face, a white glove fluttering like a small flag from the grip of her left hand.

He stood there until long after the cab was away and gone, and felt a part of him away and gone with it; a vital part and something he needed, or had needed before he had been given her goodbye in exchange for it; hence, no longer needed because given and replaced, and the replacement a pain on his heart, a ringing damned over-whelming ache, yet the void around it even more overwhelming.

And it was hard, standing there at the curb with the broad-beamed matrons and the spindle-shanked dogs going by on their collective leashes, and with the traffic and the fumes thereof, and with two patrolmen in a prowl car watching him solicitously as they might watch any wild-eyed young cleric who looked like he needed shepherding back to the good fathers superior—it was difficult to isolate what he felt for her, and to give it moment and reverence; but he looked off into the park, to the sun on the deep green of the trees, and was finally able to shut out the world sufficiently to say, knowing exactly what he meant, Yes, sweet Julie, I'll remember. And for all that he turned from the sidewalk and went back inside to his chair requiring of himself, as priestly candidate, just what the hell he meant by saying he would remember, he didn't give an inch, and stared stubbornly at the rug, and assured his holier part that he and Julie and God knew precisely what he meant, and had meant; he would remember and who the hell but the Devil himself could find room in it for accusation? And who the hell cared if he did?

He was still sitting there an hour later when Rexfordia came in and presented him with a Latin Vulgate Bible and with a large oblong gift-wrapped box which contained, he discovered, a brand-new golden military bugle hung with red and white tassels. He laughed, but Rexfordia didn't, reminding him that he'd asked for a bugle; and then laughed alone and to himself until Kermit came gamboling in, beard newly trimmed, eyes bright and full of enterprises, and as Aubrey explained the bugle, collapsed laughing into a half squat under the African dik-dik while Rexfordia called him the most uncouth man born of woman since Genghis Khan.

The ride to Southampton (after goodbyes to Eulalia in the back seat of the old La Salle—she saying, "Your mother cried all the way over! Serve you right if those Muslims captured you and married you off to a harem as a eunuch!"—Aubrey asking her to repeat that, but Eulalia refusing and telling him to go to hell on a cartwheel but then forcing ten one-hundred-dollar bills on him for, as she called it, "mad money,"—and goodbye to Roger, who shook his head and blinked tears until Eulalia told him goddamn it to get in and get her back to Fort Milligan before she caught her death of Central Park goldenrod fever), proceeded out of the bugle argument, through an argument over Aubrey's unpacked impedimenta (Nellie had promised to pack it, and claimed to have engaged the British Eighth Army to haul it out to Southampton in lorries), through an argument instigated by Solly about who the hell *said* the other housekeeper could stay on at Kermit's house while Solly was in residence, be Jaysus, and a final argument that lasted from Jamaica, or thereabouts,

538

all the way to the end of the Northern State Parkway concerning Arnie's burial, Kermit saying that Arnie was a Strycker, by name and by inclination and by God, and should have been buried in Strycker ground, and Rexfordia saying that Arnie was her son, that she had suffered to bring him into the world and therefore she had the right to say where he would rest, and saying, too, that the side of the Breesvort cemetery where Arnie was buried was consecrated ground, and that no part of the Strycker cemetery was consecrated ground, and that Kermit had better start looking to the state of his soul before he fell on his face with a heart attack, or worse, and died. Kermit took spirited issue with what Rexfordia might mean by "worse," and the ensuing discussion, with strident interjections from Solly, covered everything from gout to the Sligo shingles and saw them clear through to the other side of Quogue, when the argument about Arnie's grave site was renewed and carried on simultaneously with a dispute about Kermit's intention to take Aubrey on safari.

And Aubrey sat there throughout, refusing to answer questions or to take sides, even when he was being misquoted (which he frequently was), and tried not to listen, and looked out the window, and hummed grimly to himself; but he heard it all—heard it until he thought he would lose his mind. Heard it until he was plotting to leap headfirst from the car into the next available water. Heard it until, just as they got into Southampton, he could stand it no longer, and suddenly clapped his hands over his ears, delivered himself of a rocketing bellow that brought even Kermit up staring, at the conclusion of which he started to sing, at the limit of his lungpower, "Ace, we'll gather at the river!" And, not needing to attend to the words, held his face close to the window and spoke to Arnie, and to himself.

Ah, Arnie, do you hear them? Do you hear them mourning your untimely death? Listen. Dear Arnie, we are the living. Isn't it marvelous the way we love to maim one another? How we hunt one another down and drive stakes into our secret hearts? Listen to us living, Arnie, and luxuriate in your death. Listen to our pain, and rest quietly in your peace.

And then he did leap from the car as Mr. Jebb came nearly to a stop in traffic just opposite Job's Lane, and was running when he hit the street and went on running, free again, not looking back, until he was on the front porch of the Saharan Motherhouse, thumping at the door with both fists.

It was opened almost immediately by Father Paquette of the

telephone. He was smiling broadly and spoke with some excitement as he reached a hand to Aubrey's elbow and led him inside. "Come in! I saw you approach! *Alors!* Such splendid zeal! Very few of our novices come running, I can tell you." He closed the door and turned to Aubrey, rubbing his hands, chuckling delightedly, his eyes perfect little hoops of holy joy. "But I knew you would be back. Yes. Do you know how?" Aubrey, also smiling now, shook his head. "It is simple. You forgot your fine hat, and Father Bogart has been wearing it!"

And Father Paquette was still giggling when, a moment or two later at the priest's suggestion, they went into the small chapel to say a prayer of thanksgiving for Aubrey's safe arrival; and, kneeling just there in that tiny white room—the yellow shades tightly drawn, the air close, the makeshift altar almost shamefully bare and inadequate—Aubrey began to feel secure, gathered, battened against shock and pursuit. For the first time in the three weeks since he had left the Titans, there was an incipient and sudden stillness within him, an obscure but definite easing of apprehension, a kind of silence nearly forgotten but moving now toward him like an echo from the far side of memory. And he thought he knew what the silence was, having held it so often at bay, but waited for it now and bade it come on in, and promised it a lasting home. And called upon Arnie to witness this return of his vocation; this return, if not precisely or clearly or yet fully of his vocation, of the ache and the will for the serenity and order and solitude of religious life; this return, certainly and at least, of the primal force of his conviction that he and God had no positive mutual future except in the midst of a waste of sand; and the return, perhaps, of some part—some sapling root willing to try his dust again—of the holy green innocence he had so busily destroyed. This last he wanted above all, as that which, it seemed to him, would make all the rest possible; and his hope quickened as the quiet continued to take him, and as he assured himself that innocence, too, was a kind of silence.

When the hammering began at the front door, Father Paquette gave a small jump and a cry like that of a wounded bird, darted his eyes at Aubrey in alarm, waved his hands in little circles for a time, then blessed himself and went chittering out. Aubrey didn't move for a moment. He stared at the tabernacle, then closed his eyes to see if the silence was gone within as well as without. It was indeed

540

gone, and with it his certainties, and in its place a desperate, almost panicky anger, growing now as he heard Kermit roaring in the entry hall about goddamned blockheads in blockhouses, and Rexfordia shrilling about her rights as a mother, and Solly tearfully denouncing white slavery and black Africa, and he groaned aloud and went on groaning and put his head between the heels of his hands as in a vise and pressed at his temples until he felt dizzy, until his anger was down. And then he spoke to Arnie.

Ah, Arnie, do you hear them? The hunters winding their wreathéd horns? They took to my spoor and smelled me out and now they're out on the drawbridge demanding a last clean shot. Their privileged right, of course, according to the code of all honest hunters. But they're forgetting one thing. This is sanctuary. The fink of a quarry has taken refuge in a church. He is a thinking man's fink, this quarry, and he's going out there one time to say his last and final goodbyes and then hang up his yoick forever. I don't care what those hunters do. They can scream, curse, pee in the sorghum, foam at the mouth, run rabbits, or tear off their clothes and climb the walls for all I care. I'm not leaving this building. Not until I'm outward bound, Arnie, to where they'll have to work and sweat to track me down. To where they may never find me again. Fancy that. Freedom from wreathed horns? Why, the fancy boggles. Yet that desperate hope drives me on, and let it begin here, and once more unto the breach, and when the beast charges, drop it on him. Do plan to attend. It promises to be a very high-type public disaster.

He got slowly to his feet, sighing, moved out of the pew, genuflected, and went in solemn step down the aisle to the door. He paused there, touching the wood with his fingers, and spoke a last time to Arnie.

You know I love them, as you love them. You know I wouldn't hurt them if I didn't have to—to save my life. You know now that I've got to get away. So don't condemn me if I hurt them, Arnie. Stand with me in this, and stay with me. Come with me, when this is over, out to my solitude, out to where they can't follow, out and beyond to my gentle desert. Come, Arnie. Come, and we'll walk down the Sahara in the wind together, and we'll leave no footprints at all.

And then he went out.